TheTwo-Book Series of The McGowan Collection Series

ISBN: 979-8-9886604-1-5 (ebk)
ISBN: 979-8-9886604-2-2 (pbk)

Printed in the United States of America
Edited and Produced by I.E.R. Media

The McGowan Collection Series Book 1:

Wolf Laurel

A Novel by
Col. Lee Martin

I.E.R. Media
Miami, Florida

Wolf Laurel

Also by Col. Lee Martin:

The Third Moon is Blue
The Six Mile Inn
Starbright

Copyright © 2008 by Lee Martin
All rights reserved. No part of this book may
be used or reproduced by any means, graphic,
electronic, or
mechanical, including
photocopying, recording, taping or by any
information storage retrieval
system without the written permission of the
publisher except in the case
of brief quotations embodied in critical
articles and reviews.

ISBN: 979-8-987-2241-0-6 (ebk)
ISBN: 979-8-987-2241-4-4 (pbk)

Printed in the United States of America

Edited and Produced by I.E.R. Media

And Then:

The McGowan Collection Series Book 2:

PROVOCATION:
Return of the Weatherman

ISBN: 979-8-9872241-3-7 (pbk)
ISBN: 979-8-9872241-5-1 (ebk)

Printed in the United States of America

I.E.R. Media

13874 SW 151 Lane

Miami, FL 33186

tbyrnes@ierworld.com

786-525-9487

Wolf Laurel

A Novel by
Col. Lee Martin

o West Virginia ...

... where the moonlit meadows ring with the call of Whippoorwills, always you will find me in my home among the hills. And where the sun draws rainbows in the mist of waterfalls and mountain rills, my heart will be always in the West Virginia hills.

"And made ready against them all you can of power, including steeds of war, to threaten the enemy of Allah and your enemy who you may not know. The Gates of Paradise are under the shadows of the swords.. A martyr's privileges are guaranteed by Allah and he forgives with the first gush of blood, protected from the test of the grave and assured security in the Day of Judgment. Declare war with your hearts and your bodies against the Great Satan and cause the blood of every man, woman and child to run in its streets."

وأعدوا لهم ما استطعتم من قوة ومن رباط الخيل ترهبون به عدو الله وعدوكم وآخرين من دونهم لا تعلمونهم. إن أبواب الجنة تحت ظلال السيوف. امتيازات الشهيد مضمونة عند الله، وهو يغفر عند تفجر أول نقطة دماء، ويحمي من عذاب القبر ويجعلك تأمن في يوم الدين. أعلنوا الحرب بقلوبكم وأجسادكم ضد الشيطان الأعظم، واسلكوا دماء كل رجل وامرأة وطفل يجري في شوارعه.

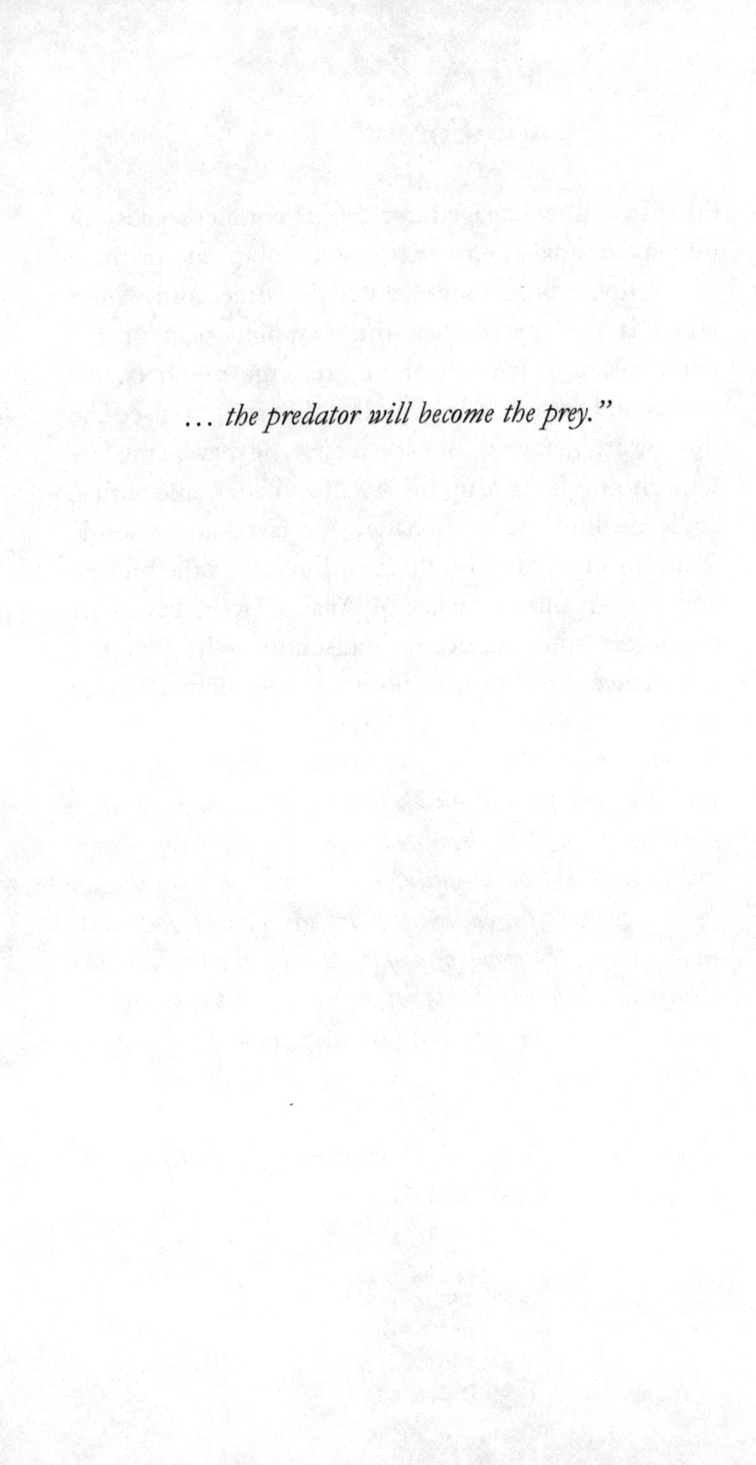

... the predator will become the prey."

Foreword

So we are now engaged in a global conflict against an unconventional enemy that may number one or three or twenty, whose battlefield is the street and whose target is the sky scraper, the shopping mall or the marketplace. Anywhere there are large numbers. He strikes and then shields himself within the populace like the coward that he is. But conversely, he may be the one who chooses to give up his *own* life willingly and with a, smile on his face in exchange for favor and rewards from his God. He may think of himself as the blessed and chosen one, a seeker of Allah's favor; but as he slaughters the innocent indiscriminately, without conscience, he is instead nothing more than a bilious disciple of *Shaitan*, the Evil One.

"A martyr's privileges are guaranteed by Allah; forgiveness with the, first gush of blood, he will be shown his seat in paradise, he will be decorated with the jewels of belief, married off to the beautiful ones, protected from the test in the grave, assured security in the day of judgment, crowned with the crown of dignity, a ruby of which is better than this whole world and its contents, wedded to seventy-two of the pure Houris and his intercession of his relatives will be accepted."

Osama bin Laden, 1996, Dark Prince of Terrorism from the Qur'an, Suras 44 and 61

CHAPTER 1

It doesn't matter. It could be pouring one of those bone-chilling, mind-numbing rains. Or in the dead of winter, the landscape may be painted brown and gray with dirty patches of snow hanging on until that first warm and hopeful spring morning. I don't care. Whatever the weather, the temp or the season, I am good there. It is the place I have always called home. I have lived a great number of places in my life, seen every state and worked and played in most of Europe and Asia. I have been intrigued, fascinated, enticed and enchanted by so many of these places. Author's always go home. Not often. But when I do, it's my needed shot in the arm.

Each time I cross the state line into God's country, my heart bristles and swells as I sweep my eyes along great defiant mountains that finally level off to the west into lush, peaceable meadows. In the summer the hills can change color, from hazy blue to violet, from deep green to gold, depending on where the sun is positioned on any given day. The land, rich and munificent in its bounty, is now left relatively undisturbed by those who would defile it in their search for gas, coal, salt and iron. The environmentalists and entreating lobbyists have seen to that. Still, this beautiful state so greatly advanced the by those industries that have often spoiled the air and earth, never fails to provide for the comfort and prosperity of its people.

Well, I'm not exactly a poet. Although I can *get* pretty poetic at times, you won't see it coming out very often. But there are still a few things that continue to bring out the Robert Burns in me. One of those is Caroline, the love of my life, who happens to be my daughter; another, an ice cold six pack of Heineken that when sucked down my swallow pipe on a hot day, cools my arteries as well as my jets; and lastly, my Austin Healey 3000, to which I have visitation rights once a month while it sits in my ex-wife's driveway. But the odes and sonnets that sometimes dance in my brain are never more prolific than when I do go home from time to time to the extraordinarily beautiful land called Greenbrier.

I know it sounds all dramatic and clandestine, but I simply can't tell anyone what I do, who I work for or where I'm going from one day to the next. Not even my daughter, my ex-wife or my brother. What I *can* say is that I'm a contractor and these days my services are pretty much in high demand. It's not really one of those jobs where if you asked me what I did, then I would say "if I told you skyscraper kill you." Well ... maybe it is; but I wouldn't necessarily go through with it.

It's a hell of a lot more dangerous world we live in now; and seeing as how we're slammed into World War III, a war like no other, you could say I'm a modern day battlefield soldier ... a for real Army of One. The difference is I don't wear a uniform, have a sophisticated, high-tech weapons system at my fingertips nor do I take orders from skin-head Colonels. When I was in the Army's Special Forces a hundred years ago, I used to carry a card for fun that listed my job responsibilities like *'villages plundered, despots exterminated, terrorists castrated and virgins deflowered.'* The card that I carry now provides no information about me or my job responsibilities as a government operative. It's actually pretty generic. Across the top it reads *United States*

Department of State, over which you will find the department seal, and under which is my name. The only other items on the card are my State Department web site and the main office phone number which patches the caller directly to my cell phone.

Let's just say I fix things ... and people ... both good and bad. But the thing I'm most proud of is that I do my damnedest to facilitate life, liberty and the pursuit of happiness for American citizens. My tasks and methods, however, are a little unorthodox. Call it skyscraper ... deactivation, extermination or perhaps a fancier word like *extirpation.* But if you're fishing to know exactly what I do, please don't ask and I won't tell. It may end up, changing your impression of me.

I'm in kind of a sales and service business for the government. Actually, mostly service. Here's how it works. I get a call from my boss at the Counter Terrorism Team (CTT, not to be confused with CTC or Counter Terrorist Center), an elite, covert and classified department of the Bureau of Intelligence and Research. He has no name on his door nor supervises a department known or recognized by ninety-five percent of all government law enforcement organizations. He has a code name like Falcon, Condor or some other freaking bird ... that is in times of crisis ... which would make one think he's James Bond or the Man from U.N.C.L.E. This is a sapient guy with steely eyes who walks and talks like Joe Friday and would never ever admit he was breast-fed by his mother ... that is if he ever had one. But I have to admit he is a good guy; and as tight-lipped as this distinguished, silver-haired dude is, whenever he speaks, anyone in CTT had better listen. To everyone else in the State Department, he is the Preceptor of CTT. But to us on his Special Ops field team called Zulu, he is affectionately known as *Birdman.*

Officially, our mission is to collect and analyze intelligence about foreign state-supported terrorist groups and warn appropriate government agencies and branches of impending terrorist operations or threats. As necessary, we will employ 'defensive' measures to prevent terrorist attacks from occurring or at the 'very minimum weaken the enemy's infrastructure. Selected members of Zulu will be fluent in a half dozen languages, and depending on their ethnicity, may actually infiltrate the terrorist organization.

There are six of our strategically located teams throughout the Continental U.S., mostly situated in or near the larger metropolitan areas. Four additional teams are in Europe, the Middle East, Asia and South America. Each team is comprised of four to seven agents who mostly operate individually but will come together as a Special Reaction Team (SRT) when a threat is realized. Our goal will first be to capture the subject or subjects, conduct preliminary interrogation, assess the threat, and then transfer the element to the Company's (CIA) Counterterrorist Center in Langley Guantanamo Bay.

The Preceptor will tell one of us he was contacted by an operative or informant who has secured information about a customer of the 'imported' persuasion with a product that will unwittingly attract our services. But unfortunately for the customer, he will not appreciate these services. It will be up to one of us to approach the customer, give him our sales pitch and insure that any concerns he has are extinguished forever. I must be good, because so far, I have never heard back from any of my customers. Furthermore, neither has anyone else.

My twenty years with the Bureau behind me, I had planned to settle down, rust away and become a slug, operating a bar in the tropics somewhere or growing some tobacco on a little farm in North Carolina. But after my first week in retirement of doing absolutely nothing except eating and drinking everything I could get my hands on, I decided that as this FAG (Former Action Guy) would soon end up either in a funny farm or on a fat farm, I would make some calls. One of the calls I made was to another recent Bureau retiree by the name of Charlie Green who I knew had gone through the same post-partum blues and took on an afterlife with the government of different capacity. Sending up the old S.O.S., huh fella?" "Help me, Charlie," I replied. "I feel like a '58 Edsel, broken down, unloved and upon blocks. I need something to do. And I don't mean handcuffed to a desk, my friend."

He laughed. "So, a case of the D.T's, huh? All right, I know a guy, okay? All I can tell you is that people are being recruited for this new kind of organization that operates out of the State Department. It's still on the drawing board and has been for quite some time from what I understand, but they plan to implement it sometime this year."

That's when I was put in touch with a man named Brent Sawyer who ultimately got me an interview with Birdman. I guess because I was a true FAG and knew a thimble full of Arabic, not to mention being pretty astute in English, I was in. In three weeks I was undergoing training with the Del at Ft. Bragg in the Close Quarters Battle (CQB) course. The Combat Application Group was doing much of the training which included modules such as terrorist profiling and assessment, Intel ops, sniper M-24 certification, selective targeting and what is called double tap engagement (making sure the target does not get up). We were to be the first line of defense where it came to counterterrorist warfare. The CTC and other global counterterrorist groups would still do their strategic stuff, but *our* ears would be closer to the ground. And by the time we sought out and destroyed the element, the spooks and FBI would just be getting out of bed. For the most part, we would only share our information with them when the action was over, if in fact it was a matter of national security, and then we were selectively resistant. That meant we wanted no Mostly, especially large bureaucratic Intel groups who were in competition with one another and who were compelled to run their plans and operations by special congressional panels to determine whether something was indeed of national security interest, a violation of the Geneva Convention or human rights, congruent with U.N. concupiscence or politically correct.

Well anyway, what it comes down to is that I'm sort of a government cop, but I carry no badge. I do have an ID with a barcode on it that can be read by select people at certain federal agencies; however, I will not necessarily be recognized by other law enforcement, especially the local yokels. Basically, breastfed rank, title or position. One other thing; it is imperative in my work that I have zero visibility. For this reason I am not always the person I appear to be. Let's just say there would be fewer questions if my vehicle were stopped by a *federal* cop versus a *local* ... especially if they found my deadly accurate cryogenic-treated Remington 700, .308 complete with sniper scope. And then also somewhere on my person are usually my Glock and .380.

My name is not a code (except when I'm on a mission) or a number, like Mr. Bond. But although I sometimes change my name temporarily to protect the innocent (me), I generally go by the name my Scottish-American parents laid on me some fifty-four years ago, Bruce McGowan.

It wasn't but a month after I joined in up with CTT that the Birdman dropped my first mission on me. The intel came down the chute in April just a year ago where two young Islamic Idealists, both disciples of the militant sheik Omar Abdel Rahman, the convicted mastermind of the 1993 World Trade Center bombing, had been spotted reconning the Sears Tower in Chicago. Their mugs had appeared just once too often on cameras in the vicinity of the building, looking around suspiciously, scratching notes and crotches, and taking photos. As there was nothing incriminating about their activity, there would not be enough cause for law enforcement to pick them up for questioning. These guys would argue that besides them, a great many people pass by or stop and look at the building day after day, which was true; and if they, the Islamics, were hauled in just because they had been admiring the building, that would be a case of ethnic or religious profiling and a complaint would immediately be filed to the Council on American-Islamic Relations.

Anyway, I staked these guys out for about three weeks, finding also that a Chicago FBI team was on their case. A self-made problem for the Feds was that their black Ford Crown Vic with plain wheels was just a wee bit too conspicuous. The suspects' casing of the Sears Tower then suddenly stopped cold. But knowing where the Arab boys lived, I rented an apartment in the same tenement just two doors away. When all they had to do was look out their window to spot the Crown Vic, they did as I expected them to do... took the fire escape down the back side of the building. Each time they did, I trekked down my own set of stairs, followed them at distance and recorded their activities.

And then there was that cold, blustery evening in early April when I tailed the suspects' Pontiac Grand Am from a parking garage to the empty lot at Soldier Field. I watched from about fifty feet away through my, telephoto lens while they made contact with another Middle Eastern man in a white cargo van. The boys disappeared through t doors of the van and then reappeared about three minutes later with a large suitcase. I snapped shots of the license plate on the van as it pulled away, then advanced quickly on the Grand Am. They never saw me coming. Before the driver could throw the car into *drive*, I jumped into the back seat, cracked him on the head with the butt of my Glock and stuck the muzzle into the passenger's ear.

"Touch the suitcase and a .40 caliber round will split your head open like a ripe watermelon," I barked. The would-be terrorist didn't go for the suitcase, but instead reached down under the seat for a handgun. Since I had thought in advance to attach the silencer, it wasn't a very loud report.

Instantaneously, the passenger's head exploded, coating a section of the windshield with a smattering of goopy red and white stuff. I retrieved the bloodied suitcase from the man's lap and to my car. In case it was booby trapped, I did not open it. Popping the cover of my cell phone, I called Ramon, the team leader for Zulu Chicago.

"Ramon, this is Scorpion. Cleanup on Aisle C10 at Soldier Field. I have one DOA and one sleeper. Bring an EOD expert and a disposal unit."

Well, we *did* find that it was an explosive device which was meant for the Sears Tower. As for the would-be terrorists, the dead guy disappeared altogether. The *driver's,* brain, scrambled as it was from my whack, and somehow still remembered the names of the two cohorts in the van. And a few days later, after further interrogation of all three at Gitmo, they seemed happy to give up details of the plot. I drove back to my tenement, got out and strolled up to the Crown Vic, still parked in plain sight, and tapped on the window. When the startled driver dropped the window down, I said, "Give it up Bureau Boys and call your office. Your boss has something to tell you." I just love spreading good news. So, anyway, most of the time, thanks to guys like me, the general public never finds out that a threat like that even exists nor that the purveyors of such plots suddenly and rudely exit from society. We Zulu guys not only keep Americans from developing unnecessary fears about their security, but our way of doing business keeps us from being subject to all those pesky civil rights concerns.

But then something happened a few months ago where for the first time in the year and a half since I had hired on with CTT as an operative, not only did certain members of my family find out more about me, I ended up breaking my policy of secrecy. And I also found myself compelled to collaborate with people and agencies that I usually keep in the dark. But I needed them … and they sure as hell needed me.

I drove slowly over the old bridge on Route 136, glancing down occasionally at the now unused and broken tracks, then pulled my Suburban onto the dirt shoulder at the end of the guardrail. Sitting for a few moments with my wrist propped atop the steering wheel, I allowed the sweet memories of childhood to fill my head. In the past thirty years I had been home, as I still called it, perhaps a dozen times, but the visits had generally been short. Short except for when I came back for the funerals of my mom and dad and the one-time fishing sabbatical I took at my brother's cabin up on the Greenbrier River. I reckon I needed those days in the woods on the water to recuperate that year just after a perp's bullet drilled my lung out. And scantly a month after I was released from the hospital, my divorce was final. Not a good year, to say the least.

I stepped out of the Suburban to greet the sweltering afternoon sun and adjusted my Ray-Ban flight glasses to shield my eyes from its piercing glare. In late August the mountain air is generally tolerable and even down-right cool, especially just after a front has passed through. But that afternoon, the dog-day haze was heavy and consuming after the rain, after the sun began again to heat up the soggy earth, making it hatefully humid if you will, making it difficult for me to suck enough oxygen from the atmosphere into my damaged lung. Summer just didn't want to give up.

It was peacefully, even deafeningly quiet on the bridge which allowed me to barely pick up the noise of whining tires and tractor rigs running through their gearboxes on I-64 near the Lewisburg exit. Obnoxious crows called and answered one another from the white oaks that towered over magnificent mountain laurel, some of which had crept cautiously toward the tracks over the years. It had been twenty years or more since the last coal train passed under the bridge on those tracks on its way from the Raleigh mines, over the Alleghenies, through the Shenandoah, and then on to Norfolk. I placed one of my Tony Lamas onto the lower abutment and leaned over the railing to spit out a gnat that just had to find a moist cavern to fly into. Fortunately for my sinus cavity, it hadn't flown up my nose. My chest hurt a little that day where six years before, an emergency room doctor had cut a hunk out of me. But otherwise, I felt pretty good. I'm still in fairly good shape, considering both knees were blown out by shrapnel from an NVA .122 rocket back in 1970. Oh, and did I mention I had actually been wounded when I was with the Bureau … *twice;* once in a shootout with a bank robber and then by a mob henchman (ergo the sucking chest wound) after my partner and I cornered him in an alley. And then there was that time I rolled a Bureau Crown Vic and banged up my head when I was chasing an escaping wife killer.

By the way, the bad guys I mentioned got the worse end of the deal. But at least I can say I'm proud to be an American economist at heart; no taxpayer money is generally shelled out for trials and incarceration. *My* services are both expedient and cost effective. At six-two and a hundred seventy-five pounds (with Glock), I can still hold my own in any scuffle, damaged goods and all. Except I choose not to do that anymore. Cause if you *are* the bad dude and you run on me, two of my rounds will take out each leg at the back of the knee. Of course, I would warn you first. The law mandates that. But if you continue running after the warning, ten yards is all you get.

Anyway, I'm still a pretty good-looking guy who hasn't let age ravage his body, although Heaven knows I've beaten it up over the years by allowing bullets, booze and babes to have their way with it. The babes and booze, of course, I allowed into my life voluntarily. One thing is, though, I can still run … bad knees, bad lung, bad years and all. Five, six mornings a week you'll see me pounding the pathway on the D.C. Mall, from the Capitol to the Lincoln Memorial, or maybe some trail off the beaten path wherever I happen to be.

Upon hearing the limo approach, I turned my head and watched the car pass by. I kept my eyes on it until it pulled off the road to the right and to the front of my Suburban. For a few moments the driver stayed put, but then the door eventually opened and a man of fifty with hair as black as the coal in them thar hills, wearing a black suit and tie, exited the Lincoln.

He approached me slowly, but with purpose. "Special Agent McGowan, I presume." I took off my glasses and shook my head.

"Not anymore."

"You're not going to jump, are you?" he asked, gluing his eyes to mine.

"Any reason I shouldn't?"

"Yeah, you'd probably miss the ground. I know what a bad shot you are. Dad always said you couldn't hit water if you fell out of a friggin' boat."

I smiled wryly. "Contraire, little brother. I could drill a hole in your belly button at two hundred yards. And that's with a .45." Joe McGowan outstretched his arms and walked over to embrace me. We patted each other's back and then separated.

"You look good, Brucious. Obviously, even with all the holes in you, you're still running. Either that or you've been shacking up with some split-tail who's giving you a good workout."

"Definitely not the latter. Still making it on my own. I just can't seem to get a woman to accept my being gone ninety percent of the time. I had a goldfish once, and it lived, I think, three days. I found out you have to feed the little bastards."

Joey laughed and turned to the railing to look down. A couple of the N&W tracks were missing, but mostly, the rails remained intact. He followed them with his eyes until the rails grew together at a point a half-mile away. "I miss the old trains, Brucie. Gawd, it had to be forty or more years since they ran the last of the steam engines from the coal camps through here. We'd stand and watch them come under the bridge, black smoke puffing with every chug, and then after the train was gone, the gray fog laid in the trees. I remember that smell of the burning coal." Joey closed his eyes and drew in a deep, nostalgic breath.

"Yeah, I know," I said. "And do you remember when we used to bring our model planes up here and pretend, they were WW II fighter-bombers. We'd hold our P-51 Mustangs in one hand and drop cherry bombs with the other down into coal cars as they passed under. They'd go off and scatter bits of coal like shrapnel."

Joey grinned. "The thing I most remember like it was yesterday was when you thought the train was longer than it was and dropped a bomb on the caboose when it went by. Man, the brakeman jumped out of the back and started cussin' and shaking his fist. We took off like a couple of scalded dogs."

We both had a good laugh with that. I also remembered that the brakeman reported us and somehow it got around that it was *us* on the bridge. That was one of the few times I wish I had been wearing asbestos underwear. Dad sure as hell lit our britches on fire.

I found my smile quickly fading when I thought of how simple and innocent those days were and then how complicated we had all made our world since. Those childhood years were stocked with good times. And although there would be many more good days to come in my teens and twenties, bad days were soon to follow. Days of heartache. Days of pain and disappointment. Some of which would be thrust upon me by fate. Most of which, however, was of my own making.

It was McGowan and Sons Funeral Home for more than seventy years. First there was my grandfather and his three sons. Then when Pops died, Dad took over and kept the name, hoping both his sons would go to mortuary school, become licensed funeral directors, and settle into the family business with him. Little Joe did; I didn't. Dad thought it was family treason to reject the business, and considering the business was our very life growing up, he never understood why I hated being around the dead. It was just a natural thing for him to embalm, bathe, dress and primp corpses in preparation for viewing. When Dad married Mom, she knew that to be his wife, she had to become comfortable with it all. And that she did. She washed and set the women's hair, helped loved ones pick out just the right burying clothes and held the trembling hands of the bereaved at wakes. I ignored the whole sordid atmosphere. I had too much living to do to spend my life with the dead. Anyway, corpses always gave me the heebie-jeebies. The first time I saw Dad push that needle up under somebody's arm to drain the veins, I passed out cold on the floor. Dad just smiled, checked to see if my heart had stopped, then went on flushing.

And then there was that one day I remember with shocking exactitude when I was feeling sorry for myself, being an outcast like I was, I was bound and determined to join the family business. I also guess I was tired of my dad calling me a pansy or a pantywaist. It all started with ol'man Cunningham who up and died of a heart attack after he climbed on top Prissy Purcell, the town whore. Although Dad was normally tight-lipped about picking up people who expired in such compromising situations, I did overhear him telling Mr. Bartholomew, the barber, that he had to strap the old man's erect penis to his leg with duct tape. The damn thing wouldn't go down, he said. Of course you can't tell the town barber, bartenders or butchers anything in confidence. You might as well set up a PA system in the middle of town. Old man Cunningham's wife gave Dad the devil for inadvertently spreading the story around and even threatened a lawsuit. But after a few days it all simmered down.

My point here on the Cunningham corpse is that right after Dad brought him in and dropped him on the embalming table, he received a phone call and left me in the room by myself with the stiff, telling me, 'don't let him go anywhere.' Dad smiled and patted my head before going to his office, like he was elated that it was finally going to be *McGowan and Sons* after all. And when little brother Joey would get into *his* teens, the 's' on Sons would be for real.

It was deathly quiet in that room (no pun intended). Just old man Cunningham and me. I could swear the corners of his mouth were turned up. I guess he had every reason to smile when he drew his last breath. What happened next Dad says occurs sometimes by reflex, but *that* didn't make it make it any easier for me and my stomach. One moment ol' Cunningham just laid there with a sheet up to his neck and then the next … well, suddenly he sat straight up and exhaled a burst of air. Then his head plopped back down hard on the metal table with a clunk. I let out a scream that brought Dad back into the room and then I yelled *"He's alive, he's alive!"* Sometime thereafter I recalled I must have sounded like Dr. Frankenstein just after he jolted the monster to life with channeled lightning. Dad laughed like I'd never seen him. Mom whisked me out of there quickly and held me while I muttered and sputtered something unintelligible. At twelve, that was the last time I set foot in a room with the dead. I still don't hang around the dead. I've *made* quite a few of them that way, but don't usually stick around to pay my respects.

Back to the bridge.

"So, what's up, Joey? Why the phone call?"

"Well, you haven't been home in more'n two years, Brewster. Thought maybe you'd like to take some time off … maybe go up to the cabin again."
He had called me the day before and said he had something

I needed to see and that I should get there as soon as I could. But he was reluctant to tell me over the phone what it was. I *knew* Joey, he being my brother and all, and it had to be more than a concern that I was working too hard and needed a vacation.

"You'd better have a more compelling reason than *that* to get me back here, Joey Boy. You said on the phone you had something to show me. Something that would interest me because of what I do for a living. With the urgency in your voice, I thought somebody died." He nodded and shuffled a bit.

"Somebody did, Bruce. And I thought you'd like to go to his visitation."

"What are you talking about?"

"Well, I know you've really never told me what you got into after the FBI, but it *does* have something to do with hunting down subversive types, doesn't it?"

"Let's just say I investigate people suspected of planning or conducting activities against the United States. Does that sum it up for you?"

"Okay, then you *may* be interested in this. I've got a dead Arab on my slab."

"A what?"

"An Arab."

"And?"

"Well, I think he may be connected to some kind of terrorist organization."

"Because he's Middle Eastern?"

"No … look. I know you had been working in some kind of counterterrorist organization and were on the USS Cole bombing. And I know you've been involved in bringing a number of the Arab guys to justice."

"Yeah, but that was when I was still with the Bureau. The Arab… er, Arab, Joey. What about him?"

"Well hell, Bruce, these kinds of people don't live around here or hardly anywhere else in the state for that matter.

Then one ends up prostrate, face down on Washington Street."

"Uh huh. So how did he end up that way?"

"The stupid bastard stepped off a curb and got flattened by a UPS truck."

I had to stifle a smile, listening to the way Joey was prone to put things. "And you think I'd be interested in him *why?*"

"Well, as I said, when did you ever hear of any Middle Easterner visiting or taking up residence in good ol' Greenbrier County?"

"The world's a global community now, Joey. People can live anywhere. But you think he lived somewhere around here?"

"I don't know. Rufus Morgan, you know, he still runs the Western Auto, says he thought he saw the guy two or three weeks back at Spurlock's Grocery. You know old Griffin Spurlock, right?"

I nodded, even though I really didn't. In fifty odd years of compiling information about people, places and things, stuff has been steadily seeping out of the seven holes in my head. But maybe I did remember the Spurlock girl. Nobody ever looked better in a knit sweater.

"Go on."

"Anyway, the EMTs picked him up and took him to the hospital where he was then transferred to the county morgue. He had no ID on him and no one has claimed the body in over six days. A public notice ran in the paper a couple of those days."

"You're still the assistant coroner, aren't you?"

"Yes."

"Did you or anyone do an autopsy?"

"Yep. Harvey Tucker the M.E. did it. No alcohol or drugs in his system and he obviously died at the scene, according to the paramedics.

I shoved my fingertips into my jean pockets and shrugged.

"I still don't see anything suspect here. This is why you

called me? About a dead, unidentified Middle Eastern man? And by the way, how do you know he's of the Arab persuasion?"

"He just looks like it … like he's from Iran or Libya. Maybe Iraq, I don't know. He doesn't look like he's from India or Pakistan. We've got a couple of them in the county running motels between here and Ronceverte. They're more chocolate in color and have glossier hair."

"The next time I see an ad in our system for a bigoted government profiler, I'll be sure to give you a call, little brother."

"Very funny. I *can* tell the difference in ethnic origins, you know."

"I still don't have my question answered, Joey. What's so special about this John Mohammed Doe, other than him not blending in with you mountain WASPS here in Greenbrier County?"

"Tell you what. Follow me down to the shop and let's finish our conversation there."

"Why do you have him there and not at the morgue?"

"I dispose of all the unclaimed and indigent in the area. The county pays me. Before I cremate him, I wanted you to have a look."

I shuffled a bit, kicking a loose stone over the bridge to the old tracks below with one of my roach killers.

"Look, Joey. I don't know if this is a carcass, I'd be interested in. Hell, I thought somebody killed somebody and that's why you called me."

"You're not far off, Bru. I think somebody was planning to kill a hell of a lot of people. And there *is* something about this guy that will interest you."

"What?"

"You'll see when we get to the shop."

"If you have suspicions about the man, why haven't you taken this to the State Police or Feds in Charleston?"

"Hey, you're the only anti-terrorist guru I know and I

thought you'd like first crack at him. Anytime I can help my big brother get another feather in his bonnet, especially if this turns out to be something, I want to call you."

"You're being way too mysterious and dramatic about this. Whatever you've found out about this schmuck better be worth my trip out here."

He grinned. "Wouldn't you have come here just to see me, Cora and the girls?"

I squinted my eyes at him and shook my head. "Let's get it on with it, Joey Boy." I turned to walk toward my vehicle and he followed.

The butter-bright sun was oppressive and the piercing heat radiating off the Suburban created a shimmering effect, making the trees in the distance lose their clarity. I suddenly needed a burst of air conditioning. It's really hell to get fragile like this. I do love my comfort.

Before I entered the SUV I said, "So you have reason to believe he's a terrorist, huh?"

"Was. *Was* a terrorist. Now just a stiff. Just follow me to the shop. You can make up your own mind. By the way, is this how a G-Man dresses these days? Jeans. Golf shirt. Cowboy boots."

"Not a G-Man anymore, Joey. I'm just making a living fighting for truth, justice and the American way."

"Right," he replied with a smirk.

"I don't see you wearin' any blue underwear on the outside of your pants and that shirt doesn't have a big 'S' on it. But come on, Mr. Kent. I may actually have an exclusive for you."

CHAPTER 2

I have never forgotten how incredibly beautiful this Eastern West Virginia landscape is. The low hills between the Alleghenies and the Appalachians slope gently into green velvet pastures that on most crisp mornings lay blanketed with a haunting fog. When the ten o'clock sun floods the valley and dissipates the opaque wisp, the colors of summer and fall are then gradually and vividly magnified. Almost Heaven, they call it.

I followed the McGowan family car west along the highway for four miles until it turned left at Saturday Road. Small, white-frame houses with ten to fifteen year old sedans and pickups sitting in gravel driveways popped up on either side of the narrow two-lane. Further along, the terrain widened again into rolling, majestic farmland stocked with fine, brawny Herefords and Guernsey's, owned by Greenbrier's more affluent barons. What they call the opulent society.

The covered bridge over Nathan's Creek appeared to be standing as strong as ever. A few of its panels were missing and it needed a coat of paint, and although it creaked a little, it had never given an inch after sixty five years. I did see where it had been reinforced by new timbers and pylons some time back. The bridge was an important piece of the county's history. It had carried both the living and dead to points of destiny since the days of my mortician grandfather.

As the road curved uphill and to the right, Rest Lawn Cemetery, a veritable city of monuments stood silhouetted against the hazy late summer sky. Beyond the grave markers was the old board-and-batten church where I was baptized eons ago by Pastor Billy Tompkins back when God used to smile on me. I guess I've been a major disappointment to the Great One over the years.

Joey finally turned into the mortuary ... the shop ... as he called it. For some reason Dad's weathered face and guttural voice popped into my head as McGowan and Sons Funeral Home came into view. Dad used to crack corny one-liners about the business that made Joey and me nearly gag. When someone would ask how business was, he'd say "dead" with a straight face. "People just die to get in here." And "*rest* assured, we're the last people to let you down." Yet, the man actually committed these quippy atrocities wearing a dead-pan face.

I sat in the Suburban for a while as Joe went to the left of the building to unlock the large double doors out from which a thousand coffins had rolled to the hearse parked under the huge carport. I hated this place, mostly for the reasons mentioned earlier, but also because I took a lot of heat from my friends growing up around the area. Most every other kid's dad was in the farming business, but the only thing my old man planted was bodies. Hell, I couldn't get a date on a bet. No girl wanted a guy to touch her if he had touched dead bodies. Even when I tried to convince them I didn't ... ever, I guess they thought I was lying. One of my buds, Bobby Crawford, even joked that I was into necrophilia. I was nineteen before I learned *that* meant having sexual relations with corpses. I was thirty before I actually did. But it was with my ex-wife, Darlene, and she only pretended to be dead.

Joey motioned for me to come on, but he stayed by the door without going inside. His face appeared urgent. He yelled to me, "You got your piece on you?"

"My piece?" I knew what he meant but didn't know why he asked.

"Why? Aren't people already dead in there or is business slow and you want to kill old Lester?"

"Lester's off today. The door's been rifled. Looks like someone broke in here." I reached across the glove compartment and took out my Glock. Holding it at my side, I moved in toward Joey.

"Stay here."

After assessing the broken lock and the chewed up facing, I swung the left door open and propped my gun atop my left wrist. I scanned the lobby through the sight and swept the Glock around the room. Joey was right on my heels, the disobedient little shit.

"No one's ever broken in here," he said. "What would they want?"

I didn't answer but continued my canvass of the lobby. It was quiet, as it should be in a funeral home, and no sign of a fleeing burglar. I moved from room to room, Joey with me all the way.

"I thought I told you to stay."

"I'm your brother, not your dog."

The place seemed to have been left intact. Joe didn't readily see that anything was missing. But what would someone take from a funeral home? No money was kept around. People didn't buy caskets and funerals with cash. Of course, if it were kids, they probably didn't know that. In Joey's office, two desk drawers were half open and papers strewn about. The safe was still locked and anyway it would only temporarily contain valuables, like dead people's jewelry, mostly costume, until the family claimed it. There was no attempt to pry it open or blow it. I told Joey not to touch anything; he needed to go ahead and call the locals to dust for fingerprints.

"If our stiff had a friend, I believe I know what he'd be

looking for," Joey said.

"What?"

"I'll show you later. But first, come take a look at the body."

I had searched every room, including the viewing rooms to see if an intruder was hiding out. We even popped open the caskets in the selection room. Only *the* room remained. *The* dreaded room of my psychological pain and childhood nightmares. The room where I last saw Mr. Cunningham, the old letch.

Joey pulled out one of the refrigerated body drawers, number ten. Fully expecting to see a corpse, I was surprised when he grabbed a bottle of Evian and tossed it to me.

"Would you like a snack? Let's see here … got some cheese, beef stick … how about a boiled egg?"

"You've got to be kidding. You made a refrigerator out of one of these drawers?"

"Yeah, why not? Embalming makes me hungry. Some people whistle while they work; I get the munchies."

"Sheesh! You're sick, man." I let that picture filter on through for a moment.

"So, is your John Doe in one of the drawers?"

"Number Six there."

"Anybody in any of the other condos?"

"Nope, he should be the only one."

"Should be?"

"Unless our intruder decided to take a nap." I smiled.

Joey had a pretty good sense of humor, but he was still not as funny as me. Or maybe as funny as I *used* to be before bullets and ex-wives scarred me for life and made me rather grumpy.

"Pull him out," I said, shoving the Glock into my pants at the butt crack. "Whoever broke in here is long gone, now."

Joe opened the fridge drawer. John Mohammed Doe was still there. He hadn't been stolen, but I could see the alarm in Joey's face.

"Obviously, our intruder was interested in our friend here. The sheet I covered him with is now down around his ankles."

"Maybe your perp is into necrophilia."

"No, that's *you*, remember?"

"Damn. You talked to Bobby Crawford." Joey just looked at me with a confused expression on his face.

The John Doe looked to be about twenty five, had light brown skin and a half dozen black moles on his face. The body was well-developed without an ounce of fat. He did look Middle Eastern and could have been from twenty different countries across the pond. And he looked very dead. Actually, angled. But you would expect that, being kissed by a big brown truck. The head was swollen and one eye was partially open and puffy. There were comminuted fractures of the humerus and tibias on both sides, and major torso bruising. I took out my Nikon and snapped several shots of his face.

For whatever reason, I started becoming intrigued. Obviously, the intruder or intruders could have been kids, breaking in on a dare. It was the same kind of challenge they may pose to one another like in spending a night in a haunted house. And that's what I told Joey.

He shook his head. "I think the intruder was likely another Arab, looking for something. And that *something*, big brother, is in the safe."

"Okay, I'll bite. What?"

I followed him back into the office and he went directly to the safe. "Eh, eh," I chided. "Fingerprints."

Joey reached into a box on his desk and pulled out a single latex glove. Snapping it on his right hand, he began fiddling with the combination. After some left and right spins, he pulled the lever and the door popped open. He pulled out a box which did contain some unclaimed jewelry, several envelopes, some photos and a pistol. He withdrew the photos and one of the envelopes.

"Here are several police photos taken at the scene. You may want to see these. Most of them are of Mohammed back there. He was killed instantly and dragged about twenty feet before the driver got stopped."

I looked them over.

"Okay. Nothing unusual here."

"Inside this envelope is what was found in his pocket. No one's seen this except for the medical examiner. As I said, there was no ID or green card on him. Just what you see here."

Inside of the envelope were a small pocket knife, a twenty and about two dollars in change, a green capsule and a small photo of a young woman in headdress, probably his wife or girlfriend. There was also a sheet of printer paper on which there were some words scribbled in Arabic and a hand-drawn map. I studied the paper for a few moments, then turned to Joey.

"My Arabic is a bit rusty, but one of the words here is *factory*. Whoever sketched this put a lot of detail in it. That line there is a road and has a 6-0 on it. Maybe Route 60. There are two gates indicated, seven, no eight buildings, and two circles which could represent storage tanks which have internationally recognized radioactive symbols by them. Well, I can see why you'd find this interesting. A map of a factory on a Middle Eastern man who by the way was found dead in Podunck, West Virginia, with no ID."

"My thoughts, exactly," Joey replied, looking pretty proud of his detective work. Then I believe I must have scowled.

Joey gave me a funny look when I held up the sheet of paper to his face. "If you recognized the importance of this map and had suspicions about this guy being some kind of terrorist, why didn't you take this immediately to the FBI or State Police?"

"I called *you*, didn't I? And the state cops didn't act much interested in the man. They took one look at him and thought he was a derelict. I knew that you being Bureau and all, you'd be the guy to look into this."

"I'm *not* the FBI anymore, Joey. I'm retired and doing contract work for the government, only."

"Which some day you're going to tell me *what* kind of work. Of course, I have it on good authority that you're some kind of terrorist hunter."

I gave him an irksome glare. "Don't concern yourself about that, little brother. I'm making a living and the government pays me what I'm worth, which isn't much on either account. You actually broke the law, you know. They call it *suppressing evidence*. Getting this information in the right hands on a timely basis could be the difference in whether a very real plot is choked off. Something could have already happened in the time it took for me to get over here."

"Well, apparently it didn't, or we would have heard about it."

I dropped the sketch map back in the envelope. "I need to get this to the Bureau as soon as possible. First, I'll call the Charleston office and see if I can meet with one of the agents this afternoon or tomorrow morning."

"So, should I go ahead and cook this guy?"

"No. How much longer can he stay in the fridge before he starts to … you know …?"

"He can go another two days; then, he starts to melt. We don't embalm those destined for the cooker. You should know that, or did you forget your Mortuary 101?"

"Probably. Look, Joey, you need to go ahead and report the break-in to the county or state. I'd say this is up the sheriff department's alley." He nodded and picked up the receiver at his desk.

I needed to call the boss, so I pulled my cell phone from its holster and hit 2 on speed dial.

"Hello," the familiar voice answered. "Is this Vulture?"

"Very funny. Where are you?"

"Home."

"In D.C.?"

"No. Home, like as in *boyhood*. West Virginia."

"What are you doing there?"

"So, what kind of bird are you today?" I answered his question with one of my own.

"Never mind. Where are you exactly?"

"I'm still wearing my locator chip. You should already have me pinpointed with that sophisticated satellite toy you've got."

I had almost convinced myself that during the psychoanalysis performed on me by CTT that first day of service when they put me under with sodium pentothal to check out any deviancies in my personality, they injected a chip in my forearm. A chip that is both a listening and a locator device. That's the only explanation I have for Birdman ringing my cell phone immediately after I get too engaged with a vixen over a couple of drinks in a bar or if I wander too far off his radar screen. And then every time I hear his voice on the other end, the lump under my skin becomes irritated.

"You taking a few vacation days?" he asked.

"You need to tell me these things, if you are. Give me your location."

"Should I send it in the clear?"

"You're not in a combat zone nor are you on assignment, Bruce." He paused.

"Ah, there you are. You went to a military school near there, didn't you?"

I was just kidding about the satellite toy. He really *did* have me located. Damn chip. And then I wondered how he remembered the military school.

"You're either psychic or have the memory of an elephant. But I suspect you're reading my file."

"It does make for interesting reading. Okay, enough small talk. What's going on there?"

"I'm looking at a dead Middle Eastern male in my brother's freezer drawer … you remember me mentioning Joey … has a bad habit of draining blood from people and sticking them in the ground …"

"Yes. Go on."

"Well, the Arab schmuck tried to make love to a delivery van going 30 miles an hour. Found on his person was a hand-drawn map of a factory which appears to be on the Kanawha River near Charleston. Looks like he or someone else sketched in great detail the interior of the factory, specifically highlighting buildings containing radioactive, possibly nuclear or chemical material. Also in his possession was a capsule. It's not for acid reflux or high cholesterol, either. I suspect it's cyanide."

"Hmmm."

"Is that a reply of interest?"

"I assume you'll be nosing around, then."

"I thought I was on vacation."

"Okay, then. Combine a couple of days with this. Yes, do some digging. I suspect a colony of roaches. Where there's one, you know there's a nest somewhere."

"So, do I put out bait or just pull out my can of Raid and start zapping?" Joey rolled his eyes at all my gobbledy-gook while he was waiting for a deputy to come on *his* line.

"Your mission," began the boss, "should you decide to accept it, would be to take out the colony if one does exist. But I need to know beyond any doubt there is good evidence. Of course, we would disavow any knowledge of your activity." For a stoned-faced, no-nonsense ex-CIA chief, he enigmatically loved to quote those lines.

"Got it, Preceptor. I do need a Bureau contact in the city. They have to know I'm here in case I misbehave and get taken for a Company man. You know all too well the two families don't get along. But I can show them my Junior G-Man barcode card and decoder ring, and I'm sure they'll let me keep my peashooter. Will have to avoid the locals, however."

"I'll make the call to Charleston for you."

"Thanks, Chief. Now warble me something soft and melodic." I heard the click, and he was gone.

"I stayed on the phone and continued a one-way conversation for Joey's benefit.

"This cell phone will self-destruct in five seconds. Phelps, out." Joey, who was still waiting on his line for somebody, anybody… had a pained expression on his face.

"That was the weirdest conversation I ever heard. Do they call you Phelps?"

"They do, Bro," I replied.

I remembered that Joey was probably too young or too disinterested to watch *Mission Impossible*. When that show was on, he was only into *Captain Kangaroo* and *Romper Room*.

"I take it you got the green light to stay and check out our Doe, huh? What are you going to do with the map?"

"Let the Bureau see it and then try to find out where the factory is. Maybe the map itself will provide clues as to what 'dead guy' was up to and if there are anymore out there like him."

"You think there are?"

I shrugged. "Maybe. By the way, when you do get hold of the locals, ask if anyone has seen any other Middle Eastern types around the area. That question would much better come from you than me going to them. An undertaker and assistant coroner would have reason to follow up. I can't afford to get into a dialogue with anybody."

"I don't understand why you have to be so mysterious around me as to what you do."

"Don't concern yourself with it, little brother."

He sighed in resignation about the time a deputy came on the line. Joey began filling him in on the break-in and then was told a car would be dispatched in about twenty minutes. After he hung up from the call he returned all the contents to the safe except the map and capsule, which I kept. I would have the powder inside the capsule tested.

"You *are* staying at the house, aren't you? Cora and the girls will expect that."

"I don't think so, Joey. I'll need to be in Charleston early in the morning, so I'll probably go on in and stay there tonight. Maybe tomorrow night I will. But my lodging gets paid for with my government credit card and as I'll be coming and going at a lot of strange hours, I don't want to disturb anyone. I'll likely get a motel between town and the interstate."

"Okay, but it won't be a bother."

I swept my eyes around the 'shop' and realized that I didn't miss the place one iota. Missed the old home place and countryside, though.

"By the way," I said, "are you planning to drag the girls into the business? You'd have to change the name to McGowan and Daughters, you know."

"I haven't decided yet. Molly has some interest, but Casey gets the willies, just like you used to do. She definitely wants no part of it."

"Smart girl."

"Not exactly. She's decided to be a gourmet chef. But what does *she* know; she's only sixteen."

"Well, I think that's a good thing. Maybe I'll be visiting *her* more than *you* if I don't one day find a wife who can cook."

"But I remember visiting you and Darlene a couple of times when you were in San Antonio and I thought she did okay on the meal."

"Ha! She thought *Cook*ing and *Bak*ing were cities in China." Joey laughed.

"Man, you could never hang on to a good thing. Speaking of good things, how's Caroline?"

"Super. She graduated from Columbia last year with honors and is now in Quantico."

"In the Marines?" he asked, grinning ear to ear. That was

Joey … once a jarhead, always a jarhead. Could it be his only niece was joining the Corps?

"No. Don't get excited. She's in the FBI Academy."

"Then I guess she'll soon be following in her old man's footsteps."

Not finding myself particularly elated about her being there for any reason, I replied, "I sure as hell hope not."

CHAPTER   3

Around five I set sail west on I-64 toward Charleston. Almost immediately after climbing a long five mile grade and reaching the apex of the mountain just east of Beckley, the temperature cooled a bit. It had actually turned into a pleasant afternoon; so I continued the two hour jaunt with my driver's side window down. On hot days, I have to admit, I'm a wuss. I run the air conditioning most of the time during the hot months, especially in D.C. where it can get into the mid-nineties with no breeze any given summer's day. The blacked-out windows also do much to keep the Suburban comfortable inside. But I love the mountain air … invigorating to the lungs and smells delightful. Every once in a while, there's a whiff of wood smoke or the sweet scent of lilac, tweaking the olfactory sense that much more. The state's stunning beauty is promulgated by showy rhododendrons, towering blue spruces, and majestic waterfalls that splash over huge black boulders alongside of twisting roads. I heard say that Bob Denver, you remember Gilligan, having moved to the Bluefield area, once told a reporter 'they ought to put a fence around the whole state and charge admission to get in here.'

After another hour on the WV Turnpike, and reluctantly paying that 'admission' at a toll plaza near Cabin Creek, Charleston loomed ahead. The area was much as I remembered: cracker box houses crammed together from the base of the mountains to the banks of the Kanawha. People had better be able to get along under such close conditions. The few who actually own little more than postage stamp front yards would be considered land barons around there.

Then there's the Kanawha. It begins way up stream at the Gauley, that treacherous tourist attraction with Class Five rapids, mellows out and runs gently through the locks at London and Marmet, snakes past the Capital City and its factories, and finally works its way to the Ohio.

Soon the familiar gold dome of the Capitol building, a somewhat smaller replica of the U.S. Capitol, came into view. It is clearly the most recognizable feature of the city. I jumped off at a Holiday Inn in Charleston, took a quick shower and put the old jeans back on. I did change into a nice pink polo, however, which by the way is not a threat to my masculinity. After sitting down for a light Italian dinner of ravioli, a side of spaghetti, salad and hunk of garlic bread, I sipped on a glass of Merlot on a neat little terrace over-looking the city. After that glass was gone, I ordered another, taking a good bit of time to do a little reminiscing.

I had visited Charleston a few times when I was a boy, mostly when my dad went there to pick up the body of some poor bastard from Greenbrier County, who had left home to find both his for- tune and a new family, only to be planted back in his hometown bone yard. I had remembered Charleston as being a rather dirty and old looking industrial town. Factories to the east and west along the Kanawha emitted a retching font of chemicals that stunk up the city air with that rotten egg smell, then passed over the river valley, finally settling into the surrounding hills. There was the seedy red light district called Fry's Alley, where scantily-clad whores sat in the windows of seamy bordellos, and Capitol Street, the only real shopping area around, both of which venues kept Charleston on the map. I didn't recognize the newly-rejuvenated Capitol Street with its tree-lined sidewalks, modern curbing and sprightly store fronts. Somewhere along the line, Charleston went from old and feculent to modern chic. Hip coffee houses, quaint epicurean-style restaurants and neato book stores had sprung up here and there, all within the past twenty years. It almost reminded me of a minute Greenwich Village. And although many of the factories and mills still remained, the air ultimately got cleaned up. Like in Pittsburgh. I guess the EPA had a lot to do with that.

The lights of Charleston were now on, which did not exactly give me the impression of a New York night life scene. But what did I expect in a small river city? I went back into the bar and had a cold draft. Sweat from my frosted glass formed and drained into a pool on the mahogany bar. The barkeep seeing this egregious violation of bar room protocol quickly plopped down a cardboard coaster and placed my glass on it, giving me a stern, silent lecture with his steely blues.

It was just me, a couple of businessmen talking about plastics over their scotch, and a lonely-looking redhead in a tight skirt stirring a fruity drink in a martini glass with a swizzle stick. Ten years ago, I might have hit on her with my "I think I can make you very happy" routine. I don't do that anymore. The last time I tried to be bar room suave I opened a dialogue with a very svelte vixen with this line: "Hi. I'm a photographer and I've been looking for a face like yours." Her reply was, "Hi. I'm a plastic surgeon and I've been looking for a face like *yours*."

My eyes left the redhead and returned to the TV screen behind the bar where Kramer was having an animated dialogue with Seinfeld and Elaine. The sound was down low or even off, which was a good thing. And I was damn glad there was no mediocre lounge singer with a guitar and stool singing overly done renditions of *Margueritaville* and *Brown Eyed Girl.* Please!

I returned to my five diamond room around eight, stripped to my tee shirt and boxers and sat down with a carafe of spring water at the desk. Retrieving Dead Arab Guy's (DAG for short) map from my valise, I unfolded it flat to study the drawing again. Why would a sketch-map be on DAG unless he and others were plotting to blow up the place and kill a lot of people? That factory could be one of five or six such plants that lay along the Kanawha. It had to be somewhere around Charleston as there was a river drawn, represented by wavy lines with a 'K' on it, and a road that tracked along beside it bearing a 6-0 (Route 60). I guessed that tomorrow I could drive by each plant to see if I'd recognize the buildings as they were positioned in the sketch. If DAG did have designs on some kind of terrorist act in the Kanawha Valley, why was he in Greenbrier County? Perhaps he and others thought they'd attract more attention staying in and around Charleston's factories. On the other hand, Middle-Eastern men would certainly be more visible in the state's rural areas, living among the farmers and shopkeepers versus a conglomeration of people. But I stopped thinking about it all for the evening as I had fallen victim to the devil wine that I had consumed earlier. I snapped off the desk lamp and lost consciousness on my pillow in no more than thirty seconds.

The seven-thirty sun poured its dollop rays rudely through the vertical slats on the window blind, painfully opening my eyes. While still working for the Bureau more than a year ago I would bounce out at five-thirty, drain the lizard, and run my five miles. Then I would shower, drown myself in a pot of java, and was at headquarters by seven with a breakfast bar in my hand. It helped having an apartment seven blocks from J. Edgar's place. Now-a-days in semi-retirement, I'm out of bed a little later, run less far, and go into the D.C. office probably three days a week. The breakfast bar is still part of my routine, but my stomach rarely allows me to go beyond a second cup of coffee. But the good thing is, my agenda is no longer structured. I'm no longer attacking each day with a tenacious sense of purpose. Mostly, I just make it up as I go along. Granted, I can be up any time of the day or night, canvassing, following, questioning, probing or exterminating, although the latter thing kind of ruins my day, not to mention the exterminee's day.

After I donned my light blue oxford and khaki slacks, I threw on my Navy blazer, looking rather G.Q. in the motel mirror. This is about as dressed up as I get. I haven't worn a suit since I used to be *known* as one of the 'suits.'

I arrived at the Charleston FBI Headquarters at 9:30. A lovely young thing greeted me with a sweet smile and asked me to wait. I had hoped Birdman had telephonically introduced me yesterday, which would prepare him for our meeting. In a couple of minutes Special Agent Jack Fuentes appeared in the reception area with his hand extended. I took it, finding the grip a little wimpy, not to mention clammy. It has always made me think that a guy like that was either a Nervous Nellie or perhaps had a glandular problem.

"I'm Jack, Mr. McGowan. Please come back to my office." Jack was a nice-looking chap of Hispanic descent, I later learned to be Cuban, but he was as stiff and uptight as they come. He motioned for me to sit down in the chair facing his desk and then he quickly retreated behind it to his leather wingback. I always hated the scenario. It made me feel like I was either in the principal's office or interviewing for a job. In *my* office, I had always made it a point to sit in the companion chair adjacent to my guest.

"Well, Mr. McGowan, I did get a call from your boss in New York. He told me you're retired Bureau *and* a West Virginian to boot."

Jack had gotten right to business, so I suspected he was not one who was comfortable with small talk. He neither asked me how my trip was or if I got lucky last night.

"Call me Bruce, Jack. Yes, I finished out my twenty. I was

twelve years with the Army before that."

"Special Forces, right?"

"You *did* talk to my boss. But … right."

"Where did you go to college?"

Did I say he was not comfortable with small talk? "WVU."

"No kidding. Same here. I graduated in '88. How about you?"

"Let's say we weren't in the same class." He chuckled.

I figured it was because he knew I had twenty years on him. Jack was a handsome dude with his black, thick hair and square jaw, but a little paunchy in a couple of places. A picture of his wife and two kids, boy and girl, was on his desk. She looked like a typical former high school cheerleader, blonde, beauty pageant smile with perfect white teeth. Even the kids were blonde, and the little girl, who looked to be seven, was in a miniature cheerleader getup. Perfect family. I'll bet he even had a white picket fence around his house in South Hills, a Honda Odyssey in the driveway and a Jack Russell that wears an Izod sweater in the winter. His daughter, he said, was into ballet and tap, and his son who was five was an All-American soccer player. There's some sarcasm in there, but maybe I was just jealous of this golden boy and his sublime, ideal life.

"Beautiful family, Jack."

He looked at his photo and beamed proudly.

"Thanks. My wife's name is Diane, and my children are Jessica and Jack, Jr."

It just suddenly hit me and I almost giggled out loud.

"So you kids are from the heartland and doin' the best that you can."

"I beg your pardon?" Jack said, looking very confused. I finally laughed.

"I'm sorry, Jack. It just made me think about *Jack and Diane*, you know, the song?"

"No," he searched his mind, rolling his eyes around

thoughtfully. "Can't say as I know that one."

"You're kidding, right?"

"*Jack and Diane* was a song?"

I just kind of stared at him with my own dumbfounded look, but then nodded. I finally changed the subject because right about then I was feeling very old.

"Well, I guess you know why I'm here." He nodded.

"I got the gist of it from your boss."

"He told you about the Arab John Doe and the map."

"He did. Do you have the map with you?"

I pulled it from my inside coat pocket and handed it to him across the desk. Before looking it over, his expression changed like he had just performed a social faux pas.

"Hey, Bruce, where's my hospitality? How about a cup of coffee or a pastry?" Obviously, this guy was not your father's Oldsmobile … er, FBI agent. He looked like some light-loafered accountant or stock broker at Smith Blarney with not one ounce of macho in his entire body. In my day we Special Agents were a cross between Robert Stack and Sean Connery.

"By the way, Jack, what is your degree in?"

"Accounting. Why do you ask?"

"Oh, no reason. Just small talk." *Damn, I'm good.*

Jack looked back down at the map on his desk. He studied it for more than three minutes. I thought he was going to diagram it like a sentence or dissect it like a frog.

"Hmm. I would agree that finding this on a deceased Arab gentleman would create a concern or even a suspicion of a potential terrorist threat." *Brilliant, Jack.*

I pulled out my digital camera and showed him the photos I took of the corpse. "This man died when?"

"About six days ago."

"Why is this information just now coming into our hands?" I definitely didn't want to give Joey up for his evidence suppression indiscretion.

"I think it may have been overlooked by the locals or just

not been given that much attention when first found. My brother got hold of it and called me. He's a mortician and has the body." I have this unique way of filtering my lies so that a little truth will squeeze out every once in a while.

Jack looked at me over the map as though he didn't quite believe me. And with good cause. But then he replied, "You know, that's just typical of local cops. Many don't have the nose or investigative insight that government cops do. Does your brother still have the body?"

"Yes. The mortuary is in Greenbrier County, McGowan and Sons."

"McGowan. Like you."

"Family Business."

"Interesting. Did you pick up anything significant about the body? Tattoos? Birthmarks?"

"No, not really. He has a bunch of facial moles. But he won't have them long. He will soon have a pauper's funeral and be put in the oven. The county M.E. has the stiff's prints and DNA sample for posterity purposes."

"Well, I'm glad *somebody* over there is on the ball. Your boss said you believe there could be a network of these people in Greenbrier County or here in Charleston. Do you have any evidence to support that?"

"No, none. But it only figures that if the dead guy had a map of a factory on him, he's not the Lone Ranger. In my experience, these guys work in packs, three or four together."

"That's right," added Jack.

"As you know, we have developed profiles on these types of elements. Their purpose is to assimilate into the American society and then find opportunities to wreak destruction. And even though their determinant is terrorism, paradoxically they're deeply entrenched in their Muslim faith. It is the most troubling of all paradoxes."

"That's all well and good, Amen and Hallelujah, Jack, but you failed to mention that they're ruthless cutthroats, have no value as to human life, kick their women around, and are programmed and committed to annihilating the infidels, namely us. Their mission is to demoralize Americaand bring down our economy, our government and civilization as we know it." Jack nodded.

"We know they're out there … trying to blend into the mainstream."

"Yeah. They integrate our society by pretending to be students and business people, all the while plotting to kill Americans in mass. What makes them dangerous and difficult to stop is that the bas- tards are willing to sacrifice their own lives. And all it takes is one suicidal son-of-a-bitch and one bomb to take out a building, stadium or marketplace. We're long overdue in this country, Jack, to experience the same type of activity we see in Israel or Lebanon."

"I see you're very passionate about this, Bruce."

I did realize I had stood on my soap box a little too long and was actually preaching to the choir. And, hell yes, I'm passionate about this. So, I thought this was a good time to inject a little levity into the conversation. Maybe then Jack would void the corncob he was sitting on.

"Hey, Jack. Listen to this. Two Islamic terrorists are chatting. One of them has his wallet out and is flipping through pictures. He says, 'Yeah, this is my oldest. He's a martyr. And here's my second son. He's a martyr, too.' Then there's a pause. The second terrorist says, wistfully, 'Ah, they blow up so fast, don't they?'"

Jack sat there with a slight frown between his eyes. No guffaw … not even a smile.

"Well, how about this one," I tried again. "Why don't Muslims celebrate Valentine's Day?" No response.

"Because camels couldn't care less."

Well, I laughed at my jokes, but there were no yuks from Jack. He just stared at me, eyes transfixed like he was looking into a kaleidoscope at complex patterns. Listening to what was coming out of my head, maybe he was.

"Yes, well that was entertaining, Bruce," he said. I took it that Jack had no sense of humor and was all business.

"Were you this frivolous when you were with the Bureau?"

Fair question, I guess. I think early on in my career I was quite a bit like Jack … professional, matter-of-fact, dignified, anal. But then I answered him.

"I suppose I've let my hair down in my old age, Jack. I think somewhere along the line I got tired of being a regimented stuff-shirt for twenty years."

I actually believe Jack took offense to that and felt maybe it was directed toward him.

"It *is* expected that at our level we must maintain a certain decorum."

He was beginning to bore me now. This thirty-four year old kid sounded like somebody sixty-four. Obviously, his training officer was from the days of J. Edgar and had instilled in the little bastard an unhealthy degree of self-purpose and demeanor. Nonetheless, I was determined to give him the respect of his position. When I occupied a similar office in Hooverland, I may have been put out with some 'frivolous' guy making light of *my* demeanor. But I still couldn't imagine I was as stiff as this kid.

"So, Bruce, what are your plans from here?"

"I'm going back to Greenbrier County and look around for any other Middle Eastern gentlemen who merits watching."

"And if you find any, then what?"

"If I see something that deserves my attention, I will provide it."

"And what does that usually entail?"

What's with the twenty questions?

"Surveillance, information gathering. You know, the usual sneaky-peek stuff."

"What will you do with the information you obtain?

You're not a federal cop anymore."

"Jack, I'm still in law enforcement working for the Department of State."

He eyed me with what I thought to be a look of contempt … or something like it.

"I'm pretty sure I know what you do, Bruce."

"Really? I'm glad *you* do, because half the time, I don't." He kept his third-degree eyes on me.

"Let me tell you what I know about the Counterterrorist Center. It has a collaborative alliance with the FBI, but responsible only to provide intelligence information about suspected or known terrorist groups for Bureau use. It does not 'dish out' justice; its purpose is to help the FBI to wield justice."

"Jack, I am *not* CTC. My organization operates independently from other intelligence groups. We are a smaller Special Ops organization with a specific purpose."

"Which is?"

"To take whatever measures are necessary against terrorists and other subversives to assure the protection of the American people. In other words, my friend, the predator becomes the prey."

"You know what I think, Bruce? I think you're some kind of government-directed renegade who will flirt with crossing the boundaries of the law whenever it suits you or your boss. And I further believe you would take somebody out, just on suspicion. You know, 'kill' em all; let God sort 'em out."

Wow! This guy is insightful. And that impresses me.

"No. That was my motto two jobs ago, Jack. You know, the Special Forces."

"Right." He kept his steely blues on me for a moment, then added, "I'll ask that you keep this office informed about any findings, Bruce."

"Okay, Jack. Right after my boss is apprised of whatever it is I find, you'll be the second to know."

"Can we trust you to not go off on tangents and killing

sprees, Bruce?"

"Cross my throat and hope to choke." He actually half smiled and I thought his face would crack open like a glazed donut.

"And before you leave, I need a copy of the map. We're going to work on this on our end."

"Fine. Now Jack, would you do something for me?"

"Okay. If I can."

"Do you have a secure fax line?"

"Of course."

"I want you to fax the Arabic message on the map to this number. The recipient, Mr. Abu Narziz, one of our operatives, will translate it and send it right back. I'll write a note to Abu so he'll know this is from me. Then, guess what? *You'll* be the first to receive that information."

I knew Birdman would call me right away with the translation, but I wanted to make good ol' Jack feel important in the matter. He would get the impression of willing cooperation on my part. And I *would* give him that, at least partially. I may at some point need his unwitting collaboration, not to mention backup.

"No problem. Anything else?"

"One other thing." I took the green capsule from the envelope.

"Can you have your lab check the contents of this? It may be some kind of cold capsule, but as there are no trade letters or markings on it, I suspect it's a cyanide capsule."

"That was found on the dead Arab?"

"Yes it was." Jack's eyes widened.

I don't know that he'd ever seen one. "If it is cyanide, then we'd know for sure that he planned never be taken alive and submit to interrogation. The average law-abiding Joe Citizen would have no use for one of these, would he?"

"No, Jack, he wouldn't."

Jack continued. "I may skip away tomorrow to take a look at the body. Will you be accessible?"

"Probably."

"When will you return to Washington?"

"I don't know. Maybe two or three days. It depends on what I find out nosing around. Anyway, I would go to New York to brief the boss. He always wants a face-to-face when it comes to things like this."

Jack pulled a business card from his desk and I reciprocated with one of mine. He looked it over. "It's pretty plain, Bruce. It has the Department of State Seal, your name and a web site. No title indicated, like Assassin or Terminator."

Well, the junior G-Man did have a sense of humor after all.

"Funny, Jack," I replied.

"You know … I think we're going to get along just fine. Beneath that tight-ass Jack Webb exterior, I actually think *you're* a bit 'frivolous.' Maybe in twenty years, you could even be me."

"Not likely," he replied.

This time the half smile was rather smug. "You've got my number, Bruce. Stay in touch. Oh, and see you tomorrow."

C H A P T E R   4

Hey it's good to be back home again.
Sometimes this old farm seems like a long lost friend. Hey
it's good to be back home again.
—John Denver

I caught a burger at the Cedar Top and started back toward Lewisburg. I do a lot of driving across America, but I find that few states broadcast the grandeur beauty of West Virginia. For nostalgic reasons, I decided to stay on Route 60 and go the way of the Gauley and Sewell. These are majestic mountains with hair-pin curves, some so sharp that the brake lights you see in front of you may in fact be your own. Occasionally, one catches a glimpse of the New River snaking through its chasm two thousand feet below and it is both frightening and humbling to think that allowing one wheel to drop off the pavement will send one tumbling through firs and hemlocks to the gorge below … and certain death. After descending eight to ten percent grades and negotiating challenging, seemingly impossible turns, the driver levels off into quaint little towns inhabited by sweet, unpretentious people. Then after the last wood frame house or store front is passed, the wayfarer starts yet another climb to do it all over again. The land, a perfect wilderness of rapturous rhododendrons and garish Virginia bluebell, is so wild and wondrous that once afforded a taste, it remains forever ingrained in the soul.

So why here, I thought? Why West Virginia, a state that should be far removed from terrorist interests? It's not Washington, New York or Los Angeles. But I also realized that one of the goals of terrorists is to demoralize a people by striking where least expected with the element of surprise. So then, why not a place known for its innocence and simplicity? To get to the throat of America, attacking the very heart of its people, the terrorists make their statement ... "we can attack you anywhere." An attack plan involving a Charleston factory was *very* plausible. I reminded myself that since the beginning of the Cold War, the area around the capital city had been known as the Chemical Center of the World. Depending on what kind of chemicals the plant manufactured, a bombing on any one of them could release a lot of nasty pollutants into the air. Some of the stuff would be deadly.

The ride back had made me even more determined to get to the bottom of why an unidentified Arab with a detailed hand-drawn map of a West Virginia factory in his possession lay dead in a Greenbrier County mortuary. That is, other than getting mashed by a big brown truck. If there were others out there, I would find them. I called Joey and told him I was on the way. He said he had to finish up on a teenage girl from Alderson who was killed in a car wreck just south of town. She had just gotten her license and had become the victim of inexperience and speed. She had misjudged a curve at over seventy miles an hour and T-boned the driver's side into a large oak. Joey was doing his best to wire her back together. As feverishly as he was working on her face, her casket would still likely have to be closed. It saddened me to hear that. I remember as a teenager looking down on the dead faces of two of my friends after they had failed to realize that youth was not invincible. There was nothing that pained my father any more than having to work on the body of a child. And I knew that my brother was feeling the same pain, especially considering he had two teenage girls of his own.

"You're coming for dinner tonight, aren't you big brother?"

"I wouldn't miss it, Joey. It's been weeks since I've had a good home cooked meal."

"Good. Go by the house anytime. I'll be there a little later. Dinner is usually at six."

Joey's wife, Cora, was a fine-looking woman at forty-five. About an inch taller than her husband who stood five-nine, she was a little humped over like many tall women are. I guess they think by lowering their stature, their partners will not look so conspicuously short beside them. But she had a pretty face with her high, chiseled cheek bones and full lips. Their two girls, Casey and Molly, sixteen and fourteen, were cute, but tall like their mother. And they were personable and talkative around adults, unlike most teenagers. As they were six and eight years behind Caroline, they had not gotten an opportunity to know her very well. Of course, the fact that Caroline had mostly lived with her mother in Maryland, distance made it even more difficult for the cousins to know one another. One of my biggest regrets.

Cora and I had a nice conversation in the kitchen to catch up while she was chopping up carrots and peppers on the carving board. She was a sweet gal with a marvelous personality and genuine smile. Her eyes were happy eyes, sparkling nearly as brilliantly as the diamonds on her earlobes. She and Joey were perfect for one another. Had been since the day they met more than twenty years ago. Their utopian little marriage had made me quite envious, not jealously so, but in a good way. Sometimes, though, seeing them go on with each other like they did summoned remorse within me for not trying harder in my own marriage.

Joey bounded in the back door after an hour or so, bellowing lively that he was home. I don't know how he did it … working every day with corpses and bereaved families seven days a week, then turning on the laughter and jocularity with his family when the day was over. But I knew Cora and the girls were his end-of-day catharsis. His sanity. And I did admire and respect him for hanging in there with the business.

We all sat down at the dinner table and about the time I picked up my butter knife, Casey put my left hand in hers and Molly picked up my right. "The blessing," Casey said.

As Joey was talking to God, I tried to remember the last time I said 'grace' or was in the presence of someone who did. More than anything, it made me not only realize my heathen status in this world, but that I never said a blessing over a meal with my own daughter. And then instead of listening to Joey pray, I thought about the probable terrorist lying in Joey's drawer and all the other jihad and al-Qaeda types who pray religiously … excuse the play on words … then go out and blow-up innocent Americans. This kind of hypocrisy I will never understand, and I have had tons of courses in Psychopathology, Criminology and yes, even Religion.

"… amen."

I didn't hear much of the sermonette, mainly because of my A.D.D, but it did make the vittles taste that much better.

"Joey says you're not going to stay with us, Bruce," began Cora. I chewed and swallowed the bite of roast beef before answering.

"I told Joey I'd stay tonight but will go to a motel tomorrow."

"Nonsense. We have plenty of room and you know you'd be more comfortable than in some stinky motel room."

"Thanks, Cora, I really would like to, but I need a kind of

base to work out of, to come and go without bothering the girls." I winked at them and smiled.

"The type of work I expect to do may require that I stay out part of the night or even all night. I'm used to it. Don't think I've had any decent circadian rhythm since before college."

"What kind of work do you do, Uncle Bruce?" asked Molly.

"Well, sweetie, I still work for the government. I locate and investigate people."
Casey was now interested.

"What kind of people?"
Joey shot me a glance and formed a half-smile, like "talk your way out of this one, Brucie."

I hate explaining things to children, especially *these* inquiring minds. I definitely wanted what I do to remain in the dark where they were concerned.

Joey bailed me out. "Your Uncle Bruce hates talking about work, girls. And he's been traveling for two or three days and tired. Now let him be. Look at the bags under his eyes."

All three women looked at my suitcases and didn't say anything else.

I nodded my thanks to Joey.

After dinner Joey and I stepped out onto the front porch. He lit a Swisher Sweet which I'm damn glad he finally went to after those nasty Marsh Wheelings. I propped a foot up on the railing and inhaled the cooling air. Joey was still thinking about his young wreck victim he was working on just before dinner.

"She was the same age as Casey, you know. The whole time I was working on her, I thought about the horror of seeing one of my girls lying there. It made me almost demand the keys to Casey's Honda."

"I'm with you, Joey. I think of Caroline every day there in Quantico. A hundred different things could go wrong. She could get hurt or even shot by accident in training. I can't even call her except on certain evenings. Trainees can only receive calls if there's an emergency. Hopefully, she'll call me tomorrow."

"Caroline will be fine, Bruce. She's in great physical condition and she's smart. She'll take care of herself and she'll make a good agent." I nodded, but didn't respond.

I was afraid the lump in my throat would give me away. Real men don't bawl like little girls. Joey changed the subject.

"Well, the deputies came out and gave the shop the once over. They did dust for prints, checked the door, looked at the Arab and said if I find out I'm missing anything to call them."

"In hindsight, maybe the State would have been more thorough. Maybe you should have called *them* instead."

"Maybe. But these guys thought it was just kids who broke in."

"What did they say about DAG losing his sheet?"

"Dag who?"

"Sorry. Dead Arab Guy."

"Good acronym. They thought it was still kids. The kids likely took a peek and left out screaming. Some guy was probably showing his girl what Arab equipment looked like."

Joey grinned; then it went away. "So, how will you find out if there are other people of his persuasion in the area?"

"I'll take DAG's picture and float it around the shops downtown, the post office and all motels in the area. Believe me, if there are others and they look like him, they'll be remembered by some- one."

"Yeah, but you know that people don't often recognize ethnic differences. They may see a darker-skinned Mexican or Italian and think he's the kind of guy you're looking for. And there are scores of Indians, you know, from India, around here running Seven-Elevens, Dairy Queens and motels." I nodded in agreement.

"After Pearl Harbor, not only Japanese Americans were rounded up, but Chinese, Koreans and Siamese were as well. Let's face it, Joey; we all tend to profile when a person doesn't look like you and me."

"Well, I don't envy your task. Good luck." He paused for a drag. "By the way, what motel are you going to stay in?"

"I haven't decided. I was thinking about the General Lewis or the Best Western."

"Not the Greenbrier?"

"Yeah, right. I'm lucky my expense account allows me to stay at a Motel 6."

"Why don't you stay at Wolf Laurel?"

"What's that?"

"It's a Bed and Breakfast. I don't think the cost is extravagant, although the accommodations are."

"I can't say that I remember such a place around here."

"Actually it was the old Wolf estate. I don't think it became a B & B until the early '70s when the owner died. He left the house to his son, Mason, who turned it into a country inn of sorts. And do you remember Adrianna Randolph? She now owns the place. She was three or four years in school behind me. Ended up marrying Mason. Then Mason died a couple of years ago of an aorta dissection at forty-eight. Was as healthy as anyone I've seen his age and he just dropped over one day. No warning."

Bummer. Yeah, I remember her. Pretty little girl. Pretty name. I'll never forget when I went off to WVU, she was about ten. I used to kid around with her and do some innocent flirting. I cut her dad's grass for an entire summer when Mr. Randolph got hurt in a saw mill accident. Then one day we were coming out of church, the day before I left for Morgantown, and she said out of the blue, "Skip McGowan, I'm going marry you one day." I thought that was really cute.

I winked at her and said, "Okay, I'll wait for you to turn eighteen. Can *you* wait that long?"

"You know, I haven't seen her since. That must have been more than thirty years I reckon. So what's she look like now?"

"Forget it, Brewster. She weighs over two hundred pounds, got bleach blonde hair and a huge mole or wart on her upper lip."

"Cute little Adrianna?"

"Cute people can grow up and become beasts, Bro."

"Well, whatever. Maybe I'll go by there to see if a room is available. That is, if I can get Birdman to pay for it."

"Birdman? Who's that?"

"You know, the guy I spoke with on the phone."

"Oh." Joey was still puzzled by all the bird references.

Our old house was a handsome looking place with its white frame and bronze cedar-shake roof. It was built in the early Twentieth Century by our granddad when he was a young man fresh back from WW I, the war to end all wars. Joey had done a lot of work on the house, like replacing all the distorted windows, adding R13 insulation throughout and overhauling the decrepit wiring system. There was a fair amount of acreage around the old home place. Some of it was being farmed by Homer Ridgeway just down the road and the rest of it was being mowed continuously by a herd of Joey's Billy goats.

I remember going there on weekends as a child with my parents, listening to Dad and Pops talk funeral business. It wasn't enough that they talked it all day at the shop, but they brought it home with them. Mom and Grandy, as we called her, just sat in the kitchen snapping green beans or husking corn, saying very little to one another, but hanging on every word the men had to say in the parlor. Sometimes there was stuff talked about that pricked their ears, like what they found on the decedents or what the dearly departed were doing when they kicked off. Like old man Cunningham, for example. When it came to men talk, Mom and Grandy were sure to keep the door between the kitchen and parlor open.

I remember a movie that came out way back when called *The Loved One*. It was based on a book by Evelyn Waugh and was a kind of satire about the funeral business. Jonathan Winters played the part of twin brothers. One mortician owned a very respectable business while the other, a kind of black sheep brother, ran a pet mortuary. My dad, who took us to see it, mostly for curiosity reasons, was incensed about the movie. He said the mortuary service was one of dignity and shouldn't be parodied and degraded by cartoonish comedians. Dad was serious about the business. But I guess death *is* pretty serious business. I don't remember much about the movie, but I did like looking at Anjanette Comer. Can't believe I actually conjured up her name. She must have made a hell of an impression on a kid like me slammed almost overnight into puberty.

Well, back to the old house, Joey and I would be camped out in front of the black and white Zenith watching Paladin and Gunsmoke if it were a Saturday night and the Ed Sullivan Show on Sundays. Joey was just a tot and didn't pick up much of the dialogue, but still sat in a trance just like his older brother, never taking his eyes off the snowy picture, even when grabbing a handful of popcorn from our bowl. He just groped and dug until he got enough to shove into his mouth to make himself look like a chipmunk.

And now back to the present, I followed Casey up to my old room which was now hers. She had insisted that I sleep in her bed, which actually was *my* old bed, so that she could rough it on the couch in the den and watch old movies on AMC until the wee morning hours. Joey and Cora were good with that if it was weekend or non-school night. Casey ignored my protests and began putting together her pillow and comforter to set up camp downstairs.

"Goodnight, Uncle Bruce. If you need a nightlight, there's one on the wall by the bathroom," she giggled.

"I'm a big boy now, Casey. I haven't needed a light on since … well, since maybe a couple of years ago. And I don't wet the bed, either."

Now she was laughing. "That would be a *good* thing. Then I guess you don't want me to tuck you in or read you a story."

"Only if you want to."

"What will it be … *Goldilocks* or *When Harry Did Sally*?"

"Get out of here, little miss, before I report you to your dad."

Casey was a McGowan, all right, with her zealous frivolity and lusty sense of humor. She grabbed an armful of comforter, formed her lips into a kiss and said, "Love, ya, Uncle Bruce. Sleep tight."

After she closed the door, I was thrown back to ten years ago and my own beautiful daughter. Although Caroline was always more serious than Casey when she was her age, there was still that same sweetness and winsome spirit that delighted me every moment I was with her. I shed my clothes, brushed, plopped onto my old bed and turned the switch on the bedside lamp. As the pale light of the half-moon cast ghostly shadows of monster-like creatures on the wall, actually made by a gnarly oak outside the window, I realized a smile had broken out. I was twelve when Pops died and Dad moved us in here with Grandy. I saw similar figures on the same walls then and although I would never admit being afraid at that age to my parents or little brother, I refused to take my eyes off those abominable shadows until my heavy lids finally closed.

Lying in my old bed, I felt like John Boy Walton, returning once again to the home of his youth and to the remnants of his loving family. The house creaked and popped much as it did forty plus years ago as though it were saying to me, 'welcome home,' kid. I missed you. Goodnight, Joey Boy.

CHAPTER 5

I did need a place to stow away and remain inconspicuous. I also needed a plan, although it probably would amount to a lot of gum- shoe work. Out of curiosity, I thought I would at least drive by Wolf Laurel and check it out. Thought it would also be good to see an old face which was very much a young one the last time I saw it. I drove back across town, following Joey's directions, until I came to Seven Bridges Road (obviously renamed from something else after the group, the Eagles, made it famous) where I turned and took the second gravel driveway on the left. It was a charming house with more grace than grandeur, white with stylish lattice and millwork, cedar shake roofing, and a looming turret on the right side within what appeared to be a pentagonal room. The B&B was set down off the road about fifty yards and nestled under several large oaks and sycamores. Pink mountain laurel and feathered ferns graced either side of the wide veranda and lavender clematis climbed and intertwined along the banister.

I dropped down from the Suburban, tweeped my security system with the remote, and slung over my shoulder my tote which contained a toiletry bag, my Glock and other such essentials ... just in case I decided to stay. Over the door was a historical marker bearing the B&B's original name and birth date: *The John Mason Wolf House, Circa 1869*. And on the right side of the door, a shiny brass marker read *Wolf Laurel, 1939*. A guy could enjoy such a place for a few days, I thought. But again, I may be coming and going a lot, and maybe I would be best suited to stay in some flea bag, considering what the place was going to cost. I doubted the Birdman would spring for this.

When I stepped up onto the veranda, a large Abyssinian came to greet me and began rubbing its tail on my pant leg. Cats generally avoid me, like I carry the scent of dog on me or something, but this one was obviously not going to be afraid of anyone or anything, weighing close to twenty five pounds. I reached down to pet the varmint which made it all the more amorous.

I opened the screen door that creaked and sang like one would expect and made my way to a high, rustic desk in the small lobby. My new friend zipped through the door with me. A dining room that would seat about eight people lay off to the left that also adjoined a small kitchen. Beyond the dining room was the hallway that appeared to have five guest rooms, three on the right, one immediately on the left and one at the end of the hall across from the last room. The place gave off a scent of cedar from the wood flooring which lay throughout, roughhewn but glossy smooth.

I dinged the bell which immediately brought out a very lovely thirty or early forties-something angel with silken, light brown hair pulled back behind two perfectly-shaped ears adorned with dangling diamond earrings, gorgeous eyes and a lovely smile emanating from somewhat full, pouty lips. She had on a sleeveless blouse with the name *Wolf Laurel* embroidered over the left of two very nicely-shaped breasts. Other than that, I didn't notice much about her. Whatever the cost, I thought, I would definitely be staying. But then I glanced at her left hand and, sadly, she was wearing a simple wedding band.

"Hi," I said in the sexiest Tom Selleck voice I could cough up. "Do you have a room for the weekend and maybe a couple of days longer?"

"I didn't until about a half hour ago," she replied in the same soft, sultry voice I would have expected. "We had a cancellation. Looks like you're in luck."

"I would definitely say that I am," I replied, then looked at her finger again. Maybe it was just a costume ring with some kind of stone that got turned around.

"I see you met Burt." She eyed the fur ball as he disappeared into the office behind the desk.

"Sure did. Friendly cuss."

"He's that way with everyone ... even with people who don't like cats. But they eventually come around and end up petting him."

Okay. Enough about Garfield. "Say, I used to know your proprietress several years ago. Would you know if Adrianna Randolph is around? I think she may have the last name Wolf, like the inn."

"Well, who might you be, just so she'll know who's asking?"

"Bruce. Bruce McGowan."

Cutie Pie looked at me a moment like she was undressing me with her eyes, and then stepped around the counter to my side. For the first time I got a glimpse of her legs under that clinging skirt. They fit the rest of her very well. Suddenly, she threw her arms around my neck and pulled me into the firm bulges on her upper torso. Somewhere in my sex-starved brain, which incidentally was enjoying every sweet second of the hug, I realized she must be Adrianna.

"Well, hello." That's all I could say.

She backed up at arm's length and held my hands in hers. "*I'm* Adrianna, Skip. God, you look good. I knew there was something familiar about those eyes. There may be a bit of snow on the rooftop, but I swear you're much the same."

There's also still fire in my furnace, sweetheart. Of course, you have no way of knowing that. At least, not yet.

"So you're Adrianna. The last time I saw you I think you were ten. You were a doll." I paused for dramatic effect. "Of course, I see you *still* are."

She flushed a little. Her blue eyes glistened from the tears of nostalgia that had formed. But the eyes were dazzling, moist or not. "You're sweet to say that. And you … you're as good looking as ever."
Now my turn to blush.

"My brother, Joey, told me you ran this place. He described you, but fell way short of doing you justice."
Remind me to kill the little rat for yet another of his practical jokes.
"Joe, yes. I've always liked him. A good-looking guy, as well, but certainly not as handsome as you." I nodded in agreement.

"I remember last seeing you the day I went away to the university. Do you remember what you said to me?"

"Mmmm, no," she replied.

"Can't say that I do."

"That one day you were going to marry me."

She flushed again. Her lovely smile revealed a full set of white perfect teeth. I was glad to see she had all her teeth. One never knows in this good ol' state.

"I said that?"

"Uh huh."

"Oh, now I'm embarrassed. I did have quite a crush on you, but I guess it didn't take me long to get over it. I remember liking a boy in my fifth grade class. Liked him enough to end up marrying him. Mason Wolf."

"I've been pretty forgettable to a lot of women in my life. Why should you have been any different?"

She laughed and flicked an errant strand of hair back from her brow. I had only been talking to her for five minutes and already I regretted not coming back from college to marry her. Of course, I would have been twenty-two and she, *fourteen.* I didn't spend four years at WVU to come back and spend eight in jail.

"So you're staying here for a couple of days?"

"Maybe longer, now," I answered.

She knew what I meant. "Tell you what," she said. "We don't do dinner here at the inn, but if you'd like to join me at Tavern 1785 around seven, that would make my evening. I'd like to catch up on the last thirty-some years."

"Sounds great," I replied with the giddiness of a five year old. I didn't want to appear too anxious, so I forewent the cartwheels.

"Then seven it is," she said. "I have someone who stays at the office some evenings from six-thirty until ten or whenever I come back in from one of my usual exciting nights out." She rolled her eyes. "We can leave together from here after that, if you want."

"Okay. Looking forward to it."

I signed her book, went over the financial arrangements and took my key from her sweet little hand. I was staying in the Pine Room.

I still had about four hours to kill, so I dropped in on the State Police detachment outside Lewisburg. Mostly, I do not establish relationships with state and local police. First, they generally don't know what to make of me, and then, since I'm a card-carrying member of a terrorist exterminating organization, packing heat, they don't know whether to assist me in my investigations or investigate *me*.

The sergeant behind the desk looked to be six-seven and two-forty, sporting a Marine high-and-tight burr cut and a face like Herman Munster. This was a guy I wanted beside me the next time a bunch of thugs want to put holes in me. I could use him for a shield because slugs would bounce off this body like BBs.

"Can I help you, sir?" asked Herman.

"Yes, Sergeant. My name is Bruce McGowan and I work for an organization in the Department of State." I gave him my business card.

After studying my card like he was cramming for an

exam, he said, "I see the State Department seal, but it doesn't give the name of your organization. What do you do for them?"

Here we go again. I'm in the extermination business, Herman. Nevertheless, I got out my ID to supplement the card and showed it to him. "I am part of a team that looks for foreign and domestic subversives." I put my finger to my lips.

"So that would be some kind of counterterrorist organization. Is there something going on around here that involves terrorism?"

Did I mention the word *terrorist?*

"I'm just following up a lead, Sergeant …" I looked at his metal nameplate. "… Storm." Well that sure as hell fits. "My brother owns McGowan Funeral Home and is also the assistant county coroner. He has an Arab John Doe on ice that got hit by a UPS truck about a week ago."

"Yeah, I heard about that. Down on Washington Street, it was. And you think he was a terrorist?"

"I have no idea what he is, Sergeant. I'm just checking him out. I do know he had no identification."

"Do you investigate every Arab that ends up on a slab without an I.D?"

Obviously, Herman attended the same redneck school my brother went to.

"Naw. I'm actually taking a few days of vacation and just passing time. Anyway, do you have an investigator in the detachment I can speak with?"

"Lieutenant Harlan Williams is our uniformed detective. Right now he's at the Greenbrier Woman's Club giving a presentation about personal safety."

"Would you ask him to give me a call on my cell when he returns? I'll write my number on the card."

"Will do, Mr. McGowan." He eyed me like he still wasn't sure about me. I guess I have one of those faces. But nothing like his; that's for sure.

I got back to my room about five and settled in with a

brewski from the Seven-Eleven. I had eyed the store clerk behind the counter with my ethnic-profiling baby blues. I told myself I was probably no different from every other white-bread, white man when it came to people of the Middle Eastern persuasion. Not that *I* thought they all looked alike.

The mattress on my bed was about ten feet high and required that I step on a stool at the bed rail to thrust myself up. I stretched out my hands behind my head and blinked a few times, realizing I still had a couple of hours before my date with cutie-pie Adrianna. With a frilly canopy overhead, tasteful Federal blue and white wallpaper, and an ancient drawer chest situated by a window with sixty-year-old distorted glass, the room boasted an elegance that was far too spiffy for the likes of me. Of course, at $155 per night, I felt I had every right to enjoy it. Birdman was going to drop a load when he reviewed the bill. Next time he would insist I stay in a place where they left the light on for me. And that would be a good thing seeing as how I'm still afraid of the dark.

I decided I would close my heavy lids for just a few minutes. Immediately the sweet face and petite body of Adrianna Wolf appeared like an angelic vision in my tired brain. Just a couple of winks and I would feel like a new man. But then similar to experiencing an electric shock, I jumped when my cell phone went off. I snatched it up, pushed *send* and a man on the other end identified himself as Lieutenant Harlan Williams, West Virginia State Police.

"Mr. McGowan, Sergeant Storm filled me in about you. Says you're investigating the Arab man over in your brother's mortuary. I'm actually the officer who happened to be on the scene when the guy got hit. We found no ID on him, and we still don't know where he's from or what he was doing around here. Are you investigating this man for the Feds?"

"For my organization, yes."

"I wasn't able to tell from your card what area of the government you work in."

"Personnel management," I replied with a dead-pan expression in my voice.

"I'll bet. Find 'em and fire 'em, huh?"

I prefer the word 'terminate', Lieutenant.

"Let's just leave it that I do State Department investigations."

"Locating possible terrorists, right?"

"Possible subversives, Lieutenant." I then changed the tenor of the conversation. "Did you know about the map he had on him?"

"Yeah, I saw it. It didn't make much sense and unsure it actually meant anything. It remained in the possession of the coroner along with other personal effects."

I sat up, now that my eyes were fully open. "Did you not think the situation warranted calling in the FBI?" I asked.

His hesitation to immediately respond fully reflected a defensiveness. I think he took issue with my tone of voice and insinuation of incompetence. I really didn't intend to suggest that; it was probably because he woke me up from my late-summer's nap.

"There just didn't seem to be enough substance to the sketch from my perspective to merit any federal investigation. But anyway, I did call someone I've known for a long time at FBI Headquarters in D.C."

"Who do you know up there?"

"A guy named Bob Tucker."

"Tuck. I know him well. We worked together on a terrorist case back in '99."

"You were FBI?"

"Twenty years."

"So that's what this is about. You think the Arab man was a terrorist?"

"We actually refer to them as extremists until we get to know them. You know, innocent until proven guilty."

"Okay then, suspected terrorists."

"Unfortunately, they're confirmed as terrorists when they blow people up. And it's my job to see they don't get to that phase of the plan." Since I had guessed this guy had now figured me out, I went along with his *terrorist hunter* theory about me.

"I take it that's when you blow *them* up. That's your real bag, isn't it?"

That's pretty perceptive, Detective. "Someday I'll tell you in person."

"So be it. Why don't you come by my headquarters in an hour or so? We can talk more about it."

"Actually, that would be a little tight. I have a date this evening."

"You've been in the area one day and you already have a date?"

"I work quickly."

"You must. Well, how about tomorrow?"

"Tomorrow it is."

"Have a good time this evening."

Well, it appeared his nose was back in joint and he was now wishing me good hunting. "Oh, but I intend to."

I hadn't accomplished much so far, so tomorrow I would devote my entire day to rubbing elbows with the town folk. First thing, the post office, then a couple of the motels, a counter lunch at Kaufmann's Drugs, some gas stations, and downtown shops. No need to look for Arabs in the bars or fast-food places. Most Muslims are committed to a wholesome lifestyle and avoiding putting impurities in their bodies, which is criminal in itself.

It was getting late, so I would now be taking a chance catching the twenty winks. I may not wake up till four in the morning. I showered, shaved, primped and stared back at the handsome dude in the mirror. Adrianna was right; there *was* a good bit of salt in the pepper. Maybe tomorrow I'd rub in some Grecian Formula. Naw. Adrianna seemed to like the gray. Distinguished looking on men, you know.

After splashing on some Bvlgari, the cologne that is said makes a woman's nipples stand up like Vienna Sausages, I put on another Oxford. This time tan. I avoided the pink, because I was taking no chances in projecting my sexuality. The tan shirt with the dark green slacks creates that military macho look. Maybe on a future date, I'd show her my soft, more sensitive side and wear the pink Ralph Lauren.

At seven I slipped on my blazer and gave my tongue a shot of Binaca. At two minutes after, I heard the light rap on my door, wondering who that could be. I opened the door, finding a most stunning specimen of womanhood. She had on a tight black skirt with a slit up both sides, a white silk blouse cut to the cleavage and medium heeled pumps beneath tanned, hoseless legs that looked as though they belonged to a thirty-year-old, although I knew she should probably be about forty-five or six. And she was also wearing that glamorous smile.

"Ready?"

"Oh, yeah."

"Let's go. I'll drive," I said.

I opened the passenger side door and watched with great delight as Adrianna climbed onto the seat.

"Thank you," she said. "Handsome and a gentleman to boot."

I can't remember anyone ever calling me that ... a gentleman, that is.

Although she didn't need me to, I helped engage the seatbelt, mostly because I wanted my hand to sweep over that tight waist of hers. *And* because I'm a gentleman.

When I pulled out onto Seven Bridges, my curiosity got the best of me, so I had to ask. "I assume there are seven bridges down this road, ergo the name.

"Yes, that's right."

"So, what body of water do they cross?"

"None."

"You've got seven bridges and no water?"

"That's right." I could see from the glint in her eyes she was playing with me.

"Okay," she confessed.

"My friends Ted and Scarlett Bridges live at the end of the road with their five children. Ted was instrumental in getting our road paved a few years ago, so the folks who live along here thought it would be fun to rename Magnolia Lane to Seven Bridges Road. Neat, huh?"

"Yeah, neat," I echoed, giving her a squint like that was all made up.

"Really. I'm telling you the truth," she grinned. "Would you like me to introduce you to them?"

I chuckled. "No, that's not necessary. I believe you."
Then like a blooming idiot, I started whistling the Eagles' song.
And that made her laugh.

CHAPTER 6

We sat on the terrace at Tavern 1785 with a backdrop of late summer red roses weaving in and out of a trellis not three feet from our table. Twilight was suddenly upon us as the sun finally gave up on our day. We didn't order right away as neither of us seemed to be very hungry. I was sipping on my second glass of Merlot while Adrianna's marguerita glass was only half full. Or is that half empty?

There was a lot of small talk and then I asked her what she had been doing all these years. Her story didn't take long. She went off to college at Mary Baldwin in Staunton, married Mason Wolf after a long courtship and then they took over his family's business, Wolf Laurel, greeting guests for the next twenty-two years. The name 'Mason' had been handed down through several generations.

"We just lived a perfect life all that time," she said. "We loved one another, made a pretty good living and kept a piece of Greenbrier history going. And then he died." She dabbed a tear from her cheek. "It was a heart issue and it was quick. I closed Wolf Laurel for six months and went to Paris to live with my cousin, Yvette. She taught English at a girl's school during the day and French to me in the evenings. Paris was … c'est magnifique.

"These last two years have been tough for me, but I've had lots of encouragement from my parents and friends. And some really nice people have come to stay at the inn. I happen to be sitting with one of them right now." She smiled and patted my hand. I may never wash it again.

"I'm sorry about your husband and am sure he was a great guy." That sounded kind of lame, but I'm really not good at these tender moments.

"I see you still wear your wedding ring."

"Yes." She turned it around on her finger a few times with her thumb, looking down at it with reflective eyes.

"Okay, your turn. What have I missed all these years in the life of the man I was going to marry?"

"Well, as you know, I finished out at WVU with a major in Criminal Justice, and then there was that nasty little war called Vietnam. I got my diploma one day and draft notice the next. I ultimately went to Officer Candidate School, got a commission and joined the Special Forces."

"The Green Berets?"

"Yep. 'Fighting Soldiers from the Sky' and all that. I did my tour in Southeast Asia as an advisor to a Vietnamese Ranger battalion, came back and spent the remainder of my Army days in the exotic lands of Benning, Bragg and Belvoir."

"I don't think I've ever heard of those places."

"I'm just being silly. They aren't lands, they're penal colonies." She looked confused. Most people are around me.

"I did have a nice tour in Germany for a couple of years. I got out after twelve to marry the lovely Darlene Eubanks who said she would not go down the aisle as an Army wife. So, I applied and was accepted into the FBI, chased bad guys, lived in places like Beirut, Nairobi and Detroit. Darlene didn't like the Bureau either and so I gave up on her. I got the feeling that it wasn't just me; she didn't like our government, either. No way I could stay married to a commie."

"I'm sure she wasn't a communist." She grinned. "And

are you still with the FBI?"

"I retired nearly two years ago."

"Are you doing anything now?"

"I'm traveling a bit here and there at government expense."

"Yeah? Doing what?"

Well, I guess I needed to sugar-coat this a bit. "I still work in law enforcement for the Department of State. I mostly do investigations, looking for immigration threats and subversives. Saving the world. Things like that."

Her eyes twinkled with amusement. "Interesting, Mr. Bond. How do you like your martinis? Shaken or stirred." I laughed. Pretty. Smart. *And* a sense of humor.

Well that does it. I'm looking for a Justice of the Peace tomorrow.

"It's not like that. I'm not a spy; nor is our New York department's assistant's name Moneypenny ... although she thinks she is. I'm just dispatched by a special arm of the government to check out people with suspicious behaviors and may have designs on harming Americans."

"You're saying you hunt down suspected terrorists." *Very* smart.

"Just illegals, that's all," I lied. "Actually, I think I've said a little too much. But you're very perceptive, not to mention inquisitive. Are you sure you weren't a government interrogator at one time, using the B&B proprietress as a cover?" She giggled.

"You're a card, Skip. Are you on some kind of mission here or just taking some time off? I would have thought you'd be staying with Joey and his family."

"Well, I guess I can tell you this; I will begin asking around tomorrow if anyone has seen any Middle Eastern-looking men in the area."

"Why Middle Eastern? Is there someone specific you're looking for?"

"Not sure." I began telling her about the Arab stiff in

Joey's filing cabinet who was probably an illegal alien and that there may be others. I didn't want to alarm her about the sketch map of the factory, so I was selective about the information. Anyway, that was not for public knowledge. "I can start with you. Have *you* seen anyone around that looks Middle Eastern?"

"Well, there's Sayed at the Dunkin Donuts."

I shook my head. "Donut shop? No. The cops would be all over that. Anyway, Sayed would probably be Pakistani or Indian. Slight difference in looks and color tone."

She smiled, then took on a contemplative expression. "There *are* two guys staying at Wolf Laurel that are definitely Middle Eastern, but I don't know anything about them. They just come and go and mind their own business, never saying anything. I think one must have left, though. I haven't seen him in about a week."

"What do they look like?"

"The one who I haven't seen lately is about five-nine, black hair of course and has a bunch of dark moles on his face."

That would be DAG. No wonder she hadn't seen him in a week.

He had been hiding in a drawer at Joey's place. "How about the guy who's still there?"

"He also has black hair, a little receding in places, light brown skin, clean cut and rather nice looking. He's probably twenty-five. I would say he's from the Gulf area … Iran or Iraq. Maybe Saudi Arabia."

Adrianna did seem to know her geography.

"What's his name?"

"I'd have to look it up."

"When did they check in?"

"Oh, about three weeks ago. It is a little strange. Most people don't stay more than two or three days. A week tops. The man staying there now did say he was a student at the community college. I know they started up Phase II of summer classes a couple of weeks ago. I'm not sure why they would be going to a little old community college here unless they were actually from around here."

"Are you sure you're not at least a private eye? You're mighty insightful."

"I guess in running an inn all these years, I've learned a lot about people and it has probably made me kind of nosy."

"Did it seem strange to you that students would be paying the kind of money to stay at Wolf Laurel just to go to a community college for a few weeks?"

"A little, but they'd still be paying $70 to $80 at other places."

"But a Super 8 or something similar would be half that and they could probably get a weekly or monthly rate."

"I guess they split the cost of the room and that would make it turn out the same. And I did agree to give them a break if they stayed a week."

"How much of a break?"

"$120 a day."

"And you're soaking me for $155?"

Adrianna smiled and winked. "I could cut you a deal if you stay longer."

"Sounds like a form of blackmail."

"Exactly."

I took another swig of the Merlot. "How long did they tell you they'd be staying?"

"Actually, I only talked to the one guy … the guy who's still there. He said they'd probably stay through the end of September, but would like to stay week to week. He pays at the beginning of each week in cash."

"That's still over $800 a week. By the end of September that will amount to about $6500. Pretty expensive board for a two-month session at a community college."

"Yes, it is, now that you mention it."

I scooted out my chair. "Can you excuse me a moment? I'll be right back."

She fully expected me to hit the pisseria and appeared surprised when I went out to the street to my SUV. Retrieving my digital camera, I returned to the table.

"Take a look at this." I said, pushing the *ON* button and accessing my photo gallery. I showed her a couple of pictures of DAG. "Could this be the man who left a week ago?"

"I think so. It's hard to tell. He doesn't look too well. Like he got beat up."

"What he got was *dead*."

"Ew, yuck. What happened?"

"He tried to kiss a moving UPS truck. It happened about three blocks from here."

"I remember that. He stepped off the street and got hit."

"I think the word is *creamed*."

She studied the photos a little closer. "I'm pretty sure that's him, but it's hard to tell with his eyes closed. At least one of them."

"Well don't look for him back."

Then it came to me that I may no longer have needed to canvass the county tomorrow as planned. It was either coincidence or sheer dumb luck that I was staying at the very place that DAG and the other Arab cohort were bunking. *And* at a B&B owned by an old girlfriend. Of course, I didn't know ten-year-old Adrianna was my girlfriend at the time and that we were in love.

I realized I had shared more information with Adrianna about me and this mission, should I choose to accept it, than I had intended. That wasn't like me. But somehow I knew in my heart I could trust her to keep anything we discussed to herself. I really didn't want to use her as a pawn in my investigation, but she was going to be involved just by virtue of her proprietorship of the inn.

After I talked to the Birdman tomorrow, she may find herself unofficially partnered with me as I undertake the investigation of her Arab boarder. I was determined to find out whether a very real terrorist plot was being hatched right under her roof.

I thought it was time to change the subject, so I asked her about her friends.

"Well, I have a few close girl friends in my book club and a very special older friend in the Lewisburg Historical Society. Involvement in civic things keeps me sane, you know. Oh, I enjoy many of the people who come to stay at Wolf Laurel. It's interesting to learn where they're from, what they do, what they love and sometimes what they're running away from. But being the hostess of a B&B gets old and mundane seven days a week and I have to get away for a few hours to be with my buddies. Mostly, engaging in community projects. Good therapy for me."

I nodded, thinking at the same time that I needed some kind of therapy. Maybe she could help me with that. Therapy of the sensual kind.

She continued. "What about you. I guess with your travels, you have friends all over."

"Not really. Most of my life I haven't stayed in one place long enough to acquire any lasting friendships, although I do still hear from a few buddies from Special Forces and the FBI from time to time. But I did fall into some very meaningful (or was it meaning*less*) friendships with some guys from Tennessee by the names of Jim Beam, George Dickel and Jack Daniels. Unfortunately, my brain stayed marinated half the time I was with them. Thank goodness I severed ties eventually with that bunch; but then I turned to the ladies … you know, Sara Lee, Little Debbie what's-her-name and Marie Calendar. And I allowed these women to do gross and sinful things to my body, many days leaving me feeling sapped and sluggish. So much for my addictive personality."

Adrianna smiled, but frowned with her eyes. "You're very strange, you know. Are you always joking around like this?"

"Joking? I don't understand."

She shook her head and smacked me playfully on my knee. I thought about returning the favor and going for *her* knee, but then thought the better of it. Maybe later.

It was now completely dark and I was getting hungry. I ordered steak and lobster, knowing full well that Birdman would end up paying for it. But Adrianna, who looked like she had eaten nothing but salads all her life, ordered of all things, a salad. What a surprise. There was even something sensual about the way she ate. She exuded sexuality and grace in every movement of her body, every engaging smile, every slow, dreamy blink of her blue eyes. Seductive blue eyes. In just a matter of hours Adrianna Randolph Wolf had gotten into my head. The wine helped put her there, as well. I knew, however, I needed to stay focused and not allow her to unwittingly distract me. And it wouldn't take much to subdue this love-starved heart.

We changed the subject again and talked about people we both once knew in the Greenbrier community. She told me more about Mason and I told her a couple of war stories, mild ones, both from Vietnam and the Bureau, to which she acted interested, but I could tell she was just being polite. So I stopped talking about myself.

After she worked through the last bites of her salad she laid her fork down, dotted her lips with her napkin, then looked at me and smiled. I smiled back, but *her* smile seemed to have a punctuation mark on it.

"Do you remember the summer my dad got beaned in the head by a 2 X 6 at the sawmill? You came over and cut our grass once a week. That may have been the last time I saw you."

"Yeah, I was just talking to Joey about that. It was the summer before I left for the university. How did your dad get hurt, anyway?"

"For a year or so he could hardly stand on his feet. Besides having a concussion, he developed a blood clot, which eventually went away; but then a bad case of vertigo ensued. He healed up very well after that, but even today he has some balance problems."

"That's good … I mean the healing up part."

Her smile returned. It was one of those smiles that I knew something was rattling through her head … like she had just summoned up some kind of orgasmic memory. And I was right.

"I'm almost embarrassed to tell you this, but I will anyway." She giggled a little. "You would take off your shirt when you cut the grass and I would spy on you from my bedroom window. It would be hot and I could see the perspiration on your chest, gleaming in the sun, making you look like some bronzed god. You tanned very nicely. I kind of thought I was in love with you. But what does a ten- or eleven-year-old know?" More giggles.

"Now you're embarrassing *me*." How about taking *your* top off later, I said to myself? Turn about fair play, you know! "I guess I was some kind of exhibitionist back then."

She laughed and so did I. I couldn't remember when I had such a nice time with someone so fresh and unpretentious.

It was a beautiful night, in more ways than one. Rays of moonlight filtered through the leaves of tall trees and settled on the sweetest face I had seen in years. A slight breeze caught up the glorious scent of gardenias off the edge of the terrace, delighting our olfactory senses with their lavish perfume. Jumping off the branch of a nearby elm a hawk took flight, beating its wings against the indigo sky.

And then at the end of that most perfect night, I realized I owed Joey big time for telling me about her. Of course, I still needed to thump him on the head for storying about the weight, the hair and the big, ugly mole.

About ten-thirty we returned to Wolf Laurel where by the way she lived upstairs in the turret quarters. When we got to the lobby, she walked me on down the hallway and to my door. I wanted most desperately to ask her in for a nightcap and steamy sex, but as she was already in my brain, I wasn't sure to what level I could afford to let myself go. We would just leave the night as two old acquaintances, reviewing old times and renewing old friendships. Obviously, she felt the same way as she squeezed my hand and gave me a quick kiss on the cheek. "I'm glad you showed up after all these years, Skip. Sleep well and I'll see you tomorrow." Then she turned and walked toward the stairs. I listened to her dainty feet on the steps all the way up and then along the upstairs hallway to her part of the house. And then I heard her door shut.

I had almost forgotten that my nickname was Skip when I was growing up. No one had called me that in years. I was always *Bruce* to my parents and Joey, but somewhere along the way the *Skip* handle started. I think it may have been when my gym teacher coach in the seventh grade began calling me Skippy from the way I drove to the basket when I played JV ball. I always felt he was making fun of me and that's why if you had to call me that, just shorten it to Skip. But the way Adrianna said my name made me not want to be Bruce anymore. And it made me feel eighteen once again. I knew one thing; she definitely made my equipment feel eighteen again.

And I have always been attracted to intelligent women, whether or not they were drop-dead gorgeous. Conversely, blonde, voluptuous-breasted, gum-chomping bimbos I avoid like the plague. I guess with me it's another one of those narcissistic deals where a guy with a cave man brain enjoys turning smart girls into his conquests. Psychological deviance? Probably.

Sitting at the antique secretary, by the light of the Tiffany style lamp I jotted down a few thoughts. DAG had moved in here with another man of the same ethnicity. Why were they students at the community college? Why not WVU, CCNY or USC? If they wanted to go to a small college because of the money, why not Glenville State or West

Virginia Tech? Then again, if they had the money to stay in a place like Wolf Laurel on a longer-term basis, why couldn't they afford a real school? So many Middle Eastern men were wealthy. Some even were princes. But whether they had money or not, terrorists, often well-funded by extremist organizations such as Al-Qaeda or the Egyptian Islamic Jihad, were sometimes covertly placed in community and college settings to integrate themselves into society as America-loving immigrants.

And then I was wondering why 'roomy' didn't go by to claim his friend's body? Did he fear being exposed? Was it he that broke into McGowan and Sons looking for something? Maybe something incriminating he needed to get back? Like a hand-drawn map of a chemical factory?

I know I promised to share any findings with Jack, but again I wasn't totally straight up with him about that. Something called *turf protection*. Each time I found out something new, I would be compelled to call Birdman; then maybe I'd feed Jack some scraps. I generally didn't share my candy when I was a kid, nor did I play well with others. I'm much too old to start now, so Jack the G-Man would just have to be patient.

Coincidentally, bright and early the next morning, Jack called me before I called my boss.

"Like I told you yesterday, I thought I'd pay a visit to the funeral home today, Bruce. I *would* like to get a look at your friend before he is cremated."

"My friend?"

"Okay," I said. "When will you be here?"

"Can you meet me there, say around eleven? And maybe we can have lunch."

"Lunch at the mortuary, huh. Could you maybe pick a better place?" I think I actually heard him chuckle. "A sandwich or something afterward."

"Fine. See you at eleven."

It was about eight-thirty and I figured by now that

Birdman would be out of the rack and getting his family ready to go to Mass at St. Peters. I dialed his cell and after five rings, he laid his grumpy 'hello' on me. Maybe he *was* sleeping in.

"Okay, what's the score down there? I thought I'd hear from you yesterday."

"I think I've found a mate to the other sock … and right under my nose. Ironically, I'm staying at the same place dead guy was also staying before he … you know, checked out. And he had a roommate of the same persuasion who's still here. I can feel this one in my gut, Peregrine. There's an ill wind brewing here. Shall I stay with it for a few days?"

"I absolutely insist. I assume you spoke with the man in Charleston?"

"I did", I said. "He appears to be on board and is meeting up with both me and the carcass today."

"Okay. You know the drill. Counterparts, big or small, get only what they need to know, when they need to know and not before."

"Gotcha."

"And let's make our conversations more frequent."

"For sure. Anything else?"

"That's it."

"Well, say hello to mother hen and the chicks for me."

There was that familiar click without a 'goodbye' or 'have a nice day.' Birdman needs to work on his telephone etiquette. I called Joey and told him I'd be there in a couple of hours with the G-Man. He said he wouldn't have much time to spend with us as he was getting ready for the sixteen-year-old's funeral at one. "How'd you find Adrianna, Brucie?"

"Like you said … obese, moles and warts, but actually has most of her teeth."

He laughed heartily. I guessed he needed that, considering what would be a very heart-*wrenching* day for everyone. I know I'd be a basket case where it came to children. I didn't know how he did it. "I had a feeling you'd like what you found," he said. "And that I did, little brother."

"Okay, gotta go. See you later."

I went to the Suburban to get more clothes. After woofing a breakfast bar, I donned a tee shirt that had a picture of Mickey on it, a pair of gym shorts and my Nikes, then went out to the veranda to stretch before my run. I was hoping Adrianna would be around to check out my Adonis body in these cute little shorts, but she had apparently already laid out the continental breakfast and retreated back to her quarters. After the thighs and calves felt primed, I walked past the five vehicles in the parking lot to see which car likely belonged to the Arab boarder. Was he there today and would I be able to accidentally-on-purpose meet him somewhere on the premises? I would be Joe Tourist coming back home for a nostalgic visit and he would be Joe Terrorist, pretending to have a temporary visa and so blessed to be in this wonderful capitalist country of golden opportunity.

My SUV occupied one space. There was a Buick Electra, obviously owned by some older couple. Buicks are only owned by geezers and blue hairs, you know. The third vehicle, a minivan, had a West Virginia tag and a sticker on the back from a local dealer in Lewisburg. That had to be Adrianna's van, although I would have taken her for a Porsche owner which would fit her sleek, sport-model body. Maybe she needed a van for hauling stuff in support of the B&B operation. A fourth vehicle was a Chevy pickup with an Alabama tag and a bumper sticker that read *I will only give up my gun when they pry it out of my cold, dead hand.* That was definitely a Bubba truck and I was set to wonder why he and his mama chose a rather expensive and classy place like this to stay in. Maybe it wasn't his wife with him and he was trying to impress her. It was pretty safe taking her to a fancy hideaway where he didn't know anyone rather than take her to a race at Talladega where he probably knew *everybody*. Anyway, he couldn't get into her underwear as easily around a grandstand full of good ol' boys all crammed in like that.

The car at the end of the parking lot was a ten year old Nissan Maxima with blacked-out glass. I continued my stretching routine behind the cars and made a mental note that the Nissan had a New Jersey tag, which didn't really mean anything. On the left side of the rear glass was a parking sticker from Valley Community College with a seven on it, indicating it would expire in July of the next year. This was obviously the Arab dude's car. Tomorrow I would get Birdman to run the tag.

I jogged out to the end of the parking lot and onto a farm road that twenty minutes later seemed to have no end. It had not taken long for the knees to start hurting and appeared to be time to turn around, which I did at a dilapidated barn. It was a beautiful lemon yellow Sunday morning, though. Birds were singing hymns, a church bell somewhere over the sweet, green-rich farmland was chiming and all was peaceful and holy. Wildflowers of blue, yellow and crimson dappled by sunlight graced the landscape in a distance meadow.

About a third of the way back to the inn a red vehicle approached from a distance … a van. Adrianna's van. When she saw me, she slowed to a stop. The window came down and there she was, smiling, obviously impressed with my athletic legs and tight butt.

"Hey, good lookin.' Want a ride?"

I was breathing rather laboriously and was afraid she would mistake that to mean I was out of shape. But I caught my breath and replied, "You're going the wrong way."

"No, I'm going the *right* way. To church."

"Oh."

"But I can take you back if you'd like. You look exhausted, not to mention sweaty."

Damn. I mean dang; this is Sunday. Now she *does* think I'm out of shape.

"Thanks, but I have to finish these five miles (actually three) and anyway, I'd ruin your seat as drenched as I am."

"Okay, then. Will I see you later?"

"You can count on it." There I go, sounding like an over-anxious puppy, with his tongue out and panting happily.

"Well, bye then." She winked and smiled, then pulled away.

I was then afraid that in the thirty seconds I had stopped, *rigor mortis* would be setting in; so I continued on at an even brisker pace. About ten-fifteen I chugged back into the parking lot and saw that the Nissan was gone. Missed him, dang it. There will be another time, Arab guy.

I then realized I only had forty-five minutes to shower and get to Joey's shop, so I zipped up the steps and down the hall to my room in anticipation of the hot, body-soothing shower.

CHAPTER 7

This was a courtesy meeting on my part with Jack. If I had blown him off, not only would he have been pissed, giving up a Sunday morning at church with his family, but he would think I was probably being rude and intentionally evasive. I still needed to keep him at arm's length in case the Bureau's services were needed, but otherwise, he would get very little out of me until Birdman gave me the green light. Again, it was also a case of not sharing my candy, being the self-absorbed guy that I am.

I arrived at McGowan and Sons a few minutes before eleven and found a government Crown Vic in a parking space in the front of the building. Jack had preceded me. Joey and sidekick Lester had already loaded the young girl's casket and flowers and were on the way to the church. I found Jack in the lobby gazing at some of the McGowan fine art accumulated through the years from Wal-Mart and Dollar General.

"Hello, Jack." I extended my hand.

"Good morning, Bruce. I didn't see anyone about and wondered why the place was left open, considering the break-in."

"My brother knew we'd be here at eleven and that you wanted to see the Arab corpse. Whatever the intruder wanted, he didn't find. I'm sure he won't be back."

He nodded. "Likely. I assume you know your way around here. You want to take me to the body?"

"The kitchen's this way." I led him back to the fridge room, eyed the dreaded embalming table and pulled out the Number Six drawer. DAG was still dead.

Jack looked over the body like he was some kind of forensic expert and knew what the hell he was looking for. But then again, he was probably just curious about the dude and this was his way to get up close and personal to the situation. "I'm sure this guy wasn't a loner. Have you canvassed the area for others?"

"No, not really." I didn't lie. When DAG's roomy is staying thirty feet from my door, why burn shoe leather?

"Do you still plan to? I think it could prove meritorious."

"It's on my list of things to do."

His expression reflected that he was not sure of what to make of that comment … or me.

I quelled his concerns, however. "I'll be looking around starting tomorrow, Jack."

"Good. If you need Bureau assistance, we can have an agent from Southwest Virginia collaborate as appropriate.

*It's **not** appropriate, Jack, I almost said aloud. I don't want any Bureau noses up my backside.*
"We'll see how it goes, okay?"

He nodded. "By the way, we received this guy's prints from the coroner's office and ran them through our system as well as Interpol. No hits."

"He probably hadn't been in this country long enough to get himself arrested. Since he had no ID or prints on file, I'd say he also had no immigration status. Of course, 'illegal' is a status."

Jack continued. "I also ran a search on all known Middle Eastern visitors to West Virginia this year, especially from Iran, Iraq, Saudi Arabia, Libya and Yemen. There were only sixty-two such legals with visas in the entire state. There were none in Greenbrier County. We also secured data on all known extremists or radical groups on government lists and potentially operating in the state and came up with zero."

"It figures. West Virginia is not New York or Washington."

"Exactly," replied Jack. "As you know, the Jihad and Al-Qaeda have an immense hatred for moral decadence such as you would find in New York or other big cities. And as they accuse Washington of being anti-Islamic in its policies, allied with Israel, D.C. remains a primary target. I'm sure they don't consider a bunch of mountaineers with their earthy value systems as immoral or a threat to their agenda."

"But Jack, this state like many others is largely Christian and the radical Islamofascist sees Christianity as hedonistic, evil and anti-Muslim. Christians are *historically* targets of Islamic extremists. So why not target West Virginians and their industry? The good people of this state represent the very core of American values. By striking fear in the heart of Americans, attacking their factories and killing the innocent, the Islamic terrorist achieves his goal of demoralizing the good people in states like West Virginia. And you know as well that Muslims believe they're commanded by Allah and the prophet Mohammed to kill men, women and children, sparing none. This assures them life in Heaven and the more infidels they kill, the greater their rewards."

"Okay, I can't argue with that, Bruce, but so far, with what we have, I don't see any tangible evidence of a terrorist network here in West Virginia or any actual threat of a terrorist strike. Yes, the sketched map is certainly suspect, having been found on a dead Arab, but short of finding more of these guys, all we can do is speculate. I'm sure the security at the gates of the Charleston area factories will be stiffened. I would encourage you to go ahead and do your canvass. But I hope you're not wasting your time, my friend."

From Jack's attitude, I sensed his highers didn't think much about the schmuck in the drawer or his map, either. Jack appeared to be one of those cynical Doubting Thomas guys I hated working with who would wait for a grenade to be dropped down their shorts before saying "Houston, I think we may have a problem here." But he also appeared to be good with me doing the leg work, and just in case I did fall onto something solid, I would be good enough to go running to him and lay out all the bits and pieces on a silver platter. That will happen, Jack.

After taking another look at DAG, Jack pulled up his stakes. "Well, at least I got a look at the guy. Now I have a mental picture to file away in case something does materialize. About the map, I will do a Google Earth or GlobeXplorer on the computer and see if I can't start comparing the layout of some of these plants with the satellite image."

"I seem to remember that the Bureau has a more sophisticated interactive satellite system than the Google thing for you to bring up photos of the area factories."

"You're talking about SpyTrek. Actually, some of the private vendors have better quality than the agency program," Jack replied. "Whatever. I *would* appreciate it though if you could give me a ring-i-ding if something matches up."

"You bet. And again, the same goes for you. By the way, are we still good for lunch?"

"Well, Jack, do you mind if I don't join you? I hate you drove two hours here to spend thirty minutes giving this non-terrorist the once over, but I need to get back and do some work." That was a lie, of course. I just didn't feel like having lunch with Jack today. I would actually be looking to have lunch someone else.

He sensed I was a little put out with his indifference on the matter. I really wasn't, because the less he pressed me about my investigation, the better. I didn't want him dogging me for information nor did I want some Bureau yahoo getting in my way. And I know first hand how they like to take over, making everyone else on the case feel subservient and stupid. I can be stupid without anybody's help.

I did promise again to inform him right away should something significant materialize and he did the same with me on the satellite search. I'll keep you on speed dial, Jack.

I pulled off Seven Bridges into the B&B parking lot and saw that the Nissan was still missing. Adrianna's van hadn't returned either. Church would be over and she was likely having Sunday dinner with a couple of her lady friends from White Sulphur she had mentioned last evening. I was famished and since I had passed up the Continental breakfast for a granola bar earlier, I turned around for Lewisburg and a hot dog at Jim's Drive-in. It was my hangout when I was a teenager and Route 60 was the strip. Wish I had that Z28 again.

The dog was as good as I remembered, so I had a second. I totally undid the three miles I had run earlier and what's worse, I needed a Pepcid.

On the way back I encountered the teenage girl's funeral parade on Highway 219. As was the custom in the earlier days, I dismounted and stood beside my vehicle as the grim procession passed. Joey threw up his hand as he went by with the hearse and I averted my eyes from the family car, dropping my head in respect. As the windows were blacked out, I wouldn't have been able to see the grieving parents anyway. Although I didn't count them, there appeared to be more than fifty cars in line. Most were classmates, I reckoned, in their pickups and pocket rockets. A few were driving nicer, later model cars, some riding with their parents.

My heart, heavy, I again thought about my sweet Caroline and what she was doing on a Sunday afternoon. Determined not to allow a mood to set in, I slid back onto the driver's seat and pressed the radio's *on* button. There was something soft and melodic playing and I didn't need *that*, either. So, I found a contemporary rock station, even though I hated the crap. And then that served to remind me that it was something the sixteen year old girl who was no longer with us would have been listening to and I shut off the box entirely.

I got back to my room, popped the antacid and grabbed a book from my bag. It would be a great afternoon to sit on the veranda, read, belch, and swig a couple of bottles of Evian. Also, I was hoping I would finally get to eyeball my Arab neighbor. And of course, I was waiting for the Lady of the Inn who had somehow managed to get into my head. I read the first two chapters of the Grisham novel and as I started the third, I realized I had no earthly idea what the damn... dang thing was about. It was still Sunday.

At just before three I heard tires on gravel and looked up to see the Nissan pull in. To my surprise, behind it was a two door white Civic. I didn't want to act too interested so I glanced back down at the book, but watched them peripherally. A very nice-looking olive-skinned man about twenty five, wearing a white shirt and dark pants got out of the Nissan, then waited at the rear of his car for the driver of the Honda to exit. Except, two people, both Middle Eastern as well, got out of the second car. The driver was a shorter fellow with a huge honker and a closed-cropped beard. The other was at least a half foot taller, somewhat older and thinning on top. In fact, he was nearly bald. None of the three was over thirty.

One of the Honda men said something indiscernible and all three laughed. As I was still in running shorts, perhaps they had gotten a look at my legs. They looked harmless enough ... even affable. But some of the deadliest serpents appear to be of the non-venomous persuasion. A coral snake can often be mistaken for a king snake.

As the three men trudged up the veranda stairs, my

presence appeared to startle them. I guess they hadn't seen me *or* my legs.

I looked up. "Afternoon," I said. "Nice day, eh?"

Nissan man, who would be DAG's roommate, returned my greeting. "Yes. Yes, it is a fine day." I noted the thick Arab accent. Getting a closer look at him, I saw that he was indeed a good-looking kid with shiny jet-black hair, dark piercing eyes and a slight build. He glanced at the others who nodded to me, but said nothing. Then they went on inside to the lobby and made their way back to the Magnolia Room.

Three of them, now. Originally four. Still, none of the three had claimed the body. I waited until I thought they were in the room, then walked out to look at the rear tags on the two cars. The Civic had a Massachusetts plate and the Nissan, of course, New Jersey. There were Valley Community College stickers on the rear glasses of both cars. Either all three were genuine students from different states and had gotten to know one another because of their ethnicity or they were pretend students and the education was a ruse. If it was the latter, I smelled rats. I went quickly to the lobby, pulled a pen and scratch pad and returned to the cars to record the numbers.

When I turned to walk back toward the inn, I looked up to find Big Nose on the veranda watching me. At first, I didn't know if he saw me jotting down the numbers, but as I approached him, his icy glare told me he did. Either he had forgotten something from his car or he wasn't convinced I was just an innocent porch-sitter. I passed him without word and his incessant stare followed me until I was clear of him. I should have been more discreet and casual about my snooping. Obviously, I had been found out.

The man did go to his car and got out a backpack which he slung over his shoulder. While he was standing there, he eyed my Suburban. I could swear he was memorizing *my* tag. His lips were moving. I had returned to my rocker, retrieving the book, and when he mounted the veranda again, he intentionally diverted his eyes. It was all rather uncomfortable, if not unnerving.

I remained on the veranda pretending to be engrossed in Mr. Grisham. But the pages may as well have been blank. Runaway thoughts bounced off the corners of my brain until I thought I was getting a headache. If tell-tale eyes and expressions accounted for anything, I was becoming convinced there was something terribly wrong about these guys. Of course, I'm no psychologist, but from my training and experience I have learned a good bit about reading faces and assessing human behavior. That would be *behavioral profiling*, in government terms.

Sometime after four-thirty Adrianna returned. She exited the van and upon seeing me in the rocker, she smiled. "Hi, there. Did you have a good day?" she asked.
"Pretty good. Mostly relaxed. How about you?"

"It was nice. I went to church … of course, you know that. Then I had lunch with a friend."

"Is she as pretty as you?"
She seemed to be uneasy with the question and then I found out why.

"Well, it was a *he* and I guess he's not bad looking." She paused before her confession, maybe because she was embarrassed to tell me or it could have been for effect. "I've sort of been seeing him. He's the high school coach, but it's all very innocent of course."

"Of course," I said coldly. I was a little hurt, but then I knew I had no right to be. Yesterday evening was nice, but it was just an evening. No real happenings.

She sat in the rocker beside me, then put her hand on mine. In a soft, almost apologetic voice she said, "He's just someone to talk to. I know he'd like us to develop into a couple, but I'm really not attracted to him."
Good.

"Adrianna, you don't have to explain anything to me. Hey, I've only really known you for twenty-four hours." I then smiled. "Actually, I've known you all my life."

"I know. But I did kind of feel something last night at dinner. I don't mind telling you that when I went up to my room, I thought about you lying down there all by yourself. I actually started to come down and knock on your door."

Now the birds were singing again and my heart was sailing on deep blue waters. I realized at that moment, she was not only inside my head, but she had also lassoed my big dumb old heart.

"I thought about you too last night," I responded like a fourteen-year-old puppy dog wuss. Here I am, a government terrorist eradicator, but when it comes to the female species, I'm a joke. God help me if this woman ever offered her body to me. I'd probably retreat to a corner, suck my thumb and wet myself.

"Anyway," she continued.

"I hope you stay around for more than a few days." She put her face close to mine and drilled me with her eyes.

"I can use the rent money."

We laughed and I took the opportunity to ask her out for a cup of coffee.

"Let me check my messages and spruce up a bit. I'll be right back."

"I'll do the same and meet you out here, say about five? Heck, we may as well have dinner again."

"Okay. Don't tarry."

I practically skipped to my room, suddenly remembering why I got the nickname over forty years ago. As I was primping, the man in the mirror told me to slow this thing down and to keep my hormones in check. I certainly didn't need any distractions and I knew this was a huge one. But anyway, I would think about that tomorrow. I brushed my teeth, splashed some Bvlgari onto my nasty body and donned a golf shirt and shorts. Before going back to the porch, I called Birdman's number. He didn't answer. Must have something going with the family. No business was ever conducted when he was with his wife and kids. I admired him for that.

I did leave a message, however. "Eagle One, this is Bruce. You're probably barbecuing in the back yard. Hope you're enjoying the family. Call me sometime. Seriously, it's important. Chao."

We drove into town and climbed the hill on Route 60 until we reached the General Lewis Inn. It was a stately place all in white sitting back off the road with majestic eighteen foot columns on the front and a two-hundred year old highway coach in the front yard covered by an ornate port. I remember the place as a teen, having gone there to check out hundred year old relics hanging on the narrow hallway wall. The rooms were quaint, much like Adrianna's place, with beds so high off the floor that you might wake up with a nosebleed. Wooden floors creaked and groaned with every step and it all made for great ghost story material if you used your imagination.

Adrianna seemed to know the owner, Nan, and after a few pleasant words, we were directed through a rustic sitting room with a fireplace and into a small dining area. There was one other couple seated in the room by a window and we were positioned close by them at an adjacent table. Shortly, a kindly Black gentleman in a snappy, red bowtie and black vest presented himself to take our order.

"Coffee for now, thank you." I replied.

"We haven't decided on dinner as of yet."

The couple by the window was elderly and still dressed in their church-going clothes. He was in a Matlock blue seersucker and she was wearing a stylish red hat. Stylish of course when Mamie Eisenhower was First Lady. She had the look of blue blood which would of course match the color of her hair.

I spoke soft and low so that the couple would not readily hear me, even though the man was wearing a hearing aid. But in my experience, a woman's hearing actually improves as she gets older. God apparently made them that way so that the art of gossip, which is actually a religion in some circles, would be perpetuated and handed down, generation to generation. My mom was a devout gossiper and her hearing was actually more acute than Superman's. It is a medical fact that in women the tongue's life support system is the ear.

I started right in with my conversation about the two Middle Eastern visitors and asked Adrianna if she had ever seen either of them or their Civic.

"I don't think so. And I believe Juanita, my maid, would have mentioned it if they had come through the lobby. Of course, we're all not always around. Is this something I need to be alarmed about?"

"I don't know. I will be focused this week on finding out who they are, where they're from and hopefully nail down their purpose in being here in Greenbrier County."

"I can tell my boarder that I can't give him another week … that I have every suite promised the rest of the month. What's the purpose of you keeping an eye on him? Oh, I forgot; you're a government spy?"

"I check out immigration issues for the government, that's all. If it's alright with you I'd rather we kept him at bay where I can watch him. If something tangibly suspicious materializes, I will get my FBI acquaintance in Charleston to secure a court order to search his room. Unless you'd like to let me in there when he's gone." I smile.

"I think I'd be in a lot of trouble if I did that. And I'm sure you would, too."

The server brought me a refill on my java and I dumped another pack of the blue stuff in it. The coffee was actually very good and I wondered why I had to doctor it up like that. A habit, I suppose. Looking over at the elderly couple again, I noticed that the little old lady had her dichotomous listening skills in full gear. Even though her husband was rattling on about some medicine he was taking, she cocked her head every once in a while in our direction to catch a word or two. She especially hung on words like 'FBI' and 'court order.' I thought about having some fun and making lewd and lascivious suggestions to Adrianna to see if I'd get a real rise out of the old lady, but I'd probably get Adrianna's full hand across my face, instead.

Speaking of my tablemate, I took notice how a ray of the evening sun, glinting off a water glass on the table by the window, high- lighted her silken brown hair. She was radiant enough without the sunlight. And then her pretty face exuded a wholesomeness and honesty that I don't see much anymore in contemporary women.

But back to the conversation at hand. "You know I wouldn't do anything at all to put you in trouble with the law or place you in any danger. That was inappropriate to suggest." I paused to take a sip. "I *would* like you to do something for me, though."
She grinned. "Have I ever denied you anything?"
I really do like her.

"Do you trust that your night person and maid can maintain a level of confidence and discretion?"

"Absolutely."

"Would it be possible for you three to keep tabs on your boarder ... when he comes and goes? And record when he has guests?"

"I think we can do that."

"By the way, did you remember the name he gave you?" I asked.

"Yes. I wrote it down forg you." She opened her purse and after digging past her compact, cell phone, checkbook, tampon and keys, she found the slip of paper on which was written the name Assad Mohammed. Well, I was wrong again; I kept calling the *dead* guy Mohammed. At least now I had confirmed that these guys were Arabs and not Sicilians or Spaniards. And don't call me a profiler. Contrary to popular belief, I don't see all the Mediterranean's Arabs, Indians and other people of olive and brown complexion as look-alikes.

"And the other guy who apparently didn't stick around (DAG); did you happen to record his name?"

"You know, for some reason I never got his name. I think maybe it was because Mr. Mohammed paid the entire cost of the room."

"I see," I said. "I will be running Mohammed's name through my system, but since it may be like running the names Smith and Jones, we'll probably get thousands of hits. But now that I have a tag number *and* a name, I can narrow it down. Of course, he could have given you a bogus name, too." And then I remembered the student sticker on the car. "By the way, do you know anyone at the community college?"

"I know the Dean of Admissions, Paul LeMer."

"Good. The very guy I would be speaking with. If he'll cooperate, I should be able to secure all names, addresses, immigration statutes and et cetera."

"Do you want me to call him?"

"That may involve you more than I'd want. If somebody came in and tortured him for information, your name may be on his lips."

"There may be torturing?"

The old lady's ears did pick up on that question. I think I saw her scoot her chair a little closer to us. Whether she heard all of what we said or not, she diverted her attention back to the boring man that she had probably been married to for fifty years. He was still going on about his drug side effects.

We had been sitting and talking for a half hour or so when other folks started coming in for dinner. It was time to stop talking shop.

"How about some dinner?"

"I think I'm ready now," she responded. "Won't be another salad, will it?"

"No, I'm up to here with salads these days." She whisked

her hand across her lovely throat.

"Good. You look like you could use a hearty meal."

"You don't like my body?" She leaned into me and flashed that wanton smile.

I wanted to sweep the table off with my arm like you see in the movies and devour that body. But I thought that might draw a crowd, so instead, I leaned even closer to her face and replied, "There is absolutely nothing wrong with your body."

Expecting her to order something like prime rib, mashed potatoes and a hunk of pecan pie, she ordered a boneless chicken dinner.

"It's kind of sad, you know," I said.

"What is?"

"Where they come from."

"Where who comes from?"

"The chickens." I pointed to her plate.

"Okay, I give up. Where would they come from other than from chicken coops?"

"Why from Boneless Chicken Ranches, of course." She stared at me with puzzled eyes.

"What?"

"Yeah, if you ever went to one, you'd remember it. It's actually pitiful watching them flop around, not having any backbones and all."

She started giggling again which re-attracted the attention of the blue hair. "You are nuts."

"I'd actually prefer that you'd think of me as funny."

"Funny *and* nuts," she remarked.

After dinner we drove the four miles back to Wolf Laurel. Upon pulling into the parking lot, I noticed the Nissan was gone again. I thought to myself, "now that I've seen you, boys, I *will* find out who you are and what you're up to."

We climbed the veranda steps and I asked her if she wanted to split a bottle of Merlot in my room. She said she really had to balance the books, as she had procrastinated the chore all day. Well, I don't call spending half the afternoon with the football coach, innocent or not, procrastination. But I left that alone.

I turned the key in the ancient lock and it clanked loudly. When I opened the door and turned to bid her *adieu* for the evening, she put both arms around my neck brought her lips within no greater than two inches from mine. She teased me with her eyes and parted her lips slightly, still not touching. I lifted her right hand with my left and placed my other hand to the small of her back.

"Wanna dance?" I asked.

She grinned, still tantalizing me with her ever so close lips. "There's no music."

"We can make our own."

"I'm very much out of practice."

"Doesn't really matter. I only remember a couple of steps, myself." I began swaying and then she started moving along with me.

"Another night, Mr. McGowan," she whispered. "You can count on it." Then she kissed me, gently. Her lips were like moist velvet… lipstick flavored velvet.

When those ten seconds of pure bliss were over, I felt like having a cigarette. And I don't even smoke.

"You're killing me. You know that, don't you?" I panted.

"Uh huh." She gave me a peck on the lips this time.

"I always wondered what that would feel like and thirty-five years later, now I know. You taste … delightful."

At that point, I was pretty much speechless. All I could do was stand there and nod like one of those little head bobbing dogs in the back window of a Mexican taxi.

She touched her fingertips to my lips this time, smiled and walked away. About halfway to the lobby, she turned and said, "Sleep well tonight, big boy."

Fat chance of that. But I knew I'd sleep hard.

C H A P T E R   8

My head was still jammed up with Adrianna the next morning and then when I saw her helping to put out the Continental breakfast with her pinned back hair and wearing a tight, accentuating blouse, I just really had to get the hell out of there. I grabbed a pint of milk, box of granola, a plastic bowl and spoon and headed for the Suburban. It was seven-thirty five and I figured that if Assad Mohammed was indeed a student at Valley Community, he would be coming out soon. Of course, I had no idea as to his class schedule, so I may have a long wait.

It was already a celestial morning. As our Supreme Being, the Almighty, had already set the glowing red ball to rise to the occasion on the eastern horizon, a full Sturgeon moon was setting beautifully in the southwestern sky. But the sun was barely peaking over the distant trees, so it hadn't quite begun its mission of heating the atmosphere to its forecasted ninety degrees on this 28th day of August.

I finished off my cereal and sat for the next forty minutes reading my copy of the USA Today that every guest gets, until my cell phone went off. I could see it was Birdman. "Good morning, Preceptor, did you get my message?" I asked first thing.

"Yes. Sorry. I was grilling out in the back yard with my kids. I also had one of our old acquaintances from the Company over."

So, he *was* grilling. Why do I know these things? Either I'm psychic or have become able in the short time I've known this bird to read him like a book.

"Hope it was a nice evening for you. Say, can you run these two tag numbers? First one is on a 1990 or 91 Nissan Maxima with New Jersey plates NR 15773. See if it belongs to one Assad Mohammed. Got that one?"

"Yes."

"Good. The second one is Massachusetts 3492BG, a 1995 Honda Civic."

"Will do. Bad guys?"

"Unsure at this point. Could be a sleeper cell. I'll snap you some shots of the subjects when I see them again."

"How many?"

"Three that I know of. There was actually a fourth and he's the Arab stiff in cold storage, soon to be ashes. I'll send you his photos along with those of his cohorts. You may not be able to match him up with any Interpol photos. His mug has seen better days."

"Roger. I'll see what I can do. These people could be infiltrators, so you have the green light to continue your plans. Try to wrap this up in the next few days and see me here on the 1st with a complete report."

"Can't I e-mail it to you and just continue my vacation?"

"What vacation? Just be here on the 1st without fail."

"Yes, Mother Goose."

He didn't reply and I had the feeling he was about to click me again.

"Boss."

"Yes."

"Trust me. These guys are viruses. I can feel it in my bones."

"I understand. You have four days to prove it or you move on to something else."

"Wilco, out." I clicked *him* this time. It felt good.

I had my Nikon on the dash cocked to fire at such time

Assad came out. That is if he ever did. I also felt that if I *was* about to uncover something heinous, it was good time to start carrying the Glock. I pulled it and the holster from the glove compartment and clipped it to my belt. The safari jacket I had on would cover the weapon, only if it did get stinky hot later, I would be uncomfortable. But it had to stay hidden so I would not be mistaken for a cop or a cowboy.

At eight forty-five Bama' the pickup owner came out with his concubine. I knew it had to be him because he was wearing a red baseball cap to match his neck, a tucked-in Dale Earnhart tee and a size 42 gut. What I could see of his belt buckle, it appeared to be bigger than his brain. His girl had mousy-brown hair and wouldn't have been bad looking had she had all her teeth. And then there were those two chins. Dressed in a pink Mickey Mouse sweatshirt and black, shiny tights, it was obvious she had consumed too many cheese pizzas. Even Spandex has its limits. Even so, the guy's hands were all over her as they walked to his truck; and because of that, I was now assured that she was *not* his wife. Maybe his sister.

No sooner had 'Bama and the bimbo pulled out, Assad stepped onto the veranda and trotted down the steps with a small olive drab backpack in hand. I nailed four close-ups with the telephoto before he reached his car. I waited till he backed out and headed south, then pulled out after him, allowing another vehicle to get in between us. We rode on Mountain View for a while and then the Nissan turned east. After two miles and a four-way stop, Assad went another 500 yards and turned into the campus parking lot at Valley Community College. Well, so far he appeared to be a student, but was this a smoke screen?

I gave him two minutes to disappear through the door at the main entrance, then I drove down every lane in the parking lot in search for the Civic. It was not there. Perhaps the two Honda men had classes at different hours or on other days, but I wouldn't think so. It was obvious that all these guys were friends and they either met in classes or came to Greenbrier County to converge and plot some type of mission … like targeting a factory in the Kanawha Valley. While I continued to canvass the parking lot in case I missed the car, I saw the Civic pull off the highway. So that they would not spot my vehicle, I drove down the aisle to the rear of the campus and waited for them to park.

From a distance I watched the men dismount and walk to the same entrance Assad used. I waited another ten minutes, until ten o'clock, when I surmised their class would begin. At a few minutes past ten I entered the main door and stopped at the glass-encased wallboard to locate the office number for the Dean. I was vigilant to look out for any of the three suspects who may have been lollygagging in the hallway, then found my way to Room 140.

A large-set bleach-blonde about thirty sitting in a pod near the door asked, "Can I help you?" Obviously, Joey was confused about his women and had described this gal as Adrianna Randolph. The sex of the two was the same, however, making it understandable how he could have gotten them mixed up.

"Is Dean LeMer in, please?"

"Yes, do you have an appointment?"

"No, I don't." I held up my State Department ID, which again, didn't tell you squat about me. But it did seem to impress the blonde. "I'm with the U.S. Department of State and need to speak with him about an important matter."

"I'll see if he is available." She continued to eye me curiously as she picked up the phone to buzz him. "Sir, there's a Mister …"

"McGowan," I finished her sentence.

"… McGowan to see you. He's with the government." She paused. "Okay." Blondie hung up the receiver and said, "Would you have a seat, sir? He'll be out in a couple of minutes."

"Thank you, Joanne." That's what it said on her nameplate.

The community college was built in 1972 (I read that on a plaque when I came in) and it had developed that same musty smell that I remembered when I was going through my elementary and secondary schools. Even the halls and rooms at WVU had that odor. I used to hate the smell. It smelled like ... education. But then, sitting in the Dean's office, I felt a bit of nostalgia. It conjured up faces of teachers, long since departed, and school chums who went to the four winds and whom I will never see again.

"Mr. McGowan." The Dean startled me from my memory trance. All of a lumpy two hundred seventy-five pounds, LeMer appeared at first to be an imperious figure had it not been for his clownish face and horrible combover.

I stood and shook his hand. It was slimy and soft. No grip at all. Like he had just laid a cold, dead fish in my hand. And I knew right off he had never done a lick of manual labor in his life. "Bruce McGowan, sir. Thank you for seeing me."

I followed him past a half-dozen people crammed into pods, looking very frenzied and drowning in a sea of paperwork. We entered his office and at his beckon, I sat opposite his desk. A Kenmore fan wound up on its highest speed sat nearby on a credenza. Each time it rotated into LeMer's face, his combover flew straight up for a few seconds, then laid back down softly on the top of his forehead. I had momentarily lost my concentration, not to mention my composure. Slyly, I covered my grinning mouth, faking a cough. Nonetheless, I finally got to the point. "Dean LeMer, here's my card and identification. I do research for the Department of State and by direction, locate individuals, such as illegals, subversives and other persons of interest. We have an interest in three of your students."

"Really? Who?"

"I only know one of their names and thought you could help me with the other two."

LeMer reflected a moment and moved forward in his

over-stuffed wingback. He then leaned to one side and killed his breathing for a couple of seconds. Obviously, a silent one-cheek sneak. I wondered if I should clear the room. Then he breathed again and asked,

"What organization did you say you worked for with the State Department?"

"I didn't say." Nor would I.

"McGowan, huh? I know of a Joe McGowan. Owns one of the funeral homes around here."

"Yes," I replied.

"Joe's my younger brother."

"You don't say. Nice guy, Joe. I assume you don't live here, working for the government?"

"That's right. Now, Dean, can you help me with these students? I need information on Assad Mohammed and two or three of his friends." I had the feeling DAG would have been among them.

"You think they are involved with something … I believe you said subversive."

Groan.

"Yes. Possibly." This guy was starting to annoy me. LeMer eyed me a moment as though he really should buzz the President … both of the college *and* the United States, but then he pulled out several pieces of paper from his left hand drawer. "This is our current student roster." He looked over the first page, then the others, one by one. I'm sure they were alphabetical, so why didn't the bozo just zip through to the M's? "Yes, here's Mohammed's name."

"While you're looking at the roster, do you see any other students' names that appear to be Middle Eastern?"

He started counting, moving his lips. "Looks like an even dozen."

"Hmm. I didn't expect *that* many in a small college like this and in Greenbrier County. Do you mind if I look at the list?"

"No, no. These students are protected under the Privacy

Act. There are addresses, phone numbers, social security numbers and other personal items on here. We have to maintain a confidentiality of this information. You would know that as well as anyone."

Don't try to school me on the law, Deano. I can have a court order slapped on your ass in less than an hour.

"Then perhaps you could just read me the names and leave the other stuff out," I replied, condescendingly.

"I think I can do that." He started reading the names of the twelve and I struck seven right away. These were obviously Black American students with Muslim names, for example, Jamal, Rashid and Kareem. The reason I knew this was because they had American last names like Washington and Johnson. LeMer wasn't exactly the genius he purported to be. I told him to forget about those.

The other five names had possibilities. "Let's try this, Dean. Of these five students, do any have Massachusetts addresses?"

He studied the names again. "Yes, two of them do." "And can you give me their home *and* local addresses?"

"Mmm, no. Not without permission from the President, Dr.Stalnaker ... or a court order. You know that, too, Mr. McGowan." He gave me one of those condescending, schooling looks over his reading glasses.
I may just go ahead and slap you.

"Mr. LeMer, as an agent of the government I am authorized to at least secure addresses. This is not privileged information. Addresses can be secured in a number of ways. The phone book, for example. Addresses are not top secret."

"I don't know about that, sir."

Ofcourse you don't, Einstein. Obviously, that's why you're just an admissions Dean and not a bio-physics professor. But I could see we were getting nowhere. It's hard to match wits with an unarmed man.

"Can you not just jot down the five names for me?" *Before*

I come across that desk.

"Let me talk to Dr. Stalnaker, first. I've probably let out too much. Students and their information need to be especially protected. I appreciate that you're from the government, but since you didn't produce a badge, I need a little more information about you, Mr. McGowan."

I came very close at that moment to putting him out of his misery. He obviously had to realize what a prodigious prick he was.

"Dean, would you mind if I zipped to the restroom before we finish this conversation? Morning coffee, you know. I'll be right back. In the interim, perhaps you can buzz your president for that talk."

"Of course, I'll do just that."

I did have to hit the whizzeria, so I made quick work of it. When I finished, I stopped back by the lovely Joanne's cube and leaned over her desk all official looking. I made sure my Glock was visible beneath my jacket. She saw it all right. I thought she was going to hyperventilate.

I took a chance. "Joanne. Dean LeMer told me to stop by here and have you print out the full student roster for me. Can you do that, Hon?"

"He said that?"

"Yes. Do you want to check with him?"

She glanced at the phone. "No, I guess not. He's on his line. I'll get it for you right away."

I watched her type in a password and hit 'enter.' The roster popped up on the screen.

She hit *print* and fifteen or so pages spit out of her printer. She then handed them to me and I folded them lengthwise in half and shoved them into my safari jacket pocket.

"You're a dear, Joanne," I said in my lowest, sexiest voice. "May I also remark how lovely that blouse is you're wearing? The color brings out the green in your eyes."

She blushed and I thought she was going to jump my bones right then and there. I winked and then ventured past the droids with the drained faces back to LeMer's office.

After dropping my body back in his chair, I let out an audible sigh. "Ah, what a relief. I was under pressure. That's one of the most underrated pleasures of life."
The Dean looked confused. "What?"

"You know." *Is he for real?*

"Oh, the potty break." He grinned, revealed some very unattractive yellow teeth.

I hoped to hell he didn't use the word 'potty' with the students. If he did, he obviously ended up with signs taped to his back, like 'Kick me' and 'Yes, I'm a turd.'

"Well, Dean, what did your president say?"

"She wasn't at her desk, but I asked her secretary to have her call me. Then I'll let you know."

"That will be fine. I respect what you are required to do in these circumstances. I can see you're a pretty sharp fellow, knowing the law and everything."

He beamed like he had just out-maneuvered a big time government agent. Then he frowned a little. "Now knowing that there are three or four students who could be in trouble with the law, should we be concerned?"

"I'm not saying they're trouble or *in* trouble, but I will say this, Dean; if you notice any strange behaviors from any of the Middle Eastern students, you have my card. Call me."

"Strange in what way?"

"Any un-student behavior. You'll probably know when some- thing's not right." *What kind of word is 'un-student?'*

"I will keep my eyes open."

Right, Paul. You don't have a clue.

Then he began some sort of soliloquy about how there had never been any trouble from students at the college. There were institutional standards of conduct, you know, and anyway, most of the kids in the area came from wonderful, nurturing family systems grounded in Christian values. I assumed he was also talking about the Islamic boys on the student roster from out of state. Paul prattled on in his nasal voice and my auditory system was remembering similarly annoying sounds such as teachers' chalk screeching on the blackboard and an old girlfriend that I had taken once to my bed who emitted shrill screams in her moments of climax. Again, that was *once*. My apartment neighbors asked me not to invite her back. "... and as faculty and administrators we do enjoy such a warm and wonderful relationship here at Valley. Most of us have been here since the institution was founded ..." Yada.

He had one of those voices that if I ever fell into the hands of the Red Chinese and was tied to a chair, forced to listen to a tape of him for more than thirty minutes, I'd spill every last bean. I tried to stifle a yawn, but embarrassed myself in letting out something audible from beneath my hand. "Hmm, yes. I'm sure," I said in my attempt to recover. But then I got up to leave and shook his hand. "Well, thanks, Paul. I appreciate your cooperation and will likely be in touch with you about things after you have a dialogue with your President."

I quickly released his moist, meaty paw, then tactfully shoved my hand into my pocket to wipe it off. He smiled and I turned to leave.

"Oh, one other thing, sir," I began, sounding much like Columbo. "Are you at liberty to tell me what classes these five or so gents are taking?"

"I think I can do that. Let me see." He went into his computer for the information. After studying the screen for a moment, he had a look of surprise on his face. "Only one class. One hour Monday through Wednesday, ten to eleven. The class is *Multicultural Issues in America.*"

Now that was a surprise to *me*. Not the class, but the fact that it was their *only* class.

"Again, thank you for your courtesy, Paul. I will look forward to hearing back from you after you talk to the Prez. I do need that information." *Not anymore, Mister Play-by-the-rules.* "And might I say you have a most accommodating staff. You should be very proud of them."

"Oh, I am, Mr. McGowan."

I left out, giving Joanne another wink as I passed by, and walked hurriedly to the front door. It was now ten forty-five and class would probably be out in five or ten minutes. I pulled my Suburban out of the visitor's spot and parked it in a row behind the Civic, sandwiching it between two other SUVs.

At three minutes before eleven according to my dash clock, the three Arab students left the building together. They stopped by the Nissan first to talk and then the two unknowns sauntered off toward their Civic. At the moment they were in proximity to their car I snapped a half dozen shots, getting both front and side views. They entered the vehicle, sat for a moment, and then when the Nissan passed by, they pulled out to follow.

I watched until they were off campus and back on the roadway, then followed at a distance of about a thousand feet. After making a few turns they entered Route 60 and headed down into Lewisburg. I thought at one point they were going to stop, but then I saw they were just slowing to allow a little old man with a cane to jaywalk in front of them at mid-block. That had to remind them how their friend got whacked the week before.

The Nissan and Civic then made right turns onto Jefferson, or Route 219, and pressed on toward the interstate. I kind of thought they'd take the expressway somewhere, but they continued on out of town past the country club. About a mile further they made a right turn onto the road leading into the Greenbrier Airport, a medium sized field that launched mostly Lears, puddle-jumpers and 727s. Why the hell were they going in there, I wondered? The airport did have a pretty good restaurant in it, according to Joey, and after parking their cars adjacent to the small terminal, that's exactly where they went .I sat outside for a few moments contemplating whether I should go in for a bite and continue my surveillance up close and personal, but them knowing I was also a Wolf Laurel boarder and showing up for lunch in the same place they were would be too much of a coincidence. Especially considering I was seen scribbling something on a piece of paper behind their cars. I thought the better about going in and decided instead to grab a slider from a burger joint on the other side of I-64. It would take them longer to order and eat than it would take me to zip to Hardees, wolf down the burger and shake, return to the parking lot, and still have time to chew up a whole roll of Tums before they returned to their cars. I did just that, getting back to the airport right at noon. The cars were still there. It was getting a little warm, so I dropped the driver's and passenger's side glasses to get a little cross-ventilation going. The sweet Greenbrier air was intoxicating to the lungs and had it not been for the gut bomb I threw down, it would have been a most comfortable stake out.

On the seat beside me I had laid *The Mountain Messenger*, a local weekend newspaper, and in flitting about here and there … mostly there … I had not read it. On page six was the Sports Section and the heading **Bobcats Look Good**. In reading further, it appeared that the AA team may even go all the way. A picture under the heading showed a player in practice nailing a tackling dummy under the watchful eyes of a coach. The coach was rather good-looking, tall and muscular, no gut, and poured into a pair of coaching shorts. I was suddenly very jealous, because this was the man who would be my competition. The caption under the photo read *Coach Dan Laramie looks on as defensive tackle Jason Matthews slams practice dummy.* So, this was the jock that had caught Adrianna's fancy, except of course she had told me he was just someone to talk with. I could readily see what she saw in him. I would be compelled to go for him myself, that is, if I went that way. Which I *don't*, okay? Well, anyway, I saw enough and hoped I wouldn't ever see the subject in person. That meant Adrianna would either be with him or with me when the other one of us sauntered along … and somebody could get hurt.

Twelve-thirty and one o'clock came and went. The vehicles remained in place. I flipped through some stations, the few that they were, finally deciding on WRON. When I was a kid, this station played elevator music, which I'm glad they changed. But now today's Top Forty affects me like a dentist's drill. I tapped the radio off and checked my watch again. One forty-five. Either the suspects were yakking it up in the restaurant or they had given me the slip.

While killing more time, I took out the student roster and began scanning the names. Assad was there and so were four other Middle Eastern names. One kid's address was listed as Tel Aviv and a second was from Miami. The two from Massachusetts were named Fayz Al-Hazmi and Ahmed Omari. These were obviously Assad's friends. There was no local address indicated. The stiff at Joey's shop was still unaccounted for, but since I was sure he wasn't Israeli, I assumed he was the student from Miami. There was a status to the far right of his information …'Dropped.' Actually, he was dropped the hard way. It appeared that Joey's boarder was named Khalid Barem.

A couple of Lears took off and I watched a Cessna do several 'touch-and-goes.' Still no Arab boys. The churning in my gut passed after the last Tum went down and the fresh mountain air nearly turned out my lights. I slapped myself and checked my watch again. Two-twenty. I turned the ignition switch to 'accessory' and ran my windows up with the intent of going into the restaurant. But just as I opened my door, I caught sight of them coming out of the terminal. Assad was making flying gestures with his hand, gliding it up and then down. I figured that after their lunch they had gone to the observation area to watch the planes come in and take off. Long damn lunch!

Without tarry, they piled into their respective vehicles and began backing out. I watched through my blacked-out driver's glass as they passed my vehicle, and wondered in retrospect if they had recognized my Suburban. But as their windows were down, I could see they paid me no mind.

I had no sooner pulled onto the highway after them when my cell phone went off. The sharp voice on the other end hardly let me get my 'hello' out.

"Mr. McGowan, this is Lieutenant Williams."

"Yes. How are you doing today?"

"Well, I could be better. I just got my ear bent by a very upset Dean at the community college." Uh, oh. Busted. I knew what was coming next.

"Really? I just left there. What's the problem?"

"Mr. LeMer, I believe that's his name, said you hood-winked his assistant into giving you a copy of a confidential school document. A student roster."

"I'd say hood-winked is a little strong …"

"No, I'd say it's not strong enough for what you pulled."

"Well, I asked politely."

"Did you ever think to try them?"

"Not enough time to go through the red tape, Lieutenant. Anyway, there was no reason he couldn't provide me with the roster, given what was on it." I watched as the Nissan and Civic turned off 219 onto I-64 east and followed a quarter mile back.

"I'm under a deadline to get as much information on someone who could be a person of interest before I leave for New York in a couple of days."

"You believe there is someone of interest at Valley Community? What kind of interest? You had mentioned you seek out suspected terrorist elements. Is that what this is about?"

"That's what I'm trying to nail down. There are several Middle Eastern names on the roster and they may somehow be connected to the dead guy in my brother's mortuary. If he hasn't gone to the incinerator yet."

"And how did you find out about these students … that

they go to Valley?"

"Long story, Lieutenant."

"Tell it to me sometime."

"I just need to do a lot more digging, but I assure you, you'll be the first to know. Maybe the second … or third. But you're on the list."

"Can you meet with me on the matter before you leave town?"

"Do my best."

"Good. And for God's sake, do me and the community a favor; stay away from our institutions and especially LeMer. The guy's a putz."

"Don't I know it? Say, you're not from New York are you? Putz is one of their words."

"Hardly. But I do watch NYPD Blue. Probably heard it from Sipowitz."

I laughed. This guy was all right. "See you, Lieutenant. I'll con- tact you before I leave."

"Please do, Mr. McGowan."

I called Joey to see if he had cooked Assad's friend, Khalid. He said he was doing the barbecuing this afternoon. I really saw no reason to delay the party any longer.

"Can we do dinner afterwards?" I immediately thought how that sounded.

"Sure. Why don't you come by the house for supper?"

"Shouldn't you check with the wife first? I think she may feel I'm a bad influence on the girls, being the renegade that I am."

"She'd love to have you. And she doesn't think of you as a bad influence. A moron, maybe."

"She always was a good judge of character," I replied.

At the White Sulphur exit the cars slowed to turn onto Route 60. I allowed two cars and a septic tank truck to pull in front of me to help block the view of my big old SUV. A slogan on the back of the truck caused me to chuckle out loud … *We Are Yesterday's Meals on Wheels*. I guess they were proud to be Number One in the Number Two business.

About a mile east the Nissan turned left into the parking lot of the Jamestown Motel, followed closely by the Honda. I zipped on by, turned around at a street about five hundred feet away and pulled off the road where I could observe them from a distance. Actually, the Jamestown was a series of a dozen or so rustic cabins, some of which were tucked in neatly directly behind the office and the remainder situated in a not so perfect alignment further back into the woods. I now assumed it was no accident that Assad and friends had purposely chosen out of the way places to stay so they could avoid a lot of people traffic. The men exited their cars and went directly to one of the 20 X 30 cabins behind and cattycornered to the office. It had a number 8 on the front.

After a few minutes, I decided I had spent enough of the day in surveillance and now that I knew where the other two suspects were bunking, I'd get on back to Wolf Laurel. I had just caught a glimpse of Adrianna earlier and hoped I would see a good bit more before the day was over. But when I pulled back into the inn parking lot about three-thirty, her van was gone.

For an hour or so I sat at my desk in the room going over what I had so far. I now knew the names of the three players and probably DAG as well. Each was keeping a low profile at hideaways in two different places and each, a community college student taking only one class, *Multicultural Issues*, which helped them learn enough about Americans to kill them. They were shelling out a good bit of cash each week just to take one class. The college scene was more than likely a way to integrate into the area without raising much suspicion. DAG (Khalid), had a map on him and obviously one or more of these guys broke into the funeral home to look for it. If they knew that Joey was also the assistant coroner in the county, it would be their guess that he had it along with Khalid's pocket contents. Of course, they had to figure the cops kept the map if it was recognized for what it was intended. If it *was* of strategic importance to them, they had to realize that the authorities would definitely be suspicious about it and the map had to be retrieved. Did each of the suspects have a copy of the map and for that matter, were there maps of other factories as well? Today they left class and spent over two and a half hours at the local airport. I wrote down the word 'why' in several places. These boys smelled. There was some kind of plot here involving the Charleston factory or I'm giving up this business to buy a bar in Aruba.

CHAPTER 9

"So, Big Brother, what have you been doing the last couple of days?"

"Thanks to you, spending a little time with Adrianna and looking for your dead guy's compadres. Is he a crispy critter yet?"

"He's done. Very well done. And what have you found out?"

As I mentioned before, I don't generally share information with anyone, except the Birdman. I did tell Adrianna just enough to enlist her into service and keep her vigilant. But since Joey found the map, got me here, and overheard conversations, I'd continue breaking my cardinal rule and fill him in. And anyway, I trusted my brother with my life and may have needed help from him before this was over. So I gave him just a little more information to satisfy his curiosity…except any knowledge about Assad's friends. For now, that is.

"Hmm. Interesting," Joey said. "It seems to me that the map is certainly the key and makes it pretty probable that there *is* a plot to blow up the factory."

I nodded. "Either that or the plan is to somehow get inside the plant and make off with something radioactive to put together a dirty bomb. Who knows what they're developing in factories right in the midst of population centers. Could be chemical, biological *or* radiological. The Kanawha Valley is still a viable target in a terrorist's playbook, just as it was in the Cold War. Remember, Eisenhower had the Bunker built under the Greenbrier for the Congress to be placed in the event of a Soviet strike. West Virginia may be just a minimally populated coal and tourist state, but few people realize how strategically important it is."

"So what's your next move?"

"I think I'll saddle up for Charleston tomorrow to scour the valley and determine which plant was featured in the sketch map. But enough about business. What's Cora having for dinner?"

"I think she said liver and onions. She knew you'd like that." He grinned and winked.

Of course, everyone I've ever known in my life knows I absolutely detest liver. I make it a point not to eat anything that used to be a filter. And then there's *escargot*. It's also my rule to never eat anything I would scrape off the bottom of my shoe.

"Liver, huh? Tell me Joey, did you put all of the Arab guy's parts back in after the autopsy?"

Joey's grin widened and then he licked his lips. "Would you like some fava beans and a nice Chianti with your liver, Bru-man?"

Well, it wasn't liver she was making. That was just more of Joey's sick humor. Actually, Cora had gone Italian, which by the way was my favorite, second only to hot dogs.

After dinner, I gave my compliments to the hostess, kissed the girls and zipped back to Wolf Laurel. Settling in with a bottle of Coors Light from my icebox, I picked up the remote and ran through the fifteen channels on my television. Twice.

I leaned back against the big, puffy pillow at the headboard and began jotting down some notes in my Day Planner about my findings. Slowly this was all unfolding in my head, but I was having a bit of trouble coming up with the story's climax. What these boys were planning would certainly have an explosive end. *When* and *how* were the questions?

And then behind me on the other side of the wall in the Cypress Room I heard the filtered voice of a woman. Except she wasn't talking. She was moaning. Not a painful moaning, although it *was* painful to my ears. She was the kind of bellowing and squealing where she was obviously engaged in something squalid. Momentarily, their bedposts began rhythmically bumping the wall and stomping the wood floor. I squinted at the thought of what was happening over there. What was worse was that our respectable little inn had suddenly become a sleazy motel, thanks to the likes of Bama and his wailing wench. I think that somewhere in the woman's salacious shrieking, unintelligible as it was, I heard her call out the name Bubba. And then it was quiet. Fortunately for me their redneck rodeo was over quicker than a nine second ride on a Brahma bull.

I hadn't noticed earlier, but the red light on my phone was blinking. No one should have been calling me on my land line as 95 % of the time I sent and received calls on my cell. After suddenly realizing who it might be, I jumped off the bed and snapped up the receiver. I touched the message button and listened to the invitation for a nightcap from the sultry voice on the other end.

I took a two minute shower, actually needing one after what I had audibly witnessed, then changed into a pair of Bermudas and a black V neck tee. After climbing the creaky stairs to the turret room, I rapped lightly on the door. In a few seconds, it opened. She greeted me with a tender smile and said, "I hoped you had gotten my message before I turned in. Did you eat yet?"

"I did … at Joey's. You didn't fix dinner, did you?"

"No. But I was prepared to throw together a fresh salad if you hadn't."

Rabbit food. I was darn glad I had accepted Joey's invitation.

Her living area was warm and tasteful with bright colors in the couch and drapes. Although the inn's kitchen was downstairs, she had in her quarters a mini-kitchen with a stove, sink, refrigerator and a provincial style dining table under a hundred piece glass chandelier. A partially-visible third room was obviously her bedroom.

Adrianna had opened a bottle of White Zinfandel which I've always considered too light and sweet, but who am I to turn down anything alcoholic … or her?

"I just thought you could use some company, tonight" she said, "and Heaven knows I do. A person could go stir-crazy doing the same thing day and night without any meaningful conversation with anyone."

I wondered if that was what I was summoned for … meaningful conversation. My expectations were a little higher. "I know what you mean. Traveling like I do gets old, not to mention all the epicurean meals I have at McDonald's and Hardees's."

"I would have guessed you eat a lot healthier, considering you jog most every day and have a hard body."   *I'll say. You should have checked me out last night, sweetheart.*

"That's mostly why I *do* work out. And obviously you do as well," I remarked, licking my lips in my head.

"Yes, up and down these stairs fifty times a day."

I looked around the room, admiring her taste in furnishing and decorating. There were Monet and Renoir impressionistic reproductions here and there, which I would have expected in the home of a lady of such culture, and a couple of numbered prints. There were also ancient pictures of a man and woman around the turn of the 20th Century with cold, harsh faces, not smiling, but dignified. The faces reflected hard lives, and except for the man's facial hair, it would have been difficult to decipher who was which. If these people were Adrianna's ancestors, it was hard to imagine they evolved into someone who looked like her.

In the dining room stood a large china closet containing several ceramic what-nots, some pewter ware and pieces of fine crystal. I picked up a beautiful blue vase which had a Blenko label on the underside and nearly let it slip through my hands. Adrianna gave me one of those bull-in-the-china-closet looks. I quickly set it down and let out an inaudible 'whew.'

On an end table was a picture of a nice looking man in his early forties. That would be Mason, I reckoned. Beside him was another photograph of a boy, perhaps seven or eight, which I took to be a nephew or other family member. It was all very nice.

I'm not very good at small talk, being a man of action and directness. But I tried. "Beautiful place," I remarked. "And my guest room is well decorated, too. You've got a nice touch, Mrs. Wolf."

Her eyes darted about here and there and then she nodded. "It's been a works in progress all these years. I'm never fully satisfied with anything I do. You may even find *your* room completely redone by the time you leave."

We settled down in the living room with the wine. She sat on the divan opposite my love seat in a pair of loose shorts and one of those tops that when she made certain moves showed about 3 inches of mid-drift. A tight and youthful-looking mid-drift. Who cares what we talk about; I had a great view and could talk incessantly about absolutely nothing until the cows came home. I never understood that saying. Why not geese or hounds?

She shifted and uncrossed her tanned, perfect legs to re-cross them, this time the left over the right. I had a passing thought about that scene in Basic Instinct when Sharon Stone blew Michael Douglas' eyeballs out of his sockets when she methodically and teasingly shared with him the fact that she had on no underwear. With Adrianna, of course, the movement was swifter and more lady-like; although I thought I caught just a hint of black underwear with lace edges and the words 'Victoria's Secret.' But I couldn't be sure.

"So tell me, Skip, is there anybody currently in your life?"

"Like my daughter, my brother, my boss?" I knew where she was going.

"You know what I mean … a love interest."

That was pretty direct. But it did tell me she was interested, if last night's lip sucking episode didn't already give me a hint.

"I haven't been in any meaningful relationships I guess since my divorce."

"Wasn't that over twenty years ago?"

"At least. Oh, I've had a few friends along the way. Only one amounted to anything, but after she figured out how much the Bureau consumed of me, I guess she felt I had little left for her."

"That's too bad. What went wrong with your marriage?" She *was* getting personal now.

"Well, I think the final straw was when she jumped on me about how much I was spending on booze and I threw back at her the $125 she had just spent on makeup. I asked her how come I had to give up my frivolities and she didn't. She said she bought the makeup so that she would look good to me. Then I told her *that* was why I bought the booze. I was pretty much toast at that point." Adrianna laughed and smacked me on the knee.

"You're bad."

"And how about you? This self-disclosure session is not going to be one-sided."

"I've been out with maybe two guys since my husband died."

"The coach being one of them."

"Yes, I guess you could include him in there."

"Hmm. You said he was just someone to talk with. Is he pressing for more?"

"He's pretty persistent. He'd be here every night if I

didn't have the word 'no' in my vocabulary. We haven't been intimate, if that's what you're asking."

"No. Really, I wasn't. That would be too personal."

Adrianna smiled, but fidgeted a bit. "You know I make it a policy to never go out with anyone staying here. I don't mix business and my social life. I don't know why I made an exception with you. Maybe having something to do with old times."

"Or maybe my dashing good looks and charming personality."

She laughed and re-crossed her legs. She had no idea what that was doing to me. "No, it's your humility." Then she laughed again. "I have just felt good about being around you these last few days. It's like I've known you all my life, which is partly true, give or take three decades." She paused. "So, tell me, Skip, have you ever been really head-over-heels, can't eat or sleep, hopelessly in love with anybody?"

I mulled that over for a few seconds, finally deciding on "Yes."

"With whom, an old girlfriend, your ex-wife or somebody since?"

"No." I rested my chin in my hand and looked away, staring reflectively out the window through the trees and deep into the days of yesteryear.

"Her name was Emma."

"Emma," she echoed.

"A nice name. Very Nineteenth Century. Maybe your first girlfriend?"

"No," I replied again.

"Someone I worshipped from afar. She didn't even know I existed."

"Oh, that's sad. Who was she?"

"A British secret agent."

There was that puzzled look again. "What?"

"Her name was Emma Peel."

"Emma Peel. Now why does that name sound familiar?"

"Well, actually, that wasn't her real name. It was Diana Rigg, you know, the actress."

Adrianna arched her eyebrows and grinned, like what is it with this guy? "Okay. I think I remember there was a TV show … a British thing …" She squinted as though that would help her remember the show.

"It was called *The Avengers*." "Right. That *was* it."

I gave her my patented charming and tender gaze. "You know, you kind of remind me of her … wide, seductive eyes, sweet, full cheeks, lips that can be pouty one moment and break out into the prettiest smile God ever put on a woman the next. And then there was that jumpsuit that accentuated every tantalizing curve of her body and drove a generation of teenage boys like me bonkers. Ahhh, Mrs. Peel, as Steed called her."

"Are you for real?" she asked, arching the eyebrows again and shaking her head. I didn't know if it was because she pitied me or she couldn't believe what a nut I was.

"You don't have a jumpsuit, do you?"

"I don't even know what a jumpsuit is."

"It's a one-piece thing with pants … a zipper starts at the neck and goes south to the belly button … you get the picture."

"Do I *ever*. No, I don't nor ever did own one. I do remember seeing *The Avengers* in syndication once or twice on BBC. And I do remember her being attractive." She fluffed her hair. "You say I kind of look like Mrs. Peel, huh?"

"Well, not anymore. The woman has to be seventy-something now."

She laughed. It was an infectious laugh. Her face shone in the dim light with magnetic radiance. Small curved lines formed at the corners of her mouth. Her eyes danced and sparkled and I could still see a lot of ten year old Adrianna in them.

"Naw, seriously," I said. "I did have an early teenage fling of sorts with a girl from over in Alderson who went to the college … you know, the old Greenbrier College for Women … last two years of high school, first two years of college?"

"I remember. Most of the girls who went there though were from well-to-do families and from out of state."

"I was all of fifteen and Laura Lynn was probably seventeen, a senior. I fell hard. We both struck it up pretty good for a few months."

"What happened to her?"

"Well, at the time, I was still a sophomore at the military school, a townie as they called us, thinking I was pretty cool, dating an older woman. But in reality, I was gawky and klutzy, wore Hai Karate and Brylcreem … you know, the whole nerdy package. And then … well, I met her dad for the first time after she and I had been going out for seven or eight months. When I shook the man's hand and bowed my head sharply, my sunglasses slipped off my ears, likely because of all the hair grease, and landed on his shoes. He was one of those big business, society stuff-shirts who owned a high-end men's store and I was the product of a lowly mortician that people like him avoided like the plague. He later told her "You're not going out with any creepy undertaker's kid, especially somebody fresh out of kindergarten." And he said another reason she was not to see me was that it looked like she was getting all too serious. When she graduated from GCW, her parents sent her off to Sweetbrier for her last two years of college. And that, my dear, was the last I ever saw of her. I was crushed, of course."

"Are she and her family still around?"

"Well, when I was a junior at WVU her dad ironically ended up on *my* dad's creepy embalming table. Is that justice or what? I'm not sure where she is now. Someone told me she got married and pregnant not long after she left town, not necessarily in that order. But anyway, that was my first love and that's how we got broke up."

"Hmm." She shook her head.

"Too bad. But you know what?" she replied.

"I'll bet it wasn't her father that broke you up at all. She probably just told you those things."

"Why would you think that? If it wasn't her old man, then why would you think she dumped me?"

"It's obvious to me. The Hai Karate, of course."

"What?"

"Hai Karate was the most *un*cool, stomach-turning cologne a kid could wear. I'm surprised your girlfriend even went out with you a second time."

I smacked her hand playfully and she laughed. "Hey," I said, "I wore other stuff, too. English Leather, Canoe, Black Watch …" She laughed at those, as well; and as I thought back to those years, those bug juices, though still entrenched somewhere in my olfactory brain, *were* pretty lame.

I do believe later in our conversation I caught Adrianna sniffing in my direction to assure I wasn't still wearing any of those nauseous brands of kerosene.

We sat and talked for the next hour about life in the country when we were kids, even though we were a half generation apart. We knew many of the same people … school teachers in junior high, Manuel and his wife at the Court Restaurant and the Presbyterian minister at the Old Stone Church. The parson had been dead over twenty years, she said. She remembered sitting in the sanctuary there and looking up at the faces of us cadets in the balcony, wondering where we were all from. Of course she knew where I was from and she mostly had her eyes fixed on me. I would have been a junior or senior at the time and well over Laura. I sometimes thought about how a century or more ago those very balcony pews were occupied by slaves brought to church by their owners to receive a Christian education. And I shared with her the memory I had watching the Bond movies at the local theater in the sixties when Black kids had to sit in the balcony at the town theater.

Adrianna reached into the ice bucket to pull out the half empty bottle of Zinfandel and poured a little more into my glass. Then instead of going back to the couch, she slid onto the love seat beside me. Her perfume was light, but just the same, intoxicating. I got the impression we had been playing a game of Chess. There was strategy involved and we were studying each other's moves. Only, in the game of romance, we couldn't decide who would make the first move. Since she had bumped her piece up against mine, maybe it was my move.

"I gotta tell you," I began. "I haven't been kissed the way you kissed me last night in a hell of a long time. Maybe never."

"Is that so?" she replied, grinning and teasing me with her eyes.

"That *is* so."

"I can honestly say the same for me. I thought maybe I was a little out of practice."

"If you were, then you recaptured your skill in a hurry."

All we could do for a few moments was sit there and grin at each other. But then in our game of Chess I put her in check. I touched the nape of her neck up under the brown silk that lay on her blouse. Her hair smelled delightful with that freshly shampooed aroma … something strawberry, I think. I kissed first her neck and her shoulder, finally moving onto her ear. She shivered as though I had touched my lips to her most vulnerable erogenous zone. She closed her eyes and began to breathe heavily. Her breath gave off the aroma of the sweet wine and I moved my mouth softy onto hers to taste its residual. Our tongues touched ever so slightly and she began to work over my lips, fervently, ravenously, like a starved animal. I could feel her hunger. She pulled back just a little to catch her breath. Then she parted her lips and moved them once again onto mine. I placed my hand inside her shorts and she moaned when I touched her. The nylon felt like warm silk to my fingertips. It was nigh time to satisfy our pent-up passion. I picked up her tiny body and carried her into the bedroom. All systems were *go*. Mrs. Peel, you're needed.

We were good together. Unselfish. Sometimes gentle. Sometimes like animals. It was amazing to me that after all this time, I was able to last more than four seconds. I couldn't believe the mind control and physical discipline I was maintaining to not only avoid sexual embarrassment, but having the ability to fulfill the desires of this supercharged little vixen. If I *had* disappointed her with a premature explosion of my single shot derringer, tomorrow and every other day I remained at Wolf Laurel, I would have to avoid eye contact. It wouldn't have been so much my system failure as it would have been a blow to my macho ego.

But as I lay motionless, spent and craving chocolate, which to me was like a smoker needing that after-sex cigarette, I watched her sleep. Her face only inches from mine was sweet and beautiful in the soft light. Her eyes pitched and roved beneath the lids. Dreaming probably. As she lay on her stomach making small wiffly noises when exhaling, I ran my hand gently up and down her spine from the base of her shapely neck to the small of her back, like a pianist running a glissando. In the calm after the fervent storm, it was as though years of bridled, unrequited passion, imprisoned much too long, had suddenly and violently been unleashed like the act itself had taken on a life of its own. I had no doubt that we could look at each other tomorrow, having no shame or regrets. But that look would be a different look, at least for me. The look of love.

I stayed with her for another hour, so as not to be charged as a hit-and-run driver, then slipped away. As I donned my shorts and tee, she woke and looked at the digital clock on the night stand, thinking it was time to get up and get breakfast started with Juanita. But then she looked at me in the dim light and smiled a sleepy smile. I took the smile to represent that I had indeed stayed with her to keep watch over her, and she liked that. It told her that I was a considerate lover and sex was more than just passion. She waved her fingers at me before drifting off again, and I quietly closed her bed- room door behind me.

I returned to my room, did my bathroom ditties and crashed onto my pillow. The black tee that I had on at Adrianna's I kept as my sleep shirt and it still smelled like her. I probably wouldn't wash it again until the aroma had fully dissipated. I smiled partly from revisiting every wonderful moment of the evening, but also from realizing what a nostalgic, sentimental wuss I was, which was in stark contrast to the calloused, calculating killer I had become from my years with the Army and the Bureau. If I had not loved those careers so much, I would have hated who I had become. One day I would leave it all behind me and settle into a sedentary life with someone like Adrianna. But as I lay there waiting to fade into unconsciousness, I knew there was no one I had ever met or would ever be with that was like her.

C H A P T E R   10

Lady of the morning Love shines in your eyes
Sparkling, clear and lovely You're my ... lady
—Styx

I arose early and looked out my window at a beautiful red sunrise, which of course meant there would be rain sometime later in the day. After jogging just over four miles, I showered and read my copy of *USA Today* all before eight. Then I actually took a seat in the dining room for breakfast. I thought this morning I would have something with a little more substance than the usual granola bar since I had worked up an appetite, both on my run and the night before. After an apple bran muffin, some skim milk and a cup of coffee as a chaser, I knew I shouldn't stray too far from my room for constitutional reasons, so I sat there a little longer.

Adrianna entered the room for a second time to greet a middle-aged couple that had come in the day before as well as a smartly-dressed, elderly Black lady with silver hair and glasses who looked to be a retired schoolteacher ... and then of course, there was *moi*. Assad did not partake of breakfast and as far as I could tell over the past few days, never had. I glanced out the window and saw that his car was still there.

The lady who tended me last night came by my table wearing a face as fresh and pretty as daffodils on an early

125

spring morning. She whisked about the dining room visiting and serving each person, including me, like a spider spinning a web, precise and methodical.

A veritable fusion of energy. An errant ray of sunlight that pierced the room caught her brown hair, causing it to take on the color of chestnut. She looked a half-dozen years younger and ever more vibrant. *Did I do that?*

"Well, good morning, Mr. McGowan. Did you have a pleasant evening?"

"Mrs. Wolf, "I replied. "I believe I had the best night of my life right here in your beautiful inn." I was loud enough for the others to pick up their ears. Adrianna blushed.

I continued. "The bed was … well let me say, erotically satisfying. And this breakfast muffin …" I kissed my fingers like the Frenchy guys do.

"… superb. Obviously one of the most gratifying places I have ever stayed. I will come back again."

As she passed by on her way back to the kitchen, Adrianna gigged me in the ribs and whispered, "You are a bad boy."

Yes I am.

About nine I dropped my derrière into one of the front porch rockers and waited for Assad to come out. I wanted to see if he would acknowledge me and if I could get an impression whether he perceived me as just a tourist from Washington, D.C. (I'm sure he checked out *my* plates, too) who was beginning to wear out his welcome or someone who in fact was dogging him. Although I didn't think he and his friends had spotted my Suburban at the airport and in White Sulphur, it was possible. And if he did suspect I was there for reasons other than fraternizing with the beautiful proprietress of Wolf Laurel, perhaps his eyes would give him away.

It was a drab day. The air was thick, even swollen, and a soft, sillvery drizzle began. But after a while the rain came down harder, beating a steady tattoo on the roof. The water poured from the roof and collected in the gutters, giving off a kind of clunky song as it rushed into the downspout near the veranda. I found it a refreshing change from the hot, sultry days of the past week. And considering I was feeling feisty and rejuvenated today, I wouldn't have cared if it snowed.

About nine-twenty the door behind me opened and out stepped Assad with the familiar backpack. I looked straight at him and said, "Good morning." I think it alarmed him as my greeting was not altogether expected. He turned slightly before stepping down from the veranda and returned the greeting with an obvious Middle Eastern accent. "Good morning, sir."

"Nice here, isn't it?" I was anxious to see where this would go.

"Yes. Yes, it is quite nice." He seemed to eye me curiously.

"I have seen you several times. Are you here long?"

His eagerness to engage in conversation surprised me. I figured he would continue on to his car and avoid any dialogue, especially if he was an American-hating terrorist plotting to annihilate infidels like me. But maybe this was his opportunity to satisfy any curiosity that he had about me and why I was looking at his and his friend's car. It could be he was wondering whether I was a Muslim-hating government agent plotting to kill Middle Eastern assholes like him. Or maybe I was just another nosy, self-absorbed tourist who had nothing worthwhile to do but pamper myself at a quaint country inn. He would be correct on both accounts.

"Yeah" I replied. "I thought I'd take a few days off from the wife and kids and come here to get the fog out of my head. Saw this place in the National Geographic and thought it would do the soul some good. By the way, friend, where are you from?" I tried to sound as folksy and common as I could. You know, just a good ol' American boy.

He paused a moment as though he didn't know whether to tell me he was from New Jersey or the fatherland, wherever that was. But he had to know I took a gander at his tag the other day. "I live in New Jersey, but I go to school here in West Virginia."

"You do? What made you decide on here?"

"I had a cousin who went to the college and he liked the area very much." Assad put his bag down to be further engaging, which surprised me even more.

"What is your work?"

I was now standing to convey to him that I was a polite versus an ugly American and extended my hand. "Hey, where are my manners? I'm Skip. Skip … White." There was only a half-dozen people in the area now that knew my real name: Adrianna, the two state cops, Paul LeMer and his accommodating assistant, and of course, Joey. There was no reason any of them would converse with him or his friends about me. As a check valve, I would tell Adrianna to refer to me as Mr. White from now on. He shook my hand and said his name was Assad. I knew that. I continued. "I'm an architect and live in Georgetown. That's up in the D.C. area."

Assad smiled. "That is much a coincidence, Mr. White. My father is also an architect and lives in Washington. He is on the board for all architects practicing in that area."

Oops. Why the hell did I pick 'architect?' Why couldn't I have said 'salesman' or 'journalist'? "That *is* a coincidence. Is your father in commercial design or homes?"

"He builds very large buildings. Also, many in New York and New Jersey. He would be sure to know you."

"Oh, I don't think so. I'm small potatoes and design houses. But I did have my fifteen minutes of fame. Maybe you've seen an article about me in Architectural Design? Frank Lloyd White. Of course, my friends call me Skip."

Assad appeared to be digesting this load of horse hockey and replied, "No. I do not think so. But I do not read my father's magazines." *Good.*

He added, "But my father is a contributing editor to that

magazine and I'm sure he would have heard about you."

Not so good.

I had to get off the subject and *quick*. "What are you studying at the college?" If I were a lying sack of government waste and hot on his case, which I was on both accounts, he would know that I would find out.

"I am studying American culture, Mr. White. I have believed it important to know much about the country I live in. It is sometimes uncomfortable to live where people have different laws and customs from where I grew up."

"And where was that."

"Syria, Mr. White."

"I do understand what you're saying, Assad. You can go to different parts of the United States and find a difference in culture, even among Americans of the same race and ethnic background."

Well, this conversation was certainly amiable enough. Of course he had been more truthful with me (except that he was plotting a terrorist act) than I with him. I hoped the counterfeit expression on my face was not giving me away. Then he said, "I have to go to my school now. I will see you again, Mr. White."

If I didn't know he was just being cordial, I would have taken that as a threat. Maybe it was.

"Call me Skip, Assad. It was good talking with you."

I watched him move at quick-time in the pouring rain all the way to his car. As he backed out and passed by me with the blacked-out windows up, I was sure he was looking my way and giving me the finger.

A moment later Adrianna came out to the veranda and nudged close to me. "Did I just see you talking with Assad?"

"Yes. And by the way, I am now Skip White from here on."

"White? Why?"

"As I am sure it was he and his friends that broke into the funeral home, I didn't want him to associate the name

McGowan. I'm taking no chances on him targeting Joey and his family if he ever finds out that I'm onto him and his buds."

"Are you really onto him for that?"

"Maybe. We'll see."

"So, what are your plans today?"

"I'm going to Charleston, but should be back by six or seven."

"I'll be here," she said, pinching me on the butt at the very moment the little old schoolteacher lady opened the screen door behind her. Timing is everything.

I went to my room and punched in Jack's number on my cell. A woman who identified herself as Jane Myers and Jack's assistant, said she would buzz him.

Momentarily, Jack came on the line. "Good morning, Bruce. I have been wondering about your progress there in Greenbrier County."

"Got a few things going. Thought I would come your way today.

Did you score with the satellite images?"

"Not sure. There are maybe three or four possibilities. The images aren't all that clear. I pulled up both government and private sites. I think you just about have to fly over all of them to get a true perspective."

"I guess for now I just need to drive around the area, take the map and canvass all the factories in the valley to see if anything matches up with the sketch."

"That will be a huge chore, Bruce, with the number of plants. I'm still not so sure there's credibility to the map and that we have a genuine threat here. Neither does Washington. By the way, I had an analyst do some research on each of the factories, what chemicals and propulsions are produced and whether any of them manufacture parts or products for the military. Although the Belle plant used to produce rocket fuel, there's nothing on the surface that would be of strategic or intelligence value and that would make any one of them a target for any reason. But the FMC plant still manufactures military vehicles and hardware. Could be some threat there."

"Is there a chance there is something Top Secret manufactured in any of these plants that you and I wouldn't know about?"

"Not sure, but I can check it out. I have a Top Secret clearance, as you know, and would think you still do as well. You and I would be privy to any such information we request. I can't imagine any terrorist network would have knowledge of something like that unless …"

"Unless there's someone on the inside who's feeding it to them or even drew the map."

"A possibility. But our sources will keep after this."

"Good," I said. "Do you have the time to ride around with me today? If I need to get inside any of the plants to talk with site man- agers, you have the credentials to get me in."

"I can't today. I'm leaving for a meeting in Washington in an hour."

"Hooverland. I'll be in D.C. tomorrow evening. Still live there, you know. I'll be stopping by Quantico to visit my daughter and then on to my condo for the night before driving on up to New York on Thursday."

"Will you be back?"

"I'm sure I will. The boss is intrigued about this sketch map and I hope to put the pieces of puzzle together soon. My experience, intuition and investigative nose tell me there is a plot here, and I'm not hinging it all on the map."

"What else have you uncovered that reinforces your suspicion?" he asked.

"Nothing really. Just a bad feeling, that's all." I didn't mention Assad and his companions, still thinking the better about sharing anything about them for two reasons: I needed to first report my findings to Birdman. After all, he pays my salary. Secondly, I *knew* guys like Jack … competent and effective, but aggressive climbers on the ladder to the top. If I clued him in, he'd have a team of Special Agents swarming like bees all over Greenbrier County and the suspects would be gone in a skinny minute. And although their plot may be foiled or abandoned, like a mess of Georgia fire ants, they would pop up in a mound somewhere else.

"Well, again, keep me informed if something tangible materializes."

"Okay, Jack. Have a good trip."

"You too."

In the uncertain shadows of my brain I was still bothered by the suspects' two and a half hour visit the day before to the airport just to eat lunch and watch planes take off and land; so before leaving for Charleston I decided to stop off at the airport office to inquire if anyone noticed their activities.

After entering the small terminal building, I noticed an information desk in the center of the lobby where I found a young man in a dark uniform with a plastic identification badge clipped to his shirt pocket. I identified myself, this time as Bruce McGowan, State Department agent extraordinaire, and asked him if he was on duty yesterday about noon.

"I was, sir. Is there something I can help you with?"

"I was wondering if you noticed any men of Middle Eastern background in the building?"

"If they're the men I'm thinking about, yes I did."

"What were they doing ... Mike, is it?" I asked, looking closer at his ID.

"Taking flight lessons."

The surprises keep coming. "Flight lessons?"

"Yes. Over yonder at Ross Flight Academy." He pointed through some glass double doors, leading outside and to an adjacent building about two hundred yards toward the end of the airport campus. This, I couldn't figure. These guys were students taking only one course at the community college and then they go to the flight school for instruction. As this was baffling to *me*, it would not raise the average cop's eyebrow. But I'm not the average cop. I've got enough conjecture and paranoia in me to suspect everybody as capable of doing anything at any time.

"Is the academy run by the airport?"

"No, sir. It's not connected at all. The school just rents its space from the county, but it has use of the runway."

I thanked Mike and made a beeline across the way to the academy office. Upon entering, I found a man, perhaps forty-five in a tan flight suit and a red ball cap sitting on the edge of a desk talking to a stern-looking woman with short-cropped blonde hair that had the texture of henna. She was thin and gangly, also wearing a jump suit, appearing somewhat masculine-looking and giving me the impression of a former Soviet Block Party member.

"May I help you?" asked Red Cap.

"I brought out my ID again and replied, "Bruce McGowan, Department of State. Are you the flight school proprietor?"

The man stood and held out his hand. "I'm Jed Ross, the owner. What can I do for you, sir?"

"There are three Middle Eastern men who I've learned are receiving flight lessons here."

"Oh, you must mean Assad, Ahmed and I can't remember the other guy's name."

"Probably Fayez."

"Yes, that's it. What about them."

"I'm just doing the standard background check that the FAA requires on foreign nationals. Just routine stuff. What can you tell me about them?"

"You know, that's strange. You're actually the first investigator I've ever had come by here to do any backgrounds on anyone." *Go figure.*

"Well, anyway," he continued in a uninflected monotone

which I found rather annoying. "They give me a hundred dollars a piece each time they take a lesson and Helena here and I take them up for the lessons."

"How many lessons have they had?"

He walked to a filing cabinet and pulled out a manila folder. "They've had … let's see … six, seven, eight lessons so far. Yesterday was the first day they actually took the controls."

"How did they do?"

"Okay. Each one of them seems to grasp the concepts well and I actually think they'll be qualified in a couple of weeks. You know, there were four of them initially. One of them apparently dropped."

Actually, dropped off the world.

"What kind of planes are they training on?"

"One of my planes is a Cessna Skyhawk and the other a Cessna 172."

"Ah, great little birds." Of course, I knew absolutely nothing about crappy little airplanes.

"Where do you take them?"

"Well, so far we've just flown around the county. As I said, yesterday was the first time they actually piloted the planes. We just did some touch-and-goes. They were nervous and made the usual mistakes with air speed and yawl. But after a while, they seemed to get the hang of it."

The blonde then spoke up. "Except the student I had kept bouncing the landing gear. I'm surprised the Skyhawk is not sitting on its fuselage right now." There was a gruffness in her voice much like I had expected would come out of her mouth. I'd hate to mix words with her.

"May I review their information packet? Just need the usual stuff, like the application, driver's license, et cetera. Better yet, can you make me a copy of all the documents?"

"I guess," replied Red Cap. "Who did you say you were with again?"

"State Department, Mr. Ross. Do I need to show you my

ID again?"

"No, no. That's not necessary. Helena, can you make Mr. McGowan copies of the material?"

She glared at him like she could pull out her Saturday Night Special and nail him between the eyes. I'll bet she didn't get coffee, either.

Ross immediately realized the error of his ways and trotted to the filing cabinet to retrieve all the packets, then retreated to the copy machine.

Helena's eyes then turned to me. "You don't *look* like a government agent." The eyes were piercing and I considered running from the room.

"Don't let the fact that I am not in a black suit and tie deceive you, ma'am." Maybe it was my face that threw her. It certainly wasn't as mean and hard as the face she looked at in the mirror each morning. Red Cap finished his copying and brought the folders to me. "Here you go, sir. Is there anything else you need to know about the students?"

"Mmm, yes. How much longer will their lessons last?"

"The flight program is set up for fifteen lessons or until I feel they're ready to be tested. Could be sooner or require more lessons. It's a 'pass or fail' course."

"So, if one of them took a nose dive into the side of a mountain that would be a *fail*."

Neither Ross nor his Nazi sidekick thought that was funny. It was like a pall fell over the room.

"Well, I guess that's all I need," I said. "I appreciate your time. But I do need to tell you one thing. My background investigation is confidential and if divulged to anyone, especially the subjects, it is punishable by imprisonment for not less than one or more than three years and a $50,000 fine." Actually, I just made all that up. I just liked saying that stuff.

Ross replied, "We understand, sir. You were never here."

When I turned toward the door, a thought occurred to me. I was prepared to drive to the Kanawha Valley and try to somehow get a panoramic view of the nine factories from the road or bargain my way through the gates and compare map with buildings. But in a fraction of my time on the road and zipping around all the plants in the Charleston area, I could fly over and view layouts of the factories more accurately. It was suddenly obvious that this was what the map artist probably did as well, unless again he somehow gained information from within.

"Mr. Ross, did you or Helena happen to fly any of your students down over Charleston at any time?"

"No, sir. As I said, they've never been out of the Greenbrier Valley in my airplanes."

"Will your students be in here today for lessons?"

"No, the next lesson is tomorrow. I'm giving a lesson to our local Chamber of Commerce director this afternoon."

"Oh. I thought maybe I could get you to fly me over the Kanawha Valley today. I'd like to snap some photos of a couple of things from the air. A little project for my boss."

He didn't press me for what it was all about. "Well, I won't be able to, but Helena doesn't have anything going. She could take you."

Oh, great. I wondered if they had any parachutes to rent. "Sure, that will be fine." I looked at Helena who had obviously just finished eating a box of nails. She was still bearing down on me with her eyes. "What will it cost me for say three hours, Mr. Ross?"

"Normally that would be about $200, but for a government agent, gas money. How does $100 sound?"

"Sounds like you're singing my song."

Within a half hour I was in the air with the lovely Helena, headed west over the mountains. The sky had cleared out and it was becoming a pretty nice afternoon, weather-wise. Within another thirty minutes we were approaching the Kanawha Valley. All the factories around Charleston were within about ten linear miles, first to last, and I would be able to cover them fairly quickly. My pilot had not said a word until we hit the chemical valley, mainly because I was scared to death to ask her anything. Every once in a while I gave her a quick peripheral glance and the Ice Queen returned it with a look of her own that made the hair stand up on the back of my neck. Her mouth was half open and frozen in a scowl. Actually, the last time I saw a mouth like that, it had a hook in it.

Nonetheless, being the reckless risk-taker that I am, I decided to break the ice. "Are you from the Greenbrier area, Helena?"

"No."

I actually prefer that people elaborate a little more when they answer such an open-ended question.

"Then where *would* you be from?" Her ice blues locked onto mine like an air-to-air missile. There went the neck hairs again.

"Is this an official question?"

"No, just making conversation." Sheesh. She took about ten seconds to respond and I initially thought there would be none at all. "I live in Alderson, Mr. McGowan. But I grew up in Germany about fifteen years before that."

Well, there you have it.

I was just about out of small talk, but thought I'd keep it going. There was still the flight back and that forty-five minutes back to Lewisburg would seem double. "I hope you didn't mind taking me up today, Helena."

"No. I am always happy to help out the United States government," she replied abruptly.

I was glad she was happy. I'd hate to be on this bird if she was *un*happy and it was one of her bad PMS days.

We were snaking the Kanawha between two mountain ridges now at about five hundred feet, having just passed over the small burgs of East Bank and Cabin Creek, where again one of my Mountain State heroes, Jerry West lived and played ball. When we approached the DuPont plant at Belle,

I asked her to slow the air speed and make a couple of passes. She looked at me curiously as to what our ride was all about, but said nothing. I pulled the sketch from my pocket and compared it to what I was seeing below. Although the map was roughly drawn, it still had enough detail for me to determine whether the buildings, storage tanks and overall layout matched up. I also took a couple of shots out of my window. After reviewing what I had, it seemed fairly clear that the first of the factories that lay between Route 60 and the Kanawha was not the one in the sketch.

I then asked Eva Braun to fly further down river to the Union Carbide plant in South Charleston. Again, I could readily see that Carbide's overall layout was not congruent with the map nor was it on the Route 60 side of the Kanawha. I waved her on.

That left FMC, which had five, not *two* storage tanks, a couple of factories in Nitro, Union Carbide in Institute and the Monsanto and American plants further west. As we flew over American, the factory layout seemed strangely familiar. After having studied the sketch map for four days, its image had become burned in my brain. The adrenaline began to pump through my arteries as I compared map to plant. If I had traced the hand-drawn map onto transparencies, it would have overlaid what I was seeing below verbatim. The two buildings indicated on the map with radioactive symbols were situated on the ground exactly as drawn. Each was connected by a series of pipes and conduits to two large storage tanks. The railroad distribution point and two large depots by the river, perpendicularly placed, were exactly to scale as well. It was clear that the map found on the Arab John Doe was not only of American, but had been drawn from aerial observation.

"Helena, can you get me a little closer to this plant without raising the suspicions of everyone down there?"

"May I ask now what this is all about, Mr. McGowan?"

I fully expected that if I did not tell her something, she

would next fly me to some desolate air strip in New Mexico, bind me with duct tape, and stake me out in four directions with rawhide, pour honey over me and let the ants have a picnic. I looked closely to see if the insignia she was wearing on her jumpsuit was aviator wings or an iron cross.

"I'm on a *couple* of missions here, Helena. The series of back- ground investigations is just one of them. I'm also doing a study for the State Department on factory pollution in the Kanawha Valley. As an example, see the liquid pouring from that culvert there into the river? And notice the smoky haze laying like yellow fog throughout the valley. People have to breathe that stuff. Did you know that the incidences of lung cancer and silicosis in this part of the state are twice as high as any other chemical area in the country?" I was even beginning to impress *myself* with this load of horse hockey and wondered where all this crap I make up comes from?

"And you are now a government scientist working with the EPA?" The scowl was now actually more of a sneer.

Well, it was obvious Helena knew I had thrown her a line. She glared at me, then banked the plane around to the right, dipping my side to where my face was stuck to the passenger's side glass and I was looking at the ground. At that moment, I really wanted to be just about anywhere but in a flimsy contraption, hundreds of feet up with Frau Helena. But I was pretty damned sure I could take her. And there was no way in hell my ass was getting dumped out of that airplane.

After I had clicked off a few shots of American, we winged our way back to the east. We touched down at the Greenbrier strip about four-thirty and my underarms were soaked. With as many near misses I had had from errant RPG rockets and AK-47 rounds while doing recons and combat assaults in Hueys back in Vietnam, for the first real time after landing, I felt like kissing the good old Greenbrier earth. "Thanks, Helena. Might I say you are an excellent pilot? I've flown with a number of aviators in the bush and in hostile environments. They were good, but I believe you're the best." I was so glad to be down, I could have told her anything. "Here, don't tell your boss, but please accept this." I placed a $100 bill in her hand.

"But you already paid for the trip," she said. The scowl was strangely gone now.

"I know, but this is something extra for *you*."

It was like the sun had come out from behind the clouds. She smiled and it was actually a pretty smile. I thought her face would shatter in a thousand pieces.

"You should do that more often, Helena."

"What?"

"Smile, of course." And there it was again.

CHAPTER 11

*And I found out a long time ago What a woman can do
to your soul ...*
—Eagles

Back at Wolf Laurel, I sat at my secretary reviewing the
photos I had taken of American on the three-an-a-half inch
screen of my digital Nikon. I had clicked off about a dozen
shots of the factory from different angles as Helena was
dipping and banking the Cessna, turning my stomach inside
out. The pictures served to reinforce my earlier convictions,
that I had located the probable terrorist target. If indeed
there *was* a plot. And I was increasingly sure there was one.
On the way back to the B&B, I had seen a One Hour Photo
sign at the Walgreen's on Taylor, so I lit out again and
deposited the film card at the store. While it was in process,
I grabbed a cup of coffee and a newspaper at a Seven Eleven
next door, returning to my Suburban to catch up on what
was happening in the world. Same tragedies and heart breaks
going on, whether you were in the Middle East or in
Hollywood.

When I pulled back into the lot at Wolf Laurel, I noticed
Adrianna's van was not there. I hadn't seen it earlier, either.
But I did hope she would be back soon so that we could
have dinner, starved that I was. I zipped through the shower,

threw on a pair of khakis and a golf shirt and went out to the veranda to plop into my favorite rocker. As the rain had stopped hours earlier, it was still rather cool and damp. Shrill tree frogs were going nuts in all of the still-wet landscape. Twenty years from now I could see myself porch-sitting like this with a shawl wrapped around me and eating vanilla pudding.

Off to the left side of the porch a hummingbird whirred in one spot for several minutes making love with its beak to a rhododendron bloom. I thought how amazing that was for the tiny critter to stay suspended for that long, beating its wings several hundred times in a mere five seconds. I also thought about one other of God's amazing creatures, Adrianna. It was nearly six and she had yet to return.

About ten after six, the little schoolteacher lady, who had arrived at the B & B the day before, stepped out onto the porch, smiled at me and sat down in the rocker to my left. She had on a black, loose hanging dress, black hose and short-heeled dress shoes. Looking very sweet and proper. As she appeared to be in her early seventies, I took to wonder how many years she might have taught school and again how many children's lives had been changed from studying under her.

"Hi, I'm Skip." I stood to take her hand.

"Well, good evening, Skip. My name is Lottie. Lottie Throckmorton. Fine evening, isn't it?" I took a deep breath and exhaled.

"I love evenings after the rain. So fresh and exhilarating to the lungs."

"You sound like a poet, Skip. Are you a writer?"

"No, ma'am, although I have written the equivalent of a half dozen books in memorandums and correspondence over the years. I've worked for the government all my life." I hoped Assad wasn't listening on the other side of the screen and I knew Mrs. Throckmorton had no reason to spill the beans about me to anyone. I needed to get her disinterested in *me* and put the focus of our con-versation on *her.*

"Are you still working or retired? You remind me of a schoolteacher I once had.

"Well, I've never taught school, although I wanted to at one time. I retired last summer after twenty four years as a New York congresswoman."

Sometimes I scare myself as to how accurate I am in guessing peoples' professions. Schoolteacher ... congresswoman. I was pretty close.

"That's very impressive, Mrs. Throckmorton. I'm sure you represented your district well."

"Call me Lottie, Skip. Yes, I guess I did all right. A lot of people even wrote in my name on the ballot last fall, but I was tired and needed a permanent vacation."

"Are you here on part of that vacation?"

"Well, yes. My staff went together when I retired and gave me two weeks at Wolf Laurel. Jackie, my personal assistant had stayed here a few days a couple of years ago and loved it. But I don't know what I'll do for two whole weeks. I don't have a car to go anywhere and don't need one; I only eat breakfast and then just have snacks for lunch…and anyway, I have no desire to gad about town. But I do like to read and this place is very conducive for that. I had told my staff I needed to go to some out-of-the-way place to catch up on all my reading. Guess they took it to heart. It's so relaxing and beautiful here."

The place did indeed have some lovely amenities. And one of them was missing. Where *was* Adrianna, anyway?

"It *is* pretty here." I settled back in the rocker and sighed.

"A guy could get used to a place like this."

"Yes." She nodded and settled back as well. As she rocked and hummed some old song, the wood creaked beneath the runners of her chair.

I liked Lottie. She seemed genuine and straight-up ... obviously, a complete paradox to the typical politician. We talked a while about really nothing and then the light of day began to fail. She pulled her sweater tightly into her bosom, excused herself and stood to go back inside. I stood to show my politeness and thanked her for a pleasant conversation.

Burt joined me for a while. After I scratched him a couple of times behind his ears, he jumped into my lap. I hadn't been much for cats, but this guy had a unique personality.

"So, where's your mistress, old boy? Looks like we both got abandoned today." He answered with a mew and cranked up his motor. After a couple of turns in my lap he settled down for an apparent nap.

The sun had long gone. The dark, colorless leaves of the large maples allowed just enough of the waning twilight to peer through. But within minutes, the day finally gave up the ghost and the grounds were totally dark with the exception of the mellow light cast by a gas coach lantern at the end of the walkway. I rocked a while, feeling a bit like a geriatric porch-sitter, listening to the crick-crack of the runners, wood on wood. The crickets and tree frogs were making music together. A kind of *night* symphony. There was a bullfrog somewhere close by being answered by the female, which is sometimes called a cow. It all made for a pretty night, the cool air, the critter sounds, Burt's warmth on my lap. But I was getting a little sleepy, not to mention bored.

At eight forty-five I gave up on the mistress of Wolf Laurel, dumped Burt and went on to my room. I had no sooner puttied and turned on the TV when I heard soft footsteps in the hallway. I immediately recognized them to be hers. They stopped at my door and then I heard the gentle knocking.

I opened the door and started my routine. "Well, I'd say it's about *time* you came home," I chided, looking at my watch.

"Your mother and I have been worried sick that you were in an accident, but more-so worried that you may not have clean underwear on. I may just have to punish you."

She smiled and pushed her way by me. "Does that mean you have to spank me?"

I shut the door. "I'm afraid so." My smile was more like a diabolical grin.

She sat on the edge of my bed, kicked her shoes off and laid back. "Did you eat?"

I sat spread eagle and in reverse on the desk chair within a few feet of the bed. "No. Nothing since breakfast. I thought we would be having dinner together."

She sat up. "I'm sorry, Skip, but we didn't talk about that or else I would have."

"I just assumed we would. Oh, well. No big deal. Where'd you go?"

"Well, my friend, Dan, called me this afternoon and asked me to go to the team's first scrimmage with Beckley. Then after the game, which by the way the Bobcats won, I had a bite with him."

I took a moment with this. "A bite," I repeated rather sardonically.

"Yes, and that's all." She was suddenly very defensive.

"That doesn't bother you, does it Skip?"

A pain shot through my chest. I knew it wasn't cardiac arrest.

More like cardio-jealousy. "A little."

She swung her legs off the bed and leaned into me. "Skip, listen. Last night was … absolutely wonderful. Since you have been here, every cell in my body and every facet of my soul have been fulfilled. But my point is, we've only been together a few days. I've just gotten to know you again, but I still have friends I've known for years. I do have a life outside of the inn … and that of my guests."

Well, that just about did it. I had been reduced to a 'guest.' What a difference twenty-four hours make. Last night may have been the most passionate night of my life. But tonight? The only passion I was feeling was something between anger and resentment. But being the trooper that I am, I swallowed hard and bit the bullet.

"Okay, I'm sorry. I'm just feeling a little jealous, that's all. And I don't have the right."

She jumped down from the high mattress and stood at the rear of the chair, pressing her tight lower belly against my hands. She then leaned down and kissed me on the forehead. "That's sweet. *You're* sweet."

I didn't want to be *sweet*. I wanted to be mad as hell. I guess I'm still in the fifth grade when it comes to my continuing education in Women 101.

Standing up, I took her hands in mine. "Well, I suppose this is goodnight and goodbye for a while. I'm leaving for D.C. early in the morning tomorrow and will be in New York on Friday."

"Oh," she responded, looking not only surprised, but a bit pained.

I *felt* like saying, "Now you can spend all the time you want with Mr. Macho Jock. So I'm just going to go away and may not even come back, nanny nanny boo boo." But that would be my five year old child coming out. To save myself a great deal of embarrassment and maintain my dignity as well, I thought the better of it.

"You *are* coming back, aren't you? I had blocked out your room for as long as you needed it, thinking you would be staying a while longer. At least until you were through with your investigation. Are you done with it?"

I get it, now. It's all about keeping the rooms rented out. I began to boil under my collar again. In a low enough voice so that Assad would not hear me, I said "No. There's still work to be done. I'm still focusing on your Arab boarder down the hall and what he is up to."

"So you *are* coming back here?"

"Either here or I'll stay at Joey's."

She appeared very vexed about my answer. "Well, I would like to know for sure. The Labor Day weekend is in great demand and I have at least two couples on stand-by for your room."

"Then perhaps you should go ahead and give it to one of them." As all this was escalating well beyond our levels of comfort, we both knew that this was really about Dandy Dan. She stood looking at me with disappointed eyes. There was a degree of hurt in them as well.

I wasn't about to let this go any further, so I took her hands and said "I do plan to come back on Sunday. Go ahead and rent out my room; I don't mind. I'll just stay over at Joey's. Anyway, Assad thought I was just here for a few days of R&R. If I show back up after leaving, he may get suspicious."

Her eyes softened. I knew my terse tone of voice had indeed hurt her. She was trying to keep them from spilling tears down her cheeks.

"You can stay with me when you come back," she said in a near whisper, trying to keep her voice from cracking.

I pulled her into me and crisscrossed my hands around her back. "That, my dear, is very tempting, but I should go ahead and bunk with Joey and family. I think they felt slighted because I didn't stay with them. And my staying with you would not only draw attention, but would probably not be a good Public Relations scenario for Wolf Laurel."

"Okay," she replied.

"But I'd like you to spend Labor Day with me if you can. A bunch of my friends and business associates are having our annual picnic at the State Forest. There'll be people from the community college and the high school who will be setting up venues and games to help generate scholarship money for the county's underprivileged kids. It'll be fun. So how about it?"

"I'm not sure, but will think about it." So I did for a couple of seconds. "Oh, hell. Why not?"

"Good. Now that that's settled, would you like to come up for a glass of wine or cup of coffee?"

"No. I'd better not. I have to throw my things together and hit the sack. I'll be leaving out around five thirty." Anyway, I was still pouting about how the evening had turned out, the knuckle dragger that I am. She caught my expression.

"Are we okay here?"

"I'm okay. How about you?"

"You just seem a little distant, that's all."

"I don't mean to be," I replied, taking her in my arms. "You'll have to forgive me. I'm … just a very complex human being."

She put her lips on mine. "You don't taste complex."

"Well, that's not my complex flavor. That's my licentious flavor."

She laughed. "Guess that's it for tonight, huh?"

"I guess. Gotta pack and clean out my room."

"Then I'll see you Sunday." She capped off our rather doleful evening with a wet, sucking kiss. She definitely did not fight fair.

I was greeted by the first light of the golden sun just as I reached the crest of a long mountain grade near the exit that turned off to Goshen. Adrianna had pierced my brain more than a dozen times in that first hour and I was soon regretting my episode of juvenile jealousy the night before. I felt like turning around and going back to Wolf Laurel to spend just five minutes with her to assure that we were indeed okay. And I was not happy with myself for another reason: I had let her inside me and she was unwittingly causing me to lose my focus. It was just as well that I would be away from her for a few days. Perhaps now I would be less flaccid and weak-minded and return to my old impervious, despicable self. Just thinking about it, I was already feeling heathenish.

Going a full twenty-four hours without food and totally famished, I had breakfast in Lexington with an old Vietnam buddy. We whiled away a couple of hours reminiscing and swapping war stories. As many times as we had coughed up these old tales, it was sometimes difficult to separate fact from fiction. There was one story we left alone, however. It had haunted my dreams so often, I had no desire to revisit it while still conscious.

After a bit of manly embracing, I moved on to Richmond and then up to Fredericksburg where I pulled over to call yet another friend, John Esposito, a former Bureau partner I had served with in Phoenix for a couple of years. He was now teaching at the FBI Academy and one of my daughter's instructors. As it was not yet the weekend and Caroline, along with her candidate peers, had no life outside the academy until Friday evening, I had to perform a little hook and crook with good old Johnny to get a dinner date with my little girl. There was also a bottle of Scotch in it for him.

I went on to my apartment in Georgetown to look at my mail and clean up for the evening. I did have a couple of hours to kill before I joined the I-95 South parking lot. Caroline's training would end at 1800 (that's 6 PM to civilians) and she would be ready about seven.

I called for the boss and got his assistant. "Virginia, is His Spyness in?"

"He's on the phone, darling."

"Then I guess I'll make love to *you* for a while. How's my favorite sex symbol?"

"Still waiting for you to ask me out, big boy."

"I'll be there Friday. Where do you want to go?"

"How about my place," she replied. "I could make you a candlelight dinner of pasta and wine, and then you and I could sit by the fire in something skimpy and see where the night takes us. Twenty minutes with me, Brucie, and you'd never look at another woman."

"You're a tease, Virg. You know Tom would never go for that."

"I don't mind if Tom watches; do you?"

"I don't think his heart would take it. You'd better give up on that idea."

"Well, okay then. But five minutes after he's planted, your bones are mine, lover."

At sixty-two, Virginia de Hussey (yep, that's her real name) was the only live wire among an otherwise anal New York CTT group and the glue that kept everything together. And she was neither shy about what she said or how much of her voluptuous bosom she revealed. I know she drove Birdman nuts, not because she was still a well-preserved, histrionic middle-aged woman, but largely because she was often disruptive to office decorum. But she was very good at what she did. Left over from the Cold War, she had been the personal assistant to two CIA Directors and knew enough about foreign affairs to be an invaluable resource to the boss and the team. The Bureau wanted her and the Company wanted her *back*. But she liked working for people with integrity and moral soundness ... and that was Birdman.

We finally ended the telephonic foreplay when the boss got off his call. In a moment, his raspy voice was on the line. "What do you have, Bruce?"

He was always to the point, not 'Hello, how's it hanging' or 'I missed you, big guy.'

"I've got some names and addresses for you." After spelling the names phonetically, I began filling the boss in on the suspects' activities. I added, "I also need for you to find out everything you can on American, a factory west of Charleston."

"I assume you matched up the sketch map with the plant."

"Building for building. Even the dimensions were accurate."

He took a moment to write down the information. "So what's the deal with the flight lessons?"

"Beats me," I replied. "Either they intend to continue reconnaissance of the factory or drop something nasty on it. Or maybe they just want to learn to fly airplanes like some people want to sky dive or bunji jump."

"I don't think it's the latter, Bruce. You're doing good work. We'll of course talk more about this when we meet up. You *are* planning to be here Friday?"

"I'm halfway there now. I'm having dinner with Caroline tonight and will drive up tomorrow afternoon."

"Good. Tell her I wish her good luck in getting through her training. I know she'll make a splendid agent. She's the kind of personality I'd like to see on our team one day. Maybe replace you, old man."

"Not even funny, Hawk. I want her to have a nice long career behind a desk bagging dirty accountants and CEOs, only drawing her gun once a year to qualify."

"I don't blame you, Bruce. Give Caroline my best."

"Will do. I'll be at the Dorsett tomorrow evening if you want to have dinner."

"See you Friday, Bruce."

I had on my pink Polo again, mainly because Caroline likes me in it. I'm not really a GQ kind of guy, but Ralph (Lauren that is) and I have been pals for years. He should be paying me for all the advertising I do for him. I've got to admit I look pretty good in his stuff. Caroline said it's a preppy paradox to my tanned, rugged looks. We met at *Steverino's,* a restaurant and bar where Steve Allen played eons ago when he started out. The guy at the piano even looked like Steve, big funky glasses and all. He was actually pretty good and if you didn't know Steverino was dead, you'd think for sure it was him.

Caroline was there before me at a table set off by itself on a kind of balcony over-looking a second level of tables. She stood and hugged me and I noticed that she was a bit thinner than the last time I saw her … about three weeks ago. Her beautiful brown hair was now cropped short.

"Are they not feeding you, Sweetheart?"

"I'm eating well; they're just working it off me."

"I remember when I went through your training, ten

years older than you are now. I thought being thirty-three and out of Special Forces, all the physical crap was long behind me."

"So, what kind of physical requirement is there for what you do now?"

"Being able to drag my sorry butt out of the rack in the morning and maintaining a normal heart rhythm after two cups of coffee."

She laughed her little girl laugh, something I missed terribly. "If I know you, you're still religious about your five miles every day."

"Religious is a good word. By the end of the third mile I'm praying there won't be a myocardial infarction at the end of my run."

Caroline smiled. Funny, I hadn't really noticed before, but her big brown eyes had a hint of warm honey in them. Maybe it was the light. "You look good, Dad. You must be doing *something* right."

I winked and smiled back. At five-five and a hundred fifteen pounds, I wondered how she was able to compete with her male peers. But since she was my only child, I raised her to respond like a girl *or* a boy, depending on what life threw at her. Actually, I've got to give her mother credit for the girl part. The beauty and brains may have come from her mom, but by Gawd when she was with me, I taught her to prepare herself for the real world … the dangerous world. By age ten she had a black belt in Tai Kwon Do and on the firing range could match me shot for shot with a 9 mm. Her mother hated me running interference into her plans for Caroline to become Miss Americaand a concert pianist. Although I didn't discourage her undertaking these things, I felt they were distractions in the real game of life. More recently, however, in realizing that Caroline would ultimately be facing danger in the vocation I practically pushed her into, I knew that if something bad ever happened to her, I would not only have to face the wrath of her mother, but the face in my mirror each morning.

I ordered a carafe of Merlot, but as Caroline was concentrating on keeping her head and body sharp, she asked only for water. After each of us had a salad, then my New York Strip, medium well, and her scallops would follow whenever. Stevie was singing and playing Chevalier's *Thank Heaven for Little Girls*, which was ironically the very thing that was on my heart tonight.

I noticed that an older, conservative looking couple at the next closest table would look at Caroline and me and then work their lips. Obviously, they thought the young chick at my table was out with her Sugar Daddy. I leaned down toward their table and offered an unsolicited explanation, pointing at Caroline, "My daughter … *really*." The woman turned her head quickly back to her husband, exhibiting both a degree of disdain and embarrassment.

"Dad! Behave."

"Yes, sweetheart."

"Are you seeing anyone these days?"

"Not exactly. Who has the time for a social life when I'm gallivanting from here to God knows where? Actually, I don't even know why I keep an apartment."

"Isn't it time for you to settle down into a nine-to-five gig, get married and join the Elks?"

"In other words, you want them to find where I left my bones after I jumped off a cliff in some remote area of Idaho."

"Don't you think it's time, Dad? You're fifty-four years old and been running too long."

"Who says I'm running? This is what I do. This is all I know. As long as I'm healthy enough to still knock down bad guys and remain in complete control of my life and faculties, I'm doing okay, Kiddo."

"Sure you are," she said, sardonically. "I still worry about you."

"As I do you. And how about you, Missy. Is there a love

in *your* life?"

"Right now it's the Bureau, I guess. But rest assured, Father Dear, one day you will have some grandbabies to bounce on your knee."

"I will definitely be looking forward to that."

The dinner arrived and I started digging. Two days in a row I had missed lunch, and then dinner the night before, but I wasn't telling Caroline. She would worry about me and a lecture would follow.

"How are Uncle Joe and his family?"

"Good. The girls are beautiful. I don't guess you've seen Casey and Molly in over five years. You wouldn't know them."

"I guess not. Love to see them. Have you been taking a few days off or working?"

Between bites I filled her in on the Middle Eastern boys and their suspicious activities. She agreed the whole deal appeared stinky. Of course, I left out my sexcapade with Adrianna.

"So how's your mom?"

"I guess okay. She had never had any meaningful relationships since you guys divorced ... except now for Ned."

"Of course, where would she find anyone as wonderful as me again?"

Caroline shook her head slowly, like one does out of pity. "Still the same old dad ... narcissistic, egotistical and self-absorbed."

"You left out handsome, hunky and humble."

"No wonder Mom gave up on you. There wasn't room for anyone else in your life but yourself."

"You're being pretty critical of your old man, aren't you? You have no earthly idea what kind of ill-tempered nag your mom was when we were married. And when it came to the wedding vows ... love, honor and obey ... she totally ignored the last one."

I knew it was wrong when it came out of my mouth. Caroline laid down her fork and fired a laser beam with her green eyes. I recognized that look. It was one her mother used to wear. One that could melt the chrome off a trailer hitch. I really must be an absolute Dodo, managing to piss off two women in as many nights.

"Don't malign Mom like that," she retorted sharply.

"Sorry, sweetheart. You're right. Maybe you should add 'stupid and insensitive' in describing me as well."

I thought the smile would come back, but no such luck. Although we still had about a half hour left in our father-daughter rendezvous, I wondered if I had enough time to surgically remove my size ten Weejun from the inside of my mouth. I pushed back my half-eaten steak and drained the last drop of Merlot from my glass. There were no words exchanged for a while, then I broke the ice and smiled at her. It was my apologetic smile.

She heaved a sigh. "I'm sorry too, Dad. I just want you to realize that Mom's had a tough time and she's a really good and sweet person."

"I know she is. Probably *too* good for the likes of me. I'll say one thing: you've got her integrity and stamina. And did I also mention 'feistiness'? Those make for a good cop."

"Like you," she said.

I shook my head ever so slightly. "*You* be the good cop in this family and make up for all your old man's shortfalls. I'd be proud as a peacock to see you one day becoming the Bureau's first female Director."

The smile finally came back. That let me know she was no longer angry at me, although I'm sure she still thought I was a derogating egomaniac. Obviously, the *one* good thing she inherited from me was her keen and accurate perception.

I pulled out from Steverino's parking lot and took a slight detour off the main highway onto a secondary road that would not only still take me out to I-85 North, but also by Darlene's house near Woodbridge. The road was narrow and a bit twisty, but a good deal less traveled.

Darlene had married a guy named Ned who looked and sounded about as nerdy as his name. He was also as bald as a cue ball with a forehead that belonged on a Neanderthal. But who am I to be critical? I don't think she latched onto him because he had a lot of money and owned a twenty-some acre farm off the road, but she certainly didn't marry him for his looks. I suppose he was a nice enough guy and treated her well. And maybe after me as a husband, he was the kind of fellow she needed … someone who would dote on her and give her the time and attention she deserved.

After coming to a stop at the end of their driveway I pulled off the road into a small turn-around area. Although it was purely dark, with the aid of their yard security light I could still make out the details of their huge, looming farmhouse perhaps fifty meters back from the road sitting majestically on a small hill.

"You finally did all right for yourself, Darlene," I whispered to no one. "And I'm okay with that."

What I wasn't okay with was my Austin Healey sitting unloved on the gravel driveway off to the right side at the garage. At least Ned had the compassion to put a car cover on it. He probably had a Ferrari in the garage and there would be no way he would allow Darlene's ex-husband's sports car to share floor space with his ride. The bastard.

They had a nice spread and I had every right to feel envious. But I didn't. Places like that required a lot of money and work. Even if I *could* afford it, I wouldn't be home more than twenty-five days a year to enjoy it.

My driver's side window down, I sucked in the cool night air. It was very peaceful, way out there in the Virginia countryside. The full moon stunned the northeast horizon, rising blood orange against a blackboard sky and spreading its haunting glow softly across the pasture. Harvested bales of hay, dark and colorless, were scattered irregularly over the dimly lit field, appearing as centurions, sleeping, even dead.

It all made me feel damn lonely and suddenly I realized these feelings were all about missing Adrianna, desperately and painfully. I sat there hating myself for having pursued her in the first place. I was feeling that same old gnawing pain of love that I probably hadn't felt since I was sixteen and when Laura Lynn's old man made her dump me. I already had enough physical pain going on in my body, like in my knees and my chest, to have this achy love thing going on as well. It was like having a kind of sweet poison running through my arteries.

After a while and another look at the lonely little 3000 sitting under wraps, I shook my head, dropped the shifter into *drive* and accelerated slowly from the side of the road. My unpretentious little apartment awaited me.

CHAPTER 12

Late Thursday morning I was fighting the Battle of the Potomac on my way to Reagan National. Somebody was changing a tire on the shoulder on the Beltway and as thousands of rubbernecking drivers had never before seen such a phenomenon, I was stalled. My frustration soon eased when my cell phone rang. It was Adrianna.

"Well, good morning," I answered.

"Did you have a good evening with your daughter?"

"It was very nice. And I did my best to improve her knowledge."

"About FBI stuff?"

"About her father being a complete jerk."

She didn't laugh, not because she didn't think it was funny; she probably knew Caroline was a good judge of character.

"Oh," she replied.

"Well, I'm sure you loved seeing her again." She paused.

"I missed you yesterday."

"You missed seeing me before I left or you actually *missed* me?" Another pause.

"I miss you."

Those three words sent a shot of adrenaline through my arteries. "I miss you, too," I echoed in my best eighth grade schoolboy voice.

"Where are you now?"

"On the Beltway headed for the airport. My plane arrives in New York at two this afternoon ... that is, if I can ever get out of this parking lot. Wish I were there with you instead." The Saccharin tone in my dialogue was beginning to make me sick.

"Me too. Another rainy day here and they always make me blue. By the way, you asked me to take note of anything having to do with Assad's activities. Besides the two Arab men who have been hanging out with him, there was another, older gentleman here yesterday evening."

"He was Middle Eastern as well?"

"Yes. A little more dark-complected and older ... maybe 45 to 50."

"Hmm." Definitely a network of some kind, I thought. An older man wouldn't be a student. Why would they have any association with him? "Were they engaged in any unusual activity?"

"No. I heard them talking loudly in the parking lot and again as they passed by the desk. I couldn't understand what they were saying. It wasn't English they were speaking. The older man was angry about something."

"What kind of car did he have? Were you able to get the tag number?"

"I didn't go out to get the tag, but I think he was driving some kind of van. It looked a lot like mine. I don't mind telling you, this all seems to be rather unnerving."

"Adrianna, I'd like you to just go ahead about your business and not record any other activities. I don't want you to feel uncomfortable about this and I certainly don't want them to get suspicious. Tell your maid to stop her mental notes as well. I shouldn't have asked either one of you to do that."

"I'd feel a lot better if Assad would just go ahead and leave. But I can't ask him to leave without cause. And he's already paid for next week."

"Yeah, booting him will definitely raise his antenna."

"He has refused maid service ever since he came here. He just asks for fresh towels when he stops by the desk each day. Juanita, my maid, has never been in his room."

"That's probably a good indication there are things in his room he doesn't want anyone to see."

She was silent for a moment. "When is it you're coming back?"

"Probably Sunday night. Like I said, I'll be going to Joey's."

"Did you decide for sure if you're going with me to the Labor Day picnic at Greenbrier State Forest?"

"Only if you bring some fried chicken."

"I'll be sure to make some."

"And chocolate cake?"

"That too."

"I'll bring a bottle of Merlot."

"I don't think they allow alcoholic beverages in the park."

"You're kidding, of course."

"No. Those are the rules and the event committee reinforced that in bold letters on the flyer."

"Communists."

"Maybe I'll clink glasses with you Monday evening here at my place if you'd like."

"I'd like."

"Be careful in your travels."

"Okay, sweetie. See you in a few days."

"Bye, Skip. I ..." She didn't finish.

I thought maybe she was about to say the 'L' word. I wished she had. It would certainly hold more over until I saw her again.

My plane landed in Newark just after two and I got a taxi to the Dorsett in Manhattan. The hotel was ancient, but grand. Not the same grand as one would find at the Waldorf Astoria, but quaint and nostalgic 1940s grand. It was especially nostalgic to me, because nearly twenty-four years ago one Caroline Ann McGowan was conceived there in Room 240 on my wedding night. And it was also a time when I was in love with Caroline's mom. But that was then and Adrianna was now.

The Birdman knew I would be staying there *and* in Room 240, as he had already left me a message. "Just wanted to remind you … nine o'clock sharp, tomorrow. Don't be late."

I saluted the red flashing light on the phone and deleted the message. He could have just as easily called my cell, but I think he just enjoyed being anal and let me know he could anticipate my every move and routine. I was determined not only to piss him off, but let him know his dictatorial powers didn't work on me. I'd show *him*. I'd be in his office at 9:05.

When I stepped off the elevator onto Birdman's floor, I bumped into Abu Narziz, our Arabic translator. I had met him on a couple of occasions within the past year … once in a meeting at Zulu Headquarters and then again at Ft. Bragg two months after. The reason for the second meet-up at Bragg was to suck out the brain of a man known as Khallad, the architect of the U.S.S. Cole attack. The Yemenis had arrested Khallad for the bombing and after President Clinton, the CIA, CTC and NSA had tried diplomatically and 'otherwise' to take custody of the terrorist, Zulu moved in and appropriated him through less than diplomatic means. Delta Force had a little to do with it as well.

Abu, an Iranian army commander, who Khomeini called the Hero of Sousangerd, when he successfully repelled an Iraqi attack sending Saddam Hussein's forces back across the border, was later imprisoned by the Ayatollah for refusing to employ chemical weapons in answer to Saddam's own chemical use. Abu, who was exiled in the sixth year of the eight year war, ultimately escaped and sought asylum in the United States. Immediately establishing his loyalty and trustworthiness, he became an invaluable asset to the CIA as an Arabic translator. When Birdman was tasked by Washington to start up CTT, he brought Abu with him.

"My friend Bruce," he said, embracing me about the shoulders and kissing me on each cheek. I didn't know we were that close.

"My friend Abu," I echoed. "Great to see you." I took a moment to fill him in on Assad and the others.

He lowered his voice into a near whisper. "Ah. You may be onto something there in West Virginia. This man, Assad, may be just a student, but I do not think so. I take him to be an Islamic idealist like many who have come here, but he could also be one of the Jihadist young lions of which there appear to be many in this country now. As you have learned, some are in the universities, but others have gone to work in the factories, the airports and the financial institutions, each of the venues being significant targets for terrorists."

"You know about the American possibility?"

"Yes. Preceptor told me you had done a reconnaissance of the factory."

"There could very well be a lion on the inside."

"Yes, perhaps. That is often the plan. Someone on the inside will feed information about security weaknesses to those who plot from the outside. The insider may work there for months, even years. They are very patient. The subversives plan and wait ... wait for the day and time. Then the orders will come down."

"Years?"

"These are all people who dream, Bruce ... dream of achieving glory as martyrs. They begin as young boys receiving their indoctrination in schools, mosques and especially their family systems ... learning to hate, training to kill. It is all very sad." Abu's face took on a somberness that I did not see in our previous meetings. I suspected that he knew first hand what Jihadist poisons were injected into the brains of young Arab children concerning the Great Satan. "Our enemies are all around us, Bruce," he added. "Our eyes and ears must always be open."

And then his pager went off. Abu checked the number

and said, "I must go, now. I will be interested to see what will happen with your case, Bruce. *Assalamu alaikum*, my friend."

What little Arabic I knew, I did remember 'peace be unto you.'

"*Wa barakatuhu,*" I returned the blessing.

At precisely 9:05 I stopped by Virginia's desk. I didn't have a hat to throw on the rack, but in keeping up my Bond image, I humored her with the Moneypenny handle. And as this always tickled her, she would respond by referring to me as 007.

Today Moneypenny had on a plunging blouse that revealed unusually perfect cleavage for an older gal and I stuck around a couple more minutes to appreciate the royal magnificence. And as if on cue she said, "Go on in, 007," then winked.

I reciprocated with a quick double eyebrow raise. I tapped first on his door and then entered.

"Come on in, Bruce, and have a seat at the conference table. You're late."

Lionel Byrd sat engrossed in something on his desktop monitor, but when I approached his desk, he stood like the gentleman he was and extended his hand. Did I mention that it was actually *me* who coined all the bird code names? It just sounded Ian Fleming-ish and the 'Byrd' name made for good fun. Byrd, always dapper-looking in his three piece gray suit made of a faint, light wool herringbone and characteristic unlit pipe in hand, did look like an M. Only he looked a bit older today and that would make him a P or a Q. Birdman was one of the good guys I had known in all of this law enforcement business. Not an ounce of pretentiousness or obliquity.

But there was a carriage of pride in his demeanor, devoid of arrogance and conceit.

"Good trip?"

"So-so."

"Did you give Caroline my regards?"

"Of course." Not. I had forgotten.

"She's a beauty," he said. "Favors her mother." I caught the sarcasm. *My good looks are in there somewhere too, Birdman.*

Byrd decided after thirty seconds of small talk to cut through the chase. "Okay, lay this all out for me. What's new about the suspects since we talked?"

"Before I begin, what did you find out about American?"

"Well, it's a plant of strategic value that produces several toxic chemicals, including GB, Chlorine and Hydrogen Cyanide gases. The GB is an isopropyl agent, Sarin that would be used as a last resort by the U.S. military. Naturally, our government's *official* position is that there is *no* use of chemical or biological agents in the event of war."

"Naturally. I do remember most of my NBC education and training from Special Ops days. GB and other nerve agents, once released into the air, cause immediate constriction and secretion of mucous from the mouth. Then there are the convulsions, the paralysis of the nervous system and death in a matter of minutes. Nasty shit."

Byrd nodded. "GB has been around for decades, but only recently reproduced in uncertain quantities for stockpile, and only to be used in retaliation of a chemical strike on the battlefield. Of course this is Top Secret information and even at my level, the State Department didn't want to release that to me. I'm only passing this on since you have the same clearance."

"Don't worry, I won't tell more than two or three people." Birdman eyed me sternly.

He continued. "American is owned by U.S. and Canadian companies, ergo the name. And here's the clincher: it's also partnered with an Israeli organization. That's why we can indeed speculate at this point that the factory is a very real target by your little nest of Middle Easterners, given the detail of the sketch. My boss is very interested in this now and wants you to stay the course."

"And your boss would be who?"

"Sorry. I can't tell you that, Bruce."

"Okay then, let's say you get knocked off. Would my paycheck suddenly stop? And furthermore, who would I have my silly little conversations with?"

"Let's say I *do* get knocked off, as you so eloquently put it. You would be contacted by my replacement."

"Who is?"

He gave me that look again without responding. Now I really *was* starting to worry about future paychecks. I'd have to make sure Byrd stayed alive.

I laid out the photos I had taken of DAG, the three suspects and American. I had ordered 8X10s of the factory.

"Yes," began Byrd.

"These will be most helpful. I'll run these faces through Interpol and the FBI database to see if there are any hits. Perhaps we'll find them among our compiled list of subversives in the Muslim Student's Association, which is a very radical student group, well indoctrinated and propagandized. One of their goals is to establish an order of caliphates by grooming these young Muslim men for a kind of Islamic priesthood. A dollar to a donut that's who these boys are." He spread out *all* the photos and studied them a little more in depths. "You did well, Bruce. It's astounding that the sketch map looks like an overlay to this photo here. They have identified these two buildings and tanks where the gases would be stored. I agree the map had to be drawn from the air, so obviously either one or more of these men flew over the factory or someone else did and supplied them with the sketch."

"Likely someone on the inside," I added. "How else would the average terrorist schmuck know about what a strategic type of factory like American would produce?"

"Indeed," he replied, reflectively, stroking his chin.

"Your brother did right to call you about this. I trust he

will maintain a high degree of confidentiality."

"Joey? Of course. Undertakers are sworn to secrecy by the National Mortician's Board."

"Are you making that up?"

"Yeah," I grinned. "But think about it. Sometimes they find out things on dead people that family and friends would never suspect. They're held to standards and codes like any other profession, and in some ways, such responsibilities are even more fiduciary in nature. That's when families are the most vulnerable. Dead men tell no tales and neither does my brother."

"Okay."

"What did the auto tags turn up?"

"The Nissan is registered to Assad Mohammed. No surprise there. The Honda's owner is one Afain Shareq. That name is nowhere close to either of the two men's names you provided. Could either belong to one of their fathers or a friend?"

I nodded. "There's another interesting item. I talked to the owner of the Bed and Breakfast where I've been staying and she said a man between 45 and 50 visited Assad Mohammed two days ago. The man was having an animated conversation with the three younger suspects in the parking lot. Could be he is running the show and I wouldn't be surprised he was upset about the missing map. Either they need it for whatever raid is being planned or the man fears it has fallen in the hands of the authorities. I'm pretty damned sure that was what the break-in at the funeral home was all about."

"Then you need to find this man." He crunched on the pipe stem and bore down on me with trenchant eyes.

"This B&B owner … is she the woman with whom you have struck a special friendship?"

How the hell does he know about her?

"Special friendship?"

"How much does she know about you and what you do?"

Well, somehow and for some reason the greatest currently living spy man in the world has kept private tabs on little old me. He apparently knows my moves, both business-wise *and* social-wise. This was going to rattle me. I knew he trusted me and was complimentary of my work; so was he still required to know my activity every moment? And who required that of him? I didn't readily respond to him.

He continued. "It's my business to know everything about you, Bruce, even when it involves acquired relationships."

"So you think I have a relationship?"

"If it's not one, you missed your chance. Now for the answer, Bruce."

"I have engaged Ms. Wolf as an informant, given her capacity as the inn's proprietress. She only knows I work for the government and some kind of investigator."

"As she is not a professional, you can trust her to be discreet?"

"She has no reason not to be, boss."

"But things could slip out."

"Not with her."

"You must be careful about this, Bruce. The suspects can't pick up on her. Cease any activity on her part to watch the men."

"I already have."

"Good. So, go ahead and get on back to the inn to continue the surveillance. Your intuitions have been dead on. Get the goods on them any way you can."

"So, you now want me to continue staying there."

"Actually, it has always been okay for you to stay there. I'm also glad you rekindled an old friendship with Adrianna."

"You know her name and about our friendship years ago?"

"There's nothing I don't know, Bruce."

"Oh yes there is."

"Oh no there isn't." He paused for effect. "Just be careful not to mumble in your sleep." His eyes had a more patriarchal tone now.

Birdman was good ... and obviously sneaky. Now I was *embarrassed.* I wondered if there was some external video or listening device in proximity to the inn. Maybe in my locator chip. And I now assumed he had been privy to our secret interlude. *Damn!*

I broke away from that subject, quickly. "You don't care about the bill there?"

"How much is it per night?"

"I thought you knew everything."

"For some reason, not that."

"$300."

"*What?* That's not going to fly."

"Well, would you approve half that? $150."

"That sounds more in line."

"Good. I'll negotiate for that or press for a special Government rate. Anyway, she's a special friend, remember?" I figured if I told him up front the place was $150 per night, he'd blow a gasket and insist I stay at a $40 a night Motel 6.

"So, tell me again what she knows about you?"

"Again, not much. She thinks I'm some kind of immigration cop," I lied. He probably knew I was lying since he knew everything else.

"Okay. Keep it that way."

"How long should I stay on this?"

"Right now? As long as it takes. I have a feeling something's on the move and hopefully you'll be in position to out-wait them."

"When will you expect the profiles from Interpol on these faces?" I asked.

"This is Friday and it's tough to secure information over the weekend, especially holiday weekends."

"So I return there and wait."

He nodded. "Hopefully there will be increased and significant activity that you can monitor and evaluate. It would also be good to get a look inside both the B&B suspect's room and the bungalow where the other two are staying. There would be no way, however, without a court order, but we don't want to go that route. Understand?"

"I understand," which meant I would use my own discretion and means. "Anyway, getting a court order would make them disappear in a hurry."

An immediate problem was that I was no longer staying at Wolf Laurel and I sure as hell couldn't take a room at the Jamestown Motel. That would be a dead giveaway I was on their trail.

I continued. "Don't we need to get American alerted for a possible terrorist attack?"

"Your phone call the other day was enough to get the ball rolling. They've increased security on the gates and there will be observers in strategic locations outside of the factory as well."

"And the airspace around Charleston?"

"Covered. The West Virginia National Guard will be patrolling the skies in that area. Every small plane in the area will be monitored and if there's one up there without a flight plan, it will be shot down. Of course, I don't know how long this vigilance can be kept up. It may be weeks or months before any plan they have is executed."

"In Charleston, every Labor Day weekend, the city puts on their Stern Wheel Regatta at the Landing. They bring in a couple of big names, block off the boulevard and let the beer flow. They even have a New Orleans-style funeral parade. There may be as many as two hundred thousand there over the weekend. A prime venue for a dirty bomb." I shook my head. "Don't even want to think about it."

"I know all about that, Bruce."

"Of course you do," I said to the man with all the

answers. "Looks like as always you've done your homework, boss. What then do we do about the Bureau? The Charleston agent is pressing for any new and continuing information."

"The Bureau, the Company, CTC. They're all looking for a piece of the pie … and all the credit," he replied. Byrd swiveled around and looked at me glumly. "Jack Fuentes and his post have been alerted to anticipate an attack on American or somewhere in the Kanawha Valley, but we have not given them everything. You know the area and your one face is better than five Bureau faces out there beating the bushes. I agree with you. We don't need a bunch of hot shot agents running amuck without a plan rounding these people up. Just have some random dialogue with Charleston and keep their number on your speed-dial in case you need to engage them. And don't hesitate to bring in the locals as necessary. Stay close to the suspects, Bruce, but not *too* close as to garner suspicion."

"Roger that. These maggots will spook and run at the first sight of a Crown Vic."

Byrd nodded, then swiveled in his chair facing the window. As he bit on his pipe and scanned the rooftops of commerce below him on Wall Street, he was silent and reflective. After a few moments he spoke. "We're vulnerable, Bruce. You know, I look out over this city some days and think how easy it would be for just one hatemonger with a suitcase device to wreak havoc, bring down buildings and kill thousands of people. Islamic radical factions thrive on hate. They don't believe hate is a bad thing … that it is necessary and is justified by the Koran. Any people who are outside of the Dar al Islam or House of Submission are infidels, and violence is the only resource."

I didn't respond. I have always been struck by this man's philosophical and spiritual nature, not to mention his intellect, political and otherwise. Any attempt on my part to have an engaging dialogue with Lionel Byrd would be like a seventh grade Civics student conversing with a Harvard

Political Science professor.

He continued. "These radicals also instill in their youth a hatred of the West, a degrading of women, and a belief that the one true path to Heaven is to lose their lives by killing as many Americans as possible. It is the necessary combination that will lead to Muslim unity. They literally follow the words of Muhammad and Imam Muslim: *The gates of Paradise are under the shadows of the swords.* As a Muslim's deeds are on a balance scale, his good is measured against the bad, and although they wait until the Day of Judgment for the final tally, they believe that Allah does guarantee he will admit the true Jihad into Paradise for giving up his own life to kill infidels.

"The Jihadis are like Nazis in Kaffiyahs. They are a radical form of Wahhabi Islam, undergoing a kind of inquisition, who want to finish the Holocaust and destroy not only Israel, but Jews everywhere. They ultimately want to control all of the Middle East, to include OPEC and the entire world's economy."

I nodded like if he hadn't offered up these profound observations, I would have. Byrd was indeed a scholar on this stuff and it was always an education for me just to be around him. But I had to add some of my own reflections to show him I was not a *total* ignoramus on the topic. "And then there is that obsessed hatred of Western depravity. Islamic ideology mandates that immoral secularism must be eradicated. To do that, all of Americaand its entire population of men, women and children, the epitome of immorality, must ultimately be exterminated. These people are not just ruthless, but they have no value of human life. To the Jihad, if you are not Muslim, you may as well be a piss-ant mashed on the sole of one of their sandals."

Birdman sat a while longer, fingers formed prayer-like under his chin, and gazing from his window beyond the clutter of skyscrapers toward the Hudson. He was quiet for the longest time. I thought he had fallen asleep after I had begun to chime in with my observations. But then he slowly whirled his chair back around and affixed his eyes on mine. "We need more tangible information on this nest, Bruce, to find out for sure whether they are Al-Qaeda, Hezbollah, Aden-Abyan Islamic Army or even Jaish-e-Mohammed. You know what to do and how to gather it."

"Okay," I replied, like I knew what the hell all these Islamic organizations were. I would definitely need to do some Googling.

"Remember what I said about your friend. I hope you can keep her out of danger. She's a very pretty lady, Bruce."

Okay now, that *did* it. How the hell would he know what she looked like? How was he doing this and what kind of toys did he have at his disposal? I felt at that moment like I was in the room with a reincarnated Ian Fleming and J. Edgar, all wrapped up in one. "Yes, she is," I agreed.

"So are we done, Boss?"

"We're done," he replied, maintaining his reflection.

"Lunch?"

"No."

As usual, Birdman was short on his goodbyes. He pretty much punctuated the end to all conversations with one or two words, leaving his fellow converser hanging like a dangling participle.

So I had lunch with Moneypenny. We had a nice conversation, but I had trouble making eye contact with her since breasts don't have eyes.

CHAPTER   13

After getting back into Georgetown at two thirty on Friday afternoon, I took a nap, then dined at my favorite Italian haunt, Mariano's. As I had enjoyed Georgetown this past year, complete with its university flavor, nifty shops and riverfront restaurants, for some reason I again felt very alone. Although I had tried all evening to expel the feeling, it was all about missing Adrianna. Just in one week, this woman had inadvertently caused me some very real inter-personal distress. I thought I actually enjoyed being me, having a very focused and uncomplicated life; but just as I had realized the other night on the road outside Darlene's house, I was a very lonely person with no real future in sight … at least a happy one.

I sat by myself listening to a pretty young thing at the piano bar singing some ballad in her awful beauty pageant voice, strained, cracked and loaded with false vibrato. Then images of another lovely woman and her soft, Southern voice penetrated my brain. I guess I had always thought I would one day meet someone that I felt good about … good enough to marry. But I still had contributions to make to our country. And as I was still in pretty good shape and healthy enough to continue doing the work of law enforcement, helping to keep our country safe and free from those bent on destroying it, I didn't need the responsibilities and distractions of a relationship. But, of course, I hadn't counted on Adrianna coming into my life. If she expected more from me, I knew I would end up hurting her and feeling sorry for the both of us.

After dinner, I stopped off at *The Cat's Meow*, a nifty knick-knack shop down the street, and found a most lovely crystal vase which I thought would look nice on Adrianna's dining table. I shelled out $250 after whittling the little lady behind the counter down from $300, although I was sure it cost her something like $49.95; but for some stupid reason I felt I had made a great deal. As I walked out of the store, I caught the reflection in the storefront window of some poor, lonely and sentimental shmuck who had allowed a little time and distance away from his girlfriend to develop a mushy mass in his brain and at the same time lighten his wallet. If they saw my moony eyes now, both my old Special Forces buds and new Zulu pards would be laughing their asses off.

I went on back to my apartment and dipped into some Merlot, feeling even sorrier for myself than before. I thought a lot about how and why Byrd was keeping tabs on me. I knew it was nothing personal and there was no lack of trust. Was everyone in his peep sight? How about the couple sleeping in the Lincoln bedroom? I suddenly felt very naked, not to mention paranoid. But after catching a little of the tube, sleep came over me just after nine-thirty and put me out of my misery.

The TV that had partnered with the wine in knocking me out woke me up the next morning with the early edition of Fox News. I was still slumped in the over-stuffed sofa chair where I had passed out and my neck hurt. A car bomb had gone off in a Tel Aviv marketplace, killing more than twenty people. A PLO extremist group had already taken credit and the face of Arafat, looking more like Willie Nelson than Willie did, was all over the tube half-heartedly condemning the blast. It would not be long until the Israeli government would retaliate with a raid on some known terrorist stronghold, vindicating the deaths. Wonderful, I thought.

Saturday morning I ran the Mall from where I parked my car near the Capitol building to the Lincoln Memorial and back. My shadowy twin running alongside kept perfect pace with me. I did catch a breather and some water at the Vietnam Memorial where I ran my fingers across the names of four of my Special Forces compadres. It had become a ritual of mine each time I ran. I knew precisely where each name was as I had visited them scores of times since the emplacement of the wall.

Back at the ranch I did a week's worth of laundry, showered and went again to Mariano's for supper. Strangely enough, the beauty queen sounded better than the night before. It may have had something to do with the carafe of wine I gulped. But then later when she started singing that one song that at least one contestant always did in every pageant ever held, *I Feel Pretty*, I knew at that very moment my life sucked.

I couldn't wait for the light to hit my eyes around 6:15 on Sunday morning, so having awakened at five, I swung out of bed, showered, grabbed my bag and suitcase and hauled ass for West Virginia. This time I went west to pick up I-81 and the northern neck of the beautiful Shenandoah. If God ever decided to come back to earth and take up residence, I was sure He would settle somewhere in that part of Virginia. There's a good thing about having a job where you set your own hours and get to travel. You can take your time getting from one place to another and zip off the highway to see anything you want. And I did just that. I first visited the site where the VMI cadets fought a battle with Yankee troops at New Market and then I exited at Staunton for a superb country lunch at Rowe's.

Further down the pike I stopped at the Washington and Lee campus to visit the Lee Chapel. If there was ever a place that gave me such hallowing serenity and peace, it was here. Sitting in the front pew, I gazed for several minutes upon the magnificent marble statue of Robert E. Lee lying in repose on the battlefield. The sanctuary was deafeningly quiet as I was the church's only visitor. After a while I closed my eyes, blocking everything from my mind, including Adrianna, Arab terrorists, arthritic knees and other annoyances. I listened for a message from God, but I had been such a heathen over the years, He probably wanted to take me out to the woodshed instead of giving me His valuable time. But He finally showed up, showering me with a sudden spear of sunlight through the leaded glass window. I looked up at the sun-dappled cross above the General and it was purely the first time I remembered having such a religious moment since I was a kid. That is, except for last Monday night at Wolf Laurel.

Driving long hours on the interstate opens up the brain to thousands of thoughts that interweave and run onto one other, often making no sense. But ultimately they will all dissipate which will in turn allow me to settle onto one of them. In the process, I will sometimes dwell on some pressing matter or some regret, like my divorce, or maybe on Caroline. And sometimes it may be a gnawing, even fearful thought that will engross me to a point where I don't remember passing an exit or a town, then suddenly finding myself two counties away.

Sometimes I may even begin second-guessing myself on theories I had earlier solidified. I was convinced that the Arab vermin were planning to somehow attack American. Then I began thinking if this was all just speculation on my part … that I had made too much of the map and the boys' behavior. But I always trust my instincts and they usually don't disappoint me. Again, what if I was wrong and we took this too far and I took out an innocent Arab student? You see, those are the kind of fearful flip-flopping thoughts I can have. I guess I just think too damn much.

But then, there was that compelling picture in my brain of a car driven by a young Islamic terrorist with a Russian-manufactured suitcase bomb on the seat beside him crashing through a barricade and taking out the American factory. Although these compact weapons of mass destruction that the Kremlin had intended to be detonated in American cities during the cold war weigh less than 40 pounds, they could easily cause damage equal to the bombs dropped on Hiroshima and Nagasaki. Even a suitcase bomb could create a fireball reaching 10 million degrees. A bomb exploded within a factory that manufactured hydrogen chlorine gas would be devastating enough, but with a nuclear device, there were sure to be few survivors in the entire Kanawha Valley. Anyone not immediately consumed by the fireball and shock wave would still expire within three days from radiation poisoning.

I shut off my festering brain, turned on a classical music station and listened to something by Mozart, I think. I pressed harder on the accelerator as though it would help me expel horrendous images in my head of people screaming and dying. No, goddammit, I would *not* second-guess my instincts about these bastards. I was right. I was *definitely* right about them. And I would stop them. I called Joey just east of Clifton Forge and told him to expect me somewhere around four. He said he saw Adrianna at church as she was coming out. He was going in to set up for a one o'clock funeral and asked her if she'd like to come to the house later for dinner, knowing of course I would be coming back. She said she'd like that, but her assistant was off and there was a new couple coming to Wolf Laurel between five and seven. She'd take a rain check.

At ten minutes till four I turned north onto South Ivy Road and then down the lane that led to the old McGowan place. Hearing the unmistakable drone of a small plane, I looked to see a small red-and-white Cessna buzzing the landscape about a thousand feet up. It circled the farm once and then disappeared over the tree line. I wondered if it was Assad out for a Sunday drive.

Cora had prepared yet another wonderful dinner and I made sure to compliment her. Joey couldn't begin to realize how good life was for him. A pretty wife who could actually cook, two sweet girls who adored him and a business that … well, two out of three isn't bad. After stuffing my gills with the heavy spaghetti supper, I slipped out to the porch and called Adrianna on my cell.

"Hi, stranger." She looked absolutely stunning over the phone. I could tell that from her voice.

"Hi yourself," I replied, trying not to sound too anticipatory about seeing her tomorrow, which I'm sure would be a fabulous day, and which at day's end, if I was lucky, may conclude with a nocturnal rhapsody. "Did you miss me?"

"Yes," she said.

"I'm anxious to see you."

"And I'm anxious to see you. Breathlessly so." She then changed gears. "Did you accomplish everything you set out to do?"

"Been busy, all right. I've kept my nose to the grindstone, shoulder to the wheel and ear to the ground; but baby, I only have eyes for you."
She laughed. "Seriously, what all did you do?"

"Well, in all my time away, I only spent three hours with my daughter, three hours with the boss, and the rest of the time either on the road or doing my laundry or in bed."

"By yourself, of course."

"You mean while I was on the road or doing my laundry?"

"You know what I mean, silly. In *bed*."

"And what did *you* do these last few days?"

"Behaved myself," she replied.

"Will you behave tomorrow?"

"It depends."

"On what?"

"On you. If you give me anymore trouble, like a few nights ago, I may have to punish you." She let out a soft giggle.

"You mean spank me?" *My* turn to say that.

Now she laughed. "Only if you're naughty. And I hope you are."

"You can count on it."

"Pick me up about eleven?"

"I'll be there. I don't mean to change the subject, but have you seen Assad today? Not that you're supposed to keep tabs on him now."

"He left out yesterday morning, but I don't think for good. He only had his knapsack with him. The older guy in the van came by and Assad followed him in his car. I happened to be snipping some roses for the vase in the lobby. Assad has always greeted me when we pass one another, but yesterday he just gave me a cold look and didn't say a word. It kind of gave me the willies."

"So his car is still gone?"

"Yes."

"Who do you have staying there now?"

"Well, besides Assad, Lottie Throckmorton is still here; she has another week or so. I also took in a nice middle-aged couple from upstate New York and there's a younger couple from Virginia Beach now in your old room."

"How *dare* they!"

"You're funny."

"You're cute." Starting to make myself sick again.

"See you tomorrow, Skip. Kiss. Kiss."

"Bang. Bang."

I took a little walk to melt some of the calories away. The fresh evening air electrified my lungs and re-vitalized my tired brain. It was now seven-fifty and the sun had begun to fade. The remnants of its orange glow still filtered through the trees on the far horizon. When I returned to the house, Joey was standing on the front porch with a half-smoked stogie.

"Beautiful evening. I think I worked up a hankering for that pie now."

"Better hurry, Brewster. There may be one piece left and if you don't snag it, I will."

"Why don't you go ahead? I've got to go out anyway. Don't wait up."

"It didn't take you long, big brother."

"What?"

"To hook back up with the Lady of the Inn."

I faked the kind of sheepish smile like when one is found out. "Who said I was going out to see *her*?"

He just shook his head and waved me off. "I'll leave the light on for you, Casanova. Don't wake me when you're slippin' back in about three o'clock."

I nodded, still smiling. The thing was, I would *not* be seeing Adrianna where I was going. At least I hoped not.

I changed into my black cargo pants and black tee, donned a black baseball style cap and left the house in my black Suburban in the black of night. Obviously, I was going for concealment when I parked my SUV along the road behind some trees adjacent to Wolf Laurel. The Nissan was still gone, but in the driveway there was a Buick (the older couple), a Mustang (the younger couple) and Adrianna's van. I remembered Lottie didn't have a vehicle. It was just after ten and the lights were already off in Adrianna's room. There was a light on in one of the two front rooms. I scanned the grounds for any movement and waited for my purple vision to set in.

After about ten minutes, I snapped my Glock in its holster, shoved my black metal flashlight in *its* holster and moved carefully around to the back of the house. Assad's suite, the Magnolia Room, at the far end of the house had windows at the side and back. I wondered why he got the Magnolia Room and I only rated the Pine. Through the blinds I could see there was no light on in the room. I had to assume he was still not there.

Assuring that all was quiet inside, I entered the dimly lit lobby after unlocking the front door. Adrianna had not asked me for my room key when I left and this same key also worked in the front door lock. With as much stealth as I could manage, I crept down the creaky hall floor and located the door to the Magnolia Room. I checked the door for a wire that may have been connected to something that would go off and mess up my handsome face. It appeared there was none. From my belt I then took out my handy-dandy burglar kit and with the two picks, worked my magic on the lock. After a few seconds the deadbolt clicked open. The lock below the ancient doorknob was a piece of cake. Slowly, I pushed open the door and listened with my eyes tightly shut for a click or a boom. Finally satisfied the entrance was not booby trapped, I entered the room.

I switched on the flashlight and first shined the beam onto both beds to assure they were unoccupied, then quickly scanned the main room and bathroom to reaffirm there was no one about. It was time to go to work.

The room smelled like a mixture of curry and incense, which was pretty damned nauseous. At least it didn't smell like B.O. or dirty socks. Carefully and methodically, so as not to disturb the turf, and still being cautious to look for explosives, I began checking out Assad's closet. I rifled the pockets of his clothes and sifted through several plastic bags. One of the plastic bags contained only dirty clothes and another, some cans and boxes of food, the labels of which were printed in bold Arabic. A nice pair of Mediterranean-looking roach killers caught my eye and I shook them out.

In two dresser drawers were a half-dozen folded shirts and rolled socks. The guy was a neatnik; I gave him that. Maybe even obsessive-compulsive. A copy of the Qur'an laid dead center on the desk, beside of which was an 8X10 notebook and pen. His textbook, *Multicultural Issues in*

America was to the left of the Qur'an. The drawers to the desk were for the most part empty. The left drawer contained an Innkeeper's Guide like the one I had in my room (or used to have) and in which was a picture and description of Wolf Laurel in the West Virginia section. In the center drawer were two more pens and some B&B stationery with an image of the inn at the top left.

I checked between the mattresses and under the beds, as well as the bathroom medicine cabinet, finding nothing. A rolled-up mat was in a chair by the door which I unfurled and inspected. It appeared to be Assad's prayer blanket.

After five minutes in the room, I was convinced that if he had anything of suspicious nature in his possession, it had to be in the backpack he was never seen without. The man traveled light, likely didn't eat much, and probably spent his time in the room reading and praying.

I put the beam of light back on the notebook and opened it. Counting seven pages of neatly penned hieroglyphics, which appeared to be Arabic, I pulled from my pocket my digital, set it for flash and photographed each page. I then opened the Qur'an, finding a loose sheet of paper behind the front cover on which was written four paragraphs, at the end of which were numbers, some kind of message I took to be scriptural verses. Also in the book was a picture of a young, beautiful Middle Eastern girl who was perhaps his sweetheart or sister.

Making sure the two texts and notebook were aligned on the desk top just as I found them, I made another sweep of the room in case I missed something. I apparently didn't. Just as I reached for the doorknob to leave, I heard the front door to the inn shut and footsteps in the lobby. It was just one set of footsteps, so I figured it wasn't the newer boarders. Switching the flashlight to *off*, I turned the deadbolt lock to the right and the doorknob to its locked position. The footsteps were now in the hallway and I knew it must be Assad returning at a most inopportune time. How rude is that?

Quickly, I slid under the near bed and unsnapped my holster. If it was Assad and he decided to check under the bed for vermin (like me), I'd have to plug him. The footsteps stopped at the door. For a moment there was no sound at all from the other side. I wondered if he had heard me. Just in case, I pulled out the Glock and screwed in the silencer. Finally, I heard the deadbolt click, followed by the second lock. After Assad pushed the door open, the room illuminated. He then shut the door and the locks clicked again. I watched his sandals pass by the bed a couple of times and then disappear to the closet. It was a stroke of luck that I chose to hide under the bed; my first inclination was the closet. Of course, that was also *his* good fortune. He could at this very moment been lying on Adrianna's floor with a nasty hole in his head, changing the color of her rug.

The sound of a bag unzipping and the rattle of a plastic bag told me he was transferring something from his canvas tote into one of the two Hefty's ... maybe more dirty clothes. I then watched the sandals approach the bed again where he stopped. He was so close to my face I could see the toe with the ingrown toenail sticking out of the sandal. Go ahead and look under the bed, Assad, I thought. There's a boogeyman under here. Your worst nightmare, as a matter of fact. But he didn't. He only stopped to drop the backpack on the mattress. Then, as I hoped he would, he trotted off to the bathroom.

I heard the commode seat clatter against the tank and then the audible urination, right in the center of the water. It was certainly loud enough to drown out any noise I would be making crawling out from under the bed and scrambling for the door. I prayed for his sake his bladder was full as I quickly turned the locks, opened the door to step out and re-closed it gingerly. I continued my escape softly down the hallway, thinking that by this time, his lizard was fully drained. In the morning, when he left his room, he would discover the unlocked door and wonder why it was so.

On the way to my car I checked for anyone lurking about who may have seen me, then slipped away from the parking lot to my vehicle. My work is often a matter of luck. And I was lucky I had not stopped the unfolding plot before I could figure out its particulars. Not to mention having to kill Assad Mohammed prematurely.

CHAPTER 14

A lazy fog hung over the green hills and fields early Monday morning, the 3rd, as I ran along South Ivy on my second mile. Pockets of the cottony mist lay like hosts of ghosts left over from the night, refusing to go away until chased by the sun which had not yet peeked over the far tree line. White farmhouses and ancient barns of chestnut plank filtered by the fog appeared opaque in the morning twilight. The air was fresh and cool and the warm vapor from my lungs spewed like cigarette smoke, which incidentally had never passed through my lips. As it was quiet and seemed that nothing in the world was stirring on this Labor Day morning, it tended to magnify the steady pound-pounding of my Nikes on the pavement. This Greenbrier morning, like many others early on in my life, created in my soul a religious, even holy experience, mollifying my spirit, and seemingly defying the evil that lurked in the shadows of our liberties ... an evil whose mission it was to infiltrate and violate our beautiful land. Images of radical Islam fascists wreaking tragedy upon this state's people and industry, demoralizing and horrifying the innocent, angered me, shattering the peace that had abided in me when I began the morning. I ran harder as though the physical act itself was a way to unleash my anger upon the malignancy that sought to destroy America. I was now more determined than ever to find out if a real threat existed, as I was sure it did, the scope and depth of that threat, and at all costs choke it off. Was I kidding myself that I could do it without engaging the FBI? Maybe. But if and when I did get the goods on these guys, I knew all I had to do was press 2 on my speed-dial. Birdman would have Zulu on site in a flash if needed. It's good working for an organization that provides same day service.

Cora had a country breakfast waiting for me when I returned from my run. Today's granola bar would lay in my bag yet another day. The aroma of flapjacks on the griddle, bacon and rich, black coffee brought back sweet, nostalgic memories of life in the 1960's at the McGowan Homestead. I loved the old place. The house *and* the funeral business had been left equally to Joey and me; but I didn't want either, much to both Joey's *and* my ex-wife's protests. But I did reluctantly accept a share of the life insurance proceeds and Dad's 30.06 as my inheritance. The money went to a college fund for Caroline, which I later found was only a drop in the bucket. Thank God for the student loan program.

Dad taught Joey and me to shoot ... rifles, shotguns, pistols ... even the bow. He was an avid hunter of anything that crawled, moved on four legs or flew. Although Joey and I never really took an interest in hunting, we allowed Dad to drag us into the woods during quail, duck and deer seasons. I learned that it wasn't enough to go out in the wild when it was just plain *deer* season; there was a separate *doe* season as well. I asked him one time if there was a *Bambi* season and the man of a million cornpone mortuary jokes didn't think that was a *bit* funny. Hunting was serious business.

Nonetheless, every year in mid-December when the leaves were all gone, he'd take Joey and me out to the woods behind our house and direct us to shoot clumps of mistletoe out of the trees. We collected the shot-up foliage and then Dad gave it to Mom who hung it on the overhead door facing between the parlor and dining room.

Before long they were standing under it doing suck face. I never understood why two people got romantic under a clump of fungus that was formed from bird crap. I also never understood why Dad was the one that got smooched from this deal and all I got was a raspberry on my shoulder from the recoil of the twelve gauge.

But those were great times … innocent times. I sometimes wonder why and how I turned out to be me. I was a nice kid growing up, meek and timid, wouldn't hurt a fly, a respecter of all people. How did I go from an undefiled, inoffensive little kid to a smart-tongued, imperious, sometimes bigoted, heat-packing exterminator? I *have* been analyzed by Army, FBI and private practice psychologists along the way and always checked out okay. It sure as hell didn't say much for their assessment skills.

I know Dad favored Joey, anyway, as he knew his younger son would ultimately take over the business. I was the squeamish one, remember. When Dad took us out there to hunt, I couldn't pull the trigger on a deer. I still can't. *Human* vermin? Now that's another story. Perhaps it was all a matter of preserving the innocent. And maybe I also felt there was no challenge in hunting down four-legged critters that threatened no one and couldn't shoot back. Anyway, I think it all came together for me when I joined Special Forces and went to Sniper School. There I found my niche. Contrary to popular belief, I was neither indoctrinated nor brainwashed. I just learned from that experience who I was destined to become: a purveyor of the good and an exterminator of the evil.

Anyway, this was the morning of wonderful smells: the intoxicating aroma of a Cora McGowan breakfast, and yes, even the pungent stench of cow piss and manure in the countryside, which by the way to me is nature's perfume.

We finished breakfast about eight thirty and I showed my appreciation to Cora by planting a kiss on her forehead. Joey told me to watch that stuff and I retorted with some noise about stealing her away one day. After the playfulness, I excused myself and went to the den to call Adrianna about the day's events.

She seemed a bit upset when I answered. "It's been a most interesting morning around here. Not long after Juanita arrived she came to me in tears. It seems Mr. Mohammed accused her of being in his room. He said that things had been disturbed and he found his door unlocked this morning. She told me he was screaming in her face and mixing 'American and foreign' words, as she put it."

"No kidding," I remarked in forced amazement. Actually, I *was* a little amazed that he found anything disturbed. I thought I did a good job putting everything back. That's an obsessive-compulsive for you.

"Did he say anything to you?"

"Well, I was getting ready to go down and ask him why he jumped on her, when he came up and started banging on *my* door. As soon as I opened it, he started on me about invading his privacy and violating his space. Says he now doesn't feel safe, because either someone was in his room over the weekend or tried to get in with a key while he was sleeping."

"What did he say was disturbed?"

"He didn't. He just said things were not in the same order they were when he left on Saturday morning."

Hmm. *I* thought things were in good order. I must have left a hair under the bed or the commode seat up.

"Gee. Sounds like your boarder is the sensitive type. Makes one suspicious about him, doesn't it?"

"I assured him no one was in his room as I was emphatic that he had gotten no maid service, respecting his privacy. He still ranted and raved and threatened to move out."

"We don't want him to do that. I *have* to keep an eye on him."

"How are you going to do that staying at Joey's?"

"Well, I could move back in, but you booted me and gave

away my room."

"I did not. You left, remember?"

"I just took a vacation from my vacation, remember?" She was silent for a moment.

"Skip, you didn't by chance …"

"Break into his room?"

"Well …"

"I thought that was what you were going for. Look, I've been a law enforcement officer for over twenty years. What do *you* think?"

"I'm sorry. I didn't mean to insinuate … anyway, you were in Washington and New York until last night and I know you went to your brother's."

"Right." I hated lying to her. Actually, I didn't. Sometimes impressions are perceived as lies, however. And I make impressions on everyone I meet.

"I guess I'll just have to keep an eye on his room so he doesn't have a reason to pop like that again."

Lucky for him I was in a good mood last night. *He* was the one who nearly got popped.

"Be careful about watching him and his room too closely. He may misconstrue your intent."

"I just wish he *would* go away."

"Just hang with him as a boarder for a while and keep your distance. See you in a couple of hours."

I had stepped out on the porch with some coffee to take a deep drink of the still cool morning air. Joey joined me.

"I forgot to ask you how Caroline was."

"Good. Sends her love."

"And back *to* her." He came over and plopped his butt on the banister.

"Do you have any more information on the dead guy?"

"Neither his DNA or photo set off any alarms with the Bureau. I'm running his mug through Interpol. And I did find that the map you secured was a near perfect overlay for a plant in Charleston."

He slammed his hand down on the banister. "Damn! I knew it meant something. Do you think he may have planned to blow it up?"

"Who knows? We may never know."

"You think there are more Arabs out there?"

"Could be, Joe. That's one reason I'm back and sticking around for a few days."

I still didn't want to clue him in on *everything*. I wasn't worried he would let anything slip out, but for his and his family's safety, he didn't need to know.

"And another reason would be Adrianna, I take it."

I didn't answer, but took a sip of my coffee and just smiled. I wondered if Birdman would know that I had added my brother to my list of confidants. The boss now obviously suspected that his star agent just can't keep a secret. I talked into my locator chip and said, "Only a couple of people know about all this. Really."

"What?" responded Joey.

"Sorry, Joey. Just talking to myself." He shook his head and went back inside.

What happened later that morning was what I feared might happen. The very moment I pulled into the parking lot at Wolf Laurel and stepped out of my vehicle, Assad appeared on the veranda. We would be passing one another again. He knew I had left, so why was I back if my vacation was over? Obviously, he would now think I was more than just a tourist. Maybe I was the guy who broke into his room.

As I reached the steps, I forced a fake smile and greeted him with a "Good morning."

There was no return smile. He just nodded, gave me a cold look and passed on by.

Hmm. Something I said? Something I did? I started to ask "What the hell's your problem, you Islamic fascist prick?" But it's not like me to be sarcastic. And anyway, I wanted to be in a good mood for the day. I didn't want to go to Adrianna's picnic upset that I had to pop someone. He gave me a parting shot with his eyes, then ducked into his Nissan. I guessed that we were now on an even keel. I suspected *him* and he suspected *me*. The difference was that I was a world-class burglar and he was a world-class terrorist asshole.

After we both discreetly said *Aloha* in sign language with our middle fingers, he pulled away. I went on up to Adrianna's suite to help her carry down the picnic items. She opened the door to me, gave me some wonderful lip service, and dragged me inside for seconds. "Missed you," she panted.

"Me too." That wasn't quite the response she was looking for, but that's the patented male answer to many amorous declarations, such as "I love you." Maybe I should be more specific and say something like, "Yeah, what *you* said."

I placed my gift in her hands which had been wrapped in white, slicky paper and garnished with a dainty pink bow.

"For me?" she said.

"How thoughtful." I nodded in agreement. She took the box to the dining table and began gingerly separating the scotch tape from the paper, careful not to rip it. I shuddered to think she would be saving the wrapping and someday I would get it back on my birthday or at Christmas. She finally opened it and placed her hands over her breasts, exclaiming "I love it! I love crystal." She then turned and gave me a powerful hug and another peck on the lips.

I was kind of waiting for more, but she quickly let go and said, "We have to load the car and get on out to the State Forest. Things will be cranking up soon."

After a couple of trips up and down the stairs, I wondered if in fact we were picnicking for the afternoon or camping out for a week. It would be tight, but the rear of my SUV may just be able to hold the picnic basket, quilt, table cloth, yard umbrella, king sized cooler, ice tea cooler, four plastic bags of chips, cookies, condiments, a chocolate cake, container of fried chicken and a badminton set. I can just see me out there batting around a shuttlecock like some big fruit.

As we loaded the last of the inventory, I gave Adrianna the once over ... maybe the twice over ... as she walked around to the passenger's side to get in. She was wearing a black sleeveless top tied in a knot at the waist, revealing two soft, shapely shoulders, two firm, tantalizingly pointed breasts and two tight, slightly muscular biceps that had obviously been conditioned at a gym. And the gams? Such a treat for *my* sore eyes. Perfect all the way up to her Gloria Vanderbilt shorts.

Fifteen minutes later we entered the Greenbrier Forest and drove along a winding park road into a large, grassy picnic site. A family shelter constructed of redwood and a tin roof was already filled up as were a dozen or so benches scattered throughout. We pulled in between two walnut trees and began to unload Adrianna's stuff. She found a shady spot near a huge sweeping willow and spread out her quilt. We sat down and then I leaned back with my hands folded behind my neck and gazed into the swaying tree tops as they met the blue sky. Adrianna cast off her tennies and low-cut socks, working her toes into the cool grass. May I say they were lovely toes with perfectly manicured nails painted with blood red polish?

I scanned the arena, estimating about a hundred people so far. She was expecting over three hundred. "And who all is it that's supposed to be here today?"

"Mostly, it's just a community thing," she replied. "It's sponsored by the Chamber of Commerce, the Osteopathic School, Valley Community, and several clubs and organizations. The theme is "Labor for Youth." A lot of kids will be here today, many of which won't be able to afford college."

"Kids. Oh, great."

"Most of the kids will be from the high school, but a few

from the college as well. There'll be venues set up by local businesses with brochures and information about them."

"Like a job fair."

"Sort of. Only there won't be any interviews going on. The vendors will give the kids insight about what they do. As you can see, *The Greenbrier* is set up here along with the Sheriff's Department, Zanzadyne Pharmaceuticals, and others. Over there in that booth is Valley Community."

I looked across the open grassy area where she was pointing and sure as hell, there was Paul LeMer. So let me get this straight. Not only was I going to spend my day avoiding ants and kids, but Paul the Putz as well. Since I had committed the 'mother of all faux pas' in his office the other day and made him look silly, I doubted very much if he wanted to be my badminton partner. So, being the master of disguise that I am, I put on my black ball cap with the Special Forces logo and flight glasses. I think Adrianna liked the look.

A clown came by juggling some balls, followed by a pasty-faced mime, imitating a mechanical man. He was definitely annoying. It set me to wonder that if you shoot a mime, do you use a silencer?

Adrianna put out the fried chicken and trimmings, then poured us some iced tea. I no sooner stripped a leg when a glum-faced, well-built jock about forty-two or three sauntered up to our blanket with such determination, I thought he was intending to plop down with us. He was a nice-looking chap with a Marine haircut, which unfortunately for him accentuated two huge ears that stuck out from his head, resembling a taxicab coming at us with its doors open.

"Hi, Dan," greeted Adrianna. She gave him one of those finger waves.

He in turn gave *me* a penetrating look that would make a lesser man seize like an epileptic and wet his pants.

Obviously, he was none too happy to find his squeeze sharing bed covers with the likes of me, handsome as I was.

"Hello Adrianna. I *thought* that was you across the field. I actually hoped you would be here. Who's the *old* guy?" He stood with hands on hips looking rather ominous, not to mention, pissed.

Although a bit indignant about the 'old guy' slam, I stood and thrust out my hand. "Name's Bruce, sonny." That's about all I had in me for the guy.

Dan was not going to let this go, much less shake my hand. He gave Adrianna a cold look. "I kind of thought *we* would be spending the day together."

She tried to disarm him with a smile. "We never talked about that, Dan."

"Well, I thought it was pretty much understood." Now he looked *hurt* and pissed.

"I'm sorry, Dan. We don't have that kind of relationship where one of us assumes …"

He interrupted her. "That we have something going between us? Well, I certainly believed so."

I thought I'd try to clear up the confusion. "Well, Dan, let me explain how things are …"

Now he interrupted *me*. "Uh … I wasn't talking to you, sir."

Adrianna was now beyond embarrassed. "Dan, that wasn't necessary." It was like we were all in the ninth grade and she was a cute little cheerleader sandwiched between two jealous jocks, vying for her attention.

"Yeah, Dan," I added.

Adrianna shot me a poisonous dart. "Skip, please."

Dan stared me down for a couple of seconds like he could mop the blanket with me. But I glared back with one of those laser-fired, penetrating beams that could burn through the hull of the Queen Mary. *Okay, Danny Boy, the pipes are calling. Now get lost.* He stood for a few moments in silence with his Popeye arms folded across his chest. He must have been reading my mind because he then put up one hand as if to say, "forget it," turned heel and strode away.

"*That* went well," I remarked.

"He didn't have to act that way," she said, dolefully.

"I've never given him the impression that we are an item. All we've done is have an occasional dinner and talk."

"Have you kissed him?"

"Okay, dinner and a onetime kiss. Well, maybe two. But nothing beyond that."

"Nothing carnal?"

"Absolutely not," she replied indignantly.

"Sorry. Can we eat now?"

She sighed and shook her head. I wasn't sure if it was me or good ol' Dan that ruined her day. But anyway, she went ahead and refilled my tea tumbler which was a good sign it wasn't me.

About a half hour later Danny Boy, who had been watching us from a distance, trekked back across the field to our blanket with considerably less piss and vinegar and with his wounded ego obviously shoved up into where the sun don't shine.

"Hey, Adrianna … Bruce. I really have to apologize for my behavior earlier." He grinned a cheesy grin. "You know how we boys are sometimes, right Brucie?"

No. I pride myself in being rational and mature in such scenarios. Not like you, schmuck. Watch the Brucie shit. But to be polite, I nodded in agreement.

He continued. "Say, if you two are interested, we have a Labor Day tradition of getting a bunch of guys and gals together for a friendly game of flag football. About a dozen players from my senior squad are here and it would be great if you all join us in a few minutes."

Well that sounded a heck of a sight more interesting than badminton. However, I replied, "To tell you the truth, Dan,

I was never that much of a jock …"

Adrianna jumped in. "Hey, that's okay, Skip. I don't know the first thing about football, but I used to like playing 'touch' with the guys when I was younger. Come on. It'll be fun."

And I used to play 'touch' with the *girls* when I was younger. As a matter of fact, I still do.

"I don't know," I replied reluctantly.

"I probably wouldn't last three plays."

"We'll take it easy on you, old sport," offered Dan. *Should I just go ahead and punch* **you***, old sport?*

Adrianna stood and reached out her hand to pull me up from the blanket. "I'll protect you out there, sweetie. If you get a boo-boo, I'll play nurse later."

I thought Dan was going to burst a blood vessel. And after what Adrianna just said, I was left feeling like a complete wuss.

"Oh, all right," I said, rising.

"You shamed me into it." Actually, she did.

Well, here I was, lined up with Adrianna on my right, a three-hundred-pound heart attack waiting to happen on my left, and a mixed bag of volunteer boys and girls, aged twelve to eighteen on my team. Opposite us weenies were Coach Dan, six of his players from the varsity squad and two girls from the school soccer team. I think a junior high team playing the Dallas Cowboys would have been a fairer fight. And then there was the taunting and jeering from Danny's boys across the line of scrimmage. Like *that* was going to intimidate me.

Our center pitched the ball to our twelve-year-old quarterback, who after seeing Dick Butkus barreling toward him, panicked and fumbled. I scrambled to recover it about the same time Coach Dan and his two hundred-ten-pound frame plastered me from the side and drove my chin into the grass.

"Whoa!" I yelled. "I thought this was flag football, not a

Tough Man contest." Dan stood over me like Thor while I laid there checking to see if I still had all my teeth.

"Sorry, Skippy." I detected a bit of sarcasm there.

I got up and brushed myself off, taking both my banged-up pride and tailbone back to the huddle. I had lied to Dan. Bad knees and all, one thing I could do was run. And I not only knew enough about football to be coaching the Steelers, I was an all-conference running back my senior year at the military academy.

This time I called the play and lined up behind the quarterback, telling him to just turn around and give the ball to me. I'd handle the rest. After the handoff, which was clean this time, I started left which drew in the entire defense like a magnet, spun and zipped right. I got behind Adrianna, thinking no one would dare crunch her, being Coach's girl and all, took a couple of stutter steps to avoid a flying defender and sailed undeflagged past the marker for a touchdown. The kid had tried to stay with me, but I smoked him like a cheap cigar. When I turned around to bask in the glory, I saw an angry Dan standing with hands on hips and sporting a scowl. He then put a finger in the face of three of his All Stars.

It was Dallas' turn on offense. On the first play, Dan's quarterback faked an end around and short of crossing the line of scrimmage, he fired a bullet to the tight end just about the time I got there. As we both went up for the ball, we collided and knocked ourselves out of bounds. The kid sprawled onto the turf, but Murphy's Law which had followed me around all my life, caused me to cream an innocent bystander on the sidelines. Paul LeMer.

Bruised and highly irritated, he crawled out from under my frame. I think I hit him so hard, his mama felt it. As I reached out my hand to help him up, he then saw for the first time who it was that had ruptured his spleen. "You!" he yelled.

"Are you okay?" I asked, helping him up.

"Yes, but …"

"See ya," I said, scooting back to the game. I glanced back in his direction. He was holding his head and yelling something unintelligible.

On the next play, I was attempting to run down a very fast kid who was firmly cradling the ball like Coach taught him, and just as I reached for his flag, I was blind-sided again by my new friend Dan. This time it was my eyeballs that hurt.

I was getting pretty beat up about now and began to second-guess myself about the noble game of badminton, played by kings and other royalty. About the time the birds in my head stopped chirping, on the next play another golden boy started a run up the middle with Dan ahead of him, poised to give me another shot. I faked a head-on counter-block, then at the last second threw a roll block that upended Dan, tossing him on his head. Adding insult to injury, I yanked the flag off the runner.

Out of the corner of my eye I saw Dan coming at me, yelling something about a cheap shot. He actually pushed me like the sore loser he was. So I pushed him back. He didn't much like that and threw a round-house punch, which I blocked with my left, then cocked and fired a straight punch that caught him on the bridge of his nose. He dropped like a rock. Stunned, he stumbled to his feet about the time Adrianna stepped in between us. The squad gathered around their humiliated coach to check him out, then the grumbling started. I think I may have heard the word 'kill' in there somewhere. One of the heroes brushed her aside and stuck his face in mine. The lip ring was all I saw. There were expletives spewing from this kid's mouth that I had never even heard at a Special Forces reunion.

I stuck my pinky finger through the ring and pulled the kid to his knees by his lower lip.

"There are ladies present, Sissy Boy. Now lose the language or lose the lip. Your choice." The boy threw up his hand as if to say 'uncle.' I helped him up and after a perforating glare, he walked away nursing the lip.

Meanwhile, Adrianna the referee sent me to my corner and pulled a hanky from the pocket of her shorts to stop the blood flow from Dan's nose. I actually didn't mind her tending him as it served to humiliate the prick even more. Anyway, I needed to retreat to my blankie to nurse my own wounds from Dan's body shots. When I plopped down, I looked around and then started talking into my chip in my forearm, "How'd you like that, boss?"

In a while, Adrianna came back to our picnic spot and sat quietly on the blanket beside me.

"And are *you* all right?" There was definitely some snootiness in the question. She wasn't just cool; she was downright frosty.

"I'm sorry, Adrianna. I guess my competitive nature got the best of me."

"It had nothing to do with game, Skip. It was about me, and I don't like it one bit."

"But he started it," I replied, sounding very much like a six-year-old being scolded by his mama.

Adrianna wanted to be angry, but as I nuzzled her neck, she couldn't quite quell the smile that broke out. She turned her head so I couldn't see it.

I put my face up to hers and said, "I fought for you."

The smile turned into a grin. "No, you idiot, you fought for your stupid ego."

CHAPTER 15

To keep *rigor* from setting in, I stood up to move around and then walked through several of the venues. Large and small business owners from Lewisburg and White Sulphur had the ear of teenagers and young adults alike. Four community colleges from a two-county area, including Valley, had administrative personnel and counselors set up in booths talking with high school juniors and seniors about life after graduation. A few kids were hanging out at the Greenbrier County Sheriff's display asking bright questions like 'what kind of gun is that?' and 'did you ever shoot anybody?' And there was even something for *me* at the end of a long series of booths … a coffee stand.

I stood at some distance eyeing the big and lumpy Paul LeMer with his comb-over flapping in the warm breeze. Beside him were a man and a woman. The lady looked to be a senior administrator of sorts, perhaps even Valley's president, and Paul was sucking up to her shamelessly. The man was about forty-five, with a dark olive complexion, slightly balding and sporting a neatly trimmed black beard. I couldn't tell from the distance what nationality he was, but he was definitely Middle Eastern. I wondered if he was on staff and if he had any relationship with the Arab students. Perhaps he would be worth checking out, although I was not happy with myself for profiling the guy. For all I knew, he could be an Israeli-American patriot or a respected, long-time professor in the West Virginia Educational System. But stereotyping or not, it was my job to be suspicious. I turned a moment to pay for the coffee and when I looked up again the man was gone.

Adrianna waltzed back to where I was standing, accompanied by a pretty, petite blonde with shoulder-length hair and eyes the color of golden brandy. She and her friend were jabbering on about the woman's recent divorce, but when they got in closer proximity to me, the volume went down.

But then the blonde eyed my huskiness and nudged Adrianna's arm. "Are you going to introduce me?"

"Oh, I'm sorry. Skip, this is Lisa."

Well, I obviously looked a sight, like I had been playing a blood-letting game of rugby.

But maybe she liked that sweaty, dirty, banged up look. When I held out my hand, she cocked her head to one side, smiled wantonly and took it. If I read the body language correctly, she would be asking for my phone number the moment Adrianna was out of sight. But Adrianna read the signals, too, and sent her a subtle message by slipping her hand into my freed-up hand. So there I was, both of my hands clamped onto the hands of two honeys.

"Hello. Good to meet you," I said to Lisa rather matter-of-factly, in turn reading *Adrianna's* body language. Lisa finally released her grip.

"And good to meet *you*," she replied, eyes dancing and lips smiling.

Adrianna seemed to notice how honey-dipped her friend's voice had become, so she jumped in. "Lisa and I have been friends for eons; of course, she was a few years ahead of me in school."

Of course. Rather catty comment, I thought. Jealousy can do that to even the sweetest and most consecrated of souls.

The blonde kept her eyes on me, anyway. "You don't

remember me, do you, Skip?"

"Should I?" I grinned like a Cheshire cat.

"I used to be Lisa Ramsay. We went out once or twice when you were home from college."

Then the light bulb finally came on. "Oh yeah … Lisa!"

"Remember that time we were driving around and your car quit on you? You said you were out of gas and I thought 'can't this guy get more original than to try that line on me?' But then I found out you really *were* out of gas and we walked for nearly two miles looking for a station."

"Hey, I *do* remember that."

I guess Adrianna was taking no chances on me getting re-enamored with my former squeeze. She edged even closer to me to make it perfectly clear that Lisa was definitely not welcome to renew our old friendship. It felt good to see that old jealous shoe on the other foot for a change.

Lisa got the picture, all right. She checked her watch and feigned it as though she had something else going. "Well, anyway, Skip, nice seeing you again after what … thirty years?"

"Must be. Great seeing you again, too."

With that, she shook my hand again, this time rather business-like and without that extra little squeeze. Waving bye-bye to Adrianna, she sashayed off. I hoped the little messages given off did not put a dent in the two women's friendship. But I knew they'd be all right with each other … that is, just as soon as I left the state.

Adrianna and I walked arm in arm back to the blanket. I took notice of her smile … a rather sardonic smile at that.

"*Well*, Romeo, you *did* get around in those days, didn't you? Any other old girlfriends I should know about?"

"Mmm, no, but if you'll wait right here, I can go check around." She didn't respond; but she did pinch me on my left buttock.

We packed up the Suburban about three and headed back to the inn. It took another fifteen minutes to unload all the cargo, most of which we didn't use … including the badminton game. Once settled inside, Adrianna went to take a shower. I grabbed a cold brewski from her fridge and plopped my sore bones in her leather recliner.

The steam filtered out of the shower and rose like a ghostly wisp from beneath the bathroom door, then dissipated when it hit the coolness of the living room. I listened to her humming and heard the clunk against the shower floor when she dropped the soap … and then dropped it a second time. I wanted in the worst way to be in there with her. And then I thought, 'just as well.' As beat up as I was, I wasn't sure I could muster up anything … including my body from the chair.

I was just getting comfortable, remote in hand and ready to click, when she called from the bathroom. "Skip, can you come here for a minute?"

My body protested, but at the possibility of seeing her naked, I managed to coax it out of the chair. I bargained with it by telling it that if it cooperated, it might be richly rewarded. It didn't care. But the brain, the largest sex organ in the body, won out.

I peeked gingerly into the bathroom and said loudly above the beating of the shower spray against the stall, "Okay, I'm here!"

She stuck her head out and said, "Can you do my back?"

"I can do anything you want, my dear."

She laughed. "You may want to take your clothes off; otherwise, you'll get soaked."

The tee, the shorts, the underwear and socks came off in just under three seconds, a new world record. Gradually, the bathroom was becoming even more humid and steamy as though a dense fog had settled in, making it difficult to see. But I had no trouble finding the shower since King Richard had his radar out and happily pointed the way. I opened the shower door and slipped in behind her. She handed me the soap and I lathered her up. Working with both hands, beginning at the nape of the neck just under her pent-up hair, I gently caressed and massaged her shoulders and then her beautiful back as it cascaded down, down, down. Slowly, lovingly, I worked over nearly every inch of her skin. She moaned and writhed, backing into me, grinding, even dancing, until we were enjoying the mind-numbing passion of sexual love. Obviously, she had forgiven me for my adolescent behavior at the Super Bowl today.

After our twenty-minute shower we looked like two albino prunes, she the more succulent prune. We dried off with large, thirsty towels and she handed me her over-sized terry bathrobe to put on, which still didn't quite close in the front.

"Why don't you relax in the living room while I throw our clothes into the washer? Can you pour me a glass of Chablis?"

I was feeling salubrious about now. The hot shower and furious ardor did much to soothe my wounds and the soft bathrobe made me feel like a newborn babe again. All I needed was a little massage with some baby oil. Aside from getting knocked around a few hours before, I was having the best Labor Day of my life. I was in the company of a woman, feeling after all these years something deep and penetrating to the soul. If it *was* love, I wasn't sure I wanted it to be; but it surely felt like it. I was actually feeling sorry for poor dumb old Dan who was probably still sitting somewhere with ice on his nose, trying to stop the bleeding, not to mention the bleeding going on in his heart. Maybe I was just relishing the fact that today was a day I won for a change. I won the game, I won the fight and I won the girl.

About seven-thirty as the red-orange sun finally dipped over the horizon, its last rays fading on the living room wall, Adrianna brought out some cheese, crackers and summer sausage. We shared a new bottle of Chablis and she turned on the tube. CNN was broadcasting a special on the Taliban in Afghanistan and its continuing threats against the United

States and Israel. The most dangerous man in the world was not Putin or Arafat, but a man resembling a Twelfth Century tribesman, Osama Bin Laden. He had taken responsibility for a myriad of terrorist acts in the past few years, resulting in the loss of American lives, all in the name of Allah.

Not thirty seconds into the broadcast, Adrianna switched channels. "Enough of that. It frightens me to even think there may be terrorists in this country and right under our noses. You've even got me scared about my boarder. The more I think about Assad and the way he blew up, I want him out. He may *be* just another Middle Eastern man who wants to assimilate in our society and take advantage of the quality of life in America, but he doesn't act like it. He's defensive and reclusive. So, before he pays another week, I'm giving him notice."

"If you can just hang with the guy a little longer, I need a bit more time to determine if he is an immigration concern. Don't worry. Now that he knows I'm back around, I will purposely make myself more visible. Hopefully, it will make him force his hand and expose anything he may be up to." I came very close to spilling all the beans about him, but I didn't want to alarm her; neither did I want him to be tossed out … out of my sight.

Ultimately, I knew the wolf would leave the lair, bare his teeth and position for some kind of attack. And I knew what it was and where it was; I just didn't know when. I would do my damnedest to be there when he made his move.

"By the way, do you have a room coming back open for me?"

"Your old room will be available Wednesday for you if you want it."

"And I'll take it. I can remain at Joey's until then."

"Except tonight?"

"Is that an offer to stay here?"

"You can stay here as long as you want. You know you don't need to rent the room."

I pulled her down onto my lap. "Thanks. Maybe I'll stay with you tonight, but for the sake of your guests and because of the surveillance and other work I need to do, I will start bunking downstairs. I wonder, though, what your guests may imagine about me."

"I'm not worried about the guests. Mrs. Throckmorton knows about us."

"Knows about what?"

"That we've been ... together."

"You told her?"

"No, silly. She didn't become a congresswoman without having acquired good perception skills. She sees the way we look at each other and says we make a cute couple."

"Hmm. Maybe *you*. But *cute* doesn't quite fit *me*."

Adrianna gave me a warm, wet wine-flavored kiss. "*I* think it does."

"Hey," I said. "Can I use your computer tomorrow? I need to send something to my boss."

"Sure."

I reached for my cell and called Joey. I told him I was staying back at Wolf Laurel for the night, to which he replied, "You *dog*."

"But I'll be back over some time tomorrow."

"Great. Come for breakfast?"

"No thanks, little bro. I've got some early things to do but will catch up to you later after you leave the shop."

"Then supper?"

"You bet."

"Tell Adrianna she's welcome, too."

"I will."

When I finally stirred, Adrianna was already up and in the downstairs kitchen putting out the sweet rolls from Clingman's Diner. There were muscles and ligaments that hurt I didn't even know I had. No run this morning. After the bathroom chores I settled down in the leather recliner in my freshly laundered tee and BVDs with Adrianna's laptop on my knees. I inserted the disc from my digital camera and downloaded the photos of the notebook entry Assad so graciously provided. I sent them as an attachment to the following e-mail:

Dear Condor,
A friend of mine wrote the attached, but I'm unable to decipher much of it. Can you have it translated? Will anticipate your call.
Merci

At nine-thirty I joined Adrianna in the dining room for some coffee and toast. Either the other boarders had eaten earlier or weren't interested. If I had known I'd be alone, I could have just stayed in my briefs. I was on my second cup when I heard the sound of footsteps in the hallway. It was Assad. Our eyes met briefly, but as he continued past me, he looked away. I couldn't let this moment pass. It was time to engage him and this time it would not be casual conversation.

"Assad," I called. He froze in position at the door, then turned slowly around.

"Yes?" he replied coolly.

"Good morning."

I thought for a moment he wouldn't return the greeting. His eyes, resolute and steady, never blinked.

Then with a response as icy as his stare, he said, "Yes, good morning."

"You're off to school, huh?"

He paused a moment, then in a very unfriendly tone, said, "So, you have returned. It was my understanding you were going back to Georgetown and your job."

"Well, I liked it here so much, I thought I'd take a few more days."

"It must be very nice to have a job where you can work whenever you choose." There was snootiness in his delivery.

"I have a very understanding boss ... me."

He moved closer to my table, which surprised me a little. I got the impression he was trying to intimidate me with his deliberate stare, and if he was, he'd better go back to Terrorist School. "Why do I not believe you are who you say, Mr. White? Tell me again about your business."

Adrianna glanced at me and shifted uneasily.

I wanted to be sure I gave him the same vocation as the other day, so I had to hit my recall button. "I design homes. Why would you say such a thing, Assad?"

"It is very strange considering that architects are a small and very close group of professionals. Neither my father nor his friends have heard of you. My father is on the Virginia Board of Architects and has data on all people in the business in the Northern Virginia area. He does not know your name. He would know about you if you are who you say you are, big fish or small fish."

Busted. The bastard actually checked up on me, so obviously he had his suspicions.

"Is that so, Assad?"

"Yes, it is so."

"Don't I look like an architect?"

He was back to the penetrating stare. "I do not believe you are an architect."

"What's the deal, Assad? Why are you questioning my integrity?"

"I do not like people who tell lies. *That* is the deal, Mr. White, or whatever your real name is." I could swear Assad's English was getting better.

"If I'm not who I say I am, then who the hell am I?"

By this time, Adrianna, showing considerable apprehension, was apparently afraid the conversation would deteriorate further, and said "Excuse me." She removed herself to the kitchen. But twenty feet away, she would still be able to hear the tête-à-tête.

Assad turned his attention back to me when she left. "I do not know who you are, but you seem most interested in me. I have seen your vehicle at places I have been. That is too much of a coincidence."

"Really? Like where?"

"At my school, at the airport, and in the next town toward Virginia."

"I don't know what to say, Assad." I really didn't. "I thought we had a nice conversation last week and can't imagine why you would be telling me these things."

"Because you are … I believe the word is … deceptive. I want to know at this moment why you checked my car and my friend's car … and why you follow me."

Maybe I'm just your typical bigot and hate all camel jockey assholes who come to this country to kill Americans.

"If you believe that is the case, you tell *me.*" Obviously, I had underestimated his perceptiveness.

"I think for some reason you and that woman seem to make me and my friends your business. I believe she has invaded my privacy and gone into my room to look for things. Either her or the Spanish woman."

No, that was me, dingleberry.

"I can't imagine that either of those women would have done that. Let me say this. If you don't believe I'm an architect and merely extending my vacation in this beautiful Bed and Breakfast, then you and I have a problem, Assad."

"I have no problem, but if I find that you are following me again, *you* will."

I settled back in my chair and dropped the half piece of cold toast I had been holding onto my plate, rather defiantly. I thought about smacking the boy around and re-designing his face, the architect that I was. But I let him have his say, making him think he was intimidating me. If I acted like a tough guy or otherwise gave him the impression I was a cop or government agent on his trail, he would walk out that door, gather up his friends and find another nest deeper in the hills until he was poised to execute his plot. Maybe he would anyway. I wouldn't push the envelope. Not this time.

"Sorry you feel that way, Assad. I thought I was being friendly. I hate that you think I'm a phony and a snoop."

He didn't respond, but slung his knapsack over his shoulder, warning me again with a cold, pendant stare. Whatever it was I needed to connect him and the target, American, I suspected was in that bag. But he always had it with him and getting a look inside was not going to be easy.

As soon as he had shut the door behind him, Adrianna came back to the dining room and sat down.

"That made me very nervous, Skip. Do you think he's onto you about being immigration?"

"No, I don't think so. He knows I'm not an architect, but maybe he thinks I'm just some poor lying American slob trying to impress somebody. Of course, he *has* seen my Suburban at places he's been and he's trying to figure that one out. Maybe he thought if he pushed my buttons a little, I'd get pissed and slip up. I know he'll be more vigilant now and make it a point to know what *I'm* doing. I'll have to stay two steps ahead of him. Assad is calculating. Conniving. But you know what? So am I."

"Tell me again, Skip. Why are you spending so much time and government money checking out this guy? Is it solely because Assad is Middle Eastern? I mentioned the word *terrorist* last night and it seemed you were taken aback a little. Is there more to him and his friends than merely being suspected illegal aliens?"

"All I can say is there could be. Any illegal from the Middle East could be subversive. I hate to say it that way. I'm not in the profiling business, Adrianna. There are a great number of very respectable Arab people of the Muslim faith who are here on visas and have even become naturalized citizens. They love their new country and are respecters of America's mainstream culture and religions. But from day one, *this* guy has bothered me. You see how defensive he is. Innocent people with nothing to hide don't go around vehemently accusing their proprietors of going into their rooms. *And* refusing free maid service. He is beyond just being a very private person. Subversive or not, he bears watching."

"Just be careful, Skip. I saw the look in his eyes. It was the same look I saw when he confronted me. Can I now give him notice?"

I picked up her hand and kissed it. "Again, please give me a couple more days, okay? Not to worry. I'll watch my backside. And I'll be watching yours, too." I did my Groucho imitation by raising my eyebrows a couple of times.

After my little chat with Assad, I went back upstairs to Adrianna's computer and Googled information about American. There was no reference to its Canadian or Israeli ties, perhaps for political purposes. Neither did the information go into any great detail about its products. Obviously, from its chemists right down to the snuffy on the line, many of the employees would have government clearances. It was certainly not public knowledge that highly toxic gases were being produced at the plant. Fears that some kind of chemical accident could happen would result in a massive public outcry, considering the nuclear disasters at Three Mile Island and Chernobyl. And now *I* knew that the erupting of any one of their tanks would send up a gas cloud that would exterminate 100,000 people in a short matter of time. For all any Joe Citizen knew, American produced run-of-the-mill household chemicals like ammonia, boric acid and hydrogen peroxide. But how would four terrorist lads know this or that the great Zionist whore was partnered with the Great Satan in the American enterprise? The knowledge had to come from the inside or from a much underestimated Al-Qaeda Intel system.

Adrianna came back up and told me that Juanita was readying my quarters. The Virginia Beach couple had departed a day early. Maybe she told me that because I was wearing out my welcome, sitting around in my boxers, banging on the computer and making like Freddie the Freeloader. I thanked her for her hospitality, grabbed a beer from her fridge to put in my icebox for later, and went on down to my room.

Juanita had just laid a chocolate on my pillow when I walked in. By her side and always underfoot, was her pet Chihuahua, Garcia, looking much like a nervous little rat. Adrianna's cat, Burt, made it his career to terrorize the little bastard unmercifully, and I was sure that one day he would have Garcia for breakfast. The pooch wasn't too sure about *me*, either, as he sat staring at me with those huge glassy eyes and baring his little rodent teeth.

I tried striking up a conversation with him. "Yo quero Taco Bell?"

Juanita giggled. "He's a good little dog and keeps me company while I'm cleaning the rooms."

"He doesn't leave any brown jelly beans in any of the rooms, does he?"

"Jelly beans?"

"I'm sorry, Juanita. Just a little attempt at humor."

"Oh," she laughed, although she had not the slightest understanding of what I was talking about. But I did quickly scan the corners of my room just in case Garcia left me a package.

"I hope your stay has been good here and look forward to serving you again, Senor Skip. Any time you need fresh towels and sheets, you call me, okay?" Her accent was as thick as molasses and so was her body. She was certainly a jovial, accommodating sort, not to mention a very hard worker.

I shoved twenty bucks in her hand. She smiled widely and gave me a slight curtsy. "Gracias, Senor."

"And thank *you*, Juanita. I looked down the hall to assure Assad the Arab asshole was not lurking around, then softened my voice. "Say, I caught wind of the tongue lashing the gentleman in the Magnolia Room gave you. I'm sorry you experienced that."

"I don't know why he say those things. I do not go into his room. I respect his wishes."

"Don't worry about it. He's a jerk."

She then moved closer to me and whispered, "I did as Ms. Adrianna ask. I see him come and go and make notes. She put it in her book. I am not sure why she want me to check on him, but I ask no questions."

I whispered back. "It was I who asked Adrianna to do that, but I also told her not to do that anymore."

"Are you police?"

"No, but I do work for an organization that tracks illegals and foreign nationals who act suspicious." I put my finger to my lips so that she would keep it under her hat, not that she would tell Assad. She may not ever even speak to him again.

Juanita displayed a bit of apprehension. "I do have a green card, Senor."

I put a reassuring hand on her shoulder and smiled. "I know, Juanita. Please don't think that was reflected on you. It's the man down the hall I'm concerned about."

She nodded. "He is very strange, that one. I don't know about your job, but am glad you stay here."

"I should be here for a while longer. You come to me anytime you see something he does that concerns you or if he gives you any more trouble."

"I will, Senor Skip. Thank you for the money." She placed it in her apron pocket and closed the door behind her on her way out.

Joey called and said Cora wasn't feeling well. She had been prone to migraines over the years and this was one of her bad days. She begged off for dinner and asked if Adrianna and I could make it either tomorrow or the next evening. I told him I'd check to see if that was all right with Adrianna and get back to him. As neither of us had pressing agendas in the evenings, we should be okay for any night. Unless of course, Dandy Dan needed Adrianna to help heal his fractured ego. I smiled, wondering what size his honker was today.

Adrianna and I had a casual dinner at a new rib joint about seven and then returned to the ranch. Being the good B&B hostess that she was, she saw me to my door, kissed me goodnight and climbed the stairs to her pad. I suppose both of us thought about a little 'nocturnal delight' before lights out, but as we all know, sometimes a little time and distance between interludes makes the next encounter all the sweeter. And it was just as well; neither my mind nor my body was focused in that direction. I was a bit tired, even though I had not done squat all day. Could be I was still feeling Dan's shots from the day before. I hoped he was still feeling mine.

CHAPTER 16

I was flying over the Mekong in the first Huey as Command and Control of the first assault wave on the village of Phan Le, a known Vietcong stronghold. We were taking pretty heavy AK-47 fire and two RPG rounds zipped within ten and twenty yards of the blade and skids, respectively. The chopper to my right took a direct hit in the tail rotor, causing it to go into an uncontrolled spin and explode into a sandbar on the south edge of the village. The blade continued to spin and whip violently until the riverbed killed it.

The helicopter company consisting of twelve Hueys and three Cobras enveloped the village, firing twenty millimeter rockets and a steady 7.62 barrage from the M60s. Like ants the VC scurried from hooch to hooch, but since many of the thatched roofs were set afire by tracers, which accounted for one in five rounds, the enemy was resigned to gather their families and disappear into the jungle.

As we circled back around the river's edge, the door gunners cut down the few remaining holdouts, allowing my A Team to dismount and begin a sweep of the burning huts. From two spider holes we began to take AK-47 fire which wasted three members of my team. We immediately returned fire and the snipers were quickly neutralized. My light weapons NCO dropped a grenade into both holes just in case there were more rats further down.

At my two o'clock I detected a glint off metal inside one of the mooches. I grabbed the M79 off my RTO and shot-gunned the 40 mm grenade through the open window. A brilliant flash accompanied the expected *whumph* and grey smoke from the explosion began to pour from the doorway. A few seconds later a girl child about six or seven stumbled through the door and down the ramp. She was bleeding profusely from the head, waving a stump which a few seconds before was her left arm. As she stood frozen for a moment, I saw the pain and horror reflecting in her eyes. And then she fell face down in the mud. Her blood gradually began to turn the water in the mud hole a bright red. I ran to administer to her, but she was already dead. As I fell backwards from my haunches and sat down in the red mud, the monsoon rain which began to pour harder added insult to my emotional pain and misery. I stood and then stepped onto the ramp that led to the door and was greeted by the faces of Assad Mohammed and his friends, Fayz Al-Hazmi and Ahmed Omari.

I blinked open my eyes to the flute of morning sun that had pierced the opening between the blind and windowsill. It was a dream that I had had a hundred times in the past thirty years. It was always the same. It was a haunt that I could not shake from my unconscious … a reliving in my dreams of the one horrific event in my mental scrapbook that had stayed with me since the Phan Le incident. I had gone into the hooch after killing the child and found the shattered body of her mother. At the end of my dreams she was there, just as I found her. But over the years the final scene in the dream had changed. While wading into that often-predictable stream of unconsciousness different faces sometimes emerged. I would find in place of the mother the faces of old friends, my ex-wife or a boss at the Bureau. Some would still be alive while others were as dead and as bloodied as the child's mother. Now in this new dream there were three new faces. Faces of my prey. I was surprised to wake up and actually remember the names of Assad's cohorts.

As I lay there, drained and drenched in sweat from my fitful night of dreams, I realized I had over-slept by an hour … the hour in which I was used to rising. The digital clock on the nightstand read seven-forty. After bargaining with my body, we decided this again was not a day I would go on a morning run.

I allowed the stinging spray of the hot shower to beat upon my head and shoulders for a full five minutes. After shaving and dressing in a pair of khaki slacks and a blue and gold Mountaineers golf shirt, I sat at the desk to call Birdman. It was after eight and he would probably have been at his desk for over an hour. I had a 'missed call' from him on my cell while I was in the shower.

"What do you have, Boss? Were you able to get the material translated?"

"Do you have access to a secure fax machine?"

"Yes, at my brother's business."

"The funeral home?"

"Yes."

"Do you have the number?"

"I think it's on his card in my wallet. Wait one." I found it and gave it to him.

"I want you to be at the fax machine when I send it. For your eyes only. When can you get there?"

"I was going to slide by the funeral home about four. Then I think I may be having dinner at his house later."

"Make it sooner. I'm leaving right at four."

"Banker's hours?"

"We need to talk."

"Okay. What's wrong with right now?"

"I want you to read the translation first. Why don't you go on to your brother's place now?"

"Okay. Can you give me a preview of coming attractions?"

"I'd rather not." He paused. "All I can say is, it may be time to send in the assets."

"Which assets?"

"You know which assets." And I did. He wanted to dispatch Zulu.

"It's not time yet, Preceptor. I've got a bit more leg work to do and we need to know for sure about these guys."

"Go now, Bruce. You need to read the fax. This is now officially a matter of national security."

"All right. Give me an hour. I will be at my brother's place at exactly nine-thirty. Let's 'sympathize' our watches." I guess he and a hundred others were getting sick of my play on the 'synchronize' word.

"Nine-thirty," he reiterated. My phone then lost the signal. He had hung up on me yet again without saying 'bye.' I will still have to work on his telephone etiquette one day.

I went to the breakfast room and said 'good morning' to Adrianna who was whisking about helping Juanita put out more sticky buns and fruit. All I wanted was a cup of coffee. Lottie was having oatmeal and no one was touching the buns. So that Adrianna would not be offended, I broke down and had one.

"Good morning, Skip," greeted Lottie.

"I haven't seen you in a few days and didn't know whether you were still here or not."

"I had to go back to Washington on business. But here I am again, like a bad penny. How long is it you are going to stay?"

"Another week. I'd like to stay forever, but I need to get on back to South Carolina and my little place in Ninety Six."

"I remember passing through Ninety Six one time years ago," I said. "I stopped off at a souvenir shop on the main street and bought a piece of jewelry for my wife ... now ex-wife. It was a necklace with a nicely made pendant with a colorful stone in it. I thought it was pretty unique, but when she quizzed me about what the stone was made of, I came clean."

"What was it, Skip?"

"It contained quail droppings."

"Oh, yes. I know about that. Quails make very colorful … droppings, and someone made a bundle back in the '70s enclosing them in glass or plastic, making earrings, necklaces and the like out of them. Haven't seen any of them lately, though. It was only a fad, you know. So, what did she think about the necklace?"

"She actually liked it until I told her what it was. She said she as much expected something like that from me. It wasn't enough that I *treated* her like crap; now I wanted her to *wear* it."

Lottie smiled. "I'm sure she didn't mean it like that."

I nodded. "I'm sure that's the case, too." But … she really did mean it. I changed the subject. "Well, Lottie, do you miss serving in congress now?"

"Sometimes. It's like I wake up some mornings thinking I'm playing hooky; but then I go to my kitchen, get some coffee, and go out to the garden to tend my roses. Then the *missing* part is over. And I get to see my grandbabies a lot more. No, I don't miss it, Skip."

"Well, I imagine your constituents miss *you* and were fortunate to have you represent them.

"She took my hand in one of her brown, long-weathered hands. "You're a sweet boy, Skip. Nice of you to say that. I'd like to think they do."

I let her go back to her oatmeal and walked out to the veranda.

Adrianna followed and slipped one of her hands in mine.

"Hmm, nice morning," she remarked.

I nodded. The air *was* fresh and pure. We both stood for a while and allowed the morning sun to warm our faces. It was all very electric.

"I see Assad is already gone this morning," I finally said.

"He probably didn't want to run into *you.*"

"With good reason."

"Where are you off to today?" I'm going out to the funeral home to see Joey and then … who knows. I'll check with him to see if we're back on for dinner tonight."

"I hope Cora is better."

"Me too. Well, see ya." I leaned down and kissed her lips. It was like kissing warm honey made right in God Almighty's own bee- hive.

I pulled into McGowan and Sons about nine-twenty. I wondered when Joey was going to drop the 'Sons.' I also wondered when I was growing up why they called it a funeral *home*. Who the hell would ever want to *live* there? It wasn't even a home for the dead. It was sort of like a motel, a very expensive motel, where they stayed a couple of nights till they went to live in the City of Stones. Oh, well. Who was I to question these things? I went AWOL from the business eons ago.

As soon as I closed the front door, Joey thought it was a customer and came out to greet me. "Hey, this is a surprise. Figured I'd be seeing you this evening."

"Are we on for dinner? I was wondering how Cora was."

"So far so good today."

"Say, Joey, can I use your fax machine? My boss is sending something over?"

"Sure thing. In my office."

At precisely nine-thirty Birdman rang my cell. "Fax is on the way. Call me." Click. I wish he didn't go on and on like that in his conversations.

In a few moments, the fax machine began spitting out paper. Apparently, Assad had been in some kind of meeting with the other players after which he penned the material. Although no names were mentioned, I understood immediately that someone important was directing that meeting. The six pages in Arabic had been condensed to two. There also appeared to have been some paraphrasing by Abu, our translator.

"Our leader gives us hope today that the soft under belly of Americawill soon be cut open by the mighty sword of Allah. May he be praised. Bear witness there is no god but Allah, and Mohammed is his messenger. The blood of Americans will give us vindication because the Great Satan and its infidels have shed Islamic blood for over a century.

Allah has surely blessed us. The Qur'an and the fatwa give us our spiritual nourishment and make us strong against the infidel oppressors. We have learned from our training at Imam Ali how to integrate into the infidel society and wage war on them. To know them we must pretend to fall into sin and become like them. But Allah knows our hearts and our mission as he has set us on course. He will forgive our sins because we only take them on to fool the infidels to make them trust us.

Our leader is also Allah's messenger. He established himself among the Americans many years ago to do the will of Allah. He has been like the ant who moves obstacles many times its size and weight for long periods of times, over miles of ground, to prepare for the big mission. As the ant's mission is to survive when the cold approaches, it prepares cleverly for that mission. Our leader is strong and stalwart."

Assad Mohammed continued his praise of Allah and went into detail about the content of his morning prayers alone and those at sunset with his friends. "... *my brothers give me the support and sustenance which also comes from Allah himself* ..."

"Our leader has educated us about the devices and the missile. He himself is all wise and understands the principles of the devices. The explosions will devastate the city of the Great Satan. There will be many cities affected and other brothers commanded by Allah will carry out similar missions. Our devices will only be the catalyst that will set in motion the secondary explosions. From those explosions a greater horror will be realized by the

infidels. By the wings of man, we will achieve martyrdom. We will sacrifice our blood to spill the blood of the infidels. By the wings of Allah we will then enter heaven. I swear before God I will do what I must to assure the massive death of all infidels. We will shake the Roman Throne. They will die in the thousands and the world will see the power of our God, Allah the Almighty.

"God is great. He is my refuge. He is my strength. The God of Abraham and Moses and the great messenger Mohammed gives me many blessings. He will reward me when our battle is won. The battle is soon."

He stopped there as though he was interrupted or perhaps tired. I dissected the document and underlined words and metaphors that directly or passively referred to the explosions. The devices were obviously bombs, maybe dirty bombs. There was also reference to a missile or missiles and attacks on several cities. I knew that Bin Laden had purchased as many as forty bombs from the Chechen Mafia for $30,000,000 and several tons of heroin. None of the bombs had turned up to this day. Assad and his friends were obviously lieutenants dispatched by Bin Laden or people like him. They had become Jihad or students of Islam waging their holy war. They had trained in Tehran in the terrorist training camp, Imam Ali. I learned about the camp from some of the radical Muslim extremists we detained and erased after the World Trade Center bombing.

The secondary explosions would be the erupted tanks of chlorine gas and cyanide and these gases would be propelled throughout the Kanawha Valley annihilating literally thousands of innocent, God-fearing West Virginians. It was unthinkable to even speculate how horrible the devastation would be. The bomb or bombs would not need to have radioactive components, but I expected they would anyway. I wasn't sure what the missile or missiles would be used for unless they couldn't get the bombs into the plant. A shoulder fired missile from the high ground to either side of the river would give the gunner a visible target within American. It could alternatively knock airplanes out of the sky, especially Air National Guard aircraft patrolling the skies.

There also had to be someone on the inside. Time would be of the essence to pinpoint who he or they were and in what area the person or persons worked. And when plant officials were notified of our suspicions about such insiders, all employees and their cars would be searched by security for suitcase bombs, explosives or other devices. FBI agents would also rove the grounds outside the plant as well as inside.

Now we had two important documents: the map and the proof of a plan to attack American. But if they had bombs, how would they be delivered? Would the terrorist element drop them from planes, set them off after crashing the gate or would the insiders try to smuggle them in? Then again, would some type of system be fired from a missile off an adjacent hillside? And finally ... when would it happen?

I knew that Assad and company hadn't ventured far on any given day, except perhaps the weekend I was gone, and I expected his leader was within the county or a few miles across the border in the backwoods of Virginia. I was sure it had to be a local Middle Easterner and not Bin Laden or one of his immediate subordinates. The tone of the document alluded to meetings which just about had to be local as I suspected none of the men had been out of the country recently. I was hoping Byrd, the Bureau and Interpol could confirm that.

I leaned back in Joey's plush leather desk chair and allowed a hundred thoughts to zip through my brain like a meteor shower. Byrd was ready to bring the Zulu team in to take these guys out. In doing so, however, we may only choke out a few of the weeds. It was obvious they were only a small part of a vast terrorist network. I wondered if all the elements within that network had planned to stage a series of attacks all at the same time or over a series of days or weeks. It seemed more logical that given the element of surprise, they would be on the same day. After a singular major attack, the country and all its factories, infrastructure and government buildings would be shut down and thereafter maintain high standards of alert. Zulu would be effective, but I was convinced that the terrorists would not be taken alive to be tortured into confession. As disciplined and committed these local terrorists were to their religion, they were prepared to die. DAG's cyanide capsule was proof of that. Given the terrorists' deaths, we would have only slowed down the entire network. But one way or another, it would be up to Zulu to take down this element.

The longer I stewed about whether it was actually time to bring in Zulu, the more I became convinced Birdman was right. At least we would stop the American mission. I had worked with a military version of Zulu when I was in Vietnam. It was an elite, but deadly faction of Special Ops called the Provincial Reconnaissance Unit, only there was very little recon to it. It was made up of a Vietnamese Dirty Dozen type element with the sole mission of true counterterrorism, which in fact *was* terrorism. The mission, whether covert or overt, was assassination. It got the job done … and cleanly. The targets were known or suspected Vietcong to include key officials, dirty village chiefs and the like. Bad guys just disappeared without leaving a hair. It was like they never existed.

But whether Zulu was engaged or not, the Bureau needed to be apprised. If we didn't give them a piece of this, the Director would not only have a good case of the red-ass, but on a strategic level the FBI would never again cooperate with or trust us.

I studied the message in depth, finding most of it pretty straight forward. The reference to 'shaking the Roman Throne' I had heard before and knew that it meant killing Christians whom the radical Muslims perceived not only heathenistic, but a threat to the very tenets of their religion.

I got the boss back on the phone. Although I knew he was ready to send the boys, was he willing to partner with the FBI? Again, not only did I believe we were compelled to do so, I felt an allegiance to an organization from which I was drawing retirement.

"Before we chat, Scorpion, we need to invoke Krypton. I'm sure my line is secure, but am not sure about your cell or any land line in your area. People now have new, sophisticated eavesdropping devices that can compromise both mediums."

This was Byrd's notice to me that our dialogue had to be in cryptographic format. In other words, nothing could be said in the open and we had to talk in metaphors. I always liked playing this game. I was always Scorpion. He had asked me to pick a code name under these circumstances and I thought 'Scorpion' made me sound dangerous.

"First of all, do you think there's any way you've been breached?" (that means *found out*).

"No. I don't think so." I replied; although Assad knew I was no architect. And that's for *damn* sure. All I can draw are stick people, stick houses, and stick dogs …
"So what's your take on the thesis?"
"Well, it's obvious now that the bull's eye is what we thought it was and the big bang is no longer a theory. I agree we need to order take-out."

"Who's the kingpin?"

"Don't know. Could be someone local; could be Public Enemy Number One … you know, from the Old Country."
(Bin Laden)

"My money's on the latter."

"Maybe. But the tone of the manuscript indicates an ongoing relationship with someone local."

"Okay, whatever. We still need to kill the weeds. I'm sending in the Roundup team."

"More will spring up elsewhere, you know."

"But the chore is to stop the growth where *you* are. We'll deal with the new pop-ups."

I love this spy code stuff.

"We need to inform Fabulous Boys Incorporated," I replied. I made that one up, meaning of course the FBI.

"Not sure I follow that one, Scorpion."

"Think phonetic alphabet; only substitute new and improved letters."

"I get it, now," said Birdman. "I don't want them bumping into the Roundup folks. But you're right. I will work on setting up the Tango Foxtrot."

"Okay, but it may take more time than we have to unite all the egos. We know where the weeds are, but we need to corral them and snuff them all out at once."

"I can have everyone at your location by Saturday morning. You will be their contact and make yourself accessible to receive Pest Control at coordinates Mike Delta 37964451. Refer of course to your guide book." He meant my Cryptographic Super Duper Spy Handbook.

I checked September's pocket Signal Operating Instructions, having just shredded August, and we were to meet and greet ... let's see ... somewhere near the Greenbrier Hotel in White Sulphur. I wondered if he was actually going to put these guys up at the Greenbrier. I liked where I was staying, but I'd be more than pissed if they got to stay in five star lap of luxury.

"Did anything turn up from the major landscaper (meaning Interpol, I think) on the weeds?"

"Nothing. Either they are all new crabgrass with no history or they've been very careful to blend into the lawn. There *has* been some activity in the old country (meaning Great Britain). A couple of cells were uncovered recently by the Big Bobs (MI5)."

"Did you check out the subject's daddy? (Meaning Assad's father)"

"Affirmative. He's clean."

I figured as much. Assad was one of Al-Qaeda's young lions. Older, Middle-Eastern professionals who had been in this country for many years were enjoying the fruits of capitalism and not trying to blow up their potential clients. "Should I go ahead and contact my new friend in the big city?"

"Your Fabulous Boy counterpart?" *Hey, that code name was mine. Get your own, Turkey.*

"Yes," I replied.

"No. Not right away."

"Professional courtesy, Condor. I promised to share."

"Then give him my number. If his location wants in, my rules apply. Turf protection, you know. They need to concern themselves with the lawn; we'll take care of the weeds. I'll be having a dialogue with their CEO."

About that time I was getting a little tired of the daffy dialogue and suspected we wouldn't be fooling anybody anyway with all the hooey.

"I'll see him first thing in the morning and will plan to meet your boys Saturday. In the meantime, I will be looking at the personal effects of the other two where they live."

"Good. I will be looking for heavy take-down. Stand by for further tomorrow." He clicked me again before I could click him.

I had an idea. "Joey, can I borrow your car this morning. Maybe one of the family cars?"

"What for?"

"I'm too visible in mine."

"Oh, I see. Sneaky peek stuff, huh?" "Something like that."

"Okay, take the Lincoln. But no bullet holes," he warned, pointing his finger at me. "And be careful. I've gotten all the business I need this month."

"I'll get it back to you this afternoon. Looking forward to dinner. What's cooking?"

"I don't know. But you know Cora. She'll be puttin' on

the Ritz."

I left McGowan's Pickup and Layaway and drove out to the Greenbrier Airport to see if the suspects were still on routine … the one hour class at Valley followed by the two plus hours of flight lessons at the flight academy. It was eleven-fifteen and I figured the time was about right for them to be driving in. But when I arrived, I found both the Maxima and the Civic were already there, side by side between the restaurant and the entrance to the small terminal.

I had the goods on Assad and although I was 95% sure Ahmed and Fayz were in the conspiracy as well, I like all the pieces to fall into place without any doubts before people are terminated. So, getting a look at the stuff inside their cabin while they were flying the friendly skies may prove even further enlightening as to their roles in the American plot. I may even find that there were others in the equation. Nonetheless, I had just over two days to set things right in my mind and complete the puzzle before Zulu swept in.

The Lincoln was nice and I thought to myself maybe I ought to get rid of my big black box and start styling and profiling in something like that. The windows were also tinted black smoke, and as I could see out, no one could see me inside clicking off shots with the Nikon or picking my nose at a traffic light. It's a proven statistic that seven of ten guys explore the nasal cavity on a regular basis while they're behind the wheel, digging and burying up to and including the second knuckle.

After trekking the ten miles out to White Sulphur, I pulled the family car into one of the parking spaces to the rear of the office at Jamestown and eyed Cabin Eight for any activity. After about five minutes I tucked my Glock in the back of my pants, grabbed my digital, looked around for any snoops, then got out. Just in case one of the boys had stayed back, I rapped on the door, at the same time eyeing the lock system. There was no answer or bumping around inside and the door did have a dead bolt. For the second time in less than a week I was committing the crime of B&E. Of course, I could have waited until people came home, hoping they would let me in to look at their stuff and then they would naturally admit to me they were Amim Ali trained terrorists up to no good. That would put a bow on it for me, and then I could ask them to wait there a couple of days until their new Zulu friends came by to kill them.

I pulled from my pocket my handy little kit and fiddled with the tumbler, all the while checking over both shoulders for nosy people. I heard the click and immediately tried the doorknob. Fortunately, for time's sake, there was no lock on the knob and the door creaked open. After quickly closing the door behind me, I pulled my Glock to sweep the room.

The cabin was probably 20 X 30 with twin beds on the right, separated by an eight-foot armoire. A blue velvet couch and two sofa chairs were in a sitting area on the left. A TV hung on the wall adjacent to the bathroom door. It was a kind of cheesy place and even smelled like cheese … limburger. Not quite the pristine quaintness of Wolf Laurel. Obviously, either Assad's bankroll exceeded that of Fayz and Ahmed or he was higher up in the food chain and rated a nicer place.

I began my search of the usual places, the armoire, a small closet which housed three pairs of pointy-toed Arab roach killers, two rolled up prayer blankets and some clothing which I frisked. Then I performed thorough searches of the bed linen, the couch and chairs and the bathroom. Inside of the medicine cabinet were the usual toiletries and a prescription for Benadryl with Ahmed's name on it. The pharmacy was in Binghamton, Massachusetts, which fit. A small desk with two drawers on either side sat under the TV.

On the desk were two books … again as in Assad's pad, the Qur'an and an Arab-English dictionary. A myriad of ash and trash lay in the two drawers: pens, pencils, Certs (for the limburger breath) and some Lance crackers, among other items. In the bottom left drawer was some sort of device with a crank and two wires connected to a timer. It didn't take a genius to figure out it was the catalyst to an explosive device. After placing it on the desk and snapping several shots, I put it back in the drawer.

I then looked under the bed. You always check under beds for stuff … monsters, dust bunnies, bombs, people hiding and the like. A backpack similar to the one Assad had surgically attached to his shoulder was shoved about a foot back. I checked the pockets first, finding a paperback in Arabic, a folding pocketknife and a tri-fold transparency containing pictures of Big Nose and Baldy, looking a little younger, somewhere in a desert scenario and holding AK-47s. In the background of the photos were burning oil wells and I wondered now if these guys were Iraqi and the pictures were from Desert Storm. There were also photos of young Middle Eastern women in burkhas.

In the main compartment was a notebook containing several pieces of loose paper, two magazines, *Alneda* and *Waaqiah*, Azzam pro-Taliban publications by a press in Saudi Arabia, and to my alarm, a Department of Defense field manual on Chemical, Biological and Radiological effects and dispersion. Among the loose papers was an identical copy of the American map. On a second sheet was a diagram with numbers reflecting distance from Point A to Point B and a series of inner circles or fans from the targets depicting radiuses of speculative, probable and actual collateral damage. On the left side of the page was an X from which there was a line to the target reflecting trajectory and it was obvious this would be a shoulder-fired missile situated on high ground.

This was the icing on our cake. I laid out all the material on the floor and took more photos, being careful to return everything to its proper compartment. As this was an illegal search and nothing I had found could be used as evidence in a court of law, it would still be fruitful to a tribunal. Illegals or combatives in this country plotting terrorist activities are not subject to the U.S. Court system nor would be considered enemy soldiers protected by the Geneva Convention. So, this illegal search didn't really matter when it came to disposing of these guys. And why the hell would vermin like this be protected under the Constitution? Anyway, my job is more about protecting the American people than preserving the Constitution. Especially where it comes to abominable subversives. We would be sure to do our work swiftly and efficiently when it came down. There would be no opportunity for the press, the Congress or ACLU lawyers to catch even the slightest breeze about this going down.

Just in case the boys came home early, I peered through the Venetian blind to scan the parking lot. Satisfied there was no one about, I opened the door, snapped the lock and stepped out onto the gravel walkway. Suddenly, my eyes caught what appeared to be a young Middle Eastern woman in a blue maid's uniform with towels in her hand closing the door to the cabin next to Cabin Eight. Had she seen me actually leaving the cabin? As I continued walking, our eyes met briefly, but we did not acknowledge one another. The less engagement, the better. I made my way back to the Lincoln, feeling the woman's eyes on the back of my neck. I wondered whether she was allowed to clean the men's quarters or did they also refuse maid service like Assad.

After sliding under the wheel of the Lincoln, I saw that the maid was still looking suspiciously in my direction. Perhaps she had become acquainted with the Cabin Eight occupants and was maybe even collaborating with them. I figured if that was the case, she would only be their pawn to keep a watchful eye on the place. In their culture, a woman would not be partnered with men on any venture, much less a terrorist plot. Women were the subservient gender, having not the role, the intellect or the capacity to partner with men. Anyway, my question to myself regarding her license to clean Cabin Eight was answered. She inserted her key in the lock and went inside.

I really didn't have anything else to do until it was time to pick up Adrianna for din-din at Joey's, so I decided to sit for a while. When the boys returned, they should not be suspicious about the Lincoln and would likely pay it no mind. At least they wouldn't associate it with me. If the Jamestown men were still on routine, they would either accompany Assad to Wolf Laurel or come back here. It was a 50-50 shot and I decided to take this one. I also wanted to see if the maid would say anything to them. And here I was again missing lunch. I'd be starved by suppertime.

The maid came out of number eight after about a half hour, carrying a bundle of soiled towels, which she threw into the laundry basket still sitting outside the door. She cast another glance at the Lincoln, then moved on down to Cabin Five further back in the trees. I called Birdman to let him know what I had done and my findings, being careful to send the information in my clever code that even 007 would have trouble deciphering. I also called Jack Fuentes to alert him that some information was coming down though his channels of major significance that involved the subject of our previous conversations. He asked pretty please if I would come to see him Thursday morning. We could also do lunch. I told him it was a date.

I knew once the scenario was laid on the Bureau, that would generate a great deal of political infighting about who should take out the terrorists and who should get all the kudos. Fabulous Boys International would just have to take a back seat on this one, if Byrd was as powerful as I thought he was. And although Birdman had refused to divulge the name of his boss, I knew it was none other than the President himself. I had figured that out on one of Byrd's weekly trips down to Washington when on the tube the next day I saw a press photo taken in the Oval Office of Mr. Bush with Mr. Byrd and the directors of the FBI and CIA. I had heard that Birdman was angry that his mug had been photographed, the super-secret spy that he was.

At two-thirty, as I had hoped, both the Honda and Nissan rolled into the parking lot in front of Cabin Eight. This time not only the driver's door of the Nissan opened, but the passenger side door as well. The passenger was a man about forty-five and had a dark beard. *It was the same man I had seen with Paul LeMer at the Labor Day picnic.* My instincts rarely fail me. There was now officially a fourth figure and I would have two days to find out who he was.

That meant I would have to re-establish my friendship with the good Mr. LeMer.

I snatched my professional Nikon off the seat, dialed in the telephoto and zapped a half-dozen shots of the man. Then I continued my watch as all four players stood outside of the door conversing. The three younger men were positioned together, standing erect, almost at attention, listening respectfully to the older man. His manner appeared instructive and he punctuated his dialogue with animated gestures. I wondered if this was *Fearless Leader* indicated in Assad's treatise. It seemed that *Multicultural Issues* was not the only class these kids were taking. I had no doubt this was a session of yet another, more important class to them called *Terrorism in America101*. I wish I had learned to read lips somewhere along the way.

The pow wow seemed to be breaking up and the band of confederates went inside the bungalow. I sat there for a few more minutes and about the time I reached down to turn on the ignition, the maid came out of Number Five, looked in the direction of the Lincoln, then went to the door of Number Eight. I saw her knuckles rap twice, after which the door opened and she went on in as though she were expected. Within ten seconds the door opened just a crack and I knew then that someone was checking out the Lincoln. I also saw the blind move at the window. I began backing out slowly past the office and toward the road, being careful not to let them see the license plate. They wouldn't be able to tell that the Continental was a funeral home family car, but I didn't want to take a chance they would connect Joey with the break-in and surveillance, putting him and his family in jeopardy.

And now they knew for sure that someone or some government entity was onto them. After backing onto the highway, I headed back to McGowan and Sons to get my vehicle. As I was taking no chances the suspects would break for one of their cars and follow me, I put the pedal to the metal and began straightening out the curves on old U.S. 60.

CHAPTER 17

I dropped off the Lincoln and told Joey I'd see him in a couple of hours. Back at Wolf Laurel, I saw that Assad hadn't returned. Adrianna's car was there and that meant she was not somewhere with Dan nursing his wounds from Monday's fracas on the gridiron. I had the feeling Dan was not interested in going out with either one of us again.

Anyway, I grabbed a shower, a Diet Coke and a pack of nabs to tie me over. Juanita stopped by to bring me fresh towels and another bar of soap. I think she had become enamored with me as she stayed a while to tell me about her mother in El Salvador and that more than half of her wages went to support her and three siblings. Maybe she was just trying to get me to warm up to her in case I was really INS. As she was leaving my room, we heard someone enter the hallway and saw that it was Assad returning from his bombing rehearsal. Although we were clearly within a couple of feet from him, he looked straight ahead, avoiding eye contact. He looked pissed about something. I'm sure the Jamestown maid gave him and the element a full description of me. Or maybe he thought I was doing Juanita and that supported his notion that I was a lying, whoremongering infidel. Being the religious zealot that he was, he probably thought I was servicing *all* the ladies. I heard his door shut and Juanita made a face that included eye-rolling. Obviously, that was an international expression practiced by all women.

Jack called me just after five, probing for any new information I may have. I asked if he was available tomorrow instead for the sit-down and he said he was. We'd meet at nine.

Just before six-thirty I knocked lightly on Adrianna's door, which she quickly opened. I could get used to being greeted with that sweet smile at the end of my nine-to-five workday.

"I'll be ready in a second," she said, giving me a succulent kiss on the lips. "Need some lipstick."

"Good. I like the taste of lipstick. I'll take seconds when you come back, if you don't mind."

She smiled again and retreated to the bathroom. Be careful what you ask for. She returned with the appetizer, only it tasted more like dessert. She looked marvelous in her white 'skorts', pink shimmering blouse and white sandals with three-inch heels that accentuated her perfectly-shaped size six feet with the pink-coated toenails. But again, who's noticing?

We didn't share much about how each of us spent our day as we zipped to the other side of town. Hers was the same old routine at the B&B and mine, I couldn't tell her about. She'd think I was some kind of low-life burglar, and I didn't want a little thing like my criminal activity to taint her fond impression of me.

"That's my church there," she said, pointing to a small, white building with a steeple that looked straight out of a Norman Rockwell print. It was set back off the road among four or five gigantic willows that metaphorically served as a vanguard against all that is evil and which would threaten its parishioners. As I cruised by the church with my window down I heard the little congregation from the Wednesday night prayer meeting belting out *"O victory in Jesus ..."* Their voices rang and reverberated throughout the grove and into the adjacent meadow as though a choir of angels had descended upon the valley called Greenbrier. I reminded myself that there were people plotting at that moment to destroy this perfect peace, this simple and beautiful picture of Americana, and I would be damned if I let that happen.

"You haven't said much since we left. Is anything bothering you, Skip?"
I turned my head and gave her a half-hearted smile.

"Naw. I was just trying to remember. I think I went to a couple of funerals there when I was a kid. Not that I knew any of the deceased; but Dad used to drag me to most every funeral."

"I guess that had to have an effect on a kid, to always be around the dead and the grieving. And then the cemeteries …" She shook her head.

I winked and broadened my smile. "That's largely what made me the psycho I am today. I probably lived the macabre life Stephen King writes about."

"Oh, come on. You're not a psycho. You're sweet and funny, and maybe sometimes a little serious. But you seem perfectly well-adjusted."

"Defense mechanisms, my dear. What you see on the outside isn't necessarily what lies deep in the dark recesses of the soul."

She took her fingertips and placed them between the buttons on my shirt and made tender circles over my chest hair at the heart. "I know what's in there and it is nothing but good and right. I also know you're a tough guy, hardened by experiences that the average person would never ever realize. And I'm sure that if you ever had to be violent, it would be because you are protecting someone or something you love from a terrible happening."

"Like when I punched out Dan?"

"Let's not go there, you bad boy."

"Now I'm *bad*. I was *good* a minute ago."

She gave me a playful punch in the arm, then leaned into

me, placing her arms around my waist the rest of the way.

When we arrived at Joey's, we were greeted at the door by Cora. "Adrianna, hi. We have both lived in this area all our lives and have yet to run into one another. I'm glad it's finally happening." They hugged.

"Me too. It's funny. We've probably passed each other a hundred times somewhere in Lewisburg."

"Well, anyway. It's wonderful to finally meet you," Cora said. "Joey has mentioned you on occasion ... more lately than in the past." She looked in my direction and smiled.

There was a lot of pre-dinner small talk, mostly about who knew who and who's doing what now. We sat down at the table and the family joined hands for the blessing. As Joey was speaking to God, I again was made to realize I hadn't talked much to the Creator over the years or showed Him the appreciation He was due. He had certainly gotten me out of a hell of a lot of scrapes in my lifetime. Sorry about the *hell* word, God.

It was a superb dinner as usual ... pork loin with gravy, mashed potatoes, green beans, hot, buttered rolls, and peach pie for dessert. I should go to this restaurant more often.

After supper, the women cleared the table, loaded the dishwasher and retired to the living room for coffee and more talk. The adult women carried on like old friends, and after a while, Molly and Casey disappeared with their cell phones, one by one, into their rooms for more meaningful conversations with their friends.

Joey and I took our usual places on the front porch. He sucked on a Dominican and I sucked in the cool evening air.

"What's going on now, Bruce? Not that I want you to leave, but you're sticking around a long time on this dead Arab case. I know it's not just because of Adrianna, unless you're thinking about retiring for good and settling down. Don't you have a job to get back to?"

"My job is not just in Washington, Joey. Anyway, I'm still officially on vacation, thanks to my boss."

"Okay, be that way," he said, exhaling a three second stream of blue-grey smoke. "But I know different. I know *you*. Don't get me wrong; I'm sure there are things you can't discuss. Top Secret things." He paused for a drag. "You did tell me about American in Charleston and shared a couple of things with me that you told the FBI guy. If there's more you can't tell me, no problem. But you know I won't go out and blab to anyone."

"You're putting me in a tough spot, little brother." I turned my head away and gazed out over the meadow for several moments. Then I looked back at him and smiled. "Okay. Maybe a smidgen. Before this is all over, you'll probably know, anyway. Your stiff led me to three, maybe four more of his kind. I found out they all have the same map in their possession. And don't ask me how I know that. One of these guys is actually staying at Wolf Laurel, and if I have to stay there as long as he does, I will. The others are bunking at a location in White Sulphur Springs."

"Ha! I *knew* there were more of them. And I wager they're planning some kind of suicide mission on American. I'm right, aren't I?"

"Can't go any further with this, Joey." He looked away and shook his head.

"What would make people like that want to blow themselves up, Bruce?"

"Well, put yourself in one of these guy's shoes, little brother. You have no Jesus, no Christmas, no TV, no football, no Dallas Cowboy Cheerleaders, no Wal-Mart, no hot dogs or beer. You wear rags for clothes and towels for hats. You can't shave. Your wife can't shave and by the way, she smells like your camel. Do you really want to live any longer?"

That fueled a bit of laughter. "I see your point."

We were silent for a while and then he pressed me a little more. "So, how're you planning to stop them?" I didn't answer.

"Come on, Bruce. What's your plan?"

I looked at him, thoughtfully, then leaned over the banister and spat onto the ground below. "Let's just say we've got people lined up to make this all go away in the next few days."

"Will my business suddenly pick up?" I shrugged.

Joey stuck his finger into my chest and with succinct articulation said, "Just make sure *you* don't become my business, Brucie. If these men are as dangerous as you make out ... just be careful, that's all."

We locked eyes. Serious eyes. Then I nodded. "Let's go back to the girls," I said.

We all sat in the parlor chatting for a few minutes more, balancing our peach pie and cups of coffee on our knees. One custom both Joey and I picked up from the old man was pouring the hot coffee from the pot into our cups and allowing it to overflow into the saucer. Our first sip of the java was always *from* the saucer. As the spilled-over liquid would have cooled nicely, the roofs of our mouths would not get scorched. Adrianna watched us both suck out the saucers and smiled. She loved folksy traditions.

On the way back to the inn, Adrianna put her hand on my thigh and squeezed it. "Nice people, Joey's family. I loved the girls ... so cute and perky."

And then it happened. I wish to God I had never asked my next question ... that one, probing, and evening-ending question. "So why is it that you and Mason never had any kids?"

There was no response. I thought at first she didn't hear me. Then she released her hand from my thigh and turned toward the door.

"We did," she replied softly.

"Oh." I was afraid to go further, sensing that somewhere inside her was an old wound. I suspected perhaps she had miscarried.

But she continued. "We had a son. His name was Johnny

… John Mason, to be specific." There was a long pause. "He lived to be nine." Then the sobbing came. I quickly pulled off into a school parking lot.

"God. I'm sorry." I placed my hand on hers and squeezed sympathetically.

"It was leukemia. We tried everything … transfusions, treatments, even the Mayo Clinic. He was gone in only eight months after the diagnosis. But even though it's been five years now, every day I think about him. Some days are better than others."

And now that I had reopened that wound, today was one of the worst.

"I … had no idea, Adrianna."

She turned her face toward me, and even in the dim light, I could see that her beautiful, glistening eyes were full of pain.

"Didn't Joey ever tell you?"

"No," I answered softly."

"It was he who buried Johnny in the little cemetery behind the church."

I couldn't respond from welling up myself and all I could think to do was pick up her hand and kiss it. Now tears were streaming down both of our cheeks.

I suppose out of respect for Adrianna, Joey decided not to tell me about her Johnny. He learned to be tight-lipped from the old man. When the dead is buried and gone, perhaps for their own emotional health, undertakers choose to talk about the living, not the dead. And I am sure that knowing I was establishing a very nice relationship with Adrianna, he did not want me to go into it with pity.

There was little more said as we continued back to the inn. I took her to her door, held her for a minute, tightly and lovingly; then she went inside and closed the door behind her.

I was determined not to go to bed depressed, so I slumped into the Queen Anne chair that sat in a corner of the room and picked up my copy of *The Far Side*. Soon I was yakking away and feeling a hell of a sight better about myself and my big, freaking mouth. I got through the paperback in fifteen or twenty minutes and tossed it on the end table. Not being the least bit drowsy, likely due to three spilled-over cups of caffeine, I turned on the TV. Two or three times I ran the remote up and down, trying to find something palatable besides the half dozen mindless sitcoms violating my brain. Where were the sophisticated comedies of yesteryear like *The Beverly Hillbillies*, *F-Troop* and *Gilligan's Island?* I clicked on ESPN and it was re-running the 1997 Tyson-Holyfield fight where they showed Iron Mike munching on Evander's ear. I wondered if Mikey had also gotten Van Gogh. And then they put on a ringside interview of Don King ... the perfect example of what you get when you mix Rogaine and Viagra.

Anyway, my attention was suddenly diverted by the sound of tromping feet on the wooden hallway floor outside my door. I counted three sets. The voices were muffled and indiscernible, but I could tell they belonged to my Arab neighbor and his comrades. In a few moments their noise dissipated inside Assad's room.

Leaving the TV blaring, I grabbed my keys, slipped out of my quarters and crept stealthily outside to my Suburban. Both the Honda and Nissan were in the parking lot, serving to confirm that the boys with Assad were not two new and different terrorists. I glanced up to Adrianna's turret room and saw that she was still there. The ghostly motion of her shadow passing in front of the window was apparent through the blind. From my cargo compartment I took out my latest spy gadget, a portable parabolic dish. It was a handheld listening device with a pistol grip on one end and a bell-shaped amplifier on the other resembling a miniature satellite dish. To accessorize my snoop toy the manufacturer, *Nostradamus*, had built in a mini tape recorder with earphones. *Nosy*, for short, had a listening range from operator to target of up to fifty yards. Now if it could only see through walls …

I moved through the flower garden and positioned myself by a large tree in the dark shadows approximately fifty feet from Assad's room. Blinds on the east and south windows were room-darkening and positioned tightly against the facing. As I did not see crack one, there was no opportunity to peer in anywhere. When I turned Nosy on, Arabic speaking voices immediately faded in.

My Arabic is weak at best. I'm not that good in learning other languages, which often makes me wonder why I was selected for this type of business in the first place. I took a year of German in military school and a second at the university. I thought I had nailed it down pretty well until I started a flirtatious conversation one evening with a pretty German lass serving drinks at the Infantry Bar at Ft. Benning. Although I had no idea what she was saying, I rattled off a few words from memory. Unfortunately, I must have mispronounced something that came out sounding like the German word for 'slut.' Not only did I get an earful of Bavarian brimstone, but a face full of the scotch she was about to serve me.

Anyway, I was deciphering only a word or two from the boys in the room. I thought I recognized the Arabic words for prayer, Heaven, fire and fight (or struggle). And then there was *Insha'Allah* or 'God willing.' After a few moments of trying to talk over one another, they got quiet. One of them then began a chant which I took to be a kind of prayer. And then there was silence. I thought at first they may have skedaddled; but since I did not hear them shuffling around or a door closing, it came to me they were probably kneeling on their prayer blankets facing Mecca. Whichever direction that was. I wondered if my hand-held listening device was interfering with their prayer signal. But whatever they were asking for, I was determined they wouldn't get it.

I remained at the tree line for perhaps another fifteen

minutes and then their dialogue started up again. Funny, I didn't hear anybody say Amen. There was some noisy scurrying and then a door shut. I took it that Ahmed and Fayez were now leaving, so I zipped around to the front corner of the inn to observe them to assure they were returning to their car. They were. When they pulled out I checked the veranda to see whether Assad was waving bye-bye to his buds or had stayed in his room. Satisfied he was nowhere in sight, I returned Nosy to the Suburban and sauntered back to my room. Tomorrow I would overnight the tape to Byrd and Abu.

As I lay in bed that Wednesday night, I pushed Assad and the other terrorists well back into some obscure corner of my brain, returning my thoughts instead to Adrianna. There had been enough loss and sorrow in her life these past few years to last a lifetime. And although on many days I'm sure she wrapped herself in that cloak of grief, she somehow managed to generate enough emotional strength to carry on life and business while wearing a face filled with joy and happiness.

I hardly saw it coming. I had let this woman inside my head at a point in my life where it was more important than ever to keep it clear … and all the while she was running mission interference. It was the one thing for over twenty years in law enforcement I said I would never let happen. And it was my own fault. I had let my defenses down and fallen in love. Well there it is; I finally said it to myself.

Sometime after midnight I ultimately lost consciousness. From out of the dark and troubled recesses of my brain, I had the dream again. Same village … same hooch. This time the bloodied child stumbling from the doorway was little Johnny Wolf. I knew it was him somehow. It was the face of the boy in the picture on Adrianna's end table. When I went inside the hut, I found the body of a dying Adrianna. The horror of my dream awakened me with a jolt. With blurry eyes I looked over at the clock on the night stand.

Two-fifty. Again, as was the case so many nights in the last thirty years, I did not get back to sleep.

My morning, which really began at three, actively began at six when I showered, donned a polo shirt, jeans and my Tony Lamas, then locked the door behind me, all in a half hour. At a quarter till seven I hit the drive-through at Hardees's for coffee and a biscuit and set out on I-64 west to Charleston. Within the two hours it took to get there, Jack Fuentes would already have had his coffee, kissed his beauty queen wife, dropped the young'ns at school and be dutifully sitting at his desk. I should be his first customer.

It was a cool morning, feeling almost like October, but the fresh mountain air whipping through my open glass was invigorating. I needed it to keep my dopey brain awake. But the brain was too busy to sign off anyway. For one thing, Adrianna's sad eyes kept flashing through it. I wondered if the night was good to her … if she slept or if the sadness that she had so carefully camouflaged, up until I opened my mouth, consumed her night.

But as much as I was beating myself up, I really couldn't keep blaming myself. How could I have known?

My cell rang as I left the toll booth on the turnpike just east of Cabin Creek. It was Adrianna. I took a deep breath and answered. "Well, good morning," I said as cheerfully as I could fake it.

"Where are you?" Her voice seemed a bit shaky.

"Almost to Charleston. I'll be at the Bureau in about twenty minutes. Anything wrong?"

"I've got a little problem here, Skip."

"What? What is it?"

"Someone broke into my office last night … probably when we were at Joey's. But it could have been during the night."

"That's doubtful. I'm a light sleeper and my room of course is only a dozen feet away. Was anything taken?"

"The place was ransacked. Drawers spilled out and papers

strewn about. The only thing that appears to be missing is my ledger, which has the names and addresses of all my guests."

"*That's* not good."

"No. The last two years of guest information are in that book. I used it as a mailing list *and* I have to have it in case I'm ever audited."

"I'll give you one guess who took it and what he wanted with it."

"You mean Assad."

"Assad," I repeated. "Now he has matched up my *real* name with the room and will also have my address in Georgetown. I'm also afraid he will now associate the name McGowan with the funeral home he broke into. This may well have put Joey and his family in danger. You did list me as Bruce McGowan, didn't you?"

"Yes, I'm sorry."

"Why be sorry? It wasn't your fault. You were just keeping records as you're supposed to do."

"Why would you think Joey and his family could be in danger from learning your name?" she asked.

"Like I said, I don't trust Assad. Who knows what ulterior motives he has?"

"The strange thing is, I had a money box with about eight hundred dollars in it. I saw where someone opened it, but left the money."

"It was Assad, all right. In his warped value system, he's not a common thief, but he would not blink an eye but to cut the throat of an infidel American."

"Skip, that's horrible," she responded in a frightened tone. "Why would you say that?"
I ignored her question as I already had said too much. "Did you call the police?"

"They're here now. A couple of deputies from the sheriff's department. They're dusting for prints."

"They're wasting their time."

"I don't mind telling you I'm a little scared, Skip."

"I'll be back later this afternoon. Maybe you should go somewhere for a few hours."

"I don't want to leave the place without anybody here. When Juanita found out about this, she went home. The poor soul was frightened to death."

"Okay, then. Is Lottie still there?" "Yes. I guess she's in her room."

"Go ask her to have some tea with you and engage in some lengthy conversation. Tell her what happened and that you need some company. Is Assad there?"

"No. His vehicle is gone. I haven't seen him all morning. He was gone when I came downstairs at seven."

"Okay. Just be careful today."

"Come back soon."

"I will. Call me if you need me."

Jack Fuentes opened the door to his office and came out to greet me, hand extended.

"Come in, Bruce."

I followed him in, closed the door behind me and plopped into the chair facing his desk. He lowered himself into his leather chair and sat with hands folded. People who sit behind desks tend to think of themselves as in situational control, holding the cards, several rungs higher than the lowly serf in the straight-back chair. Except *I* was the guy holding the cards today.

"I guess we do need to talk about all this, Bruce. I had a conversation with Washington which had earlier been talking with *your* organization. Sounds like you've been a busy guy. You found three more suspects connected to the dead Arab, and even know their names, addresses and routines. When were you planning to tell me all this?"

"Today."

"And I understand your guys have organized a task force to capture and as necessary neutralize the threat."

That surprised me. I didn't realize CTT, meaning Byrd,

had let the cat out of the bag. I would have to counsel with him about being so loose-lipped.

"If that's the information you got. Has your office been tasked anywhere in the equation?"

"We're focusing on American. We have a Task Force profile team on the inside looking around and checking out employees from the plant manager right on down to the guys who sweep up. Uniformed and private security has been doubled, and there are roving guards on the perimeter."

"Do you have the south hill area covered that overlooks the plant?"

"No, why?"

"I have cultivated some new information that they may be planning to shoot a shoulder fired missile into the plant, probably to take out one of the storage tanks if a bombing or other attack fails."

"And how did you *cultivate* that information?" I smiled and did my Groucho eyebrow thing. "You didn't."

"I did what I had to do."

"And without a court order, I presume. I guess that was the way you conducted business when you were with the Bureau. I have heard about the old days and you guys who bent the rules to the breaking point."

Don't be anal, J. Edgar.

"No. You've got the wrong guy here, Jack. But it does frustrate the hell out of me to have in my possession probable cause only to be refused a warrant by some liberal judge."

Jack spun a half-right and looked out his window. "Whose abode did you burglarize."

"Everyone's"

"Wonderful," he said sarcastically. "Okay, I'll bite. Why do you think there may be a missile involved?"

"I found what appears to be a trajectory and dispersion diagram. The trajectory begins at a point that looks like high ground in the sketch and ends at the target ... the factory."

I took the card from my digital Nikon. "Can you do me a favor and have this printed out?"

Jack buzzed his assistant who promptly materialized. I like well-trained assistants. My last one made *me* get *her* coffee.

"Any idea from your 'investigation' when a strike may take place?"

"No, but I've got to believe soon. The Arab staying at the place I'm staying is planning to leave October 1st. these guys will just hit-and-run or disappear for good when they blow themselves up."

"Suicide bombing. What do you think … car bomb crashing the gate or missile?"

"You need to prepare for both."

Jack reflected a bit, stroking his chin. "When is your team arriving?"

"Saturday morning, 0900 at or near the Greenbrier."

"The Greenbrier?"

"Go figure. Nothing's too good for *our* boys. Actually, they're driving down earlier in the unit van and will call me for a meeting place."

"And the mission?"

"The usual. Capture and interrogate. If they resist capture … total erasure. They never existed."

"You know these people vow never to be taken alive."

"And I respect people with those vows. As a matter of fact, I would do anything in my power to help them *keep* their vows. Anyway, if we take them alive and hold them for prosecution, they will lawyer-up and some ACLU prick will complain that the poor immigrants had their civil rights violated. But I'm less concerned with that right now; we have to stop them from getting to American. When American is safe, the good people of Charleston live."

Jack looked at the pictures of his family on his credenza. I knew this all rattled him and he would do everything he could to support us on this mission, even if it meant the

Bureau would take a back seat. His assistant came in with the prints and Jack studied them intently. He nodded but said nothing.

I placed my hand on Jack's shoulder and smiled at him. "One way or another, we'll take them down, Jack. I promise you that."

It had become personal with him, now, given the fact that he, Diane and the kids were Charlestonians and would be among the victims of any deadly chemical cloud. And it chilled me to the bone to imagine a scene where possibly a hundred thousand people would suddenly begin choking and convulsing, where every failing breath was petrified, people would be crashing their cars or littering the sidewalks with their corpses ... like something out of a 50's sci-fi movie.

I asked Jack to send the scanned photos of the older man I took the day before to our office in New York, giving him Byrd's e-mail. I knew that Interpol had to have something on the man who appeared to be the terrorists' leader. I also asked him to overnight Nosy's tape. Tomorrow I would find out the older man's identity from Paul LeMer.

Jack and I had lunch at a dive on Quarrier Street famous for its fried chicken and black-eyed peas, but definitely not its atmosphere. The walls were a dirty white, the tables and chairs were circa 1950s and the cook was of your greasy spoon version ... tee shirt, tattoos and obviously ate at his own restaurant ... every bit of 300 pounds. I couldn't make him out clearly where he was in the back, but either he had a moustache or a half-smoked unlit cigar in his mouth.

A very large waitress with fiery dust mop hair, plopped a plate down in front of me containing two pieces of glistening chicken, a volcano of mashed potatoes with red-eye gravy and corn bread with a slab of unmelted, artery closing butter sitting on top. For whatever reason, I had actually let Jack talk me into eating at the Cardiac Café. But since I was a runner and in pretty good shape, I could handle garbage like this. Jack, however, was choking down country-fried steak and milk gravy; and given his sedentary lifestyle and cute little pouch he was developing above his belt, I feared for his life.

I finished the breast and after gnawing on the thigh for a few seconds, I laid it down in what was left of the potato mush. "Don't you like the lunch, Bruce? You look a little green."

"It's okay. But I think I now have *ticker* shock. You don't happen to have a fibrillator in your car, do you?"

He laughed. "Hey, the body needs a little grease like this every once in a while, for system regulation."

"I hope to hell you don't make this place a regular pit stop."

"Of course not, Bruce. I'm fortunate to even get out of the office for lunch once or twice a month."

Almost on cue, Miss America, whose Jungle Gardenia perfume made me even more nauseous, came back to our table to deposit the check. Jack snatched it up quickly, the gentleman that he was.

"How about some dessert, Jack?" she asked.

"You're usual or would you like to try some of our lemon chess pie?"

I had just sucked in a swig of coffee and nearly spewed it all over the waitress. And Jack, the big liar, appeared to be right embarrassed. He smiled sheepishly. "Okay, maybe more than twice a month."

The waitress shrugged when Jack didn't order dessert and sashayed away.

"You know, Jack, I remember a grill in the Bronx a few years back and getting served at the counter by a gal in a tank top built a lot like this one. I had ordered a hot dog and some fries, and the guy on the stool next to me ordered a double cheeseburger. The waitress then took two frozen beef patties out of the freezer and slapped each one of them up into her armpits to thaw them out. I sat there with my mouth open for a few moments and then the alarm went off. 'Oh, Miss,' I said. 'Cancel the hot dog, will you?'"

Jack *wanted* to laugh, I could tell; but his dignity got in the way. After pursing his lips together to regain his composure, he said, "I'm gagging here, Bruce. Not a good story to tell at lunch."

I was sure he couldn't wait to tell my joke around the water cooler when he got back to the office. And I was also glad to see a more relaxed, even human side of this uptight kid.

Jack cleared the bill and I thanked him very much. I told him I was stopping by the American factory on the way back to talk with the plant superintendent. I was mainly interested in finding out if there were any Middle Eastern types working there in some capacity who could in fact be 'insiders.' It may be a long shot, but still worth checking out.

"I need you to go with me, Jack. Without credentials, I may not be able to even get past the gate, much less get in the see 'the man.'"

"I have a ton of things ahead of me today, Bruce. How about doing this some other time?"

"I may not *have* another day for this. Can't you spare a couple of hours?"

I must have been wearing my beggar face. He sighed and shook his head. "All right. Let me make a couple of calls. Are you always this convincing, Bruce?"

"Always. Not to mention charismatic."

He gave me one of those looks ... you know, like I was something between a knucklehead and a nuisance. But I could tell he liked me, bad jokes and all. He pulled out his cell, called the office, and after a couple of *okays*, he nodded to me and clamped the phone shut. *Atta boy, Jack.*

With his badge and ID and my captivating, good looks, we made it through the female guard on the gate. She gave us a site map which took us to the administration building. At the information desk we were directed to the superintendent's office. Carl Hamner, the boss, came out to greet us. He was a nice enough guy and once we got acquainted, he wanted to know the purpose of our visit.

"Have you been contacted in the past few days by anyone from the government?" asked Jack.

"Well, we've had government people *all over* the place lately. I got clued in there's some kind of threat in the area, although no one really wanted to go into specifics. Said they're combing all the plants for possible security breaches."

That's what he was supposed to think. Obviously, the FBI was keeping a tight lip about any *specific* threat at American.

Hamner continued. "But I did have a peculiar conversation with a gentleman with the State Department in New York by the name of Leon … no, Lionel Byrd." He then looked at my card again. "Hey, *you're* with the State Department. Is he your boss?"

"One and the same."

"He asked me several questions, mostly about what we manufacture here, how our products are used, et cetera. I'm afraid I wasn't too informative. I'm not used to talking with people on the phone about such matters without being sure they're who they say they are."

"Yeah," I replied. "For all you know, the guy could have been a telemarketer or Jehovah's Witness."

Jack gave me another one of those looks. So did Hamner, and he didn't even know me.

"Ahem … yes. Well, anyway, I made sure I didn't tell him anything that wasn't common knowledge."

Jack's turn. "I'm going to ask you a question, Mr. Hamner, which may sound a bit irregular. How many Middle Eastern employees do you have here?"

"Your government guys have already addressed that with me, too, Mr. Fuentes. They've been through all their personnel files. We have several employed here. Most are from Israel, though … Tel Aviv, to be exact. But I take it you all are interested in other nationalities. So, why should I be concerned about an employee's ethnic background?"

"There are subversives aloof in the area and we're afraid they have infiltrated various facets of our society, sir," Jack replied.

"So that's why you government guys have been swarming all over the plant. You think there could be some type of terrorist infiltration here at American?"

"Perhaps, Mr. Hamner. Please keep that confidential. Remember, you have a secret clearance yourself."

The plant manager settled back in his chair and folded his arms. "I'm not surprised at your theory considering what we manufacture. But everyone here has had a thorough background check done on them. Most have some type of security clearance. But, yes, we do have several *Arab* gentlemen working here … three of which are from India and Pakistan, I think. Chemical engineers, gentlemen; not subversives."

"You know that for sure? How many is *several?*" I asked.

"Four, to be exact. Look, they don't hire just anyone at Ameri-Can or any other strategic plant, especially those contracted with the government. I'm very confident about the men. Anyway, before hiring these people, as part of the background check, the FBI performed an exhaustive investigation on them and turned up nothing. Two of the engineers were working for the government in Washington before they came here and another began his career with a sister factory in Nepal. Same parent company and ownership."

Hamner did allow Jack and I to review each of the four personnel shields and although we were not permitted to make copies, I took notes. On the surface the men did appear clean. Two of the four graduated from M.I.T. Another, a Jordanian, had been educated in England at Oxford. There were no immediate red flags, unless we chose to look at the men through profiling eyes. I would have Byrd run their names, descriptions and histories through Interpol and both the FBI and CIA intelligence systems.

But who knows what the face of a terrorist looks like these days? I remember as an American advisor to ARVN and Peoples Self Defense Forces in Vietnam, some of the same smiling faces of the villagers whom I trained and trusted during the day, turned up as dead Viet Cong infiltrators at night, killed when they attempted to propagandize or terrorize the people of other villages.

Hamner offered us a tour of American which we happily accepted. Jack and I donned hardhats and goggles and followed the superintendent along the factory streets past buildings where machinists, scientists, equipment operators and millwrights labored. Over twenty-five hundred employees went in and out of the plant every day. Obviously, Hamner and company had been wary of the employees with Middle Eastern background as he had come up with their names immediately. I would call that ethnic profiling at its best. Did he also know the other twenty-four hundred and change by name as well? He explained that he made it a point to know who the plant's key scientists were. Of course, there were over *four hundred* chemical engineers working there. *Nice try, Hamner. I'll bet you don't know all **their** names. You're just like the rest of us WASPS.* We strolled past the two large storage units which I already knew contained the hydrogen chlorine and cyanide gases. Hamner, however, never divulged their content. And just as most all the factories up and down the Kanawha reeked with either the gagging rotten egg smell or that pungent, noxious odor that nearly takes one's breath away, I wondered how much of the pollution pouring out of the smokestacks at American had just the tiniest bit of escaping poison. The kind that would stop your breath entirely. And like it would do some good, I capped my hand over my mouth and nose as I walked along.

Hamner, amused by my discomfort, remarked "It's all

very safe, you know. In the past year we have had zero accidents and illnesses stemming from any incidents here." I wondered if that meant *before* last year there were people dropping like flies because something bad had sprung from one of those tanks.

The tour was over in about twenty minutes and not a second too soon for me. It wasn't necessarily revealing, but it *was* educational. I gained a hell of a respect for the plant's men and women and what they did. Of course, I wondered what their life expectancy was. I reminded myself to check out the obituary in the Gazette before I left town. If a great number of the dead were listed as having worked at American or another plant, expiring at forty-five or fifty from silicosis or lung cancer, I would not be back. I may not even cross the Alleghenies again. Either that or I would stop off at an Army Surplus and buy an M1A1 protective mask.

When Jack and I returned to his office, I asked him if there happened to be any decontamination showers in the building. He said *no* as I expected he would. I did fax from his machine the names of the four Arab engineers to Byrd, asking him to run them through his Intel sources. We then bid *adieu* and I lit out. Once departing the Kanawha Valley and reaching the safe side of the Alleghenies, I lowered my window to suck in the fresh, uncontaminated mountain air. My mouth wide open, I hung my head out of the window like a dog and to passing traffic I'm sure I resembled a gasping guppy that had just popped out of its bowl.

C H A P T E R   18

Just before pulling off the interstate at Lewisburg I called Joey, telling him not to be alarmed, but it appeared Assad Mohammed was the primary suspect in the break-in of Adrianna's office. It wasn't enough that he knew I was dogging him, but if it was he who stole the ledger, he could easily associate the McGowan name. I suggested that to Joey that he keep a close eye on his girls and otherwise stay vigilant. I hated the fact that because of me, he and his family may be in danger. Joey understood, but although I could hear the concern in his voice, he said not to worry; he would take the necessary precautions. And Cora knew how to use the home security service … Smith & Wesson.

I beat it back to Wolf Laurel, arriving about four-thirty and catching Adrianna at her desk in the office. She stood and thrust her arms around my neck as soon as I appeared in the doorway. It had been a tough night *and* morning for her, considering she had conjured up the sad memories of her son and her office was rifled, both because of me.

"I'm so glad to see you …" she whispered in my ear. It wasn't a romantic whisper. More so one of relief and release. "So, the ledger is all that's missing? Nothing else?'

"I think that's it. God, Skip, he could have broken into my residence. I'm glad I have a second deadbolt on my door."

I looked at the office door and obviously the perp wasn't as neat and professional a burglar as me. The door frame around the lock was chewed up as though an angry crowbar had been at work. The lock was old and had given away easily. One thing I noted and wondered if the sheriff department had as well: the lock on the front door of the B&B had not been jimmied or broken, which meant someone entered with a key and only boarders had keys. Only Lot- tie, Assad and I were the current boarders; so there you are. Of course, any previous guest could have made a duplicate key before leaving and come back to rifle the office. But I wouldn't think so.

"It's obvious that your burglar knew you were out yesterday evening and likely saw us leave. Like I said on the phone, I'm sure it didn't happen during the night. I definitely would have heard wood splitting." And I *knew* it didn't happen while I was listening in on them. "Did the deputies say they'd look for Assad?"

"They said they would question him here and I'm to call them when he returns. They did talk to Lottie. She said she had gotten a cab and went out to dinner the same time we were gone."

"Well, if no one was here for a couple of hours, it wouldn't have mattered how much noise he made breaking in. Obviously, he was watching when we all left. I'd sure like to have a go at Assad, but he'd jack rabbit and we'd never see him again. I wonder if he knew he'd be under suspicion and has already flown the coop. I still need him to be here just another day or two."

"For what?"

"Just … surveillance at this point. I'm still working up a profile on him."

"What's specifically going on with Assad that you can't tell me, Skip?"

If I told her everything, she would want him out in the street the moment he came back. A terrorist living at Wolf

Laurel? Not only would she boot him immediately, she'd toss me right along with him.

"It's an immigration matter, like I said before. Look, I've got it under control. I *will* know where he is from now on at all times. Maybe we ought to check his room."

"No, Skip. You know how he blew up the other day when he thought someone had been in there. Of course, nobody did."

"Of course."

"And anyway, with instructions never to go in his room, he could have the Better Business Bureau or Association of Country Inns down on me."

"We wouldn't want that. But what if there would be an emergency … like a fire or Martian attack?"

"I'd just rather leave his room alone, Skip. Okay?"

"Okay." I put up my hand in resignation.

She sighed and sat down at the dining table. "I just don't like what's going on here. This has always been a place where we didn't even used to lock the front door. The guests were trustworthy and brought in no problems. This is the first real time I haven't felt safe. I guess there'll be another night without sleep."

"You'll sleep tonight," I said. "That is if you'll invite me to stay with you."

The anxiety seemed to leave her face almost immediately. "I think that's a good idea. I'll make us some dinner this evening."

It was a light dinner and portions were small. Of course that's the way she ate, and that's why she wears a hundred-ten pound frame. Considering the last thing I had in my mouth was lunch's fried chicken and potatoes, it was like having a hors d'oeuvre supper. But the fact that I didn't jog at daybreak balanced things out. Still, I knew I'd be raiding the fridge by midnight.

We sat up for a while watching TV. There was this stupid sitcom, which I had always hated, but after my second glass of Chablis, I thought it was hysterically funny. I let out a few guffaws and Adrianna just stared at me like I was some kind of bleeping goofball in a fraternity house. By ten-thirty I had settled down, finding again both my dignity and suave demeanor.

But jocularity then turned to conversation of the more serious persuasion when she said, "You know, I've been wondering ever since we had our first conversation; why did you all those years ago decide on a life of danger and violence? First the Special Forces, then the FBI and now whatever mysterious thing you're doing. Couldn't you have gone into insurance or something?"

"Insurance? Me?" I laughed. "Now that *would* be dangerous to me. I'd be dead inside two years. Of boredom."

"But do any of these things you've done make you apprehensive about facing death?"

"Ohh-kay, kiddo. What gives? What's with the morbid talk?"

Her green eyes then took on a more melancholy hue. "Nothing really. I'm just a kind of a worrier, that's all."

Then it became clear to me that having lost a husband and a son in a matter of five years, the subject of death and the possibility of losing someone like me, her new squeeze, was really preying on her. And to me that was bitter-sweet. On one hand she made me feel as though I was in the same company of love as Mason and Johnny, yet it was obvious that itt their deaths would continue to haunt her.

I patted her hand and smiled. "Hey. Not to worry. I *do* look after myself; but yes, I think about death sometimes. I just don't dwell on it. I'm not like these people I hunt who are more than willing to take their celestial dirt nap at twenty-five or thirty just to gain the favor of Allah. They actually love *death* more than we love *life*. And they give up their lives with smiles on their faces, so sure of where they will be going when they cross over. I'm not giving up my life with a smile and sure as hell am not taking innocent people with me. They may *think* the place they're going is Heaven, but in my opinion their new abode will make Death Valley feel like Alaska."

"It sounds like you're talking about Islamic terrorists … the kind I've been reading about. Is that what you think Assad is? A terrorist? Was that what you meant about … you know … the throat-cutting of Americans?"

That caught me flat-footed. I guess in mentioning 'these people' in my little soliloquy, I slipped and inadvertently alluded to the fact that 'these people' (obviously describing Islamic terrorists) were 'the people I hunt.'

"Beats me," I replied. "But from Assad's erratic behavior, he does bear watching." That's as good as I could do and not spill all the beans. "Anyway, why did we get on the subject of death and the afterlife?"

"I think about it sometimes, that's all," she replied. "Do you?"

"Do I what?"

"Think about it much."

I could tell she really needed to talk about death and this life after death business, maybe as a catharsis or perhaps she was looking to see where I was in my spirituality. I think it may have been the latter, 'cause if I turned out to be a Darwinist or agnostic, being the spiritual person that she was, she would be wasting her time with me.

But I kept the heavy topic going. "Well, I *have* had occasions to think about it. Death is so … final …" As soon as I said that I realized how stupid and redundant it sounded. But I continued, "… like one moment I am breathing, talking, enjoying my state of consciousness and awareness, and then I get taken out of this life, suddenly and so rudely the next. I have to admit I've wondered at times if it will all just fade to black and I cease to exist. If that is so, then what was my purpose in being born and living a life in the first place? And I think, since I am a being of higher intelligence, why should I be cast into the same state of nothingness as a dog or a cockroach?"

She added, "How anyone could ever think we all just hatched from some piece of matter that formed on a rock is beyond me. Each of us was born with a purpose in life." Her eyes now had that faraway look. "Even when life is over all too soon."

But then again, all this caused me to think about something that happened in my mom's life a very long time ago. As I paused and allowed my eyes to wander around the room in obvious contemplation, she took my hand and said, "A penny for your thoughts."

"You want to hear something bizarre? I haven't thought about this in years. When I was four and Joey was born, something happened to Mom. She had a very difficult delivery. It seems that right after my little brother popped out, Mom started bleeding. Something about a placenta abruption. Her blood pressure suddenly dropped and then her heart stopped. The doctors worked on her more than two minutes, but her body didn't respond. The last paddle shock and cc of adrenaline administered, the doctors shot glances at one another, shook their heads and began pulling off the gloves. But suddenly there was one beep on the monitor, then two and then a series of irregular beats. After a while her heart was beating rhythmically. They said it was amazing and had never seen anything like it.

"I was too young to realize what was going on, except I remember Dad bringing Joey home from the hospital without Mom. Even though Dad told me she was coming home, she didn't for the longest time. I just kept thinking she wouldn't be back and that it wasn't a very good trade Dad had made … a pukey little bald-headed guy that cried all the time in exchange for Mom. But after about ten days, several units of blood and restored blood pressure, Mom came back to us."

Adrianna's eyes were attentive, even inquisitive. "Amazing. Two minutes without oxygen … I can't imagine. I assume she had no brain injury as a result?" She then paused for a moment. "But how does that relate to what we've been talking about … you know, life after death?"

"I was getting to that. I think I was about ten when I overheard Mom telling another woman over a cup of tea in the parlor about those two minutes she was, well, legally dead. She said about the time her heart stopped she felt herself rising from her body and floating up to the ceiling. She actually looked down on her pale body and although she knew she was probably dead, she was really okay with that. She said there was such a wonderful peace about the experience. She watched over her body for a while longer, then felt herself smile as she passed through a dark tunnel, drifting silently and softly toward a brilliant light that seemed to be drawing her to it. The light was warm and reassuring. She said she felt like an angel she had seen in a picture show, all in white, glowing, flowing.

"And then another woman who had been dead for five years appeared before her, holding out her hand. 'Mom!' my mother called. Her mom then put up her hand like a cop at an intersection. She was smiling and shaking her head. 'Go back, sweetheart,' she said. 'It's not your time. You have a new baby to care for. Bruce needs you, too.'"

I suddenly felt moisture on my cheeks, not even realizing my tear ducts had been leaking. Adrianna took my hand again and squeezed it.

I continued. "And then my mom said she saw herself rejoining her body. She heard the joy and celebration erupting in the operating room and opened her eyes to a host of smiling doctors and nurses."

"Wow," Adrianna exclaimed. "What a deep and wonderful story. But did you ever think that was all a dream?"

"While she was clinically dead? I wouldn't think so. As

far as I know, dead people don't dream."

She turned her head slightly and squinted her eyes at me. "Smart alec."

And then suddenly she became quiet. Her eyes moved from mine to the floor and back again. She was reflecting, I thought. About something. All I knew was … it was something sad. And then my suspicions proved correct.

"I had a similarly strange experience the night Johnny lay dying. He had lapsed into a coma and as I was sitting by his bed holding his hand, a kind of vision of him appeared on the opposite side. It was crazy … scary even. Here he was lying nearly lifeless and yet he stood beside himself, smiling and mouthing the word 'mom.' He nodded a kind of reassuring nod and suddenly the monitor stopped beating … along with his heart. Then the vision was gone. And I knew right then and there that he had gone to Heaven. All that remained was me. And that horrible flat line sound."

She swallowed hard to fight back the tears. "I didn't even summon the nurse. Somehow I knew it would be useless. I just sat there holding his hand.

"I dream about him so often. He is standing there just like that vision I saw of him, saying 'mom … mom.' I always feel so helpless. I can't save him in my *dreams*, either."

I nodded and kept my eyes fixed to hers. "Yeah. I know about such dreams."

We said nothing further to one another. I guess we had poured out enough melancholy between us to last a year. At least I had.

After the heavy conversation, she settled in close beside me. We sat for a while and it started to storm. It was quiet in the house, which magnified the sound of the blowing rain against the clap- board siding and the thunder that clapped sharply and rolled throughout the valley. I had just shared with her my mother's religious moment, just as Adrianna had shared hers with me. And now sitting with this very beautiful woman, feeling her soft breath on my face, I was having one myself. It had been good to reminisce and philosophize about things. And in conjuring all this up again … well, I was feeling especially good about God, family and the lovely Adrianna Wolf, all whom I loved. In a while we walked sleepily to her bedroom. I don't know whether my lights went out before hers, but the next thing I remember, a brilliant shaft of the September sun through the window drilled my eyes open. It was ten past eight. Immediately, before taking on any other thoughts of the morning, my mind compelled me to recall the nightmare I had only minutes before I awakened. When I dream, it's like experiencing a Hollywood production in vivid Technicolor, complete with complex plot, spectacular cinematography and surround sound. Some parts of the dream I find have already escaped back into crevices of my unconscious, but I'm generally able to retain the more significant, sometimes horrific pieces that will haunt me the rest of the day.

I was ten years old again and riding shotgun with my dad in an ambulance down Capitol Street in Charleston. People were bustling about, in and out of the *Diamond* and *Stone and Thomas*, jaywalking at intersections and brushing by one another without making eye contact having determined agendas in their brains. Suddenly, a woman grabs at her throat and falls face down on the sidewalk. The child holding her hand goes down with her, then convulses. A man in a fedora stumbles into our car and falls over the hood. His face is painfully drawn and milky saliva spews from his mouth onto the windshield. He tries to form the word 'help,' but nothing comes out. He falls off the hood and onto the street by the car. When I look back, bodies are lying everywhere, their faces silent and ashen white. Suddenly a hand forms over my nose and mouth. My dad is trying to keep what is in the air from consuming me, but I then see that he begins to seize as well. Blood pours from his nose and ears and then the car careens onto the sidewalk and into a building.

This is the kind of nightmare that should have awakened me at its climax and I was surprised my brain allowed me to actually finish it out. Except I didn't stick around to see myself croak. Since Assad and company were clearly planning to achieve this catastrophic scenario, that was obviously the reason for my dream. After I finally awoke I lay in gooseflesh with my arms locked behind my head and under the pillow for several reflective moments, then sighed, and swung my legs off the mattress. At least it was a different nightmare for a change, but one of proportionately greater tragedy. And as I had been responsible for some of the deaths of the people I usually dreamed about, I was determined not be responsible for failing to stop the deaths of a hundred thousand or more people as depicted in this new dream.

Adrianna had been up for a couple of hours and was already downstairs preparing the breakfast. She hadn't been putting much of it out the last few days, considering Lottie ate like a bird, I wasn't around half the time to eat it and Assad never partook of *iftar* (breakfast). I hit the potty, dragged myself down the stairs past the dining room where Adrianna and Lottie sat talking and drinking coffee. They both smiled, for different reasons, and I gave them a wave on the way to my room.

I had fully expected Assad would have returned the favor and break into *my* room last night, especially if they knew I was keeping the lovely Adrianna Wolf company. But everything was intact. Since he now knew who I was, I was sure he would go through my stuff trying to find out more about me. Except there would have been nothing to find. My weapons, cameras, notes and *life* were in the Suburban and all someone had to do was sneeze while passing by it and the bells and whistles would wake the town of Lewisburg four miles away.

I looked out and his car was still not there. It wasn't there all night, either. I suspected that he somehow knew the cops wanted to interview him about the break-in and intentionally stayed away.

I changed into my cute gym shorts and parka and began pounding the pavement past the rows of white fencing, fields of stacked hay and bold, stately farmhouses set back off the road. The sun was warm on my face even though the cool morning breeze made the hairs on my legs stand up.

As I do a hell of a lot of thinking when I jog, I wondered if one day soon I could really hang everything up and come back home to spend my waning years with someone like Adrianna. God wasn't playing fair, tempting me with mornings like this.

From behind me I heard the whine of tires on asphalt and at first, didn't pay much attention to it. The vehicle then slowed. I assumed that it was because the driver was coming up on a jogger, although I was on the proper side of the road; but then I saw who it was. It was a black Nissan Maxima with blacked-out windows. A sudden surge of danger hit me as the car slowed to a near stop when it came even with me. I didn't know whether to expect the Nissan to suddenly swerve and bounce me into the meadow or if the left side windows would drop down after which a hail of bullets would rip my carcass apart like you'd see in old Eliot Ness TV shows. The car stayed with my steady eight mile an hour pace for a few seconds and then it finally moved on. It was obvious that Assad was making a statement. He knew from my routine I'd be jogging and could get to me any time, especially when I was the most vulnerable ... without my Glock. But his day was coming and that day was tomorrow.

When I got back to the B&B it was just after nine. A thought came over me and before I returned to my room for a shower, I stopped to visit with Adrianna. I felt we needed some time together away from the inn. Tomorrow would be a difficult day and the mission could go down in several ways. It may be the last time we would have a day to just kick around. Juanita was back and had apparently realized a day's pay would help her cough up a degree of courage. She could manage things at Wolf Laurel till we got back.

I pulled Adrianna off to the side. "Say, how about you and I taking off for a few hours and going to Joey's cabin by the river. We can pick up some KFC or something and make an afternoon of it."

"Oh, I can't do that. I've got to look after this place today. And under the circumstances, I don't want to leave Juanita by herself. She'll be spooked all day."

"Juanita overheard our conversation. "No, please. Go ahead. I can take care of things here. You should take a day for yourself. If anything happens, I have the deputy's card and he will be here quickly."

"I don't know," Adrianna said. It was one of those 'I want to, but I shouldn't' replies.

"Sure you do," I coaxed. "Look, I'm going to get a shower and will be ready in half an hour." I pushed her forward to the door.

"You'll be okay, Juanita?"

"Yes. Yes. Please go and have a good day."

"You call me on my cell and let me know how things are going. Promise?"

"I promise."

Adrianna discarded her apron. "Maybe it'll be fun. See you in the lobby in a few minutes."

I noticed that Assad's car was still not in the parking lot when we left. It wasn't there when I went for my jog either, which told me he definitely anticipated my morning run and waited from a concealed position for me to get on the road.

"Do you mind if I stop first at Valley Community?" I asked. "I need to talk with Dean Le Mer."

"No problem. I'd like to chat with him myself."

I wanted to chat with LeMer alone, but she would get suspicious if I told her to wait in the SUV.

I skimmed the parking lot for the Nissan and Honda in

their usual parking spots, but they weren't there. I couldn't remember if they had class on Friday or not. It was ten-ten and they should have been in class.

When I approached Joanne, LeMer's blond assistant, did *I* ever get the cold shoulder? I was the guy who obviously got her in trouble last week. But I was glad to see she didn't lose her job over it.

"Is he expecting you?" she snipped.

"No. But if you tell him Ms. Wolf is here to see him, I'm sure he'll come right out."

Joanne told him and he did. Of course, he wasn't expecting me and the sight of me nearly stopped him in his tracks.

"Ah, there's *His Immenseness* now," I said. Adrianna gigged me in the ribs with her elbow.

"Paul," she greeted, approaching him with an outstretched hand.

He took it and smiled at her. Then he looked at me and scowled. "What's *he* doing here? Or should I say, what are you doing with him?"

Adrianna gave me a puzzled look. "I don't understand. Is there something not right between you two?"

"I think you should ask Mr. McGowan who seems to have no respect for institutional regulations."

"Skip?" She turned to me. I shrugged like I was completely in the dark.

"Well, anyway, Paul, I need to ask you something."

"Go ahead, my dear. I will certainly listen to *you*." Good ol' Paul. Always the gentleman.

"Lisa Ramsay, an old friend who is a supporting patron of the county library, is doing a book drive and is looking for any textbooks and books of both fiction and non-fiction to increase their inventory. Do you all have books from time-to-time you discard? I'm helping to make contacts with schools and private citizens who'd like to donate."

"For you, Adrianna, I will check with our librarian to see

what we have. I will also make a few calls to peers at other two and four year colleges in the state. We're all good about helping one another out."

Whoop-T-do.

"Thank you, Paul. I'll call you in a week or so to see what you've been able to gather."

"Wonderful, my dear." He picked up her hand and kissed it. The Frenchy do that a lot. Makes you sick. "Now, Mr. McGowan, do you have a question for me?" He pushed back his nerdy glasses and peered through them with two beady little eyes.

"May I speak with you in your office?"

"I suppose so." He then turned to Joanne and tried to make a joke. "If I'm not back in five minutes, I've probably been taken hostage by this man and you can call 911." And I think she'd do it, too.

Adrianna stepped into the hall as I followed LeMer back to his office. His clothing smelled sour from underarm perspiration and cheap cologne. I actually started feeling sorry for the big lug. He couldn't help it that he didn't have anything going for him. But then, ashamed of my cynical attitude, I thought it was high time I was nice to him.

"What is it, Mr. McGowan? Do you have more deceptions for me today?"

"Look, Dean, I apologize for the shenanigans the other day. The government really did need the information I appropriated, and believe me, it is very grateful. If the investigation we're doing is successful, there may even be a commendation for you for making it all come together."

"Really?"

"And your United States Government needs something else from you."

"What is that?"

"This time its information on someone else. Someone you may know. We're looking for an older Middle Eastern man about forty-five or fifty, slightly balding, but with a beard. He may even be a teacher here."

"We do have a visiting professor here from Saudi Arabia who teaches a couple of classes."

"And his name would be?"

"Navab Abouzar, I believe how you pronounce it."

"Thank you, Paul. Do you have his address?"

"It's a Crows, Virginia address, as I remember. Let me see." He accessed the faculty information on his computer. "You can get his Bio online, you know, by accessing the school's web site. Yes, here it is … Star Route 58, Crows. That's all it has. Funny, there's no box number."

"What classes does he teach?"

"He teaches Physics and a class called *Multicultural Issues in America.*"

Bingo.

"How long has he been on staff?"

"I'd say about a year."

"Paul, we may need to subpoena his personnel file. You have one don't you?"

"Of course. Has this man done anything wrong?'

"Not that I know of. An immigration investigation, that's all."

"I see." He allowed his black glasses frames to slide down his greasy nose again as he appeared to be digesting the information. I knew he wouldn't give the man's personnel file up without the subpoena and me doing a B&E on a state institution? Well, I just wasn't about to go there.

"Is Mr. Abouzar here today?"

"Let me see. No, he doesn't teach on Fridays."

"And logically, there is no *Multicultural* class today."

"Correct."

"The professor will be here Monday, I assume." "Yes, he will."

"Well, my five minutes are up. Paul, I do thank you for the information. Again, I will give your name to my highers in Washington, so one day, expect to see a plaque or something with your name on it signed by our State Department Director."

I thought Paul was going to pee his pants. "That would be wonderful. I have just the place for it on that wall."

I was certainly leaving the Dean's office on better terms than I thought. Paul would relish the idea of getting some kind of recognition from the government and I would remain in his good graces, until one day months or years from now when the space on his wall was still empty, he would figure out once again that he had been duped.

Adrianna was still hanging out in the hallway talking to a few girls whose parents she knew. "Did you get what you needed from Paul?"

"Sure did."

"What was going on between you two when we came in?"

"You know how these liberal college commies are. They hate everybody that works in government."

She had that confused look on her face which she wore a lot when she was around me.

Joey's camp was not much to look at. A rustic, flimsy cabin house, poopy brown in color and needing a new roof and porch, it listed a little to one side. On several occasions after torrential rains, the Greenbrier River had gotten up to the front porch, threatening to turn the cabin into Noah's Ark. But it had somehow stayed the course over the years and hopefully would stay the day while we were in it.

The river's bank was littered with fallen trees, resembling decaying wooden giants. Barren branches, extending into the water and catching a variety of natural and manmade deposits, served as a feeding haven for redeye bass and trout.

Adrianna was quite the angler. She, her husband and little Johnny had fished the Greenbrier often, but after she lost both of her men, she sold the boat. However, she still had Mason's gear. I was down-right impressed that she had no problem cutting up bloodworms or handling crickets and could cast out and drop her line within three feet of her intended target. I was still trying to get past the bloodworms.

But there was nothing like spending the day in God's woods to take one's mind off of things. Everything that was bad seemed so far away and what would happen tomorrow … well, that was tomorrow. I watched her with admiring eyes as she worked the rod and reel. Her face had that determined look, but there was also a smile, frozen, intense-like. She was like the water … fluid, energetic, constant, full of history and life. Never ceasing. A light breeze kicked up, catching her hair and making her appear even more goddess-like than she was. I smiled and she returned it.

"It's beautiful out here," she said.

My smile deepened.

"It sure is." She knew what I meant.

Another cast and the sinker plopped about forty feet out just beyond a large branch. She was like a surgeon with the rod.

"If you could conjure up one, what would be your perfect day?"

"Well," I replied. "This would be one of them."

She nodded. "But besides today, just to get away on a vacation to relax, letting go, making every care in the world disappear. Where would that be?"

"Oh, I don't know. Maybe I'd be sitting in an Adirondack on a beach white as sugar, looking over pristine blue-green waters, smelling the salt air, drawing the sea breeze into my lungs, listening to the screeching gulls as they circle an electric blue sky, and sucking down cold, cold Heinekens." I paused for effect. "Of course, you'd be in the picture. You'd be with me on that perfect day."

"Mmm, nice. Take me there tomorrow."

I turned my head away, reflecting solemnly in advance on 'tomorrow' and what it would bring. "Wish I could, my dear."

Reality checked back in and I watched as Adrianna continued to work her magic in the waters. I was impressed how the fish jumped on her bait within only minutes after she dropped in on them. And after she had reeled in several good-sized trout, she cleaned them, fried them up in some butter, olive oil and paprika, and added some sliced potatoes and onions in the old iron skillet we found beneath the stove. They went down nicely with a couple of cold Coors.

It wasn't long and I was ready to kick back on the rickety porch in one of the well-worn rattans and watch the gentle Greenbrier flow by. Its crystal waters sparkled and gleamed like thousands of little diamonds in the five-thirty sun. In short order, I found that Adrianna had other things on her mind. She knelt at my legs, ran her fingers over my knees and locked her dreamy eyes on mine. Obviously, she was over the fear and sadness she had experienced the past couple of days. I hoped Joey had changed the sheets in his last two or three trips to the cabin.

Just after seven, the sun was casting the last of its golden rays through the oaks and sycamores. A whippoorwill chanted a repetitive version of *September Song* and after our own song, *Afternoon Delight*, and a nap, we agreed it was time to pack up. It had been a good day and we both certainly needed it.

C H A P T E R   19

I arose early Saturday morning, skipped the run, but stepped out to see if Assad's car was there. It actually was and that was a surprise. Considering what would go down during the day, I did want him there … and everyone else out. And I hoped that the cops were not still interested in questioning him about the office break-in. That would throw a monkey wrench in our plan.

I went through an equipment check, then drove out to partake of a light breakfast at the Shoney's breakfast bar. After the winding nine mile drive on Route 60 to White Sulphur Springs, Old White, as the Greenbrier had been known for a couple of centuries, came into view. I compared the map coordinates with the topography and discovered it wasn't the Greenbrier where Zulu was staying; it was The Roche Motel just down the hill. Sorry, boys. From the looks of it, it should have been called The Roach Motel. Rather than talking Roundup, we should have been talking Raid.

I pulled into the parking lot about eight. As it was too early to expect the team, I cast off my Glock and shoulder holster and walked back up the hill approximately five-hundred yards to the famous resort with its spectacular gardens. It was right damn peaceful there. I took a seat in the gazebo, leaned back on the bench and allowed the sun now peeking around a huge magnolia to warm my face. A couple of morning joggers, a middle-aged man and a much younger woman, greeted me with nods as they negotiated the meandering path. The man was puffing a little, attempting to stay even with his gazelle girlfriend. She obviously wasn't his wife as he was desperately trying to impress her.

After I took a twenty-minute stroll down a pathway flanked by hydrangeas and brilliant chrysanthemums, I ended up back at La Cucaracha just in time to see the team's Ford Expedition pull in. All four doors opened and out came what looked to be two guys resembling X-men in black SWAT attire and two others that looked like Wesley Snipes and the Rock. I had no doubt they could engage a battalion of Red Chinese, kill half of them and send the remainder back across the Great Wall screaming for their mommies. Two of the goons I recognized right away. The Wesley Snipes character was Chuck Robinson, code name *Viper,* who was also ex-Bureau and on a team with me when we took down Manny the Mouse Carbone that day in South Manhattan. Another one of the X-men was Ty Marshall who worked out of the CTT office in Washington. I hadn't gotten to know him very well. In the year-and-a half I had been with CTT we had been on separate assignments, off to the four winds ninety percent of the time. Anyway, Ty was a very private, sometimes distant son-of-a-gun and hard to get to know. The other two guys were Jeff Palmer, a Brit who as I remembered would rather golf than eat, and Burt Candellera or Candy for short. I knew Palmer would like to go ahead and get this thing underway, take down the scum buckets, and be on the first tee at the Greenbrier by noon. And then there was Candy, lean and chiseled, sporting a buzz haircut, and still moving with ramrod exactness, just like the Marine captain he was in Desert Storm.

We all shook hands like a bunch of guys at a college frat reunion. They went by the motel lobby for their keys and then we piled into Chuck's room for the strategy session. His elegant quarters quickly became a mini situation room.

The boys then went right to work. I was hoping we'd have a couple of donuts, tell a few war stories and get slap-happy, but these guys wanted to get down and dirty immediately.

Chuck, being the Zulu commander on this gig, kicked off the meeting. I began my briefing, starting from when DAG, who I believed to be Khalid Al-Barem, as deduced from the student roster, was discovered. I filled them in on my surveillance as well as what I found in their rooms. They already had a transcribed, translated copy of Assad's notes, my photos and my report to Byrd. They did not have the more recent photos I had snapped of the missile diagram and trigger device. Neither did they know of my tête-à-tête with Assad when he accused me of being a fabricator.

Chuck, however, had something for me to see. Last evening, Byrd had faxed to him a transcript of the tape Nosy and I recorded from outside Assad's window of the chatter going on inside. Our interpreter-translator, Abu Narziz, had quickly converted the Arabic dialogue to English script.

One huge revelation surfaced that reinforced my earlier suspicion about the burglary of Adrianna's office. The perp was indeed our favorite Arab boarder. And he knew my name. I took the script from Chuck and began reading:

Subject One: *My friends, I have new information for you. While the hostess had gone off with the man called White, I went into her office. There were notes about each of us recorded by her and the Spanish woman. It was obviously the man who engaged them. From the guestbook I learned the man's name is McGowan, not White. He must be a policeman as we suspected.*

Subject Two: *Then he must know who we are and what we plan.*

Subject One: *No. I only think he suspects things about us. I do not believe he knows anything for sure or we would be*

arrested by now. It had to be him who came into my room, but there was nothing here for him to find. The short time we remain, I will be sure to watch him.
Subject Three: *Does our leader know we are being watched?*

Subject One: *I told him. I asked if I should kill McGowan. I see him out running on the roadways and I could erase him at any time. But he said that would bring others to investigate and the death of this man is not our mission.*

Subject Two: *McGowan makes me fearful the way he always appears where we are.* He has to know something (the man's voice becomes anxious, almost argumentative). *I say we kill him now!*

Subject One: *Please calm yourself, my friend. We will not move against McGowan. We must not allow him to distract us. We must remain focused.*

Subject Three: *Assad is correct, Fayez. Be patient. In only days we will become immortal. I have long dreamed of this. We are lions from the desert crouched for the fight.*

Subject One: *I too had a dream three nights ago. I saw the explosions clearly and our spirits rose above the fire and smoke. I saw many people fall. Even the trees seemed to wilt and the mountains quaked and tumbled, signaling the greatness of Allah.*

My friends, what we will do is not about emotions; we are driven by our strong Islam belief and we have faith in the Judgment Day. I am sickened with the Americans. They are spoiled, lazy and fat. But most of all they are ignorant. They place their faith in the material things of this world and in false gods. There is only one true God.

(The sound of chanting by all three subjects)

Pray with me, my friends, for it is written that we should worship God and his messenger Mohammed. We must struggle for jihad for the cause of Allah with our very persons and he will forgive our sins. Admit us into the Heavenly Gardens, Allah, where there are flowing streams and allow us to enter the pleasant Garden of Eternity. Oh, Allah, we will not be afraid to give up our lives. Our faith in you defies our fear. Our cause goes beyond jihad. We welcome quital and will trade our lives for the hereafter.

(There is now silence and the subjects appear to be engaged in silent prayer for a period of time).

We stood stoically, looking at one another with staid eyes, fully convinced that the terrorists' mission was not only substantive, but tentative as well. We knew our raid was going down none too soon. "Well, we know *what* and *where*," I began, "but *how* and *when* are the questions. They make it very clear they will kill themselves in executing their mission. Do they plan to break through the gate at American and explode a device into one of the storage tanks or drop devices on the plant by aircraft and in doing so, blow themselves up?"

Chuck responded. "Probably the latter. I guess that's why they're taking the flying lessons? But why the missile, Bruce … that is if they have one?"

"Well first, in regards to the planes, I'm pretty damned sure these guys have not been taking lessons for recreational purposes. Sometime earlier they likely flew with someone over American to do a recon and map out the plant. They didn't fly on their own because the flight instructor at the academy said their training had been limited to the county. I agree with you, Chuck. They've been learning to fly with the intention of chartering planes and dropping explosives onto the plant. They'd have to fly low in order to shove the bombs out onto their target with some degree of accuracy. The targets would be Buildings A and B here (I pointed them out on the sketch map) and the adjacent storage tanks of cyanide and chlorine gases." And then I thought for a moment.

"Maybe they even plan to fly the planes *into* the tanks, I don't know. These people don't mind killing themselves and I suspect their mission includes suicide. Even if they did shove the bombs out of the aircraft, the explosions below would knock the planes out of the sky.

"Now as to the missile, that could be a check-valve if the bombing attack fails. Someone could be positioned on the hillside above American to either fire on the target or knock down any fighters that may try intercepting the planes."

Candy added. "They could also be targeting a commercial airliner either on approach or leaving Yeager to make some kind of statement."

"Possibly," I replied. "But a missile bringing down a 747 or a military aircraft in a more metropolitan area like New York or L.A. would be more impactive and kill a hell of a lot more people. Now *that* would be a statement."

"We seem to have most of the puzzle pieces laid out, but there's no way to connect them for a complete picture without knowing for sure what means they'll use in their attack," said Palmer, checking his watch.

"Hopefully, we'll find that out at capture. So how do we do this, Chuck?" I asked.

"We'll leave here in two vehicles. Bruce, you and Candy will go back to where you're staying and take Assad Mohammed into custody. Ty, Jeff and I will raid the Jamestown lair and nail the others. We'll blindfold them and then take them to the Wolf Laurel location for preliminary Q&A ... Bruce, you need to clear everyone out of there. Then we bring in our chopper to the local airport to transport them down to Ft. Bragg and on to Guantanamo

Bay by C-130 from Pope for a more intensive interrogation."

"Of course they'll not go down easily," I remarked.

"I'm sure they've been extremely vigilant, expecting me or the FBI to make a move on them. It's obvious now that Assad Mohammed has been watching me as much as I have him, especially the last couple of days."

"Well if they won't go down friendly-like," replied Chuck, "then we'll take them *out*, no questions asked. A disposal unit will then be dispatched. Of course, the value of this operation is to gain knowledge of not only their plans, when and how, but about other elements that are part of a larger scenario. Merely wasting these guys won't get it done for Byrd."

I nodded, but added, "You know that hardcore Islamic militants will definitely not give of up *anything*, even under extreme duress. These creeps are suicidal and whether it's part their plan or not, they will blow themselves up along with their targets. The more infidels killed, the greater the favor from Allah. And whether they die by their own hands or by ours, they will be dying for their God."

Chuck smiled. "Then we'll hasten their meeting with Allah, if it comes to that. But I wonder if they believe that being killed by an infidel will send them to the furnace in disgrace."

"And I wonder if instead of harps, like they give you in Heaven, you get accordions in Hell?" I replied. The Zulu boys actually laughed at that.

The smile then quickly vanished from Chuck's face. "Okay, any questions?"

I raised my hand. "When's kickoff?"

"1100 hours, which is in …" he looked at his watch.

"… nine minutes. Any other questions?"

The guys shook their heads, but I asked one more.

"Where're we doing lunch afterwards?"

Chuck seemed a bit irked with my trifling. "Just watch

out for collaterals," he added, which meant 'don't let any friendlies get in the way.' I would be sure that didn't happen at Wolf Laurel.

At one minute till the hour Chuck's cell went off. It was Byrd. "Viper, are you set?"

"We are."

"Begin deactivation in six-zero seconds."

"Wilco."

"I want a SITREP (situation report) as soon as this goes down."

"No questions. Just do what I asked, okay?" "Roger."

I gave Chuck the directions to the Jamestown venue and after performing a radio check with our high-tech Dick Tracy walkie-talkie ear and wrist pieces, we lit out promptly at 1100.

I then called Adrianna enroute to Wolf Laurel. "Why were you gone at the crack of dawn again?" she asked. "I thought maybe we could have breakfast together."

The nerve of her. She was beginning to sound like somebody's wife.

I blew off the question. "Are Juanita and Lottie there this morning?"

"Yes, why?"

"Did any other guests come in yesterday or today?"

"No, but tomorrow there's a couple coming in from Missouri for four days. Why all the questions?"

"Listen carefully. This is important. I want you to quietly get Juanita and Lottie out of the inn. You all go somewhere and stay until after three."

"You're scaring me, Skip. What's going on?"

"No questions. Just do as I ask, okay?"

"Does this have to do with Assad?"

"Yes. Is he still there?"

"I think so. His car is here."

"Okay. Go now!"

"You're not going to shoot up my house, are you?"

"Go!" I repeated. Within ten minutes, Candy and I were pulling into the gravel lot at Wolf Laurel. I checked to see if Adrianna's van was still there. It wasn't. But there *was* a figure leaving the last step of the veranda. Assad had come out of the inn with a large duffle bag slung over his shoulder and was walking toward his car. What happened then seemed in retrospect as a choreographed slow motion were right out of an old Six Million Dollar Man scene. Just as Candy stepped out of my Suburban, Assad was within five feet of getting into the Nissan. Apparently, he saw Candy's black uniform-looking non-uniform, complete with gun belt, and panicked. As Candy stepped toward Assad's car, gun drawn, Assad jumped in, cranked the engine and gunned his vehicle toward Candy, throwing gravel forty feet behind him. Unfortunately for Candellera, he didn't jump out of the way fast enough and the front bumper of the car bowled X-man ex-Marine over.

I had already exited the driver's side, but as Assad sped by me, nearly clipping my door, I too had to jump out of the way. I drew my Glock and fired three shots through the back glass of the Nissan, one of which apparently struck Assad somewhere other than the head. I could see the outline of his body jolt when the round hit him. The car cut erratically to the right and plowed into a grove of scrub pines. After taking out several saplings, Assad accelerated back onto Seven Bridges and headed north.

I keyed my mike. "Agent down! Agent down!"

Chuck immediately responded. "What's happening, Scorpion?"

"Candy Man is hit. The suspect saw us coming and ran him down with his car. I need to tend to him. Send the paramedics and get the locals on your freak. Tell them to intercept a black Nissan Maxima with a shattered back glass heading north on Seven Bridges within two miles of Highway 60."

"I copy. Is Candy all right?"

"I'm seeing to him now,"

I said, running toward him. Candy was not moving and I observed that one leg was badly mangled.

Blood was now pouring from his nose and mouth, and he was choking on it.

I carefully turned his head to the side and let the blood drain into the gravel.

"Candy, can you hear me?" He nodded.

"Don't move. I'll be right back."

While running to the Suburban to retrieve my first aid kit, I summoned Chuck again. "He's alive, but he has facial lacerations and what appears to be a comminuted fracture of his right leg."

"Goddammit! What else will go wrong?"

"Why? What's going on there?"

"Nada, man. The Jamestown targets had already abandoned ship. Their cabin is cleaned out and the manager says he doesn't know when they left. They were here last night and that's the last he saw of them."

"All right, then look for the Middle Eastern maid I told you about. She's a player and unless she skipped with the boys, she's around somewhere."

I went back to Candellera and applied a compress to his head. The blood had stopped, but although he was tougher than a two dollar steak, I could see the pain in his eyes. His face, however, refused to show it.

The paramedics were on the scene within minutes and once Candy was addressed and loaded, I accompanied him to County General.

What began as a slick, well-planned operation ended with three terrorists missing in action, a G-man in the hospital and serious wounds to the rest of our egos. As I was sure Assad took a bullet, I alerted the staff in the ER to look out for an Arab man with a big hole in him.

The extent of Candellera's injuries was as I expected, a badly displaced fracture of the lower leg, a concussion and of course the deep facial wounds. The good news was that he would survive and to a rough-and-tumble guy like him, they were just flesh wounds. As soon as I was allowed, I paid him a visit in ICU.

I stood at the foot of his bed and picked up the clipboard that contained his chart. Like I could actually read the physician's hen-scratching.

I must have startled Candy from a good dream brought on by the morphine, as his body jolted. He opened his eyes and in a guttural voice said, "What the hell are you doing?"

"Oh, nothing," I replied. "Just checking to see if you were going to die."

He closed his eyes again for a moment. "You're a shit head, McGowan."

"That's what they tell me, marine. Hey, you looked good out there today. Do you plan to take your act to the circus?" Candy didn't appear to be amused. "I heard your shots after I went down. Did you nail the bastard?"

"I'm pretty sure I did, but he got away."
He brought his fist down hard on the mattress. *"Son of a bitch!"* I could tell he was not happy about the deal. "I thought you Special Ops guys were supposed to be crack shots."

"I thought you marines were supposed to be quick and agile."

Candellera shook his head, dismissively. "How about the other targets?"

"Gone before Chuck and crew got there."

"Well if that isn't a fine crock of monkey shit."

"Exactly."

Candy raised himself up on the pillow and apparently knocked off one of his EKG hookups. The machine let out a high-pitched signal and the monitor flat lined. A gaggle of nurses suddenly flew into the room and converged on the bed, thinking his ticker had stopped. When they discovered the problem, they re-hooked him, then turned and gave me dirty looks.

"*I* didn't touch a thing. I swear."

The head nurse who closely resembled Ernest Borgnine in drag jammed her finger into my chest and pushed me out the door. "And do not come back in here, sir." Not on *her* shift, I wouldn't.

I went down to the cantina for a bottle of water and sat mulling over the fiasco. Blaming myself as much as anyone, I knew I could have handled the thing a hell of a sight better than I did. I wondered where the little prick went. For that matter, where did they all go? Hoping they didn't reorganize at Wolf Laurel, I called Adrianna on her cell, telling her to remain away. I would still meet her there at three. She again wanted to know why and I said I would explain later.

The next call I made was to Jack. His office said he had just left. His normal schedule was to work only half days on Saturdays. I did reach him on his cell and from our conversation, I got the impression he was laughing his ass off. I'm sure he was thinking that if it had been an all Bureau operation, it would have gone silky smooth. The terrorists would have all been where they were supposed to be, given up peacefully and sang their hearts out about their plans to blow up American.

As I was still talking to Jack, Harlan Williams from the State Police showed up. The look on his face did not reflect a pleasure in seeing mine. I signed off and stood up to greet the lieutenant.

"Okay, Mr. McGowan, what the hell do you Feds think you're doing coming into this area taking on such a mission, putting the civilian populace in danger, and keeping every state and local authority in the dark about it? Have you people not ever heard of professional courtesy, not to mention law enforcement decorum?"

Well, I guess not. That's a new one on me.

"Look, Lieutenant, this mission was classified. Besides the President, the State Department and Attorney General, no one except this task force knew the particulars." I didn't tell him I had clued Jack in on the deal. But Jack needed to know so that he could set about protecting American, the citizens of Charleston and Diane.

"Uh *huh*. I think that's a pile of horseshit. When were you planning telling us what's going on?"

"Well, you did get a call didn't you? We asked you to run down our escaping terrorist."

"I see. You botch your operation, let three suspects escape and then you call us to help you find them. Like we're the Lost and Found department."

Well it just seems all crazy when you say it like that, Harlan. "Okay. Maybe it *didn't* go so well; but now is not the time to mix words. So, is there any luck finding the Nissan?"

Williams looked at me derisively and sighed. He then took two quarters from his pocket and dropped them in the vending machine for a cup of coffee. "Nothing yet. We have the APB out. I understand you may have winged the guy."

"I'm pretty sure of it. I alerted the ER here. Can you do the same with clinics and doctor's offices as well? Also, we'll be looking for a Valley Community professor named Navab Abouzar. We believe he's tied in with these guys if not their leader."

"You'll have to spell that for me. Do you have his address?"

"Just somewhere in Crows. We have a route number, but no box number. Perhaps you can check with the Virginia State Police."

"Okay," replied Williams. "But you see how this works? You tell me things; I help you catch bad guys." *I got it, Harlan. Don't be so condescending.*

Chuck, Jeff and Ty and I sat on the veranda at Wolf Laurel licking our wounds and lamenting our failures. Our morale had been quelled, our confidence defeated. With the team listening in, I took the opportunity to break the news to Byrd. As gingerly as I could, sugar-coating my capsule of the events with words like 'unfortunate' and 'unexpected,' I dropped it all on him. The score was terrorists-3 and Zulu-0. Actually, we were minus one, considering Candy was in the hospital. I thought I actually heard the gears grinding in Byrd's head, but suspect it was only the sound of his teeth chewing on that old pipe of his.

"I had hoped this would have gone down cleanly and successfully, Bruce," he said. "I suppose you now realize these people will remain underground until their planned day of attack. We had our opportunity here; now you tell *me* what we could have done differently." Byrd was never a man to berate or to point a finger of blame when exercises failed to achieve results; but his well-minced words and intonation had a way of making one feel lower than snake poop. And we did, anyway.

"I have no excuses, sir." That was the response I learned years ago in the Army after I had screwed something up.

"Timing is everything. We probably should have raided the nests a couple of days ago. Obviously, they were onto me, and as I knew they *would* do, they jumped ship. Assad Mohammed had apparently loaded up and was on his way out to leave for good when we intercepted him. His room is cleaned out."

"Lovely."

"Another thing, boss, airplanes will be used somehow in the terrorist attack. I'm convinced of that, given the lessons. Suggest the FAA and FBI be alerted so that all airports and private operations are placed on notice to watch for these guys."

"Done." He paused for a moment.

"Find them, Bruce. Engage all counterparts and turn over all the stones. This thing got away from us in a hurry. My boss will not be happy about it. The team will go to the capital city to hook up with friend Jack by 1700 tomorrow if the element does not materialize in your area. Keep this tightly wound and tell the locals to not engage the media. We don't want an epidemic of panic. Call me with your results ASAP. Got it?"

"I copy." I would've said 'Have a nice day, boss,' but he was already gone. I closed my cell phone and looked at the other three who had taken on the appearance of statues while I was getting reamed by Birdman. "We need to get out and beat the bushes, guys. If we don't find them by tomorrow evening at 1700, you all are to dispatch to Charleston to collaborate with the Bureau and wait for further from Byrd."

"Where do you think they went, Bruce?" asked Chuck.

"I have a feeling they're in some kind of staging area with this professor guy. They could be back in the woods somewhere or on their way to Charleston. Every cop in the state is now looking for them and their cars. I think we need to start combing the Crows area to look for any evidence of a residing Mr. Abouzar. It's possible that with the cursory address he gave the school, he may not even live around there. But they're all somewhere they can hide their vehicles, such as a barn or residence with a garage. Chuck, we need a chopper in here to recon the entire county as necessary. Look for a white and a black car together and check out any vehicles under tarps. We may be wasting our time in Crows, but suggest we go house-to-house first and ask around. I'll check the White Sulphur post office to see if he has rented a box. I'll also get back with the college Dean and perhaps Valley's President to see if I can gather more information about him."

"I'll go on ahead with Jeff and Ty," replied Chuck.

"Suggest we meet up back at my room at 1900 and then we'll do this again tomorrow. Bruce, I guess you'll stay in touch with your Bureau and State counterparts for their updates."

Team Zulu dejectedly set out for White Sulphur Springs and a rendezvous point to meet the chopper which was dispatched out of Washington at 1345 hours. I stayed at the inn and called Paul LeMer to obtain contact information on the President, Dr. Angela Stalnaker. His information was short and sweet. Mostly short.

Upon securing the address, I drove immediately out to the President's house, finding it to be a large, grand Victorian set high on a hill off of Route 60 in Lewisburg. I introduced myself and told her up front that Professor Abouzar was a suspect in a police matter. She seemed surprised at hearing that, but said unfortunately she knew very little about him. She did say that he was a very bright and pleasant man, passionately committed to the education of his students, but otherwise very private, socially. He had a Doctorate in International Studies and the kind of credentials that would allow him to teach in most any major university. Immediately before coming to the community college he was on the faculty at Seton Hall. I wondered if he had had previous contact with the New Jersey boys and arranged not only for bringing them to the area but their admission to Valley as well. He would see to their continuing education in Terrorism 101.

Dr. Stalnaker gigged me for a little more information about why I was after the professor, but I side-stepped her questions with questions of my own. I could see the concern about Abouzar in her face. She asked if she should go on to the college, pull his personnel shield and see if there was any other information of significance. Of course, I already *had* his information. All she knew was that he lived in the Crows, Virginia area, but didn't know where. Shaking her head she added, "He seems like a very passionate and precipitate man ... working one-on-one on his own time with students outside the classroom, especially those teetering on a failing grade. He even helped us out in our booth at the Labor Day picnic."

"Do you ever monitor any of his classes to ... you know ... review the content of his teaching? A course like *Multicultural Issues* opens up a myriad of possibilities when it comes to filling young people's heads."

"Is that what this is about, Mr. McGowan? Is our government afraid he may be poisoning our students' minds with some kind of political or Islamic propaganda?"

I dodged the question and fired another. "Is he required to teach in harmony with a specific syllabus and curriculum?"

Obviously I was being rude in not responding to her question as she shot me a glare. "Yes, we provide the text and generic syllabus for all instruction and require adherence. And no, I personally have not sat in on any of his classes." I could tell she was getting a little testy with me, so I needed go in a different direction to keep our dialogue flowing.

"Doctor, these are just questions that will enable me to learn a bit more about the man. Do you know anything about his life outside of the college?"

"As I said, Professor Abouzar is a very private man, Mr. McGowan. He teaches his classes and goes over-and-above with some of his kids *after* those classes; but then he leaves the campus. I guess he goes home like every other brain that's been picked and drained by our students. I don't know much else about him." She paused a moment.

"May I ask again why you are looking for Dr. Abouzar?" She was not about to give up on her inquisition.

"It's a matter of about a hundred unpaid parking tickets, ma'am." I lied.

"What? But you said you work for the State Department. Why is the Federal government interested in parking tickets?"

A good question indeed. Now if I could just think of a good answer.

"Interstate flight to avoid prosecution, which is an even more serious offense for a foreign national. It will affect his visa status, you know."

She reflected on that. "Oh." Her eyes took on a bit of a frown while digesting the information. "I suppose that could be a big deal; but now you have me fearful there may be more to him than meets the eye." *Very perceptive, Madam President.*

I really thought at that time I needed to bring our little conversation to a close before I started running out of fabrications *and* credibility.

"I understand your concerns, ma'am, but I don't believe he'll be back to finish out his classes."

"How do you know that?"

"He knows we're after him and keeps on the move."

"To avoid prosecution for parking tickets?"

"Sounds ridiculous, doesn't it?" And it did. I was surprised someone with her education was swallowing this pony poop.

If for some reason he does materialize, I will ask that you call me right away. And be careful, Dr. Stalnaker." I reached into my pocket. "Here's my card."

She nodded. A renewed look of worry clouded her face. "Thanks, Mr. McGowan; I will." Then she mumbled, "I must say, this is all very confusing, not to mention disconcerting …"

It was *more* than disconcerting to me. *Exasperating* would be a more appropriate word. But there was no question; we had to pull out all stops to find this guy.

I met Adrianna back at Wolf Laurel on the veranda at three as planned and she had Lottie Throckmorton with her. There were looks of fear and apprehension on both of their faces. I was still dressed in my SWAT looking garb and both women stared at the Glock in my shoulder harness. I'm sure to them it was like they were looking at a different person than they had gotten to know … like the old Skip had died and come back as the Terminator.

"Okay, what's going on, Skip? You have scared us half to death." She quickly checked over her place as if to look for bullet holes.

"Please, ladies. Have a seat. I do need to explain to you

what came down this morning."

Adrianna and Lottie did as asked and took up two adjacent rockers. I pulled up a straight-back chair and sat backwards in it, facing them.

"First of all, I need to come clean with you all about some things. I do work for the government, but I am a counter-terrorist agent, working in the Department of State. Adrianna, I did tell you that I investigate possible subversives, but my job actually goes beyond that. I not only hunt down terrorists, but I *bring* them down as well... anyway I can. I've been watching the Arab man who occupied the room down the hall from you, Lottie. We suspected from the onset he was a terrorist and I have been attempting for the past week or so to gain information on him as regards a possible plot against the American people. I just hope this hasn't upset you ladies."

Then I specifically looked at Adrianna. "There are some things you really don't need to know. But I *will* tell you this. A team of my folks came here today to take Assad Mohammed into custody along with the other two, and maybe a fourth, who are, or were, in a motel in White Sulphur. Unfortunately, they were a step ahead of us and cleared out before we could get to them. But another agent and I did drive upon Assad as he was leaving here. He struck my partner with his vehicle and put him in the hospital. The good thing for you all is that Assad is gone and apparently so is the danger."

Adrianna sat without word and stared at me. I couldn't tell at first whether she was angry or just disappointed with me, but she was certainly stunned. She knew pretty much about what I had been doing, but I'm sure she thought I was just gathering enough information on Assad to get him deported ... if in fact I found out that he *was* a bad guy. I knew she didn't like the idea of a possible raid on her place, but mostly, I think it was both my deceptiveness and the scope and depth of my position with the Department of

State that surprised her. She pulled on her lower lip and looked away from me.

"I'm sorry, Adrianna. I didn't intend to put you all in danger, but this thing just developed as I went along. I really didn't know how it would turn out … whether I would find nothing or whether we'd find that he was in fact a terrorist."

"Fine, Skip," she replied with a soft but biting tone. "I guess you were just doing your job." She then paused. "Was I just part of that job, too? A means to your end? You convince me to keep him here so that you would gain enough time to set something like this up? I don't like being a pawn on your State Department chess board."

The questions stunned me a little. "If you're thinking that way, Adrianna, then you've got it wrong. I didn't stay here to get to know you as a means or convenience just so I could get the goods on Assad and this sleeper cell. It was purely incidental that I chose to stay here. And then you … we … happened. You have to know I really do care about you, Adrianna … I think even more than you may realize." I picked up her hand and held it tightly. "I hope we're still good here."

Lottie spoke up. "Of course you are, dear. Adrianna, I know the way this man looks at you. And you, him. He's doin' his job, that's all. And you, my dear, are in no way part of his job."

I looked back at Adrianna and smiled, devilishly. "Yeah. What *she* said."

She looked away for about ten seconds, then back to me. "I'm not okay with this by a long shot, Mr. McGowan. You have a lot of making up to do, you know. But I guess we can talk about this later. That is, unless you intend to remain … how shall I put this … less than forthcoming?"

I gave her a reassuring smile and then turned back to Lottie. "Sorry you were exposed to all this, too, Lottie."

"Don't you worry none about me, Skip. I'm just glad you found out about this man. I hope you eventually hunt him down and bring him to justice. And the rest of them, too."

I think Adrianna *was* okay with it all … or at least *would* be once she thought about it. I told her I had to get out and continue my search for the suspects, but would be back later. One thing I had to do was get her out of my head for a while. She was in there enough as it was. I didn't need to add her displeasure with me to the list.

From the look of Assad's room, it was obvious he was prepared to leave anyway. I think he and the others had actually planned to vacate about the same time. The room had been cleaned and was spotless. His soiled linens and towels had been neatly stacked on the floor by the bed. When he left out, whether or not he had affirmed that I was moving in on him, obviously seeing Candellera spooked him and that's when he reacted. The question was … did each of the suspects leave to consolidate in a staging area? The attack on American could go down over the weekend or perhaps early the next week. I knew the Air National Guard would be scanning the skies over Charleston. The FBI would have American covered and the State Police would be patrolling the roadways in the Kanawha Valley looking for the terrorists' vehicles.

LT Williams called me back about six and told me that Abouzar's vehicle was registered in Virginia and was a 1999 Dodge Caravan, blue in color, tag number TAY-513. His address was again listed generically as the star route with no house or box number. I called Chuck and gave him Abouzar's vehicle information. They were still canvassing on Highway 202 also known as Star Route 58, going house to house and now looking for the van as well. No one knew of anyone with the professor's description living along the route or on any of the intersecting county roads. Chuck said he and the boys would give it up at dark and begin again on Sunday morning. I begged off on meeting them later at the Roche.

I swung back by the hospital to check on Candellera. He

looked pitiful, bruised and battered, and his right leg suspended by a pulley and cable. But he was in a hell of a sight better spirits, all things considering. Ernest Borgnine was off shift, so I knew I would live yet another day. I filled Candy in on our canvassing activity. And then I told him that Byrd was going to have him airlifted to Walter Reed on Tuesday, providing he was able to be moved. He wasn't too happy with that. I guess he thought his leg and head would heal overnight and he'd be joining us for a power breakfast in the morning before we took down the terrorists.

After driving around aimlessly, looking for the three vehicles, I returned to my quarters at a little after seven. I think Adrianna had been worried about me, because when she heard my Suburban pull into the parking lot, she came out to meet me. I threw off my shoulder harness and carried it and the weapon in my left hand. I then took hold of Adrianna's dainty pinkies with my right. She eyed the Glock again and since she hadn't seen me with it before today, I'm sure it was all very strange and uncomfortable for her. Her image of me had obviously changed. I was no longer the frivolous, good-natured romantic interest wearing the slightly older face of a long-departed hometown boy. Of course, I wasn't around her when I was with the Bureau. She would have understood then that because of what I did, I had a badge and a gun and she would have taken me for what I was. But I had projected myself quite differently over the past ten days and she obviously didn't know what to make of me.

I accompanied Adrianna to her room and as she went to the fridge to get me a beer, I slipped in behind her and placed my arms around her waist.

"Why do you do this, Skip? Why this kind of work?"

I sighed and pulled her tightly against me. "Because … I'm only one of a few who *can* do this."
She didn't respond.

"Look, sweetheart, whatever or whoever you think I am

now, I'm still the same person I was. And I'm still crazy about you."

She gently leaned her head back into my chest and I kissed her hair. It smelled freshly shampooed. She then turned around in my arms and kissed me tenderly, playfully, and gently bit my lower lip. Her body was warm and I began to heat up; but the cold air from the still open refrigerator provided a counterbalance.

"And you, sir, are all I think about these days. Why does the guy I'm falling for have to be some kind of government spy?"

"You're falling for me?"

"Maybe," she replied, smiling and teasing with her eyes.

"Well, maybe I can say the same for me."

She giggled. "Do we sound like a couple of high schoolers?"

"Hey, I'm still a high schooler inside, you know."

"I know. Especially inside here." She thumped me on my noggin. "And here." Then she pressed her lower body into my stiffening loins. We were compelled to take the conversation down the hall. In our close encounter of the blissful kind, I found her immensely satisfying considering this had been a most *un*satisfying day.

"Well, so much for the dessert," she said, smiling.

"How about some supper?"

I rolled over and checked out the clock on her night stand. "Eight-thirty? Where did the evening go?"

She pulled me back into her and said, "If you don't remember, I will just have to show you the instant replay."

"Oh, yeah. Now it's coming back to me."

A little after nine and craving chocolate for some strange reason, I asked Adrianna if she had a Hershey bar or a Snickers.

"Not up here, but I keep candy bars behind the counter downstairs for kids sometimes." She jumped out of bed.

"Let's go get one."

We threw on our clothes and went to the lobby where we found Lottie in the dining room munching on some apple slices.

"Hi, kids," she said. "Hope you don't mind, Adrianna, I got an apple from the Frigidaire. I got a little hungry a while ago."

"Not at all," she said. "We're a little hungry, too. Both of us missed supper."

"But," I added.

"We had dessert." Adrianna gave me her *don't go there* look.

"Why don't I grill us up some pancakes? I like breakfast sometimes for supper."

"Oh, that sounds good, "Lottie replied. "Of course, that will lay heavy on my stomach for hours."

"No problem. We'll just all sit up together and talk."

That's easy for you to say, Adrianna, I thought. I'm the one here that needs beauty sleep.

I actually did sit up talking with Adrianna and Lottie until well after eleven-thirty. We talked some about the events of the day, but I soon changed the subject. I don't pick at old scabs. I was more interested in Lottie's history. She grew up in Prince Edward County, Virginia, and the year after the schools were integrated in 1954, the county suspended all public education. She was a junior in high school when that happened and was not able to finish out her education. All the White kids had opportunities to continue their education at Prince Edward Academy at a very reasonable cost. Blacks were not invited to apply nor were approved when they did. For five years, until the Federal government stepped in, an entire generation of Black children went uneducated. One of those who escaped was Lottie Nelson. Her church was able to make arrangements to have her placed with a Quaker family in Iowa who saw to her education.

Years later, Lottie had become an advocate for civil rights and was photographed with President Johnson just after the passing of the Civil Rights Act of 1964. Shortly thereafter she moved to New York, became a councilwoman and was ultimately elected to a New York congressional seat. As she had told me a few days ago, she relocated to Ninety Six, South Carolina to be close to her grandbabies.

"So, Skip, do you intend to be with the government the rest of your working life?"

"Not sure, Lottie. I'm getting tired of being a government man. I've actually been one in some capacity since I was twenty-two years old. I'm thinking I'd like to only work a couple more years and then chuck it all. What I'd like to do is maybe something completely away from government work, like hiring on as a swimsuit model photographer for *Sports Illustrated.*"

She laughed. "Can't quite picture you doing anything like that. But I'm sure whatever you finally retire doing, you'll be doing something worthwhile. You've got a lot of work years left, so you'll figure it out. I remember a quote by George Eliot: "It's never too late to be who you might have been.""

"Unless you're a *has been* like yours truly. But you, Lottie … you have lived a significant life. You have fought nobly and selflessly for people of color."

"I have worked so hard in doing my part to assure that *every* American enjoys every freedom that the Constitution guarantees its people and that we can live without fear and persecution. And I tell you one thing, Skip. I may not be as strong and influential as I once was, but I'll be damned if I will condone any son-of-a-bitch to come into this country and threaten the freedom and safety of U.S. citizens. I would fight like I have never fought before to keep that from happening. You find these bastards, Skip, and you stop them from hurting even one American."

My heart was exploding with admiration for this woman, the beacon of freedom that she was. And then I couldn't help but smile, hearing all that profanity spouting from the sweet little woman. For the first … no, second time today, I felt good … not to mention *full* from the hot pancakes. But it was the warm conversation I had with Lottie that allowed this day of 'unfortunate events' to end on a high note.

I stayed the night again with Adrianna. Now neither of us cared how it looked; and certainly Lottie didn't. If Birdman knew he was paying for a room I wasn't occupying, my next lodging on the road would be the rear compartment of my Suburban. But we laid together talking, holding and caressing one another for an hour or so. And then after she was quiet awhile, from out of the blue came a subject that had ended abruptly a few nights before.

"He was a wonderful child, Skip. Sweet, always happy, loved puzzles and could solve the Rubik's Cube in five minutes. He wasn't athletic, which somewhat disappointed his dad, but he made up for it as a brilliant student."

She went on about Johnny, this time without the tears, and as I held her, I almost felt the catharsis in her body. She said that Mason was never right after their son died and although the official cause of her husband's death was a heart dissection stemming from rheumatic fever when he was a child, she almost knew he had died from a broken heart instead. She had been alone since Mason died. Within weeks of his funeral, her parents moved to St. Petersburg.

"I had a beautiful life once … like a lovely and colorful stained-glass window. But then it got shattered. I've tried piecing together all the broken fragments and making some kind of mosaic out of them to fill up the big, gaping hole in my life. I really don't have very much to do that with. I have my friends and I have Wolf Laurel. Somehow that's not enough." She paused. "But I do still have all the beautiful pieces in here somewhere …" She tapped her heart.

All I could do was nod. Any words of consolation I had would only sound trite and empty anyway.

After a moment she continued. "Our minister said that it was God who chose the time for Johnny to go. Why would

God do that? Why a child … a sweet and precious little boy who had an entire life to live? Why couldn't God wait until he was old and I was long gone?"

For a long while, as we lay face to face, scarcely a foot apart, I kept my eyes steadfastly on hers, still silent. And then when my words finally came, my voice seemed to crack a little. "I used to listen from another room in the funeral home the breaking of people's hearts as they spilled out their grief onto one another … and onto Dad. They wondered 'why', too. Some of the people who had died were younger … husbands, wives, adult children … although I can't recall if there was ever a child. I would have remembered that."

Her eyes remained stoic and glistening in the wanly light, but she didn't reply.

I went on. "Maybe … God just loved Johnny so much, He wanted him to go and be with Him. I guess that's His choice, although we can't understand it."

"I'd say that was rather selfish of Him, if that's the case. He gave our son to us and then, just like that (she snapped her fingers), He decides He doesn't want us to have him any longer. How cruel is *that*?"

She turned her face away. "Every morning I get up asking Him that. Every Sunday I go to His *house* and ask Him that."

I searched her eyes again, allowing her vexations a moment to digest. I had no more words. It was as though someone or something had crept inside my throat and stolen my voice. With the backs of my fingers I brushed her silken hair, following it down to the point where it lay on the pillow.

Adrianna smiled, weakly. "Okay, McGowan, enough of this sad stuff. I go there too much as it is." She then rose up and reached for her bathrobe, wrapping it quickly around her as though the baring of her soul had made her feel self-conscious.

She went to the bathroom for a few moments and then returned and sat back down on the edge of the bed.

"Thanks, Skip," she said in a low voice. "For what," I whispered back.

"I guess for just being here … for coming back into my life once again. You spending these few days with me … it's been like a fresh breath of air. Things that I have shared with you I haven't even talked about with most of my girlfriends. You make it so easy for me to let out things that have lain on my heart these years."

I smiled at her. In a strange way, I didn't mind exposing my seldom seen soft side and serving as a special 'girlfriend.' I thought at that moment I had never felt so close to anyone as I was her. I pulled her back down beside me and scooted my body up against hers.

We were both silent, but still holding one another, watching the soft moonlight through the window create a beautiful and sensual ambiance especially for us. Then after a while as she slept deeply I watched her chest swell and retract. Her lips were slightly parted and her warm breath smelled sweet, feeling much like a light tropical breeze on my cheek. If this wasn't love, I would never in my life know what it felt like.

CHAPTER 20

Lieutenant Williams called mid-morning on Sunday just after Adrianna left for church. He volunteered there had been no sightings of any of the three vehicles and we both agreed they were probably parked under a canopy of trees back in the woods or in someone's garage. The APB hit all wires and there were pullovers everywhere from Lewisburg to Charleston. What few Arabs there were in the adjacent counties had unfortunately been profiled and stopped by law enforcement; some of the people were found to be Hispanic and even Native Americans. The word as to why Middle Easterners were being sought was not explained to law enforcement, much to their frustration; but I was pleased that Harlan Williams was true to *his* word that information about the probable terrorist plot was not being revealed.

Chuck and boys did spend the day covering the White Sulphur-Crows area by chopper as planned and I combed Lewisburg and Western Greenbrier in my Suburban. Still nothing. Not a trace. It was as though the terrorists had dissipated into the atmosphere.

I had suggested earlier to Adrianna that she get a locksmith in to change both the lock on the front door and on the Magnolia room. Assad had neglected to turn in his key before he left out, the bozo. He didn't even have the courtesy to tell his hostess how much he enjoyed his stay.

At four the Zulu team met one last time on the veranda at Wolf Laurel. Needless to say, we were not sitting around with joined hands singing *Kumbaya*. We were all a bit solemn and for the umpteenth time we rehashed what we had, but mostly what we *didn't* have. It was like a replay of the old TV show *Where Are They Now?* But more like *Where Were* **We** *Now?* After a while we were reduced to talking over old times at the FBI. We sounded like a bunch of old VFW bench warmers telling war stories. Chuck then announced that he had had enough and after they would swing by to check on Candy at the hospital and draw little hearts on his cast, they would take off for Charleston.

It was time to give Byrd an update. He wasn't going to like our Day Two results. Again.

"You want to call him or shall I?" Chuck said.

"You have to get your marching orders before lighting out for Charleston, you know, so why don't *you?*" I replied.

"Yeah, but you have a way with words; and anyway, he likes you better than me."

Why did I suddenly think it was 1960 again and my little brother and I were trying to agree who would own up to our dad for something we both did? In this case, what we didn't do … locate the targets.

"All right. *I'll* call Dad," I said.

all but disappeared. "What?"

"Never mind." I speed-dialed Byrd's number and he answered, gruffly.

"No luck, Boss. They've all but disappeared."

Charleston as well?" I asked Mr. Byrd.

"That's not good news, Bruce."

I assumed we could now talk in the clear without metaphors as the mission got declassified in a hurry. "You know, I've been thinking. I believe it was their plan all along to leave their quarters yesterday morning and reconsolidate in hiding to gear up for their strike.

They may already be in the Charleston area, but somehow I

don't think so. Unfortunately, Eastern West Virginia is so rural, mountainous and covered with triple canopy foliage, an army couldn't find these guys. And did I mention Greenbrier County has more caves than any other area of the state? Of course, a cave may make them feel right at home."

"Seems there's really nothing more you can do there. I can't allow you to remain there forever, you know. Who knows what their timetable is. It could be six months before they strike. These guys may also have set up a rural training base to rehearse their plan as they generally do over and over. If they can't be found, then our best recourse is a good defense. The Southern West Virginia Bureau has the Kanawha Valley covered and more specifically, American. They will pick up the hunt. Plan to pack it in on Tuesday, Bruce. I want you here for a full brief at 0900 on Wednesday. Is Chuck there with you?"

"Yes, he is."

I switched the phone over to Chuck and after a few seconds he replied. "Yes, sir. Yes, sir. We're leaving right now." He then pushed the phone to me.

"Should I not go to Charleston, as well?" I asked Mr. Byrd.

"No. Chuck and teamand the building have it covered. If the targets aren't found by the weekend, I'm sending them back to Washington. You, I need to see."

"Okay, I'll get back to Georgetown Tuesday and take a red eye out first thing Wednesday for your location."

He was silent for a while. I could hear the disappointment in his breathing. "Bruce, you do good work. Sorry you folks were not able to get a slam dunk on this."

"No sorrier than me, Boss."

I lost the call and knew he had hung up. I didn't even mind it this time. I hate failure and whether this was all or partially my fault or not, I did not like telling that man I couldn't get closure on the mission.

We all stood and after a group hug, the Zulu guys piled into their SUV.

"Stay in touch," said Chuck. He formed a gun with his thumb and index finger and made a clicking sound with his mouth. I returned fire with mine. As soon as their trailing dust rose and dissipated, I went back inside to my room to brood some more.

Monday I visited Candellera again and then drove around without design, hitting the community college parking lot, the airport and other places I had seen them frequent, but knowing they wouldn't be stupid enough to risk being anywhere near them. It would be a stroke of needed luck if I even saw one of their vehicles. I wondered how badly Assad was hit and who had treated him. The wound was probably not that serious or he wouldn't have been able to zip down Seven Bridges and out of sight.

Knowing that I would be leaving for Washington the next morning, I asked Adrianna out to dinner at Tavern 1785, where we had gone on our first date. It was there I told her that I'd be leaving in the A.M. She was quiet the rest of the evening … not a pissed quiet, but a sad quiet. It was like it was the last day for us on campus and we would be going our separate ways after graduation. We went back to her place and after a nightcap, turned in. Neither of us wanted me to sleep in the room I had abandoned a few nights before. We made love again, but it was bitter-sweet love. And neither of us seemed to be into it.

She was so quiet and still, I thought she was asleep. Her face was faintly illuminated by the waning moon, but it was still light enough for me to see that her cheeks were moist. I kissed them and told her I *would* be back, somehow, someway. She turned over away from me without response and in only a couple of minutes she *was* asleep, breathing deeply and peacefully. It took me a while to get to sleep, and then at some point in the early morning hours I had the dream again. This time I saw that the child who stumbled out of the hooch was not a child at all. It was difficult at first to see the face through the smoke and fire. But gradually, as the face took form, I heard a helpless cry escape from its lips. It was the horrified face of Lionel Byrd.

Tuesday morning dawned cool and clear. I took a pre-breakfast jog around seven-thirty, showered, packed, and then joined Adrianna and Lottie for a bun and some coffee at the dining room table. As I would be leaving in a few minutes and Lottie would check out tomorrow, a mood of melancholy hung over the room like a pall. Adrianna was still quiet, but she did mention that a couple would be coming in later in the afternoon and she would place them in the Gardenia Room. As of Wednesday, her two favorite guests *ever* would be gone. Lottie patted her hand and said she *would* be back one day, and may even bring her grandkids with her. I would miss Lottie too. I felt we had struck up a special friendship as there were few people I had met in my life who were so genuine and humble. Of course, that was largely due to the circle I was used to running in,

But I knew that five minutes after I was on the road to Washington, I would be missing the beautiful mistress of Wolf Laurel. By the time I hit Georgetown, I would be ready to turn right around and come back. And the next day, when I was sitting in Mr. Byrd's office, likely receiving new marching orders, I would be thinking seriously about chucking it all and coming back to Greenbrier County to love and family and maybe some cushy security job. On the way out of town, though, I would stop by to see Joey and promise to make my visits more frequent. And that I would, primarily because of one Adrianna Wolf.

While we were sitting and talking, Lionel Byrd called me on the cell to fill me in on the most recent Interpol report he received. It seems one of the American employees' names that I supplied him *was* on the hit list. Mouri Abasi, a chemical engineer and M.I.T. grad, happened to also be a graduate of the Dar al Islam 'school of terrorism' at the Beit

Jalla Palestinian training camp in 1996. Obviously, this is one background check that had slipped through the crack. He was arrested the day before and in process of being interrogated in Guantanamo Bay. There were no documents or other information found on him or at his residence in Charleston's grand South Hills to connect him with any of *my* subjects. Whether he had repented of his sins since working at the plant remained to be determined. I suspected, however, his co-workers would not see him again. Maybe nobody would.

Seven days a week, the television on the wall in the dining room brought a dose of Fox News to the guests partaking of breakfast from as early as 6:30 until Adrianna shut it down sometime just after nine-thirty. We were actually paying little attention to the tube as its volume was down and the commentators, two men and a lone woman, appeared engaged in some friendly bantering. Adrianna was asking me about Caroline and perhaps when she finished her training, I could bring her back with me some time so that she could meet her. I glanced back at the screen and was alarmed to see smoke pouring from one of the World Trade Center towers.

"Hey, look at that," I said. "Looks like there's a fire at the World Trade Center."

Adrianna went over to the TV to turn it up and about the time she touched the volume button, I was stunned to hear from the commentators that a commercial aircraft had struck the tower. "Holy shit!" I exclaimed. "Did you hear that?"

Both women gasped. "Is that for real or a movie?" said Adrianna. I couldn't respond, because I knew it was real. Then the female network anchor confirmed again our worst fears. "Oh, my God, people," she exclaimed. "An airliner has just slammed into one of the World Trade Center towers. We can only speculate that it was either due to pilot error or mechanical problems. There has to have been significant loss of life in both the airplane and the building."

"Those poor people," lamented Lottie. "I always feared a plane would someday go down in a highly populated area like New York."

But as we watched the tragic scenario unfold, suddenly we saw the second plane strike the other tower. The massive fireball carried completely through the depth of the building and out the other side. My brain initially refused to accept the fact that this was actually happening. And our faces frozen solid in horror reflected that denial.

It took me about three more seconds for it all to register. "God Almighty, it's a terrorist attack!" And three more seconds later, the last puzzle piece finally fell into place. I jumped to my feet and ran to my room for my Glock. Hustling back through, I tore past the women and yelled, "You all stay here and lock up. I'll be back when I can."

"Why? Where are you going?!" Adrianna exclaimed.

I didn't answer, but ran out the front door to the Suburban. Snatching the .308 from the rear compartment, I laid it on the passenger seat and spun out onto Seven Bridges. My first thought after digesting the New York tragedy was that Assad and the others had degassed the area on Saturday for a major airport, boarded two commercial jets and took control of the cockpits to crash the aircraft into the towers. Yet, would they be able to assume control of 747s when they only trained on Cessnas? That's why on second thought I believed that the hijackers in New York were not them. But as it was all too clear that American was going to be a target today, likely along with several other targets, I couldn't think of any place to go but to the Greenbrier County Airport.

I figured that Assad and his confederates were smaller fish, piranhas if you will, partnered with the school of sharks that attacked New York. But instead of *bombing* American or crashing through the gate to explode their bomb, it was even more apparent that they had planned all along to fly the

Cessnas *into* the deadly storage tanks, sending them and 100,000 Charlestonians into eternity. I didn't know why my gut sent me to the airport, but somehow I knew something would be happening there. If it wasn't already too late.

As my breakneck speed carried me there in less than ten minutes, Assad's words recorded in his journal nagged at me from the periphery of my brain. I had wondered about the significance of one sentence … a sentence I earlier thought was pure metaphor … *"By the wings of man we will achieve martyrdom …" Now* the meaning was all too clear. Why in the hell I had not interpreted these words was already haunting me. If the terrorists did reach Charleston and carry out this catastrophic mission, these mere haunts would eventually dump me into a state of permanent abasement.

I slid into the parking lot and across the field directly to the flight academy. Holstering my Glock to my belt, I also grabbed the .308 from the seat and ran to the door. Given my warning to the FBI and FAA through Byrd, I thought there would have been guards or officers posted outside of the academy, but they were probably somewhere in the airport terminal.

With the .308 cradled in my right hand, I threw open the door to the academy with my left. The first thing I saw was a trail of blood which appeared to have been created by the dragging of a body through the back room doorway. Kicking open that door, I found a man dressed in security guard uniform. He was older, perhaps 65 or 70 with a crew cut and looked like he could have been a former Marine. The man's throat had been cut and blood still drained from the nasty gash at his jugular. His eyes were frozen open, reflecting the horror of the last moment of his life.

I then ran to the academy office where I found the bodies of both Ross and Helena. The brutal scene sickened me. Their throats had also been sliced. Helena's wound was so severe, she had been nearly decapitated. Her head remained attached to her neck by only a strand of muscle. I would have guessed that she put up one hell of a fight. I hated the grisly scene before me, but I hated these god- damned terrorists even more. I deduced from the still gushing blood that the butchery could not have occurred more than a couple of minutes before. My stomach turned over and my brain was suddenly rendered impotent. The immense adrenaline hit my heart with a burning flush, causing it to pound vehemently and my blood to thunder in my ears.

Tearing through the back door that led to the tarmac, I caught sight of two men, one making his way toward one of the Cessnas approximately two hundred yards away and the second already entering the cockpit of another plane. And that second man was Assad. He looked in my direction before closing the plane's door and signaled the man still walking. The second man appeared to be the one I referred to as Big Nose. Suddenly, as he spun around in my direction, he pulled a pistol from his belt. I quickly raised the .308 and fired a single round that caught the man squarely in the throat. Flesh and blood exploded violently between his jaw line and chest and he dropped like a brick.

Meanwhile, as Assad had already engaged the starter, the prop began buzzing. I fired one round through the Cessna's right door and then as it began to move away from me, I fired again, striking the tail section. I ran by Big Nose, not pausing to see if he was dead. I knew where my bullet had struck and didn't need to further inspect my handiwork.

Spying something resembling an open golf cart that pulled a train of baggage units, I jumped in, hit the starter and sped away at neck-jerking ten miles an hour across the tarmac to the runway where the Cessna would set up for takeoff. Rather than following it to the end of the strip, I drove in the opposite direction to intercept it as it took off. I was able to make the middle of the runway just as the Cessna started its takeoff run. When the wheels lifted off, the bird blasted across the eastern margin of the field, its noisy prop shredding the still air. I fired the first of two rounds into the engine compartment. After the second one hit, the plane immediately spat black smoke and sputtered. It was going nowhere. Assad was able to glide the plane off the end of the runway where it crashed into some scrub brush and flipped over.

My little cart was doing all it could as I pressed on in the direction of the wounded plane. When I was within a hundred yards, one of three bullets struck the cart, each arriving a split second before I heard three distant reports from what appeared to be a handgun. I swerved right and then left to make myself a more difficult target, and then caught sight of Assad running into the woods toward the highway. I stopped and fired several shots that I heard ricocheting into the oaks, unsure whether I nailed any part of him at all.

I figured he would be making a break for the road, so I shanked the cart off to the right across a small field, suddenly finding myself on the state highway and in the path of an oncoming semi. Pucker time. I swerved and the semi swerved after laying on his locomotive horn. It was a good miss. The truck went on, still blaring its horn and I rode further down the road looking to see if Assad had come out. About the same time a white Buick approached fifty or more yards to my front, Assad busted out of the tree line into the path of the car. The Buick skid to a stop and Assad brandished his handgun in the face of the driver, a woman. He quickly opened the driver's door and tossed the elderly woman onto the asphalt. Quickly he slid behind the wheel and gunned the car in my direction.

As I knew he was coming for me, I brought up the .308 and fired two rounds through the windshield. His head well below the steering wheel, my rounds zipped harmlessly by. As he was still bearing down on me, I grasped the rifle tightly and jumped out of the cart into a ditch, a split second before the car slammed into my ride. The impact catapulted the cart over me within inches of my head. By the time I crawled back out, the Buick was gone.

And then Farmer Brown came along in his '84 Dodge pickup. After he slowed cautiously to a stop to see what the commotion was, I ran to the driver's side of the truck and shoved my ID in his face. "Sir, I need your truck. There's a fugitive on the loose about a quarter mile ahead."

"But … I can't give you my truck. I don't keer if you are the law …"

I didn't have time to argue. "Get the hell out of the truck, sir!" I opened the door, grabbed him by his bib overalls and politely sat his ass on the road.

"You can't …" That's the last thing I heard from the man as I tromped the accelerator, laying rubber for fifteen feet.

After setting sail to the west on 219, I saw the rear end of the Buick exiting onto I-64 toward Charleston. I pulled my cell from its holster and dialed 911. A female operator answered promptly.

"Ma'am, please either 'patch me through to the West Virginia State Police or give me the number for the Lewisburg detachment."

"Sir, would you please identify yourself?"

"I'm a government agent, Bruce McGowan, and need that contact right away."

"And for the record, is there anything you need to report?"

"Yes, I will report your *ass* if you don't get them on the line and NOW!"

A wounded pause. "One moment, sir."

After a few moments I heard the voice of Herman Munster on the line. "Sergeant Storm here; how can I help you?"

"Damn, finally," I said. "Sergeant Storm, this is Bruce McGowan, the State Department agent from a couple of weeks ago. Do you recall?"

"Yes, sir, I do. What can I do for you?"

"I am in pursuit of a confirmed Arab terrorist who

commandeered a white Buick Century traveling at a high rate of speed on I-64. I am in a blue Dodge pickup about a half mile back approximately five miles west of the Lewisburg exit heading west. You need to intercept the Buick and suggest you set up a roadblock near the Alta or Sam Black Church exits. The terrorist is enroute to Charleston, possibly carrying a bomb."

"Does this have anything to do with what happened at the World Trade Center and Pentagon today?"

"The Pentagon?"

"Yes. You didn't hear? Terrorists flew a plane into the building killing a great number of people."

"*Son-of-a bitch!*" I screamed. But after a moment I calmed down a bit and replied. "I didn't know that, Sergeant. I've been busy chasing *this* asshole. Yeah, I think there *is* a connection. You will find three DOAs out at the Ross Flight Academy at the Greenbrier Airport and a terrorist on the tarmac with my bullet in his throat. You need to get people out there to secure the scene. And get the road- block set ASAP, please."

"Roger, sir. I'll dispatch units to intercept."

"Tell them he's armed, but to watch out for an explosive device also. He may set it off if he gets cornered." "Got it. Out."

The old pickup was doing all it could, but the Buick was not a Vette either, so I managed to stay with him at just over a hundred miles an hour.

My cell phone rang and it was Chuck. He was calling from Jack's office in Charleston. "Bruce, I assume you've been following the WTC event?"

"I just saw it earlier and took off to the Greenbrier Airport, Chuck. I got there in time to stop two Cessnas from taking off. One bad guy is KIA and I'm chasing the other one. The locals are setting up a roadblock west of Lewisburg on I-64."

"Bruce. Byrd would have been in the World Trade Center

north tower."

"Oh, Jesus. I didn't even think about that." I let it sink in a moment. "Since his office was on the fifteenth floor, maybe he got out."

"Knowing him, he probably stayed to help people out and went down with the building."

"What do you mean 'went down?'"

"Both buildings collapsed, Bruce. Thousands were burned or crushed. Al-Qaeda has already taken the credit for the thing."

I felt at that moment I couldn't get my breath and found myself sobbing.

"Bruce?"

Suddenly at the Sam Black Church exit Assad must have spotted the stopped cars in advance of the roadblock. He swerved onto the shoulder, passed the cars, struck a State Police cruiser on the exit lane and continued west on Route 60 toward Big Sewell. I snapped my cell shut and gave pursuit past the damaged patrol car and onto the two-lane behind him.

I flipped open my cell and got Storm on the line again.

"Sergeant, I'm still in pursuit. He blasted past your roadblock and is going west on Route 60 toward Rupert. He's determined by hook or crook to get to Charleston. Need to set a new roadblock before he gets into the more congested areas in these small towns. Set up somewhere before Rupert."

"I copy."

About a mile further west, as we approached a hill, the Buick slowed behind a coal truck going about thirty-five which allowed me to close the gap. Each time Assad attempted to pass him, he found a curve and an on-coming car. Thank God for West Virginia mountain roads. I felt this was the time to make my move. Now within two car lengths, I waited until his vehicle entered a left- hand curve again and plowed into the left rear corner of the Buick, sending it into a spin and carrying it down an embankment off the right side of the road. The car then T-boned a large oak on the passenger side, expelling Assad through the open back glass that had been shattered when my rounds I had fired earlier into the windshield had gone on through. The remaining shards of glass lacerated his body in a dozen places. He first landed onto the trunk lid, and then slid off onto the ground, leaning partially against the rear wheel.

I stopped the pickup on the shoulder of the road and with Glock drawn, moved cautiously down the thirty foot embankment. Assad lay writhing in pain, partially covered by a clump of weeds. His white shirt was torn half off, revealing a large section of gauze taped to his left shoulder. I *knew* I had begged him at Wolf Laurel.

Around his waist was what appeared to be an explosive device strapped onto him with duct tape. On his left side was a triggering mechanism similar to the one I had found in his compadres' cabin. He was also laden down with C-4. Seeing that he had in his right hand a Beretta, I commanded, "Lose the gun, Assad!"

Weakly, he raised the gun and swung it in my direction, but I fired a round into his *right* shoulder, causing the Beretta to drop from his hand. Blood immediately spurted from the wound and I suspected I had hit an artery. He grimaced in pain and grit his teeth together. Then he began to drill me out with his steely, hateful eyes. It was a battle of stone-cold stares for a few moments. And for some reason there was a strange anticipatory stillness in the air.

Now bleeding profusely from the cuts on his face as well as from the .40 caliber round in his shoulder, Assad spoke in a feeble, garbled voice. "You are a filthy bastard, McGowan, and I will see that you are in Hell, just like the New York infidels are this very day."

"Hell may be waiting for me, prick, but I will guarantee that you *and* your chieftain, Bin Laden, the Son of Satan himself, will get there long before I do." Blood from Assad's right shoulder wound was now pooling beside him. "Where's your leader, the professor, and the other asshole."

"I would die before I tell you anything, infidel."

"I can arrange that at any time. Tell me where they are, Assad. You're running out of time *and* out of blood. I can save your life with just a couple of words."

"I am not afraid to die. Allah has many rewards for me."

"Like those 72 virgins? Tsk, Tsk, Assad. Have *you* ever been fed a load of camel shit. There's a very good reason they're all still virgins, you know. They're ugly as hell and covered with boils. Your Allah has a hell of a sense of humor."

"You blaspheme the name of Allah by the very opening of your mouth." With that, he lifted his left hand in the direction of the triggering device.

"Don't do it, Assad, or in two seconds you will be riding your horse straight *into* the gates of Hell. You failed in your plot to kill thousands of innocent people, so no reward for you. No Jesus, no Allah. But, when you stand before the one true God, you will *damn* sure get what's coming to you."

"Brave words for a dead man," he replied. His face wreaked of pain as he continued the hand across his body. But before he could place his fingers on the device, I pumped two rounds into his heart just inches above the C-4 body wrap. His torso flinched with each thud and his hand dropped harmlessly back to his side. I heard him exhale one long, sighing breath and then he was still.

"*Ma'assalama*, Assad," I said, maintaining my stance and aim for a few seconds. Then I moved toward his body to assure he had not been wearing a bullet-proof vest that may have stopped my slugs. Bright scarlet plumes of blood gushed from the tight shot group right at the heart. He was dead, all right, and likely catching his first whiff of Sulphur.

The coal truck driver, who in his side mirror had seen Assad's vehicle plunge down the embankment and had obviously later heard the report of my two shots, stood at the top of the hill. He called to me, "What's going on down there?"

"Don't worry about it, sir," I replied, holstering my Glock. "Just dumping some garbage, that's all."

What continued to bother me was that the man I called Baldy and the Valley professor were still out there and likely positioned to continue the strike on American should Assad and Big Nose fail, which they did, dead that they were.

I called Jack's office and although his assistant tried to put me off, saying he had been on the phone for the past hour with Washington, I explained who I was again and that I had just taken out two terrorists. I got the impression she thought I was some kind of nut or glory hound and made the whole thing up. "No, really," I told her. "Just put him on. He'll want to talk with me."

Jack finally came on the line and I filled him in on my day so far at the office. When I conveyed my concern about the third terrorist and the teacher, he said not to worry about one of them. A man identified as Ahmed Omari was spotted and taken into custody by an agent on a rocky pinnacle overlooking the American plant. He looked just a little too suspicious sitting there with an SA-7 missile on his shoulder. The man had somehow evaded the locals while driving Assad's Nissan the night before on back roads from Lewisburg to Charleston. Jack said if it hadn't been for my brilliant analysis of the plot, my speculation about the check-valve gunner and my dogged persistence, they would never have thought to add the high ground on the south to their protective barrier around the factory. Well maybe the word wasn't 'brilliant,' but it was something similar. Ahmed had been taken out with a single sniper's bullet through the shoulder that had supported the missile. But he did manage to survive. Unlike Khalid (you remember DAG), they did find identification on him ... his student ID from Valley Community.

It was now close to noon and after the State Police

arranged for road kill removal, I thought to call Joey's cell to ask him to go by and check on the ladies at Wolf Laurel, but he didn't answer. I also called the inn for Adrianna, but there was no answer on her cell or the house phone. It caused me immense concern that I was unable to reach both of them, considering the Arab teacher was still out there somewhere.

Just after twelve thirty, I limped the old truck back onto 219 and to the airport where I had left my farmer friend sitting in the middle of the asphalt. The parking lot was flooded with State and County vehicles plus two government cars which likely belonged to an agency team from the Southwest Virginia FBI. Obviously, everyone was either inside the terminal or the flight academy working the grisly scene, except two troopers, one of which stopped me as I pulled into the lot. I flashed my State Department ID, told him I was looking for Lieutenant Williams, and he said to park "over there," which was ironically the space beside of my Suburban. The trooper eyed my Dodge Ram, wondering, I'm sure, as to what a State Department agent was doing driving a beat up old pickup.

I took another moment to ring Joey's and Adrianna's cells and there were still no answers. I then called Cora at the house and she said Joey was at the funeral home as far as she knew. So, I called the shop. Lester Basham, Joey's associate, said he arrived about noon at the shop and both Joey and the family car were gone and didn't know where. It did seem rather strange that I wasn't able to reach either Joey or Adrianna, and now that Lester told me Joey was missing in action, I began to get concerned.

And then something else entered my brain as I sat waiting to go in to talk with Williams. I knew Assad had discovered my true last name from Adrianna's ledger ... and that had stayed with me. I had no doubt he and the others had figured out my connection with the funeral home and Joey. My blood was running cold again.

C H A P T E R   21

Instead of going into the flight academy to give Williams a personal account of my day's work, I transferred to the Suburban and drove out to Wolf Laurel. Upon entering the parking lot I saw that the McGowan and Sons Continental was there. My mind now eased that Joey had thought enough to go by and check on Adrianna, I strolled on up to the front door and flung it open. When I entered the lobby and saw Joey, Adrianna and Lottie sitting in the dining chairs, the urgency of the matter didn't immediately register in my brain, mostly because my eyes had to adjust from the bright sunlight to the darkened room. But then a sudden sensation of stark dread came over me. I saw that they were all seated in a straight line and bound to their chairs with duct tape.

"What the hell?" I exclaimed, reaching for the Glock.

"Bruce, watch out!" Joey yelled, unfortunately too late. I first saw the shadow cast across the floor by the figure behind me and then I felt the cold muzzle against the back of my neck beneath the left ear. At least I assumed it was a gun, but I wasn't going to ask questions right about now.

The man shoved me toward the center of the room before I could grasp the handle of the Glock and yelled

"Take out the gun with your fingertips and place it on the table, McGowan!"

Turning around, I came face-to-face with *Fearless Leader*, Navab Abouzar. In his hand was a 9 mm and it was still pointed at my head. Carefully, I grasped the Glock at the grip with my fingers, pulled it from its holster and laid it on the edge of the dining table.

"Now lock your fingers behind your head and sit in that chair." While digesting the imperativeness of the moment, I was struck by the fact that his English was very good.

I did as instructed and looked at my brother and the two women. None of them appeared injured, but they were sure as hell scared.

"Sorry, Bruce," Joey said. "He came into the shop and put a gun to my head. Then he made me drive him over here."

"Shut up, infidel," said Abouzar, now waving the gun in Joey's direction. He then picked up my Glock from the table and shoved it into his pants. Turning his attention back to me, the professor stared a while before giving me an evil half-smile. "So you are the man called Bruce McGowan."

"And a very good reason I'm called that, asshole. It happens to be my name."

"You have a profane mouth, McGowan. I suggest that you curb your sharp tongue or I will take great pleasure in cutting it out before I kill you." The grin turned into a snarl.

"You are the government man responsible for the destruction of our plan."

"Well, I do what I can, you know."

Calmly, he switched the 9 mm to his left hand and slapped me across the face with the back of his right hand. I immediately tasted the blood that poured from my lower lip.

"Enough with the jokes!"

I stared at him fiercely. He was right. This was not a time for frivolity.

At that moment, Burt the fur ball, who had apparently just awakened from his midday nap on the office couch, sauntered in. Although he took notice of the scenario, he obviously did not understand or appreciate the predicament we were all in. Nor did he sense the element of danger. After all, he was used to strangers being around. He went to work as usual on my pant leg, whisking his tail back and forth to solicit some stroking. I did start scratching the old boy behind his ears, then apologized to him under my breath, "Sorry about this, Burt."

Grabbing a handful of Burt's skin and fur behind his neck, I flung the cat straight into Abouzar's face. Burt, of course, had extended his claws to latch onto anything in preparation for a landing and Abouzar yelped. Unfortunately, the gun went off and I immediately felt a fiery pain shoot into my left side. The ladies screamed, Burt bolted from the room and Abouzar shoved the hot muzzle into my forehead. I thought for sure he would pull the trigger again and this time repaint Adrianna's dining room wall red. But I guessed he wasn't through with me just yet. His face was a bloodied mess as nearly every one of Burt's claws had dug in.

The bullet seemed to have gone into my washboard abdomen at an angle, out my side and into the floor. But the blood was pouring and I grabbed a cloth napkin from the dining table to press it first onto the entry wound and then the exit. Abouzar also grabbed a napkin to press against a series of lacerations around his right eye, nose and mouth. His black beard had caught much of the blood and had turned a bright red in places. Burt and I had obviously pissed him off as he suddenly kicked me in the left side right on the exit wound. I think I screamed like a little girl from the pain. The corners of Abouzar's mouth turned up into a snarling half-smile. I guess if Burt had still been in the room, his nine lives would have been used up at the expense of a 9 mm slug.

"How does that feel, infidel?" Abouzar continued applying pressure against a half dozen cuts, a few seconds at a time.

I didn't respond, but my gut hurt like hell. I straightened up in the chair and laid on him my most squalid glare. "What do you want here, Abouzar?"

"Ah, you know my name; but I do not think you know everything about me."

"I know you're a goddamned sheet-head … or should I say Muslim *shit* head who likes killing Americans. I thought you Islamic bastards were supposed to be peace-loving. Well, guess what, prick, all I've seen out of you assholes is violence. Islam is nothing more than a religion of hate-mongering psychopaths."

"Such language and blasphemy from a man who is about to die. Maybe you should pray to your God for forgiveness." I didn't respond.

Abouzar studied me a moment, like he couldn't believe I wasn't blubbering and begging for my life. Then he continued. "I will tell you who likes to kill. It is your government who continues to make war on the people of Islam. You kill our religious leaders, our women and our children as though they are nothing but maggots."

"Mmm … maggots, you say? Yeah, that's about right."

I believe he wanted to go ahead and kill me then and there, and here I was making it easy for him. How stupid is that?

"I should first cut out your blasphemous tongue, McGowan. Then you will beg with only grunts for me to end your life."

I figured then I had better back off with the insults and stall for both time and opportunity to rush him.

"Where are you from, professor?"

He looked puzzled from my question, but answered anyway. "My home is Saudi Arabia, if you must know. Which is where I will be returning within hours after you are dead."

"So, when is the last time my country invaded your country and killed your people, genius?"

"Do not worry about where I am from, infidel. I am a brother to all of Islam in all countries. Even those here in the United States. Your country persecutes my brothers in all lands."

"And for good reason."

I winced after that retort, fully realizing that the comment was not exactly 'backing off.'

Abouzar placed the 9 mm within inches of my forehead and cocked the hammer. Adrianna gasped and let out a cry that sounded much like a small bird. I probably shouldn't have pushed him like that. We had been having such a nice little conversation.

He smiled again, mirthlessly, and softened his eyes. "You think that antagonizing me will cause me to become irrational and I will lose my composure. And in my weakness, you will try to take advantage." He walked casually around me several times, all the while keeping the gun trained on my head. Working the muzzle over the back of my neck, he taunted me, and on one occasion bumped it into my skull. He then circled me like a wolf paralyzing its prey with fear. I may have been a bit afraid, but unlike the defenseless lamb, I waited for just that one opportunity to spring onto *him*. However, it wouldn't be easy. He had the gun and all I had was my cat-like agility and wit. Again, he seemed to take great pleasure massaging my forehead with the muzzle of the 9 mm. The hammer was cocked and with crossed-eyes I was taking note of the pressure of his forefinger on the trigger. All I would have to do is flinch and my brains would be laid out on the dining table for everyone to examine. I felt little beads of sweat breaking out on my face as Abouzar continued to smile that demonic smile and ridicule me. Somehow, though, I knew he wouldn't pull the trigger ... not just yet. He had plans for me. I knew he would eventually plan to kill me, but he first wanted me to watch him kill Joey, Adrianna and Lottie. And maybe even Burt, if he could find the feline. One by one he would put a bullet in their heads or cut their throats, taking his time with each, relishing the look on my horrified face. But he had to figure that after the first killing, I would lunge for him and then he would have to go ahead and end my life.

Suddenly, he moved away from me and stepped behind Joey, pulling a large knife from a sheath that hung from his belt. I turned and froze in fear, contemplating what he was about to do. He held the knife high in the air as though he was prepared to plunge it into Joey's neck. The blade gleamed like a mirror as it caught a ray of the afternoon sun peering through the window. But then he lowered the knife and laid the blade across Joey's throat. "You killed my brothers today, McGowan, and now I will kill yours. His blood will be on your hands."

Adrianna cried out, "No, Mr. Abouzar! Please don't do this."

And then Lottie spoke. "Please listen to her, Mr. Abouzar. I beg you. If you must take a life, then let it be mine. I'm seventy-four years old and have had a good life"

"Shut up, old woman. I am talking to the infidel. Do not worry; your time will come. Before the hour is over, your blood will soak into this floor along with the others." The blade now made an indentation in Joey's neck and Abouzar's mouth drew up into a wicked smile again.

"McGowan. You will get on your knees to beg for your brother's life. You mock my religion and my prayers, so you will now pray to Allah, the one and only god. Perhaps *he* will have mercy on your brother."

Slowly, I got down on my knees and watched as Abouzar tightened his grip on the knife. He now grinned gleefully at the thought of seeing me humbled. A small amount of blood oozed from Joey's neck. I knew Abouzar would still kill him whether I prayed or not. He would kill us all. I bowed my head until my nose actually touched the floor. Muttering some words that included the name Allah, I dropped my hands to the floor in front of me as I had seen Muslims do in their prayer rituals. "Please," I begged. "Please don't do this. Spare his life."

"That's it, McGowan," Abouzar said, smiling. "But, alas. Allah does not hear you. How can he answer the prayer of an infidel? You have failed. I will now take pleasure in watching your brother's head fall to the floor. Look at me, infidel. I want you to see it, too."

I brought both hands back along my side and then slid my right hand up under my jean cuff until it touched the .380 holstered on the inside of my boot. Slowly I formed my fingers around the grip of the gun, knowing I had only one chance, one shot. And it had to be accurate. Then I called to him. "Abouzar."

"What. What is it, infidel?"

"Do you love your God?"

"You have no right to ask such a question, but if it is important for you to know before you die ... yes, I love Allah with all my heart."
"Then you will be prepared to give him my regards."
"What?"

I raised up quickly, still on my knees, and fired without aiming the one shot that struck between his thick eyebrows. The report was so deafening in the small room, pain shot through both of my ears. Abouzar's head snapped back and the knife fell harmlessly from his right hand. The body then disappeared behind a terrified Joey.

"Son-of-a-bitch!" Joey yelled. "I think I felt the bullet whiz through my hair. Do you realize how close that was?" He was a little pissed.

"You're welcome," I replied.

I stood and went first to Adrianna, who was now crying and shaking, cut her loose with Abouzar's knife, and gave her a quick hug and a kiss on the forehead. Then I cut the tape from Lottie and hugged her as well. I thanked her for her bravery and for offering up her life for Joey's. Both ladies quickly ran to the veranda for a breath of fresh air and to get away from the D.B. who was now leaking all over the floor.

"I suppose you want loose as well, little brother."

"If it's not too much of a bother."

I looked down at Abouzar who was now wearing a very large eighth hole in his head. Black-red blood slowly pooled beneath him. In his death stare the look of surprise remained. He was getting Adrianna's beautiful wood flooring all goopy, bleeding like that. But so was I. The cloth napkin I had jammed between my belt and entry wound was totally soaked with my blood. Anyway, I sliced the duct tape off of Joey and ruffled his hair.

"Thank God for the backup gun, Brucie. Cut it pretty close, didn't you?"

"I live for drama, Joey boy."

He didn't respond to that, but went immediately to a mirror on the hall wall to check out his hair. "Damn, I do believe I have a new part."

Joey doctored me up temporarily until he could get me to the hospital. Before we left, I shoved Abouzar's body into a broom closet down the hall and asked Adrianna and Lottie to go along with us. I was concerned about both of their emotions, and just in case, hoped the Greenbrier Valley Hospital had a psychiatrist on staff. They sat in the waiting area like zombies, saying nothing, while I was getting patched up.

I hate hospitals. There's always an atmosphere of funky, nauseating smells … like disinfectant, not to mention the odor of hospital food as it rolls by on a cart waiting to be gagged down by the patients. And people are sick. People are in pain. People die. Of course I was *one* of those people. Sick with nausea and experiencing throbbing pain in my side where by the way I started leaking again. I was sure as hell hoping I wasn't one of the *dying* people. But I pretty much figured that wouldn't be the case, considering these were mosquito bites compared to the bullet that had smacked me in the lung a few years back.

A TV on the wall continued to broadcast WTC

commentary, showing the same videos over and over of the towers burning, then going down. Joey called Cora, finding her safe and unaware that anything at all had happened at Wolf Laurel. He didn't tell her, either. And wouldn't, that is, provided everything that had happened the past three hours or so in Greenbrier County were temporarily contained by the locals until further notice.

When I came out of the O.R. I smiled at Adrianna to ease her fear that I had somehow crashed and expired from my gut wounds. She jumped up to hug me and the tears began. Joey gripped my shoulder and winked. "How do you feel, big brother."

"Like an idiot. I should be more careful and look for people with guns when I walk into a room."

While I was at the hospital I decided to check in on Candellera. I made my way down the corridor past the double doors that led to X-ray and Radiology and then by the door that said *Maternity,* under which was a brass plate at the door edge that read *Push.* For some reason I thought that was a bit funny and broke out into a smile. A pretty nurse happened by and returned the smile, thinking it was for her. It kind of was. For a while I paused at the nursery window to make faces at the newborns. But lollygagging like I was, I wasn't getting any closer to the trauma ward and Candy's room.

Expecting to see Candy on his back with his leg hoisted on a weighted pulley, he was actually sitting up in a vinyl chair by the bed in the process of yanking an IV from his arm. When I appeared at his door, his eyes immediately started to glisten. Tough guy was having a tender moment.

"Bruce ..." That's all he could say. He had been watching the endless footage of the burning WTC towers on the TV. "How're you doing, man?" I replied.

He just nodded *okay,* and bit his lower lip to regain his composure. My shirt was still open and he noticed the surgical wrapping around my waist. "What happened to *you?"*

"More holes, Candy, thanks to Professor Abouzar."

"You found him."

"He found *me*. Saved me a lot of time and trouble." "Well you're still here. Where's he?"

"Stuffed in a closet, bleeding all over the floor back at Wolf Laurel."

Candellera gave me a puzzled look, so I filled him in on the events of the day. He listened intently like a wide-eyed child at storybook time.

"Damn good job, Bruce."

"Just another day at the office," I replied.

He became sullen again and diverted his eyes back to the TV on the wall. "I got a call from Chuck earlier. Said he thought the boss went down with one of those towers. Virginia, Abu, everybody."

"I heard," I said. There wasn't much more I *could* say.

This was the first real opportunity I had throughout the day to watch the footage other than when the tragedy first unfolded. I was stunned speechless. With one sweep of the death scythe, an estimated three thousand innocent people had disappeared. Although I had seen a number of horrific aftermaths while with the Bureau … to include the Branch Davidian inferno and the Oklahoma City Federal building bombing … what I was seeing on the screen was well beyond my capacity to not only comprehend, but accept as reality. My heart would not leave my throat. My blood felt like it was frozen.

Candy and I didn't say more than a half dozen words thereafter. But momentarily I stood and shook his hand and said I had to go.

Adrianna and Joey were waiting outside for me. And it was time for the professor to come out of the closet.

On the way back to Wolf Laurel I called Harlan Williams to inform him of what went down at the inn and he arrived within ten minutes with a squad of troopers. We pulled

Abouzar out of the hall closet, finding him looking as dead as I had left him. Maybe a little paler.

The lieutenant let out a whistle, followed by "Good God Almighty."

I turned to him and planted my steely blues on his. "This all has to stay sealed for a while, Harlan. I know the flight academy massacre will get out, but the official account can't contain the word 'terrorists.' We have to keep a lid on it for now until the Bureau and State Department *make* it official. If we don't, there will be more panic and paranoia in the streets than this country can handle. My team will ultimately dispose of all the Arab bodies, including the one at the airport. My brother, Joey, will put them on ice for now. And we'll square it all away with the Bureau. The fracas that went down here ... never happened."

"Then how the hell do we explain all this, Bruce? How will the murders at the flight academy be explained to the media and everyone else?"

"Some crazed loon went on a killing spree, distraught with what happened in New York and you're still looking for him. I don't know. Use your imagination. If that doesn't work, just say everything is classified."

"That's not fair to the families of the flight school people and the security guard."

"There are a lot of things about today that are not fair, Harlan." I grasped him by the elbow and drew him away from the troopers. "My boss and members of my unit were in the World Trade Center today. *That's* not fair."

We studied each other a moment and he nodded slightly. "Sorry, Bruce. I didn't mean to ..."

"Look, Harlan. Let's say people around here learn there was a terrorist nest right in the heart of good old Greenbrier County. Everybody who bears any resemblance to a Middle Easterner will be suspect. That may lead to a hell of a lot of undue persecution and maybe even vigilante-ism. Remember, that happened right after Pearl Harbor. To

America, every Asian was Japanese. Innocent people got hurt … even killed. A lot of innocent people could get hurt right around here. Let's keep a lid on all this. Once the Bureau and State Department agree on what to put out, it will then be official. And that will be *your* story as well."

"Guess you Feds thrive on making shit up, don't you? Is any of what trickles down to the American people and us poor slobs at State and Local ever the truth?"
I smiled … actually, rather sheepishly. "Occasionally."

Harlan was not humored. "Then you guys get us something soon, Bruce. Okay?" I didn't respond except with a slight nod. He walked away shaking his head.

"Come on, fellows," he said to his troopers.

"The coroner will clean up here. I'll explain how we will handle this on the way back."

I called Jack again to fill him in on what had transpired and that the last piece of the puzzle (Abouzar) was now in place. There didn't appear to be any other players. That is, except the Jamestown maid. Ahmed had been taken to the Kanawha County lockup to await the Zulu boys who would interrogate him before his transfer to Gitmo. His brain would be siphoned for every minute detail of the plot as well as his affiliation with the bastards who brought down the

World Trade Center. I still had a hard time accepting the reality that such attacks had actually occurred on American soil, not to mention the resulting death and destruction. I could swallow such horror and devastation happening in places like Beirut or even Paris, but not in our safe, free and protected land. Was this just the beginning? Will Americans now live in constant fear? A nauseous tremor suddenly formed in the pit of my stomach, but it was not from my wounds. It was from pure consternation.

Adrianna and Lottie had gone on to their respective quarters. When Joey carted Abouzar's corpse off to McGowan and Sons, I trekked upstairs and rapped on

331

Adrianna's door. After a few moments it opened. Her expression was stoic. Her eyes, reddened. I could tell she was still visibly shaken, if not traumatized.

"Are you okay?" I asked.

She nodded and turned away. I followed her to her bedroom.

"I … just think I need to lie down a while," she said almost in a whisper. The ordeal seemed to have sapped her strength *and* her voice.

I sat on the edge of the bed and held her hand. We didn't say anything for a long while. Her clock read ten past four. Funny. It seemed later. The day had been long … and arduous.

"Will you be all right if I leave you for a while? I need to take a drive and clear my head. I also need to try getting up with my team."

"I'll be fine. Just tired, that's all."

"Okay. I'll be back after a while." I kissed her on the forehead and slipped from the room.   I drove downtown along Route 60 and took account of what initially appeared to be a ghost town. There were a couple of people here and there talking to one another on the sidewalk, but most of the businesses had closed up and the spaces by the parking meters were hauntingly void of vehicles. I guessed that people were sent home by their employers earlier in the day to be with their families and they were all glued to their tubes. One would have thought there had instead been a nuclear strike and what few citizens were left were wandering the streets aimlessly or huddled together in the safety of someplace underground.

I wasn't able to reach Chuck and the others on my cell phone and there was only a recorded message on the land line at my Washington office. Suddenly, I felt very alone and thought about calling up Jack or Harlan again to reassure myself I wasn't the only player left. My blood was running a little cold again.

About five-fifteen I turned down Seven Bridges and back into the Wolf Laurel parking lot. Pulling in behind me was Joey in the Lincoln. I got out of the Suburban and waited for him to dismount.

"You're back," I said. "You worried about me?"

"Not *you*. You're the guy with nine lives, remember?"

"No, that's Burt."

"Did you find Burt? Last time I saw him, he was a little pissed."

"No, he's probably cowering under a piece of furniture somewhere."

"I was actually checking on the ladies."

"I guess they're okay. I was just out for some air and some deep thinking."

I walked toward the south side of the inn and into a small garden. Joey followed.

"Cora wants you to come to the house for dinner tonight."

Where are you? "You didn't tell her anything about today, did you?"

"Nope. But I did tell her that members of your group were in one of the Trade Center buildings and you haven't heard anything." I walked deeper into the garden and Joey sensed somehow that I wanted a little solace. He stayed back a bit and leaned into a masculine elm. As I digested this day of carnage I thought again about Lionel Byrd. What really happened to him, Virginia and the other members of our team? I had to wait for news about them as did thousands of family members about their loved ones. I settled down on my knees amidst the beautiful mountain laurel and wood poppies to not only say a prayer for Byrd, but also to give thanks for our deliverance from the jaws of death today. Then I stood and looked deeper into the forest past the green-black cypress and ever reddening Japanese Maples and on into the haunted crevices of my mind where I saw a city burning. I closed my eyes to dispose of the vision.

"Are you coming, Brewster?" Joey called from behind me. "The wind's picking up and with all those holes in you, I think you're starting to whistle."

"Yeah," I replied. My voice cracked a little.

"Why don't you go up and ask Adrianna and Lottie to join us at the house. There's plenty of food and Cora wouldn't mind."

I thought perhaps that was a good idea. It would probably be what all of us needed. A little love. A little family time.

We went inside and sought out the ladies. At Joey's insistence they reluctantly accepted the invitation. They didn't need to be alone. And family … anyone's family … would be good medicine.

There were feeble smiles all around as we sat at the dinner table. It was a good country meal of Salisbury steak and milk gravy. But there was a hollowness deep inside of our stomachs that food just wouldn't satisfy. Cora said *grace*, but it was more of a prayer, like you'd hear in church. Adrianna and Lottie still appeared to be in shock from not only their horrific experience at Wolf Laurel, but what happened in New York, Washington and that field in Pennsylvania as well. But there was no mention of any of it at the table. The room was quiet save the clatter of forks on china as we ate.

And then from the open windows of the dining room, across the meadow and into the valley, we heard the faint tolling of the Methodist Church bell followed by the melodic pipes ironically chiming out *Great Is Thy Faithfulness* and a song from the Civil War era called *The Vacant Chair*. I wondered if there would be a vacant chair at the Byrd household this evening. We all picked at our food for a while and then Lottie, Adrianna and I thanked Joey and Cora for the dinner. We left just before seven for Wolf Laurel.

The ladies went on inside, but I pulled out my cell phone and remained a while on the veranda. I tried calling the Byrd house and a couple of guys I knew that were still with the

Bureau in New York, but there was no service. So many emotions were tearing away at me … anger, frustration, immense sorrow and even fear. Fear that people I really cared about were dead. Fear that we were now facing a future of terror in our country wielded by a faceless, conscienceless enemy, bent on causing our streets and gutters to overflow with American blood. I felt helpless, even lost. And I couldn't even begin to imagine how helpless and horrified the people of New York were.

I laid on Adrianna's couch trying to get comfortable in a position where my wounds wouldn't hurt so badly and trying to digest everything that had happened this senseless day, September the 11th. We both watched the network news and shook our heads in disbelief at all the stories coming out of New York. President Bush had made a compelling statement and vowed swift and terrible retribution for the attacks. No mention was made by the media about the plot on American or the taking down of the terrorists in our area. The West Virginia Bureau and State Police had obviously adhered to my direction that these events would be considered classified for the time being and not parlayed in any fashion or form to the media. It was unfortunate and ironic that on the same day thousands of American citizens fell victim to the worst terrorist attack in history, two employees of a flight school and an elderly security guard in a rural area of West Virginia were murdered by an unknown assailant who tried to rob the academy. The story of these murders, as horrendous as they were, would be greatly over-shadowed by the 9-11 tragedy, buried somewhere on page ten in the Gazette and mentioned as a side note on network news, soon forgotten.

While I was in deep contemplation my cell phone went off and I saw a familiar number on the screen. I took a breath and exhaled slowly.

"Darlene."

"Hi, Bruce. Just wondered if you were okay. Where are

you?"

"Not in New York, if that was what you were wondering." I immediately thought how abject that sounded and shook my head at myself. "Good of you to call. What's the matter … you worried about your ex-husband?"

"Something like that."

"Well, I am okay. I wasn't in New York or D.C. when the planes hit. My boss may not have made it out of one of the towers, though."

"I'm sorry, Bruce. That's … awful."

How are you managing? "Yeah." I paused.

"You doing all right? It's been … what, six months since we talked?"

"I'm doing well. That is, up until today. This is all so surreal. God I hate the people that did this."

"Real bastards, they are. I hope they're frying in Hell right about now."

"My mind is totally blown today, seeing it all on TV, hearing everyone talk about it. As a matter of fact, *I* don't even want to talk about it."

"I know," I replied. "Enough said. What are you doing these days?"

"I'm working down in Fredericksburg for a CPA. Exciting, huh?"

"Very. You been taking care of the 3000?"

"Ned keeps it up. He had to put a master cylinder on it recently."

Damn, I hated that. Another man driving my Austin Healy. He can drive Darlene all he wants, but not my baby. It's just not right.

"When do I get it back?"

"With all that's happened, you want to talk about your old car?" That did not merit a response.

She continued. "The car is mine, Bruce. You remember it was the only tangible property you had and I had to get something."

"You got the apartment … and the TV."

"We didn't *own* the apartment, Bruce. I still had to pay the rent for months, you know. And the TV was ten years old. Anyway, you always cared more about the stupid car than you did me. It doesn't surprise me you're bringing it up again."

The car is not stupid.

"Okay. Let's drop it," I barked. "Sorry I brought it up."

She was silent for a while, then said softly, "I do wish Caroline wasn't entering the Bureau. This is *definitely* not good timing, Bruce. She'll be exposed more than ever to danger. And I can thank *you* for that, you know."

"Believe me, Darlene. You're not telling me anything I haven't thought about … and not just today."

She sighed. "I know. I'm sorry. You may *be* a lot of things that have irked me to the end of my rope, but you've always been a good father and I respect you for that. I won't lay any guilt trips on you." She says that, but let something happen to Caroline, God forbid.

I may as well go ahead and put a bullet in my brain. Before Darlene puts one there.

I needed to end the conversation as I was getting even more depressed, what with the talk about Caroline and my 3000.

"Well, gotta go," I said. "Be safe. Thanks for the call."

"Goodbye, Bruce. Would be good to see you sometime again soon. Stop by when you're in Woodbridge."

"Yeah. Maybe someday I will."

I checked my cell phone again and saw that I had missed a call from Caroline while I was talking with her mother. Quickly, I returned it.

"Hi, Sweetheart."

"Dad, I was worried about you. I knew you had been chasing leads on Middle Easterners in your area and when those planes hit… I just didn't know whether you were still in West Virginia or had gone to New York before …"

"I'm fine, still here in West By Gawd. How are you managing?"

"We're all on edge here. They've briefed us a couple of times, but otherwise, we're watching TV like everyone else."

"Are you sure now that you want to continue on with the Bureau?"

"More than ever, Dad. If I ever thought about quitting before, today gave me new resolve. I want these people to pay and hope to hell I'll have a shot at bringing people like that to justice one day."

"Good for you, Caroline. But that won't make me sleep any better."

"I know." She paused for a few moments.

"I love you, Daddy."

"And I love you, sweetie. Take care."

I dabbed a tear from my cheek.

Lottie left about noon on Wednesday after her son arrived from South Carolina. Over the breakfast table, she said she'd never forget either one of us and thanked me for saving her life. And again I thanked her for offering up *her* life in exchange for *ours*. She replied, "A lot of things ran through my head while I was sitting there, Skip. I just kept praying and thinking about what Jesus would do. And then I remembered what Jesus *did* do. He gave up His life, so why shouldn't I do the same for my loved ones?"

I hugged her and kissed her forehead. She hugged me back and then embraced Adrianna, telling her that she'd try making Wolf Laurel a yearly event. She then pulled me off to the side and whispered in her softest, folksy voice,

"That little girl loves you, Skip. I see it in her eyes every time you walk into the room. Sweet as fine Muscadine wine, she is. Now don't let her get away from you. You hear, boy?"

"Yes, ma'am," I replied obediently. "I'll keep that in mind."

She kept her eyes on mine, cocked her head to one side and nodded quickly in that stern manner of hers. And she was gone.

I then looked down and saw that Burt was back and rubbing his face on my leg, looking for a bit of scratching or a piece of bacon. Obviously, he had forgiven me for tossing him onto a man with a gun.

Later, Jack Fuentes, along with an agent from Southwest Virginia and I went to McGowan and Sons where we found Abouzar's van. From papers and other contents we were able to determine the exact location of the professor's house which wasn't in Crows at all. It was further east and north in the woods near Goshen. A bounty of findings to include a blueprint written partly in English suggested that it was the intent of the Cessna pilots to fly directly into the chlorine and cyanide tanks. They would simultaneously fire the blasting caps with a hand crank, exploding the C-4 strapped to their waists a split second before impact. As I suspected, the lone terrorist was to be the check-valve. If the Cessna missions failed for some rea- son, Ahmed would fire the SA-7 missile into Storage Tank B which would set off the secondary explosion of Storage Tank A. Ahmed was in position to perish either way, as were they all.

And in checking all of the terrorists' vehicles and Abouzar's house, we were able to establish there were no suitcase nuclear devices, thank God. There was just some good old-fashioned C-4 strapped on the two would-be aviators … and lots of it.

In a back bedroom of Abouzar's house we also discovered the body of a woman, the young maid, naked and sprawled across the bed. Her throat had been cut and the sheets were soaked red with her blood. In the Islamic balance scale of good and evil, Abouzar had committed his one last sin at the expense of this young woman before his plan to kill us all at Wolf Laurel, the act of which would allow him to gain his ultimate reward. The maid's body was ravaged and debased, sexually. Her horrified expression revealed the last traumatic moments of her life as the blade slid across her neck, jugular to jugular. She was no more than a subjugated pawn, a necessary means to their end. Women not only are disempowered, but are in fact an enemy. As they are responsible for the sinful lust that men have, they weaken and bring down the moral man. Her punishment in death would acquit the man; he would be vindicated and his sin forgiven through her blood.

Professor Abouzar was one of Bin Laden's hand-picked lieutenants who was to methodically over the next several months execute one of several planned missions. The targets would be key population centers, towering plazas, shopping malls and of course industries that manufactured armament and munitions to supply the U.S. military as it made war on Islamic factions. There was literature that suggested Abouzar was not only an Al-Qaeda strategist, but had also taught in the Afghan training camp, Derunta al-Ghuraba.

It would be weeks later when we found out that the nineteen Islamic hi-jackers of Flights Eleven, One Seventy-Five, Seventy-Seven and Ninety-Three trained on aircraft like the Cessnas in several flight academies like the Ross Academy at small airports in the Eastern and Southern regions of the United States. Mohammed Atta, for example, learned the controls at Briscoe Field in Gwinnett County, Georgia, and in Venice, Florida. Although the controls on the small aircraft differed from a 737, the principles of operation were similar. Atta would have practiced buzzing Atlanta's Peachtree Plaza and Bank of Americabuilding in rehearsal for the WTC attack. I don't know why I hadn't seen the kamikaze attack coming. The puzzle pieces had been there all along … the map, the flight lessons, the plan. Unfortunately, I just couldn't connect the dots. Thank God I finally woke up and took down the terrorists just in the nick of time.

But then what would haunt me forever was the fact that

if I had figured out the actual aircraft attack plan, I would have sent the information through channels which in turn would have alerted every airport to tighten up its security. Then again, who would have known these maniacal bastards would have taken over airplanes with box cutters. Still, I would continue for weeks and months to feel in some way responsible and it would make me a very disconsolate and brooding soul.

At five-thirty Wednesday evening, my heart received that *good* shot of adrenaline that I had needed the last couple of days. My cell phone rang and the voice of Lionel Byrd was on the other end. He had made it out of the first tower just seconds before it fell. Gathered up with him were Virginia and support members of the team. Covered with debris and the blood of other people, they had walked out of Manhattan along with thousands of others. I told him I had worried and prayed about him and he thanked me for that. And then he said it was time for me to get back to Washington. He had already talked with Chuck and boys and they were leaving as we spoke. Candellera was scheduled for transport to Walter Reed on Friday morning.

There were pockets of Islamic terrorists still out there to hunt down. Zulu would reconsolidate and collaborate with several other CTT teams to be part of a task force made up of select operatives from the CIA, NSA, NSC, CTC and the FBI to strategize in seeking them out. With all those egos in the room, there were sure to be all the dynamics you would expect to find on a high school girls cheerleading squad or back stage in a beauty pageant … jealousy, back-biting, in-fighting, dirty looks. Not good when everybody in the room packs heat.

C H A P T E R   22

My cell rang again just before seven. It was Jack.

"Bruce. We have a situation over in Mingo County I'd like to get you in on."

Well, Jack was certainly living up to *his* end of the bargain where it came to the 'information sharing' code that he had earlier established with me. I can't say that I had been totally forthright with the guy along the way, being the covert, not to mention selfish butt that I am. But it kind of goes with my job. Of course, I had come around in the eleventh hour just before our world started to cave in.

"Yeah, Jack. What gives?"

"We have a report from State Law Enforcement that a Middle Eastern man did not make it home yesterday from his job at a gas company. He was involved in some kind of altercation at work with a couple of other employees Tuesday morning a few minutes after the terrorist attacks. He left the building and his wife and two children have not seen him since."

"Sounds like this one could go either way. The guy could have fallen victim to some good ol' boy profiling who helped him drop out of society. Or he could be part of an actual terrorist element, and not taking any chances on being found out, decided it was time to get the hell out of Dodge."

"Perhaps, but these folks are really family-oriented and I

would doubt this guy would just abandon his wife and children."

"Did the wife report him missing?"

"Yes, and according to the locals she seems legitimately upset he didn't come home."

"So, Jack, what would you like me to do?"

"Can you meet me over in Mingo? I'd like to talk with the wife, the gas company foreman and some of the employees."

"Now?"

"First light tomorrow."

Well. Just when I thought my Tour of Duty was over in the great WV, it appeared there would be yet another party for me to go to.

"Okay. I *was* planning to head back to Washington tomorrow, but this could be worth a look."

"That's what I hoped you'd say, you being the only Terrorist Czar I know. Meet me at Lovejoy's Shop-and-Go at 0630 on Highway 3-8, eight digit grid coordinates Sierra Lima 82503742."

"I love it when you talk all official like that, Jack."

"Goodbye, Bruce."

Adrianna and I sat in the car that afternoon like a couple of teenagers at Jim's Drive-In just west of Lewisburg. Being a sensible eater and connoisseur of the more healthy fare, she was struggling with her hot dog. Of course, I had already wolfed down two. The aroma of these puppies took me back a few years … thirty-five or forty to be exact. The grilled weenie, the ground chili, coleslaw and steamed buns all worked together to tantalize and delight my olfactory senses.

For the first time in a couple days we were actually enjoying ourselves. "You're a cheap date, Skip McGowan," she said. Her giggle was back and so was my smile. For some reason, the grieving City of New York seemed so far removed from my mind like the whole thing was a product of one of my nightmares. The attack on our nation was only in a new movie I saw called something like *World War III in America*. Funny when you're sitting and eating the All American hot dog in the front seat of your car with your honey, the plights and tragedies of the world seem safely far away. Like we will always be pampered and sheltered in our perfect little Utopia nestled in the small hills of West Virginia. The defense mechanisms were at work. Denial, repression, displacement, reaction formation … you know, all the Freudian escapisms.

That evening we took in more TV, saying very little, depressing ourselves watching the continuous network footage of human interest stories intermingled with recovery efforts. We finally turned off the tube and sat in drained silence like two old married people, then went to bed. We kissed each other good night and lay quietly until I heard her slow, heavy breathing. Then sleep came over me as well.

I jumped up at four, took my shower and sat at Adrianna's desk in my jockey shorts, plotting my route and coordinates. It would take me a couple of hours to make the rendezvous point, so I had to zip. I kissed my sleeping bunk mate on the forehead and closed the door behind me.

It was six-twenty two on the Suburban's digital clock when I pulled off Route 38 into the gravel parking lot at Lovejoy's. Coming out of the minute saver with two cups of coffee in his hands was Jack in a ball cap of some kind. A briefcase was slung over his shoulder. Even though all he would be able to see was my headlights, he walked directly toward my truck. I was not only impressed with his punctuality, but his recognition skills in the morning twilight as well. When I stopped and threw the shifter into 'park,' he opened the passenger door and got in. "Black, right?"

"Right," I said, taking the cup from his hand. "How are the wounds?"

"Sore, but I'll live." I waited for some kind of smart Alec retort like 'what a pity.' But that wouldn't come from Jack. Jack was not me.

He tapped the right side map light and opened his briefcase to retrieve a notebook and map. "If we take 38 to Barksdale and go right at the stop sign in town onto 213, Taggart Natural Gas will be on the right. They start work at seven. The foreman is a guy named Bill Hanley and the CEO is Dennis Mazeroski. There are twenty-four operators, surveyors and site crew that work there and in the field. Three female employees are in the front office doing the dispatch and bookkeeping functions."

"Holy Horse Turds, Batman. You've done your homework. So, what kind of underwear will the women be wearing ... cotton or nylon?"

Jack ignored my smart-ass question and continued on. "Although the State investigators have already interviewed several of the employees, we'll hit them again. We know the Arab employee's name is Yaheem Barat. Some kind of altercation went down Tuesday on the gas company grounds and we need the blow by blow account."

"You want to play good cop or me?"

"Neither good nor bad, Bruce. We're just here to obtain facts and assess the information. And ... it would be good to learn Mr. Barat's whereabouts."

"Gotcha," I replied, making a finger and thumb gun, then pointing it at him.

Agent No Nonsense motioned me on with a flick of his hand.

At five minutes past seven it was fully light when we entered the gate to the gas company. Jack dismounted first and re-arranged his gun and shoulder holster inside of his jacket. He was dressed in a tan golf parka, black Levi's and a Nike ball cap, appearing rather GQFBI, if there is such a thing. No suit and tie today. We both looked almost like we fit in around these backwoods. Almost. I was similarly dressed, but if either one of us resembled a good ol' boy, it would be me. Jack was too pretty and his duds, too perfect.

We entered the door that read 'office' and were immediately greeted by an ancient looking woman with a cigarette drooping from a pair of prunish lips. There were so many wrinkles in her face, I felt an urge to return to Wolf Laurel and iron something. And I was not the least bit interested what fabric her underwear was.

"What can I do for you," she barked in a raspy smoker's voice. Jack flashed his ID and badge and responded,

"I'm Special Agent Fuentes of the FBI and this is Mr. McGowan of the State Department. We need to talk to Mr. Hanley or Mr. Mazeroski."

"Is this about that Arab feller? If it is, the State cops were here yesterday about him." She accidentally on purpose allowed a stream of smoke to engulf Jack's head. He was definitely annoyed.

"That's something I will discuss with the two gentlemen, ma'am," Jack retorted curtly.

Way to go, Jack.

The woman looked him over with indignant eyes, then pressed a buzzer. "Just a minute," she replied gruffly. "Bill, the FBI's out here. About Yaheem." She glared at us for a moment and then turned sideways toward her computer screen. She made it quite apparent she was done with us.

Directly, a large balding man appeared in the interior doorway and approached us with an out-stretched paw.

"Bill Hanley," he began.

"You're FBI?"

"That's correct." Jack introduced himself again and then me. "Both the company president and I gave our stories to the State Police, Mr. Fuentes. You don't have them?"

"I do. But we want to hear it from *your* lips, sir. Not second hand."

Hanley sighed and sat down in one of the lobby chairs. We took two others. "All right, then. Shoot."

"Tell us about Mr. Barat."

Hanley settled back, exposing a humongous gut. His

flannel shirt was under enormous stress and between the buttons, three gaps formed, exposing his white tee shirt. At any moment one of the buttons could go and put an eye out.

"Well, he's about thirty, has an engineering degree and been with the company about a year. Got referred to us by a guy at West Virginia Tech. He went to school there, you know."

"I understand he has a wife and two small children."

"That's what his personnel file says."

"Have there been any problems with him?" I stepped in.

"Nope. Good employee. He's in the office here about a third of the time, but spends most of his workday checkin' out the gas wells or followin' up on leaks."

"Can we get a look at his file?"

"Guess so. There're some HIPAA stuff we gotta consider, but you all bein' Feds, it don't matter none."

Hanley disappeared for a couple of minutes and returned with Barat's personnel shield. "I got some things to do. Can I leave you fellas with that?"

"Before you go," began Jack, "tell me what kind of altercation went down here on Tuesday."

Hanley sat back down on the edge of his chair, putting even more stress on his Dunlap *and* the buttons. I think it was Jack who was in the line of fire.

"Well, Tuesday morning, nine-eleven, you know, all of us was here and Yaheem and a couple others were ready to hit the field. Somebody heard about the planes flyin' into the towers and we turned the TV on. Bad, bad deal." He paused and shook his head. "We were all just stunned and nobody was doin' any work. After we heard who was responsible for it, one of the guys, John Sisko, started spoutin' off about Arabs and towel heads and all these Muslim bastards were a bunch of goddammed camel fu ..." He stopped short. "Well, you get the picture. Then he said the U.S. ought to put a bomb on the whole Middle East and vaporize every one of them. I didn't even think about Yaheem when John was goin' off like that. I looked at him and could tell he was gettin' hot under the collar. Well, anyway, Yaheem said something like, 'we are all not terrorists, Sisko. Most Muslims love peace and do not condone violence and especially murder. Perhaps you should consider your own people like Timothy McVeigh before you begin condemning Arab Americans.' I guess that set John off even more. He started yellin' and told Yaheem to get his f'ing ass out of his sight. Then Yaheem said he was going out to a site anyway and away from bigots like Sisko. He left and didn't return on Tuesday and still hasn't. We just thought he quit. Then the cops came by my house Tuesday night and told me Yaheem never went home."

I was studying Barat's file as Hanley was talking. Yaheem appeared to be clean on the surface. He came to the United States from Libya on a Visa when he was twenty-three, worked in Pittsburgh as a carpenter's apprentice, brought his young wife over, apparently then had some kids, moved to Montgomery, West Virginia, and began pursuing an Engineering degree, finishing out in three and a half years. Unlike Assad and boys, this guy was a for real student and appeared to be seeking the American dream. I seriously doubted there was any connection to an Islamic subversive group from reading about him, but I could be wrong.

Jack continued his questions. "Is Sisko here today?"

"He called in sick. Second day in a row."

"Uh *huh*.

"Funny," replied Hanley. "A couple of other guys called in as well."

Jack and I looked at one another with raised eyebrows. About that time Mazeroski came out. He was tall and slender, silver-haired, and wearing a suit. Obviously he didn't run in the same circle with Hanley or eat the same foods.

"Gentlemen, Bea (the receptionist) told me you were here. Is Bill giving you what you need?"

"Yes, sir," said Jack. "What is your take on the missing Barat?"

"I don't rightly know. He's been a good employee ... very smart and very dependable. I think a couple of our boys may have come on too strong with him. It was uncalled for. Yaheem doesn't deserve that, no matter what happened on 9-11. I expect he's probably quit… and wouldn't blame him. I talked to the State fellows yesterday and told them my feelings about the boy. He's not of the same fiber as the people who made these attacks, gentlemen. He's just another hard working immigrant trying to make a good living in the land of opportunity."

"I'm sure that's the case, sir."

We continued with our barrage of questions and it became more and more apparent that something ill had befallen Yaheem Barat. Maybe he had everybody but John Sisko fooled, but I had a feeling that it was Sisko or one of his buds who somehow made this guy disappear.

Satisfied we had what we needed, we thanked the Taggart fellows and left the office. When we were just short of my Suburban, we turned to see Mazeroski on our heels.

"Gentlemen, may I add something else? I didn't want Bill or Bea to catch any of this, but I felt I needed to share something else with you about Sisko."

We were all ears.

"I've heard he and one other of my employees, Jarod Cummins, are involved in some kind of paramilitary group they say is nothing more than a hunting club. I've seen some of their Klanish looking propaganda floating around in the past about Blacks, Jews, Mexicans, Muslims and anybody that doesn't look like a WASP."

"And you know they're connected how?" I asked.

"Talk, Mr. McGowan. I may be isolated from everyone around here because of my position, but some things still get to me."

"Okay. So where does Mr. Sisko live?" asked Jack.

"Not far from here. Go north on this road about six miles and you'll see a dirt road on the left. I think it's called Farley Road. There should be a sign. He's about the third house down that road. I've only been there once and that was two or three years ago, so I could be wrong. You should see a blue Ford pickup in the driveway."

I asked "Would you know where this paramilitary camp is located?"

"Not really. I hear they call it a hunting camp. And I do know there's some kind of hunting camp on Jewel Mountain. I imagine someone in that area could clue you in. Near a town called Petersville about fifteen miles further north."

"Is Cummins here today?" I asked.

"No. He called in yesterday and said his aunt died and would be going to Huntington for her funeral."

"Imagine that."

"I don't check up on employees when they say they have a death in the family. I just wouldn't think a man would lie about something like that."

"Maybe not about a guy's mother, but aunts and uncles don't have the same status and are expendable," I added.

"Thanks, Mr. Mazeroski" Jack stood and put out his hand.

I thrust mine toward him as well and asked one more question. "What about Sisko? What do you think of him?"

Mazeroski shuffled his feet in the gravel and looked down. "On the job, generally dependable. But he's a rogue and we have had a couple of problems with him."

"Such as?"

"Has come in drunk or hung over a couple of times. And he invited one of the other men outside one day after some kind of argument over a gambling debt."
"Salt of the earth kind of guy, huh?" I responded.

"Not my blend of salt. I expect one day I'll have to cut him loose and then all hell will break loose."

"I guess that's it, then," Jack said. "Thanks. If you think of anything or hear anything else, here's my card."

We entered Farley Road a few minutes later and on Mazeroski's best recollection found the third house on the right. There was no blue pickup in the driveway. I figured it was Sisko's place, all right, since there was a large Rebel flag on the double wide attached to a flag stand by the door.

I got out first and led Jack to the door. After I rapped sharply, we heard the thumping of footsteps on the trailer floor. The door opened and a frail 40-ish woman in a housecoat appeared. Her left eye was swollen and blackened and when she opened her mouth to speak, I could see she was missing some teeth ... either knocked out by her husband or she had never owned a toothbrush.

"Yeah?" she greeted.

"Good morning, ma'am," I touched the bill of my cap. "We're with the State Highway Department and are talking with homeowners about the State's plan to blacktop Farley Road. Is your husband in?"

Jack looked at me and turned his head. I think I saw a bit of eye rolling.

"No, he isn't?" Her eyes widened. "You all really gonna pave this road?"

"Well, that's the plan, but we have to run it by everyone who lives on this road."

"Damnation! I've been prayin' for that to happen. When you gonna do it."

"Well, we have to get everybody's permission. I'll need your husband's signature." I looked at my faux notebook.

"Your husband's name is ..."

"John. John Sisko."

"That's what I have written here. So, he's not around today?"

"No, he's ... at the doctor's."

I suspected Mrs. Sisko had been ordered earlier in the morning by the mister to tell anyone and everyone that, given that he was 'out sick.'

"Oh, I'm sorry. Hope it's nothing serious. There's some bad stuff going around."

She nodded, deciding not to say any more. I expect she didn't like lying as she seemed a nice enough soul, but I had to dig a little further.

"Well, we have to get on. Got several other people to see and then get over toward Jewel Mountain. There's a road going up to some kind of hunt or fish camp there that people have been after the State to improve."

"Oh, yeah. My husband goes up there to hunt most every weekend all year long."

I actually think she did not know that hunting season is *not* year round and although I hate taking advantage of people who are not as bright as three watt bulbs, I had to do it today. "You know, I've been looking to get back into hunting and maybe I'll check out the hunt club. What's the name of it, do you know?"

"I don't know much about it. When John leaves the house for the camp, he don't say too much. I think it's just called The Jewell, you know, after the mountain?"

"Great. Do you know if anyone's up there today I can talk with?"

"Prob'ly. You may even catch John …" She stopped, knowing she was about to give her husband's whereabouts away. "… maybe this weekend, if you wait and go then," she recovered.

"Maybe I will wait and check out the road at the same time. That way I'll kill two birds with one stone. Well, thank you, ma'am." I touched my bill again.

When we turned to walk away, she yelled after us. "I can't wait to see this road paved. Thanks."

I actually hated the deceit I had wrought on this little lady. She would be looking in vain every day to see the road crew set up with their equipment only to realize that one very special prayer in her life would never be answered. I felt bad about that. Then I thought about something else. I hoped she would not see that my Suburban sported a District of Columbia tag when I was pulling away.

At about nine-forty, we stopped at a gas station at the base of Jewel Mountain for fuel … another cup of coffee. Jack sat in the SUV while I went in. I guessed that he about had his fill of my fabrications. There was a good ol' boy behind the counter who looked as though he could belong to the Jewel Mountain Boys Club, so I had to be coy about my questions. After paying for our coffee, I struck up a conversation.

"Great country, man. A guy could retire here."

"God's country, we call it. Where you from?" he asked.

"Over in Virginia, up D.C. way. I don't get to see this part of the world much. When you're stuck behind a desk six days a week and all you see is buildings, this is like driving through the Garden of Eden. Is there some good fishing around here?"

"Yep. We got Moon Lake up Kettle Creek not too far and a couple of pretty nice streams just off fifty-seven. You fish?"

"Don't have time for it; but I have done a little hunting, mostly up in Pocahontas County."

"Yeah, I've been up there. Snagged an eight pointer about five years ago."

"Much hunting around here?"

"When the season opens up, man, it's like Grand Central Station."

I took a sip of my coffee and chose my words carefully. "I'm just returning from a family reunion over in Matewan. My uncle said he's come over this way and met up with some guys at a hunting camp on Jewel. I guess he meant somewhere around here."

The man looked at me from beneath the bill of his Red Man cap and placed his paws on the counter. I figured right then and there I had somehow given myself away. He stared for a few seconds and then said, "Yeah, they's some kind of camp up Hog Hollow a couple of miles from here. I heard there's some fellas that go there all times of the year and hang out. Don't know if it's really a hunt camp, though." I wasn't quite sure why he was sharing all this with a stranger.

"Hmm. Maybe it's just a place to get away from the wives and do a lot of drinking," I replied.

"Well, I really don't know much about anything up there." He knew he probably said too much to me in case any of the other store patrons were listening. Obviously, he wasn't a charter member of the 'club.' And if these people *were* backwoods militia, they wouldn't take kindly to store keeps spreading any idle gossip around about them.

"Anyways, good talkin' to you, sir." He quickly broke off the conversation and turned his attention to a burly man behind me in camou who by the way was eyeing me rather suspiciously.

I returned to Jack and the Suburban and handed off one of the coffees … the one I was not drinking from. "What did you find out, Bruce?"

"I think we may have found the area we're looking for. If my suspicions are correct, we may have some home-grown militia camped out in them thar hills. Will any of your boys be ready to roll if we find a bunch of guns up there?"

"May be difficult to scrape everyone together at once without an Op Plan or rendezvous time. Better chance to draw in the State for something like this."

"Let's see how this goes and if there is evidence of either some illegal activity or we find that Sisko and Company have snatched or disposed of Barat, we'll back off and bring in the locals."

I think this excited Jack. He looked over at me and nodded. "All right. I'm game. Let's go."

I found Hog Hollow Road at the base of Jewel Mountain rather handily and after throwing the Suburban into 4 wheel drive, started up what appeared to be an old logging road.

There were no signs indicating we were on the way to a hunting camp or any other kind of camp. Soon, however, we began to see some *No Trespassing* signs. The road quickly deteriorated and some of the tire track ruts actually turned into trenches.

After covering what seemed to be two miles, we came upon a gate on which there was posted a much angrier sign than the others: *Absolutely No Trespassing. Violators Will Not Be Prosecuted. They Will Be Shot.* About as angry a warning as I have ever seen. I was getting ready to get out to open the gate when suddenly a figure dressed in authentic military woodland camouflage stepped from around a thick oak and bore down on us with an AR-15. He was about six feet tall, had a full black beard and two fierce peepers.

"Stop where you are and turn off your engine. Now!" he barked.

I did as commanded since I already had enough guns trained on my person in the past couple of days. And some of them were spitting stuff at me.

"Excuse me, sir," I said. "Please lower your gun. We were looking for a fish camp up here."

"There isn't no fish camp up here and you're trespassing. Assume you assholes can read."

I looked over at Jack and said, "Looks like we got a bum steer about this place, Jack." I then turned back to the guard and added, "We were told there was a lake up here … Moon Lake, I think."

The man edged closer to the truck and eyed me menacingly. "That's over near Coalburg, more'n ten miles from here." He looked past me at Jack and then back at me again. "And you faggots don't look like you're up here to do any fishin.' So, what are you sweethearts really up here for, huh?"

I ignored the comments and spread my map over the steering wheel, pretending to mull it over. "I don't know, Jack. I think we took the wrong road." I then looked at the guard. "Sir, will you please point out where on the map we need to go?"

The man lowered his rifle and pushed his head half through the open window on my door. No sooner had he made the mistake I hoped he would, I reached over with my right hand and slammed his nose down on the door frame. Blood immediately spurted from his nostrils. I released the handle with my left hand and kicked open the door. As the man went sprawling onto the ground, he dropped the firearm. I jumped out and kicked him in the groin as he rose to get up. Although he yelped in pain, he still tried to upright himself. Swiftly, I swung the knife part of my hand across his throat and hit hairy meat. As the man lay on his back, gasping for air, I pounced onto him, pulled my Glock and placed the muzzle against his forehead. It felt good turning the tables for a change. Two days ago a now defunct professor had a gun against *my* head.

"Put your hands behind your head and interlock your fingers!" I ordered.

The man appeared to be choking on his blood and as a result of my shot in his Adam's apple, he was getting very little air. I turned his head to the side so that the blood would drain. Jack came up from behind to join me.

"What's your name?" I barked.

"H ... Horace," he coughed.

"Horace what?"

"Tim ... mers. Timmers." More coughing.

"Where's our camp Horace?" He didn't answer.

I pressed my left thumb against his Adam's apple, still training the Glock on the forehead area between his eyebrows. "You have three seconds to tell me, Horace, or your brains will be feeding the crows. One two three," I counted very quickly and cocked the hammer.

Horace immediately unlocked his fingers and pointed to his left. "Just over that hill ... about a hundred yards ... (cough). You're ... hurting me, sir."

"Trust me, I'm *not*. Now, are there any more guards like you?"

"One," he rasped.

"Is Sisko in there?"

Timmers looked surprised and his eyes widened. "You … you know Sisko?"

"I know him and people like him. Is a man named Cummins there with him?" He hesitated, then nodded.

"How many total men are in the camp?"

"Four … five. No, four."

"For your sake, we'd better find four. Now I have one more question, Horace. And you'd better give me a straight answer. If you believe I won't kill you, better think again, asshole."

He nodded again. Jack knelt down by us and I believe he was actually ready to stop me if necessary. Now *his* eyes had widened.

I looked at Jack. "And you know I will."

I returned my attention to Timmers' wanly face. "Is a Middle Eastern man named Barat there as well?"

Timmers' eyes were now showing fear. "Yes, sir."

"Is he alive?"

"Yes, sir."

Amazing how one can command such respect when the muzzle of a 40 caliber Glock is laying lovingly against a person's forehead.

"You've been very courteous and helpful, Horace," I said. "My sweetheart here and I now wish you sweet dreams." With that said, I cracked him on the right side of his head with the butt end of my gun. The ugly thud made Jack wince.

I stood and turned to Jack. "Let's go ahead and call for troopers and then move in."

"Move in before they get here?" "Yes. Are you still game?"

"I am."

Jack's Bureau phone was still hanging on his dash back at Lovejoy's, so he used my cell to contact the 911 operator, asking to be dispatched to the Mingo detachment. After getting the unit sergeant on the horn, I heard him explaining the scenario and giving directions. Meanwhile, I had secured my .308 from the cargo area of the Suburban and moved into the woods around the gate. Leaning against a tree that sported a sign with a skull and crossbones painted on it, I peered into my binoculars through a patch of maples, spotting the other guard, also in woodland camos. Beyond him approximately fifty feet further downhill into a clearing was a small shack that appeared scores of years old, perhaps made of chestnut. A number of pickups were parked off to the side, one of which was a blue Ford. No other bodies were in sight and I assumed they were inside the building.

Jack slipped stealthily behind me and I handed him the .308. "Have you ever used one of these?"

"Just once, in a weapons familiarity class."

"Good enough. Follow me down at a distance. You've got my back. There's a guard at seventy-five yards. A shack is beyond that. I'll take the man out, but if someone else materializes … well, you know what to do. Once I take down the guard, come down the hill quickly."

Jack nodded. If I were him, I'd be questioning me as to who was actually in charge of our little covert deal. But Jack knew he had been scarcely more than a desk jockey and dealing mostly with white collar crime. I'm not sure he had ever even been in the woods; and then knowing what I was capable of, he likely chose not to challenge me for the command job.

The guard near the shack was certainly not expecting anyone to get past Timmers and appeared to be less than vigilant. He had set his rifle down and was sitting on a tree stump, digging into a pouch of Red Man. As quietly as I could, careful not to step on any dry twigs, I moved at a crouch around behind the man. He may have heard me make some kind of noise as he turned his head sharply in my direction. I immediately dropped down and after a few moments, he returned his attention to jamming the wad into his mouth. His AR-15 remained propped against a tree.

Slowly I moved to within five feet of the guard. At the same time he heard the cock of my hammer, I said softly, "Don't move." I was pretty sure he had swallowed his chaw as I thought I heard him gag. "Now stand up and keep your hands where I can see them." When he stood and put his hands up, I grabbed his rifle. "Now turn around."

Slowly he turned and I holstered my Glock, now training the rifle on the guard's head. "How many inside?"

"Three," he replied.

"Three plus the Arab man?" He nodded.

"Thank you," I said, then gave him a horizontal butt stroke on the chin with the stock of the weapon. He dropped with a groan and didn't move again.

Jack came up behind me, eyeing the sleeping guard, and looked at me with a frown on his face.

"He's not dead, Jack."

"So, what now, Bruce?"

"We need to go ahead and move in on them. If they come out and find the two guards in a supine position, they'll shoot first and ask questions when the smoke clears. We can take them, Jack."

He nodded.

I went through the guard's pockets and found his wallet. It wasn't Sisko. The man's name was David Burke. I had an idea.

"Jack, position yourself by the door and be ready to take down anyone who comes out."

"What's the plan?"

"I'm calling them out."

"What? Bruce, they're not in a saloon and this isn't the Wild West."

"Not far from it."

Jack frowned and rolled his eyes again. I was sure he got that from his wife.

He moved next to the door, leaned against the siding and brought up the .308 into position. I checked the magazine in the guard's AR-15 and sought cover by a nearby tree facing the shack. I figured the people inside wouldn't be able to detect the difference in the voice. I then yelled, "Hey, Sisko. Hey, you guys come out and see this!"

Shortly, the door opened and all three men tromped down the steps and onto the turf. They had no weapons in hand, thinking that the camp was still secure. Obviously, the guard had seen something interesting, like a UFO. I stepped from behind the tree and Jack got the drop on them from behind.

"What the hell ...?"one of them exclaimed.

"On the ground! Now!" I barked. The men dropped, automatically placing their hands out in front of them.

"Jack, go check on Barat." I then tossed the rifle and drew my Glock. One by one I placed the muzzle of the Glock against the men's cheeks and searched them for weapons. Two of them had .45 automatics in their leg pockets, which I confiscated.

Momentarily, Jack came out of the shack with a very frightened Middle Eastern man, hands bound with duct tape. He had been beaten badly and both eyes were nearly swollen shut.

Jack took out a small Buck knife and cut the tape from Barat's wrists. "Mr. Barat, I presume. I am Special Agent Jack Fuentes, FBI. We're pleased to find you."

The man could hardly speak, partly from his tears, but also because his mouth was cut and swollen. "Thank ... you."

"All right, which of you is Sisko?" I began barking again.

One of the men, apparently scared peoples, pointed to the bearded one in the middle. I then pressed the Glock into the back of Sisko's neck. "Get the hell up!"

Sisko stood, looking rather indignant. "What do you people want? We isn't done nothing."

I walked up to him and started what I thought would be a meaningful dialogue. "Your militia days are over, asshole. How does kidnapping, assault and battery and terrorism charges sound to you? Jack, would you like to read them their rights?"

"Love to, Bruce."

When Jack approached Sisko, the man spit in Jack's face. "How's that, Spic? They let anybody be FBI these days. Next thing you know, towel heads like Barat there will be agents. I guess what happened on Tuesday don't mean shit to you, you Muslim-lovin' pricks?"

Jack took out a handkerchief and slowly wiped his face. Then he did something that absolutely rocked my world. Obviously, he was impressed with the way I had handled the guard by the shack. He smiled and said "Hey, Sisko. Lights out." Suddenly the butt of my .308 swung up and crashed into Sisko's jaw, certainly shattering it into several pieces. The man sunk to his knees and fell on his face. I saw *nothing.*

We then heard the sound of vehicles, one of which crashed the gate. Blue lights were flashing and reflecting all through the woods. The troopers had arrived, not that we would have ever needed them. An ambulance was called in for Sisko who had resisted arrest.

The two guards had awakened from their naps and were presented silver bracelets by the posse. Jack and I then walked with Barat back to my Suburban.

"Mr. Barat, we need to get you to the hospital," I said.

"No. I just want to go home to my family."

"You could have some internal injuries, you know."

"I don't think so," he replied. "I am all right. Just flesh wounds as your TV cowboys say."

We smiled. "Committing hate crimes is a Federal offense. You know you will have to testify against these men. Will you be up for that?"

"I will. You know I will." He paused before getting into the truck. "Thank you for coming to get me. You restore my faith in American people. I want you to know, no matter what these men did to me, I am proud to be here in this country. I would never say or do anything to hurt the American people. I hate what the terrorists did in New York and Washington. I believe all people have a right to live and worship, but I know that some of my people don't. My family and I will stay here and enjoy the freedom given to us."

"We wouldn't blame you if you didn't, Yaheem," I said.

"What these men did to you took away your freedom …"

"And you both gave it back to me." He held out his hand. I actually felt like bawling … not only for him, but for the 3000 plus people who were also victims of terror and weren't so lucky. And when Sisko spouted his bigoted venom, it was like he held a mirror up to my own face. It made me think of some of my comments about the Middle Eastern society over the past couple of weeks. Guilty as charged.

We took Yaheem home. When his wife heard the vehicle approach, she ran from her doorway and into his arms. Two toddlers followed. He looked at us and smiled the best he could, given his swollen lip. He also mouthed the word, "Thanks." Tomorrow he would go back to work and things would be different. I was sure that Mazeroski would see to that. On the way back to Jack's Crown Vic, hardly a word was spoken.

Then Jack cut the stale air. "Good job, Bruce."

I didn't respond for a moment, but then said, "I guess you saw me at my worst."

"No," he replied. "I saw you at your *best*. I learned quite a bit today from you. This may have gone down differently if we had a Bureau team running the show. There likely would have been loss of life and we may not have gotten Barat out alive. It's amazing these guys were taken out without us firing a shot."

"You're a good wing man, Jack."

We shook hands and I do believe that his grip had improved since the first time we met. He actually popped a couple of my knuckles.

We stood for a couple of moments leaning against the Crown Vic, arms folded and looking down. I really liked the hell out of Jack and I do believe he reciprocated the feeling. But, over the past couple of weeks I'm sure he had reason to ponder how complex, enigmatic and confusing of a guy I was. Ruthless, yet compassionate. Austere, yet affable. Obnoxious, yet delightful. Sometimes, all at the same time. I'm often even confusing to *myself*. But I do believe Jack learned something from me at any rate … it's neither a Bureau requirement nor emotionally profitable to be a tight-ass 100% of the time.

We seemed a bit awkward saying goodbye, shuffling the toes of our shoes in the gravel. But then we nodded and turned away from each other. When he opened his driver's side door, I called out to him. "Hey, Jack."

"Yeah."

"Say hello to Diane for me." He smiled and nodded again.

"You bet. See you in the funny papers, Bruce." And *I* smiled.

The troopers found a roster in the cabin of the militia numbering twenty-three men. Each was later rounded up and charged, although it was apparent that only the five men on site had actually kidnapped and assaulted Barat. A cache of about twenty rifles and handguns was found, which did not include the weapons that the men had in their vehicles and at home. Obsolete U.S. Marines training and field manuals were also located in the shack, along with a variety of pyrotechnics and ammunition. Beyond the clearing where the cabin sat the militia had cleared off brush to build a 100 meter known distance range complete with targets. A few days later the cabin was bulldozed and signs were posted, *No*

Trespassing by Order of the Federal Government.

C H A P T E R   23

And yes, I know how lonely life can be The shadows follow me
And the night won't set me free
But I don't let the evening get me down Now that you're around me.
—Don McLean

Sometime around seven I turned down Seven Bridges and into Wolf Laurel. I was hungry and because I had had my cell phone off all day, I hadn't talked with Adrianna about any dinner plans. I hoped she hadn't succumbed to any invitation from Dan. Of course, as long as I was in the picture, he was going to steer clear of me. I'm sure he wasn't ready to get smacked around again.

As soon as I reached the top step of the staircase, she opened her door. "Well, how was your day today?" she asked. "Have you been off saving the world?"

"Something like that. Have you eaten?"

"Waiting for you. I tried your cell a couple of times. I thought you just blew me off."

"No way, my dear. How about you and I making this a special night out? Dinner and a little dancing at the Greenbrier?"

"Really? Why? Is this some kind of special night?"

"I don't know if you'd call it special, but I *am* going back to Washington tomorrow."

Her eyes sank and she turned to go back inside her room.

"If you don't mind, Skip, can we just stay here? I'll fix us a nice dinner." In five seconds she had gone from *bubbly* to the *ice blues*.

I followed her to the kitchen where she took out a roaster. I could see the melancholy in her face clean through the back of her head. "Come on, now. You knew I'd be leaving. Remember, I was all set to go a couple of days ago." She nodded without reply.

"I *do* have a job in D.C., you know."

"There are damsels in distress around here, too, as you have found out. I think I saw an advertisement just the other day in the paper for a knight in shining armor." She actually smiled. A little.

I smiled back. It was the first set of smiles of the evening. "But I think the kind of job you'd *want* me to have would make me a knight in shiny Armani, you know, politician, professor, used car salesman ..."

"Used car salesman dressed in Armani?"

"Well, I'd have to show these people around here how to dress, wouldn't I?"

Her smile widened. Now just a little more, but still all not that much.

While she busied herself in the kitchen over the next hour, I slipped into the sofa chair and dialed Birdman's cell.

"Just checking on you, boss. How is everyone?"

"We're managing, Bruce. I moved my family temporarily into an apartment down in Alexandria. I have a meeting with Mr. Big (I took it to mean the President) on Saturday about the people who did this and to determine if there are any remnants out there. By the way, congratulations on taking out the element in *your* area. You were right on the money about that nest, the factory, everything. That would have been catastrophic."

"The least I could do."

"And I also got word through the Fabulous Boys system that you handled a home-grown threat in Mingo today."

"Jack and I handled it."

"Good work. Assume you'll be back tomorrow? I want you in on the Saturday meeting to brief the boss."

"Should I wear a coat and tie?"

"I insist."

"Okay. Turtle neck it is."

"See you in a couple of days, Bruce."

I didn't even turn on the TV that evening. I could only take just so much of the scenes of rubble and smoke in New York, the hole in the ground in Pennsylvania and that missing section of the Pentagon. Anything I needed to know beyond that would come to me through official channels.

Somehow, Adrianna's mood had managed to retrogress as the evening wore on. We sat picking at our food, not saying much and it appeared that the emotions associated with fear, separation and loneliness would rule out in the end. Occasionally, we would lift our wine glasses to take a sip (or a gulp in my case), but most of the beef and greens remained uneaten.

I broke the ice. "You do know how I feel about you, don't you."

"I think so," she replied softly. "But what does it matter? I'll be here … you'll be there."

I didn't respond, but kept staring at my plate.

I guess she took that as apathy. She scooted her chair back and picked up both of our plates. A moment later I heard them clamor inside the sink. I couldn't leave it at that, so I finished sucking down the wine and as she was facing the kitchen window, looking out into the night, I slipped my arms around her waist. Laying my cheek against hers I whispered in her ear "I do love you."

It had been years … maybe never … since the last time I

said that to a woman. That is, other than my daughter.

The night was again bittersweet for us. We made love to one another with such fervor, it became at one point volatile, even desperate, like there was a finality to it. We lay spent and perspiring, gently stroking, talking, laughing, and then silence. Her eyes glistened in the soft light and occasionally she would dab them with a corner of the sheet.

"Is this *it* for us?" she asked.

"You know it's not."

"I don't want to go back to being lonely. I've kind of gotten used to having you around."

"Well, there's always Dan."

She slapped me playfully on the abdomen, careful not to bust open my new stitches. "That's not nice," she chided. Then she paused a few moments and shuffled her body, turning away from me. "But, he *will* always be around, you know."

And I wouldn't.

For the longest time after that we were silent and still. I began to make love to her with the tips of my fingers, running them lightly over the back of her neck, shoulders, breasts and tight belly. Where the side of my head crushed the pillow, I could hear my heart thumping in my ear. My brain came within inches of asking her to marry me. But then I knew I'd have to seek out some meaningless vocation that was foreign to me, and for a hell of a lot less money. The community college was now looking for a new teacher, but I'd have to become buddies with Paul, and that made me very afraid. Afraid I may become just like *him*. But at least people would not be putting holes in me.

I placed my lips close to her ear and buried my nose into her hair. Inhaling deeply, once, I drank in her sweet scent. "It's impossible right now, you know," I whispered.

"What is?" she asked, still facing away.

"Coming back here anyway soon.

" She was quiet again for a moment, then said, "a coeur

vaillant rien d'impossible."

"What?"

"Nothing is impossible to a willing heart."

I didn't respond. My heart was truly willing, but for now and likely years to come people like me would be needed by our country. I did know that I wanted to spend the rest of my life with this woman, somehow, some way. She would never give up Wolf Laurel and never condone being married to a counter-terrorist agent who flitted around the world ninety percent of the time at a beckoned call. And anyway, I would miss the excitement and action, now that our world was ever more dangerous. My kind was needed out there. The kind of evil we now experience in this world has the determination of a cockroach colony. As we knock down two or three, hundreds more will spring up.

Nothing more was said. She wriggled into my body and I held her tightly against me. It would be so easy to love this woman and take her into my life. She may even domesticate me to a point where I got used to living an uncomplicated life. A safe life. But whereas I would be happy with *her*, my mind and my body would begin to die inside. I would be like a stone-sober drunk going through the DTs. She would sense that and soon come to realize our mistake. We would both feel guilty for different reasons. She, because she coaxed me into a safe and sane relationship; and I, because I would ultimately leave her.

Sometimes I dread the thought of sleep taking me over. One of the last thoughts I have before losing consciousness is whether the dream will come that night, and if it does, will it give me a break and wait to materialize until at least five or six. That night, however, the dream monsters invaded shortly after one-thirty, and as usual, it opened my eyes and left me in a cold sweat. The badly mangled Vietnamese child stumbling from the burning hut this time formed the word *why* with her horrified lips. It was strange; she had never done anything but scream before. Now, she confronted me.

As I knew I wouldn't get back to sleep right away, I arose and eased myself quietly into Adrianna's cushy sofa chair near the bed. It began to rain, which served to perpetuate and further memorialize the dream, reminding me of the monsoon rain that fell on the village that horrific day. I closed my eyes, finding the girl and the rain still affixed to my brain like an appendage, but with special effects going on outside my window. The girl just wouldn't let this thing die. For thirty years she and her mother had haunted me and now it was my turn to ask *why*. Considering the number of people I had sent to their graves, not just in Southeast Asia, but in the last few years in the good old USA, why hadn't any of *them* materialized in my dreams?

Adrianna stirred, reached over to find my side of the bed empty, and then sat up.

"Skip, is anything wrong?"

"Naw. Just having trouble sleeping, that's all." I looked toward the window. "The rain puts a lot of people to sleep, but sometimes I just like to sit up and listen to it. It's like experiencing a nocturnal symphony, sweet and intoxicating."

Although I couldn't make out her face in the darkened room, I knew she was smiling. I heard the smile in her voice. "There's that *poet* coming out again. I love that about you, Mister Tough Guy."

"Sorry I disturbed you," I whispered. "I'll go sit in the living room for a while."

"That's okay. If you're still going to sit up, then you can keep watch over me while *I* sleep. You make a pretty good protector, you know."

"Yeah. Gotta keep guys like Dan Laramie away from your bed."

"Goodnight, bad boy." I heard the mattress creak and groan as she settled back under the sheets.

I squared my bill at the front desk on Thursday morning,

said goodbye to Juanita, and took Adrianna's hand in mine as we strolled out the screen door and onto the veranda. We stopped for a moment and turned to one another in silent reflection. Then she threw her head back and smiled. "Take care, hero. Keep away from bad guys, okay?" She picked up my right hand and placed something in it. It was a small box wrapped in some very familiar paper with a pink bow.

I laughed. "I knew somehow I'd get it back. What's inside?"

"Something you'll need. I searched high and low before finding it. Open it later."

"Okay."

We stood for a few more lingering moments, looking into each other's eyes. Then after a parting, almost emotionless kiss, I left her standing on the veranda. She leaned her body into one of the porch support beams, keeping her sad, unwavering eyes on me as I loaded the Suburban. I stopped before entering the vehicle to look back at her and threw up my hand. She did the same, then turned and went back inside.

I swung by the funeral home once again to visit with Joey before leaving town. He was already at work draining the darkened blood from an old codger who after eighty-nine years gave up on living. I waited in the office until Joey had finished pumping in the formaldehyde, after which he came out to give me a bear hug. "Bye, big brother. I'm proud of you." Then he drove his index finger into my chest. "Next time, don't cut it so close. I've always liked parting my hair on the left side. Seems like you do everything with a dramatic flair."

I smiled. "I live for drama. It is only the drama in my life that saves me from the throes of apathy. Call me anytime, Joey boy. Kiss the girls for me."

"When will you be back?"

I shrugged. "Maybe Christmas. I plan to spend a lot more time with Caroline after she gets through her training. But then they'll probably assign her to Boise or Waco, and I'll be off spanning the globe even more looking for subversives."

"Well, don't be a stranger around these parts. We love you and I *know* the beautiful Mrs. Wolf does."

"See ya, Joey." I gave him a playful shot in the shoulder with my fist and walked away.

As I passed the sign at the apex of the long, upward grade that read *Thank You for Visiting West Virginia. Drive Safely*, I felt a sudden sense of loss. A part of it was leaving my family, the lovely Adrianna and her Wolf Laurel; but also, today I was leaving beautiful Greenbrier. During the first twenty years of my life its velvet farmland, grand hills and genuine people had become indelibly ingrained in my blood. And in these three weeks, as paradoxically passionate and tragic as they had been, I felt like an alcoholic, having been over thirty years off the bottle, suddenly falling off the wagon of the world to enjoy yet another taste of Greenbrier's sweet nectar.

I knew I was getting close to Covington as the pungent odor of the old paper mill filled the cabin of the Suburban. After running the door glass up with my left index finger, I reached onto the seat for my Evian. Instead, I found the silken paper of the present Adrianna had given me. For a moment I just held it in my hand, wondering what was inside, like a kid studying an interesting looking package with his name on it under the Christmas tree. My curiosity finally getting the better of me, I opened it with my right hand and immediately began laughing out loud. It was a box containing a bottle of Hai Karate.

And there was a note attached.

"Something to keep the girls away. Love, A"

I then drove further east and north, and after the smile had long dissipated from my face, I allowed the TV images of the smoldering ruins of the fallen towers to once again haunt my brain. Although the tragedies had made us fearful, causing us to question our safety and vulnerability for the first real time since Pearl Harbor, they had also summoned within many of us an anger and a thirst for vengeance. And for the first time in many years all of us will have had a rekindled sense of patriotism. But then I wondered how long *that* would last, being the fickle and complacent society we had become. When the World Trade site and the Pentagon were restored, Americawould go back to business as usual. The horror may never be totally forgotten, but it wouldn't take long until Americans were lulled back into a false sense of security.

There was still a ravenous craving in my soul that would go unsatisfied, unrequited, until my country no longer needed me and I had nothing left to contribute. But my country would indeed need me and people *like* me in CTT, the CIA, FBI and other agencies, to seek out and destroy America's new enemy. Who knows? There may even one day be a new department in the government dedicated to securing and protecting our homeland.

I fully intend one day to return to Adrianna and Wolf Laurel. She will be the one person who can help me get beyond myself; and I pray to God that when I am through serving my country *and* myself, she will still be there.

There are stars in the Southern sky And if ever you decide you should go. There is a taste of time sweetened honey Down the Seven Bridges Road.
—Eagles

PROVOCATION

Return of the Weatherman

Col. Lee Martin

I.E.R. MEDIA

Miami, Florida

PROVOCATION:

Return of the Weatherman

The Sequel to WOLF LAUREL

To fully appreciate the primary character in this novel, Bruce McGowan…his history, his enigmatic personality and where we last left him…the reader is encouraged to first read my critically-acclaimed novel, Wolf Laurel, available at Amazon.com in paperback, Kindle E-Book and Audible.com in Audio format A young woman named Starr Ravenel from my third novel, Starbright, also resurfaces here. As the reader's interest in these characters is sure to be piqued, one may wish to acquire copies of both novels.

NLM

A Forewarning

When I come for you, I will not be hiding behind a woman or a child. I will come at you head-on, with full force and without reservation. I want you to know that I am very good at what I do and can snuff out your life in a split second with a forty-seven-cent bullet. You may not hear me or see me. You may run to any corner of the earth to evade me, but I *will* find you. I may not be as eager as you to give up my life; but by God I will gladly sacrifice it for my country to protect my people from people like you.

—Bruce McGowan—
U.S. Department of State

*"War is an ugly thing, but not the ugliest of things:
the decayed and degraded state of moral and patriotic feelings
which thinks that nothing worth war is much worse.
A man who has nothing for which he is willing to fight,
nothing he cares about more than his personal safety,
is a miserable creature who has no chance of being free, unless
made so by the exertions and blood of better men than
himself."*

John Stuart Mill

CHAPTER ONE

We are again at war. But it is a different war this time. An unconventional war of terrorism where the enemy may be seen every day on our streets and beside us on the freeway, yet we will not recognize him. There are no enemy troops massed at our borders preparing to invade. It is those who call themselves the enemy of the Great Satan who have either come to our country under the pretense of education or have been recruited here to band together in small factions under orders to inflict maximum casualties against innocent citizens who bear them no ill will.

My name is Bruce McGowan. I am a hunter. I am one of those whose job it is to covertly stop this enemy before he places his terrorist plan into action. And not only will I find him quickly, but I will just as quickly make him disappear, no questions asked or answered. If he is part of a network or organization, I will help them downsize…through the process of elimination, of course. I have both means and methods to do so. And I do so with swift and violent execution. Few know who I am or *what* I do. And there are few *like* me. Where it comes to the terrorist enemy, there are no rules of engagement and no laws to which my team and I must adhere. This enemy is not a soldier protected under the Geneva Convention nor subject to the laws of this land and due process. So, he is fair game for me. And when I kill him, do not ask me if I will have any remorse.

My father was a hunter as well…but a different kind. The usual kind. He had dreamed one day that I would also take to the sports of the woods and streams, but I had no interest in them. How challenging is it to shoot at helpless creatures that cannot shoot back? Where is the sport in that? Although the killing of bad humans is not exactly a sport, it is however a contest where either party's blood could get spilled. It is both the unknown and the unpredictable that makes my game a sport. No, it doesn't thrill me to do it. If it did, I would likely be the first to realize that I was indeed some kind of psychopath. But some people *need* killing… people like rapists, child molesters and the aforementioned terrorists. And somebody's got to do it. The liberal court system seems to have no interest in doing it. But don't get me wrong. I don't go around looking for opportunities to be judge, jury and executioner; but if somebody who *is* somebody drops that mission in my lap, who am I to disobey orders? I *am* a loyal servant of the government.

Okay. You now have the picture. For the most part, I investigate and run down factions of a foreign enemy that plans to methodically destroy Americaby murdering its people, disrupting its infrastructure, and planting fear in the heart of every God-fearing citizen. And when I do, I for the most part make sure that law enforcement does not get its hands on them to read them their Miranda rights. And then the courts will, after a laughable trial, sentence them to life in a jail cell that is a hell of a lot more cushy than the tent or cave they're used to living in. But then there is also an enemy within our country of the *home-grown* type. He might be an American citizen who was raised as a child in the most utopian of all societies to have ever existed on this earth. Then along the way as he fell in with a subversive lot, brewing up a maelstrom of dissent and contempt for

America, he grew up to hate our government and its laws. Yet he still enjoys those blessings of liberty and freedom that good men and women have shed their blood to protect. It is fine that he protests and demonstrates in our streets. That is his right. But when he plots to bring down government buildings or set bombs in market places to kill his fellow citizens in the name of peace, he is the worst of the lot. And I will kill him just as dead as I will the foreign invader.

I had a lot of thinking to do. In mid-September, 2001, scantly days after the most horrific attack on our country in its nearly three-hundred year history, I arrived back at my Georgetown pad sick at heart, emotionally spent and smarting from yet another bullet wound to my body. Still in my head was the lovely Mrs. Wolf, inn proprietress, friend, lover and the most wonderful distraction a counter-terrorist operative like me could ever hope to be bothered with.

The wonderful memories of our tender moments together those days in the late summer had continued to haunt me. Memories of that first night we spent together when we sat in the courtyard of a quaint Greenbrier restaurant talking over a carafe of wine, watching the brilliant full moon break through the trees as pure and white as I had ever seen it… and when we later walked the uneven streets of Lewisburg past lighted windows that showcased antiques and what-nots, her small, velvet hand in mine. Maybe I fell in love with her that very first night, I don't know. But I do know that she was *the* woman who had re-fired the molten lava in my loins that had lain capped for entirely too long.

So, therein lay my conflict…spending the remainder of my days with a woman more embraceable and beautiful of heart and body than anyone I had ever known or continuing on as a State Department Counter-terrorist operative. I was a man caught up in two love affairs…one was my love for Adrianna Wolf and the other was for country, freedom and yes, I admit, myself.

She didn't play fair, being as naturally sweet and perfect as she was. But she couldn't help it. And I couldn't stop the rush of feelings I had for her anymore than I could stop a train. Adrianna had made it succinctly clear what she wanted. And for better part of three months, I had argued with myself over two agonizing scenarios: having the blessed fortune of being married to Mrs. Wolf and becoming a for *real* FAG (Former Action Guy) working a humdrum nine- to-five job *or* continuing my service with the government as a covert agent doing my part as a member of Zulu, code name for the State Department's Counter-terrorist Team (CTT), to help keep the threat of terrorism away from our soil. Last September, being faced with that dilemma, I chose the latter. Danger has its own intoxicating smell. And I love it.

And just who are we? Probably 99% of the State Department doesn't realize we are even on their payroll. Those who *do* know we exist think we do some kind of research or dabble in government contracts. The latter would actually fit the bill. However, the government contracts we effect are never mutually binding nor do they ever benefit the contractee. But they do benefit America and its citizens. And because we are technically not, shall I say, authorized on paper, we don't operate with any sophisticated, gee-whiz gadgets and toys. Our team communication consists only of our Blackberries, which the government *does* spring for, and our weaponry which could come from a variety of sources that are not necessarily Government Issue.

For all of us in the organization whose mission had suddenly become even more intensified, it would be a good while before life returned to normal. If it ever did, that is. My boss, our Prefector, Lionel Byrd, AKA the Birdman as I have referred to him, had lost his office and nearly his life when the second of the twin towers went down. So, for a while, he was homeless. And so were people like Virginia, his Girl Friday, and Abu, his trusted Middle Eastern advisor on terrorist factions, who by the way speaks nine languages.

But the first week in December the Birdman's supervisor, who I found out was none other than the Prez himself, relocated him and his New York staff to an old two-story complex in the Washington burbs near the switch yards which had been rezoned commercial a dozen years before. The sign on the front of the building ironically read *Terminal Enterprises, Inc. Terminal* being the operative description of our organization's responsibilities. The place, by the way, had become *my* new digs as well.

A person couldn't just walk into the building from off the street since the cast iron door on the brick abode was locked to the outside world…and even to the inside residents. Bars covered the windows all around. Surveillance cameras were positioned on the porch and a half-dozen strategic places on the house, which of course made the place seem all the more friendly. Behind the building was a small lot where Mr. Byrd, his staff and the four of us who make up Team Zulu parked our cars.

One of the cameras, we affectionately called *Voyeur*, which was motion-activated, continuously scanned the parking area and zoomed in on the subject driver or passenger as quickly as he or she exited the vehicle. If Voyeur was familiar with the face, it continued on about its business. When it saw *my* face, however I'm sure it just sighed and fed information back inside that it was just that smart-ass, Bruce McGowan. I sometimes waved at the nosy little bastard with my middle finger and smiled pretty for him. If for some reason he did not recognize my charismatic smile or the finger, he might automatically transmit my photo to Interpol which would then appear within seconds on Birdman's or Virginia's screen.

It was December 22nd and I was feeling particularly blue, being companionless and a bit lonely. And having promised my new squeeze, Adrianna, that I would be back in West Virginia and into her arms at Christmas, I had to call and give her the bad news.

"Sorry, but I'm not going to be able to make it in, sweetie," I said.

"What? But I had plans for us, Skip (my nickname). My book club is going to the Greenbrier for a dinner and dance tomorrow and I've already bought tickets. *Now* what do I do with them?"

"Is Coach Dan still around?"

"You're suggesting I go out on a date with someone of whom you were insanely jealous? Jealous enough to punch him in the face?"

"I think he learned his lesson, so I'm sure he would be the perfect gentleman with you."

There was a long pause.

"So what do I do with your Christmas present? Mail it to you?" she asked.

Somewhere in there I detected a note of sarcasm. "You got me a present?" I replied all bubbly like.

"Did you expect I wouldn't?"

"No," I responded. "I knew you would. I have something for *you* as well."

"Uh *huh*. Maybe we ought to just return them and call it even."

More sarcasm.

"I'm sorry, Adrianna. I had planned to be there tonight, but am heading to Boston as we speak. I was pulled in a few hours ago to take part in an interrogation of this bozo shoe bomber you probably heard about on the news. I guess if he had been successful, he thought he would be greeted in Heaven by 72 virgin sole mates."

" I chuckled at my own joke. But Adrianna was not amused.

"Well then, I guess as long as you're doing what you do, there's less and less of a chance I'll even see you again."

I knew she was pissed and feeling low, and the guilt was settling into my brain like an emotional flu.

"It's just that right now my team is terribly consumed with the business of the country's security. If we were sure at this point that all threats and factions were compromised, maybe things would be different. But it's too soon after 9-11 and our work has only begun. I've had to put my travel agent on speed dial…"

"Meaning you'll be out of the country a lot." "Some," I echoed. There was then that uncomfortable silence again.

"Which further means I need to take my life off *hold* and get on with it." And then it was my turn for silence.

"Merry Christmas, Skip. I guess I'll see you when I see you." And she was gone. She had never hung up on me before, and I really felt badly about it.

Considering my lack of credentials to show people (no shiny badge or official paraphernalia other than a generic ID revealing myself specifically as a State Department takedown artist, I either had to fly commercial without my Glock or the Birdman would send me out on missions in the department jet. If there was a chance my trip would end up being 'terminal' (our business, remember) for the other guy, I'd fly the latter. Which is exactly why Byrd flew me to Boston on Delta. There would be just too many guns in the room when Richard Reid, AKA Abdul Raheem, got smacked around. And the boss knew there was a very good chance my gun would not stay in its holster. I would have enough of a chore anyway explaining to the Boston FBI team who I was and why I crashed their party.

Reid proved out to be a real genius. Fortunately for the passengers and crew of Flight 63, the low-life shoe bomber didn't have the technical knowledge to even light a match, so the plane landed safely at Logan, ironically the same airport where the 9-11 hijackers launched their mission. It was one of al-Qaeda's chieftains, Khalid Shaikh Mohammed, who had ordered Reid to carry out the shoe-icide mission.

My counterparts' interrogation techniques were, well should I say, candy-ass at best. I kept saying…"in my day at the

Bureau"…and they kept looking at me like I was some sort of dinosaur whose J. Edgar Cold War interrogation tactics were straight out of the *Attila the Hun Playbook for Hard-asses*. In my day, we used to call it 'enhanced interrogation techniques.' Where was the water boarding and electroshocks, not to mention hanging the perp from the ceiling with a meat hook stuck to his ribcage?

So, after the Bureau boys had shared tea and crumpets with Mr. Reid and bought him a shiny new pair of shoes to replace the ones he had tried to light up, I called the Birdman and told him I wasn't allowed to play with them anymore. I told him he was just going to have to get me a badge or some other kind of G Man identification that would get me into the same fraternity with people from the Bureau, the Company, NSA and the like. We could all get to know one another, play interrogation games like 'good cop, bad cop,' or even exciting board games like *Terminal Jeopardy* or *Win, Lose or Die*.

Unfortunately, even after only three months following the air assault on New York and the Pentagon, the liberals were at work to assure the rights of our brother terrorists, bless their hearts, were not violated when apprehended. If we *must* interrogate them, the temperature in the room had to be a comfortable 70 degrees and the music we let them listen to must be something smooth like *Osama's Rhapsody in G Minor* or the popular Afghan hit, *Can't Get Enough of My Camel*. After watching the Bureau play their gentleman's game with Reid, I had had enough by the end of the day and broke camp. Byrd then pulled me back in to Washington the very next day.

Anyway, after the Wolf Laurel incident in September back in good ol' West by Gawd Virginia, ironically the place I was fetched up in the first twenty or so years of my life, I was sort of getting antsy to go back there to see the woman with whom I was pretty damn sure I was in love. So, on Saturday, two days before Christmas, a couple of hours after I had flown in from Boston, the old slave driver Lionel Byrd actually closed our office until the 28th. The flirtatious and tawdry Virginia DeHussey then wondered what I would be doing for dinner on Christmas Day. She made some noise about baking a succulent ham for the two men who were the dearest to her…hubby Tom, bald, cranky and too old to cut the mustard, and hunky Bruce McGowan, fifty-four year old government hit man and the heart's desire of sexually frustrated women everywhere. I admit I made that last part up. But I thanked her just the same and told her I had made other plans.

Actually, the boss had also invited me to *his* place for Christmas dinner. But I knew it would just be him and his family together and told him I had some fence mending to do back in WV. As I previously thought I would be spending Christmas in Boston, I told Lionel I would now be swinging over to God's country to surprise my brother and his family.

Chomping on the stem of his pipe, the muscles in Byrd's cast iron jaw flexed and hardened. "To see your brother or your girlfriend?"

"I'll probably find some time to see her as well."

"I'll bet you will," he chuckled. "Do you think she'll still be speaking to you now that I ruined those dinner plans she had for you last night?"

"I think my showing up to be with her at Christmas will make her forget all about that."

"Mighty sure of yourself, aren't you, Romeo?" Byrd quipped, rather uncharacteristically.

"Not really. But I do owe her, seeing as how I kept promising all month long I'd be there."

Byrd then became reflective. "Bruce, I want you back here on the 28th. I need all of Zulu present on that day. We received a new communiqué this morning from NSA and Bureau sources that al-Qaeda has something planned for New Year's Eve in Time Square. I don't have to tell you how catastrophic something like a dirty bomb would be in that crowd. I've been tasked to station CTT with sniper rifles on rooftops along with New York's finest and government agents from multiple branches and to filter throughout the crowd. You'll be on one of the roofs.

"I'll make sure I'm back here the evening of the 27th," I promised.

Byrd leaned back in his chair and drilled his steely grays into my baby blues. "Look, Bruce. I know you've done a good deal of soul-searching about staying on with CTT after the West Virginia incident. As badly as I need you on Team Zulu, I don't *want* you if your head is not in the game. If thoughts of going back to the lovely Mrs. Wolf affects your focus in doing this job to any degree, I can't use you. My operatives have to be clear-headed and 100% mission-dedicated. That's why none of our agents are married with children."

"You're telling me that Caroline's not my kid? Oh, hell."

Byrd's unwavering stoicism coupled with his lack of immediate response, made me squirm in my chair. I should watch the things that come out of my mouth.

"Sorry, boss," I said. "I'm just being my usual smart-ass self. I understand what you're saying. But I'm *here*, aren't I? It would have been very easy for me to hang up my spurs a couple of months ago and settle in as a domestic. But I didn't."

"I don't think you could easily have done that, Bruce. You've always been a man who needs action in his life as much as he needs food and drink. And anything that threatens to deprive you of that, I believe would be poison for you."

"Somehow I can't think of Adrianna Wolf as poison," I replied.

"Not just her, Bruce. It's the living a domesticated life that would kill you within a year."

I stared back at the man who for going on two years now I had grown to admire and respect like no other in all my years as a government servant.

"As long as I'm doing this job, mien furher, my brain belongs to you…100%. You can depend on it."

"And I *do*," he said. "You've never disappointed me." "Except that day Candy and I let Assad get away from Wolf Laurel."

We all have our bad days. Ultimately, though, you took him and everyone else down before they could wipe out an entire city.

By the way, the docs will be releasing Candellera for duty on January 2nd. He should be completely healed."

"Good deal. I wonder if his big Marine ego also got healed."

No reply to yet another one of my quips. But then he switched gears to talk about my favorite topic.

"So, Caroline's all graduated from the academy and assigned out in Denver."

"Yep, and loving every minute of it. She sent me a clipping from the Denver Post which capsuled her assignment. It even mentioned that she was following in her retired father's footsteps. Mentioned me by name."

"They put things like that in the paper?"

"The Bureau issued a press release on her. Not only that, but people can actually go online and see who their resident FBI agents are in the area. I guess it's not all a big secret anymore."

"I guess not," he said.

"Is she still a right wing conservative like her old man?"

"Somewhat. I think you could officially classify her politically as a middle-of-the-roader. And although she *is* sold on a strong military and foreign policy, she's also passionate about supporting the country's social welfare programs. Her heart especially goes out to the indigent. She was not only a Peace Corps worker, but several Christmases in her teen years she spent the holiday season working in soup kitchens and collecting blankets to give to street people."

Byrd smiled. "The kind of woman I pray my girls will grow up to be."

"I couldn't be prouder."

He didn't say anything after that for a few moments, but just stared at me, chewing on the pipe stem and rocking ever so slightly back and forth in his big leather chair. "You know, Scorpion (my code name), I wouldn't at all blame you if you just went on back to that little lady and lived that simple life in the country. Forget what I said earlier."

"Naw, boss," I replied without batting an eye. "I'm good where I am. Maybe someday."

"What is it…you're afraid some day you won't check out of this life in a blaze of glory?"

I was suddenly seized by an attack of laughter. "No, Preceptor. Not at all. I want to die in my sleep like my grandfather did, not screaming in terror like the passengers in his car."

He actually laughed at that. It looked good on him.

"That's why I keep you around, Bruce. I never know what's going to come out of your mouth."

He then rose and stretched out his hand. "Tell you what, my friend. Let's go on home to our families and I'll see you back here next Thursday morning." I nodded, pushed myself out of the chair and got to my feet. "Merry Christmas, boss." I then laid a box of Cognac on his desk that had a small red bow on it. Cognac was his only vice…except chewing on that old pipe, which he seldom lit. The man didn't even cuss, God bless him.

"Merry Christmas, Bruce. Give your family my regards. And when you talk with Caroline, tell her to come by and see me sometime when she's up in these parts."

"Will do. Best to Miriam and the girls."

I understood what the Birdman was saying about my 'keeping my head in the game,' that is. I think I saw in his eyes for the first time the look of fear. Fear that I, his 'ace,' as he called me, might return back to my old stomping grounds to something or some*one* over the Christmas holidays that may just keep me there…if, in fact, Adrianna Wolf had anything to do with it.

CHAPTER TWO

I left my Georgetown flat on Sunday morning, Christmas Eve day, with Adrianna's present on the seat beside me, a set of cultured pearls, which of course I *didn't* take back. Also lying in the passenger's seat was a large basket of meats and cheeses from Hickory Farms for my brother, Joey, and wife, Cora. In my coat pocket were envelopes for his girls, Casey and Molly, which contained gift cards from the Gap. Joey, one of Greenbrier County's most respected businessmen, had developed layaway plans for a great number of people in eastern West Virginia, the vampire that he was, draining their blood *and* their bank accounts. But even so, they knew he was the last man to ever let them down, as dear old Dad would say. McGowan and Sons Funeral Home had been in our family for over seventy years.

It was beginning to spit snow in the northern neck of the Shenandoah, although there was no accumulation expected. So far, it had been a dry but cold winter in the Virginias and to the dismay of all the 'dreamers', the forecast did not call for a white Christmas. I had called Joey earlier to tell him my plans were back on for a short holiday visit since my unexpected Boston jaunt a couple days earlier was short-lived. I didn't, however, call Adrianna, thinking I would just drop by Wolf Laurel and surprise her, hoping I didn't get surprised myself in finding Dandy Dan Laramie there. But I did call my best girl, Caroline, whom I found working on some files at her desk in Denver. "Hi, Dad. How are you?"

"Zipping down 81 on my way to Joey's for Christmas. Kind of a spur of the moment thing."

"I thought you had planned all along to do that," she said.

"I did, but I was sent up to Boston to collaborate with your Bureau cohorts who were having a tea party with the shoe bomber."

"You were in on that?"

"Not terribly much, I'm afraid. Your folks had it completely in hand and made sure *my* hand got nowhere close to his face."

"I haven't heard the results of the interrogation through our network as yet. Did they get anything out of him?"

"He didn't give up much. He mostly played ignorant, which was easy for him. But he *was* caught red-handed. Anyway, if you want the official story, turn on CNN."

"Hmm, okay. Say, I'm coming back to Virginia for a few days after Christmas. Will you be there?"

"I'll be in dubya-vee until the 27th and then in New York at New Years," I said.

"You're going up there to get in all that hullabaloo?"

"Not for fun and pleasure, that's for sure."

"Oh, then business."

"And you *know* the kind of business."

"Yes. I heard what al-Qaeda has in store, whether or not it materializes."

"Well, sorry I'll miss you," I aid. "Love you, Dad."

"Back to ya, sweetheart. What are you doing tomorrow?"

"Since I haven't made a lot of friends here, except for

a fellow agent, I thought I would go down to the Union Mission and be Santa's helper with the kids. You can't believe the number of entire families that are on the street. I'm going out today before the stores close to buy up a bunch of dolls. The Broncos have donated several dozen footballs to the Mission, so maybe, collectively, we can put smiles back on the kid's faces…at least for the day."

"That's my girl."

"Will you be seeing Adrianna?" she asked.

"You bet. I'll be stopping by there in a couple of hours."

"I'd like to meet her someday." She paused a couple of seconds. "Is she the *one,* Dad?"

"Maybe. We'll see." "Don't wait too long."

"That's what *she* said. Have you all been conspiring against me?"

Caroline laughed. "I've never had an occasion to speak with her."

"Well maybe someday I'll hook you up. You'd like her."

"And I can tell that you *definitely* do. Anybody who could tame the heart of the elusive wild man, Bruce McGowan, I've *got* to meet."

"Looks like I'm coming up on traffic now. A wreck, I think. Guess I'd better get off the phone. By the way, I mailed you your present today. Sorry it won't get to you on time. But I got yours and will open it tonight."

"Okay, Dad. Take care. And give my love to Uncle Joey and Aunt Cora."

"I will. Be safe, okay?" "Always," she replied.

Regrettably, I had missed out on a lot of holidays with Caroline, except of course in those early years before her mother flew the coop with her. During her teen years, when I was still with the Bureau and knocking down bad guys, I missed a great number of her recitals and soccer games, not to mention Christmas Eves. But then, following her year in the Peace Corps when she started William and Mary, just about the time I was able to settle down with a desk job in my waning years, she was too busy to find time for *me*. There were a lot of missed opportunities along the way about which I have immense remorse. When you've lived a self-absorbed life like I have done, a lot of distance can get between you and your kids, emotionally *and* geographically.

The sun, out bold and radiant on Christmas Eve day, was so brilliant that it hurt my eyeballs clean through my flight glasses. Even so, it made little impact on the 22 degree wind chill that seemed to penetrate my bones and crystallize my blood. It's hell to get that fragile. When I had finished pumping the twenty-five gallons that seemed more like fifty in the frigid elements, I cranked the engine and advanced the temperature on the heater control to a balmy seventy-five degrees. Before pulling out, a vision of me tending to customers in my bar somewhere in the Caribbean zipped through my brain. I was wearing Bermuda shorts and a tank top, trying to separate a couple of babes who had gotten into a fight over me. What a dreamer, eh?

Then I snapped back to reality when I heard rude honking behind me where a little old blue hair wanted my spot at the pump. I waved to her and said, "All yours, dear lady. Be careful you don't freeze your nubbins off out there."

About eleven-thirty I pulled off of Seven Bridges and into the gravel parking lot to a spot directly in front of the stately inn. Wolf Laurel looked much as I left it in September except there were no chrysanthemums or bougainvilleas gracing the footpath leading to the veranda. But Adrianna had festively draped the banisters with pine branches accented with bright red bows at each point where the greenery dipped. Strands of Christmas lights, which I'm sure were stunning at night, adorned the roof line and turret. I wondered if Adrianna had climbed up there herself to string and staple them down or did she engage the services of Super Jock Dan Laramie, the man who desperately wanted to play house with her.

I left my Glock in the Suburban this time so it could keep company with my trusty Winchester 700, assuming that the lovely proprietress had learned her lesson to refrain from offering rooms to Muslim terrorists and I wouldn't need them. It was hard to believe that it had only been three months since I had taken out a would-be suicide bomber and his Islamo-bastard leader. I wondered if Adrianna had gotten all of Professor Abouzar's blood removed from the grains of her hardwood floor. I can get pretty messy sometimes in my work.

When my boot heel hit the porch steps, the clonk startled old Burt the Cat who lay curled up on one of the veranda rockers, basking in the warmth of the sunlight. Then when he saw it was just me, he closed his eyes and rolled back up into a big furry ball. Good to see you too, old man.

I had noticed there were no other cars in the parking lot except for Adrianna's van. It not only meant Danny Boy was not there, but likely no boarders as well. Of course, it was Christmas and people were generally at home enjoying the time with their families. I figured, however, Adrianna would probably get some customer business at New Years.

I found the door unlocked, which meant she must have recovered emotionally from September's terror, enough maybe to trust the world again. It would certainly be unusual and even uncanny that there would be such a happening again in the out-of-the-way B&B. It was pretty much a freak thing that it had occurred *at all.*

When I entered the lobby area, I found no one about. I figured that Juanita, the maid, was home with her daughter, and Adrianna was probably upstairs in her apartment. So, I dinged the bell at the front desk. In short order, I heard footsteps in the hallway which prompted me to look into the hallway mirror to again check for leafy green things in my teeth or for any uninvited guests in my nostrils. I was wearing dark green cords, a starched khaki shirt and my Bvlgari, not the Hi Karate she had given me as a joke (at least I hope it was), so I not only *looked* good, but *smelled* good as well. And in my hand was the small, beautifully-wrapped box that contained her Christmas present.

When she saw me, her face turned a ghostly white. But she herself was an apparition…of the gorgeous kind, looking ravishing in her tight red sweater and parochial school style red and black plaid skirt. Her dark chestnut hair was pulled back behind her ears revealing two glistening diamond earrings that adorned her two succulent ear lobes.

"Skip!" she exclaimed. "I thought you…"

"Had abandoned you at Christmas? Not a chance."

She ran to me and I embraced her tenderly, immediately working my lips over hers.

"Oh how I've missed you," she panted in my ear.

With my juices surging like they were, I wanted to sweep her up in my arms and take her upstairs at that very moment to unleash my three months of pent-up passion. But I still had my travel bag in one hand and her gift in the other.

"You were supposed to be in Boston over Christmas. What happened?"

"It didn't quite work out. I was going to show the bomber the correct way to light his shoe and then make a Roman candle out of him. My compadres at the FBI were not amused. So I came home unappreciated."

She grinned and her perfect teeth dazzled as brilliantly as her earrings. "You're still a bad boy, aren't you? Just when are you going to get away from that kind of work and come back to me? I hear they're looking for a bus boy down at Clingman's Diner."

"Mmmm. Tempting, but I've never washed a dish in my life. Anyway, I'd probably break a couple and then my boss would yell at me, prompting me to shoot him."

"He's a *she*."

"Then I'd slap her around a couple of times." "She's every bit of ninety years old."

"Okay, then, I'd hide her walker. But I won't take a job where I can't pack heat."

Adrianna smiled. "Are you packing heat today?"

"Always," I replied, winking.

"I mean are you wearing a gun, bad boy?"

"It's in the Suburban," I replied. "I didn't think I needed to bring it inside this trip. Oh, wait. Is Danny here?"

"No he is *not*! And, I didn't take him to the dinner at the Greenbrier event, either."

"Good. Then I won't have to shoot him."

Adrianna held onto my hand and I thought for a moment she was going to lead me upstairs. But instead, she squeezed my fingers and then let go. "You want to have lunch or have you eaten?"

"Granola bar about seven. I'm famished. I was supposed to eat lunch with Joey and family. Will you join us?"

"No, no. They wouldn't be expecting me, and…"

"Nonsense. Come on. They'd love to see you again. Cora will have her homemade chicken soup simmering about now. It was my mom's recipe. Goes great with grilled cheese sandwiches. It takes me back to those snowy Saturdays when Joey and I went sledding. We'd be out in the white stuff for hours. Mom would have soup and sandwiches ready for us when we came in and we'd sit watching TV westerns the rest of the afternoon."

"Memories," she said, smiling. "How they sustain us. But if you don't mind, Skip, let me beg off. I've already arranged to meet some friends at the hospital. Santa will be there in the children's wing to hand out presents and a few of us are going to help."

It compelled me to think about my other darling who would also be devoting her Christmas to those in similar unfortunate situations. And it warmed my heart.

"Then will I see you later?" "I insist on it," she replied.

"What are your plans tomorrow?"

"I guess *you're* back on. A friend of mine who teaches at the community college invited me to her place for the afternoon. Her husband also died a few years ago and she was going to be alone. I half-promised her I'd be there. Will you spend this evening and tomorrow with me, then?"

"You bet. But tomorrow I will be having Christmas dinner at my brother's. You're invited, of course."

"Well then, I'll accept. But…I'll have you know that Cora had already called and invited me for Christmas dinner a week ago. And then when you bailed out, she told me it didn't matter whether you were here or not; she still wanted me to come."

"That was nice of her."

Adrianna then eyed the present I had laid on a chair. "Is that for me?"

I nodded. "You want it now?"

"Tonight or tomorrow at Christmas will be soon enough. What is your family's tradition? Opening presents on Christmas Eve or Christmas morning?"

"Actually, we exchanged gifts on Christmas evening as a family, but then Santa would come during the night and leave stuff for us kids under the tree. I carried that same tradition into my marriage, doing the same with Caroline until she was seven or eight."

"Then that's what we'll do," she said.

So, Santa's coming here tonight? And he'll leave me something under the tree?"

She laughed. "Your present is already under the tree. Tonight, I'll open your gift and you open mine before I go to bed."

I then gazed down at her with my serious Clark Gable eyes. "My dear, there's only one thing I want to unwrap tonight."

She put her arms around my waist and laid her head on my shoulder. I then buried my nose and mouth into her freshly-shampooed hair. She smelled delightful.

"And I believe I will let you," she replied softly.

She pushed herself away and held my bulging biceps in her hands. "You *have* been a good boy these three months, haven't you? Santa will only leave you a lump of coal, if not."

"I've been *very* good and have been saving up all that goodness for you."

"Well," she said, flushing a little. "I expect this will turn out to be a good Christmas after all. For you *and* me."

I hadn't noticed the tree she had placed in the corner of the dining room by the front window. It was decorated in a taste I would have expected from her. Pink and white balls and clear lights. A lovely white, silk garland began at the top of the tree and cascaded down the branches in a half dozen places. Under the tree were three beautifully-wrapped presents, at least one of which I was sure belonged to me. Seeing them, prompted me to take my gift for her and place it under the tree with the others.

"Nice touch on the tree," I said.

"Thanks. I try to have a different theme each year. I guess I felt kind of pink this year. Last year I was all alone and blue. So was the tree."

I smiled and squeezed her hand. "I'm glad I was able to be here to share Christmas with you this year."

"I wish you could be here every Christmas…and the other 364 days a year."

I dodged that bullet without batting an eye, telling her I had to get on out to Joey's. Lunch was supposed to be on the table at noon and I had ten minutes.

"Okay, then, when will you be back?"

"Not sure. When will you be through at the hospital?" "Oh, I guess around five. If you want, I can make dinner for us."

"How about if I buy you dinner at the Greenbrier? I owe you that, you know."

"That's pretty extravagant," she replied. "You don't have to make up for the other night."

"I want to. It's Christmas Eve. We'll dress up a little. Maybe there'll be some music there to dance to."

"Okay then. Sounds like fun. Do you want me to make dinner reservations?"

"If it's not too much trouble…and not too late," I said.

"Then it's a date."

"I kissed her and then turned toward the door. "By the way, are you not locking the door these days?"

"It would be a real deterrent to any walk-in guests, not to mention unfriendly. I do lock it when I leave, however. I'll be sure to leave the key for you in the usual spot."

"There's nobody staying here, I guess. I didn't see any other cars."

"Just you," she said. "Do you want your old room back?" She grinned.

I smiled back and winked. "I want my old *bed* back. The one upstairs."

On the way over to my brother's house, I was set to thinking how lonely it must be for Adrianna on holidays like Christmas. With no family left in the area, all she had were her memories of sweet times with her husband and little boy, both now long departed. She had told me before that she tended to avoid visiting her friends on holidays who still had young children at home. It just served to remind her of those happy days when little Johnny scampered about Wolf Laurel mingling with the guests or bugging her in the kitchen while she was making gingerbread men and chocolate chip cookies. She told me in September she would give up the rest of her life to have just one of those days back with him. But this Christmas she would have me and the company of my family who would hopefully take her mind off both the good and the bad that still haunted her.

"My darlings!" I said enthusiastically as I greeted Joey's girls, sweeping each under one of my arms and spinning them around a full turn in the foyer.

"We were hoping you'd be here, Uncle Bruce," said Molly. "How long are you going to stay?"

A voice then came from the hallway as a younger version of my old man appeared. "Not long, girls, if I know your Uncle Bruce. I'm sure he'll be spending much of his time at Wolf Laurel…for some reason."

"Yeah," I replied. "Just two or three days. But I intend to see a lot of you all while I'm here."

"You look a bit thinner since the last time I saw you," said Casey. "Have you been eating?"

"Let's just say I've been trying to watch what I eat, considering it's the time of year when we start packing it on."

"Well, lunch is ready," said Joey. "Let's go on to the kitchen."

It actually felt good for once to have *nothing* going on at Christmas. No one to be hunting down and no terrorist pricks to make disappear. This trip, anyway. Assad and Abouzar were long since put in their graves, and even if I *were* after anyone, I do have sets of rules and scruples about me. I don't kill people at Christmas. Unless of course they're trying to kill *me*. So, I was getting a small dose of what it would be like to retire from the government assassin business and have a normal holiday like most everyone else.

Looking across the table at Joey, his lovely wife, Cora, and their two adorable daughters, I had to smile. Their eyes laughed and danced as they talked. They were obviously happy and loved life to the fullest. A portrait of Americana straight out of a Rockwell print. It made me a bit envious, if not remorseful that I had made decisions in my life that left me feeling very much alone and living without purpose. A situation for which I could only blame myself. Hearing the girls giggle and tease their father was like listening to a piece of my favorite music…something classical with a dynamic tempo, punctuated by French horns and lilting strings. They were altogether a symphony of love and laughter. I closed my eyes and listened as the music of their words seemed to escalate into a climax. Their lyrics then faded as the image of one Caroline McGowan lit up my brain. She was nine again and was sitting across from me at the table, telling me about the dreamy new guy in her class. I was afraid for her then, just as I was now…only in a different way. She carried a gun. And at some point in her life, she may in fact find one pointed at *her*.

"I think he's fallen asleep." Molly giggled. "Is everything okay, Bruce?" Joey asked.

I opened my eyes. "Everything is…beautiful, Joey. I didn't actually fall asleep. *And* I'm not quite yet at that point when food will start falling out of mouth, either. I was just thinking what a wonderful family you are and I'm blessed to be sharing this Christmas with you."

Joey lifted his water glass. "Here here, brother. Great to have you."

I returned to Wolf Laurel around four-thirty, finding the key that Adrianna had left me, and went up to her apartment which was above the dining area. The place was quiet and lonely without her. But her fragrance was there. Sweet and sensuous, just like her. I took the liberty of showering, and as the steaming water sprayed out, an automatic smile broke out on my face. My big brain and little brain were remembering the day I joined her in the shower and…well, it was simply one of the most beautiful and intimate moments of my life.

Since we were dining at the Greenbrier where coat and tie are required, I knew I was in trouble. I hadn't brought with me anything but a couple of oxford shirts and pairs of slacks. I thought perhaps I could run downtown to Yarid's or some place to get a jacket, but then I realized nothing would be open on Sunday and especially on Christmas Eve. On a whim, I checked Adrianna's closet. No, I wasn't going to wear any of her clothes and go in drag; I just thought perhaps she had not discarded all of her dead husband's clothes.

Pushing aside scores of hanging garments, which also had her smell, I almost missed the Navy double-breasted blazer at the right end of the closet. Under the jacket on the hanger were also three neckties. The man had taste. I had to give it to him. I could tell he was well into the social scene, dressed all preppy in his silk Forzieri tie which was too spiffy for the likes of me, so I chose another one…a cotton-polyester Italian model with the name Renato Balestra on it.

I checked myself out in the mirror. The six-two, hundred seventy-five pound dude with the salt and pepper hair smiled back at me. He surely didn't look his age and if I do say so myself, he could still turn many a pretty head, the handsome yet humble brute that he is. The blazer was just a bit tight in the shoulders and upper arms, which supported the thin image I had of Mason from the photograph on the dresser. But the coat would do. The pair of gray slacks that I brought with me would work out just fine with it.

Adrianna came home about five-twenty just in time to

catch me modeling the jacket and tie in her free-standing floor-length mirror. Immediately, her rosy smile diminished and her eyes froze over.

"Skip," she said softly. "Why are you wearing Mason's jacket?"

The tone of her voice actually said, 'why did you get into my personal things and violate my past?' I hadn't even thought about it. Her seeing me in her dead husband's blazer and tie had to be a shock to her…a shock to her sacred memory of him. I then suddenly realized that for her the past and the present *had* to stay separate.

Quickly, I slipped the jacket off and said, "I'm sorry, Adrianna. I just didn't think how you would react, seeing me in the blazer. I'll put it back. I didn't bring one with me, and…"

"No, no. Don't give it another thought, Skip," she interrupted. The smile was back on her face and her eyes had softened. "It was just kind of a shock seeing you in it. Please, go ahead and wear it. It looks very nice on you."

"Are you sure? I can borrow something from Joey. I don't want to…"

"Nonsense. I'm okay with it. As a matter of fact, I prefer that you wear it."

I placed the blazer on the frame of a straight-back chair and swept my hand along its shoulders to knock off some lint. "I used to have a suede Navy blazer like this. It was a nice jacket, but it picked up everything except women." I paused and waited for her laugh at my joke, but I think it went by her. "Well, anyway, thank you. I will feel honored to wear it."

She gave me a peck on the lips and then quickly zipped off to the bathroom to run the shower. "I'll be out in a few minutes," she yelled. "Our reservation is at seven, so we have a little time. *And no, you can't shower with me.*" She then closed the door.

"I've already had my shower!" I yelled back. "I see that now! Sheesh, but you're messy."

Under my breath I said, "It could *really* get messy if you let me in there."

CHAPTER THREE

One could readily understand why the Greenbrier, a Five Diamond joint, is easily the swankiest, most picturesque resort in the United States. And right there in little old West by God Virginia. Sitting majestically for over two hundred years at the base of the Alleghenies, it is an impeccably beautiful place, unrivaled in its elegance. Being from the area and all, I had been there scores of times before, to include three years in a row to our military school's Graduation Ball in one of its elegant ballrooms. I have never failed to be in awe as I walk through the dozen or so grand sitting rooms that are decorated exquisitely with colorful wall patterns, furniture and carpets.

The sixty-dollar steak and lobster combination, however, was hard for me to swallow, even though they could have been the most succulent varmints that I had ever sunk my teeth into. I had stayed a week in motels for the same money I spent on both our meals and the order of drinks. But, I did get my money's worth, savoring every morsel of the fare and every second of the time spent with the beautiful Adrianna Wolf. How I had missed her those three months. A call or two each week had done little to satisfy my longing for her. And she had been good in not making me feel guilty about choosing my service to *all* the citizens of the United States, rather than just her. Of course, I was looking forward to servicing *her* a little later.

Back at the inn before nine, after she had *ooed* and *ahhed* over the pearl necklace I had gotten her and after I unwrapped the nice Seiko she had gotten me, we had a glass of Merlot, talked a while and turned in. Merry Christmas to *me*!

We slept a little late the next morning…me, till seven and her, just past eight, which was the hour I woke her after returning from a frosty Christmas morning jog down Seven Bridges Road. Afterward, it took a full ten minutes for my lungs to thaw out. I then showered while she made breakfast. When we had finished eating, she said, "Okay, let's get dressed. We don't want to be late."

I looked at the face on my new watch which read ten minutes past ten. "What's the hurry," I said. "Cora won't have dinner ready till two…unless you had planned to go earlier to help her."

"No, we're going to church."

"What?"

"My church is having a Christmas Day service.

"Today? When families are at *home* doing Christmas?"

"Well, I just figured if we're going to be sinners, we need to go and make things right with God." Ouch, I thought to myself. Hitting a guy where it hurts…right in the old conscience. "Don't you think that would be a bit hypocritical?" I had to somehow come up with a *de*fense as shallow as it sounded.

"Church is a hospital for sinners, my darling," she said. "What other place is so appropriate to go and pray for His forgiveness?"

Feeling lower than a snake's belly right about then, I was trying to wrangle myself out of it. "But I haven't been in a sanctuary more than three times in as many years."

"Then wouldn't you think it's about time? I need this, Skip. It's my spiritual vitamin."

Well, who was I to argue with her, and I really couldn't say, 'Just go on without me.' I knew God had been mad at me for a long time, and I also knew that if I in any way impeded one of His children from communing with Him, especially on His Son's birthday, the next time I went for a run, He might leave my carcass on the side of the road for the devil buzzards to pick up.

"Okay, I'm going," I said emphatically. "I've got to talk with Him about a couple of things anyway."

"*That's* my guy," she said. "But you can talk with Him anytime, you know, not just in church."

"Do you think He'll hear me?"

"He hears *all* of us, no matter how bad we are."

"And unfortunately, I'm as bad as they come," I said. She rolled her eyes.

It was the little white Methodist church on the hill where she had not only been sprinkled as a child, but where she had also mourned over the coffins of her son and husband. They had been buried in the ancient cemetery just off the east wall of the building.

I was correct in assuming that most everyone would be at home on Christmas Day with their families. But a few of the faithful, mostly the elderly whose kids were probably older than me, were already sitting quietly in the white wooden pews on red velvet cushions. Several turned their faces toward our direction and smiled as we passed by on our way to her usual pew three rows back on the right side. I'm sure they were wondering where Adrianna had found the likes of me…the heathen and scoundrel that I was.

We sang a few hymns and then the minister, who wore a white robe with black sergeant stripes on his sleeves, delivered a short sermon about the Spirit of Christmas. He was an old dude and I chuckled under my breath when I thought of a funny line I heard some time ago. '*When he was a boy, the Dead Sea was merely sick.*' Adrianna looked at me and noticed I was smiling. I guess she thought it was just a smile of happiness and joy, considering the spiritual setting we were in. But then during the remainder of the service I noticed that Adrianna was patting dry a tear or two that had run down her cheeks. And that set me to wonder if they were tears of joy about the Christ Child or of sorrow. Maybe both.

About forty minutes later, Adrianna's minister gave the benediction and another song was sung. And then all the old people stood up and began chattering warmly with one another. Some of the ladies had on hats of 1950s vintage, and the men, suits that they had obviously *worn* since the 1950s. Another picture of Americana. It all left me with a nice feeling. "I enjoyed this, Adrianna." I said afterward. "Thanks for bringing me. In a way, it makes me feel like a child again."

"You are, you know. *God's* child."

She was absolutely too good for somebody like me, the Godly spirit that she was.

It all seemed perfectly natural, us sitting at the Christmas dinner table with Joey and brood, like we belonged together, she and I. And we did look good together, if I must say so. Cora said so, too. Joey even nodded in agreement while still chewing his mouthful of ham and yams. Over dessert, we told funny stories about our childhood at Christmas, like our worst Christmas present ever and about the tree that fell over after our cat scampered through the branches to the top. Adrianna added one about her very large father who when playing Santa at her school play, lost his pants on stage in front of three hundred kids and parents. It was a day of laughter and merriment where no one was embalming corpses or weeping over the loss of a child or putting bullets in bad guys. Our hearts and our stomachs full, the women practically fell onto the parlor couches as Joey and I hit the front porch rockers.

As it had warmed up to a balmy forty degrees, our light-weight jackets were comfortable enough. Joey, as usual after a huge meal, cranked up a Columbian, which actually smelled fairly aromatic in a pungent sort of way. I almost accepted one, but being a non-smoker all my life, my Christmas dinner would probably be lying in the bushes.

"When are you going to settle down with that girl, Brucious?"

"Now don't *you* start on me."

"Who else is on your case?"

"Well, there's Caroline, who says she just wants her old man to be happy and not die alone in a geriatric facility."

"And?"

"And Adrianna herself, although she's been fairly passive it this trip. But I know what she wants."

"What does Bruce McGowan want?"

I leaned back in the rocker and interlocked my fingers behind my head. "I admit there are days I'd like to come back here, get married, and wake up next to her. But…"

"But what?"

"It's…just a little too comfortable for me right now."

"At fifty-four years of age? Shouldn't you be thinking about cashing in IRAs and joining a country club? After thirty plus years as an action man, don't you deserve a little comfort in your life? You've got a lot of miles on you, old man. I'd think you would be pretty road weary by now."

"Everything you say makes good sense, Joey. But I feel good about what I do. Like I'm useful. Making a contribution. I'm still in good shape and can do anything a twenty-five or thirty-year-old can do."

Joey blew out a silver plume of smoke. "But there are a lot more of those twenty-five year olds than there are dinosaurs like you. Let *them* take over."

"Ah, but they don't have what I have, little brother."
"Which is?"

"Which *are* experience, wisdom and a hell of a lot of things they don't teach young operatives today."

"Like forty-nine ways to kill a man with just one finger?"

I had to laugh at that. "You've been watching too many Bond flicks."

"What I'm saying is, if I had a good looking chick like you've got in there, I'd chuck it all in a skinny minute."

"But you already have a good looking chick."

"I mean if I were *you*."

"You can't be me. *I'm* me."

Joey grinned and shook his head. "Why do I feel I'm playing straight man to Groucho Marx?"

"Wait a minute," I said. "*You're* the one with the cigar."

I think Joey was getting a bit disgusted with my grade school dialogue. His eye rolling told me that. Or was it his Groucho imitation?

"Talk to me about Caroline. Is she still in Denver?"

"Yep. She graduated from the academy in October and is now learning the ropes of the Special Agent."

"I guess Darlene didn't take to her joining the FBI, huh?"

I nodded. "She'll come around. Right now, she's hardly speaking to me, thinking I was the one who encouraged her to apply. Actually, I didn't. Caroline made that decision on her own."

"Well, whether you did or not, I know you have to be worrying about her."

"More than you know, Joey. Believe me, I've spoken a lot with the Creator about her lately."

Joey nodded a couple of times and then we both became reflective for a few moments. And right about that time, a sudden feeling of gloom came over me that lasted for the remainder of the afternoon. I wouldn't call it a premonition or anything foreboding, but I get these feelings every once in a while just before something calamitous occurs. Magnum used to call it his 'little voice.'

It was just after four and although I didn't want to rush

Adrianna with her visit, I thought we should be getting back to her place. When Joey and I went back inside, I could see that she was ready to go as well, thinking she should not over-stay her welcome, especially on Christmas Day.

When we arrived back at Wolf Laurel and settled in, Adrianna picked up on my mood.

"Is anything wrong, Skip? You're so quiet."

I smiled at her and shook my head. "Naw. Everything's fine. It was a nice day, huh?"

"Nice people, Joey's family. I love the girls. They're so adorable and full of life. And I can't get over how polite they are. Most kids won't give grown-ups the time of day."

"It has something to do with good genes. They take after their uncle, you know."

She grinned and kissed me on the lips. "Their uncle also *tastes* pretty good."

We sat on the couch the remainder of the evening and watched TV like some old retired couple, pausing to swallow a few bites of the apple pie we brought home with us. I really wasn't hungry for anything else. Later, I pulled a cold Heineken from the fridge and nursed it until I fell asleep on the sofa. I think I woke up briefly when Adrianna pulled my Weejuns off and covered me with a blanket.

At mid-morning on Tuesday the 26th, my cell phone rang. It was the Birdman.

"Hey, Condor," I said. "A belated Merry Christmas. You're not working today, are you?"

"Always. I may have shut the office down for a few days, but I'm always on the clock. And so are you, by the way. That clause was also on *your* contract as I remember." He chuckled.

"Funny. Did you and Mother Hen have a nice Christmas?"

"Splendid, Bruce. And were things good with your family there in West By God?"

"Splendid as well. So, what gives?"

I heard his pipe chomping on the other end. "Well, I'm not sure. I got a call from the Bureau's Assistant Director… you remember Sean Leary?"

"Yeah, I remember. He came on with the FBI the same year I did. Fast tracker. I wasn't surprised when he went to the top as quickly as he did, brown-noser that he was."

"Well, anyway, he said the Denver office sent up a communiqué which ultimately got to him, that someone slid an envelope under the door that was addressed to you. The security camera picked up the image of a man dressed in a Broncos ball cap, jacket and sunglasses. He zipped the envelope under the door and was gone in two seconds."

"To me, huh? Did anyone open it?"

"The Bureau people took it to their lab to check for any white powdery substance, and finding none, did open it. A single white piece of paper was inside with one line typed on it, probably by a computer keyboard. It read: *"Dear Bruce. How's the weather where you are?"* It was signed simply with a 'W.'"

"A 'W'? Like in George Bush?"

"What do you think that means, Bruce?"

"That the President is wondering if I'm having a good time on my mini vacation?"

"I have absolutely no clue."

"I wonder why someone would send me something like that by way of the Bureau?"

"Well, it's probably someone from your past who doesn't know where you are or where you work now and took a chance that the Bureau would still know how to get in touch with you. Sounds like some kind of taunt to me. Maybe someone you put away a few years ago?"

"That's what comes to my mind as well. What did it say on the envelope?"

"To Special Agent Bruce McGowan."

A dozen different thoughts and questions began to dart through my mind.

"How did Leary know to call you, Lionel?"

"He knows you're part of my team. People at *his* level know the names and whereabouts of every operative, covert or not, in *all* organizations."

"Scary."

"He *and* the Director are wondering what this is about."

"They're not alone." And that's when the laser-like pain shot through my heart. "Does this sound to you at all coincidental that Caroline is assigned to the Denver Bureau?"

"I had thought of that, Bruce. But it could be just that…a coincidence."

"I'd like to talk with Denver's agent-in-charge. Do you have his name?"

"I don't, but can get it for you."

"That's okay. I'll just call there and let them know who I am."

"Call me back if you need any help with that. See you Thursday, Bruce." He then clicked me off without so much as an adios, as usual.

Adrianna said she had to run a couple of errands, one of which was to take back a blouse that Maid Juanita had gotten her. Several sizes too large. Her absence would allow me to mull over the alarming message from some secret admirer who was probably concerned I was not freezing my gonads off, wherever I was. But, considering that the message had a threatening ring to it and delivered by a man who appeared bent on remaining both anonymous and disguised, I didn't have a good feeling about it. Especially since it was shoved under the door where my little girl worked. Which prompted me to call her cell.

"Hi," the sweet voice began. "I am currently unavailable at this time; but if you would leave me a message, I will get back with you as soon as possible."

After the beep, I left my message. "Hi, sweetie. It's your dad. I hope you had a nice day yesterday. Call me when you get a chance. Love ya. Bye."

I then called her number at her apartment, getting the same message.

As soon as I hit END, I called information for the Denver, Colorado Federal Bureau of Investigation. I was then connected by my cell provider as a courtesy. After two rings, a woman's voice answered.

"Denver FBI. May I help you?"

"Yes, thanks. My name is Bruce McGowan from Washington, D.C. May I speak with the Special Agent-in-Charge?"

"May I ask what it is about, sir?"

"Sure. It's about an envelope with my name on it that was slid under your door this morning."

There was a pause. "Just a moment, please."

I waited for what seemed like a minute and then a man's voice came on the line. "This is Special Agent Pettyjohn. Are you Mr. McGowan?"

"I am."

"And you already know about the envelope? How did you find out?"

"I still have Bureau connections."

"I'm sure. I do know that you're a retired Special Agent. I have your entire dossier printed out in front of me."

"Don't believe everything you read."

"Actually," he replied. "You had quite impressive career. Several commendations…one for valor."

"Yeah, yeah. All that and a quarter might buy me a cup of coffee. Hey, is my daughter Caroline there today?"

"No. She took leave until after New Years. She's supposed to be going where you are. Virginia, right?"

"Actually, I'm not there now and will be in New York by the time she gets into the area. I tried reaching her by her cell to no avail. Has she called in today?"

"No," replied Pettyjohn. "I didn't expect her to. When people are off, I try not to bother them. Our folks put in enough time, twenty-four seven, as it is. You remember those days."

"Mmm, yeah. Well listen. If she happens to call in before I get to her, will you have her call me?"

"Sure thing. So, how *is* the weather where you are?"

"Do you have any idea what that's about?" I asked.

"No, I don't. Not a clue. Could be just a prankster or could be someone you nailed in your past life who wants to make a statement."

"I wish the message was a little clearer. Were you able to pick out any distinguishable features from the video tape?"

"Not really. The man appears to be at least fifty as there was a tuft of white hair showing from beneath his ball cap. The collar of his coat was up around his neck. There was no facial hair that we could make out, and we could see his eyes. His jacket was open, however, and holding his jeans up was a belt with a large silver buckle."

"That's it, huh?"

"He definitely didn't want to be recognized which indicates he may be a threat."

"What I'm worried about, Agent Pettyjohn, is that if he does have some kind of vendetta against me, does he also know that Caroline is one of your agents?"

"It's possible. Our web site lists our agents now. It's not a secret who they are. But even though her last name is McGowan, how would he connect her with you?"

"I don't know," I said. "But these days there is so much information out there on people, anyone can find out practically anything on anybody. That's what bothers me. There *was* that piece on her in the Post which mentioned her dad was retired FBI."

"Don't worry, Mr. McGowan. We'll look out for Caroline. This guy, whoever he is and whatever his agenda is, will be on our radar."

"Thanks. That eases my fears. I know you will."

"What are you doing now that you're retired, sir?" "Still in government service," I replied.

"Doing what?"

"Oh, personnel management. You know, procurement and terminations."

"Hmmm. What you're *not* telling me is in fact telling me *something*. I won't press that any further. I think I know now how you found out about the envelope so quickly."

"Is it possible that you can scan both the envelope and letter and send it over a secure fax line?"

"It's possible. When will you be at your fax machine?"
"Friday morning."

"Then call me when you get back there and let me know the number."

"Will do. Thanks."

"I'll have Caroline call you when I get up with her. And again, don't worry. She can take care of herself. I have no doubt."

"I hope so," I said. "Goodbye."

After Adrianna returned, we had a quick lunch of some chicken salad she had made, then I tried Caroline's cell a couple of more times. I still got her recording.

As much as Caroline enjoyed the outdoors, I kind of thought she might have hooked up with a new beau or some girlfriends she may have acquired and gone hiking or skiing in the Rockies. She had sent me a photograph in November of her and two other young ladies, also appearing in their twenties, standing in some high country real estate with a backdrop of aspens, firs and snow-capped peaks. As she wasn't due at her mom's for a couple more days, I figured she was taking advantage of her days off with some fun and leisure.

And as Adrianna could see that my last evening's moodiness had not subsided, she sat down opposite me in her sofa chair and took my hands in hers.

"Okay, Mr. McGowan. What gives? You're as jittery as a mouse trapped in the corner by old Burt downstairs."

I didn't want to tell her about the note addressed to me, but I didn't want to lie to her either. So, I told her just a few pieces.

"It's just that I've been trying to get hold of Caroline all morning. She's not answering her cell or home phone."

"Well maybe she's out having fun and is in a bad cell area. Colorado, isn't it?"

"Yes, I thought of that as well. Maybe you're right. But I've never known her to be inaccessible more than a couple of hours. She always checks her phone and never fails to call me back. I've tried reaching her for over six hours."

"I'm sure she's fine," Adrianna replied. "You're just a typical dad. Believe me, kids have more stuff going on in their lives to occupy their time these days…versus keeping up with their dads."

"Yeah. Maybe you're right. I'll wait a while and then call her back. I'm sure she'll be calling me any time now."

I waited until just before nine, seven her time, before trying Caroline's cell and home phones again. Maybe she did take off on a camping trip, which in fact added a new concern, considering footage I saw on the Weather Channel of sweeping unexpected snowstorms out there, not to mention avalanches. But I think she would have told me her plans. She always told me about trips and activities she was planning. But, I sat stewing yet another hour.

At ten sharp I called her mother. It had been over two months since I had talked with her…at Caroline's graduation from the FBI Academy. She had given me the cold shoulder, although her husband, Ned, was quite affable. He always reminded me of an excited puppy waiting for his bowl of Kibbles and Bits.

"Darlene. Bruce."

"Hi, Bruce. How are you?" She actually sounded up-beat, to my surprise. It must have been the holidays and her anticipation of seeing Caroline.

"Fine and dandy, and you?"

"Okay, as well. Is anything wrong? I'm just wondering why you're calling so late."

I didn't want to alarm her about not being able to get hold of Caroline…now for *twelve* hours. It would set her off and I didn't need that. In her subtle way, she had promised that if any harm ever came to our daughter while she was performing her agent duties, harm would be inflicted upon *my* person tenfold.

"Everything's okay. I just wondered when Caroline was coming to Virginia."

"I thought you knew that. She'll be here on Friday. I'm picking her up at Reagan at two-something in the afternoon."

"Oh, that's right. Have you talked with her today?"

"No. I did yesterday morning before she went to the shelter. She was helping out with Christmas and the meals there, you know."

"Yes, I know. I did try calling her today, but whatever she's doing, she must be out of cell range."

She paused a moment before responding. "You sound… different, Bruce. Are you sure nothing's wrong?"

"Nothing's wrong. I just miss our little girl, that's all."

"Well, I guess you'll be seeing her sometime around New Year's."

"Unfortunately, I'll be in New York during her visit to Virginia."

I heard her sigh. "Well, that sounds like it's *your* problem, then. As always, job before family."

One of her unkinder shots. The *old* Darlene was back. "I won't go there," I replied, snottily.

"Is there anything else?" she asked, even snottier.

"No, I reckon not. If you're talking with her the next couple of days, tell her that her old man called."

"Fine," she said in a tone that sounded like 'I'm not your secretary, you know.'

"Okay then. See you."

I then heard the dial tone without a goodbye, which told me she was either still harboring ill feelings after all these years about our marriage going sour or because I called too late. Maybe I had committed *coitus interruptus* between her and Ned.

CHAPTER FOUR

Wednesday the 27th I waited until about ten-thirty to call Caroline's numbers again…and again getting only her voice message. I hadn't slept much during the night, still feeling the dread that had manifested itself inside of my bones, given what I considered to be the threatening note coupled with the fact that I was still unable to reach Caroline. It was just not like her to be unavailable. And what if her office had been calling her? She was an FBI agent, for goodness sake.

Not standing it any longer, I told Adrianna I was going for a run and would be back hopefully before my ticker stopped. I did some of my best thinking, beating the pavement in my Nikes. A wispy, lazy layer of low, gray clouds moving across the morning sky was little by little being melted away by the ever warming sunshine. And then it was not long until the sun was finally out in all its glory, once again painting the Greenbrier countryside a beautiful gold and brown. Vapor spewed from my mouth with each breath, and after my first mile, steam began rolling off my forehead. The temperature, still hovering around thirty, was actually bearable the further I ran, thanks to a calm breeze and the radiant warmth of the sun on my face. I also had on two layers beneath my jogging suit which prompted me to unzip my jacket.

I then heard someone coming up behind me and turned to see that it was another runner. The muscular-framed woman about thirty-five or so jogged past me at light- year speed, making me feel like I was a turtle stampeding through peanut butter. So, I picked up my pace. She might have had a tight body, but danged if she wasn't an ugly cuss. However, she appeared to be enjoying her run and loving nature, in spite of what it had done to her face.

Making the turn at the gate of the old McGill Farm, I began what I believed was my third mile. A red Ford F-250 of the seventies vintage with wooden sideboards approached from my front and began to pass by me. Three small Hispanic children hanging onto the boards, looking as frozen as popsicles waved and smiled at the poor man running on the road and whose face fully revealed the pain he was inflicting upon himself. I waved back. No sooner than they had passed, the cell phone in my jacket pocket rang. I slowed my pace and looked at the number.

"Thank God," I said between pants. "Caroline."

I hit the *send* button. "Hey, sweetie, I was wondering about you."

There was no immediate answer, so I pulled up to a full stop to listen. An electric jolt suddenly fired through my arteries when I heard the man's voice.

"So, I am now 'sweetie' am I, Bruce?"

"Who the hell is this?" I shouted.

"An old friend, Bruce." The man's voice was mealy, sounding somewhat like Truman Capote. "How's the weather there?"

My heart began racing and thudding well beyond what I had just put it through.

"Who are you and why do you have my daughter's cell phone?"

"How's the weather, Bruce?" he said again. Now I was getting scared…for Caroline's sake.

"I've had about enough of this!" I shout back. *"Now, I'll ask you again; why do you have this cell phone?"*

There was an unearthly, even diabolical pause, and then he replied. "You mean Caroline's phone?"

I then thought my heart would pound right out of my chest.

"Goddam you son-of-a-bitch. What have you done with my daughter?"

The caller's voice did not change. It was still calm, monotone and nasally. "She's a pretty girl, Bruce. My, my, my but you did well siring this beauty."

I was now suddenly choking back tears along with the anger. But somehow, I managed to get a grip on myself *and* my voice to ask the next question. "Have you taken my daughter?"

He laughed. It was almost a cackle. "I will be back in touch with you, Bruce. But, for now, I want you to suffer, thinking what I might have done to her. Paybacks are hell, which is where you will *be* as you ponder Caroline's fate. Goodbye. Until tomorrow." And then the phone went dead.

My knees suddenly went weak and I sank into the ditch beside the road. A vortex of pain tore through my chest with every wild beat of my heart. I was actually sick, feeling spasms of nausea, like I was going to heave. And then the tears finally came. Sitting on the bank behind the ditch, I buried my head in my knees.

It seemed like a thousand voices were feverishly whispering all at once in my head, creating a kind of white noise that would at any moment cause my brain to explode. "Who was this devil? Why did he have Caroline? But did he really have *her* or just her cell phone?"

I couldn't think anymore and wanted to deny that the conversation even took place. But then I hit the redial button on the phone. Three, four, five times it rang and then her recorded voice kicked in. "Hi, I am currently…" I let her voice continue until the beep and then I yelled like a mad man into the phone. *"Answer the phone, you son-of-a- bitch! Let me talk to my daughter!"*

But the man neither answered nor called me back. He had said he would call tomorrow and I supposed that he meant it. I sat on the edge of the bank for a full five minutes, still weak-kneed and feeling I was unable to get up. Several passing cars slowed, their drivers gawking, likely assuming that I was either drunk or a derelict. No one stopped.

And then I saw the red truck again preparing to overtake me from the opposite direction. I stood and then stepped into the lane to flag him down. The driver braked to a full stop, thinking that I might actually step in front of him, as I was *prepared* to do whether he stopped or not. The man shouted to me in Spanish which told me he spoke very little or no English.

"Es usted loco?" (Are you loco?) "Lo siento, senor,"

I replied. "Por favor. Yo tiene una emergencia. Llevame a los Siete Puentes Road?" (I have an emergency. Can you take me to Seven Bridges Road?)

I'm sure the man was thinking I could be an axe murderer, causing him to fear for his kids who stood peering over the back of the cab at me. He paused for a moment and looked me over. I had no weapon in my hand and *did* have on a rather expensive jogging suit to match my Nikes.

"Okay. Si, Señor. Entre."

I was shaking and obviously had the look of fear in my eyes. The Señor was either wondering if I was being chased by someone or on hallucinogens. He didn't say another word the rest of the way. After he dropped me off at the end of Seven Bridges, I uttered a quick 'gracias' and then ran wildly the few hundred feet to the steps at Wolf Laurel as the kids in the back of the truck waved goodbye.

When I charged through the front door, I startled Adrianna who was in the inn's kitchen making brownies to take to a reading event at the library. Seeing the frenzied look on my face, she exclaimed, "My God, Skip. What's wrong?"

Finding it difficult to say the words, I blubbered something, which probably caused her to wonder if I was having a seizure or cardiac arrest from pushing myself too hard. Finally, I got it out. "It's Caroline. Somebody's kidnapped her!"

Adrianna dropped the glass platter she had in her hands on the wooden kitchen floor and it shattered into a dozen pieces. "What are you saying? Who? Where?" That's about all that came out of her mouth. I paced back and forth, wringing my hands.

"I don't know. *I don't know!*"

"How do you know this?" she asked.

I tried catching my breath, but continued to hyperventilate. "A man…a man called me on her cell and told me that. Somehow he *knows* me. Maybe some vendetta…maybe a ransom, I don't know."

Adrianna wrapped her arms around herself as though she were cold and leaned against the wall. "I can't believe it. Why? Why would someone do this?"

I shook my head and sat down in one of the dining chairs. She came to me, leaned down in front of me and held my hand. I shook loose and grabbed my cell again, dialing the operator to connect me with the Denver FBI. This time the Bureau's assistant, noting my sense of urgency, sent me directly to Lewis Pettyjohn.

"Yes, Mr. McGowan. What is it?"

"The man who left the note at your office yesterday morning has Caroline."

"What do you mean…*has* her?"

"He called me on her cell phone and said he had kidnapped her somehow, somewhere. It had to be Christmas Day. Tell me she's called in to you all the last couple of days.

Maybe he just stole her phone."

"No, she hasn't called in," Pettyjohn said. "I'll get a couple of agents out to her apartment right away. This is uncanny. I've never known an agent to have been kidnapped."

"I'm flying out to your location as soon as I can get a flight."

"I understand. Let me know when you arrive and I'll send a car for you. I'm also putting this on the wire to all law enforcement. The Director will also be apprised immediately."

"Okay. Until I get there," I said. "Keep me updated. My cell number is…"

"I'm looking right at it, Bruce."

"All right then. Do what you can do to see how valid this thing is. I hope to be there in a few hours."

Adrianna heard my conversation and said, "I'll help you get your things together while you make your flight arrangements."

"Thanks," I said, still trying to calm myself down. "I'll call to see when the next flight goes out from Charleston."

"I'll drive you to the airport."

"No, that's okay. I'll get Joey to take me." "I insist, Skip. Really."

"All right," I replied while dialing Information again for Yeager Airport.

There was a flight leaving at three-forty for Cincinnati with Denver as the ultimate destination. I booked it and called Joey to fill him in. He was, of course, horrified and told me that maybe it was all just a big joke. A sick joke at that. I told him that that was unlikely, considering the creep knew me and knew where Caroline was. It was possible that he was merely taunting me and hadn't taken Caroline, but I didn't think so. Joey said he and Cora would pray hard for her and then he told me to be careful.

My next call was to Lionel Byrd. I told him I was not

going back to D.C. or ultimately to New York, giving him the whole story.

"Was there a ransom demand, Bruce?"

"Somehow I don't think this is about money, Lionel. It's about me."

"Somebody from your past life?"

"No idea. The way he was talking to me, I must have done *something* to piss him off."

"I will do what I can at my level to help the Bureau, Bruce. Even lend my resources if necessary."

"And I will do what I can to end this man's life,"

I said. "Just be a father, Bruce, and stay out of the investigation. Let the FBI do its job. She may be your daughter, but she's one of their people."

"You know I won't." Byrd sighed.

"I know. But whatever you do, don't expose CTT."

"I'll be careful not to do that. You know you'd be all over this yourself if this were one of *your* girls."

"Yeah," he replied. "But try to take a back seat and let them handle it."

"I hear you. I have to go, now, Lionel. But first I have one more call to make. The one I dread the most."

"Darlene?."

"Yes."

"Do you want me to do that for you?"

"No, it has to come from me," I said.

"I don't envy that task. Telling a mother her daughter is missing and may have been abducted…well, there's only one piece of news that's worse."

"Don't say it, Lionel. I don't want to even *think* it."

"You say the man was going to re-contact you tomorrow?"

"He said he would."

"You know the Bureau has ways to triangulate the call with the cell towers in the area to determine where he is within about fifteen miles."

"I know all that. Goodbye, Lionel. I'll keep you apprised."

I quickly collected my clothes and kit bag and then Adrianna and I walked toward her van. I had three weapons in the Suburban and knew I couldn't get them past airport security, not having a badge. Even before the new policies had gone into effect, my State Department ID alone would not get me through security if I was packing anything more dangerous than a ballpoint pen. As I didn't want to leave my arsenal on wheels at Wolf Laurel, I asked Adrianna to follow me to McGowan and Sons where Joey would lock the vehicle and weapons in his garage along with the hearses.

It was normally two hours to Charleston, but braving the icy patches and Turnpike police, I actually made it in an hour and a half. Adrianna and I said very little to one another along the way. But what *could* we say. It was neither a time for small talk *or* fun talk.

I pulled her van to the curb at the small mountain terminal and hurriedly kissed her goodbye. I told her to be careful going back and she said she would pray that Caroline was returned to us unharmed.

My Christmas holiday had begun with the promise of love, joy and family. But now the year would end for me experiencing the angst of fear, worry and uncertainty. And I hoped to God it would not end in sorrow.

As soon as I touched down in Denver, I called Pettyjohn who said his S.A. would be at the passenger drop point at 1830. I would have just enough time to deplane and zip through the terminal. As I only had a small roll-along and a hanging bag, I would not find myself stalled at Baggage Claim.

When I stepped through the sliding glass doors onto the sidewalk, the agent's car was not hard to spot...a black Crown Vic with black walls and no hubcaps. But just to be sure it was not an unmarked Denver P.D. unit, I walked up and tapped on the passenger side glass. The window then came down and I peered inside, finding a very pretty young woman with auburn hair about twenty-eight or thirty. I thought I had the wrong car for sure.

"Mr. McGowan?" she called.

"Yes," I replied, opening the rear door and tossing in my bags. I then slid onto the passenger seat and held out my hand. "I was…"

"You were expecting a male agent I can tell. Maybe somebody in his fifties wearing a black suit and a forty inch waist."

She was a spunky-sounding girl who I was sure could put the other SAs in their places.

"I…really didn't know who to expect," I said.

She instructed me to fasten my seat belt, like I didn't know any better, and then she pulled the shift lever into 'drive.'

"Caroline has your eyes," she said. "Is that a compliment?"

"Just an observation, that's all."

I studied her for a couple of moments which she picked up on with her peripheral vision. She was naturally pretty even without any make-up, and had a healthy, wholesome look about her.

"I didn't catch your name?"

"Sorry," she replied. "I'm Starr Ravenel." She held out her hand again which I took.

"My name's Bruce, Starr. Some people call me Skip. You can call me either."

"Then *Skip* it is. Are you holding up all right?"

"Pretty much on edge right now, as you can imagine, not knowing what happened to Caroline."

She shook her head. "It doesn't make any sense. Obviously, this is not a random kidnapping, considering the note and call to you. Has he called you back?"

"No. It's like waiting for the other shoe to drop. I have never felt so helpless."

"I will be working on the case along with Lew Pettyjohn, Skip.

Everything else goes to the back burner. We're getting our heads together as soon as I get back to the office. It'll be a late evening for us."

"I'd like to be in on that. I'm ready to roll with you." "Only as a private citizen and concerned father, Skip. You'll be staying out of the investigation business. I know you're a retired agent and had a stellar history, but you can no longer act in an official capacity."

Her warning did not set well with me and I thought about taking issue with her on the spot. I *had* to be involved in the investigation. This was apparently about *me*. Ideally,

Pettyjohn and folks would review all my cases over the twenty years, pick my brain about any perps that may have stood out, we'd find him and Caroline, and I would put a bullet in the prick's head. Pure and simple. I kept my tongue, however, and gave her a generic response. I would pick my battleground at such time anyone attempted to shut me down.

"I understand what you're saying, Starr. But you *do* need me involved to a degree for information purposes *and* for my law enforcement expertise."

I thought I caught a slight nod. She knew I would not stand for being shoved off into a corner somewhere to twiddle my thumbs.

"What do you do now, Skip?"

"I still work for the government…for the Department of State. My card."

Taking one from my card holder, I placed it in the cup holder.

"So, what do you do for the State Department?"

I desperately wanted to give her my full job description complete with responsibilities that were not necessarily included on the State Department list, but I had to respect the Birdman's request that I not broadcast my association with CTT. Our little club needed neither the visibility nor any adverse publicity, especially considering that the liberal press, the ACLU and even members of Congress didn't even know we existed.

Anyway, I'm used to going off on my own little killing sprees with no one but Birdman and my Zulu cohorts the much wiser.

"Oh, just a desk jockey shoveling papers from eight till four," I lied.

"Are you part of Tom Ridge's new organization?" "Homeland Security? No. But some of my work has to do with national security."

Which was the truth. "So, where are you from, Starr?"

"Georgia. A little town you never heard of near Savannah."

"Why did you join the Bureau?"

"Well, my dad was a cop and I had always been intrigued with law enforcement. I majored in Criminal Justice at UGA, and then applied to the FBI. The rest is history."

"Go Dawgs," I said. "Criminal Justice was my major and Caroline's as well."

And then just mentioning her name returned me to the reality as to why I was sitting in Starr's car. She picked up on my sudden somberness.

"Who went by her apartment today?" I asked.

"I did, Skip, along with another agent. Caroline's red Nissan was still sitting in the parking space in front of her apartment which is 16 A on the second floor. We got hold of the Super and he gave us a spare key. First, we found nothing had been disturbed. No sign of a struggle. Then I went through several drawers, ultimately finding a set of keys which had a spare key to the Altima on it. I checked inside of the car and the trunk. Nothing. No blood or anything, thank God.

Since the car was still in its spot, we figured she was probably abducted between her apartment and the car sometime after she returned from the Union Mission.

"We talked to the neighbors on the upper and lower level, and no one saw her or heard anything. Then we checked the stairwell and the area around it to see if there was evidence of her being drugged…looked for needles, chloroform cloths and etc. Nothing as well.

"Finally, we went by the Mission. They said it was nearly dark when she left there. I guess it would have been redundant to ask if anyone saw any suspicious characters hanging around, considering a great number of folks there are derelicts and troubled people. But the manager said no one appeared to follow her when she left."

I shook my head and grunted. "Like she just totally dissipated. I can't tell you the anguish I'm going through."

"We'll get this guy, Skip. And whether or not he does have Caroline, we'll see her soon…safe and unharmed."

I nodded and looked out of the right side of the car toward the city lights. "I pray to God you're right."

Starr pulled the Crown Vic into a parking garage around the corner from Stout Street and then we walked the short block to the building. After being buzzed in, we passed the receptionist I guessed was the young lady with whom I had spoken. She smiled a rather understanding smile, and then I was ushered into Lewis Pettyjohn's office.

Pettyjohn, a dapper-looking Black gentleman in his mid-forties was well-groomed and wore spectacles that made him look more like a professor than a G Man. Tall and big-shouldered, he looked as though he could have played some kind of ball, college *or* pro. When I entered the room he rose and extended his hand. A reassuring smile was on his face.

"Hello, Bruce," he greeted. "Lewis Pettyjohn. Call me Lew."

I took one of the chairs opposite his desk and Starr took the other. Standing off to the left of us was another man, who a bit portly, was wearing a K Mart suit. Pettyjohn introduced him.

"Bruce, this is Detective Wendell Rogers with the Denver P.D. I have engaged Denver's services to collaborate with us on Caroline's alleged abduction."

Rogers then walked to where I sat and shook my hand. "I believe you can throw out the word 'alleged,' Lew,"

I said. "I think it's for sure that this wacko did take my daughter. He has her cell and she's missing."

Pettyjohn seemed to want to slow everything down now that I had sprung my horse from the starting gate. "Let's get acquainted and start at the beginning, folks. Detective Rogers, Mr. McGowan is a retired Special Agent…what, two years now, right? He works for the Department of State and lives in the D.C. area. I shared with you that an unknown suspect who signed his name 'W' slipped a note in an envelope under our door that simply read, *"How's the weather, Bruce?"* And as Mr. McGowan has not been able to reach his daughter the past couple of days, and neither have we, we believe the same man who wrote the note possibly abducted her. The man called Bruce's cell phone using Caroline's phone. He claims he has taken her, but did not provide either the particulars or circumstances. So, let's talk this out. What did the man mean by asking Bruce how the weather was? Is there any significance to the word 'weather?'?"

"Maybe he simply wanted to know where Mr. McGowan was at the time, so that he could get a fix on him," offered Rogers.

"I don't know," replied Starr. "I think it goes deeper than that. Generally, nut cases like this like to play psychological or word games by throwing in puzzles or symbolic jargon that will frustrate the game show contestant. He won't come right out and say what the ransom is or whatever else he wants. Like a cat toying with a mouse before he eats it."

I didn't like the analogy, but had to admit she could be right. My turn to talk. "I'm thinking that somewhere along the way I nailed this 'W' guy for something and he's on some kind of vendetta. He's probably turned over every stone to try finding me and thought he could do that through the Bureau. Maybe he thinks I still work for the FBI."

"I agree, Bruce," said Pettyjohn.

I continued. "But if he does have Caroline, how did he manage to get the drop on her. She's a tough kid and extremely vigilant. I taught her to be that way early on. She's a Black Belt and was on the Olympic shooting team."

"Maybe an accomplice or perhaps he somehow gained her confidence at the shelter Christmas Day," reasoned Starr.

"Maybe. And maybe that is the place we need to start and back-track."

Pettyjohn shifted forward in his chair and locked eyes with me. "Let me lay this out for you, Bruce. There is no *we* in this investigation. You're too close to this *and* you're no longer in law enforcement. You're important to us as a witness and as someone this guy will be contacting. You're a valuable resource only…not John Wayne. My team will find Caroline and take this man down. Am I clear?"

As I don't like being lectured to as to what I can and can't do, I was getting pretty hot under the collar about that time. "Let me make *my* position clear. I will do whatever I need to do as a father and as a quite capable policeman, *Lew*."

"Ex-policeman, Bruce."

"Whatever. Let me ask you, Lew. What would *you* do if Caroline was *your* daughter? Sit back and just wait for the situation to unfold?"

"I realize it would be difficult for me. But, yes. I would rely on law enforcement to do its job. And we will, Bruce. This thing will be my office's primary focus. I have set up a Task Force on the case which includes Agent Ravenel and Agent Bob Murphy. You'll meet Bob tomorrow. Detective Rogers here and CBI Lieutenant Harriman, who has also been apprised of the matter, will join in. I'd like you here in our office as much as possible so that when this nut case, as Starr calls him, calls you back, we can listen in. And when he does, we can work with Caroline's cell service to try pinpointing his location. Her file indicates her cell service is with Rocky Face Communications."

"I'll be here," I said. "What time?"

"Just in case he calls early on, how about seven?"

"Fine."

Pettyjohn then picked up a file from his credenza. "This is *you*, Bruce. Twenty years of you. I had it sent over the wire to me earlier today. I have summaries and After Action Reports on every case you were on." He leaned back and smiled. "You were a real action figure. You either nailed or were in on the apprehension of several mob kingpins, both Mafioso and Russian. You were wounded twice, once seriously when you took down two bank robbers in an alley."

"I feel the effects of that one every day."

"And you served on several Task Forces that took out both domestic and foreign terrorists. Very impressive. And no black marks anywhere in your record. The kind of file that should serve as the example for all young candidates going through Quantico."

"You're making me blush," I said, which brought a smile to Starr's face.

"Here's what I'm going to do, Bruce. You and Starr will sit down tonight and go through every one of your cases to see if that creep is in there anywhere. Anybody who made even the idlest of threats against you, I want to know about it. If necessary, we'll run down every perp you put away, threat or not. Detective Rogers will field a team to look through every file on known and suspected molesters in the area and cross reference any of those names with our files.Off the top of your head, do you know of anyone, especially in the State of Colorado that you put away?"

I cringed at his use of the word 'molesters,' but then

took a deep breath and answered. "I'll think about it. A couple of cases do come to mind, and I'll visit them when I peruse through the file."

"Then I'd like you to get off somewhere with Starr and see if anybody clicks. This man definitely has it in for you and is using Caroline as a pawn. Where are you staying tonight?"

"I thought I would go to Caroline's apartment. Who knows? This asshole could even be in her building."

"I have a list of all occupants from the Superintendent. We're already checking them out," said Pettyjohn.

Starr then added, "I'd like to go with you to her flat if you don't mind. He might even call you back tonight."

"He said he would call me tomorrow. And he will, all right. I know this kind of creep. He's getting his jollies knowing that I'll sweat it out tonight and not get any sleep. He wants me to feel like a hungry little bird with its mouth open, waiting for him to drop in even the tiniest morsel."

"Then you all go on," said Pettyjohn. "And Bruce, here's my card with my cell phone number on it. You all call me as soon as you hear from him."

Rogers gave me his card as well. "Sorry this happened, Mr. McGowan. I'll also be in touch."

Pettyjohn rose and put a vice grip on my hand. "Bruce, I don't mind telling you that the very thought of someone having abducted Caroline makes me ill. But, rest assured, every law enforcement agency in the state has or will have this on their radar. I sent Caroline's picture around. No press is to know about this until I say so. We don't want this guy to go underground."

CHAPTER FIVE

Starr was one of the girls in the Rockies photo Caroline had sent me. They had skied together once and on a couple of occasions gone swing dancing with some guys. Over Thanksgiving, Caroline flew down to Savannah with Starr to spend Turkey Day with the Ravenel family. As Starr had become rather close to Caroline in their two months of service together, I knew she was nearly as upset as me about the probability that she had been abducted.

I realized I hadn't eaten since about ten-thirty, so Starr and I picked up a pizza at a joint called Dino's and then took it back to Caroline's apartment. The apartment complex, called *Sundowner*, sat off of Highway 58 down over a hill among a grove of pines and hardwoods. There were six two story buildings all in a row off to the left side with a large parking lot on the right. In front of Building 6, I immediately saw Caroline's red, two-year old Altima in a parking space directly across the sidewalk from the walkway leading to the concrete stairs. Her apartment was the end unit on the back side of the building on the second floor. A balcony which I presumed to be Caroline's jutted out toward the far end of the parking area, over-looking a good bit of the parking lot and a row of pines. I stood for a moment outside of the building looking around, trying to envision how Caroline could have allowed herself to be taken. Even though I realized that Starr and fellow agent, Bob Murphy, had scoured the entranceway, the stairs and the second floor landing, finding no evidence of either a struggle or items that may have been utilized to render her unconscious, I still shined the beam of my mini- light over every foot of the area.

Off into the far corner of the parking lot I spotted a white Impala which appeared to be an unmarked police unit. Detective Rogers had said he would place a plain-clothed officer in the parking lot to watch the place. He would also give the officer our descriptions so that a hoard of squad cars would not be down on us in two minutes when we entered Caroline's apartment. Starr lifted a finger to signal him.

Starr had also kept the manager's key. When she turned the knob on Caroline's door, I was praying that my daughter was inside waiting for us after all. That somehow this was all just a cruel joke perpetrated by some asshole who had found her phone where she had dropped it on a hiking trail and then decided to have some fun with her old man. Perhaps a friend had picked her up and that was why she left her car at the apartment complex. I even considered that Caroline had met some guy and had gone out with him a couple of times. And then maybe she dumped him, but not before he learned enough about me to begin his campaign of harassment. But then there was the 'weather' note, and its author knew too much about me for it not to be real. I knew deep inside that *he* was the man who had her and no one else. We found the apartment dark and eerily quiet. Reality finally set in. Actually seeing that Caroline was not there caused my heart to sink. I was almost sick to my stomach, which on top of my hunger pangs made me feel weak and dizzy. I handed off the pizza to Starr as thoughts of eating even one bite worsened my nausea. I hadn't felt that way in years. I had faced the business end of a gun several times, been shot, clubbed and faced death in other ways. I had seen bodies riddled, blood splattering against walls, and flesh melting away from napalm. But I had never been as afraid as I was at that moment.

Starr turned on the light switch, put down the pizza and drew her Glock, cradling it with both hands and pointing it around the room. It was doubtful that the creep would be there waiting for us, knowing that the apartment was probably being watched. But Starr was a careful cop and I could see that she did her job by the numbers. As she went off toward Caroline's bedroom, I walked deeper into the living room. Immediately, my eyes fell on the red, flashing light on the phone sitting on the end table by the couch.

I waited until Starr returned to the room and then pressed the message retrieval button. The generic voice said, "You have five messages." The first three were from me and the fourth from a telemarketer selling life insurance. But the last voice sent a chill through my neck and down my spine.

"Hello, Bruce. I knew you couldn't stay away. How did you find the weather here? I guess you're dying to know who I am and where your precious little girl is. She's right here with me, Bruce. A little sleepy, but she's perfectly fine…at least for the moment. Sleep well tonight. Me? I'm going to sleep like a baby. Don't worry, old man. You're not out of time…yet. But your time is coming. Believe me, you *will* pay dearly." And then we heard the dial tone.

The pain tore through my chest again and I balled up my fists. Starr and I then looked at one another, saying nothing for a few seconds. I saw the ire in her eyes. And I'm sure in my bitter grimace she saw the hatred in mine.

I played the tape again and then a third time. After writing down the words so that I could analyze them in more detail, I switched the answer machine to its back-up tape and took out the one with his message on it. I realized that my hands were shaking, but I knew it was from anger and nothing else. The prick did not scare me, except what he might do with Caroline.

"Sit down, Skip," Starr said. "I'll get you something from the ice box. What do you want?"

"A beer if you find one. Thanks."

When she left the room I eased my buns into the sofa chair and then closed my eyes for a moment, trying to realize what must be happening with my daughter. Where in God's name did he have her? And why? Just to get to me? Did he want money?

"All right, Skip," Starr said after returning with a long-neck Coors. "Now that you've heard this guy again, what are your thoughts?"

"Well, he still sounds like Truman Capote and the statement he made…"you will pay dearly"…is either a reference to a ransom payment or that I did something to him and he wants revenge."

Starr nodded in agreement. "And, he insinuated he's drugged Caroline when he said she's 'a little sleepy.' Maybe from chloroform or via a needle."

I closed my eyes again and tried to visualize from his voice who he might be…the voice that had by now become embossed in my brain. My own inner voice was desperately trying to remind me of something, but I just couldn't put my finger on it.

"This dweeb's voice," I said, "I keep thinking I've heard it somewhere before. Especially the way he pops his P's…"

"What do you mean…pops his P's?"

"You know…when he said 'perfectly' and 'precious'? He sounded like he was spitting the P out from between his lips. I can imagine a wad of spittle flying out of his mouth."

Starr nodded and then laid my file on the coffee table between us. "I think we need to start going through this and see if your 'dub-ya' is in here somewhere."

I picked up my file and pulled the contents from the fasteners, giving Starr half of the material. It had been put together by Pettyjohn in chronological order beginning with my first year of service.

In 1980, after twelve years in the Army with the Special Forces, I hired on with the Bureau. The first couple of years were rather uneventful, which generally happens with newly-appointed Special Agents. The Bureau likes for its S.A.'s to groom themselves before getting their feet wet. In early 1982 I was on the team that took down Russian mobster Sergey Gaponecko for running a protection racket, strong-arming small shop-keepers to cough up obscene amounts of cash every week to not only stay in business, but stay alive. Shots were fired in a Hoboken spaghetti joint and when the smoke had cleared, two hoods lay dead, both having eaten bullets from my service automatic. The third man, Sergey, was captured and got life. I guessed that he was still pulling time. But neither his given or surname began with a W.

And then in 1986 I had left two other heroes dead, the bank robbers I mentioned, who were trapped in the alley a block away from the bank. One of them plugged me before I could empty *my* gun on them. Could be that a family member with the first initial 'W' was out for revenge, but I didn't think so.

My Denver gigs were more white-collar than anything. On one case, after I had spent hours going over literally a ton of bank and payroll records, I got the goods on the Vice President of a national Savings-and-Loan operation, one Lawrence Persinger, for the embezzlement of more than three-hundred thousand dollars over a four year period. I popped in on him with a cohort and arrested him without incident. He had no hard feelings about it as far as I knew. And I wouldn't think his type would pull anything like kidnapping his arrestor's daughter to get even.

I was feeling a bit frustrated at this point. In the forgotten attic of my brain there was something or someone that wanted to come out. But, nothing readily materialized.

Was the kidnapper *anywhere* in my file? Unless we just happened to stumble onto something, I felt our efforts for the evening may prove futile. And one thing for sure… before we found out *where* he was, we had to find out *who* he was.

I watched Starr work over the other half of my arrest records as she continued to nibble on pizza. She was smallish in build, but just like Caroline, I would have bet she was a stick of dynamite if her fuse were ever lit. Her green eyes were fiery and she definitely said what she was thinking. In another life I might have gone for her. Maybe even in *this* life, had it not been that I was over twenty years older and at the moment consumed with getting my daughter back. And then there was the Lady of the Inn back in West By Gawd Virginia.

"Okay," she said, swallowing a bite of the pizza. "I may have something here. Remember the guy, Jonas Karn?"

I then slapped my hands together and clicked my fingers. "Yes! That's it! That's the correlation. The Weatherman Underground. He's the guy with the voice."

"I remember studying about this group," Starr said. "They were mostly active back in the sixties and seventies. Home grown terrorists that sprung out of the Students for Democratic Society. They actually issued a Declaration of War against the government, blowing up banks and government buildings. *The Days of Rage* they called it. They even bombed the Pentagon in the early seventies to protest American bombings on North Vietnam."

"Yeah," I added. "Most of these subversive clowns like Ayers, Robbins and Tomashevsky gave themselves up or were taken down by COINTELPRO long before I hired on with the Bureau. But Karn was never found. He was the most violent-natured of the lot. In 1975 he set off a bomb in a restaurant in Colorado Springs near Peterson Air Force Base, specifically targeting aviators who were known to frequent the place. Two pilots were killed and a slew of others, injured. One of the aviators I knew from Vietnam.

Karn then dropped off the face of the earth, but the Bureau never closed out the case. When I was assigned to a resident office in Detroit in 1986, we got an anonymous tip about him. We found him working in an auto factory in Dearborn. I'm sure, as the file must read, I was not too gentle with him."

"I *see* that," Starr replied, eyes wide and eating up every morsel of the report, seemingly with glee. "He testified at his trial that you used harsh even criminal apprehension techniques. "…*and then Agent McGowan threw me into a corner in a room at the factory and jammed his fist into my throat, cutting off my air. As I lay gagging on the floor, he kicked me in the ribs, breaking two of them, and then smashed my testicles with the toe of his shoe…*"

"Ergo, the Truman Capote voice," I said. "He's now wearing orthopedic underwear."

Starr smiled and tried to stifle a giggle. She obviously got into this stuff. She continued. "…*and then he put his face close to mine yelling about one of the aviators being a friend of his. The beating was brutal. I will never be able to have children or even an erection. Sexually, I am dead below the waist…*" "And when I find him," I added, "He will be dead all over."

Starr was still grinning. "I don't know why I think this kind of thing is funny. It really isn't."

"Especially not to men," I said. "You were a pretty brutal bastard back then, McGowan."

"I did what I could for justice and the American way."

She shook her head slowly, obviously trying to figure me out, then returned her eyes to my file.

"Looks like no charges were placed against you, though."

"Back in those days, during the Reagan years, no one would do so."

"Says he got thirty-five years and was eligible for parole in thirteen. Apparently, if this is our man, he got out. Thirteen years for the murder of two servicemen. Justice, huh?"

"It *is* him. I'm *sure* of it, now," I remarked. "And we know that it's purely a vendetta."

"So, this 'W' initial means what? Weatherman?"

"I'd say that's a good guess. Again, word games. I think he was testing me to see if I was smart enough to come up with the 'weather' correlation with his little riddle and his 'dub-ya' sign-off. He definitely wants me to realize who he is."

"Do you think he's back in Colorado Springs?"

"That's where we…uh, you all can start. But I suspect he's more local, considering that he abducted Caroline here and now knows that I've come to her rescue."

She glanced up at me and then back down to the file. "There's something else here, Skip. A post script in the file provides that Karn's wife, Elaine, who was active in the WUO but was not arrested along with her husband, committed suicide about a month after he began his sentence. Sounds like this may be what the kidnapping is all about."

"Hmm, I think I remember that. I suppose he blames that on me as well."

"You took something from him and now he has something of yours."

I then realized that taking away his masculinity was only a small part of his vendetta against me. The physical pain I caused him was personal enough, but losing his wife…

Starr laid her part of my file aside and a look of perplexity formed on her brow. "I'm still wondering how Karn would know about Caroline…that she was your daughter and serving with the Bureau here in Denver."

"As we talked, he likely pulled up the FBI site on the internet, and seeing the McGowan name, and the fact that her father was a retired Special Agent, he put it all together. I also think this bastard made it his business…his passion to learn everything he could about me. He might even know

I'm in D.C. A few questions here and there would do it. He probably even kept tabs on old J. Edgar and knew what style of dresses and ladies underwear he wore."

Starr laughed. I hadn't seen her brilliant smile to this point. It looked good on her.

I continued. "And if he truly remembers me, he knows I'll be coming for him. I assume that's what he wants so that he can lay a trap for me."

She shook her head.

"Like Pettyjohn said, Skip. Leave it to us. We'll decide what the best course of action will be. We need your brain…not your muscle."

I didn't respond to that, but gave her a dismissive flick of my hand. Then I got up and went to the fridge for another Coors.

My daughter kept a neat place, obviously taking after her mother. There were several pictures of her and another girl stuck to the refrigerator door by magnets. There was also one of her FBI graduation class and then a larger one with her, her mom and her mom's Pekinese. Butt ugly mutt. But there was none of ugly, dear old dad, however. It made me realize that it had been years since I had even had my picture taken with her. I would certainly fix that once Caroline came back to me.

A flurry of emotions kept taking hold of me the entire evening. I seemed to alternate between anger, fear and sadness. Having just about convinced myself that it was indeed the creep, Jonas Karn, who had taken Caroline, I tried to remember his face. I knew he was not only a dangerous psychopath, but an unpredictable one as well. Most of them are. If what he said at his trial was true, I figured he had not raped Caroline. Anyway, I had blocked *that* image out of my brain to this point. But I had no way of knowing if there was second or even third accomplice. Who he would have commit such an act. Maybe he would get his jollies watching. And it was thoughts such as these that were leaving me feeling even more helpless than I felt before.

Around nine, Starr announced that she was leaving to go back to her place, but would return in an hour.

"Return?" I asked.

"Yes. I'm staying here tonight. And I get Caroline's bed. You get the couch. It's a sleeper."

"Why?"

"Why do you get the couch? For obvious reasons. I'm a girl…you're a guy. It works like that."

"No. I mean why are you coming back?"

"Because this guy might come back here and try something."

"Like what? He sure as hell knows what I can do to him."

"Perhaps he drew you here so that he can take you and the entire apartment complex out with a bomb."

"And of course you would like to be here to die with the rest of us."

"Let's just say I want to be here in case he does show up or calls back," she said.

"Whether you're here or not, Karn could probably get to me anytime he wanted. He could be sitting somewhere out there with a sniper rifle ready to plug me as soon as I hit the bottom stair. I appreciate you staying here to protect me, but I'm a big boy. It's not necessary."

"It's just as much for the rest of the people in the complex that I'd be here. I'll be checking under the stairwell and elsewhere around the building as I go out to see if he's planted anything. And the city detective is sitting out there as well. But we'll still need to be super hypervigilant."

"It's Karn's game, Starr. And he's the game show host at this point. I don't believe he'll come after me. He wants me to find *him*. Catch me if you can…that's the name of his game. It makes him feel powerful and in control."

"I'm coming back just the same." "Suit yourself," I replied.

After Starr left, I began going through Caroline's things to see if she had any notes lying around that could somehow be connected to her abduction. Maybe she received a phone call from Karn where he pretended to be someone else or someone from one of her social projects. I checked the kitchen cabinet drawers for bills and letters, her clothes closet, and the old Army foot locker I gave her, which she was using for storage. There was nothing out of the ordinary. I then checked the drawer in her night stand and found the 9 mm Beretta she told me she had purchased as a back-up. Locked into the grip was a loaded clip. I then took it into the living room and shoved it in my coat pocket, hoping that I would ultimately find good use for it.

I suddenly realized I had forgotten to call Adrianna to tell her I had arrived in Denver. And I had also forgotten that it was eleven o'clock her time. She had been in the periphery of my mind all the time, but I had had a more pressing matter to deal with.

"Oh, Skip," she said. "I can't imagine what you must be feeling. I'll keep praying you'll find her soon and that she hasn't been harmed."

Actually, she *did* have an inkling what I was feeling, having lost her own child under different circumstances, but to the grave. And I was praying that Caroline didn't end up the same way.

"Well, I just wanted to let you know. Sorry I called so late. Guess I'd better go now."

"Take care, Skip. Call me tomorrow. I'll be praying all night. I love you."

"And I love you," I said. It was a good time for each of us to say that. There are generally two circumstances guys find themselves in that make it easy to say the 'L' word…in the heat of passion and when he or his mate is troubled.

After we had hung up, I finally made the call I most dreaded. It was a quarter past eleven in Virginia, and the ringing of the phone alone at her time of night would be alarming enough.

After the third ring, a man's voice answered.

"Ned," I said. "This is Bruce McGowan. Can you put Darlene on?"

"Yeah, sure." I heard him call "Darlene!" She then apparently answered him from another part of the house. He replied "It's your ex. Pick up."

I heard a click and then her voice. "Bruce, why do you keep calling this late at night? What is it this time? Is anything wrong?"

"I'm afraid it is, Darlene. Now don't go to pieces on me, but Caroline is missing."

"What do you mean…missing?"

"I think she's been abducted by someone," I replied.

"What? Oh, God! What are you saying? Who? What?"

"I'm out in Denver now…at her place. There's a man who called me yesterday and said he has kidnapped her."

There was then only an unholy silence on her end; but after a moment I could hear her shuddering breath followed by a series of sobs.

"Oh, Bruce. Why? Does he want money? Just tell me… tell me something. Tell me she's all right."

As calmly as I could I said, "I don't know if she's all right, Darlene. He says she is…that she's sleeping. I think maybe he drugged her."

"Oh God, oh God! You have to find out! You have to go get her! You're a government agent, for God's sake. You should know how to do it."

"I'm working with the FBI on it. Maybe we'll know something more tomorrow."

The sobs were now more frequent. "I can't believe this is happening. If it weren't for you, she wouldn't be doing what she is and would be somewhere else."

And that's what I *didn't* want to hear out of her. "This is not the time to lay a crippling guilt trip on me, Darlene. I'm suffering here *too*."

"Just find her, Bruce, goddammit. You get our daughter back. You hear me?!" And then she hung up.

In my anger, I flung my cell phone across the room into the seat back of Caroline's couch and slammed my fist into the kitchen cabinet door. I knew Darlene would be upset and then predictably turn her anguish onto me. Right then, I despised her more than I ever had. But I also despised *myself* for despising *her*. Then at the same time, I felt sad for Darlene. Her daughter…our daughter…was in the worst kind of danger. Darlene had to strike out at somebody, and I was the only target she had at the moment.

Suddenly, my cell phone began ringing. I froze. The weatherman, Karn, was calling again. Or maybe it was Darlene calling back to apologize. For a moment I just looked at the phone like it was some kind of noisy, blinking monster that if I picked it up, would devour my hand. However, I walked over to it, saw the number and breathed a sigh of relief. I actually wanted it to be the creep, which would in fact get me that much closer to getting my daughter back.

"Hello, Lionel," I said.

"Tell me what's going on, Bruce."

"The man with the note does have Caroline, Lionel. We think he's a guy who was with the '70s terrorist group The Weather Underground. I took him down in '86 for the murders of two Air Force officers in Colorado Springs. Obviously, he's out now and wants to make me bleed…at Caroline's expense."

"I remember the group well. They're still on our radar even after all these years. A revival of the old Weatherman group is known as Prairie Fire, although now they claim to be peacemakers. What's the suspect's name?"

"Jonas Karn. At least I'm 90% sure it's him. I need you to do me a favor, boss. Run him through your system. And

Interpol. I need to know when he was released and where. I want to know who his family and associates are and what brand of toothpaste he uses. Everything you can get."

"I assume the Bureau is doing the same on your end."

"I'll be meeting with their Task Force tomorrow.

You have as much information as they do at this point. Concentrate especially on the Colorado Springs area. He was *from* there, blew up the restaurant there and was incarcerated there. Somehow he found out that Caroline was my daughter and here in Denver with the FBI."

"Perhaps he knows you're with the team," Byrd commented.

"I doubt it. Otherwise, the note would have found its way under *our* door. That's the one good thing about all this."

"Okay, Bruce. I'll get on it first thing in the morning. You know the team will be on mission at New Years, so I really don't have anyone to spare to come out and work on this with you. If we're uneventful in the Big Apple, I'll send Chuck and Palmer to dig out this Weatherman character. I know that it's nearly a week away, but it's the best I can do. Maybe it'll all be over by then with a good result. I hope and pray that it will, anyway."

"Okay, thanks, Lionel. I'll keep you apprised of any developments."

"Good. The Mrs. and I will say a prayer for Caroline… and for you. Goodnight, Bruce."

"Goodnight, sir."

Just after ten-fifteen, Starr returned with her kit bag containing her toothbrush and skivvies, and a change of clothes.

"So," I said. "Do you intend to shack up with me the entire time I'm here?"

Obviously, the smart-ass question did not set well with her. She gave me a disgusted look and zipped on to Caroline's bedroom. When she returned to the living room a few minutes later, she had on a set of pink, woolen jammies that intentionally made her look very *un*provocative. I assumed she was taking no chances with the likes of me. But, whether she realized it or not, she didn't have anything to worry about even if she had come out in a baby doll French maid outfit. She was only slightly older than my daughter and womanizing was the last thing I had on my mind.

Taking a few moments to call Pettyjohn at home, Starr filled him in on the findings from my Bureau arrest file that the '60s hippy terrorist, Jonas Karn, AKA the Weatherman, just moved to the top of the food chain on our list of one. As he and his nouveau underground organization, the WUO, were already under the FBI's and CBI's radar, now they would be placed under the microscope. There would be more talk about it tomorrow.

Starr then plopped down in the sofa chair opposite me to where I was sitting on the couch and again picked up the section of my file on Karn. Without looking up, she said, "So, Skip. What did you do with Caroline's Beretta?"

I was becoming more and more impressed with this little gal. She had me dead to rights.

"You're very insightful," I replied. "Not to mention nosy."

"Remember, I was here earlier today and went through every inch of this apartment. What do you plan to do with it?"

"There's a creep out there who's gunning for me. Is that a good enough answer?"

"As long as you don't go gunning for *him*."

"The thought has crossed my mind."

"I *know* that. And that's another reason I'm here." "You think I'll accidentally shoot myself?"

She looked up from the file and placed her green eyes on me. "Do you have a carry permit?"

"No. I don't need one."

"Explain that," she said. "You're now retired from the Bureau. So, why wouldn't a private citizen need one?"

"Let's just say my current job requires it." "Okay, then. Tell me more about what you do. Something tells me you're not the paper pusher you claim to be."

"Let's just say I'm still in law enforcement. Can we not leave it at that?"

"If I'm going to spend however long it takes to find Caroline and the Weatherman character, I need to know everything there is about you."

"Why can't you just be satisfied I'm only your

co-worker's father who's here trying to get his daughter back?"

"Because I don't know if that father is some kind of renegade who will go off like a cannon and get my butt fired."

"I won't do that, Starr. I won't do anything that will embarrass you, jeopardize your job or get you killed. Any action I take will not be implemented with you anywhere around."

"Which means you intend to do your own groundwork."

"I'm not going to sit here or park my ass in your office all day long waiting for this maggot to come to *me*. He may want me to squirm a while and then when I can't stand it any longer he'll wait for me to make a mistake. He wants me to go looking for him. Don't you see, that's his game?"

Starr tossed my file back onto the coffee table.

"I guess you're going to do what you're going to do. But let's get something straight; when you're with me, you do what I tell you. When you're at the division, you play it by our rules. If you go off on some tangent by yourself and break the law, you'll be treated as any other criminal and we will take you down." I glared at her but knew I had to swallow the words that wanted to come out.

"Understood. Your rules."

She nodded. "Okay, then."

"By the way, I need to use Caroline's car."

"All right." She reached down under the chair for her purse and produced the set of keys. "There's a spare apartment key on this ring as well." She tossed the keys to me.

"Thanks," I said.

Her eyes were still on mine like two lasers. "So why can't you tell me what your job is with the Department of State?"

"I didn't say I can't."

"You won't then."

I looked back at her for a few moments and then got up to walk over to the sliding glass door. Peering down over the balcony, I saw Rogers' plain clothes cop sitting off well away from all the other cars looking rather conspicuous in the white Impala. Through the windshield, I could see the red glow from his cigarette every few seconds when he took a drag.

"Did you check the apartment for bugs?" I asked.

"Yes, we did. I ran the bug detector over every area of the place."

I then returned to the couch and sat facing her with my elbows on my knees. Why not, I thought. She was right. I would be spending the next few days with her at my elbow and she needed to know exactly who I was.

"What I'm about to tell you has to be in strictest confidence, Starr. You are not to tell Pettyjohn any of this, although he's probably figured me out by now. Tell me now if you feel you can't keep this from him."

"How can I make that promise if I don't know what the information is?"

I then leaned back onto the sofa and closed myself off like a clam, saying nothing further.

"Okay," she said. "I will promise…as long as what you tell me is not against the law. I take it that it isn't, since you work for the government…that is, if you really do. So, who are you…an American version of 007?"

I laughed. "Ironically, that's what the department assistant, Moneypenny, calls me."

She smiled…just a little. "Go on."

"I'm a member of a rather covert faction of the State Department that hunts and takes down known or suspected terrorists, foreign or domestic. We are fed information through Interpol, agencies like yours and confidential sources. Mostly, when we handle things the public, the Congress and other law enforcement departments never get wind of it. We take care of the problem quickly and quietly, and everybody in Americagets to sleep soundly at night."

Starr's young eyes were as big and wide as fifty cent pieces. "Government assassin. I guess I need to be impressed."

"Nothing to be impressed about. I do my job like anyone else. It doesn't make me feel any more important than what you do or anyone else in law enforcement does."

"Okay. Now I think I feel a little better about you having the Beretta."

"I feel better about that, too. This Weatherman character, Karn…he's a terrorist as much as any member of al Qaeda or the Taliban. He's proved that in the past, but now he's just an ordinary thug."

"So, are you out for the creep as a father or as Bruce McGowan, Terrorist Hunter?"

"Both, actually. But I have to consider which one of me will put a bullet in him. The father will kill him out- right. The terrorist operative will try to capture him to determine if he has a new agenda. These anti-government types never get it out of their system. A few may continue their campaigns in some fashion, and others may become university professors in a venue where they can spew out their poison in the classroom and propagandize impressionable young minds."

"If you must involve yourself in this beyond assisting us

capture this Karn, I prefer that you act as the government man, not the irrational father."

"That will be up to him. Okay, enough about me. Who is Starr Ravenel?"

She pulled her legs up under her and leaned to one side on the arm of the sofa chair. "Just a small town girl, and like I said, the daughter of a cop. I love astronomy and so did my mom. She used to call me Starbright which also caught on with my dad and friends. My mom died when I was two, by the way. Anyway, I never get tired of looking at heavenly bodies out there."

And neither did I. But I didn't say that out loud. "Well, you can do some real stargazing in this part of the country. When I looked out a while ago, the sky looked as though it was peppered with five carat diamonds."

"I live about ten miles from here out of the city lights on the way to Castle Rock," she said. "My telescope sits out on my balcony and few nights go by when I am not out there picking out all my little stars. I can name several hundred. Caroline came down a couple of nights to watch some astronomical happenings over a glass of wine."

The mention of my daughter's name obviously changed the expression on my face, which prompted Starr to say,

"I know this is tough on you, Skip…not knowing."

"I…just feel so helpless in all this, like this guy has my gonads in his hand."

Neither of us said anything for a few long moments.

Then Starr announced she was going to bed.

"There's extra bedding in Starr's closet. I hope the mattress on the pull-out is comfortable and you can get some sleep."

"Fat chance of that," I replied. I always wondered why 'fat chance' and 'slim chance' meant the same thing.

CHAPTER   SIX

I woke suddenly somewhere around three in a cold sweat having just had the one dream that had haunted me for thirty odd years. It was that same sleep-invidious dream that made me relive that day in 1970 when my Special Forces A Team attacked the hostile village in the Mekong that we found to contain a number of heavily ingrained, hard-core Viet Cong. It was the one moment in combat I wish I had back.

It was the day the hard rain came. We were tired, miserable and soaked to the bone. It was also a day of bad decisions. We had shot and killed nearly everything that moved. We had discovered that almost every man, woman and child had some kind of weapon. When the fire fight had finally died down and the hamlet had been neutralized, we went looking for other targets of opportunity. After spotting a glint from the window of a thatched-roof hooch, I propelled a 40 mm high explosive round from my M-79 through the opening. Almost immediately, a small child having just had one of her arms blown away stumbled through the doorway of the hut emitting horrifying screams. She looked directly at me with eyes of helplessness and then fell head-long into the mud.

Over the years as this dream continued to invade my

unconscious, an unconsciousness I wish could be stripped of its memory, the face of the little girl began to change. This night of the nightmare, it was the face of six-year-old Caroline McGowan. Although I desperately tried to wake up before she died, I couldn't. My unconscious mind would not release me. In my dream I had gone on into the hooch to check for other victims of the explosion, and there found the little girl's mother, dead. I turned her over and upon seeing her face, fell to my knees and let out a silent scream, my face resembling that horrified face in the haunting painting by Munch. The mother was not Vietnamese at all, but twenty-six year old Caroline McGowan. Both mother and child were dead and wearing my daughter's face in two stages of life.

But relief finally came when my *conscious* brain turned back on. I wheeled my body out of the sofa bed and suddenly realized that in my sleep I had been crying. My cheeks were moist with tears and my heart was racing as though I had just run a marathon. Psychologists who make it their business to analyze dreams and nightmares believe that they are manifestations of our fears…fears that we have not yet begun to conquer. In the tangled fibers of our brains we store unprocessed thoughts and trepidations, especially those conscious fears that we intentionally repress only to have them unveiled in our dreams.

As I stood at the patio door looking out into the early morning darkness, I knew there was only one way this nightmare about Caroline would never recur. I had to first find her safe and unharmed. Then I would have to put a bullet in the brain of one Jonas Karn. I should have killed the son-of-a-bitch when I took him down fifteen years before.

I did sleep a little after that, off and on, probably because I had only caught a few winks the previous night. And it had been a long day, beginning with the first phone call from the Weatherman while I was on my morning run, the long flight to Denver, and the mental anguish the rest of the day that had spent me both physically and emotionally.

About six-thirty, I heard Starr running the shower. After I drained the lizard in the hallway toilet room, I went to the patio door to see if the police officer was still there. He was. In the very same spot. When Starr came out at a quarter till seven, I hit the shower and then knocked a few whiskers off. I had to do a double-take, wondering who the haggard-looking character was that glared back at me in the mirror. My eyes were puffy and I noticed that the worry lines along my forehead were a hell of a lot more prominent than normal.

After I had donned my jeans and a black turtle neck, I came out into the living area and found that Starr had put on a pot of coffee. The aroma was intoxicating.

"Good morning," she said. "Did you get some sleep?"

"You didn't hear my snoring?" I replied.

"Was that what that was? I thought someone started up a chain saw during the night."

I smiled. It was the first inkling I had that she had a sense of humor.

"I guess if we're going to be at your office by seven-thirty, we'd better get a move on. Do you want to get a Mickey D's biscuit or something along the way?"

"Pettyjohn will probably have donuts. He usually picks up a dozen three or four times a week."

"Law enforcement's main staple…I forgot."

While Starr was putting the finishing touches on her hair, I pulled out the pair of binoculars I remembered were in the kitchen drawer, and threw on my coat to step out on the balcony. From there, I had a panoramic view of the parking lot. Besides the Denver P.D. unit, there were still thirty or more cars remaining in the lot. I adjusted the lens so that the insides of the cars were sharp and clear. Although I didn't expect to see anyone sitting there with a sniper rifle, I wasn't taking any chances. After checking each vehicle, I found only the Impala to be occupied. The officer was still sitting in much the same position with his arm hanging out the window.

Starr and I walked out together, descending the stairwell and checking all around us for suspicious packages or for C-4 stuck to the wall. After I got to Caroline's car, I dropped down on all fours to check underneath for any explosive devices. My caution prompted a smile from Starr as she entered her car. I then looked over toward the south end of the complex and threw up my hand to the cop who still had his arm out the window. But he didn't wave back, the putz. I then cranked the car, exhaling a sigh of relief that it didn't go *ka-boom*, and then drove by the police unit to get a look at the officer. Immediately, I knew something was not right.

Before Starr left out, I motioned for her to join me. She quickly pulled up on my right side and between open windows asked "What's wrong?"

"You'd better call your boss, Starr. This guy's dead."

Both of us then pulled out our Berettas and cautiously approached the Impala. Through the open window we could see that the heavy-set middle-aged man was lying back against the headrest as though he were asleep. Blood from the deep gash wound on his neck had soaked the entire front of his white shirt and green tie.

"My God!" exclaimed Starr.

"Apparently, the Weatherman, Jonas Karn, paid us a visit last night. Some of his handiwork."

As alarming as this was, it made me even more afraid for Caroline, now knowing first-hand what the psychopath was capable of. A vision of her lying somewhere cut up like the officer kept trying to invade my brain. But I kept pushing it away.

In less than ten minutes the parking lot was swarming with Denver squad cars, followed thereafter with the arrival of the EMT and the coroner's wagon. Finally, Pettyjohn pulled in with Rogers who had only arrived at the Bureau office on Stout moments before for the planned pow wow. Rogers was visibly shaken. He had served with Officer Larry

Montgomery for over fifteen years. To see his friend's wanly face and life's blood spilled into the seat and floorboard made him visibly sick. Starr patted him on the back as Rogers went off to the bushes, bent over and heaved up the donut he had already consumed.

Finally, he erected himself and said, "I don't know how I'm going to tell Fran that her husband won't be coming home this morning. Horrible."

The CBI and CSI teams arrived on the scene within a half hour and began setting up the crime scene for their investigation. Curiosity seekers from the apartment complex began edging their way to a point where they were disallowed to venture any further. A few went to their cars to go to work, but not before they were questioned briefly about anything they had seen. Just before eight-thirty, Starr, Pettyjohn and I then moved out in separate cars to make the now-delayed staff meeting. Neither Starr nor I had had an opportunity to talk much with Pettyjohn at the crime scene out of ear shot of the officers and on-lookers, believing that the information we discovered the night before about Karn was better furthered at the office.

No sooner than we arrived and I had met Bob Murphy, a tall and lanky 30 something lad with a blonde buzz cut, my cell phone rang. It was Caroline's number.

"Quick!" I shouted to Pettyjohn. "Can we get this call triangulated?"

He handed me a wire that was connected to a micro cassette player. "Here. Plug this into to your phone. I'll get on my phone to Rocky Face Communications."

I then flipped my phone open, put it on speaker, and answered with a cool "Yes?"

"Ah, you're there," the nasally voice said. "What took you so long? Are you trying to get a fix on my location? You know that's impossible."

"Hello, Karn," I replied.

There was then a moment of uncomfortable silence on

his end, and then he finally replied. "So, you figured it out, eh Bruce? I knew you were smart. A flaming asshole, but smart."

And then I knew for sure. Starr and I had guessed right.

"Where's my daughter, Karn? If you've done anything…"

"Oh, she's lying here right beside me, Bruce. A little tied up right now, though." Then he cackled.

"Let me talk with her!" I demanded.

"Oh, Caroline, your daddy wants to hear your voice."

I strained my ears to hear something from her in the background.

"What?" Karn said. And then another pause.

"I'm sorry, Bruce. She can't talk to you right now. Her lips are taped shut. I know how disappointed you must be."

"I'm coming after you, Karn. I know that's what you want. You just tell me when and where."

"So that you can kill me, right Bruce?" He laughed again. "I'm not going to make it that easy for you. You want Caroline back? Well, you're not going to get her today…or tomorrow. Maybe never. The wind is now blowing *my* way, Bruce." I swallowed hard and looked around the room at my cohorts. Pettyjohn was still trying to get through the cell phone company's menu.

"*What do you want, creep?*" I yelled. "Money? Revenge? I'll trade myself right now for Caroline. Let her go. I'll come wherever you are, unarmed."

He cackled again. "Your life for your daughter's. Well, aren't you the noble father?"

"Just set it up. Tell me where to be."

There was a long silence before Karn spoke again. Then in a low, diabolical tone he said, "Did you like what you found this morning, Bruce? In case you were wondering, the pig died quickly. And that goes to show you that this is all not just vibrato. I want you to close your eyes and imagine pretty Caroline lying in a pool of *her* blood."

"When I find you, you son-of-a bitch, God help you. You're sure as hell going to need Him."

I then heard the dial tone. He was gone. I hit 'redial' and it rang three times before Caroline's voice recording kicked in. After the last word of her recording and I heard the beep, I screamed into the phone, *"You call me back right this instant, you dickless*

bastard! You hear me?! You spill one drop of her blood and there will be no place on God's green earth you can hide! I will find you and cut you into so many pieces there won't be enough left of you for the goddam ants to find! You hear me, maggot?!

I glanced over at Pettyjohn and then Starr and Murphy who were staring at me, the maniac that I had suddenly turned into. Finally Starr walked over to me and laid her hand on mine.

"Sit down, Skip. I'll get you a bottle of water."

Pettyjohn, still struggling to get through to a real person at Rocky Face, gave up. "Sorry, Bruce. These damned menus on companies' lines drive me bonkers."

"He won't call back today," I lamented. "And…I didn't handle that very well."

"You responded like a father," he replied. "Let's all just sit down and go through this. By the way, Bruce, this is Bob Murphy. He's been around about six years."

I reached over and shook his hand.

"Hello, Mr. McGowan. I hate what you're going through. I've got a four year old girl and two year old boy at home. Even considering the business I'm in, I can't imagine one of mine…"

"Murph," Pettyjohn interrupted. "How about ordering out for some deli sandwiches. Get me a roast beef and whatever Mr. McGowan and Ravenel want."

"What will that be, sir?" Murphy asked me.

I didn't answer. As hungry as I was, I couldn't think about food. I just shook my head. Pettyjohn then leaned over to Murphy and said in a low voice, "Just get him a ham and swiss." He then stopped himself.

"Oh, you're not Jewish, are you?"

I didn't answer.

"My guess is that you're not, considering your Scottish name. Get the ham sandwich, Murph."

I flipped my cell phone open again. "Before we go into anything, Lew, I need to make a call." I then went into the break room and speed dialed the number two.

"Good morning, Bruce," greeted Byrd, recognizing my number. "Are you all right?"

"Karn just called again, Lionel."

"What's going on?"

"The bastard slipped up on a Denver detective sitting in his car watching Caroline's apartment last night and cut his throat while we were sleeping."

Byrd let out a low whistle. "That's too bad. At least it tells us the kind of psychopath we're dealing with."

"And that, sir, is what bothers me. What did you find on him?" I asked.

"He was released from prison via a Presidential pardon in early January this year and then disappeared for a few months. He reappeared on the Bureau's radar in June when he wrote and distributed a kind of manifesto similar to the Declaration of War communiqué back in the early '70s against the federal government. Karn's manifesto charges the government with the systematic oppression of the poor and all minorities with its practices of racism, classism, imperialism and homophobia. The same kind of allegations we saw thirty years ago by the old Weather Underground. He even claims he ultimately turned to homosexuality himself in prison because of the government's brutal tactics against him that left him emasculated."

"Hmm, yes. He's right about that. I jammed his marbles

so far up his ass, they landed in his throat."

Byrd cleared his throat. "Yes, well, for a while he rejoined the Prairie Fire Organizing Committee. I think they were too much about words and not violent enough for him. He apparently has founded a spin-off element from the Weatherman Underground Organization, which he calls the New WUO."

"Yeah, I learned about that from one of the agents here last night."

Byrd continued. "Karn not only has ties with suspected al-Qaeda sympathizers, but we understand there also may be two or three Islamic terrorist types actually in the organization. He has created an alliance with several young Arab students who are suspected to have collaborated with the same terrorist order that the 9-11 hijackers came from. The new manifesto has been posted in a radical newspaper called *The Subterranean* which blames 9-11 on the American government, and that the country not only got what it deserved, but says it demonstrates that the imperialistic giant has a soft underbelly. Karn was recently seen in several venues in Washington and we believe it was him who was photographed at Ground Zero holding up both hands with fingers formed in the peace sign."

"And somewhere along the way as a side mission," I added, "he put together a plan to kidnap Caroline so that he could at last get revenge on me. A multi-tasker. Ironically, learning that Caroline was a Bureau agent in Denver, he found he could execute his plan in his own back yard."

Byrd agreed. "The Bureau in Denver is also onto a commune similar to the ones back in the sixties, north of you there just west of Boulder. It is believed that Karn and a few of his former associates either live out there or frequent the habitat."

"I will take that up with Agent Pettyjohn."

Byrd then changed the subject. "Were you able to

determine Caroline's state of health from your conversation with Karn?"

"Not really. He insinuated that she was bound and gagged. Probably still drugged as well. I've got to find them, Lionel, and I'm not waiting on the Bureau to take days to analyze and dissect the scenario, and then act, like they're prone to do."

"Do what you need to do, Bruce. You know I would if it were one of my girls. Remember what I told you about the exposure, though."

"I understand. Talk later."

Pettyjohn finally convened his briefing and strategy meeting on the kidnapping around eleven just after Murph had ordered lunch. "I have put an APB out on Karn and will pull in the CBI to partner with you, Starr and Murph, to investigate this New WUO more in-depth. A Lieutenant Harriman and another agent will be here at 1400 tomorrow, but I've got something planned for you two"… he looked at his two young agents…"this evening and will tell you about it in a moment. I'm also contacting the U.S. Attorney's office to obtain a court order for a shakedown of that commune. I would doubt, however, that Jonas Karn has Caroline in captivity anywhere near that place. He may have some newly-kindled subversive agenda going on, but the bulk of his peace-nick friends would not be involved in a kidnapping. This thing against you, Bruce, is all too personal for him. Obviously, you made a lasting impression on him."

"I'm sure he's been planning this vendetta behind bars for years," I added.

Pettyjohn picked up the tape recorder and fiddled with the volume. "Let's listen to the tape again and see if we can pick out any clues from what he said. I will also have our lab tech analyze any background noises that may indicate his location."

As Pettyjohn replayed the tape over and over, he wrote down keys words. "What's with his voice? I wonder if that's his usual tone or is it his attempt to disguise himself."

"I don't know," I lied. "For some reason his voice seemed different *after* I apprehended him…higher in pitch. Then, the louder he got in court when he testified, the harder it was for everyone to keep a straight face. Especially his own attorney."

"I'm not sure I follow that," said Pettyjohn.

Starr stifled a smile. "You don't want to know, Lew."

"What did he mean by 'the wind is now blowing my way?'"

"I know that one," I replied. "When the Youth Revolutionary Movement split off to become the WUO, they coined the Weatherman name from the Bob Dylan song, Subterranean Homesick Blues. There's a line in the song that says, "You don't need a weatherman to know which way the wind blows." You see when Karn was a part of that earlier group, he was actually living in Colorado Springs and later, the Boulder area, and along with his wife, putting out that sick and twisted anti-government propaganda, trying to incite people to take part in the Weatherman revolution. He might even have been living in that same commune you all are planning to turn upside down."

"Yes," said Starr. "As you know, I was up in Boulder the day before Thanksgiving nosing around that commune. But the presence of my car, driven by a government-looking character with flight glasses caused a lot of consternation for sure. Heads turned away and kids hid their faces as their parents taught them. Some of the women and little girls were wearing sun bonnets and long dresses. Looked somewhat like an Amish settlement."

"Without the religion," I said.

Starr nodded. "They have their own religion, founded on some weird kind of philosophical socialism…like something between classless communism and existentialism."

"Again, very insightful," I remarked. "Sounds like you've really studied up on this group."

"A good bit. But now that we know this Karn character moved on to domestic terrorism and kidnapping, maybe we'll get lucky with someone in that hippy colony. Somebody up there knows where Karn is. Somebody that he's maybe alienated."

Pettyjohn then stood and said, "I'll get this tape to the lab. Now Murph…you and Starr, I want you to change into something casual…even earthy, like jeans and tie-dyes, and go canvass that area. There's a small village outside of that commune and two or three bars where a number of them hang out. Don't make yourself conspicuous by going in there and pounding them with questions. You know how to do this. And take one of the old clunkers from the garage."

"You have FBI clunkers?" I said.

"We have a couple of cars out there that we appropriated from some perps a couple of years ago. We use them for undercover work when we're in a low-life area."

"But aren't Starr and Murph here a little too clean-cut for that area?"

Starr answered my question quickly. "I can look pretty haggard when I put on a sweatshirt, let my hair down around my face and wear no make-up. I can look very 'Boulder' as they say around here."

And Murph added, "I've got an old tattered Army field jacket and can look very Aryan with this buzz cut."

"Shall I go with you on this inquisition?" I asked. "I can get me a wig and a guitar and tell everyone I'm Arlo Guthrie. Maybe lead them in a chorus of *Alice's Restaurant?*"

"No, you're out of the equation, Bruce," said Pettyjohn. "You're a civilian, now, and I will not allow you to take any action on your own nor will you interfere with any operation undertaken by this office."

We stood there a while just looking at each other.

Finally, Pettyjohn continued.

"Look, Bruce, I'm just doing my job here."

"Yeah? Then watch me do *mine.*"

He frowned and shook his head.

"You'll do me a big favor by just sticking around here and not causing me any trouble."

"My staying here won't smoke this creep out. He wants me out there looking for him. I'm the target and you know he won't come here to get me."

"I can't *let* you be a target, Bruce. You'll end up dead and Caroline right along with you. That's what happens in a lot of kidnap cases. You know that all too well. I hate to say it that way, but I'm not going to sugar-coat it for you. And I don't want either you *or* Caroline on my conscience."

"All right. But I'm not sticking around here day in and day out. But I promise you I won't do anything to get in your way or impede your investigation. You have a killer and kidnapper to catch. I have a daughter to get back. Just keep me informed. That's all I ask."

"You're an important part of this investigation, Bruce. I will *definitely* let you know of any developments."

At twelve-thirty, Detective Rogers came by the Stout Street office with a video tape secured from one of the two cameras perched on the corners of Caroline's Building Six. On the tape at nine minutes past three in the morning, a lone figure walked from between two rows of tenant vehicles in the dimly-lit parking lot and approached the police unit from the rear. The man who had on an open black coat and baseball cap moved quickly upon the car and tapped on the driver's side glass. Officer Montgomery probably thought the man was the apartment superintendent or security officer, wondering what he was doing sitting there. When the window came down, the assailant struck quickly and ruthlessly, swiping the blade of a large knife across the officer's jugular. When the man turned away from the car, the blade of the knife glinted for a second in the adjacent overhead light. And so did his silver belt buckle. And then the murderer popped a salute to the camera, taunting and mocking those who would later review the film. Quickly, he left the complex on foot, walking from left to right out of the camera's range to a car likely parked well out of sight.

We all watched the film in horror. Starr let out an audible gasp when Karn cut the officer's throat. I could see tears welling up in Rogers' eyes. His lips quivered.

"Bastard. Friggin' bastard," he said.

It was like watching a movie. But we knew it was all too real.

Pettyjohn compared the tape with the one secured from the camera posted outside the door at the FBI office and concluded that it was the same man. Same cap, same build of one hundred seventy-five pounds, same silver belt buckle. In neither tape, however, were his features distinguishable. Not much else to go on.

After we had watched the film a third time, Starr and Murphy left the office. I followed them out to their Dodge clunker in the garage. A burnt orange clunker at that, it was difficult in places to determine what paint was and what was rust. I threw up my hand to say toddle-loo and went on to my Caroline's car. Murph was going to stop by his house first and change clothes. Then he would take Starr to her place. Although it would probably be a fishing expedition, they would stop by a couple of watering holes outside of the cult's village, strike up some conversations about the enslaving government and casually mention the name of Jonas Karn. And whatever happened to him anyway?

As Karn had been pardoned versus paroled, there was no probation officer to report to; neither was he required to notify the state and local law enforcement of his whereabouts. He did not own a home or register an automobile and was not on anyone's payroll that the Bureau could find…which meant he wasn't paying any taxes. A model citizen for sure.

His mama, Sybil Karn, owned a small, one-story house on Pearl Street in a low-rent area of Boulder, so Lew Pettyjohn said. Jonas Karn had lived there with her up until the late sixties until he decided to start bombing restaurants and killing servicemen. During the entire decade of the seventies the house was not only under close surveillance, but Mama was visited scores of times by the FBI. They stopped dropping in on her, of course, after I added her bad little boy to the dance card at the Colorado Penal Colony. CBI units were now on a twentyfour/seven stake-out of the house, just in case the man with the Navy parka and Broncos cap decided to come by and check on his mommy. But I knew the bastard wouldn't be that stupid.

CHAPTER SEVEN

After wishing Starr and Murph good hunting in Freedomsburg, which as the crow flies laid about five miles outside of Boulder, I found Caroline's Altima and climbed in. Since I was running out of cell juice, I pulled my car charger from my briefcase and plugged it into the cigarette lighter. While my phone was still charging, I used it to make my round of calls. It was going on three and I figured Birdman was still at the wheel on Eastern time working on the New Year's Eve Big Apple mission. All eight Zulu teams from throughout the country, which in total numbered somewhere in the fifties, would either be taking up sniper positions from high buildings looking through night vision scopes for suspicious activities or filtering throughout the mass of bodies on the street. There may in fact be more law enforcement and security from the battery of agencies than revelers. I hoped to hell everyone that carried a gun knew how to recognize one other.

"I don't have anything new for you, Bruce, except the names of a couple of Karn's known associates from the seventies who are still in the area there. One is teaching Philosophy at Arapahoe State and the other is ill and has been drawing Disability Social Security."

"Ironic, isn't it," I commented. "He's being taken care of

by the very government he sabotaged."

Byrd gave me the teacher's name and address as well as that of Sybil Karn. While Starr and Murph were getting chummy in Freedomsburg, I would be having tea with Mama Karn. I would be Jonas's friend from the foul Weather days.

While en route to Boulder, Darlene called to see if our little girl had been found. She was unusually sweet this time, saying nothing accusatory. We could only blame the maniac that had her. I guessed that to her *I* was the best chance Caroline had in getting her back. I told her I understood her frustration the last time I spoke with her. I was frustrated as well. Darlene did ask why I thought Caroline was taken and I lied to her. Actually, I just didn't tell her it was all about me. I said there was scum out there who did these things purely because they're evil and psychotic. She again asked about money and I said the man had not yet said what he wanted. Another lie. It was *me* he wanted…in time. Not money. He just wanted to toy with me to make me bleed until he figured out how he could have me at his mercy. I didn't tell her that of course. But I did tell her that the man promised in his messages that Caroline was unharmed.

"But neither you nor I have a lot of money. At least not the kind of money they usually want…like hundreds of thousands. But whatever it is, I'll find a way to come up with it."

"There's been no demand yet, Darlene. He's just holding her as long as he can to see if I get desperate enough to maybe rob a bank."

"Well, if that's what it takes, *I'll* do it." She then became very quiet. Softly she said, "You've got to get her back, Bruce. Please."

"I will, Darlene. I promise. I'll find this guy. Just continue with your prayers, as I am doing."

As the Denver media was all over Officer Montgomery's

murder, the Denver P.D. and CBI at the request of the FBI let out a white lie that an unknown assailant, probably a druggy, killed him. Actually, Montgomery did have a couple of known dealers under surveillance earlier in the week and did in fact receive a tip about a buy at one of the apartment complexes that was supposed to be going down. The kidnapping of Caroline McGowan needed to stay under wraps as long as possible. The more media frenzy, the less likely Jonas Karn was to crawl out of his hole to meet with me. And if the media found out about me, they would clock my every move.

Nonetheless, I just couldn't rest on my laurels for one more day. If I did, I was not only furthering my feelings of helplessness, but wasting every valuable moment I had to find the creep.

Via my pocket GPS, I followed the directions north to the residence of one Sybil Karn. It was a rundown old house with broken batten-board siding and a sagging roof that was missing several hundred shingles. A cluster of chipped and weather-beaten gnomes peppered the postage stamp front yard and trash blown in off the street lay strewn about. On the front porch sat a faded, white wicker chair that had become unraveled in several places. The house was definitely not going to be featured in either *Home and Garden* or *Colorado Living* anytime soon.

I tapped lightly at first on the screen door and then turned slightly to look out of the corner of my eye at the unmarked police unit sitting a half block down the street. I was sure the stake-out officer inside the car was radioing his division about the visitor on the porch and whether I should be nabbed as soon as I left the house. I didn't fit the description of Jonas Karn and he certainly wouldn't be knocking on his mum's door anyway.

After a long minute the door opened just a crack and the hollow-eyed face of a frail woman perhaps seventy-five appeared. "Yes? What do you want?"

"Hello, Mrs. Karn. I'm sorry to bother you. I'm not selling anything, but I was just looking to reconnect with Jonas."

She then opened the door a little wider to get a better look at me. I could see that the setting sun was in her eyes and I wasn't sure she could fully make out my face.

"Reconnect? Are you a friend of his?"

"He and I were friends a long time ago back in the early seventies. We were in kind of…a club together for a couple of years. I won't go into it, but it had a lot to do with writing articles and handing out pamphlets."

She squinted her eyes and had an expression on her face as though she was trying to remember something. "I don't think I know you…and I knew all Jonas's friends." "I'm Bob Hagen, Mrs. Karn. I've never met you, but Jonas sure talked about you a lot."

Dressed in a pink robe and appearing rather sickly, she pulled her garment tightly around her to hide her gown. After she gave me another good look, she said "I'm not very presentable, but you can come in for a cup of hot coffee or tea if you'd like." She then coughed a couple of times that sounded like she was bringing up a piece of her lung. I wasn't sure I wanted to go any further. But I followed her in, anyway.

"Thank you ma'am. That sounds good." I also knew I didn't relish putting my lips on one of her coffee cups and hoped the temperature on her dishwasher was scalding hot.

"Make yourself at home. Which will you have…coffee or tea."

She definitely looked sickly and her complexion was something between ghostly and ashen. "That's okay, Mrs. Karn. I don't want to be a bother. I really don't need anything. I was just looking to see if Jonas was still around."

"Well, he isn't here. Last time I saw him was about three weeks ago."

"Does he live here?"

"Sometimes. And sometimes he stays up north of here in

the mountains with a friend. Up around Horse tooth, I think. Don't know exactly where."

"I see."

"He works a little bit at some book store is all I know. Sometimes he comes here and stays a couple of days and then he's gone."

I looked around and decided there were some things I wanted to get a look at, so I said, "You know, Mrs. Karn, on second thought, maybe I will have a cup of coffee." Knowing I was probably risking TB.

She stood unevenly for a moment and then dragged herself off to the kitchen in apparent pain. I heard her cough again, sounding kind of like a dog hacking up a bone. I felt sorry for the woman, more so because she was the mother of a psychopathic killer and kidnapper, but I actually did feel badly about causing her any trouble. However, I needed an opportunity to look around. As soon as she disappeared through the kitchen door, I went first into the bedroom on the left side of the house, finding that it was obviously hers. The bed was unmade and the room smelled sickly and medicinal. As I didn't think I would find anything there, I dashed stealthily across the living room into the second bedroom. Since the house had two bedrooms, one of them had to belong to part-time occupant, Jonas Karn.

The room was largely barren, containing only a bed that had been stripped of its covers, a small, worn green chair, and a faux roll top desk made of pressed wood. I checked quickly to see if Mrs. Karn was still in the kitchen, and hearing her getting a coffee cup down from the cabinet, figured I had a minute or so.

As silently as I could, I raised the flimsy roll top to look for envelopes or papers which might have the address of his friend's place or that of another associate, but found nothing.

I opened the bifold doors to the closet, finding a pair of boots and sneakers, a pair of jeans and some shirts. I then looked up on the top shelf and saw a shoe box which I took down. Inside I found a handful of papers which I shoved into my coat pocket. No sooner had I closed the closet door and started back for the living room, the frail-looking form of Mrs. Karn appeared in the bedroom doorway. Her eyes, though sickly, drilled into mine accusingly.

"Why are you in here, Mr. Hagen?"

"I'm sorry, Mrs. Karn. I was just looking for the bathroom. I must have taken a wrong turn."

She then bobbed her head in the direction of a door at the end of the hallway. "It's there…on the right."

"I thought that was a closet," I said. "Thank you."

I could feel her eyes on the back of my neck as I walked the few steps down the hall to the toilet room. I really didn't have to go, but it did give me an opportunity to check out the medicine cabinet and underneath the sink. The linoleum was yellowed and peeling in places and the wash basin looked as though it hadn't been cleaned in years. Grungy stains coated the bottom of the sink and the toilet bowl had rusty run streaks in several places. At least I was hoping it was rust.

I opened the door to the bottom cabinet first, finding bottles of cleaners that had obviously never had the caps off them, a couple rolls of toilet paper and a plunger that looked *well* used. I then opened the glass door to the medicine cabinet, finding a half dozen prescription bottles all with the name Sybil Karn. Except one which bore the name

Jonas Karn. It was a prescription from Kelsey's Pharmacy in Boulder for an anti-depressant.

I shoved the bottle in my pocket, flushed the commode and then returned to the living room. Mrs. Karn had sat down and was nursing her cup of coffee. Mine was set on a rather decrepit-looking table that was positioned between the couch and a sofa chair that looked as though a cat had clawed the stuffings out of it in a number of places. I nodded to her politely and sat down.

On the back wall of the living room was a fireplace which had been closed off. The mantle supported a number of black and white pictures in metal frames, one of which I presumed was of a younger Sybil Karn, and a couple more that appeared to be more than forty years old of a child with a choir boy's face. There was another of a teenager in a cap and gown which I took to be Jonas as well. In the center, between the pictures was a mantle clock. Suddenly, it bonged five times and I think I must have jumped. Its throaty chimes sounding like a mini grandfather clock seemed to reverberate through the house for several seconds.

Ancient, dingy wallpaper which had been ripped at the top on one wall hung down to about midway to a portrait of some homely Nineteenth Century character and there was a caved-in place on another piece of sheetrock where Jonas had likely bashed it in a fit of rage. The carpet was mangy and matted to where there was no form at all left to the shag.

Mrs. Karn's hands shook as she sipped her coffee and I surmised that she was probably in some latter stage of cancer. I was becoming so depressed that I thought about popping one of Jonas's pills.

"How was it you knew my Jonas?" she asked. "You said a club you were in?"

"Well, ma'am, it was more of an organization…one where we wrote letters to the government, telling them we didn't approve of the way they treated poor people and Black people. It was maybe thirty years ago."

"That long? It wasn't that group I didn't approve of, was it? You know the police kept coming here and talking to him back then. Then one day, years later, after he left the state to go to work in a factory, the police took him off to jail. I didn't see him for a number of years. I think it was all due to his affiliation with those people he knew. You weren't one of them, were you?"

Because she looked as if she could tumble off the couch dead at any time, I didn't want to upset her by getting into anything about the Weatherman organization; so as I had already concocted a tall tale, I thought I'd make my nose grow even longer.

"Naw," I replied. "That was one of those organizations that did bad things and led Jonas astray. Our group was very peaceful and nobody got into trouble. Mostly, we just hung out together, sang peace songs and played guitars. I have to admit we were a little ornery at times. We did a little drinking and smoked things we shouldn't have to get high."

"Like weed?"

I almost choked on my coffee. "Mmm, yes. I'm afraid so. Well, anyway, did Jonas say when he was coming back?"

"No. He just shows up for a day or so and leaves." "And you don't know any of his friends who might know how to get hold of him."

"I'm afraid I can't help you, Mr. Hagen. He may have told me, but my memory isn't what it used to be. I…just haven't felt well for months and sorry to say I probably won't be around much longer."

I then stood and laid down my cup. "You know, I've bothered you much too long and should be going."

"So soon? I wish you'd stay. I don't ever get any visitors… maybe a couple of people from the church."

"No, really, I have to be going…but maybe I'll come back sometime." I stretched out my hand and she took it. Her hand was weak and cold and I felt the promise of imminent death in it.

"Goodbye, Mrs. Karn," I said, opening the front door. "Thanks for the coffee and your warm hospitality. I enjoyed talking with you."

She nodded a couple of times and closed the door behind me. I glanced down the street and noticed that the black Ford was still there. When I cranked up the Altima and pulled away from the curb, I saw in my rear view mirror that the cop car hadn't moved. However, it didn't take me but a block to see that another unmarked unit had pulled out behind me to begin a tail.

Considering Caroline's Nissan wasn't a powerhouse and couldn't get out of its own way, I knew I'd have to do some fancy maneuvering to shake my pursuer. A couple of blocks down I pulled around a Pontiac on the four lane street just as the light turned from yellow to red. A second vehicle in the left lane pulled up beside the Pontiac and as I made an abrupt right turn, both vehicles had to stop for the light, trapping the police unit behind them. I heard a quick blast of the siren and by the time the car had gotten around the good citizens, I was out of sight. I knew it didn't matter if they had caught up with me. They had Caroline's tag anyway, and the fact that I was visiting Mrs. Karn was sure to get back to Pettyjohn, who would then know I was sticking my nose into his investigation. So, why was I evading the cops? I just thought it would be fun.

As it was now nearly dark and I had no idea where to go from there, I decided to find Freedoms burg, the place where my Bureau cohorts had gone. I thought maybe I could just hang out in one of the dives and grab a sandwich and a beer. Even though I didn't expect to find Karn in any of those places, I thought maybe just as Starr and Murph were doing, I could engage some of the local commies and finagle some information about their hero. But then again, I thought that too many people looking for Jonas Karn on the same night, pretending to be his friends, would raise a few eyebrows.

I started to just turn around and head back to Caroline's pad in Denver to get some sleep, but then off to the right I spotted the old Dodge rust bucket parked in front of a bar. Out front there was a marquis that read *Frankie's* under which were neon signs in the windows advertising Coors and Foster's beers. I pulled my ride into a spot in the row behind the clunker just to be sure it was one and the same car. It was.

I recognized the sticker on the bumper that read *"War is Not the Answer."* It fully fit in with the other pieces of junk in the lot that had stickers condemning the good old USA like *"Down with Imperialism"* and *"Freedom Before Fight."* Another bumper sticker simply read *"COEXIST"* where each letter of the word was a symbol associated with a religion.

I sat for a while wondering if I should go in and occupy a booth close by my new buds, listening for any words or a name I could key in on. But this was *their* deal and I had promised not to interfere in what they were doing. I hoped they were making friends.

While sitting in the car wondering why I was just sitting there in the car, I dialed Adrianna's number. It would be about nine-thirty back in West Virginia and she should have still been awake.

"Skip," she answered softly. "Are you okay?" "Yes. What have you been doing today?"

"Not much. A couple came in from Wisconsin to spend New Years and I was just downstairs spending a little time with them. What's happening with Caroline?"

"It's been three days since she was taken. The creep called me a couple of times, mainly to taunt me and so far hasn't given me any specifics as to what he wants…except to make me bleed. And he's sure as hell doing *that*."

"I'm sorry, Skip. I don't know what to say. Just be careful."

"It's frustrating for me. I don't know if she's getting food and drink or is even still alive. I know one thing…I'm going to cut this asshole into little pieces and leave what's left of him for the Colorado crows."

She didn't respond and I was thinking she was trying to digest the picture of that in her mind. "Well, anyway, I'm just hanging on here by a shoestring, waiting for his next call. He…" I then stopped my conversation to take account of the man and woman leaving the bar. It took me a short moment to realize it was Starr and Murph. I slinked down a little in the seat so they wouldn't see me and said, "I've got to go. I'll call you tomorrow. Sleep well, kiddo."

"I'll try. Don't let this get to you, Skip. She'll be returned safely. God answers the prayers of his children."

"Even heathens like me?" "Anybody who calls His name."

"Yeah, I heard that somewhere." "Bye, Skip."

Starr and Murph stood a moment outside of the door talking, but as they were preparing to go to their car, three men came out of the bar and approached them. Suddenly the agents raised their arms, turned and walked toward the left corner of the building with the men following them. In the bold light of the marquis, I caught the glint off the gun that the larger man was holding on them. When they all had fully disappeared around the side of the bar, I sprang from the Altima, pulled Starr's Beretta from my coat and injected a round from the clip into the chamber.

Upon turning the corner of the building I didn't see them any longer and suspected the men had taken Starr and Murph behind the building. Stooping to peer around the back corner, I saw that the captors had the agents down on their stomachs. By the light that hung over a dumpster, I could see there was now also a gun in a second man's hand and it was pointed at the back of Starr's head. The third apparently unarmed man was checking her coat pocket.

"Who the *hell* are you people," one of the men barked. "And why are you asking about Karn?"

The man who was rifling Starr's pockets then let out a low whistle. When he stood up he had Starr's gun and badge in his hands. "I'll tell you who they are…FBI!"

"Pigs!" the larger man yelled. "You know what we do to pigs around here? We butcher them."

When I heard the hammer cock on his gun, I knew I had to act quickly. I didn't want to fire, fearing that the bullet smashing through his brain may cause him to jerk the trigger. I then shoved the Beretta back into my coat pocket and stepped into the light. Feigning drunkenness, I stumbled into the back wall of the building and started singing, "If pigs could fly…" in a slurred voice. I then fell into a garbage can, knocking it over and coming to rest onto on the ground against the concrete wall.

The gunman then pivoted and trained the gun on me. "Steve, go check out that drunk son-of-a-bitch."

Steve then advanced on me and stood over me with a gun of his own trained on my forehead.

"Steve…Stevie Wonder," I said in sing-song. "Ma cherie amour…"

"Shut up, you piece of shit. Get your ass up and vamoose."

"I can't get up, Stevie," I said. "I think I've had a… hic…wee bit too much to drink." I lifted my eyebrows and gave him a sloppy smile.

Steve placed his .38 against my forehead and yelled, "Get the hell up, rummy!"

"You have to help me up," I replied.

He then shoved the revolver into the back of his trousers and reached down to grab me by the coat with both hands. With one solid straight punch, I landed the knuckles of my right fist into his Adam's apple, then grabbed a handful of his long hair sending his face hard into the concrete wall. Blood spurted immediately from his nose and mouth and he began making a gagging, choking sound. Jamming my foot into his mid-section, I kicked him away so he wouldn't continue to bleed all over me. He fell like a brick onto the pavement.

The two men standing over Starr and Murph had looks of surprise on their faces, but by the time the larger man had lifted his gun in my direction again, I had already swept the Beretta from my pocket and fired the one round that struck him squarely in the middle of his forehead. His gun then fell harmlessly from his hand as he sunk to his knees, landing face down.

Starr and Murphy then sprang to their feet to turn on the third, unarmed man, but he was already fleeing toward the woods off to right side of the building. I fired two shots in his direction low enough not to kill him and then I heard him yelp. The three of us converged on him, finding him lying in ankle-high weeds, nursing the wound that had entered at the rear of his thigh.

"Skip!" yelled Starr. "What the hell are you doing here? Weren't you specifically ordered to stay out of the investigation?"

"You're welcome very much," I replied. "Next time maybe you won't have me watching your back."

"Okay, I know. I'm glad you were here, but…"

"No buts. I wasn't tailing you. I just happened to see your junker out front as I was doing my own snooping around. Come on. Let's get this moron back into the light." I grabbed him by his jacket and lifted him to his feet.

"Arrgh!" he screamed. "My leg!"

I then drug him out of the woods and plopped his carcass onto the pavement under the overhead light. He screamed again and held his leg. Spying a discarded dish towel by the garbage bin, I tore it into two strips and tied off the man's leg above the wound. His face grimaced in pain.

"What's your name?" I barked. "B…Barry. Barry Rafferty."

I shoved the muzzle of the Beretta into his good leg. "All right, B…B…Barry, you have ten seconds to answer two questions. Do you know Jonas Karn and where can we find him?"

"Mr. McGowan," interrupted Murph. "You need to stop this and get the hell out of here *now*."

"Get lost, Murphy." I then growled at Rafferty.

"Now you have *five* seconds. Answer the question or I'll

blow your kneecap off!"

The man held up his hand. "Wait! Wait! I know who he is, but don't know *where* he is."

I then moved the muzzle of the gun to his right leg and jammed it hard into the wound. Rafferty screamed.

Starr then yanked at my coat sleeve. "Stop this! Stop it now!"

I let up on the pressure, but moved the barrel to the back of Rafferty's head behind his ear. "You're lying," I said in almost a whisper. "Where is Jonas Karn?"

And then Rafferty began to sob. "I'm not. I'm not lying. He's kind of an icon around here…from the old days. He comes in to Frankie's every so often and I hear he stays in a cabin somewhere north of here. That's all I know. I swear to God." And then he began crying like a three year old snot nose.

"What God is *that*, prick? I hear you people up here worship just about anything that walks on all fours."

Rafferty continued to writhe in pain. "It's…all I know. I swear. The guy you shot, Wally Tarver, he knew Karn pretty well and both of them rented a cabin somewhere west of

Ft. Collins. But I don't know where. I don't…please believe me."

"What about Stevie over there?"

"Steve don't know Karn. He's my brother-in-law just here for a couple of days from Kansas. Oh, God…I'm dying."

"You're not dying, moron. You better be telling me the truth." I then stood up, pretty much convinced that he told me all he could. "Just my luck. I kill the guy who could actually have led me to Karn. *Son-of-a-bitch!*" I exclaimed.

Starr touched my shoulder. "You couldn't have done anything different, Skip. He was going to kill us and you, too."

I shoved the still warm barrel of the Beretta into my belt and interlocked my fingers on top of my head in dismay. "I was *that close*," I said in a low voice.

"You need to get out of here, Mr. McGowan," said Murph. "We can explain this. You can't. Now go."

"All right. If you don't mind cleaning up after me." I then looked at Starr. "See you back at the apartment, roomy."

She nodded and I turned away. Before I got to the corner of the building, I overheard Murphy say in a low tone to Starr, "*Ruthless* bastard, isn't he?"

He didn't know the half of it.

Back at Caroline's place I tossed my blood-stained coat in the laundry closet on the floor and the papers I had absconded with from the shoebox in Karn's closet fell out. In the night's fun, I had almost forgotten about them. A few of the envelopes were post-marked as far back as 1988 and addressed to Jonas Karn at the Colorado State Penitentiary with his mother's return address on them. Although I didn't want to read what she had to say to him, I did skim over the content to see if any names or places would pop out at me. After leafing through page after page of her scribble and dribble, where she said she loved him no matter what, I saw I was wasting my time. But then I found a blank envelope inside of which was a newspaper clipping that appeared to be of the community persuasion. When I unfolded it, sure enough in the upper left-hand corner I read "*The Subterranean, October, 2001 Edition.*" About midway down the page was a photograph of two men standing in front of the steps of a cabin-looking dwelling. The caption read: *"Standing from left to right are Wally Tarver, Jonas Karn and Maheem Nadir at Tarver's home in Horsetooth."*

The article below it read: *"Jonas Karn, pioneer of the WUO, was released earlier this year from prison after receiving a Presidential pardon. A founding member of the SDS and ultimately the Weatherman movement, he recently led a vigil to commemorate the thirty year anniversary of the Pentagon bombing and the Days of Rage that followed. Pledging that a new world order would soon emerge with the help of his Islamic brothers, he would continue to cut out the cancer of imperial tyranny that exists at all levels within the U.S. government. Mr. Karn vows that the New WUO will rise from the ashes of Washington and New York after they are destroyed and there will be a revolution like this country has not seen since 1776..."*

And so, I thought, Jonas Karn's revival of the Weatherman Underground would not only see an outbreak of domestic terrorism throughout the United States, but the subversive group would also be aligned with Islamic terrorist cells which appeared to be operating in the rugged hills and back country at the foot of the Rockies. As subliminally conveyed in the article, he and his fellow conspirators would likely explode devices in a number of places that would reduce the Nation's Capital and the Big Apple to smoldering ruins, making the 9-11 attack pale in comparison.

But before kickoff, Mr. Karn had to first take care of some personal business. He had to get *me* out of his system. He had to get his revenge on the man who had maimed and humiliated him before placing him behind bars for over thirteen years. And the man who indirectly caused the death of his wife. And to do that, he was going to use Caroline to lure me into his sights. And I would make it as easy for him as he wanted in order to get my daughter back.

Starr came back to the apartment just before midnight. The moment she came in the door, I could tell she was pissed. Upon tossing her purse on the sofa, she grabbed hold of her Glock. I thought for sure she was going to shoot me, but instead she slammed the gun and her badge down on the granite bar.

"I can't tell you what kind of trouble you caused us tonight, not to mention the mess we had to clean up."

"You know, that's what my ex-wife used to tell me."

"Don't get cute, Mr. McGowan. I had to not only

explain to Lew Pettyjohn what went down, but *his* boss as well."

"So, how would you have explained that you and Murph took two bullets to the backs of your heads?"

"Look, Skip, I am beyond grateful that you showed up and saved our lives, but the bottom line is that Pettyjohn and his boss were wondering what a civilian was doing there interfering with the case and taking down bad guys."

"*Doing what the hell I needed to be doing to get my daughter back!*" I snapped.

Starr placed her hands on her hips, threw back her head and sighed, partly in disgust and partly in resignation. "Don't get me wrong. My highers were happy as hell you saved us from certain death. But maybe the next time it won't turn out that way. You might not just get us killed, but innocent civilians as well. You crossed the line tonight, Skip."

"In my business there is no line!"

"I'm not sure I really know what your business is. Are you government renegades or something? Do people in your organization get their jollies from killing and torturing bad guys…like shoot and then ask questions later?"

"Okay, I hear you. Let's just simmer down and talk about a few things. Look. I snooped around somewhere else, too. You might as well know about it. I'm sure the CBI told Pettyjohn by now."

She cocked her head to one side. "Oh, great. *More* exciting news. What is it?"

"I found Jonas Karn's mother and went to her house."

"I guess that doesn't surprise me. So, what did you do to *her*? Tie her to a chair and slice her throat open?"

I smiled at Starr's sarcasm. "She's a pretty nice old lady with big-time health issues and I treated her respectfully. She says she doesn't know where Karn is. Last time she saw him was several weeks ago. I didn't have any reason not to believe her. But when she turned her back, I rummaged through the room Karn stays in sometimes and found this." I then showed her the photo and the article. "Apparently, something catastrophic is being planned by Karn and his new and improved WUO. Something like what happened on 9-11, only apparently a hundred fold. Could even be dirty bombs or suitcase nukes."

Starr studied Karn's face. "Looks like an ordinary guy. And this place is supposed to be near the Horsetooth Reservoir? I've been up in that area a few times. Locating this cabin would be like looking for a needle in a haystack."

"But somebody up there has to know this Wally character, even if he was renting the place. And there's at least one person connected to this *Subterranean* piece of compost who knows where this cabin is. Like the photographer. How about you and I taking a little field trip tomorrow and visit the paper?"

"I doubt there's any actual business location. The paper could be printed out of somebody's basement. The quality looks like it."

"I'm sure your Bureau database will have some associated names and locations. We could…"

"Eh, eh…no 'we' on this, Skip. If you go off on your own tangent to do your detective work, I can't stop you. But you and I are *not* a team. I'm not going to get *my* butt fired over you."

I didn't reply. She was right. Hanging with me while I employed my ugly style of interrogation *would* get her suspended and I certainly didn't want to put her in any jeopardy with the Bureau.

She then stood up and started for Caroline's bedroom. "Get some sleep, Skip," she said. "Did you notice there are *two* officers in a Crown Vic sitting out there tonight?"

"Yeah. It's the first thing I saw when I pulled in. But Karn won't come anywhere near this place tonight. He knows they'll be ready for him."

"You're probably right." She paused at the doorway. "Are you comfortable there on that couch? It's a little over-stuffed."

"Is that an invitation?" I winked.

"You're funny, old man. Maybe I should lock my door."

I grinned and shook my head. "Get a good night's sleep, Starr."

CHAPTER EIGHT

The early morning sun streaming into the apartment woke us both up about the same time on Friday. With all that I had on my mind, I didn't think I could ever get to sleep. But after speaking with the Creator for more than ten minutes last night, more time than I had collectively spent with Him all year, He must have taken pity on me and put my lights out. It was a little past seven and being a bit hungry, I went looking for some cereal.

I then heard the shower crank up and she yelled out something.

"What?" I yelled back.

"I'm running late!" she replied.

I went to the bathroom door so that I could hear her better. "Was I supposed to go into your office with you?"

"Not necessarily! I've got a staff meeting at 8:30. I guess we'll be in there an hour or so. You can come to the office after that. *Now get away from my door!*"

I smiled and thumped the door once with my knuckles. Her spunkiness reminded me of Caroline in more ways than one.

When Starr left the apartment, I took a cup of coffee out on the balcony and breathed in the rays of the sweet, allaying sun. It had gotten down to the mid-twenties during the night, so the girl on the Weather Channel said, but the bright yellow ball which climbed ever higher over the eastern tree line in the cerulean blue sky felt like warm honey on my face. The snow that had fallen before Christmas still lay in dying drifts in the low spots. Off to my left where the snow had melted, the white bark of the aspens and deep green firs projected a stunning and salient contrast to the drab browns and yellows of winter. And then my eyes fell onto Caroline's bird feeder that hung from a roof beam over the balcony where three colorful finches pecked at the food that she had no doubt put out for her fine feathered friends. She had loved birds of all sizes and types since she was a little girl. As they ravenously picked away at the seed, I felt her spirit and presence as surely as if she were sitting there with me. And it was her spirit that warmed my body even more than the morning sun.

It was approaching nine and I wondered how long it would be before Jonas Karn would call. I expected that he wanted me to stew a while during the morning in gnawing anticipation that I would find out something more about Caroline. He would continue to feed me morsels to peck on like the little birds I was watching. And I didn't care if he called when I was or wasn't in the presence of the FBI... just so that it was soon. I hated the fact that he had control over me.

In a few moments I left Caroline's pretty finches to enjoy what was left of their breakfast and went in to take a shower.

I arrived at the Denver Division FBI office at just after nine-thirty just in time to see Starr and Murphy coming out of Pettyjohn's office. Starr bobbed her head in the direction of the office and said, "He told me when you arrived, he wanted to see you."

"Principal's office, huh? Guess I'm going to have to start behaving."

When I popped my head through the door, he didn't

quite have the expression of doom I expected.

"Come in, Bruce, and have a seat," he said.

"Are you taking me to the woodshed?"

"That's where you *need* to go, you know. Did I not make myself clear that you stay out of Bureau business and refrain from acting on your own?"

"You mean like taking down three guys who were going to kill two of your agents."

"And you did so rather brutally I might add."

"Usually I'm a lot less charming."

Pettyjohn was not amused. "Can't you be serious and dispense with the paltry nonsense? Who the hell are you, anyway, now that you're retired from the Bureau? A man who pulls the tactics you did is not just a paper-pusher for the Department of State. And you didn't learn those tactics from your twenty years at the FBI."

"I'm a very pissed-off father, Lew, that's who I am."

"Yeah, you're a father, and I appreciate what you are going through. But you're also no desk jockey. If I read you correctly, you're the kind of guy who would die before he settled down to a desk job. I suspect you're some kind of government-hired gun…maybe you went straight from the Bureau to the Company."

I laughed.

"The CIA? You've got to be kidding. I'd sell encyclopedias door to door before I'd work for the spooks. A bunch of primadonna James Bond wannabees."

"You know you killed two men last night and tortured a third."

I frowned and shook my head. "Two? I only drilled one of them in the head. The other I shot in the leg."

"No, Bruce. The guy whose head you drove into the wall died from a skull fracture and subdural hematoma."

That disturbed me. "I…I didn't know…"

"Look, Bruce. You *did* save my agents from certain

execution and that's something that will stay with me the rest of my life. And I appreciate that you're using your police skills in looking for this guy. Yeah, I know you went to Mrs. Karn's house, and that you followed my agents up to Freedomsburg. But you have to trust that we're all over this and are working hard to find your daughter, who by the way happens to be *my agent*. Do you not think we're over-turning every stone?"

"I don't know," I replied. "*Are* you?" Pettyjohn sighed and dropped his head.

I then pulled out the *Subterranean* clip I stole form Mrs. Karn's closet. "Check this out, Lew. A recent article and photo of Karn taken at the cabin where he has been staying with the guy I nailed between the eyes last night… Tarver."

Pettyjohn put on his glasses and studied the article. "Where did you get this?"

"Karn's mother gave it to me…in a way."

"Uh huh. I think I know the way you mean. I…"

Suddenly my cell phone rang. Caroline's number flashed across the small screen. "It's Karn," I said.

Pettyjohn motioned through his picture window to his technician Patrick Dawes. He then plugged his recorder into my phone.

I answered on the sixth ring. "Karn."

I heard him breathing, but he didn't immediately reply. Finally he said, "I thought you would pick up on the first ring, Bruce. If you're trying to trace the call, you're wasting your time." He paused. "I'm disappointed in you, Bruce."

"It's not my purpose in life to either please or disappoint a fudge packer like you, Karn. Now cut the shit and tell me where you are!"

"You don't want to know why I'm disappointed, Bruce?"

"Okay, prick. I'll play your game for two seconds. Why?"

"Because you went to see my mother yesterday!" he screamed into

the phone. "You crossed the line on that, Bruce. I may just have to send one of Caroline's pretty fingers to you for that."

The thought of that triggered in me both a rush of anger and nearly crippling fear. But I kept my composure.

"I was respectful to her, Karn." "Yeah, she said that."

"Now you respect my daughter and set her free, you dickless piece of monkey shit!"

"Tsk. Tsk. If you're going to call me names, Bruce, we're not going to get anywhere. Rest assured, before this is over, you're going to grovel and beg…even pray to me for Caroline's life."

"I'll meet you, Karn. Just me. You name the place and I'll be there. I'll trade her for me right this very day. I know you want to humiliate me…and eventually kill me. You can do whatever you want to me. *But let my daughter go!"*

"Easy, Bruce. At high noon sharp I'll call you and then I'll give you a verbal map. I'll tell you where to go. But you'd better be alone and unarmed. If I see a Bureau unit or any other unmarked car within two miles of you…I don't care if a cop coincidentally pulls over a speeder…you'll get your daughter back all right. In a thousand pieces." He then paused for effect. "You do understand what I'm saying, don't you?"

A shiver ran through me. "I understand. I'll make sure of it. Now let me talk to Caroline."

And then the line went dead.

Pettyjohn buzzed his technician. "Did you get that, Patrick?"

I heard the voice on the other end say "Yes. I'll play it back over the intercom. I want you to hear something."

As Patrick played the tape back, we heard Karn's mealy voice say, "…before this is over, you're going to grovel and beg…" And then we heard a clock bong ten times as the conversation continued.

"Where do think that is?" Pettyjohn asked. "A church

bong? Play it again."

Patrick ran the tape again; but he didn't have to. I had heard it before. I knew where Karn had made the call.

"Sounds like a kind of a mini grandfather or mantle clock," Patrick commented.

"I think you're right," said Pettyjohn. "Well, looks like we have a couple of hours to go till he calls again. Sounds like he plans to draw you out and make something happen, Bruce."

"I'm sure he's already had plenty of opportunities to put a bullet in me. But if I know his malignant mind, he'll want me to surrender so that he'll have both Caroline *and* me to play with."

"Well, we're not letting you waltz into that scenario. I'm sure he wants to settle a score with you, but could also be that it's money he wants to finance his new order."

"And that being the case," I said, "what would the Bureau's position be on coming up with any money? He'd want millions, you know."

"Officially? We don't make deals with kidnappers or terrorists. I'm sure you remember that. But, that's not to say we'll never consider it."

I then checked my watch and said, "I think I'm going to step out a while. I have some calls to make and would like to get a little brunch."

"Okay, but suggest you be back here no later than eleven forty-five so that everyone will be in place to field Karn's call."

"That is if he *does* call. Not calling me back could be another way he plans to screw with me."

"Just don't be late, Bruce," Pettyjohn said.

I gave him a faux salute and slipped on out past the agent desks without word to either Starr or Murphy. Starr followed me out of the door to the street and called after me.

"Skip, where are you going?"

"I'm just going to drive around and make a couple of

calls."

"Karn called didn't he? I saw how animated you were through the glass. What did he say?"

"Not much, except that he'll call back at high noon and meet me in the street for a gunfight."

"What?"

"I think he's going to set up a meeting. Without you all, of course."

"Where?"

"Don't know. I'm sure he'll tell me."

"What did Lew say about what happened last night?"

"He wants to hire me full time as your all's bodyguard."

"Very funny. I do know he was glad as hell that you showed up at that bar in spite of what he said to you. And so was I."

"Hey, I'm available anytime you need me."

"You know you won Murph over. He thinks you're some kind of super hero from the D.C. Comics."

"And Pettyjohn probably thinks I'm more like a cartoon character."

"Like Wily Coyote?"

I smiled and then glanced down at my watch again. "I need to go."

"See you back here, then," she said.

I gave her a wave and then dashed off to Caroline's Altima. In less than ten minutes I was already on the Denver outskirts and on the way back to the Karn house. As I was ninety-five percent sure Jonas Karn had called from his mother's living room, there was an outside chance I would still find him there. On the other hand, if he did plan to draw me into his sights, he wouldn't do it in the presence of his mother or the officer parked down the street.

It was now time for *me* to be in control.

At just past eleven I parked the Nissan on Carroll, two blocks east of the Karn house, pulled my P coat up around my face and walked through the back yards of several houses until I came to the rear of the Karn house. I was taking no chances of being spotted by the CBI officer. I suspected it was through the back door that Karn was slipping into his mother's shack. But then I wondered why the stake-out team didn't also position a unit on the adjacent side street just in case Karn did use the rear route.

Taking account of the narrow driveway along the left side of the house that ended at a rather dilapidated two car garage, I paused to look into a single dirty and clouded window at the side. Inside was a white Buick sedan that looked as though it hadn't moved in a while. A couple of rugs lay folded on the roof and a cardboard box sat on the right fender.

In looking at the back of the house, I saw that all the blinds were pulled. However, if the creep was still there peeping out through a blind slat, when I came through the back door, I could be facing the business end of a shotgun. But it was my only opportunity to get in.

After stepping upon the small back porch, I tried the door knob, finding it locked. Having nothing on me to jimmy the lock, I turned my attention to the garage. Perhaps I could find a screwdriver or a small crowbar. Quickly, I moved to the overhead door to the garage, but it wouldn't budge. Probably raised and lowered by a remote. At the side of the garage by the window I had peered through was a flimsy-looking, weather-beaten door that had rotted along the bottom. I found it locked as well.

I shot another glance at the windows on the rear of the house and seeing no moving slats, sent my shoulder into the door like an offensive lineman. It not only gave easily, but a large strip of the door facing came away with it. I stepped inside the garage and then returned the door to a closed position the best I could. As the small window did little to bring in the light, I moved about to look for a flashlight to locate a screwdriver. None to be found. Remembering that

Caroline had a mini-light on her key chain, I pulled the set of keys from my coat. The light, though tiny, was piercingly bright, something of the halogen quality, and served me well.

Confirming my earlier impression of the Buick, I was set to wonder how the frail Mrs. Karn got around. It was for sure that her son would no longer be chauffeuring her. Did a delivery boy bring her groceries and medication to her? Was she under hospice care where she was visited by a home health nurse? Son, Jonas, had to be slipping in and out regularly…and somehow doing so with ease.

At the back of the garage bay I found a workbench on which there were a few basic tools like a hammer, a hand saw and a flat-head screwdriver. I then shined the mini-light around the garage, looking for anything that might provide clues about where Jonas Karn was keeping my daughter. But I knew it was a long shot.

The walls were barren except for a rake and shovel that hung from large hooks that were screwed into the wall.

Several cardboard boxes that contained rags, paint cans and small plastic containers of nails and screws, sat against the back side of the room. I could readily see that save for the Buick, the garage served as a junk bay. I was pretty much resigned that there was nothing I could find that was of any value in my search of the place.

I almost missed it. Had I not shined the penlight over the floor, I would have walked out and not seen the four-by-four wooden door on the concrete slab. Taking the Beretta from my coat pocket, I then grabbed the handle and pulled the door open from the floor. Just in case Mr. Karn was waiting for me at the bottom of the black abyss, I aimed both the beam of light and muzzle of the gun into the hole. A set of wooden steps perhaps a dozen in number ended at a concrete walkway.

After wrenching myself through the opening, I allowed the penlight to lead me down the stairs a step at a time until I touched bottom. Shining the light three hundred sixty degrees, I saw that I was in a tunnel of sorts about five feet wide and seven feet high. The walls and ceiling were constructed of wood planks and the concrete flooring continued on several feet to my front in the direction of the house. The floor was wet where water had eroded a few of the planks, causing the tunnel to smell dank and moldy. Piles of dirt and mud lay in places and I was convinced the life of the passageway was not for long. It was a good thing I was not claustrophobic.

Suddenly, something fell onto my neck and scratched me before falling to the floor. It didn't take me long to realize what it was…a filthy, disgusting rat. "*God!*" I exclaimed. I knew that my skin had been ripped and I prayed the rodent wasn't rabid. Hate those slimy bastards.

After walking another twenty feet, I found that the tunnel opened up into a room measuring approximately twelve by fifteen. My light then fell on a chain on the ceiling which I pulled. As my eyes had become accustomed to the darkness which was only barely illuminated by the ever fading penlight, the sudden brilliant light of a naked overhead bulb nearly blinded me. Directly in front of me was a shelving unit that went all the way to the ceiling and on which were dusty cans of fruit and vegetables and sealed Mason jars filled with home-canned foods. The room appeared to be a fallout or storm shelter built in the late 50s during the Cold War. To the left of me on what was probably the west wall were a dozen or so yellowed and frayed posters, one of which had a picture of an angel hand-drawn by someone who was obviously on psychedelic drugs at the time. It read: *Welfare-the Exterminating Angel.* Another poster had a picture of two fists, one white and the other black, shoved defiantly in the air. It read: *SDS and the Black Liberation Movement: a Coalition for Revolution.* And yet a third poster had a photograph of a Vietcong soldier holding an AK-47 in the air with the caption: *Bring the War Home-Chicago, October 11.* Other posters boasted the accomplishments of the Weather Underground Organization, and a more recent one had been added that promoted non-violent change through *Prairie Fire.*

I then turned to my right and saw a vintage, metal Army cot with a worn and soiled mattress, on top of which were a wadded-up sheet and a haphazardly-folded, olive drab blanket. The cot was chained to a hook in the concrete wall. Hanging down from the bed frame was a set of handcuffs. A fiery bolt of adrenaline suddenly shot through my chest as though I had stuck my finger in a light socket. *The room was where Karn had imprisoned Caroline.* And not too long ago. She had been chained to that bed perhaps as recently as the day before, but he had now obviously moved her to another location. On the floor beneath the bed were plastic pouches of half-eaten slop similar to MREs or camping food. I smelled one of the pouches, finding that the contents were not spoiled. It served to reinforce that Caroline had been there scantly hours before. A mostly empty plastic jug of water lay at the foot of the bed along with used plastic forks and spoons.

I had to sit down on the cot as my weak knees were buckling. Caroline was most probably in that very room while I was upstairs visiting Karn's mother less than twenty four hours before. That revelation struck me in the heart like a bullet. But as my mind ever plays the devil's advocate, I was set to wonder if Caroline actually *had* been there. Maybe it was someone else. Maybe Karn just made it his sick business to kidnap and imprison beautiful young women and chain them up for his pleasure. A kind of sadistic, perverted ritual practiced by a man who no longer had the capacity to perform sexual relations, thanks to me. But then I realized that didn't fit his profile. Anyway, he had confessed to the world that he had been compelled to take up the life of a homosexual. Thank God for that.

As I sat looking around the room, I spotted a bottle of

liquid chlorine alongside another container that read *Acetone*. It didn't take me but a couple of seconds to realize that combining the ingredients created homemade chloroform. And that was how he got to Caroline. He must have approached her from behind in the dark at the apartment stairwell, dazed her with a blow to the head, then placed a cloth over her nose and carried her to his vehicle parked nearby. He likely kept the mixture there in the room to keep her out, especially if she decided to become rambunctious.

And then another, more horrible thought hit me. Although he had probably moved Caroline to another location because I was getting too close, what if he hadn't? What if he had ended her life and buried her someplace? A wave of nausea and cold sweat suddenly swept over me like a typhoon.

As I looked around the dungeon, I realized that it was actually a part of the basement. Light from the overhead bulb streamed through a narrow open door that led to the main part of the basement and a stairwell to the upper floor. With the Beretta still in hand, I moved through the door and onto the stairs with stealth, trying the best I could to keep the wood beneath my feet from cracking and popping. After negotiating the last of about fifteen steps, I shined the penlight on the door at the top stair and turned the knob. Opening it just a crack in case someone was in the kitchen, I allowed the muzzle of the Beretta to lead me past the door. The room stank of garbage and stale coffee. Dirty dishes cluttered the sink bowl.

And then my cell phone went off. I had forgotten to put it on 'vibrate.'

Immediately, I heard footsteps from the living room entering the kitchen. When I brought the pistol up in line with my face, Mrs. Karn turned the corner and walked directly into the muzzle. She let out a scream and placed a hand over her chest as though she were about to go into cardiac arrest.

"*You!*" she exclaimed. "Mr. Hagen!"

The phone kept ringing and I could see on the caller ID that it was the number from the Denver FBI office. Pettyjohn was obviously calling to see where I was, it being ten minutes till twelve. I said nothing, but continued holding the pistol to Sybil Karn's head. Finally the ringing ceased and I dropped the phone into my coat pocket.

"Where's Jonas?" I said in a low voice. "He's…he's not here."

"Was he here this morning?"

She nodded. "Just for a few minutes." She was haking.

"Move into the living room, Mrs. Karn. *Now! Please.*" As she led me slowly out of the kitchen, she asked,

"What do you want with me?"

"Sit down…there," I commanded, pointing the Beretta to the sofa chair. She did as instructed, seemingly in a great deal of pain.

"Stay here and don't move, Mrs. Karn," I said. I went first to Karn's bedroom, checking the closet and under the bed. Then I crossed through the living room and did likewise in her room. The last place I looked was the bathroom. He was apparently nowhere in the house. She had told me the truth.

As I could see that her hands were trembling, I put the gun in my pocket and sat on the couch opposite her. I certainly didn't want to be the cause of her premature death.

"I'm sorry, Mrs. Karn. I didn't mean to frighten you, but I need to know where Jonas is."

"I'm afraid I don't know. He never tells me where he's going. Why are you here like this? I thought you were his friend."

"Okay, Mrs. Karn. My name is not Bob Hagen and I am not a friend of your son's. I'm sorry to have lied to you. My name is Bruce McGowan." I then paused and leaned forward toward her. "And Jonas has my daughter."

"What do you mean…has her?" she asked weakly.

"He kidnapped her and is holding her prisoner some place. And I believe that up until today, it was downstairs in your basement."

"I…I don't believe that…don't believe it at all. My Jonas is a good boy. He might have some strange ideas about things I don't agree with, but he would *never* do anything like what you're saying."

"He did *time*, Mrs. Karn. For some very bad things.

You know that. I'm sure you read about what he did."

"I read about it, yes, but he didn't do all those things. The government railroaded him, he said, for the stands he took on things. And I believe him."

I shook my head. "No, ma'am. He killed some people. I'm the one who put him away for that. And the court convicted him."

She then shook *her* head. "Jonas wouldn't do that. And I know he didn't kidnap anybody."

I could see there was no way to convince her that her son was a scumbag, so I let it go.

"In about five minutes, Mrs. Karn, Jonas will be calling me. I will put my phone on 'speaker' and you'll hear him say things that will make you see I'm telling you the truth. I may say or do some things that will alarm you, but please don't take it personally. I just want my daughter back."

She took from her smock a piece of tissue and stifled a raspy cough, then placed her sickly eyes on my face. "Why…why would he want to kidnap your daughter, Mr. Hagen?"

"McGowan, ma'am. To get back at me for putting him in prison."

She didn't reply, but shook her head and dropped her eyes to the floor. I hated what I was about to do.

CHAPTER   NINE

Almost on key, after the twelfth bong of the mantle clock, my cell phone rang again. I pulled it from my packet and hit the speaker button, then laid the phone on the coffee table between us. I looked at Mrs. Karn who appeared to be shaking again. I let it ring a few more times and then touched the 'talk' button.

"Hello," I said roughly.

"Well, Bruce, I can tell you're on the speaker phone and you have all your pig buddies standing around listening."

"Mmmm, actually, Jonas, I'm not with them. It's just you and me. Now what do I do to get my daughter back?"

Mrs. Karn's eyes widened.

"Oh, but aren't we impatient. I haven't decided when that will happen…if at all."

"Fun and games are over, Karn. Now let me talk to Caroline!"

He laughed. "There's a gag order in place, Bruce, and I can't remove it."

Then his laugh became a cackle. I took a deep breath and let it out audibly. "I wasn't telling you the truth when I said I was alone, Karn. There's someone here who wants to speak with you." I motioned for Mrs. Karn to talk into the phone.

"Jonas?" she said in a cracked voice. "Mom?" Karn responded.

"Jonas. This man is here in the house. He says you kidnapped his daughter. Tell me that's not true."

"Mom, I…"

"*All right, Karn!*" I yelled. "*You have something of mine and I have something of yours.*" I took the Beretta out, placed it near the phone and pulled the slide so that he could hear the clicking action. It extracted a shell that was in the chamber and it bounced loudly on the coffee table. "Now you put Caroline on the phone or I will paint your mother's living room wall red with her blood. *Now!*"

"You son-of-a bitch, McGowan. If you touch one gray hair…"

"*Now, asshole!*"

There was a dreadful silence for about twenty seconds and then I heard, "Dad?"

I closed my eyes and said in a whisper, "Thank God."

"Are you all right, Caroline?"

"I'm okay, Dad. He hasn't harmed me."

"Yet!" Karn's voice broke in.

"All right, prick. How do we do this? Where do I find you?"

He didn't readily respond and I wondered for a moment whether we had been disconnected. But then he said, "You shouldn't have gone to my house, McGowan. You shouldn't have frightened my mother like this. Now you'll have to pay for yet another sin."

I then heard Caroline yell out, "No!"

I quickly brought up the Beretta and fired a round into the wall behind Sybil Karn. She let out a scream and cupped her ears with her hands. The report of the pistol was deafening, reverberating throughout the small house for two or three seconds.

"*What did you do?*" Karn screamed into the phone.

"I don't know what you were about to do to my daughter, Karn, but that was a warning. The next round slams into your mother's head. If you think I won't do it, you just remember back fifteen years what I'm capable of."

"Okay, okay," he cried. "Just…settle down. She's an old woman and very sick."

I picked up the phone and took it off 'speaker.' In a voice that in retrospect seemed to come from the depths of my bowels I said, "I'll tell you what we're going to do now…and I want you to listen carefully. This is not up for debate, Karn. There's an old game show that we're going to play. It's called *let's make a Deal.* Your mother is going to get dressed and accompany me to my car. We're going to drive to wherever you and Caroline are this very hour. I will trade your mom for Caroline. We both then walk away with our loved ones and that will be the end of it. Simple as that."

"I don't think I can do that, McGowan. You and I have a score to settle."

"Fine. Then the ladies will go their ways and you and I will have at each other."

He laughed nervously. "No. I'm not a fool. I realize I'm no match with you one on one. The rules have to be different. Just you and my mom will come to where I am. I'll give you directions. I will be able to see you coming for two miles. If I see a chopper in the air or any agents trailing you, Caroline and I will be gone by the time you get here. And you won't kill my mother…not as long as I have Caroline. Anyway, the FBI would have your ass behind bars. Oh, yeah, Bruce. I'd like to see that. It would almost be worth letting you kill my mother. But you play this like I tell you and Caroline won't get hurt."

"If I find a mark on her…so much as a rope burn… there will be no place on earth for you to hide. And then I will find where you stashed your mother and kill her, too. I want you to visualize that image, maggot. You can't even imagine what I'll do to her. And she won't die quickly. Do you get the picture?"

"Two o'clock, McGowan. That's when we make the switch. You don't have much time. If you're late, it doesn't happen."

"All right," I said. "Where are you?"

"Drive from the house north along I-25 and get off at the second Fort Collins exit. Take Hardscrabble Road beyond the Horsetooth Reservoir and follow that to Prince Ferry Road. You will take the second left off that road and it will lead you to a series of cabins about two miles up to the top of a long mountain grade. I'll be watching for that little red Altima…and I'd better see just the one car."

"Then we're done here," I said abruptly. I then disconnected the call.

Mrs. Karn was now crying. I wasn't sure if it was because I scared the hell out of her or that it grieved her to learn that her only son was a lying, criminal piece of shit. I put the Beretta back into my coat pocket and picked up her hand across the coffee table. What had scared me half to death a couple of minutes before was whether I was capable of ending an innocent woman's life in revenge for the loss of my daughter's life. If it came to that.

"Mrs. Karn, I'm sorry about this. I had no choice but to do and say what I did. I wouldn't have hurt you. But I would do nearly anything to get my daughter returned to me."

She nodded and smiled through her tears. "And I'm sorry, Mr. McGowan, that my son has done this."

"Can you please get ready, ma'am? I need to drive you out to where he is."

I helped her stand. "Give me a few minutes if you will," she said.

At a quarter after twelve, my cell phone rang again. It was Pettyjohn.

"What's going on with you, Bruce? And why aren't you here? Did Karn call you?"

I could have storied him, but I decided to play the stall game rather than the liar's game.

"I can't go into it right now, Lew. Just trust me for a few hours and I'll call you later."

"That's not good enough for me, Bruce. Now what the hell's going on?"

"I can't talk now. Just bear with me. That's all I ask."

"Have you forgotten what obstruction of justice is?"

"Goodbye, Lew." I then closed my cell phone.

Mrs. Karn was still getting ready and I thought I heard her voice once, as though she was talking with someone. When I moved toward her bedroom to see if that was the case, she came out wearing a light blue warm-up suit and an old pair of sneakers. The pastel color made her face look even paler.

"You'll also need a coat, Mrs. Karn. It's nearly freezing out there."

She nodded, returned to her closet and came back out wearing a long, woolen coat, mousy gray in color and frayed in places. Anywhere else, she could easily be mistaken for a street person. I left out of the rear of the house with Sybil Karn to avoid the stake-out officer, hoping that within the last hour the cops hadn't wised up about people coming and going through the back door. I helped her carefully negotiate the rougher terrain through the back yards leading to the street where I had parked the Altima. After I had positioned her in the passenger's side of the car and snapped her seat belt, I pulled away from the curb. I then retraced my route so that I would not pass by the front of the Karn house, thinking that the fuzz might recognize the Nissan from the day before. I really didn't want to take them on another chase with a frail seventy-five year old woman riding shotgun.

I wasn't entirely sure how all this would go down…or end. But one thing for sure, now I was in charge. And this had to be a real ego deflator for one Jonas Karn. However, I wasn't looking at this as 'somebody wins and somebody loses.' But most of all, I didn't want Caroline to come up on the losing end.

It took us over an hour to get to the turn-off point on Prince Ferry and by my calculations, we had two country miles and ten minutes before we reached the road to the cabin. When I had traveled less than a quarter mile along the rough asphalt road, I spotted a number of log and cedar cabins speckled sporadically fifty to one hundred yards apart among Canaan spruces and firs at the top of a hill. About halfway between the car and a large cabin just off the road in the woods, I spotted a lone figure walking at a rapid clip in our direction. I then stopped the car within five hundred feet of the figure and sat waiting. Was the person a messenger or emissary? The figure was small with a thin build and walking with obvious determination.

And then my heart leapt. I *knew* that walk. It was Caroline.

Kicking open the door, I jumped out and began running the rest of the way to meet her. When I held out my arms to her, instead of seeing a smile on her face, I saw a look of consternation. My first thought was that she had experienced some kind of psychological terror. But then she called out to me, "Dad, stop. It's a trap!" She pointed behind me.

What she said didn't immediately register until I turned around and saw Mrs. Karn standing at the front of the Nissan holding a .357 magnum in both of her hands, pointed directly at us.

"All right, McGowan. Take the gun out of your belt and drop it on the ground. Easy!" she warned. "No fancy moves."

I was flabbergasted. But gingerly, I placed my fingers

around the grip of the Beretta and laid it slowly in the dirt. Considering the muzzle of the magnum was pointed at Caroline's head and I had the feeling the old lady definitely knew how to use the gun, I wasn't looking to chance any kind of play.

Now both of you. Get in the car *now*!" Ma Barker barked.

It was probably the biggest surprise of my life. Her voice was no longer weak and her eyes now had life in them. It took me a moment to realize that not only had her voice changed, but she was not sick at all. Still old? Yes. But definitely not feeble or senile. Karn and his mum had duped us.

"She was in on it all along, Dad," said Caroline.

As we walked back toward the car, I could see the smirk on the old woman's face. "Shame on you, mom," I said.

"Don't be a smart-ass, sonny. Just get in the car. Both of you get in the front."

I slid under the wheel and Caroline got in on the passenger side. Then Mrs. Karn climbed into the back seat and trained the .357 on us.

Glancing quickly at Caroline, I said, "I should know better than to turn my back on crusty old broads."

"Shut up, McGowan, and drive on toward that cabin there." She then laughed a rather diabolical laugh. "Damn, I can't believe how easy you made this for me."

"Remind me also to start patting down these old broads, too, Caroline."

Sybil Karn laughed again. "Ah, you thought you were pretty smart, didn't you, McGowan. Well, you proved out to be nothing but a dumb-ass. I knew all along who you were when you showed up yesterday."

Caroline touched my arm. "Dad, I'm sorry. I had no way to warn you."

"Don't worry about it, sweetheart. I'm just glad to see

you…and that you're okay." I then snapped my head back to Mrs. Karn. "So, old woman. When I heard you talking in the bedroom before we left, I assume you and your asshole son were putting the finishing touches on your plan."

"You got it, boy."

"How did you and he know I'd go back to your house today?"

"We didn't, but took a chance. I saw you kind of jump when my mantle clock went off. And that's when Jonas got the idea to call you with the clock chiming in the background. And we knew you wouldn't bring the FBI to the house. Jonas…he's studied you for a long time. Knows how you think. Knows *everything* about you."

"Does he know what I do now for a living?"

"He knows where you work. Just don't know what business is. But since he knows all your friends are pigs, he figures it's got to be some government agency."

"Uh huh. So did he ever tell you that I fed his testicles to him twenty years ago and turned him into a woman?"

She placed the muzzle of the .357 against the back of my head. "And did I tell you what Jonas has got planned for *you?* When he's done, he'll be feeding pieces of you to the crows."

As we neared the top of the hill, I suddenly pressed down hard on the accelerator, getting the car's speed up over sixty-five. Placing my hand over Caroline's chest, since she did not have her seat belt on, I then jammed on the brakes. I felt Ma Karn's head hit the back of my seat…and then the gun went off. The slug from the .357 tore through the seat and entered my back with a thud. As pain quickly spread from back to front with the intensity of a kidney stone times ten, I felt myself slumping over the steering wheel. The last thing I heard as I began to pass out was Caroline screaming *"Dad!"*

When I woke up, I was lying on my stomach on a cold,

hard surface, which I figured out was some kind of metal table. I blinked my eyes open and through a window a dozen feet away saw that it was dark outside. When I tried to move around, the pain in my back shut me down immediately. And then I realized that my wrists were tied to both sides of the table legs with strips of fabric.

The first face I saw was one I didn't recognize. About thirty five with long, dirty blonde hair and a goatee, he was doing something to my back. As I was trying to regain full control of my faculties, I then figured out he was checking my bandage.

And then I heard somewhere in the room the same nauseating voice I had heard for four days on the other end of the line. "You're lucky Mr. Baines here, went a couple of years to medical school, McGowan. He dug out the bullet my mother put in you and kept you from bleeding to death."

"Then…why did you allow him to operate? I thought you wanted me dead." My tongue was so dry and thick, I could hardly talk.

"Quite the contrary. I want you alive. I want you to watch me cut on Caroline right before I start cutting pieces off *you*."

I winced, partly from the stinging pain *and* from the image of him hurting Caroline. I thought to myself that the afternoon had started off so well.

"Where is Caroline?" I groaned.

"Oh, she's with Mom in the next room. Tied up again, I'm afraid. Your daughter just can't seem to stay away from me."

"You're a real son-of-a-bitch, Karn. I'll bet you were the Queen of the Ball all those years in prison."

Karn laughed and then he drove his fist down hard on my wound. I screamed from the pain, which appeared to delight him.

The would-be doctor who saved my life said, "Whoa, Jonas. I just sewed him up. Don't bust open the stitches."

I must have passed out again after that because the next thing I knew, I was shirtless and sitting up in a straight-back chair. My wrists were bound with duct tape to the chair's arms as was my torso to the chair back.

"He's baaaack," I heard Karn say in sing-song like the little blonde girl in the Amityville Horror. I felt like I was in my *own* horror movie.

I looked around at what appeared to be the living room and saw the face of the doc who patched me up as well as that of the man I took to be Jonas Karn. It was the first real occasion I had had to see in real life what he now looked like. He did appear to be the man in the photo from the *Subterranean* rag. Prison had not been good to him. I would never have recognized him from fifteen years ago. Although he was probably late fifties, he could have passed for his seventy-something year old mother's brother. His hair was snow white and shaggy and his face had deep wrinkle lines. However, his blue eyes were still the same…cold, piercing and full of hate.

I was then able to get a better look at my doc who was wearing a green Army fatigue shirt with tears in it where the name tag and unit patch had been ripped off. He was also wearing a black arm band that had a defiant white fist on it and the letters WUO. Karn who stood beside him was dressed in a denim shirt with the same arm band. And then I saw in a dark corner of the room another man, large-set with a head of white hair and beard. Seeing my eyes on him, he stood up and walked over to me without saying a word.

"And who the hell are *you?*" I said.

"You don't recognize me, Bruce? Think back about thirty years. Picture me with short hair and twenty less pounds."

For a short while the face didn't register. But then there was something in his eyes that gave him away.

"Tom Sperry."

He smiled through the heavy beard. "You *do* remember me.

Small world, isn't it?"

"What happened to you, Tom? You were the best explosive man I ever saw in Special Forces. *And* you were a patriot."

"I still am, Bruce. I love this country. I just despise what the government has become. It doesn't care about people… people down on their luck, people living in ghettos, Black people, the sick, the vets…I could go on and on."

"So you turn to this new revolutionary guard, as you call it, bent on terrorizing and destroying the country's infrastructure, not to mention killing innocent people."

"Collateral damage, Bruce. You know about that. I remember that day in the Mekong when you blew up that hooch with a grenade launcher. Killed that woman and her little girl. I remember how that affected you. Spoils of war, my man."

The subject of a hundred nightmares.

I looked at Tom, head to toe. History hadn't been good to *him*, either. "So, Tom, when did you join up with that sorry sack of shit standing beside you?"

"Jonas? Well, I got off active duty in '71 and met him at a demonstration in Chicago. A riot cop was whacking on him with a night stick and I took the pig out. Took his baton away from him and made him eat it. Then I whisked Jonas off somewhere away from the fracas. And that's when we became friends." He then looked at Jonas and smiled. "Yeah, Jonas here is a visionary with ideals and ideas."

"Who kidnaps young women and chains them to walls in underground bunkers."

"I gotta admit. *That* I didn't like. I told you as much, didn't I, Jonas? But see, Bruce, he has this *thing* against you. You ran him in for a necessary act against a terrorist government. You can't imagine what Nixon and the CIA were doing to people. And the FBI was violating rights of citizens by pulling illegal searches and railroading dissenters.

Hoover should have been on his *own* Ten Most Wanted list."

"And were my Air Force friends that Karn killed in Colorado Springs terrorists, too?"

"You better damn well believe they were. They bombed innocent civilians in Hanoi. What did those poor women and children ever do to America?"

I stared deeply into the eyes of the man who used to be my friend. I then shook my head. "You were as good as anyone I knew in the S.F. at what you did. How could you jump ship and turn to something like this, Tom?"

He stared back at me just as intently. "I looked at myself in the mirror one day, Bruce, and didn't like what I saw."

I continued my glare, then turned my head away and spat on the floor.

Karn then spoke. "Well, Bruce. At long last it comes down to this. You, here tied up, helpless, bleeding, hurting, and wondering what's next for you and your bitch daughter in there."

"Hey, Karn," I responded. "You know your homo friend Wally who liked giving it to you in the butt? Well, it was me that put the bullet between his eyes a couple nights ago… not the FBI. Guess you'll have to find yourself another boyfriend, eh?"

Well, I know what you're thinking, and you're right. It was a stupid and provoking thing to say given the fact that I was tied to a chair and started bleeding again down my back. I could feel the warm trickle.

Karn walked slowly toward me and stopped within two feet of my knees. A glint from the overhead light was caught in the same large silver buckle I saw in the tape. Now I could see that it had a raised fist on it.

Speaking of fists, he hit me hard in the side of my head and then back-handed me across the mouth. Blood immediately poured from my busted lip.

I licked the blood and grinned. "Is that all you've got,

pussy?"

And that invited him to kick me hard in the groin. The shot momentarily took my breath away. "Ha!" I yelled. It was part laughter and part response to the horrific pain. It also made me forget about the pain in my back. The excruciating injury to my boys brought a new wave of nausea over me. Paybacks are hell I found out.

Tom Sperry held up his hand. "Hey, Jonas. He got the message, okay?"

I took a deep breath to try managing the pain. "Yeah, Jonas," I said. "Now I've got a message for *you.* Just as soon as I break loose from here, I'm going to cut what's left of your manhood away and shove it down your throat."

He came back around in front of me and placed his face within inches from mine. He was badly in need of a toothbrush, not to mention a Certs. "How does it feel, Bruce? Huh?"

"At least I've got something left to feel. And my voice doesn't sound like a fourth grade schoolgirl."

Karn's mouth quivered in anger. "You want to die now, don't you, McGowan? But I'm not going to let that happen just yet. I want you to see that little girl of yours in there take on all my Islamic friends. They love raping pretty American white women. Unfortunately, they won't be here until tomorrow morning or I'd set it up right now."

I reached down deep in my throat and conjured up a wad of spittle that I unleashed directly into his eyes. Again, not the smartest thing I ever did, but it gave me the most pleasure I had had in days. With his hand on my forehead, he pushed me back hard, toppling the chair. I landed on my back, of course, which served to split open my stitches even more.

Tom Sperry came over and immediately up-righted me. "Man, why do you say these things, bringing all this on yourself?"

I gasped for air and pressed against the chair back to

apply enough pressure to slow down the bleeding. "My mom used to say I didn't know when to keep my mouth shut."

Tom saw the blood dripping on the floor and turned to Baines. "Hey, Doc. See what you can do for him."

Baines took a pocket knife out and cut the duct tape from where I was attached to the chair back. "Lean forward, McGowan," he said. I did as instructed and he ripped off the bandage. I winced as he applied pressure to the wound for a half-minute and then he put another piece of gauze on it, subsequently wrapping me several times around the chest and back with surgical tape.

Karn, who had been watching Tom and Doc attend to me, stood back a little with a wicked smile on his face. "You *see,* McGowan? My compadres are not inhuman. I would have left you there till morning."

I re-settled in my chair and fixed my eyes to Karn. I was about to strike a nerve. "If this is about your wife, Karn, I'm sorry."

The comment prompted him to again put his face close to mine. "*Don't…*talk about my wife, McGowan. I don't want you to say her name or refer to her in any way with your filthy mouth. "You as much as killed her as if you put a bullet in her head."

"No, Karn. If anything, *you* were responsible for her death. *You* made the choices that led to your arrest and put her in the mental state…"

"*You don't know anything about her mental state!*" He shouted. "And don't make out like you do."

"Look, Karn. You know damn well why she ended up like she did. The thing is, how in the hell would a sane woman choose to end up married to a piece of shit like you?" Which was of course again the wrong thing to say. Almost as fast as an old west gunslinger, he pulled his pistol from his belt, cocked the hammer and laid the muzzle between my eyes. His hand quivered and I knew it was from a combination of anger and constrainment to keep himself from pulling the trigger.

"No," he said, releasing the hammer. "I refuse to let you provoke me. As much as I want to pull the trigger *right now*, I will be patient. And I really don't think you want that to happen, anyway. You might not be afraid to die, tough guy, but I think you don't want to exit this world at this very moment without saying bye-bye to sweet Caroline in there. But, I'm not *totally* cruel-hearted, McGowan. I will give you that last opportunity tomorrow morning to see her, right before I splatter your blood all over this building and turn my pack of wolves loose onto her."

When he was done, I looked back at Sperry. "Tom, is this what you signed up for? Is this the patriotic ideal you were just talking about?"

I could see that my questions got to him. He wasn't the psychopath that Karn was and I was banking on our former friendship as well as his value system to assure nothing bad happened to Caroline. As I knew I had pushed the envelope too far with Karn, I might have put Caroline in even more jeopardy by taunting the weasel.

Tom didn't answer me nor would he look at me. And that's when I realized there was nothing left of the man I used to know. I wasn't sure I could depend on him to be Karn's check valve. Caroline and I could be in deep shit.

Karn then looked over at Tom, chuckled and left the room without further word. A short moment later, Tom pulled up a chair in front of me and heaved his large frame into it with a lumbering sigh. Before he could say anything, I started in on him.

"I'm asking you to do the right thing here, Tom. I know this maniac bastard's agenda is to seek revenge on me, but please don't let anything happen to Caroline. If there's any way you can get her out of here, please just think about it."

Sperry motioned with his head for Doc to leave the

room. After Baines disappeared through the door, Tom leaned into me.

"He's actually not a real doc. He's a former Naval medic who went a couple of years to med school and flunked out."

"Oh, great. A medical school failure performed meat ball surgery on my back. My day just keeps getting better and better."

"He's a pretty good guy, but doesn't say much."

"I'd prefer that he was a pretty good *doctor*. To hell with the dialogue."

I could tell that it pained Sperry to see me sitting there tied to the chair and bleeding like a stuck pig. A renewed trickle of blood was seeping into my butt crack.

"I hate that you're in this thing, Bruce. And I doubly hate the fact that Jonas took your daughter as a pawn to get to you."

"He's a psycho, Tom, and you know that. I'm depending on you with Caroline."

"Nobody's going to get to that girl in there if I have any control over it. I've got two teenage girls of my own at home. Yeah, I know that Jonas has a couple of screws loose. But, Bruce, he's the perfect revolutionary…like Thomas Paine and Nathan Hale. He brings to our new order the heritage of the old Weather Underground. You would be surprised at the numbers we have all over the State of Colorado and in other venues like Illinois, Indiana and Michigan. Scores of these people are spinoffs of the old SDS and more recently, Prairie Fire. In just days this country will know the new WUO. There will be several 9-11s and people will experience terror like this nation has never seen. There will be a new swift and terrible sword of justice in this land. The eyes of the people will be opened to see that their corrupt law enforcement and weakened military can no longer protect them and they will look to the one organization that has their interests at heart."

"So, let me get this straight, Tom. From the WUO will rise a new government, new law enforcement and a new military? No longer will you just be making a statement to get the government's attention. You plan to actually *topple* the government."

"In time, yes. It's not going to happen overnight, but it will only take one night for Americato see how vulnerable it is. It will look to the very organization that brought Americato its knees for help."

"My God, Tom. Do you not realize how insane this all sounds? But not surprisingly, you have somebody insane leading you people."

"It's not as insane-sounding as you may think, Bruce. Lesser ideals and plans throughout history have succeeded."

"I still don't understand it, Tom. You're better than this. Certainly better than the nut case in the other room. I know you're a passionate American, and in some ways, still a patriot looking for a *better* America. But cut yourself loose from this 'new order' as you call it before it's too late." "I'm here because I need to be, Bruce. For me and my family. And again, I'm sorry you're sitting here tied up in this room."

"You know that Karn or maybe even *you* will end up having to kill me. And not only out of Karn's revenge, but because you have told me too much."

"I won't kill you, Bruce. Karn wants to have the pleasure of doing that himself. That's *his* deal and I don't have anything to say about it."

We studied each other's eyes for a moment. I could see the remorse and even reluctance in his face. We had old times between us. But his allegiance to this new order was more powerful than old friendships. It would pain him, but he would see me die.

"Look, Bruce. Like I said, I don't condone a lot of shit he does, but Jonas is a wounded man. *Has* been since his wife took her life. When you took him and he got sent up, she just didn't seem to have any purpose in carrying on. Like she gave up. They idolized one another. She knew he'd be out of her life for at least twenty and I guess felt like there was no reason to live. Just like you said…in his mind, indirectly you killed her."

"I did my job, Tom, in taking him out. I might not have been gentle with him in doing so, but he had to know that some government would eventually get a bead on him. It just happened to be me."

"Yeah. I guess you represented everything he hated about the government. And he had all that time behind bars to grow a personal hatred for you. You killed his wife… he plans to kill something precious to *you*."

I kept my eyes on Tom's and bit on my lower lip. "Do me one last favor and do it now."

"If I can. What is it?"

"Go in there and set Caroline loose."

A look of pure anguish crossed his brow and then he turned away toward a window. "It's a nice night out there. The stars are so brilliant. But they generally *are* here in the Colorado countryside." He paused a moment and then turned around. "It's not that easy, Bruce. You know what she'll do. It would only be a matter of hours and she'd have an army of agents down on us. I'm sorry as hell about her."

I didn't respond, but began wondering at what point both Caroline and I would die. And I think Tom Sperry feared that Karn would make him do it.

Sperry stood up and took both a .45 from his waist band and a Buck knife from the sheath on his belt, then approached me. "Et tu, Brute?" I said, smiling. "I'm not going to kill you, Bruce. I'm just going to cut the duct tape and put you in the bedroom back there with your daughter. Mrs. Karn is no longer there. She left in the car you came in."

"You'd do that for me? What would Karn say about that?"

"I can handle Jonas. He'll be fine with it as long as you don't try to escape. You're probably hungry. I've got some old

C-rations for you." He then ripped open the tape and said "Stand up."

Damn I was weak. My boys were still traumatized and I had no legs. I knew there was no way I could subdue him. With a powerful left hand, keeping the .45 in his right, he stood me up and helped me toward the bedroom.

"Thanks," I said.

When we opened the door I saw Caroline tied by cloth strips to the frame of a lower bunk bed. A piece of duct tape was over her mouth. Tom then sat me down into a wooden chair that belonged to a pine desk. Pulling a piece of cord from his pocket, he ordered me to put my left hand on the chair arm. He then secured my wrist to the chair.

"Now sit there and don't move," he said. "I'll bring you a couple of C's and some water."

"Hey Tom, can you take the tape off Caroline's mouth? She won't be able to eat, otherwise. And if she does yell, who the hell is going to hear her way out here?"

He nodded and walked to where Caroline lay on the lower bunk. Gently, he pulled the tape from her face.

"Thank you," she said.

"Don't try anything, Bruce. I left your right hand free so that you can eat. If you betray my kindness, don't think I won't kill you. Both of you."

"I understand," I replied.

Within thirty seconds he was back with two boxes of supper, two canteens of water and a younger man, perhaps Caroline's age, wearing a buzz cut. On his left bicep was the same arm band with the fist.

"This is Aaron," Tom said. "He'll open the cans for you and watch you eat. Then he's spending the night in here to assure you don't try anything. When you're done eating, Aaron will tie down your right hand."

"Hello, Aaron," I greeted. "Dining with us? Gee but I was counting on a white tablecloth and candlelight dinner."

Aaron took out a P38, which is a small military device with

a hinged swivel that cuts into the can, and first ripped open the ancient can of ham and eggs that was all blended together. Its smell immediately permeated throughout the room. Nasty stuff. He then opened up the small can of peanut butter as well as the only truly edible food in the entire C-ration inventory…peaches.

Aaron seemed to be a nice enough kid…maybe too nice for the likes of Karn and crew. I wondered how many more of these young recruits there were in the organization whose heads had been filled with the WUO garbage. He hadn't spoken at all until Caroline addressed him.

"Aaron, could you please cut the tie off my right wrist so that I can eat, too?"

"Sure," he said. He then pulled out a pocketknife. Working the blade between her wrist and the cloth, with one slice he ripped the fabric open. "Now don't you all be trying anything? I isn't never hurt another human being and I don't want to start tonight."

"Aaron, if you had any real knowledge of Jonas Karn's plans, which will involve you, you'll end up hurting a *hell* of a lot of people," I said. "Is that who you want to become? You seem like a nice kid and I don't think you'll like what he will order you to do."

"Mr. Karn is what everyone calls a visionary. He told me we're all going to be famous some day when we bring the government to its knees."

"And given the extremely remote possibility that would ever happen, thousands of people will die from the bombs and devices he plants."

"He never said that. He's a good man and a good leader. He won't hurt *nobody*," Aaron rebutted.

"If he's such a good man, Aaron, then why did he kidnap Caroline here? And why does he plan to serve us to the lions tomorrow?"

"I'm sure he has his reasons."

"You need to stop drinking the Kool-Aid, Aaron, and wise up."

"I haven't had any Kool-Aid since I was a kid. I drink a lot of Coke, though."

I glanced over at Caroline who was shaking her head. The poor bastard was as bright as a three watt bulb. We both felt sorry he had somehow ended up subservient to a man bent on becoming America's version of Adolf Hitler.

CHAPTER   TEN

We sat for about fifteen minutes awkwardly digging out the contents of the cans which to a hungry stomach tasted every bit as good as they would have in 1953, the date stamped on the bottom of the peanut butter can. I thought about hiding one of the plastic spoons, but Aaron eyed me closely. Anyway, what good would a plastic spoon do anyone handcuffed to a chair?

Caroline then decided she needed to go to the bathroom, so Aaron left momentarily to go knock on the door where Karn was busy strategizing with a couple of other subversives. I heard him say "What is it, Aaron?"

"She wants to go to the bathroom."

"All right, but you watch her do her business."

"You mean go in there with her?" he said in his childlike way.

"That's *exactly* what I mean." Which I was not at all happy with.

Aaron then returned and ripped open the second wrist tie and escorted her down the hall to the bathroom.

When they got there, I heard him say, "I'm not going to look." Which told me a couple of things. First, he was a decent boy who likely was not cut out for or smart enough for the military but saw the Weatherman order as something noble and righteous. He could then actually *be* somebody. Secondly, I saw him as an opportunity for our escape, if he was as easily duped as I perceived him to be.

I moved around a bit trying to get comfortable. The groin pain had mostly subsided, but I was sure I'd have throes and aches in the manly area for at least several more hours. While Aaron was *not* watching Caroline go potty, the light bulb in my head went off. He had not fully taken the metal lids off either my can of peaches or the peanut butter. Holding the empty peaches can between my knees, I tore off the lid and tossed it just to the underside of the bed. For good measure I also took the lid off the peanut butter can and flipped it in about the same spot.

Aaron then returned with Caroline and asked her, "Are you through eating, now?"

She nodded and then he began re-tying her wrists to the bed posts.

"I'm done here, too, Aaron," I said. "Thanks. You make a delightful ham and egg casserole."

He smiled as though he liked the quip. Or at least I *thought* it was why he was smiling. Maybe in his seventy- five IQ brain he actually thought he had something to do with making our supper.

"You know what, Aaron? Now *I* have to go." And I really did.

Like the obedient little dog that he was, he pulled the knife out and sliced through my wrist cord. Seeing that I was a walking wounded, he dutifully helped me ambulate down the hall. "You don't have to watch me either," I said. I thought about taking him down then and there, but as weak as I was and the fact that that he was a pretty strong- looking kid, I figured I could wait for at least some of my strength to come back to me.

As he was standing by the open door not watching, I emptied my bladder and checked around the room for anything sharp. Nothing to be found. I then stood at the wash basin soaping my hands and after checking to see if Aaron was now watching, saw that he was still turned around. Quickly, I opened the medicine cabinet, finding it barren. Not even a toothbrush.

Aaron returned me to my chair and seeing that the ripped-up cord was not salvageable, he took the roll of duct tape Tom had left in the room and secured both of my wrists to the chair arms.

"Is everybody good, now?" he asked. Like we were children who had just been fed and were tucked in for the night.

"We're good, Aaron, except for being all tied up like we are. Anything you can do about that?"

"No. Mr. Karn would not like that." Again, the boy was slow, but certainly courteous enough.

Speaking of the devil, Jonas Karn appeared at the door to see if we were all comfy. At first he didn't say anything. He just had that look in his eyes that matched his wild hair. Then from the back of his waist band he pulled out the Beretta I had brought with me to kill him.

"Well, is it execution time?" I asked. "If so, I ask that you not do it in front of Caroline."

"You will live another night, McGowan. Just one more night. So you and your daughter better enjoy a good night's sleep. You and she will be the stars of my demonstration tomorrow. I will show my people what's necessary when pigs like you try going head to head with our family."

"Oh, so you're a big happy family now, Queenie? What's it called again? The Homo Underground?"

Karn cocked the hammer on the Beretta and placed the muzzle in my left ear. "That's exactly why this country needs a change in its attitude, bigot. What say I get my biggest, dirtiest goon to come in here and spread your little girl's legs right in front of you?" He paused a moment. "Naw. That's my show for tomorrow."

"Have you eaten this evening, Karn? What say you untie

me and let Aaron there watch me cut out your black heart and feed it to you for dinner?"

He then kicked me in the side with his boot, which again toppled my chair, and broke open my wound. And again, it was my sharp tongue that had caused me more pain. What's wrong with me, anyway?

"Stop it!" yelled Caroline. "You're pretty damned brave kicking a man tied to a chair who just had a bullet removed from him."

Karn laughed. "That's what I like about Caroline, Bruce. She's got your mouth. A mouth that I will also personally shut forever, right after I send you to hell."

I gritted my teeth from the pain, but still had enough fight in me to say, "Then you'd better take me out right now, prick, or somehow, some way I'll personally see that *you* get there long before me."

"Tough talk from a humiliated not to mention helpless man, eh Aaron? Take a good look at the great Bruce McGowan, boy. Take a look at a dead man." He then turned to leave, but suddenly stopped. Pulling my cell phone from his pocket, he added, "You're a pretty popular guy, Bruce. Since I've had this on me, I've listened to three messages from the FBI man, Lew…one from a sweet voice named Starr…and a very bitchy message from Darlene, who I know is your ex-wife. Oh, and some guy named Lionel said you have to call him right away."

"Well, I'll be sure to do that if you hand it to me."

"Mmmm, afraid not, Brucie. He then dropped it to the floor and stomped it several times, smashing it into several pieces. "Tomorrow, Bruce. The Big Show is tomorrow."

I then grinned at him. "You know, you might even be a match for me now, considering my current medical condition. Why don't we see what kind of *real* man you are? I'll even let you tie one hand behind my back."

Karn scowled and then turned to Aaron. "Make sure the light stays on all night and you sit right here and watch them. You hear?"

"Yes, sir," he replied.

"Good. Go pull Mr. McGowan up-right, but keep your guard up. He's full of tricks. Call me if he starts to create a ruckus."

"I will, sir. You can count on me."

I then whistled to Karn. "Oh, Jon-ass. Last chance to come dance with me."

He didn't respond.

Aaron laid his .45 on his chair and pulled me back up to a sitting position. I noticed drops of blood on the carpet where I had lain. Karn saw the red drops on the beige shag. "I'll send Doc in here to plug him back up. I don't want all his blood to drain out prematurely before I kill him tomorrow. It's no fun killing dead people." He then left the room.

Momentarily, Doc Baines came in and had me lean forward. He removed the soggy bandage again and let out a low grunt. "You can't keep opening up this wound, Mr. McGowan. We don't want infection to set in."

"Tell that to your dickless dictator, Doc. He's the one that keeps kicking me around."

"Then do yourself a favor and quit provoking him." He poured more alcohol on the wound, which I enjoyed immensely, and then put another compress on it. Tightly binding me with more masking tape, he seemed satisfied it would do the trick. In less than three minutes his work was done. After Doc left, I began trying to engage Aaron in conversation over the next hour, asking him about his mother, his girlfriend and his dog. I found out he had none of the above. His mother died giving birth to him and he had only been out once with a girl he took to his senior prom. And he liked cats, not dogs. Caroline's eyes told me she really felt sorry for the boy, and if Karn's brainwashing

Weatherman group proved to be Aaron's new family, his innocence would surely be lost forever. I was actually set to wonder about Karn's judgment, allowing such a neophyte to guard us, given that Caroline and I were as he said, loaded with a bag of tricks.

"Is it okay if my daughter and I talk, Aaron?" "Sure. I don't see no harm in it."

At eight forty-five that evening, it was the first real time Caroline *had* been able to talk. The last time we had spoken was on the road that led to the cabin with the ancient Mrs. Karn.

"You look pale from the blood loss, Dad. Are you all right?"

I nodded yes, although I was actually very lightheaded and dizzy. "I'll make it. I think the gourmet dinner helped a little. If I get anymore holes in this old boat, one of them is bound to spring a leak. I've been shot by the Vietcong, a bank robber, a member of the mob, and now a seventy-something year old actress, who by the way deserves an Academy Award."

"The last bullet was an accident," she reminded me. "The gun went off when you went into a panic stop, throwing her against the seat."

"Nevertheless, I let her get the drop on me. I must be losing my edge."

"So, Dad, tell me why Karn kidnapped me. He never even talked to me at all. Just kept me tied up and sedated. I assume it had everything to do with you, since he somehow knows you."

"He didn't tell you *anything*?"

"Nothing. I only heard him a couple of times on my cell phone with you."

"I was the field agent that took him down back in the '80s for planting a bomb that killed some servicemen."

"But you were just doing your job. Why would he be

vindictive about it?"

"It was what I did to him. He didn't always have that squeaky voice."

"I'm not sure I follow."

I looked at Aaron. "Do you know what I'm trying to tell her?"

He shook his head. "I…I don't understand either."

"Of course you don't. Why would I think otherwise?

I'll give you the play by play some day, daughter. But for right now, I think I'm passing out."

"No, Dad! Stay awake! Aaron, please give him some water."

Aaron jumped up and placed the canteen to my lips. "Drink," he said.

I took two or three swallows, one of which choked me. I ended up in a coughing fit that sent electric bolts of pain throughout my back. But I no longer found myself fading to black.

"You know, Dad, next year I will not plan to spend Christmas in some underground dungeon and New Years out in the middle of nowhere. I will have to do a little more research about my innkeepers at these plush resorts."

She had my same warped sense of humor. And I'm glad it came out at a time when I needed it.

"Did Karn treat you okay otherwise? Did he ever hurt you or try molesting you?"

"No. But I did find myself living like a chained up dog. He'd throw me some scraps to eat and I had to go to the bathroom in a saucepan. And do I ever need a shower and change of clothes." She then dropped her eyes for a few seconds. "He has my gun and shield, Dad."

I think she was as upset about that as anything else. She had earned that badge and felt that losing it was like losing an appendage. She had been indoctrinated by the Bureau to feel that way. I *knew* that feeling.

"And you weren't actually harmed by Karn or anyone else."

"No. Mrs. Karn may be a bad lady, but I think she kept her son from doing anything to hurt me."

"I was alluding to anything sexual."

"No. Absolutely not."

"Good. I think you will find he's not capable of that, anyway. I was responsible for changing his sex a few years ago."

"What?"

"Never mind. A rather unpleasant thing. Right, Aaron?"

"Er, right, I guess." He still didn't have a clue, the poor putz.

We talked well into the early morning hours, long after I no longer heard any voices in the other rooms. I couldn't really get a good feel for how large the place was, seeing as how I was out cold when I arrived. I did suspect there was a room somewhere, maybe a basement that could hold a large number of people…like terrorists from the old and new Underground and people of the Middle Eastern persuasion who were sharing their terrorist methodology with Karn.

At just after two-thirty I motioned with my head to Caroline that our boy Aaron was nodding. The .45 he was holding was also starting to slip from his hand, but every time it did, he would grasp it and half open his eyes. Finally, he just laid it in his lap, crossed his arms and closed his eyes for what I hoped was the remainder of the morning. It appeared that our incessant jabbering we did about Caroline's job, her mom and my girlfriend of four months bored him into a state of unconsciousness.

"Caroline," I whispered. "Can you kick off one of your shoes and feel along the carpet with your toes for the metal lid I tossed under the edge of the bed?"

"When did you do that?" she whispered back.

"When Aaron went to the bathroom with you. There are two lids under there from the C-ration cans."

"Brilliant," she said. After pushing off her left loafer with the toe of her right, she lowered her foot from the mattress and began groping around with her toes.

"Be careful not to cut yourself," I said. "Do it slowly." After a few seconds, she found the lid.

"Good," I whispered. "Now try to pick it up between your great and second toe."

At that moment Aaron stirred and half-opened his eyes. Then he settled back down in his chair and closed them again.

It took Caroline a little while before she was able to get her toes up under the lid without cutting herself.

"When you get a firm grip on the lid, lift it over to my right hand."

I then scooted my chair on the carpet to within two feet of her foot so that the exchange from foot to hand would be smooth. When she had fully grasped the lid with her toes, she pushed her foot slowly toward the chair arm. When I felt its sharp edge on the back of my hand, I twisted my fingers around to grab it. Unfortunately, I botched the exchange and the lid fell back onto the carpet…well out of range of her foot.

"Damn!" I said, a little too loud. It startled Aaron and he looked up at both of us, clutching the gun. Both Caroline and I closed our eyes, feigning sleep. When he was satisfied that we were in la-la land, he closed his eyes again. It was not long until I saw his head roll back and mouth fly open. He was definitely out this time. I was now hoping he wouldn't snore and wake himself up again *or* anybody else in the cabin.

"Okay, sweetheart, let's try this again. There's another lid under there in nearly the same spot as the first lid. See if you can find it."

Slowly sweeping her toes along the underside of the bed

again, she came up with it. As she was now good at toe grappling, she gingerly brought up the lid toward my hand.

"I'll try not to fumble the ball this time."

Gingerly, I placed my fingers around the lid and secured it. I thought about trying to reverse my fingers toward my wrist and cut the duct tape, but given that it would be awkward and I was afraid I'd drop it, I decided to do something else. I scooted my chair a few inches at a time toward Caroline's right hand which was firmly tied to the near bed post. Gripping the lid between my thumb and forefinger, I began sawing away at her wrist binding. Blood oozed from one of my fingers where I was gripping it too tightly. But after about two minutes, the last of the threads on the cloth had been severed. Caroline quickly pulled her hand away, took the lid from my hand and began working on her left wrist. Finally, she was completely free. She then went to work on my duct tape.

Although now unbound, I found that I couldn't move. I was afraid *rigor* had set in. I looked helplessly at Caroline who nodded and motioned for me to stay put. She then tip-toed over to Aaron and went around behind him. In one swift motion she snatched the gun from his lap and placed her hand over his mouth. Cocking the hammer, she placed the muzzle against his right temple. He sat wide- eyed and motionless.

"Go back to sleep, Aaron," Caroline whispered and then cracked him on the top of the head. He let out a slight groan before his eyes rolled back. Easing his body out of the chair, she then dropped him onto the carpet. That's my girl. "Come on, Dad," she whispered, helping me to my feet. "We're going out the window."

As I was slowly getting the feeling back in my legs, Caroline went to the small window, quietly flipped the lock and tried to raise it. It wouldn't budge. The wood had apparently swollen during the summer months and it had been closed ever since.

Caroline and I both placed our fingertips on the lattice panel and after I counted out *one two, three,* we pushed up. It was enough force between us to break away the stuck window frame from the casing. It was also enough for me to feel that yet once again, something broke away at my wound. Cold air began streaming into the room. I then returned to the chair I was in and put back on the bloodied shirt. If I was going out into freezing weather, I needed *something* on my body. Unfortunately, my coat was probably in one of the other rooms.

Not knowing whether the bedroom was on the first or second story, I stuck my head out of the window to see how much of a drop we would have. After seeing that we were actually high enough up to call it a third story, I came to the conclusion that if a slip and fall didn't kill me, I would still die sometime after daybreak from a bullet to my head, courtesy of Jonas Karn.

Spotlights on both corners of the house illuminated the receding ground which made it easy to see as many as fifteen cars and pickups parked out of sight of the road. It told me there were at least that many subversives enjoying a sleep-over which would be a prelude to The Morning Show that Karn had planned for them at my expense. Beneath me and to the right were double doors that seemed to belong to a large basement that walked out onto a patio.

I asked Caroline "Could we not just go out the front door?"

She shook her head. "We *have* to go out the window. There's snoring coming from the living room and we'd be sure to wake somebody when we opened the door."

I knew that, of course, but as I wasn't sure I could make it down to the ground without breaking my neck, I thought we could at least try getting by the sleepers.

"How's the strength in your arms, Dad?"

"I guess all right. You of course want me to shinny down that downspout."

"Can you do it?"

I looked at it and given my condition I likened it to rappelling down a fifty foot cliff. "I'll make it."

"Okay, then. I'll go out first. The spout looks pretty solid and should hold. Don't worry…I aced the obstacle course at Quantico."

"And you'll be at the bottom to catch me when I fall."

She grinned. "And kill us both? No, Daddy dear. You're on your own."

"I can do it. Now go," I said. "When you touch down, I'll hop on."

Nimble and quick as an acrobat, it took less than fifteen seconds for her to get to the bottom. The spout did hold firmly. Of course, there were close to sixty pounds difference in our weight.

After swinging my legs over the window casing, I grabbed hold of the spout. Taking my time while quickly recalling my rappelling techniques from my Ranger and Air Assault courses, I negotiated the aluminum spout hand over hand and by bumping my feet against the siding. The difference was, I wasn't holding onto a rope that was being held by someone on the ground. With every movement, my wound felt like an ice pick was being pushed in and out of it. The last four feet, I just gave up and dropped on down to the ground.

"You okay?" Caroline asked.

"Yeah," I replied. "Let's get the hell out of here."

And then we encountered something we hadn't anticipated. As we stepped into the spotlight toward the left corner of the cabin, the sensor set off an ear-piercing siren.

"Quick," I said. "Into the trees."

Within seconds the lights turned on in the cabin and we saw someone stick his head out of the window from where we had just escaped.

"They're gone! Everybody up!" he yelled.

I figured that if we stayed off to the right of the road, taking full advantage of the cover and concealment of the pines, we would be difficult to spot. It was brutally cold and in several places we buried our feet up to our ankles in patches of snow. But if we kept running, as difficult as it was for me to do so, we would keep our body heat up.

It was hard to tell just how many men came pouring out of the cabin, but I saw maybe a dozen flashlights working over the area. We heard a voice yell out *"Spread out off both sides of the road!"* And that unmistakable voice belonged to Jonas Karn.

We had covered what seemed like three or four football fields when we saw that one of the men was almost upon us. I told Caroline to hand me the gun she took off Aaron and get down behind a fallen tree. After I allowed the man to get within three or four feet of me, I sprang from my position and clubbed him at the base of his skull with the butt of the gun. It was a sickening thud. He sprawled head first into a patch of snow. He wouldn't get up anytime soon…maybe never.

I then picked up his flashlight and looked for his weapon. A .45 automatic lay next to his right hand. I tossed it to Caroline and told her to follow me. We continued trudging through the snow drifts to the southeast where we began picking up the lights of Fort Collins. I kept sweeping the beam of the flashlight left and right to give the remainder of the search party the impression I was one of them.

Suddenly, the beam of someone else's flashlight hit me in the face. I shined my light into his face and then down on the pistol he was holding on me.

"Drop your weapons and get down on the ground! Both of you!" he barked.

"Okay," I replied. "Just take it easy. I have to get down slowly. I have a bullet wound in my back you know."

I laid my gun down and Caroline did the same. She was already on the ground as I was still struggling to place myself in a face-down position. When the man took a couple of steps toward me, getting within five feet, with every ounce of energy I had left, I swept my right foot into his legs, knocking him down. As he tried to get some traction in the snow to get back on his feet, I sprang onto him, knocking him down again. Grabbing him by the throat with my left hand, I gave him a straight punch between the eyes. He didn't move again. Two down and a dozen to go. The odds were moving in our favor. They could be in trouble with a father and daughter team like us.

In two hours it would be twilight. And that was important as we were sure to be spotted. It was imperative that we find a house and phone so that Caroline could get hold of Pettyjohn and team. But knowing we were still out there somewhere and with one phone call could bring FBI and CBI SWAT down on them, Karn and company would have to abandon ship. As a matter of fact, the WUO subversives would probably de-ass the area within the hour. Just another one of Jonas Karn's plans I would ruin.

A waning three-quarter moon setting through the trees still provided enough light to illuminate the landscape as we ran out of trees. We also ran out of snow, the lower we got in elevation. And that was a good thing, considering Caroline only had on flimsy black loafers and her feet were freezing. But leaving the shelter and the astringent scent of the pines and firs, it seemed colder, even raw. And then off somewhere in the distant night of shimmering stars I heard a coyote's shrill howl. Ever weaker from the gunshot trauma and blood loss, I was fading fast. And both of us were shivering, considering that we had no coats. We had to find warmth soon or one of us was going to experience hypothermia. And one guess which of us that would be.

CHAPTER ELEVEN

After dropping down into a low spot which we quickly found out contained shin-deep mud and freezing water, we found ourselves in the back yard of a large house with a wrap-around deck…the kind of fixture that provided its residents with views of stunning sunsets over the Rockies as well as a hillside view of the cabin we just left.

Caroline then pulled me up a small knoll past the east side of the house to the front porch. The lights were still off inside the house. *Some* people who live normal and sane lives are still sleeping that time of the morning.

Caroline rang the doorbell and getting no immediate response, she rang it again, at the same time rapping loudly on the screen door. Finally, we heard a man's grumbling voice and a stirring around in one of the rooms, followed by the pounding of his bare feet on the wooden floor.

"Who is it?" barked the cross voice.

"FBI!" Caroline shouted back.

The porch light came on and a man's face appeared in the door glass. Not fully believing Caroline, the man said, "Put your badge up where I can see it."

Which presented a problem.

"Sir, this is an emergency. I am Special Agent Caroline McGowan and this is my father. We were taken prisoners by a subversive group and my dad here has been shot."

Well if I were the man inside, I wouldn't buy it. Why would I believe such an incredible story made up by probable home invaders? But Caroline listened to herself and realized what he must be thinking.

"I know this all sounds bizarre, but go ahead and call the police. Better yet, call my supervisor, Lewis Pettyjohn. I can give you his cell number. Please, we are very cold and wet, and my father is hurting pretty badly."

There must have been an earnestness in her voice that finally convinced the man we were not Bonnie and Clyde. He opened the door just a little at first and then seeing the color of my face, which must have been something between paper white and Mother of Pearl, he came out onto the porch and helped me inside. However, after he turned on the hallway light and saw that we had guns, his eyes enlarged and he took a step back. Stocky and in his late sixties, he wore only a tee shirt and striped boxer shorts.

"Don't let the guns alarm you, sir," Caroline said.

"Believe me, I *am* with the FBI. My identification was taken from me. Now, please, where is your phone?"

Suddenly, a woman appeared in the hallway wielding a 12 gauge shotgun. What was it with elderly women and guns?

"It's all right, Jeanene," the husband said. "They're FBI and in a bit of trouble." He then turned back to Caroline and said, "There's a phone in my study." He pointed to the small room off the foyer.

"What's the address here, sir?"

"1540 Elderberry Lane."

"Thank you," Caroline replied.

"Could you allow my dad to sit somewhere?"

"Yes. Yes of course."

I took off my muddy shoes and the man helped me to the living room. I was shivering, but the warmth of the house was already thawing me out.

"I'll just sit on that ottoman there," I said. "I don't want to lean my back into your furniture." It was then he must have noticed the large splotches of blood on my shirt back.

"My God, you were shot. What the hell's this all about?"

"Your neighbor from up the hill doesn't like me very much."

"Who are you talking about?"

"A guy named Karn. Do you know him?"

"Can't say as I do."

"He's staying in one of those cabins a couple miles up on that ridge. I think the place may be owned by some guy named Wally something or other."

"Him? Oh, yeah. A real kook, that one. We've seen people going in and out of there all times of the day and night. Of course we're looking through our telescope from the sliding glass door back here," he said sheepishly. "Not that we make it a habit of spying on people. But a lot of cars go in there on that road behind us, Prince Ferry. I've even seen some Arab-looking guys going there. Brian next door thinks there's some kind of home-grown militia up there. Sometimes we pass by people in everything from green Army jackets to camouflage."

I nodded. "That would be the people who had us. What's your name, sir?"

"Kenny. Kenny Kirk. That's Jeanene there."

She took one hand off the shotgun and wiggled her fingers. I smiled at her, still eyeing the gun. Realizing by now I wasn't a threat, she placed it carefully against the stairwell.

"Mr. Kirk," I began, "would it be too much trouble to get a hot cup of coffee and a cookie or something?"

"Oh, no problem at all. Jeanene, can you take care of that for…"

"Bruce. Bruce McGowan."

"Both of you are FBI…father and daughter?"

"She is and I'm retired from the Bureau. I work for the

State Department."

"Geez Louise. This is all straight out of the *X Files* or *Alias*."

I smiled. "Where do you think they get their plots?"

Kirk still had a puzzled look on his face. "How was it you two ended up getting yourselves sideways with those people? You say they held you captive?"

"It's a long story, Mr. Kirk. The bottom line is, these are really bad guys and you should be careful not to get in their way."

"Well, if they were able to get to you two, then what the hell could we do anyway?"

"Mrs. Kirk there looks like she can handle that shotgun."

"Yes she can. And I have an arsenal upstairs just in case they come down here looking for trouble."

Caroline then came back into the room with a report. "I got hold of Pettyjohn and gave him a quick recap. He will have a Strike Team out here within the hour. The EMTs are on the way as well."

I looked at the rather handsome grandfather clock standing in the hallway which read a quarter till six. "Karn and his boys will be long gone." As I sat drinking a second cup of coffee and nibbling on one of Jeanene's brownies, I felt on my face the golden warmth of the early morning sun now streaming in the Kirks' living room window. It seemed to have a healing power about it. What warmed my blood even more was that I now had my daughter back. Nothing else bad could happen to me.

Speaking of Caroline, she had been slipping in and out of the patio door that led to the deck to see if there were any signs of a massive air and ground attack on the hillside cabin. At just after eight the EMTs arrived. A large young Black man with a name tag that read Ben McDuff went immediately to work, ripping off my shirt and cleaning out my wound. He appeared to be alarmed at what he saw and let out a low whistle. And when you're the victim that is *never* good.

"We need to patch you up and get you to Poudre Valley, Mr. McGowan. Your wound is infected."

"Then lead on, McDuff," I said, which I'm sure he had grown very tired of hearing through the years. But I couldn't help myself. He did ignore the quip and began strapping me onto his gurney after which he bounced me down the front porch steps.

The real doc in the emergency room had to go back in to debride and cauterize the wound. Minute fragments of bone where the bullet had ricocheted off my ribcage were still in the wound. He also found pieces of foam from the driver's seat. The doctor said that the seatback slowed the bullet down considerably stopping it from piercing my heart by a few millimeters. This time it got stitched up professionally by a pretty, young nurse and not with thread from a sewing kit which I think Doc Baines used.

When the nurses wheeled me into my room, I was greeted by the faces of two lovely young women, one of them who was freshly showered, painted and coiffeured. "How're you doing, Dad?" she asked.

"Great, now that we've got you back."

"Did I ever say 'thank you' for coming to my rescue?"

"No, but you can start now by giving your old man a kiss."

She then came to my bedside and touched her lips to my forehead for a full five seconds.

"Ah, yes," I said. "You're welcome."

After the lovely nurse checked my IV, took my temperature and was satisfied that my ticker was still throbbing away, she was replaced at my bedside by another pretty face, Starr Ravenel.

"I'm thoroughly pissed at you, Skip McGowan. You stiffed us, yesterday. I thought Lew was going to come unglued. What were you thinking?"

"About not leading a parade of law enforcement down Prince Ferry to Jonas Karn's front door. So, did you all raid the place?"

"*Oh*, yeah. Pettyjohn assembled a Task Force of three of our agents and the CBI's SWAT Team and hit the cabin about seven o'clock. They had, of course, all cleared out before we got there, just as Caroline said they would when they failed to find you. There *were* a couple of stragglers, however, that the CBI's Bell 412 helicopter chased down and shot up. Both occupants of the pickup truck were killed when the mini-gun opened fire."

"I assumed Karn wasn't one of them. Did they get identified?"

Starr pulled from her blazer pocket a small notebook. "One of them was a guy named Leonard Baines."

Doc.

"The other was a Thomas Sperry."

The latter saddened me. It was bound to come to that. At one time a good soldier, he had become disillusioned about his government and gone off the deep end. And I was certain that it was he who had kept Karn in check the night before so that he wouldn't just go ahead and end our lives.

Starr continued. "After a search of the cabin, we found the body of a young man in an upper bedroom with a bullet hole in his head."

"It was Aaron, Dad," Caroline added.

And that saddened me, too. Karn had executed him in a fit of rage for allowing us to get away.

"So," I said "Karn is still out there somewhere. Something's going down with that group, soon. Karn was bringing in all his troops for some kind of summit. But you know what? He won't let his vendetta against me go. He might put me on back burner while he puts his attack plan into action, but rest assured, I'll see him again. He's been tracking me over the past year and somehow even knows about Adrianna. Obsessed *and* dangerous."

"Which means he might try again to get to you through me or Adrianna," Caroline said.

"All the more reason you need to stay vigilant. *You* would be the more likely target, considering you're here in his backyard. He probably won't try taking me down with a sniper's bullet and I don't think he would order anyone else to get to me, although he's probably had others follow me around. He wants the pleasure of the kill all to himself. He's made that clear." I paused to switch gears a little. "By the way, Starr, did you all pay a visit to Mother Karn this morning?"

"Yes, but she's also gone as you might expect. We did find Caroline's car parked on the street near her house, though."

"With my blood all over the front seat," I commented. "So, Dad, when are they letting you out of here?"

"Supposedly in a couple of days. Mind if I spend New Years with you or are you going to your mom's?

"I'm sticking here with you, Dad. And when we get back to my place, you get the bed. I'll take the couch."

"Speaking of your mom…have you called her to let her know you're safe?"

"I did, first thing. She is actually very grateful to you for coming to get me. Of course, she still blames you for *me* getting kidnapped by Karn for something *you* did to him."

"Of course she does."

"Well, we need to make tracks, Dad. I need to hand in an After Action Report to Lew Pettyjohn by five."

"Put in your report that I knew one of the men killed by chopper fire. His name was Tom Sperry. I served with him in Special Forces thirty years ago. He talked with me a few minutes while I was still in the cabin's living room and alluded to the fact that something big may be going down, courtesy of the WUO. I guess he thought I wouldn't be around today, and that's why he got a little loose-lipped. Could be something as big as 9-11, and I think several metropolitans will be targeted."

"I'll make sure Lew knows about it so that he can send it forward to all levels of law enforcement. I guess your Band of Brothers will be all over it, too."

"You can bet on it."

"Lew may be by to see you this evening," Starr said.

"Good. I'll make out like I'm dying and maybe he won't yell at me. Old Lady Karn is not the only person in this state who can act."

"I'll prep him for you," Starr replied with a wink. "I'll tell him they sent for a priest."

"There are a couple of calls I need to make before you leave, Starr. May I use your cell phone? Mine seems to have died a horrible death."

"Sure. We'll get something to drink and will be back in a half hour. Then we *definitely* have to go."

I wanted to get the Birdman out of the way first so that I could engage in some phone sex with Adrianna and not rush it. Obviously, I was feeling a hell of a lot better. Maybe it was the drugs.

"Where have you been, Bruce? I left a couple of messages for you."

"Oh, laying around in a cabin up in the hills."

"I caught on the wire the confirmation of an FBI take down in the Fort Collins area. Somehow, it came to me that you might have had something to do with that, especially when I read that a female Special Agent had escaped from her kidnappers with her civilian father. I wanted to do a back flip."

"And I would pay real money to see that. Yep, that was us."

"You got Caroline out on your own? I'm sure that P.O.'d the FBI Agent-in-Charge out there."

"And I'm sure I will never hear the last of it," I replied.

"Where are you now?"

"In the hospital."

There was a pause on his end, followed by an audible sigh. "You took another bullet, didn't you?"

"Yeah. It was a hell of a shootout. You should see the other guy."

"Where were you hit?

"In the back."

"Running away I expect."

"Har, har, Prefector."

"I understand the Bureau only took down a couple of fleeing suspects. I didn't see where either was Karn. There was evidence from the bedding, food and tire tracks there were at least a dozen bad guys at the cabin. Maybe as many as twenty."

"And more were expected in today," I added. "It was going to be some sort of big pow wow to finalize plans for a series of terrorist attacks in collaboration with the local al-Qaeda network."

"Interesting. Anything tangible to back this up?"

"Just what I heard from an old friend."

"I don't understand."

"When I'm back at the ranch in a few days, I'll give you the complete story."

"Any indication the attack will be New Year's Eve in New York?"

"Could be, but I think it will be later. A date like 9-11 when no one will expect it. When Zulu returns to D.C. on January 2nd, I suggest they take occupancy of the cabin up in Fort Collins to use as a command post. That whole area west of there as well as the communes down around Boulder are contaminated with remnants of the old and re-tooled WUO."

"Not a bad idea. I'll work on that."

"Since my cell phone was destroyed yesterday, I've got to go get a new one. For the time being, you can reach me on this phone which belongs to Agent Starr Ravenel."

"Okay, I see the number on my screen. Talk later,

Bruce. Heal up. And oh, by the way, stay away from little old ladies with guns. Goodbye."

He heard, dammit. He was playing me all along.

My nurse, Mrs. Tankersly, was short, built like a boxcar and had no neck whatsoever. She also had the eyes of a cobra and a tongue just as deadly. I remember dating a girl one time who had no neck. When I walked into a room with her, every head would turn…except hers. She had no neck, remember?

"What are you doing out of bed, Mr. McGowan," she snapped.

"Going to the rest room. Is that not allowed?"

"Don't be a smart-alec. That's why you have a call button. I need to help you."

"But I can pee all by myself. Have done so for years."

"You are not to get out of bed unless someone is with you these first few hours!" Tank Tankersly barked. She stood with hands on her thick hips, slowly turning me into melting plastic with her eyes. "Okay, okay, I think I get it. Sheesh." Why couldn't I have gotten someone nicer, like Nurse Ratched who looked after Jack Nicholson?

"Look, McGowan. Just cooperate and let me do my job so that I can get out of here at a reasonable hour and go home. I need my beauty sleep."

"Yes, I can see that," I said. "You've never gotten much through the years, have you?"

It was a bad thing to say and I immediately was sorry. "I…didn't mean that, Mrs. Tankersley. It's was just my attempt at sick humor. I apologize. You're actually a very handsome woman."

She turned one corner of her mouth up in a snarl, then snatched my sorry ass up and dragged me to the toilet. I think she got the last laugh when she took account of my manhood. The snarl quickly changed into a grin.

After I did my bathroom chores, she left. I then flipped open the cell phone to call Adrianna.

"Hey, beautiful," I answered after her hello.

"Why didn't you call me back last night? I tried a half dozen times."

"My phone wasn't working."

"Well, you could have gone somewhere and called me collect. I was worried half out of my gourd."

"Sorry. I was tied up most of the night. Then I got busy rescuing Caroline and…"

"You got her away from the kidnapper?"

"Yeah. The dude didn't want to give her up, but then I was going to shoot his mother…"

"You *didn't*," she said.

"No, but I wanted to. I might just do it *yet*." Of course, I didn't tell her that she shot me. I was still trying to get past that.

"Honestly, Skip. I just don't know about you sometimes. Anyway, I'm happy Caroline was released. Did the man harm her?"

"She's fine. Better than fine."

"God answers prayers."

"Yes, He does." Which reminded me…I forgot to thank Him for her deliverance.

"When are you coming back? You *are* coming here before you go back to Washington, aren't you?"

"Yes. My SUV is still there. But it won't be before New Years."

"Oh."

"I do miss you, though," I added.

"And I love you," she replied.

The words felt good in my ear. Like the real medicine I had been looking for all day. It was having a curative effect. And I was more than ready to leave the hospital way ahead of schedule. First, however, I'd have to get by the Tank. I knew I could out-run her even with a hole in my back, but not sure I could take her, uno on uno.

"When *do* you think you'll be back here?"

"I'm not sure. Likely the end of next week."

"Another lonely New Years Eve," she lamented.

"I know. Wish I could be there. I just have some loose ends to clear up in regards to Caroline's kidnapping," I said.

"I understand." She paused. "I'll be anxious to get you back in my bed."

The very thought of that suddenly let me know I was *definitely* getting better by the moment. I hoped the Tank didn't pop back in and throw back the sheet to check my dressing. "You take care. I'll call you tomorrow after I get a new cell phone."

"Bye, Skip." And she was gone.

I then made my final call…to Joey. I told him Caroline was now safe and unharmed. He said 'thank God' and told me Cora and the girls would be elated.

CHAPTER TWELVE

Jonas Karn had quickly become the most hunted fugitive in Colorado and would soon make the FBI's Ten Most Wanted list. The Colorado Bureau of Investigation wanted him for the murder of the Denver police officer outside of Caroline's apartment and the FBI for the kidnapping of one of its agents. The U.S. Department of State Counter- terrorist Team wanted him for conspiracy to commit acts of terror against the government and the People of the United States. And I wanted the cowardly, terrorist bastard for taking my daughter.

Karn's band of dissidents, however many there were, appeared to be scattered in the burbs and countryside between Denver and Fort Collins. But there was every reason to believe they were wider-spread than that. The FBI knew this new order of the WUO was in Indiana, Illinois, Missouri and Michigan. Could be they were being recruited in a dozen other states as well. Was Karn their General or merely the Colorado lieutenant who was taking his orders from someone on the top rung of the WUO hierarchy? But as the new order was a compilation of the old and present day terrorist regimes, I thought he might be the BMOC.

He was seemingly revered by both generations of the

Weatherman group largely due to the rebellious tactics he and the others used against the government in the '60s and '70s. And because many of his cohorts from the old days had either surrendered or died along the way, he was the last of his kind. At least he didn't become a college professor like a few of the old WUO, bent on poisoning the minds of America's impressionable youth.

Upon his release from prison, he had openly vowed to continue his war against the American government…a war that could make home-grown terrorists like Timothy McVeigh and Unabomber Ted Kaczynski look like schoolboy pranksters. The new WUO was well forward on its mission to become a multi-ethnic backwoods militia of both radically left political progressives and America-hating soldiers of fortune.

Lew Pettyjohn did not stop by the hospital to see me as Starr said he would. Perhaps he was too angry with me for going solo and thumbing my nose at the Bureau. And here I was all ready for a rebuttal. I would pound home the argument that this was not a scenario for tactical warfare, Eliot Ness and John Wayne style. I knew the Bureau's methods and I sure as hell didn't want Caroline to end up dead because the FBI had waged an all-out assault on the cabin. And I was convinced it would go down that way. Even if the Bureau's Task Force had been lurking back a greater distance out of sight of the cabin, they would have had enough men lying in wait in strategic places to spot them and report back to Karn. So, that was the rebuttal I had planned for Pettyjohn. I would now have to save it for the next time I saw him.

Even though I had been duped and then shot by the grandma gangster, I supposed it all worked out. I was just glad old Sybil was sitting behind *me* when the gun went off rather than Caroline. Of course, although Caroline was relieved to have been rescued by her old man, she was still fuming not only about the loss of her gun and badge, but her purse, wallet and keys to boot. When Mrs. Karn returned to her house, parking Caroline's car on the street, she forgot to leave the apartment and car keys where they could be found. How inconsiderate was that? Caroline would spend most of the day of the 30th getting the super to change the lock on her apartment door and getting replacement keys for the Altima at the Nissan dealer.

I was released from medical care the morning of the 31st. Caroline, who was retrieving me from the hospital, had to do battle with the Tank as to who would wheel me down to the pickup point. I preferred to walk out, but as Tankersly thought of me as an invalid, I had to go downstairs by wheelchair. At least I was getting away from her.

As I figured I was about 90% and feeling fine, I begged Caroline to stop at a fast food joint for a big, greasy artery-clogging cheeseburger. But she wouldn't. "I just *got* you out of the hospital and now you want to go back there in cardiac arrest? I don't think so."

"Okay, then. Take me to the Pizza Hut for some *healthy* food."

"I'm taking you to the apartment. I'll fix you something to eat there."

"My dear, I stayed in your apartment. There's nothing there. Obviously, either you don't eat or you eat out."

"All right, cranky old man, I'll take the next exit and get you a salad at Bombay's."

"Indian food?"

She looked over at me and shook her head. "And to think I have to put up with you the next few days."

After we returned to her apartment, I pulled my wallet from the kitchen cabinet drawer and accompanied Caroline to her cell store. As she had no wallet, cards or cash, I paid for her phone. I also had the store contact my service provider which would give them the information to set me up with a phone. We both obviously had to change our numbers since Jonas Karn knew them and might just call us to tell us in that nasally, nauseous voice how much he enjoyed the time spent with us at the cabin and to be sure and call him the next time we were up that way. My new cell phone had lots of bells and whistles on it and so I spent most of the afternoon playing with it. Even had fun little games on it.

New Years Eve 2001 was quite different for me. As I had never been the big party guy out with the ladies, drinking and reveling, I was either always on alert with the FBI or warmly tucked away under the covers by 10:30 and the hell with Dick Clark. It felt good to sit in Caroline's comfy recliner sipping on my second body-numbing glass of Merlot while she catered to me, bringing pizza rolls and other fancy hors d'oeuvres she had bought from the supermarket. I might even make it till eleven this year, I thought to myself.

Starr was pulling duty along with agents from the Boulder, Fort Collins and Colorado Springs Bureau field offices and collaborating with CBI agents preparing to respond just in case Karn and WUO did in fact plan something nasty. City and county law enforcement were patrolling the Denver streets watching for suspicious activities around courthouses, the City Hall and other municipal buildings. Historically, these were the kinds of targets the old WUO liked to hit. There was no reason to think they would not continue doing so in the new order.

Occasionally, units from the Denver P.D. swept through Caroline's parking lot as a show of presence. I didn't think Karn would risk trying to get to me again, knowing that he and his fellow subversives were on everyone's radar.

And by golly, I did make it through midnight, even though my lids felt like they had gained a pound every ten minutes. Mainly, I was curious to see whether al Qaeda had decided to extend its agenda of fear tactics by detonating a dirty bomb in the middle of Time Square. As I watched the revelry of the masses on the tube, I was pleased to see that the people standing shoulder to shoulder, defiant, daring and resilient, were not going to let a threat of terrorism strike fear in their hearts. That's exactly what the enemy wanted. If it can demoralize the people of America, its mission is half done.

As it was apparent throughout the U.S. *and* the world that 2002 would come in without incident, I signed off in my chair about 1:30. Caroline, seeing that I was sleeping comfortably and soundly, was kind enough not to wake me even though she had promised me her bed.

It only seemed like twenty seconds had lapsed until a brilliant sluice of the morning sun had worked its way over the eastern tree line, through the patio door and into my eyes. It was eight-thirty.

Testing out my new phone, I called all the significant people in my life…Lionel, Adrianna and Joey…to give them my new number. And that set me to thinking: besides Caroline, I only had a handful of people at this time in my life that mattered. And that's sad. Of course, there was Darlene, who used to be a significant other. I would ask Caroline to give my number to her. I didn't think my ex wanted to hear from me first thing on New Year's Day.

The Birdman and I rehashed the cabin scenario and specifically what went down when I set out to rescue Caroline. "Well," he said, "one CTT agent versus fifteen to twenty bad guys? Sounds like they were at a disadvantage from the get-go." He then chuckled.

"I couldn't have gotten out of there without Caroline driving the train, though. She was brilliant, Lionel."

"I'm sure. I had no doubt when she signed up that she would make a dandy agent. So, when will you feel up to coming back to work?"

I swallowed hard before giving him my reply. "I'm not sure I will, boss."

He paused a moment to digest what he had feared might happen one day soon. "You're not going to quit on me, are you?"

"I haven't decided yet. I *am* tired of people putting holes in me. Used car salesmen may not be on the top rung when it comes to the public's respect and confidence, but not many customers would be out to kill me."

"You can't let a little thing like getting shot dissuade you from staying on. Maybe you should just take a couple of weeks off. Get your body *and* your mind healed, then come back here and let's talk this out." Another short pause. "You're the best I've had the privilege of supervising, Bruce."

Coming from Lionel Byrd, who rarely commends anyone for anything, that meant a lot to me. Pure gold. And he was sincere when he said it. He would never make such a comment merely to convince a person to stay on because of his own selfish reasons.

"Thanks, Lionel. I'll *take* the two weeks and will see you on the 15th. It will give me the time I need to get my strength back…and to think."

"I get the impression *this* bullet took something out of you, Bruce. How bad was it?"

"Let's just say that a younger man would have been back on his feet the next day kicking ass."

"That bad, huh?"

"I think it had more to do with the infection than anything else."

"Okay, well listen, Bruce. If you ever *do* quit on me and end up selling used cars, don't sell any to gun-toting old ladies.

" He then laughed. I couldn't remember if I ever heard old stone-face that jocular before. Sumbitch.

Lew Pettyjohn, who had probably been too miffed at me to come by my hospital room, actually came by the apartment New Year's Day afternoon. After we shook hands and he inquired about my wound and how I was doing, he as I expected started in on me.

"You realize I could have you charged with obstruction,

don't you? And I haven't ruled that out. You knew when Karn was going to call you and you deliberately failed to show at my office, striking out on your own like the Lone Ranger." "Hey, did I ever tell you that the Lone Ranger was my childhood hero?" I quipped. He glared at me without responding.

"Look, Lew. This guy wanted *me*. And I had to play it *my* way."

"And your way got you shot up and Karn driven further underground. Now we're back to square one with this outfit. If you had cooperated with us, we'd have taken him down and a good number of the Weatherman crowd."

"And Caroline would have gotten caught up in it and been killed," I said.

"You don't know that, Bruce. With your help we could have found a way to rout this outfit without anyone getting hurt."

"And I'll give it right back to *you*. You don't know *that*."

Pettyjohn threw his head back and sighed. "All right. What's done is done. When will you be able to come down to the office to give us your statement?"

"Caroline can probably tell you more," I replied.

"Where is she anyway?"

"At the grocery getting me some health food. She thinks salads and lean red meats will help me heal up."

"She's due back to work on Friday. Will you be up to coming in that day? I've set up a situation room and will have two field agents there from Fort Collins as well as Lieutenant Harriman from the CBI."

"I'll be there." "Good. With all we have to go over about the current scenario it'll probably be an all day party."

"I like parties. Can I bring something? Beer? Pretzels? Pettyjohn rolled his eyes and shook his head. My ex-wife used to do that a lot around me.

CHAPTER THIRTEEN

I had mostly sat around all day like a slug, and with my three day-old scraggly beard, I must have looked pretty crummy. That evening, Caroline made a couple of comments about a guy down at the Union Mission that I reminded her of. So, without further word, I hustled to the facility to shower and shave.

When I was all clean and coiffed, I returned to the recliner and watched Caroline flit around the kitchen preparing us a hearty but healthy meal of wheat spaghetti and meat balls. I couldn't believe that my little girl was already slammed into womanhood and even though she was now a hardened federal agent, looked every bit the domestic behind that counter. It gave me an immense sense of peace that she was actually there in her kitchen seemingly back to normal, alive and unharmed. She reminded me of a young Darlene McGowan from twenty-five years ago.

As the sun had long since set and evening twilight was upon us, Caroline lit a couple of candles and poured me a glass of dark, biting Chianti. It was the first real time in ages that we had such an opportunity to just sit leisurely and reminisce about things. We talked about life as it was when I was her at-home father, about her very best Christmas, teachers she remembered, and then how much she loved sitting at the dinner table watching her mom and me smile at one **another**, so much in love. I wasn't sure why Caroline threw the last memory in, but it was making me conjure up those old guilt pangs I thought were buried years ago about the divorce that left ten year old Caroline without a full-time father. But if you heard it from her mother, Darlene, I never was full time when I lived with them. But this might have been Caroline's catharsis all going toward the idea and ideal of living in the perfect, nuclear family, a family she wished we could still be today. As usual, I was careful not to say anything critical about the woman my daughter idolized. As the words had fallen from my brain onto my tongue several times during our conversation, I immediately chewed them up and swallowed them along with the pasta.

Our conversation then turned to the present and the rehashing of her kidnapping. After all the praise that Caroline had given me about her mom over the previous two hours of dialogue, she said the one thing that meant more to me than anything I had heard in years.

"I'm proud of you, Dad. You were my knight in shining armor, coming to my rescue. You even took a bullet for me."

I beamed. "Now don't remind me of *that*. If I'm going to get shot, I want it to be a situation that a guy can get a medal for."

"But the gun went off by accident."

"After I let the old hag get the drop on me. Was I stupid or what?"

"Well, just the same, you were there for me. And I sit here only because of you." She patted my hand and gave me a kiss. She used to do that a lot when she was a little girl.

"Can you do me a favor?" I asked. "Sure. What?"

"Can you check with the coroner's office to see if they've released Tom Sperry's body for burial? And if not, when?"

"I can do that. Why do you ask?"

"Pettyjohn told me there was no address for him or even any record of him living anywhere around Boulder or Fort Collins. I'm sure his wife is waiting for his body so that she can commence burying him. I used to know her... her name's Geneva. We were all kind of like family, you know…thirty years ago before he turned on his country."

"How do you know that he's still married?

"He told me so. He also has two daughters. I'm unsure of their ages, however. If we can tail her, we may be able to find other members of the WUO."

"I'll make the call," Caroline said. After identifying herself to the Larimer County Coroner's Office, Caroline secured the information I needed.

"Well, timing is everything," she said.

"They're releasing his body tomorrow at ten."

"And I'll be there when they do."

It was my only real shot…at least for the moment. Karn and the Weather crew were back underground hiding somewhere. I imagined that most had blended back into their communities and communes. Maybe a few had literally *gone* underground. Karn, of course, would not go back to the wretched house with the bunker, the home that had been in his mother's family since the '60s. And I was sure wherever he was, Ma Karn was likely with him. I found out that he was very protective of his mama.

It was certain that Jonas Karn and I would come face to face on another day. He *would* continue to worry me, however; not that I was afraid of taking a bullet in the back of the head as I walked along the street in a Georgetown crowd. But I was still afraid for Caroline and Adrianna.

A coward like him would not confront me one on one or even pick me off with a high-powered rifle. He would get to me where it hurt…through my loved ones. And just as he used Caroline as a pawn to lure me in, he would choose the method and venue that would be a test of my vulnerability.

As Karn knew about Darlene, he probably knew where she lived. Maybe he would stoop to something juvenile like sabotaging my Austin-Healy 3000 that I lost in my divorce. As far as I knew, it still sat unloved beside of her driveway while Her's and Ned's vehicles had the garage. Which brings up a sore spot with me. If she has no use for it and Nerdy Ned was not cool enough to drive it, why didn't she give it back?

Just before eight on Tuesday, January 2nd, Caroline and I left her apartment for Mickey D's and a biscuit. Afterwards, she dropped me off at the downtown Hertz location so that I could rent a car for a few days. I didn't want to inconvenience Caroline by having her chauffeur me all over hell and half of Colorado. And considering the places I would go, her car may in fact be recognized.

At a quarter till ten, I parked my rented Ford Escape outside of the Larimer County Coroner's office. I wanted to see who would come by to claim Tom Sperry's body. I suspected it would be Geneva, if in fact he was still married to her, but wasn't entirely sure after all these years I would recognize her. Although there was no phone listing for the Sperrys, I imagined that the Bureau had by now located their residence through its network if not simply through something like tax or the local municipality's records. They likely had already paid Geneva a visit. Since this was a spur of the moment thing, and I figured Pettyjohn and team were not going to provide me any information that would facilitate my own investigation, I figured this was the easiest scenario for me.

After a couple of minutes, I went inside to see if I could get an audience with the coroner, Dr. Sam Kendall. The pretty, young receptionist asked me who I was and when I presented my State Department ID, she beeped Kendall. In a few moments he came out to meet me. We shook hands. I hoped he had remembered to put on latex gloves when he went digging around the guts of his morning customers.

"Gwen says you're here to talk about the D.B. we plan to release today…Sperry. The FBI was here yesterday to check out the body. I didn't expect anyone else. What interest does the Department of State have in him?"

"I'm not sure if the agents who took Sperry down had clued you in, but he was a member of a covert group whose agenda it is to wage hostilities against the U.S. government. That would be State Department business."

"Do you want to see the body?"

"Not necessarily, but I would like to hang around for a while to see who signs for Sperry. It will likely be his wife. I'll probably be sitting in your waiting area or outside in my rental until that happens. Would you mind dinging me on my cell when someone does arrive?" I gave him my card.

"Be glad to."

We talked for a few more minutes and then I saw that the clock on the wall behind him read ten-fifteen. I shook his hand again and then went back out to the SUV to listen to some Bach on the local PBS station.

After eleven-thirty came and went, I got out of the vehicle to walk around so that my back wouldn't stiffen up on me. I was feeling pretty well, but I found the last few days that sitting longer periods of time seemed to irritate my wound. No sooner than I had stepped onto the sidewalk, a white 1960s VW hippymobile pulled up to the curb on the opposite side of the street. All that was missing on the bus were sunflower appliqués and peace stickers. A woman was behind the wheel.

For a few moments she sat motionless as though she were contemplating whether or not to go inside. But then she swung the door open and dropped down to the pavement. Smallish with long, straight hair, more gray than brown, she reminded me of a Joni Mitchell. Dressed in a peasant smock with no coat, she had the 'Boulder' look which was something on the order of retro Haight-Asbury. Although thirty years older, the face unmistakably belonged to

Geneva Sperry.

I waited until she entered the building and then went up the steps after her. Peering through the door glass, I saw that she was talking with the receptionist. Momentarily, the girl invited Geneva to follow her down the hallway. I quickly went inside and stuck my head through the hall door just in time to see Dr. Kendall greeting Geneva. When he saw me, he gave a nod and then escorted her back to the morgue. I then returned to the lobby area where I could ogle the pretty young thing behind the counter. Did I tell you that I was feeling better?

After about fifteen minutes, Geneva appeared at the door from the hallway, eyes reddened and moist, failing to take notice of the man behind the *Field and Stream* magazine. I watched from the glass door as she descended the steps and entered her vehicle. The moment she began pulling away from the curb, I bounded down the steps, crossed the street and jumped in the Escape. When the VW had cleared the stop sign at the next intersection, I made a U turn and began trailing her at a distance of about five hundred feet. After a few left and right turns, she then picked up the southbound ramp of I-25.

The VW bus appeared to be doing all it could and was smoking a little which made it easy to follow. Traffic was whizzing by the both of us like bullets. After the bus eased off the interstate at the second Boulder exit, it continued west for a few miles. When we had rounded a couple of curves and topped a hill, the splendor of the Rockies in the noonday sun suddenly opened up. It was almost so brilliant, it hurt my eyeballs. But it was unbelievably beautiful. I momentarily took my eyes off the bus and almost missed it as it turned right onto Highway 48.

We traveled a good five miles along the twisting, narrow road until the bus started slowing to make a turn into a driveway where a small eco-house mostly covered by earth sat.

As I scanned my eyes around the area, I saw that there was a cluster of these homes speckled along rolling farmland, giving it the look of a small agricultural community complete with a general store. A commune of sorts, I presumed.

When Geneva came to a stop in front of her house fifty yards off the roadway, I pulled off onto the side of the road at the store directly across the street. No sooner than she exited the bus, two young adult women with long, stringy hair came out to greet her. They embraced for several moments and then the three of them went inside.

I hadn't really thought through what I would do at this point. Even though I was going to stand out as a stranger anywhere I went in the commune, I *was* wearing a flannel shirt, jeans and a parka. In my Ford Escape and backwoods attire, I didn't quite fit the profile of the FBI. Generally, commune people are not aggressive unless provoked or in any instance where their bars are infiltrated by government types asking questions about certain domestic terrorists. But as there were a number of such communes all over from the northern neck of Denver up to the Wyoming border, the likes of me could have been from anywhere. And if I just walked up to Geneva's house, I could in fact be one of

Tom's buddies who had heard about his death coming by to pay my respects.

I sat for a few more moments to take account of the small commune. The people lived a simple enough life kind of like the Amish or the Mennonites, except without the religion. Each family seemed to have an equal plot of land which was farmed every year. Barren, symmetrical garden rows now at rest and lying dormant for the winter were all that remained from the fall harvest. Fading snow lay in the narrow ditches between the humps of soil.

At twenty minutes past noon, I made the left turn down the dirt road that led to the Sperry house. Thinking I might be disrespecting Geneva by approaching her too soon after her husband's death, I hesitated a few moments behind the wheel. Maybe this wasn't such a good idea. But, I was there, and the imperativeness of finding Jonas Karn greatly over-shadowed courtesy and any feelings of sympathy I may have manufactured.

After stepping onto the porch, I rapped lightly on the door. In a short moment, a late teen's girl with a pretty yet unpainted face opened the door. She had Tom Sperry's eyes.

"Yes?" she said, eyeing me suspiciously. I guessed that she didn't figure me for an encyclopedia salesman, considering my grungy look, but then as I considered she had likely been well-schooled in her young years to be wary of the police, she remained positioned behind the locked screen door.

"Is Mrs. Sperry home? I…was a friend of your dad's."

Her look gave me the impression she was still not sure about me. But maybe I was in fact one of Tom's friends from 'the club' and knew Geneva as well.

"Just a moment, please," she said politely.

I heard the women talking somewhere in the rear of the house and then footsteps approaching the door.

"Hello, Geneva," I greeted.

There was a confused look on her face. "Do I know you?"

I smiled reassuringly. "You did at one time. I'm Bruce McGowan. Fort Bragg? Thirty years ago?"

Her eyes softened. "Yes, I think I do remember. You were Tom's commander…Captain McGowan."

"That's right."

Then the puzzled look returned. "I don't understand why you would be here. How could you have heard about him? Did you take the path as well?"

I wasn't sure what 'the path' meant, but assumed it had to do with Tom leaving the Army Special Forces to enlist in the army of the government's enemy, the WUO.

"No. I didn't take the path. But may I come in to talk for a while? I know it may be inopportune, but it *is* a matter of importance."

"You're basically telling me you work for the government."

"Yes, Geneva, I do."

She began chewing on her bottom lip. "The Feds have already been here. I told them I knew nothing about Tom's activities." Her eyes were accusatory, like I was working for the same sorry-ass government that killed her husband. The eyes may have even said, 'you got my husband killed.' Which, of course, I did.

"I know, Geneva. But can I have just a few moments with you?"

For a moment she just stood on the other side of the door without saying anything. But then she unlocked it and pushed it open. "Okay. I'll respect the fact that Tom thought a lot of you back then. You were one of the good officers he always said. Come in."

She led me from the door into a very unpretentious living room that had neither pictures on the wall nor any what-nots lying around. Her girls were not present, but I suspected they were close by in a bedroom or the kitchen listening.

Geneva then offered me a seat on the couch while she sat very politely across from me in a well-worn sofa chair. Her face revealed some very hard years. The sun had added wrinkles that belonged to a woman ten to fifteen years older than I suspected she was. Her skin was otherwise drawn close to her facial bones, but sagged in her jaws and neck. And her hands were rough and reddened similar to that of a field hand. I took it that commune living was a pretty tough deal and she reminded me of photographs I had seen many times of nineteenth century pioneer women.

"So then you know about Tom, Captain," she said, dabbing her handkerchief at a tear on her cheek.

"Please call me Bruce, Geneva. The Army was a long time ago. Yes, I was there at the cabin a few days ago where Tom, Jonas Karn and the others were." I figured it was an opportune time as any to throw out Karn's name.

"Why were you there, Bruce, if you work for the government?"

It seemed obvious from her question that she didn't know about Caroline's kidnapping since Tom had nothing to do with it.

"It's a long story, but I will just say that I was there to get my daughter back. Jonas Karn kidnapped her"

She appeared stunned. "He did what? Why in God's name would he do something like that?"

"To settle an old score with me. He thought if he took my daughter, I would come to him. And I did."

"And Tom knew about that?"

I nodded. "Yes. But he did not have a hand in it. As a matter of fact, when he found out about it, he took steps to shield her."

She shook her head. "I'm glad you said that. I too know that Tom would never have been a part of anything like that. He only involved himself in…" She stopped short, thinking that she may be telling me too much. That he was part of the New Order of the Weather Underground.

So I made it easy for her. "I know about the group he was involved with, Geneva. His beef was not with twenty-five year old women. It was with Uncle Sam."

"And your daughter…?

"I got her back. She's fine, again, thanks to Tom. That's one reason I'm sitting here…to tell you that."

Her eyes began glistening again and she swallowed hard. "If you talked with Tom up there, it might have been the last real conversation he had with anyone from the outside."

"Probably. I won't say it was under the best of circumstances, considering I was also captured by Mr. Karn, tied to a chair and beaten. But afterwards we did talk a bit.

I wish we would have had an opportunity to reminisce about old times over a beer."

"Why did Jonas have something against you?"

"It goes back to when I was an agent with the FBI. Karn had bombed a restaurant, killing a couple of servicemen. He disappeared for a while in the '70s. On a tip, we found out where he was. I was the agent that arrested him. Admittedly, it wasn't the gentlest of take downs. But he ended up getting twenty years. And then his wife committed suicide. Apparently, he begrudged me all that time and began stalking my daughter, my ex-wife *and* me when he got out of prison. He nabbed my daughter, Caroline, on Christmas Day."

Geneva broke her eye contact with me and looked down at her hands. "I'm sorry that happened. Tom and I may have participated in a lot of demonstrations back then, but no one ever lost his life by *our* hands. And neither he nor I would ever condone taking anyone's family."

"Like I said, Geneva, it was purely a vendetta. It was personal and had nothing to do with the old *or* new Weather Underground."

Her eyes picked up and returned to mine.

"The Weather Underground is dead and buried, Bruce. There is no new Underground."

"Maybe not in its old form, but Karn has revived it and is molding it into what appears to be a more violent organization with concrete plans to kill a lot of innocent people. Tom was part of that, Geneva. He told me so. Tell me *you're* not."

She settled back in the chair and laid her hands on the arms. "So, what *is* it you do with the government, Bruce?"

"I'm no longer FBI, Geneva. I work for the State Department."

"And so you're here officially and not just for old time's sake."

I didn't readily respond, thinking I might give her an

answer that would alienate her…at least to a point where she might clam up and kick me out. "I am here to see if you know where the man is that drugged and kidnapped my daughter…and who got Tom killed."

Geneva stood up and then walked to the window. Folding her arms about her as though she was cold, she replied, "You know, Bruce, I was an idealistic and impressionable fool back then when the WUO started up. I could have even been convinced to do things like Charlie Manson's followers did. When Tom left the service, both of us immediately connected with the WUO. I bought into it all. The government was out of control. American kids were still dying in Vietnam. I looked around us and saw that the typical American citizen had blinders on and just didn't care about it, unless they lost a son. People had become so self-absorbed and complacent that values didn't matter anymore. Americahad become totally enslaved to capitalism and materialism. They had forgotten what our founders truly envisioned when they penned the Declaration of Independence and the Constitution. It was our purpose back then to open people's eyes and make them really *think* about what their government was doing to them. And we believed, Bruce that we were made of that same revolutionary fiber as the early patriots."

She then turned from the window and walked back to her chair. After folding her rough hands in her lap, she continued. "Did anyone not open their eyes during those days of enlightenment?"

"Geneva," I said. "Tell me again. Are you now a part of this new Weatherman order? Are you in fact supporting this new plan of terror from a group that is collaborating with factions like al Qaeda, the people who killed 3000 innocent Americans?"

She began to cry again. "I lost the love of my life, Bruce. Lost him to something he believed in." She still wasn't answering.

"I don't think he was 100% into Karn's plan, Geneva. That was what I picked up from him in our conversation. And I'm being truthful about that."

The tears now began to roll down her cheeks and onto her neck. "He was a hard worker down at the bottling plant. And he was a sweet and good father to our girls. But he was a passionate man where it came to this country. He still believed there needed to be changes in our government. I admit I didn't like a lot of the values that Jonas Karn brought to the WUO. Tom challenged him on some of them. But, no. I'm not involved with all that anymore. And I was trying to talk Tom into letting it go. Just be that loving husband and hard-working stiff and enjoy our simple life as it is."

I nodded understandingly.

She continued. "I'm tired, Bruce. Losing Tom has really taken the wind out of my sail. And I don't want to lose my daughters to the Feds in some kind of Branch Davidian or Wounded Knee incident. So, no. I'm not part of it. It got my Tom killed and I don't want anyone else to die. I wish the whole organization would just go away."

As she sat opposite me, I leaned over and took her rough, callused hands in mine. "I understand what you're feeling, Geneva, and I'm very sorry about what happened. I want you to help me, though. Tell me where Jonas Karn is.

Her eyes, hollow and lifeless, continued fixated on mine. "I don't know where he is, Bruce. He came by here a couple of times this year and all I know is that he stayed in that cabin where Tom was killed."

"How about Tom's and Karn's friends? Maybe if you gave me some names of people who might know…"

"You're saying I should divulge where Tom's friends are and risk them getting put in jail? Some of these people are my friends, too. We go way back. We were in the Weather Underground together and almost gave up our citizenship for being with the group. How can I betray them?"

"It's not the same group you were part of, Geneva. And Karn is not the same kind of revolutionary as eighteenth century heroes like Patrick Henry and Nathan Hale were. He thinks he's a modern-day replica of people like them. He's nothing but an insane and calculating criminal with a personal agenda. Don't have the blood of the innocent on your hands. Help me stop whatever terrorist campaign is being formulated."

Geneva pulled her hands away and cradled them in her lap. She then began to shake and sob. "I do hate him. And I know he's the one who got Tom killed."

At least she didn't blame me.

Finally, she dried her tears and in resignation, said "All right, Bruce. I'll tell you what you need to know."

CHAPTER FOURTEEN

At four-fifteen on my way back to Caroline's pad, I called Pettyjohn and asked him if he could reschedule his planned strategy meeting with the FBI and CBI Joint Task Force. I told him I had some urgent information for him. He wanted to know what, but I told him I needed to convey it in person. He told me he couldn't get everyone together immediately. He, Murphy and two agents from Colorado Springs were leaving in a few minutes to collaborate with the ATF to raid a meth lab out in the country just east of Pueblo. Would the next morning be okay? I told him that would be soon enough, considering what was being planned by Karn and the WUO…on Groundhog Day.

The information that Geneva Sperry had given up should result in a Weatherman smackdown if in fact the Task Force mission was planned and executed well. And I fully planned to be involved in both stages. I wanted to come face-to-face with Karn again. This time, he would be missing more than his gonads.

I was feeling increasingly better as the day continued. When I got back to Caroline's apartment, she was in the kitchen chopping up rabbit food to go with whatever was smelling delectable in the oven.

"Lasagna, Dad."

"Not your mom's recipe, I hope." She snapped a wet dish towel into my behind which brought back painful memories of eighth grade gym and rat tail whips in the boys' shower.

"It's my *own* recipe. And you will like it or there's PB&J in the cabinet."

"I will like it, I promise. You've set a third plate." "Starr is coming by for dinner."

"That'll be nice," I said. "I never officially got to thank her for looking after me while you were on vacation."

"She told me what a pain in the ass you were." "Well, that little…"

"She was only *kidding*, Dad. She said it was actually good to spend those couple of days with you. You remind her of her dad."

"Her dad? I was hoping I had made a little younger impression on her…like reminding her of a handsome former boyfriend."

Caroline laughed. "Here." She tossed me a corkscrew. "Make yourself useful. Open the wine."

"Ahhh. Thought you'd never ask."

Over the supper table there was first a little small talk, and then when I told them where I went, they wanted to know what I found out from the Widow Sperry.

"A good bit, actually. From out of that information, Pettyjohn's Task Force will have an opportunity to rout the entire Colorado faction of the WUO and especially Karn. But I probably should save it all for Pettyjohn. You'll be there Starr, but Caroline the information brief is on Thursday and you're not scheduled to be back until Friday."

"No, Father dear. I *will* be at that meeting. And as I have a vested interest in one Jonas Karn, I will also be involved in any planned take down."

And that bothered me very much. Although I was sure she would possibly be involved in a number of missions where she had gun in hand, I didn't want her on this one. But I didn't say anything. I would have *that* dialogue with her boss.

"How are you feeling today?" Starr asked me. "Everything healing well?"

"It feels kind of like a bee sting, now. I'm sure by the first of the week I'll feel little effects from it. Anyway, I hope to be heading home by then."

"So soon?" said Caroline. "I thought you'd be here a little longer."

"No. Gotta get back to work. Anyway, I'd go stir-crazy sitting around here all day."

I noticed that Starr wasn't saying much. She would eat a bite here and there, and then I'd catch her staring at me.

Finally, I said, "Is something wrong, Starr. Is there sauce on my chin?"

She smiled and took a sip of her wine. "I was just studying you, Skip McGowan."

"How so?" "I don't know. It's like you're one big paradox. You sit here as a funny, wisecracking and loving guy, yet the ruthless man I saw in action, shooting those guys outside the bar the other night…it was like watching the Terminator. I have never seen anyone react so quickly and so deadly. It makes one wonder to what extreme you *will* go."

"I've been told I'm a very complicated human being." "It's like you're two different people," she added.

"A dissociative personality, huh?"

"No, I didn't mean it like that. More…enigmatic."

I chewed and swallowed a mouthful of pasta and then laid my fork down. "It's something that comes with age, training and experience, Starr. We learn to separate our domestic side from our violent side. Maybe you are wondering if you could ever pull the trigger on someone?"

She dropped her eyes to her plate and picked aimlessly at her pasta. It seemed that somehow I had struck a chord.

"Starr?"

She had only been with the Bureau for two years and as I would think she had only been exposed to white collar takedowns, perhaps she *had* been involved in gunplay that ended someone's life…and it stayed with her.

"I don't have to wonder about that, Skip…that I could ever pull the trigger. I already have."

"Really?" I replied, swallowing a gulp of wine. "You've already had to shoot somebody?"

She shook her head just a little and then brought her eyes back to mine. "It was when I was a child…twelve. I shot and killed a man."

"What?" exclaimed Caroline. "Why? How? Is it something you can talk about?"

"Not easily."

I nodded. "Then we won't go there. Whatever it was about should stay in the past."

Starr gave me a faint smile. "Thanks, Skip. Maybe sometime I'll tell you all about it. But it's something I live with every day…remembering how it felt to take a life. And I admit it makes me wonder, that if it ever came to it, could I do it again?"

"Let's hope you'll never have to worry about that, Starr.

Or you either, daughter."

"Hey, let's get off this subject," Caroline said. "And I don't mean talk about 'the weather.' We've spent enough time on that group that last few days."

After I kissed the cook and told her how wonderful the dinner was, I helped her clear the table. For the remainder of the evening it was only small talk. Easy for the girls, painful for me. Shortly, I announced I was retiring to the recliner to watch some old serials on TV Land, which drove the ladies to the balcony with their wine.

The next day, Wednesday, I spent on Caroline's computer putting together a PowerPoint presentation complete with slides for my information brief on the situation at hand.

At 0930 on Thursday, all the players were in place in the

situation room at the Stout Street office of the FBI. Before Lieutenant Harriman and his CBI Swat leader arrived, I had a closed-door pre-brief session with Lew Pettyjohn to give him a quick overview of the information I had obtained from Geneva Sperry. But there were deals to be made.

"Lew, I want to make it perfectly clear that on the day the raid goes down, I will be part of it. I have spoken with my boss at the State Department and he says he will be monitoring the FBI's preparation for the plan. At this time, my team will not be engaged, but will however be on standby."

"What team is *that*, Bruce?"

"I will table an answer to that question for now. Just hear me out. The State Department will assume all responsibilities and liabilities for my actions and personal risk. I will give you my boss's number for you to verify that and to discuss any questions with him as to why I will be involved. I in turn will follow the instructions of the Task Force Commander..."

"Which will be me," Pettyjohn replied.

"...and not act on my own or step out of line. If you cannot live with me participating in the mission, then my briefing is off, and via orders from the State Department, my organization which answers to a higher power than yours will carry out the planned strike. You guys will catch the results on the eleven o'clock news along with the general public."

"This all sounds like coercion, Bruce, even a threat."

"Not at all, Lew. It's just the facts of life. Deal with it. Secondly, Caroline McGowan will not be a player in the take-down."

"Why should she be treated any differently than any other of my agents? I may not have put her on the Task Force, but it's not my job to shield the agents from danger because of their sex or that their Daddies don't want to see them at risk. As you know, there will be many other times she'll have a gun in her hand and face the possibility of death. It comes with the job. You knew that when she signed up."

"That's my deal. Take it or leave it. You don't buy the deal, then I will make sure the FBI doesn't play at all. My team gets the trophy for the take-down."

"So, let me get this straight. You would risk me charging you right now for Obstruction of Justice."

"Won't happen, Lew. Like I said. It's a matter of who out-ranks who. *I* won't pull rank, but my *boss* will."

Pettyjohn sighed, swept his hand over his forehead like I was giving him a headache and then pinched the bridge of his nose with his thumb and forefinger. I knew he was right about Caroline. I had to place *myself* in his shoes. If I were him, there would be no way a brash, deal-talking non- Bureau type would dictate to me whether or not I could engage his daughter in an operation. But I kept staring him down for an answer.

"I'm waiting," I said.

"All right," he finally said. "I'll need to leave an agent back here anyway. I'll tell Caroline that what she's been through the last few days, I'm putting her on light duty. So, who do I tell the other players you are? Hell, *I'm* not even sure who or what you are."

"Just introduce me as a State Department operative with intelligence information about Mr. Karn, his organization and its tentative mission." "And when this comes off and you end up dead, who at the State Department do I send your carcass to?"

"I pulled from my wallet Lionel Byrd's card. "This man."

"I guess I need to call him anyway to verify everything you're telling me."

"Be my guest. I told him to expect your call. By the way, on mission day, I will need a vest, an M4 Carbine and a Glock."

"You're a demanding bastard, aren't you?" he said.

"Would you like a bottle of Rothschild and a box of Cubans to go with that order?"

I think it was the first time I had ever seen him smile.

Seated in the situation room at 1100 were all FBI Special Agents from the Denver and Fort Collins field offices, Lieutenant Harriman from the CBI, his SWAT leader and the FBI Special Weapons and Tactics commander from Pettyjohn's team. "Good morning, ladies and gentlemen. You all know me, Lewis Pettyjohn, Special Agent in Charge, Denver field office, and some of you know why you're here. This is a Warning Order to apprise you of a tentative take-down operation at a site north of here which you and your teams will be conducting at my direction. To quickly bring all others up to speed, one Jonas Karn, a suspect in the murder of a Denver police officer and who kidnapped our agent in this department, Caroline McGowan on Christmas Day, is also suspected of conspiring to commit acts of terrorism against the U.S. government in the State of Colorado and possibly other locations throughout the United States. Intelligence obtained from an informant indicates that Karn, a former member of a '60s and '70s spin-off of the Students for Democratic Society, the Weatherman Underground or WUO, was arrested and convicted in the 1980s for the murders of two U.S. service officers. We have reason to believe he is the organizer and leader of the New Weather Underground which we also believe is or will become considerably more violent than its predecessor group.

"Standing here with me is retired Bureau Special Agent Bruce McGowan who is currently an Intel operative for the U.S. Department of State. Any information as to his credentials that will surface in this meeting about Mr. McGowan must stay in this room. An expert on Karn and his group, he has uncovered credible evidence of a plot to detonate explosive devices in the City of Denver, as well as other cities, that could result in death and destruction far greater than that experienced in the Oklahoma City bombing. Mr. McGowan will provide details to include the location of a planned strategy meeting and rehearsal and the date of this attack. I'll now let Mr. McGowan take over."

"Thank you, Agent Pettyjohn. Before you is a series of slides showing members of the original Weather Underground, such as William Ayers, Bernardine Dohrn, John Jacobs and Terry Robbins, who launched campaigns back in the '60s and '70s to, in their words, provide for "the destruction of U.S. imperialism and achieve a classless world or world communism." Here is a photo of Jonas Karn as he appears in the early '70s and n aged and enhanced artist's description of Karn as he looks today with long white hair and wrinkles. Here is another photo taken with an Islamic subversive, who we believe is a member of al Qaeda, and another man who owned the cabin where Karn had been recently staying.

"Via communiqués, various terrorist acts in several states and staged Days of Rage riots, they struck out against everything from the Vietnam War to the government's policies that they say perpetuated racism, gender inequality and poverty. Many of these radicals have moved on in life, such as becoming college professors, or simply just gave up their mission. Some continue to press forward with their radical ideology through another spin-off of the old WUO called *Prairie Fire*. But Karn, only released from prison a year ago where I put him in 1986, has sought to reorganize the WUO into a more violent subversive group than it ever was. Whereas the old group sent out warnings in advance of impending bombings to give the government a chance to evacuate Federal buildings, Karn believes that killing innocent citizens, who will become the spoils of war, will not only get the government's attention, but bring it to its knees at the negotiating table. The more concerning issue is the fact that Karn has enlisted terrorist elements from the American al Qaeda faction here in Colorado which will continue its agenda to create an even more dangerous scenario. They vow to make the 9-11 horror pale in comparison to the mass destruction wreaked in a number of cities.

"Incidental to Karn's plan, he has also launched a personal vendetta against me for arresting him and sending him to prison until he was pardoned on Christmas Eve, 2000, by the former President…"

Murphy then broke in. "And I heard through the grapevine he somehow became rather emasculated, shall we say, when you took him down." This raised a few chuckles, but lowered Pettyjohn's eyebrows in the direction of his young agent.

I continued without comment. "Anyway, through a fairly solid informant, I bring to the meeting some essential information about Karn's plans of hostility against the government. I have in my hands, and which I have also blown up for you on the screen, a new communiqué from Karn. It reads like communist propaganda.

"Friends and comrades of the New Weather Underground. We now awaken from this long winter's sleep…the winter of complacency. We and we alone will undertake a new offensive which will ultimately carve out the very heart of the American government. We will call it Operation Groundhog. Just as that furry little creature has spent his winter sleeping underground while the complacent world continues to ignore the festering sores of its needy and oppressed, we will rise from the underground to declare that a New State of War exists with the Government of the United States. The era of protest and demonstration is over. We will bridge the Days of Rage from yesteryear with the imperatives of the present. The American people will see blood running in all of their streets, not just New York City. The people will beg the government to concede in order to make the violence stop. And you, my friends, will be the revolutionary pioneers of our time who will set off

hundreds of attacks throughout this land. We begin here and in Chicago, and as we recruit and increase in strength and ally ourselves with our Muslim brothers, we will become <u>the</u> force to be reckoned with. On February 2nd, as most of Americais anxious to see if Punxatawny Phil sees his shadow, we, my friends, will spring from the underground and cast our shadow upon the population centers of America."

"In advance of that," I said. "My source tells me that Karn will gather his lieutenants, if not all local members of this group, at an abandoned warehouse at the end of Collier Road west of Lyons here." I pointed to the location on the screen. "As you can see, it is just on the eastern edge of where Roosevelt National Forest begins. It will happen in two days, Saturday the 6th. For the battle plan, I will turn the briefing back over to Agent Pettyjohn."

Pettyjohn thanked me and when I sat down, he kicked off the mission particulars. "I will have a recon bird in the air tomorrow and at first light on Saturday to observe the arrival and activity of the element. Once it appears all parties have driven in and have entered the building, the Joint Task Force on my command will, from these avenues of approach, converge on the target." He pointed to two routes of advance. "We will have attack helicopter support as well. Subjects are expected to be heavily armed and it is probable that the warehouse contains numerous explosive devices. We speculate the warehouse may even be a bomb manufacturing plant. It is not known whether there are any so-called dirty bombs at the site, however, so each member of the attack team will don protective masks. The source of information Mr. McGowan mentioned is not a player in the group, but her husband was. He was killed in our raid on the cabin where Karn was most recently located. The informant provided the copy of the communiqué as well as the verbal you heard. Mr. McGowan considers her credible."

"The Joint Task Force will be selected this afternoon as I collaborate with Lieutenant Harriman and FBI SWAT

Commander, Lieutenant Morrelli. There will be a supporting cast of fifteen field agents to include Ravenel, Murphy and Caudell from this office, and Agents Elliott Blanton and Joe Radford from the Fort Collins office. Including the FBI and CBI SWAT Teams, I expect our force will number sixty or more. I will also put out signal operating instructions, frequencies and call signs by 0900 tomorrow to be disseminated accordingly. We will have less than two days to put the take-down plan together. Any questions."

"Has a warrant been issued?" asked Harriman. "Federal Judge Casey will sign the warrant today. Any others?"

Caroline raised her hand. "You mentioned three agents from this office as mission participants. Were you not planning to use all of us?"

Both Pettyjohn and I knew this was coming.

"I have decided we need a field agent to man the Tactical Operations Center here for command and control purposes. I've selected you, Agent McGowan."

The look of disappointment on her face nearly broke my heart. She then looked at me and I was set to wonder what she was thinking. Did she read into the equation that I had something to do with Pettyjohn's decision?

After the meeting terminated, Caroline made a bee line for Pettyjohn's office, closing the door behind her. I moved closer in to the door to eavesdrop, but considering their voices were beginning to escalate, I could have stayed where I was.

"Why not me, Lew? This is the creep that took me and held me hostage for nearly five days. I want a chance at him. I want him in my sights."

"What you just said is part of my decision. You're too close to this. I need rational and cool heads out there, not someone whose agenda is vengeance."

"And you don't think I'm capable of acting rationally when it comes to doing my job?"

"On this case, I don't know whether you are or not," he replied. "You've only been aboard three months, Caroline. And I want you to become seasoned before you can be put into a major scenario like this."

"And that's your final say."

Pettyjohn nodded. "Yes. I'm afraid it is."

I could see her through the plate glass window, standing with hands on hips and giving him her mother's icy stare. The one thing I wished she hadn't inherited from her. Then, without further word, she turned heel and left his office. As she passed by the desk where I was sitting, the glare from her beautiful blues remained, and she said nothing to me. At least Pettyjohn was good enough not to mention I was the cause of their tête-à-tête.

My dear daughter's sullen mood continued through the day and into the evening well past dinner, which consisted of left-over Italian, which I might add was as good as it was two nights before. After the meal, we sat out on her balcony looking at the stars. The night was crisp and the radiational cooling had caused the stars to project all the more vividly on the blackboard sky. The police unit which still randomly cruised the parking lot day and night on our behalf had just moved on. Knowing Karn, however, and what he was capable of, he could easily time police presence like clockwork and get to us whenever he chose. I knew that Karn was too busy hiding and prepping for his Saturday morning seminar to focus on us. But if he did, it would only take a mere second to plant another, this time deadly bullet in me when I hit the bottom step of the stairwell. So, just in case, I still canvassed the parking lot before coming all the way down.

"Are you still miffed you're not in the Task Force?" I asked her.

"Oh, you bet. And Lew's explanation as to why I'm not? Pretty lame."

"Well, I don't think it's a matter of confidence, or lack

thereof. I believe he wants objectivity in the scenario. You have to admit, you might lose it if you personally came face- to-face with Karn. Can you tell me right now you wouldn't just blow him away on sight?"

She placed her fingers on her forehead and looked down at the balcony floor. I knew she was visualizing how that might play out. "I think I could take a deep breath, step back and allow him to surrender."

"And in doing so, in thinking about it, would you then be so focused on holding back killing him that he may put you in *his* sights? Thinking too much can get you killed, you know."

"I believe, given the circumstance and opportunity, I would react appropriate to the situation and make a sound and timely decision," she replied.

"Good text book answer, my dear, but you can never be certain how you're going to react until you're confronted."

She nodded 'yes' and I'm glad she didn't ask me the question I feared she would…like 'did you ask Pettyjohn to keep me out of the Task Force?' Hearing my truthful answer, she would send me packing immediately.

"And how is it *you* get to participate in the raid on the warehouse and I don't? You're just as close to this thing as I am."

A fair enough question. "I have over thirty years of experience as an action man, beginning with combat. *And,* I would not hesitate to pull the trigger to kill a man…something you haven't done. Something I never want you to have to do."

"But it could happen with me on any day and at any time," she replied.

"Yes it could. And I pray about that every night."

"Same here where it comes to you, old man. Why don't you give up that 'action man' life and marry Adrianna?"

I smiled at her. "Don't think I haven't thought about it. More so every day." I checked my watch. "Which reminds me. I'd better call her before she hits the sack."

Caroline was still sitting with me on the patio when I rang Adrianna. Though it was after ten Eastern time, I did find that my West Virginia sweetie was still up. I told her everything was good now that father and daughter were spending some quality time together. I also let her know that I'd probably be back there by the 15th and if possible, could she pick me up at Yeager. She said she'd find a place for it on her calendar. There was some gooey talk which started making me feel the kind of way I shouldn't, being in the presence of my daughter. But a third of the way through the conversation, Caroline smiled and went inside, stopping a moment to whisper, "say hello for me, lover boy."

Even though I was anxious for the Saturday morning mission to go down, I was equally anxious for the 15th to arrive.

CHAPTER FIFTEEN

At 0530 on the 6th, having been issued the weapons and protective vest I requested, I stood in the CBI staging area beside two vans and a dozen SUVs loaded down with the aforementioned FBI agents and SWAT teams from both the Federal and State law enforcement entities. The SWAT members, armed with Heckler and Koch MP5 machine guns and CAR-15s, also performed buddy checks on one another to see if all equipment to include protective masks were on the person. After a short send-off briefing that covered final coordinating instructions, Pettyjohn performed radio checks with the SWAT commanders and the Bell attack helicopter jockey who would precede the ground unit to perform his recon on the target at Beginning Morning Nautical Twilight.

At 0630, he announced, "The bird is in the air, team. Move out." As we convoyed out, Code Two, early Saturday morning risers craned their necks as we left Kipling, making our way toward I-25. Murphy was driving our Suburban with Starr Ravenel riding shotgun and Pettyjohn and I in the back seat. I was in good company. And so were they. As we began to exit I-25 onto 66 West, Pettyjohn received the transmission he was awaiting from the aviator. "The dogs are in the house. I say again, the dogs are in the house." Which meant all of Karn's players seemed to have arrived at the warehouse and were inside. Some twenty-five to thirty cars and pickups were spotted.

At 0650 we turned off of State 66 onto a narrow, two-lane asphalt road, then traveled less than two miles before turning left onto the side road that led to the warehouse. As the 11,000 square foot building sat off the road behind an auto salvage yard, it was not readily visible at first blush. At 0657, our teams, split between the two avenues of approach, converged simultaneously, sliding to a halt on gravel and ground, respectively, and dismounted to take up firing positions behind the vehicles.

No sooner than the chopper dropped down to hover in position above the gaggle of vehicles, with mini guns pointed at the building, fifteen to twenty men dressed in wood camouflage began scrambling like ants from the warehouse toward their vehicles. Some cradled rifles, but most did not.

"You're completely surrounded!" shouted Pettyjohn through his bullhorn. "Stand down now! Drop your weapons and place your hands on top of your heads! Drop to your knees. I'll only tell you this one time!"

He did not have to repeat the order. Each man surrendered his weapon and SWAT personnel over-took them quickly without incident. I moved in as well to look them over closely. Karn was not among them. I then advanced on one of the men and threw him face down onto the gravel. Placing the muzzle of my Glock against the back side of his right ear, I yelled, "Where's Karn!"

The man trembled, took one hand off his head and pointed toward the building. "There. He's inside…he's still inside. Please d…don't kill me."

"Then don't give me cause to," I said, jerking him

back to his knees by his jacket.

At the split second I turned to get Pettyjohn's attention across the way to tell him Karn had not come out, suddenly the warehouse exploded. It was cataclysmic. I, along with several others, was knocked off my feet. The sudden flush of intense heat and deafening concussion from the blast combined for a body-numbing shock to my system that seemed to paralyze me for a few moments. As choking dust, red cinder sparks and bits of debris continued to rain down all around us, I saw scores of fallen officers and suspects lying motionless or writhing around on the ground in pain. A few of Karn's men who had not made it much past the warehouse doors lay dead or seriously injured under heavy debris. Most of the SWAT team was back on its feet within thirty seconds, checking one another out. I looked around for familiar faces, ultimately seeing Pettyjohn and Murphy back on their feet dusting themselves off. But off to my left about fifteen yards a smallish form with an auburn ponytail hanging out the back of her helmet lay motionless, face down. Starr.

I ran to her, then gently turned her over. There were cuts and abrasions on her face and the collar on her black uniform shirt was smoking. I yelled to Pettyjohn to get her a SWAT medic and some water. She was breathing, but her breaths were shallow and irregular.

As I cradled her in my arms waiting for help, I watched as the intense fire raged, melting steel and setting off secondary explosions. It would be a while before anyone could sift through the debris for the remains of those left inside. And then it occurred to me that it would be just like Jonas Karn to set off such an explosion that would in his own warped mind make him a martyr like Jim Jones, David Koresh and Mohamed

Atta.

In a few moments, Pettyjohn arrived with a canteen of water. I first poured a few drops onto Starr's lips and then a little on her face. She blinked open her eyes and then I knew she was going to be all right when she smiled that kind of smile I had seen on a china doll. "Am I still alive?"

I smiled back. "You're very much alive, sweetheart." I then laid her back down to allow the medic to attend to her. And I was damned glad that Caroline was sitting back in the office on Stout Street.

As the Fort Collins and Lyons Fire Departments were putting out the last of the flames and smoldering embers, the press descended on us like fire ants wanting particulars of the operation. Pettyjohn, being the shrewd and coy cop that he was, not wanting the media to catch immediate wind that a domestic terrorist threat existed which would alarm people too soon after 9-11, told the reporters, "Our information is that these were some good old boys operating a meth lab. But of course we won't know for sure until we sift through things."

I stood with Pettyjohn a while talking and watching the medic work on Starr. She was a bit shell-shocked, and except for the cuts, there were no other visible injuries. However, the rescue squad, which was on the scene in a hurry, took her and two SWAT guys to the hospital for a check-over. All agents and SWAT members had been accounted for. Four of the suspects were killed by the blast. Two were of the Middle Eastern persuasion.

"If Karn was in that building when it went up, he's toast *now*," said Pettyjohn.

"When the CSI team is done and the debris is sifted through, I want to *see* that toast," I replied. "I'm now wondering if sometime during his incarceration a DNA sample was taken."

"Probably no reason to," said Pettyjohn. "And back when you arrested him there was no such thing as DNA samples. DNA came in the late 80s, didn't it?"

"I think that's right. Nonetheless, I want to find *some* evidence of whether he is dead or alive. Hopefully, this took care of the WUO reprisal for a while. But if there is merit in Karn's communiqué that elements in Chicago and other areas are planning to strike on Groundhog Day, this is definitely not the end of it. And what about the association with al Qaeda? There have to be more players out there than the crispy critters inside."

"We'll know eventually." My team will have it on their radar now. You may be seeing me more than you'd like."

"Actually, Bruce, I do like what I've seen and appreciate your assistance on this immensely. You're still a renegade, which will continue to bother me if you stick around. But you did some very nice work to make this all come together. My folks didn't get *squat* out of your informant when they grilled her."

"Often old friends, even when they become the enemy, will ultimately not betray old friendships," I said.

Pettyjohn nodded. "In this case, I'm certainly glad about that."

Starr was treated and released before most of the Task Force, including myself, had returned to the FBI building. Pettyjohn allowed Caroline to leave early in the afternoon to go check on Starr at her apartment.

As I had left my card with Geneva Sperry, she called me later in the afternoon. Some of her and Tom's male friends did not come home to their families Saturday afternoon, and as she had heard through her commune family about the FBI raiding the warehouse, knowing of course about the WUO dress rehearsal, she was concerned.

"What happened to all of them, Bruce? If they were killed, I will live forever with the guilt of having set them up."

"There were four who lost their lives, Geneva. You might know only two of them. Karn either accidentally or intentionally blew the warehouse up. Law enforcement did not fire a shot. Unfortunately, we don't know how many others remained in the building. The CSI team will be sorting through all the debris looking for bodies. I can't imagine there were many inside, since a great number came running out the front and back of the warehouse just before it exploded."

There was silence on her end for a moment. "I hope I did the right thing in talking to you. Some of those men's wives are my friends. The guys that were not killed…what will happen to them?"

"I don't really know, Geneva. They'll probably be charged with conspiracy to commit terrorist acts against the United States. Some will likely do some time; others who have clean records might skate or get probation. Nevertheless, this will hopefully stop them from grinding their axes against the government."

"I just don't want to see anyone else die," she said. "Did you get Tom's body?"

"Well, I signed for him last Tuesday. His body went to a funeral home in Boulder. There'll be a graveside service for him at one o'clock tomorrow out at Rest Haven."

"It will then be over for you, Geneva. It will be a time for you to totally break your ties to the organization once and for all. I don't believe there will be anyone left of the new order to assume Karn's role. At least for a while. You and your daughters can now live in peace."

"Peace," she repeated. "It sounds so…foreign. It is something I have not had in my heart since I was a child. Between Tom and me, things continued to be stirred up. But you're right, Bruce. It *is* a time for peace."

"Goodbye and take care, Geneva."

After I sat in on Pettyjohn's After Action brief, I returned to Caroline's apartment around six. I assumed she was still looking after Starr. I then took the opportunity to call the Birdman to fill him in on the operation.

"Sounds like the Bureau did its job," he said. "Too bad Karn wasn't taken prisoner. Perhaps they will identify his ashes."

"Karn was apparently not going to allow himself to be captured. My only regret is that I didn't have the opportunity to again come face to face with the parasite."

"It may be over in Colorado but looks like we'll need to put a team in Chicago to determine if there's merit in the communiqué. He might have been blowing smoke, but if not, I'm wondering if the attack will in fact go forward now that Karn is apparently dead…unless there's someone there equally as powerful as *he* was."

"Do you need me on that team in Chicago?"

"Take a few days more and heal. We'll see."

"I *am* healed, boss."

"Then go see Mrs. Wolf."

"I intend to. Will be there on the 15th and back to work the next day."

"Give her my regards."

"Be glad to…among other things that I intend to give her."

He sighed. "Goodbye, Bruce." And he was gone.

The CBI had left a couple of men at the razed warehouse over-night to protect the evidence until the CSI team moved back in at first light on Sunday. I slept a little late that morning, then got up and watched Charles Stanley on the tube while I downed a protein bar and a cup of java. As it had been two weeks since I had jogged, aside from the fact that I had been put through the meat grinder as a result of the ageing actress's carelessness, I wondered if my body was ready. Caroline said she'd go with me if I wanted. I actually think she did not want me out there all by myself if my body happened to go into shut-down mode.

She was a natural runner. While she cut through the frigid air with effortless grace, I stayed with her the three long blocks it took us to get to the high school track. And that's where she turned it on.

"See ya," she said. Like a cheetah, her strides were smooth and extended. In just one lap, she was sailing around the opposite side of the quarter mile track, her long brown hair waving and flapping from the rear of her FBI ball cap. It didn't take long for the traumatized muscles in my back to stove up on me and the pain cut all the way through to my abdomen. But after completing four laps, I pulled up to a walk. My body felt like it was caked with rust. As Caroline passed me a second time, she yelled, "How are you doing?" She wasn't even winded. I nodded and continued walking the rest of the way around the track to where I could go into the pits and take a seat on the metal bleachers. The seat was ice cold to the buns, but as my body had told me to 'sit,' I wasn't giving it any backtalk.

Perched there watching the girl I loved like no one else, I reflected back on another day I had watched her overtake the reigning district high school champ in the 880. The girl had broken all Virginia state track records the year before and was a shoo-in to take the day's trophy. But my little sophomore with lengthy strides and tenacious spirit *took* the girl down the stretch at the tape by a step. I remember coming unglued and slapping some stranger on the back in my elation, later finding out that it was the other girl's father I had assaulted.

In her last lap around, she kicked in the afterburners and it was like watching poetry in motion. At the finish line she pulled up and walked around with her hands on her hips, now breathing like I was a few moments before.

Except, she was not gasping for air. Any other day she might have gigged me with something like, "Did your engine quit on you, old timer?" But she knew that I was not up to my usual speed…which even on a good day about 60% was of her.

"You're feeling it, huh?" she said. "Maybe this was a little too soon for you to start running again."

"Maybe, "I replied. "But lying around like a slug without exercising and then eating like I have been, I think I've started developing a pouch over my washboard abs."

She laughed and said, "Come on. We'll *walk* back. Let me buy you some brunch."

"Yeah. Exactly what I *don't* need."

After my shower, she took me out to Macintosh's for a smorgasbord brunch, which would sure as hell last me all day and half-way through the next. We returned to her apartment about noon, after which I announced that I would be gone the remainder of the afternoon. I wanted to revisit the warehouse rubble to see what evidence had been obtained to this point. Pettyjohn had told me he would be going out mid-afternoon himself. I should already be there, I said. First, I had another place to go. At five minutes past one I dismounted from my rental and walked up the incline past the symmetrical rows of stones to a spot beneath the barren branches of a massive oak at the top of the hill. From that vantage point, I was able to observe some thirty yards away the graveside service for Tom Sperry. As most of Tom and Geneva's male friends were guests of the local correctional facility, I only counted the heads of six women gathered in semi-circle fashion around the coffin at the end of which stood the minister, Bible cupped in his hands. Off to the side stood a balding man in an overcoat, hands folded in front of him, which I took to be the funeral director. After about ten minutes, they all bowed their heads and then it was over. Three of the women then departed, leaving Geneva and her two daughters alone with the minister. Shortly after, he then left.

Geneva stood grieving for a while with her girls and then each one of them laid a single rose onto the coffin. The man in the overcoat walked over to Geneva, shook her hand and she tugged at the sleeves of her daughters to leave. When she turned in my direction, she saw me. I smiled and lifted my hand to which she acknowledged with a nod. And then they walked past me toward the family car where another mortician stood beside the open door.

When they had pulled away, I remained in place, watching the grave attendant lower Tom's coffin. Regardless of how Tom had turned out, he was still a veteran and a brother-in-arms. It was even sadder that there was no Honor Guard, no bugler blowing Taps, and not even any Legionnaires to place the veteran's marker.

When the coffin had totally disappeared beneath the ground, I trudged back down the hill to my car. What a waste, I thought. A husband and father gone because of his own stupidity and warped sense of allegiance and devotion to a cause such as the WUO. For some reason in my head I heard the '60s hippy ballad being sung, *Where have All the Flowers Gone?*, and the words… "gone to graveyards everyone. When will they ever learn? When will they ever learn?"

I actually arrived at yesterday's mission site about the same time Pettyjohn did. As we stood talking, CSI Lieutenant Jeanette Pomeroy approached us. A short stocky woman with black butch hair and the nose of a hawk, she looked as though she had just chewed up a peck of nails for lunch.

"What did you find out, Lieutenant?" Pettyjohn asked her.

"Looks like only two bodies in the ashes, sir. Not much

left of them. We can confirm they're male, however. This was on one of them." She then held up a large plastic bag that contained a mostly melted leather belt attached to a large silver buckle burnt black in places. On the buckle was a raised fist.

"Karn's," I said. "Anything else?"

"An arsenal of weapons to include three AK-47s and several automatics. It appears the secondary fireballs you saw were from exploding personnel and incendiary grenades, C-4 and ammonium nitrate. It's a wonder the entire county didn't go up. And oh, by the way, walk over here with me."

We followed her to the rear of the building, stepping and climbing over piles of twisted metal beams, charred wood framing and unidentified remnants of various fabrics. Permeating throughout was the nauseating smell of a combination of burnt wiring, plastic and chemicals.

"There," she said pointing to the concrete floor. "A door and steps leading underground. It is a way in and out that leads to a wooden trapdoor just inside that tree line… maybe a hundred yards in that direction."

Which raised my antenna. Did anyone manage to make it into the tunnel before Jonas Karn set the place off?

After walking back into the woods to take a gander at the door, we saw that its lid was lying open. I looked inside the hole and with my eyes, followed the concrete steps down to where they disappeared in the dark abyss.

"Did you folks open the door and leave it like this?" I asked.

"This is just the way we found it, sir. And if you follow that path there, you will see that it leads to Highway 168 about five hundred feet out. We believe it's possible someone may have escaped out through this tunnel."

And that set me to wonder if that person was Jonas Karn. But if that was the case, why was there a charred, unrecognizable corpse back there in the rubble wearing his belt buckle? I could only speculate that if he did not materialize in some shape or form within the near future, we could pretty much assume that it was he who died in that warehouse. Otherwise, Jonas Karn, his agenda and his ego, would not lay low for very long.

The rest of the week was quiet. I made an appearance a couple of times at the Denver FBI office to see if there was any WUO-related activity, new communiqués or a resurfacing of the presumed dead Jonas Karn. There was nothing. As we suspected, there was no record of DNA samples having been taken of Karn when he was incarcerated, so there was nothing to match to the corpse. The CSI folks even went into Ma Karn's house to try finding one of Jonas Karn's hairs in the bathroom and bedroom to no avail. They also followed up with the Colorado Correctional System to see if there were dental x-rays on file. Unfortunately, there had been a fire earlier in the year that had destroyed half the facility to include all medical records. Go figure. And then the CSI team performed a similar crime scene analysis at the cabin up in Horsetooth where I was an over-night guest, finding hairs galore, but none matching the body with the buckle. Pettyjohn was convinced Karn was dead. Ergo, case closed. Me? Huh-uh. Karn was not dead until I personally examined his corpse.

CHAPTER SIXTEEN

On the 15th, Caroline actually kissed her old man goodbye at the passenger drop off point outside the Denver terminal.

"Now would you please quit collecting bullets, Father dear? I've got other things to do besides have to worry about you. And for goodness sakes, refrain from turning your back on old ladies."

"I'll be sure to put that in my 'lessons learned' file, princess. *You* be careful, okay?"

"I will, Dad. Bye bye." She then slid back under the steering wheel, waved a final time and drove away. It would be the beginning of many days of worry for me.

During the hour I sat at the gate waiting on Frontier 1438, I allowed those horrendous two weeks of anxiety, hostility and pain to parade through my mind. I had wondered about old lady Karn and where she was hiding, now that her son was dead. If he was. She had lost not only him, but her home as well. I figured someone had to have taken her in. Her Social Security checks would be piling up in the mailbox and ultimately returned to the government. I knew she would not be stupid enough to notify the post office of an address change. But enough about the old woman.

My thoughts were mostly on Caroline. Reality was setting in

more and more about the dangers she could face as a Special Agent on any given day. Her safety would forever be in the forefront of my mind as long as she was with the Bureau. Before Christmas, I had pretty much remained in denial about that. And I sat there blaming myself for even passively encouraging her to sign on with them.

But then my mind turned to more pleasant things. Like seeing Adrianna in a few hours. And I just couldn't wait to hold that soft, sweet-smelling beauty in my arms. She would be the medicine I had needed that would take away all my mental and physical pangs. *And it was at that honest moment of untrammeled revelation that I realized I had just arrived at the crossroad of my future.*

My plane touched down at the small airport on the mountain above Charleston at three-fifteen. A gentle but wet snow was still falling as it had for much of the day, adding to the four plus inches already on the ground. As I rode the escalator down to baggage claim, I saw that she was standing, waiting for me at the turnstile. With her dark hair pulled back behind her ears and coat collar tucked up around her neck, she looked even younger than I remembered. I had never seen her eyes dazzle more beautifully or her smile more captivating. For some reason, even though it had only been three weeks since I kissed that face, it seemed like three months. And then at last, when I drew her tiny body into mine and felt her warm breath in my ear, I was sixteen again.

"Welcome home, sweetheart," she said in a honey-flavored whisper.

Home. Although it really wasn't, it sure did feel like it.

The turnpike having been salted was clear. But all around us was a winter wonderland. Heavy snow caked the barren limbs of the maples and feathery branches of the deep green spruce, causing them to droop and bow as we passed by.

Occasionally, I would see where waterfalls off the mountains had frozen over into gleaming, diamond- like sculptures, making it appear that the world itself had stopped. It was beautiful. Both outside and inside the car.

As she negotiated the winding highway and listened as I filled her in on most of what had gone down in the Denver area, her eyes danced and sparkled with wonderment. Her mouth fell agape a couple of times and I occasionally found myself distracted watching her full lips react in harmony with her eyes. And even though those expressions were not meant to be sensuous, they enticed me, summoning deep inside me a craving wantonness that I knew could not immediately be satisfied. At least for a couple of hours.

I didn't tell her everything, especially about my being shot, and of course the gruesome details of the raid on Karn's compound. Basically, I just said we were able to get Caroline back unharmed and the bad guys were shut down, thanks to the FBI. But being the inquisitive one, she wanted to know if the guy who took Caroline was captured or killed. I told her he ended his own life before we could get to him. She said that maybe him doing that had helped save a lot of lives. And she was correct about that.It felt like Christmas all over again at Wolf Laurel. The landscape around the inn was pure Currier and Ives. It had begun to snow more profusely, covering the roads yet again and creating an atmosphere of deafening quiet that seemed to shut out all the offenses of the world. As we carefully made our way to the front porch, only the crunchy squeaking of our shoes on the fresh snow was audible. As she turned the key in the front door lock, I kicked the snow off my shoes on the banister.

"No guests, huh?" I said, taking account of the empty parking lot.

"It's always slow this time of year. I probably won't see a

half dozen people between now and spring."

"Then I'll have you all to myself. There won't be anyone around to hear all the screaming and creaking of bed springs."

"Well, I see what's been on *your* mind since you've been gone," she said.

I grinned like a Cheshire cat, but to be truthful, it had been the furthest thing from mind most of the time I was in Colorado. However, it was certainly on my mind at the present as I watched her slip off her coat revealing that shapely forty-something rush beneath those jeans.

I hadn't eaten lunch, and even though the stomach juices were gurgling, my carnal juices had to be fed first. Our clothes came off in a matter of seconds and as quickly as I fell with her onto the bed, I began a feast that lasted nearly half an hour. The ecstasy I experienced satiated both my mind and body, electrifying every vessel and organ, sending me spiraling into a kind of surreal state of unconsciousness. As small and delicate as she was, I was amazed at her sexual power. The spell that she had magically cast over me took away all my strength, the good witch that she was.

It was now fully dark outside our window as well as in the bedroom when she finally left me limp and whimpering like a small boy on the playground who had just had the stuffing knocked out of him. She then turned on the small lamp on the night stand and sat up with the sheet pulled around her. I was lying on my stomach, eyes rolled back and bottom lip stuck to my pillow, pretty much unable to move.

"So, what happened to your back, Skip?" she asked, running her fingers over the three by three band aid.

I had forgotten that there might be that slim chance she would see me with my shirt off. Well, I just couldn't lie to her. With her keen perception, she would ultimately realize there was no excised boil under that patch.

"Well, it's like this. I was minding my own business when an old woman sitting in the back seat of the car I was driving just up and shot me."

The expression on her face was something straight out of the movies. "Are you being silly again? Why can't you give me a straight answer most of the time? Now, come on…the truth."

"Okay. This is a multiple choice question. What happened to my back?

       a.   I had a cyst removed.

b.   A brown recluse spider bit me.

c.   I developed an infection from where you dug your nails into my back the last time we did this.

d.   An old lady shot me in the back.

Adrianna then reached down and grabbed my ear lobe and began pinching it. "All right, McGowan, cut out the game show crap and just tell me."

"Ow!" I yelped, pulling her fingers off my ear. "Okay, contestant number one…bzzzzz! You didn't answer in the required amount of time, so you go home with nothing. The answer is…d."

And then like Paul Harvey, I told her the rest of the story. She glared at me for a long moment, not smiling at my funny story, then wrapped the sheet around her and trudged off to the bathroom without a u word. Obviously, she was unhappy with the game show host.

I heard the shower running and then stop after five minutes or so. Not long after that, she came out with a large, thirsty towel wrapped around her and sat on the edge of the bed. I then pulled on my boxers and sat with my back against the head board.

"Well, what this tells me," She said, "is that whatever the circumstance, you're going to continue living a life of danger."

"Like Secret Agent Man."

"What?"

"You know, Patrick McGoogan, '60s TV show? 'There's a man who lives a life of danger…' Johnny Rivers."

"Can't you be serious just one moment?" she scolded. "I'm sorry, Skip, but I can't be in love with someone who might go out on some kind of secret mission someday and not come back to me."

"You really mean that?" I asked.

"Yes, I do. I can't live with the fear…"

"No, no. Not that. Are you really in love with me?" "What do you think, Bruce McGowan?"

"I think its music to my ears. The kind of music I want to hear the rest of my life."

"What does that mean when you say that, Skip?"

I slid my derriere down to the bottom of the bed and dropped down on my knees at her feet. "I'm saying I want to be your husband, Adrianna Wolf."

Her eyes widened and her lips parted. I expected her to throw her arms around me and say, "Yes, yes. I'll marry you." But she just sat there looking at me without an answer. Finally, she said, "How could that ever be, Skip? I'm not moving to Georgetown. And anyway, as long as you continue to be America's James Bond, you can't be married to me."

I then picked myself up, floored that I was, and sat on the edge of the bed with her. "That's just it, Adrianna. I'm giving Lionel Byrd my notice as soon as I get back to Washington tomorrow."

For a while, her eyes worked back and forth between mine and then ever so gently, she put her arms around me and began to sob. We remained in that position for probably thirty seconds, saying nothing. And then she separated herself from me and said, "You're not just saying that are you? You wouldn't toy with my emotions on something like this?"

I smiled and held her shoulders in my hands. "I've never been more serious about anything in my life. I love you,

Adrianna. If you will have me, I will move here and help you operate Wolf Laurel."

"Oh no you won't, Mr. McGowan. I will not have you under foot, getting in my way and impeding me in my work around here. You will find a nice little uncomplicated, danger-free job somewhere."

"Hey, I haven't even put a ring on your finger and already we're having a fight."

She laughed and pinched my cheek.

"Good grief," I said. "What's with all this pinching? Is that what I have to look forward to?"

She then pushed me back down on the bed and rolled on top of me. "No. *This* is what you will have to look forward to."

I was going to like being married to her.

Adrianna was all smiles and giddy as a schoolgirl as we ate at the quaint Italian café in White Sulphur. While we sat and talked, we ended up setting the date of our wedding for June 22nd. My lease would then be up on my Georgetown apartment and that would give me ample time to clean up my affairs with CTT. We planned for a small ceremony with just immediate family and a couple of friends…hers…in the little garden on the Wolf Laurel grounds. Adrianna would put an announcement in the Greenbrier and Charleston papers and would otherwise take care of all the arrangements. I had nothing else to do but show up, say 'I do,' and fly with her to Cozumel for a five day honeymoon. But when we returned, there was that other thing…finding a job.

On the way back to Wolf Laurel, we swung by Joey's house, receiving congrats all around. After we had clinked our glasses filled with celebratory wine, we departed. I made sure to retrieve my Suburban before I left and followed Adrianna back to the inn. It was good to have my Glock and Winchester 700 by my side. I missed them. I had felt naked without them. That's why I had to get *some* kind of job that would allow me to carry at least one of them.

I awoke the next morning to another couple of inches of the beautiful white stuff which was keeping people in. I could see from her turret window that few cars had cut swaths along Seven Bridges Road. As the Weather Channel had forecast snow showers up through the Shenandoah on into the D.C. area, I figured I had best get an early start.

Adrianna was already up and had baked blueberry muffins which I found quite tasty with a cold glass of skim milk. At nine she kissed her newly-acquired fiancée goodbye at the door, giggled some more, as she had done most of the previous evening, and closed the door behind me.

By eleven, I was nearly to Staunton and following a salt truck. By three, I was finally on I-66 an hour from the outskirts of Washington. In all our excitement, I had forgotten to call Caroline to not only let her know I had arrived in good ol' WV safely, but that I was taking the plunge again. She screamed with elation. I believe it had more to do with the fact that I not only had someone to look after me, but people wouldn't be putting holes in me.

At four-twenty, I wheeled the Suburban into the parking lot behind Terminal Enterprises. Giving my usual one finger salute to Voyeur, I was then buzzed in through the back door.

Virginia greeted me with a bear hug, but this time her eyes were less erotic and more commiserate. "I'm so happy you got Caroline back, Bruce, and that she was okay. Welcome home."

"Thanks, sweetheart. Is he still in?"

"He's back there," she replied. "I think *he* thinks you're leaving us."

"He does, huh?"

"Yes. *Are* you?"

"I'm getting married, Virginia. I can't hold down two jobs."

"Well, congratulations. You're marrying that West Virginia girl, aren't you? That's a big mistake, you know."

"How so?"

"You could've had *me*."

"But you're taken. And anyway, you'd be too much woman for me."

"True. But you'd die with a smile on your face, 007."

I grinned and maybe even blushed. "I guess I'd better get back there and face the music."

I rapped twice on Birdman's door and he called for me to enter. I found him with his face in the computer monitor heavily entrenched in some matter. Without taking his eyes off the screen, he waved me to the chair in front of his desk. Finally, he said, "Good to have you back, Bruce."

"Good to be *anywhere*, Boss."

"How's the wound?"

"Healing well. I hardly know it's there."

"So, you're really going to do it, huh, Bruce?" "Do it? Do what?"

"Abandon the game for a dull, domestic life."

"You *know*, then." I had forgotten that Byrd's eyes and ears were everywhere, and what he didn't know, it wouldn't take him long to figure out.

"You just told me. But actually, I probably knew when we had that conversation a week ago, my friend. Have you looked ahead to envision what life will be like for you? Maybe suffocating behind some desk?"

"Always the encourager, aren't you?"

"Always the *realist*. How long before your marriage to Mrs. Wolf?"

"You've speculated about *that*, have you?"

"Why else would you be leaving CTT?"

"Right. Well, the wedding's in June. If it's okay, I'll work till then."

Byrd then leaned back in his chair and folded his hands under his chin. "Is it possible that you could work for the

Department after you are married on a contractor basis…join in on missions or do some spur-of-the-moment investigations for me?"

"I hadn't thought about that, but there are two concerns. My *new* employer may frown on me taking off without notice. And I think one of Adrianna's caveats in marrying me is that I make a clean break. She would prefer that I leave danger and anything having to do with guns behind. She made it clear she would not be a widow the second time around."

"I see," he replied. "Well, the offer will be there. I would be sure not to abuse your contract services. I expect we'd need you infrequently, unless there is some sort of major terrorist threat or we see a subversive network developing."

"I'll think about it," I said. "And I'll certainly have to sell it to my new bride."

"*Before* she becomes your bride, I presume."

"That would be correct."

Then, fair enough. By the way, I'll be sending Chuck and team to Chicago next week to determine if there's anything to Karn's communiqué. I received this morning from the Bureau a full report on the Weatherman suspects in Northern Illinois. One of our Chicago CTT operatives will infiltrate the organization."

"Do I assume I will be part of that investigation?"

"You will. They'll need your personal insight into the group." Byrd then picked up a piece of paper, skimmed over it and looked back at me. "I received this piece of distressing news earlier this morning from Agent Pettyjohn. A known female member of the Underground out in the Boulder area was killed some time last night. The police found her and her daughters' mutilated bodies still lying in their beds."

My heart sank. I didn't even have to say their names aloud, but did anyway. "Geneva Sperry and her daughters, Kathryn and Schyler."

"You know, then."

"Yes. Geneva was my informant. Pettyjohn would not have called you if it had been anyone else. What are the particulars?"

"It appeared to be Manson-type killings. Their throats were cut and the words 'traitor' and 'pigs' were written on the walls and mirrors in their blood."

"Bastards," I said. "Either Jonas Karn is not really dead or there are remnants of that group out there that are just as vicious and maniacal as him."

"The Bureau fully believes Karn is in fact dead and that someone else has taken up the WUO leadership. And another thing…the CBI found Karn's mother living in a boarding house on the east side of Denver. She had contacted the Social Security office to have them start sending her check to that location."

"I didn't think she'd be that stupid."

Byrd then leaned toward me. "And she gave up peaceably. No police officers were harmed in the take-down." I thought I caught a stifled smile.

"Very funny, Lionel."

"Well, do you feel like going back to work tomorrow? I need to send you to the Naval Yard down in Norfolk. Three young Middle Eastern men were spotted parked in a car outside of the main gate. NCIS and the NSA have located the car they were in, but the subjects have disappeared. I need your nose down there."

"I'll be ready to roll in the morning."

"Good. Here's the report. Let me know if you have any questions."

On the way to my apartment, a vision of that day I dropped in on Geneva popped into my head. I had sensed from our conversation that she was still somewhat passionate about making our country a better place for its citizens to enjoy life and the freedom to do so. And I knew she and her die-hard socialist friends still had contempt for the government and its policies that affected the minorities, the poor and other special groups. But she was also abhorred by the violence that was often a part of the Weatherman agenda. Turning in violent radicals like Karn was something in good conscience she needed to do. But then it cost her and her daughters their lives. Thinking about how they died made me want to return to Denver to find the bastards. And when I did, I would make them suffer unmerciful pain before I finally killed them.

I didn't sleep very well that night, finding myself up at two in the morning sitting in the dark in my recliner fielding the myriad of thoughts tumbling around in my brain. First, the reality of this old boy getting married a second time was actually sinking in. Was I ready for it? Was I ready to make a radical change in my life for it? Would I be living a counterfeit life? When I committed last night to Adrianna, had my body been that hungry for love that it turned off my brain? I thought I was perfectly happy living on my own and sitting around my apartment with the 3 Bs: beer, boxer shorts and batteries for my remote control. My needs are simple.

And then I thought again about Geneva. Did I actually set her up for her own murder? Should I have thought about that and found another resource to bring Karn and his fellow subversives down? So, how was she found out? Did a neighbor see me at her house?

Considering I was not going to get back to sleep, I also wondered if I would be in any condition to make any sense to anyone when I met with the NCIS and Virginia Bureau of Investigation in less than six hours.

CHAPTER SEVENTEEN

One of the three Middle Eastern boys who was traced to what the authorities thought was an intentionally abandoned car in a parking lot, possibly filled with explosives, had just left the vehicle there because it was a piece of junk and wouldn't restart. The car was stripped down by agents of the NCIS, however, and found clean as a whistle. After a warrant was issued by a Federal judge, the boy's apartment was searched. Nothing was found that would indicate that he and his buds were terrorist maggots bent on blowing up the naval base. He was finally located and as he sat across the table from the NCIS agent shaking and bawling, he swore on Allah's throne that he was only sitting in his car with his friends waiting to pick up his girlfriend who worked as a housekeeper at the small motel across the street. *She* checked out as well. Although there was nothing to hold them on, the boys' names would be added to a profile list that would make it difficult for them to get loans or make it past the TSA folks at the airport. All was well that ended well in Norfolk. After a couple of days, I was back on the road to Washington.

On Monday, the 22nd, Chuck, who we call the Rock, because he is the spitting image of Dwayne "the Rock" Johnson of action movie fame, Jeff "rather be on the tee box" Palmer, and I boarded the Department jet at Andrews with our armament bound for O'Hare. At ten-forty a black SUV pulled up to a stop on the tarmac a few feet from our plane just as we were disembarking. A young clean-cut man in a black suit and dark sunglasses exited the driver's side of the vehicle and signaled to us to approach.

"I'm Special Agent Kellen Thomas," he said, holding out his hand.

"Of course you are," I replied. "Bruce McGowan. The incredible hulk here is Chuck and this is Jeff Palmer." We shook hands.

"Good. My boss, the agent-in-charge, specifically said to take you gentlemen directly to him. He's already had a dialogue with your office this morning."

The kid couldn't have been much out of diapers yet. In my day, you had to be at least shaving and developing ear hair before you could work for J. Edgar. But he *had* assimilated that Joe Friday stiff, corn cob up your ass manner and matter-of-fact way of speaking they teach you at the Academy, an image that would charm Mr. Hoover right out of his dress. I just like having fun with all that speculation about J. Edgar and whether he actually ever came out of the closet…a closet which after his death was found to contain women's garments.

Anyway, back to Boy Wonder, otherwise known as Kellen Thomas, he was a polite enough kid who by direction from his boss began filling us in on the Chicago scenario.

What I learned was that he was a pretty darn good little investigator. He had been on the Bureau's task force (JTTF) that went looking for the local chapter of the Weather Underground Organization, ultimately securing a copy of the Northern Illinois version of *The Subterranean* back in Denver. Coming up with the brilliant idea of having the paper it was printed on analyzed by the research department at Georgia Pacific, Kellen was able to determine that it was of unique quality that was produced by only one company in the area…Synergy, LTD. Taking it upon himself to peruse through the purchase records there, which took a couple of days, he found a name that matched one listed in the Federal database…Mitchell Lively, one of Karn's cronies from the original WUO. It appeared to reinforce my earlier findings that the new order of the WUO was being re- developed by members of the *old* order. It also appeared that the old '70s ideology was still valued. These old radicals added a bit of a historical flavor to the new WUO's agenda, revered in a warped kind of way like bringing back on the entertainment stage icons such as Dylan and Baez.

Agent Thomas had also found out that Mr. Lively was living in an apartment on Tradd Street above a bookstore called *Yesterday's Message*, which he owned and operated. The store stocked mostly secondhand books, some of which were authored by radical activists with socialist, anti-government agendas. Kellen said he had actually been in the store looking around. He never caught sight of Lively, but did talk a bit with two equivocating clerks, a young man and woman who were reincarnates from 1968 San Francisco with long, stringy hair, beads, sandals and multiple piercings on their heads. Agent Thomas was obviously an ambitious and tenacious young man who reminded me of me as I was some twenty years ago. But I can't ever remember being as anal as this kid was. I was sure he would mellow out in time.

As we trucked along toward the Bureau field office, Palmer from the back seat asked him, "You said you didn't see Lively. Obviously, there's a photo on file in the system and you knew who to look for."

"Yes. We have his mug shot from six years ago, and unless he's been on Rogaine and managed to grow hair, he should look much the same."

"What was he arrested for?"

"Possession and distribution of heroin. Unfortunately, he pled out and the liberal judge gave him a year's probation."

"Sum bitch," Chuck muttered.

"We've staked out the place for about a week now," Thomas added. "Either he stays up in that apartment like a hermit or he comes and goes another way. None of our people have seen anybody who matches his description. We *have* seen several interesting-looking characters going into the place who one would not think generally patronized such a store. We have several telephoto shots of their faces and have been checking our face scan system to see if there are any matches."

"Is there any evidence that Lively is actually the kingpin in the Chicago organization?" asked Chuck.

"We don't know at this time, but suspect with his history, he probably is. The edition of the rag I secured simply shows Lively as the editor. The articles, as you may suspect, are mostly anti-government editorials, but do not allude to any subversive plans. It did, however, run the communiqué written by Jonas Karn. Unfortunately, we do not know where the newspaper is being printed, but suspect it's probably right there in a back room of the book store."

"Well, then," I said. "Perhaps we ought to get a look inside the building to include Lively's apartment." I looked back at Chuck and Jeff. "What do you guys think?"

Thomas shook his head. "We've already attempted to secure a search warrant, Mr. McGowan, but the judge did not think there was enough probable cause."

"Liberal bastard," I replied.

Agent Thomas then looked over at me with suspicious eyes. "You're of course not thinking of performing an illegal search, are you?"

"Mr. Thomas, we are Federal operatives with the State Department. I think your question is a bit impertinent, if not distrustful."

"I'm sorry, sir. I meant no disrespect."

"That's all right, son. We do things by the book. Just so you know." I then turned to wink at my chums in the back seat.

Our book, of course.

We wheeled into the parking lot at the Bureau field office about eleven-thirty. After grabbing our bags which contained the usual necessities…toothbrush, changes of underwear, Glocks and the like, we were escorted past security by Joe Friday to the upper floor where we stepped from the elevator accosted by the sign that read *Federal Bureau of Investigation, Chicago Field Office.*

After we entered the office, Thomas led us through a maze of desks where a half-dozen agents and staff sat with their faces trained on monitors, for the most part ignoring us. Momentarily, we stopped at the boss's door where Kellen rapped a couple of times on the glass and then opened it. "The Washington people are here, sir."

"Good," the voice from inside said. "Bring them in."

When I stepped into the office, I believe my jaw must have dropped to my knees. There, behind the desk sat my good friend from four months ago, Jack Fuentes.

"Holy crap!" I exclaimed. "Jack! What are you doing *here?*"

"Hello, Bruce," he greeted, rising from his chair and practically running to pump my hand. "I was promoted to here in December. You never know from one month to the next what's in store for you at the Bureau. Diane and the kids are staying in Charleston till the end of the school year and then we'll be buying a house in the 'burbs."

"Well, isn't that just the cat's meow? Moving up in the ranks. Somehow, I knew that it would happen to you. I just didn't know it would be this quick. By the way, these are my compadres, Jeff and Chuck. They work with me on our team."

"My sympathies, fellows," he said, smiling.

"I see you know him well, Jack," replied Chuck.

"All I know is, you'd better not be on the 'receiving' end of this guy."

"Well," I said with a tad of faux indignity. "I know a lot of women who would disagree with you on that."

"A legend in his own mind," added Palmer.

Jack then placed his hand on my shoulder. "I followed on the wire what was happening with your daughter, Bruce. Glad it turned out the way it did. A good many times it doesn't. And you know that as well as anyone."

I nodded. "Don't think it wasn't on my mind every moment of the time the creep had her, Jack."

"Assume Agent Thomas here filled you in on Lively? We believe he may be your Jonas Karn in this area."

"Yes. So, when do we go snag him?"

"Putting out an underground newspaper doesn't give us a case, Bruce. Nothing to arrest him for and make it stick."

"Maybe we can find a way to force his hand. One of our Chicago operatives is working on a way to infiltrate the organization."

"Would you be at liberty to tell me who your operative is? I'd like to know just in case something does go down that he won't get caught up in."

"His name is Carlos Gallegos," Chuck said. "About forty-five, long, shiny black hair that he wears in a ponytail. Looks kind of like a Steven Seagal. He gets tagged for a number of covert deals since he can look Native American, Middle Eastern or just plain Mafioso."

"I'll be sure to advise my stake-out team to watch out for him."

"Appreciate that," I added.

"Well, Bruce, the last time I saw you, you were nursing an abdominal wound. Assume you healed up okay."

Chuck and Palmer looked at one another and laughed out loud.

"What's so funny?" Jack asked. "Did I miss the joke?"

"Well, it's like this," Chuck said. "He's collected another bullet since then."

Jack turned to me and frowned. "What? You were shot again?"

"I'd...rather not talk about it." I then turned my laser eyes onto Palmer and Chuck. "And by the way, punks, how did you find out? Did Byrd tell you?"

Palmer grinned. "You mean that a ninety-year old grandma tried to waste you? We had a lot of yuks about that one."

I sighed, closed my eyes and shook my head. "She was only seventy-five and it was an accident. Get your story straight."

And then *Jack* grinned. "You want to talk about it, Bruce?"

"We're not going there today, Jack." I glared again at my former friends.

"I assume that since you're standing here today, it wasn't that serious."

"Okay, everybody. You've had your fun at my expense. Let's move on with this Lively character."

"You're right, Bruce," replied Chuck. "That's old business. Old, *old* business. But you're safe now. She's in custody."

"Can we get on with it?"

"We have a Bureau profile on Lively," Jack said. "I surmise Kellen told you about his drug history. He's been both a user and supplier. He's been divorced three times and pretty much stays cooped up in that apartment over the store...we think. No known social life. Appearance wise, he's six-three, two-hundred pounds, a skin head and has a tattoo on the back of his skull that reads, "Sic Semper Tyrannis.""

"What John Wilkes Booth shouted after he shot Lincoln," I said. "Thus Ever to Tyrants."

"Yes. He will be easy to spot in a crowd unless he wears a disguise, such as a hairpiece, hat or glasses. His known associates are three gangsters, two of which are Russians named Vilyam Yezhov, a man in his middle to late '60s, and Igor Gordievski, bad dudes both of them. The third is a Hoboken transplant by the name of Paulie "the Predator"

Gazzone. We've seen all of them going in and out of the bookstore a few times along with a few unidentifieds sporting beards and baseball caps. So far, all are Caucasian. No Blacks, Hispanics or Middle Eastern types."

"So, with a couple of Russian mobsters tied in, do you think Lively has some interests that go beyond the WUO like money laundering or human trafficking?" I asked.

"Could be that the mob is tied in and providing financial support. They *were* thirty years ago and I'll tell you about that in a moment. But there could be another agenda as well. Buildings getting blown up by urban terrorists will take law enforcement's focus off a lot of mob activity. We also know that Yezhov is former KGB. He operated a KGB training camp in Havana forty years ago, and guess who two of his star students were?"

"Okay, we give up."

"Not only Weather Underground leader Mark Rudd, but Mitchell Lively and one Lee Harvey Oswald."

"Interesting," I remarked.

"We've also learned that the KGB planted agents within the original WUO in the late sixties with the intent of infiltrating facets of the U.S. Government at all levels offering obscene amounts of money to select CIA operatives and FBI agents in exchange for Top Secret information. Unfortunately, a few took the money. And it's still going on. The Bureau believes that even though the WUO officially fell apart, remnants of the original group never ceased their activities. They have been waiting for the right time and the money to continue with their acts of terrorism against the government and its infrastructure. Could be that Yezhov and company are actually even equipping this home-grown element with suitcase devices and surface-to- air missiles. They have the money and resources. Thanks to the information you obtained in Colorado, Bruce, we now believe that the element here in Chicago will target the Sears Tower and several State and Federal buildings on February

2nd."

"Speculation or do you have more concrete information about that?"

Jack shuffled in his chair. I noticed that his tummy pouch was a wee bit larger than the last time I saw him. Obviously, he had already found out about the famous Chicago Dog. "Our agents have followed and snapped shots of Yezhov and Gazzone sitting on a bench outside the U.S. Courthouse, the Klucynski Federal Building and both the Sears and Tribune Towers. They gestured and pointed to specific places on the buildings and then wrote down notes."

"I suppose that would raise eyebrows," remarked Palmer.

"And where does the Bureau plan to go from here?" I asked.

"There're only two weeks till Groundhog Day."

"We will be collaborating with the Chicago Police and Illinois Bureau of Criminal Investigation to place people in and around doors of public buildings, on rooftops and in parking garages to watch for and profile individuals, especially those carrying bags, rucksacks, suitcases and the like. Most of these probable targets of course have security posts just inside of the entranceways. Our building here on Roosevelt could also be targeted. A couple of days prior to February 2nd, we'll have roving patrols in all areas looking for specific people we have identified that have gone into the bookstore."

"Do you plan to apply some 'preventive maintenance' to disrupt any plans the organization may have, instead of just waiting to react on D Day?" I asked Jack.

"At this point, Bruce, they've done nothing wrong. I can't justify stopping these people in their cars or when they enter the building, just because they *look* suspicious. Every time they go into that bookstore, they come out carrying plastic bags that look as though a book is inside. And if we do start harassing them, not only will their lawyers be showing up here, but they'll know we're onto them and go play hide-and-seek."

"So, you have a surveillance unit outside of the book store."

Jack nodded. "A van with cable company markings on it. I have two agents inside with all the latest in video and listening devices." *Brilliant, Jack. Like no one will take notice of a cable truck sitting there day after day.* "Okay, Jack. Well, tell you what. We're going to get a bite of supper and then meet our operative down at Navy Pier. I'm not sure if he's made any progress, but if he has gotten inside the organization, then we'll at least have a shot at getting a few scraps about Lively's plan."

"Right. And as usual, Bruce, let's work this thing together and keep one another informed."

"Like old times, eh Jack?"

"If it's like old times, then I'll get nothing out of you."

"Hey, you got the credit for the good ol' boy take down on that mountain back in West Virginia, didn't you?"

"But I had no idea what you were doing when the good ol' Islamic boys were taken down. Basically, I had no idea what you were doing at *any* time."

"Well, we *all* got a piece of that one, Jack."

Jack then shook his head and pointed a finger at me. It wasn't his middle one, which told me he was still my friend. "Just play it right, Bruce?" Okay?" "Okay, Mother Fuentes. Don't worry. We'll play nice."

Carlos Gallegos was already standing along the waterfront smoking a Camel when the three of us dismounted our rental and began strolling casually to the rail where he stood. After I introduced Carlos to Chuck and Jeff, who had never met him, we had some small talk among one another for a few moments. Palmer pointed to a number of ducks which had seen us coming and which started begging for bread crumbs, which of course we didn't have. We really didn't need to be discreet in our meeting since no one would know who we were or that we were even in town checking out the local WUO bunch.

It was nearly dark and the combination of wind, which was unusual for Chicago…just being facetious…and thirty-eight degree temperature began to make my eyes water.

"What do you have, Carlos?" I asked.

"I'm still nosing around, Bruce. Mr. Byrd sent me a list and photos of four members of Prairie Fire in this area, one of which I found out was dead and another who moved to Michigan last week. One of the remaining two named Pete Baumann works at a postal branch in the city and the other, Terrance Carpenter, lives in Schaumberg. I dropped in on Mr. Baumann, who works behind the counter, and told him I got his name from one of the guys you mentioned in your report, Tom Sperry. Told Baumann I hated that Tom bought it. I also said I was part of the Colorado Club and was glad I had gotten into a car wreck on the way out to the warehouse for the big meeting there near Lyons. And since things were hot out there, I decided to hook up with the people here in Chicago."

"Does he think you're credible?" asked Chuck.

"He seemed pretty cautious with me. Said he'd have to talk to some guy named Mitch, but to come back tomorrow."

"You'll find the man he's referring to as Mitchell Lively. We found out that he owns a book store on Tradd Street called *Yesterday's Message*," I said. "When you see him tomorrow, ask him if the guy's name is Lively…that Tom Sperry and Jonas Karn dropped his name a couple of times. Since both guys are dead and the rest of the Colorado conspirators have been corralled, Lively won't have anyone to call to check you out. If there does happen to be anyone left and that person doesn't remember you, then just tell him you came aboard with the WUO in December and didn't get to meet everyone. What name are you using?"

"Justin Barley."

An older couple then strolled by just after Carlos had divulged his alias. I waited until they were out of earshot.

"Okay, Justin. Give me your cell number and hook back up with us tomorrow evening. Hopefully, you can get inside right away."

We exchanged numbers and then Carlos tossed the butt of his cigarette into a culvert. He turned without further word and walked away back toward the pier. In a couple of minutes the remaining three of us broke up and walked in the opposite direction back to our vehicle.

CHAPTER EIGHTEEN

As we had no real game plan until such time Carlos had the opportunity to possibly meet and greet Lively, we checked into a Super 8 just on the fringe of the city proper about three miles from *Yesterday's News*. After my compadres woofed down some pizza while I picked at an antipasto salad at a corner Italian dive, we drove along Tradd until we came to the number 954. I thought perhaps we could sit at the curb opposite the store to watch pedestrian traffic going in and out. I did luck out and got a parking spot at the end of the curb where we could watch the place from approximately thirty feet away. Opposite our vehicle was the faux cable vehicle Jack had placed there which could definitely fool a nine year old kid, but nobody with any sense of suspicion.

At six forty-five I sent Palmer to check on the door as to what the closing time was and he promptly returned to tell us it was seven. In a few minutes, any patrons should be leaving and the 'open' sign on the door reversed.

The red brick building which appeared to have been erected somewhere in the twenties or thirties had four stories. I speculated that Lively lived on the second floor, considering there were curtains and Venetian blinds on the windows. The upper floors, however, looked barren. There were no window coverings and I guessed that if Lively owned the entire building, he likely used the area for storage…things like old books and newspapers, and other items which supported his business operation such as drugs, guns and explosives.

At ten minutes past seven, the last of the customers, a college age young lady, which could have been an employee, left the premises and we spotted a hand in the window of the door turning the sign to 'closed.' As it was now fully dark, we waited to see if the lights would go out inside of the store and on in any of the apartments above. After about twenty minutes when nothing else was happening, I was about ready to cash it in. Perhaps we would find more action going on back at the Super 8…that is if the Bulls were on TV.

But just as I switched on the ignition, a black Lincoln pulled up in front of the store and two men got out. One was a large-set, burly chap in his fifties with a heavy salt-and-pepper beard and the other a muscular-looking bozo with long, black and shiny hair tied off in a pony tail that hung down over the collar of his calf-length black leather coat. If they didn't look like Russian mafia, then I was a gay gigolo with a San Francisco escort service. We imagined that these were the two Ruskies, Yezhov and Gordievsky, that Jack had identified earlier. The big man then rapped his knuckles on the door glass and after about fifteen seconds the door opened to let them in. In a couple of minutes the store went dark and then another minute later windows on the fourth floor lit up.

Chuck, Palmer and I then settled back in our seats to wait them out and to see if anyone else showed up. After a full hour, we were satisfied there would be no further visitors.

At nine-twenty the store's lights came on again and the front door swung in. As the Russians stepped out onto the sidewalk, Jeff snapped some photos of their faces in the street light, dim as it was. I then caught just a three second glimpse inside of the doorway of a tall figure with a completely bald head. Quickly, he closed the door as the two visitors looked warily up and down the street and then across the street where we were sitting.

When the Lincoln finally pulled away from the curb, I waited until it cleared the intersection at Campbell Avenue, then made a U-turn to follow. I wasn't exactly sure *why* I was following them, but it seemed like a good idea at the time.

The Lincoln then began making a series of left and right turns for the next couple of miles which didn't make much sense. Although I was not that familiar with Chicago, it didn't take me long to see that the driver was going in circles. My clue was that we passed the same series of stores twice. And that could mean only one thing…they made us.

And then just when the light at the intersection of 54th Street and Collier turned red, the driver gunned through it and quickly turned left into an alley. I did so as well, nearly taking out two vehicles crossing in my path. At the end of the narrow alley I saw the Lincoln's taillights disappearing as it made an abrupt right turn onto an adjacent street. Obviously, the driver knew his city and that would be to his advantage. However, not to be out-done and out-run, I kept his rear lights in sight and duplicated every move. I think Palmer and Chuck were developing motion sickness.

Suddenly, blue lights were on my tail and I had one of three choices: continue chasing the Russians, give up the chase and shake the Chicago unit, or just pull over. I figured they had my tag anyway and all they needed to do was contact the rental company to nail me. So, I decided to take my chances with the fuzz.

I pulled off to the curb and waited. Per procedure, the two heads in the unmarked unit just sat there, probably waiting to run the tag to see if I was on the Ten Most Wanted list. But then the vehicle pulled up beside us and the officer riding in the passenger seat put his window down. No sooner than I had done the same, the barrel of a .12 gauge raised in my direction.

"Gun!" I yelled and we all laid down in our seats.

The gunman fired three quick blasts, two of which struck the front and back doors on the SUV as the third whizzed through the open window over our heads, smashing the passenger side glass. The fake cop car then sped away.

"Everybody okay?" I asked.

Without waiting for their answer, I squealed out after the car. Seems that not only did the Russians make us, they radioed a shadow team to take us out. I was determined that these guys would not get away. And if I saw another blue light on my tail, real or not, it had better have some horsepower under the hood. Not being a Frank Bullitt or Popeye Doyle, I wasn't used to street chases. But I was doing all right. The Crown Vic was not losing me.

But then we came to a railroad crossing where a slow moving freight train was impeding any further advance. As there were a half dozen cars in front of the Crown Vic and no side streets to duck down, the driver decided to throw the car into reverse and spin into a one-eighty. Since I was within fifty feet of the vehicle and it had not fully straightened up from its reverse spin, I yelled, "Hold on!"

At more than fifty miles an hour I T-boned the Crown Vic in the passenger's side door and drove it into the stopped vehicle to its front. Simultaneously, I saw a flash inside the car. Quickly, the three of us jumped out with Glocks in hand and descended upon the car. I could see immediately that the passenger was dead. And then when we checked out the driver, half of his head had been blown off where upon impact his buddy's shotgun discharged. There was no one else in the car.

Unfortunately, my rental was also dead in the road. It was either we walk away from the scene or just stick and wait for the real cops. I decided we would wait. It didn't matter. We'd be found anyway. The Chicago police was on the scene in less than five minutes. Since we didn't have badges, given the covert operatives that we were and loaded down with firearms, we had some explaining to do. Before they put the cuffs on us, I asked the cop who seemed like he definitely wanted a piece of me because of my attitude, if he could call my friend, FBI Agent-in-Charge Jack Fuentes.

"All right, smart ass," he replied. "I'll give you the benefit of the doubt for now on this. But if I find you're stalling or playing games, I'll throw you in the cage for a week before anyone finds you."

I already had Jack's cell number programmed into my phone from last August, hoping that he still *had* that number. After the fourth ring, I was relieved to hear his voice. I stepped away from the officer so that he couldn't hear my conversation.

"Hi, ya, Jack. Just thought I'd give you a call. Are you having a good evening?"

"Uh, yes, I suppose. Had a little dinner and just settled in with the TV. How about you?"

"Oh, fine. Just out for a little drive with the guys touring the streets of Chicago, getting shot at, taking down bad guys with my rental car, getting arrested…you know, having all the fun I can stand."

"What?"

"Well, it's like this. We decided to do a little recon on the bookstore. After we saw the Russian guys you told us about coming out of the store, we decided to follow them. They *made* us and engaged a couple of wing men in a fake cop car to pull us over. After they shot up my rental, I gave chase…and well, somehow my vehicle hit theirs and they ended up dead. And now we're getting hauled in."

"Good God! You've been in town less than ten hours and have already killed two guys?"

"Well, all I killed was one of them. As he was dying he decided to shoot his partner. Go figure."

"Still, at your hands, Chicago has two less citizens."

"Well, I do what I can to curb population booms, you know. Now, one of Chicago's finest wants you to vouch for me."

He sighed. "Put the officer on the phone."

I wasn't sure what Jack told the cop. I just noted that he nodded a lot and said, "I understand, Agent Fuentes."

After a couple of minutes the officer closed my phone and handed it back to me.

"A Federal officer, eh? Then where's your badge?"

"They don't issue us badges, sir," I replied. "All we have is our State Department IDs."

He glared at me for a while and then handed my license and ID back to me. "Well, it looks like these guys were bad dudes what with the illegal blue light and shot gunning your car. The detectives are still going to need your statements, so you'll have to go with us to the precinct. We will need to know what this is all about." He then looked at my SUV. "Looks like it's totaled."

"Yeah," I replied, shaking my head. "The rental company is not going to like this."

We gave our statements to the Chicago detectives, playing dumb about why two hoods would be randomly shooting us up. Probably some kind of gang game they were running…pulling people over with a blue light, then robbing them. As to why we were carrying guns without badges…now that required some tap-dancing on our part.

"Well, one of your uniforms talked with the FBI already," I said. "We're the law enforcement side of the State Department and are here in town collaborating with the Bureau on mob activities in Northern Illinois. We met today at their headquarters on Roosevelt and will likely be around another two or three days."

"Okay, then, let me get this straight," Detective Norton began, "you have State Department IDs but no badges. If you're law enforcement and packing heat, why no badges?"

"Let me answer that," Palmer said. "A lot of our work is

covert. We have no arrest powers or any police authority. A badge would be rather meaningless, considering what we do."

"Which is?"

"Intelligence gathering, mob infiltration and the like,"

I said. "We get in and get out, then feed what we find to agencies like the Bureau, ATF, DEA, NSA and others. They take it from there."

It all sounded good...to me, anyway. I had to stay away from other buzz words like 'terrorism, the Weatherman group' and of course us, 'CTT'. The less they knew what we were doing, the better.

While they were digesting our load of crap, a few eyebrows were raised to go along with the puzzling looks. Finally, Norton said, "I still don't know about you guys, but have to take it on the Bureau's voucher that there's no funny business going on with you. I suggest you clear up what you have to do and get your asses back to Washington. Are we clear here?" His face was merely inches from Chuck's, thinking perhaps he was in charge because he was bigger than everybody else. Norton *definitely* didn't want to go *there*. Well, Chuck wanted a piece of the detective. I could see it brewing. But I stepped in and said,

"Perfectly."

"Okay, then. You guys get out of here."

"Uh...Detective," I said. "Is it possible we could ask one more thing?"

He sighed. "What?"

"Can you get a uniform to drop us off at our motel, seeing as how our vehicle doesn't work anymore?"

"If that's what it takes to get you guys out of my precinct, consider it done."

After we were dropped off, we walked from our motel to a bar two doors down for a stiff one. It had been an exciting evening; however, for the likes of *us*, just another day at the office.

Jack swung by the next morning to pick us up and take us

to the rental agency so that we could report the accident, tell them where the SUV was and to get another one just like it.

On the way there, Jack had a few things to say. "First of all, Bruce, if you're going to work with us in investigating this bunch, how about not cluttering up our streets with bodies."

"Well, they *started* it, Jack. Hell, we're just tourists here, out for the evening to get acquainted with the town," I replied.

"Tourists who decided on a whim to chase down Russian mobsters. What was *that* all about?"

"It didn't start out as a chase, but when they tried to give us the slip, going after them just seemed like a good idea. I thought where they ended up might prove profitable. Maybe they would lead us to others in the group or a cache of weapons and explosives."

Jack shook his head and tightened his lips. "Well, in the future, would you do me a favor so that my neck is not hanging out like it is on this deal? Let me know what you've got cooking and try not to make such big messes. I know you, Bruce, and you're not the neatest guy, leaving trails of dead bodies like you do."

"Now my feelings are hurt. But, fair enough."

I really didn't want to take advantage of the fact that we had become friends back in September and certainly didn't want him exposed to any of our tactics. He was a straight- up G-man, and a good one at that. And for damn sure I didn't want him to get reassigned because of someone like me before Diane and the kids had a chance to taste some of that wonderful Chicago pizza.

After we landed at the rental agency, Jack told us he'd see us later and sped out, appearing most anxious to be rid of us for the morning.

Percival, the manager at the rental agency, acted a good bit pissed. I couldn't imagine the reason why. Why should a little thing like a total loss to one of his Expeditions set him off? I had paid thirty dollars extra for physical damage coverage; therefore, I was *entitled* to wreck it. I guess since the agency clearly got the worst of the deal, Percy tried to punish me by offering us a Corolla, which I politely declined. I then told him again that I was sorry and asked for a courtesy shuttle to another rental agency. And he politely informed me in return that his agency was not a taxi service and perhaps I should call one. Which I did. Percy obviously didn't know that we all carried guns.

Although it was a bit smaller than what I was used to driving, I rented a Tahoe. The new rental agency was a great deal more accommodating and friendly in our transaction. Fortunately, the manager did not ask me if I had had any recent accidents.

After we returned to our rooms at the Super 8, I called Jack and asked him to courier profiles, photos and known hangouts of both Yezhov and Gordievski to the front desk.

"And what *about* them, Bruce? Will they end up on slabs as well?"

"No, no. I just want to know who we're dealing with here. I need to piece together in my mind their specific association with the Weather group. It will help as we profile this entire network of subversives."

"All right," Jack sighed. "But please tread lightly with these people. They're a vicious lot and I don't want you folks to start any wars that will clutter up Chicago with DBs."

"We're just fishing, Jack. That's all. No guns, no bodies."

"I'll send the stuff over."

We were a bit hungry, so we found a superb deli down the street that drew us in its doors with a permeating, intoxicating aroma of succulent meats and cheeses. As Chuck and I savored the deli's wonderful pastrami, MI-6 alumnus Jeff Palmer had to have his fish and chips. A British thing, of course, he said. If he didn't get his fix once a week along with a tankard of stout, he would go into the DTs. And I had once too often seen his surly side over stuff like that, especially like when he missed out on a round of golf every three to four days.

At a quarter till three my room phone rang. The desk clerk announced that my package had arrived by courier and I had to sign for it. After retrieving it from the lobby, I pulled Chuck and Jeff into my room to review the material. The Interpol photos were fairly clear, even when copied. I recognized both men from the night before as they stepped from the doorway of the bookstore. It did appear that Yezhov's beard had, subsequent to the photo, turned more salt than pepper.

After the collapse of the Soviet Union, Yezhov, a Ukrainian, had settled in New York and immediately established ties with the Russian Mafia. Suspected in but never prosecuted for the crimes of the trafficking of young women for utilization as prostitutes and domestic servants, he ultimately branched out into arms and drug dealing as well as money laundering. As Yezhov was a high-ranking official in the KGB, he was part of the *nonmenklatura* system made up of a number of bureaucrats or *apparatchiks* some million and a half strong. The organization's nexus began in good old Mother Russia, but it did not take long to re-establish itself in the New York-New Jersey corridor as well as in the cities of Chicago and Los Angeles. Apparently, Yezhov felt more comfortable in the Windy City where its brutal winters reminded him of home.

Their hangout was called Ivanov's, three streets off Wacker within sight of Grant Park. Jack had hand-written a note beneath the name 'Ivanov's', the place Yezhov and Gordievski were known to frequent nightly. An upscale restaurant and bar specializing in Russian, Greek and Romanian fare, it catered to not only those ethnic groups, but Chicago's politically elite as well. Around seven, it would also cater to Team Zulu's elite. We not only had a bit of a score to settle for last night's carnage, but I wanted them to experience in person how easily their little hideaway could be compromised.

Chuck spoke a little Russian, but when he spoke in English with that marvelous, thick Russian brogue he had cultivated, one would swear he was definitely from the old country. The classic Black Russian.

Considering the ambiance, white table cloths, elegant chandeliers and a string quartet playing Rachmaninoff in a corner of the dining area, we felt a bit under-dressed in our jeans, cowboy boots and golf shirts. But in looking around, we saw that less than half of the restaurant's patrons were without jackets and ties. A few of the ladies were in pants. Apparently, most any attire went.

As we had no reservations and were looking at a twenty to thirty minute wait, we scooted onto three bar chairs at the far right end. Momentarily, a heavy-set bartender with greasy, slicked-back hair and a short-cropped goatee positioned himself in front of us. In his own thick Russian accent he said, "What will it be, gentlemen?"

Chuck ordered first in his faux accent, "I will have a vodka straight up."

"Ah, my friend, where are you from?" Dmitri the bartender asked. His name was on his pocket.

"I am from the region called Kirovskaya oblast, specifically Yaransk."

"I *know* it," Dmitri replied. "I am from across the way…a place called Zuevka."

Just our luck. I hoped Chuck knew enough about the province to continue carrying on a conversation.

"And I know people from there. The Karishnev family." Chuck appeared to be doing fine.

"Ah, yes. How do you know them?"

Chuck smiled. "My friend, if I told you that, you could no longer be living."

Dmitry then laughed aloud with gusto. Obviously a

story they both were in on. I would have to ask Chuck later what the hell that was all about.

The bartender then turned to Palmer and me. "And you gentlemen. What is your pleasure?"

"A Guinness for me," replied Jeff.

"And I'd like a Jack and Coke," said I. "But first, can you point me to the rest room?"

He pointed. "Go to the rear of the restaurant and you will see the gentlemen's room on the right just before you reach the kitchen."

"Merci," I said, not knowing a word of Russian except Smirnoff.

I really didn't have to go, but I wanted the opportunity to canvass the entire restaurant, table by table, to see if I could find my new Russsky friends…the ones who tried to get us whacked the night before.

After cruising by every table to the rest room and back, the faces of Yezhov and Gordievski were not among the patrons. I really didn't expect them to be, but figured they were somewhere in another part of the building. Perhaps in a back room.

We finished our round of drinks within a few minutes and when Dmitry came back to ask if we wanted refills, I replied, "No refills, but I would like a bit of information. I've got a fifty dollar tip for you if you can tell me in which of those back rooms we can find Vilyem Yezhov and friends."

Dmitry lit up and he looked at me and then at Chuck. Then he placed his two large paws on the bar in front of me and said in a low voice, "Where it comes to Mr. Yezhov, his information is not for sale. Now you must leave."

From my jacket pocket I quickly pulled out my switchblade, hit the blade release and dug it into the second layer of epidermis on Dmitry's right hand. With my left hand I firmly clamped onto his wrist, pinning it to the bar. "Let me give you a short anatomy lesson, Dmitry. Just under that trickle of blood is the median nerve. It runs through the carpal tunnel back up your forearm and into the bicep. If I sever it, you will never again be able to grasp a shot glass or a woman's boob again. Now, I will ask you but one more time…where can I find Yezhov?"

Dmitry looked fearfully at his hand and then back into my eyes which bore down on him as sharply as the knife. He then quickly tilted his head to the right to indicate the direction of the room. "Not good enough. Tell us specifically where the room is, not the direction."

"It…it is beyond the gentleman's room down the hallway opposite the kitchen. The second door on the right. The door has a red star on it."

I smiled. "Not a hammer and sickle? Tell you what, Dmitry. We're going back there, but if you pick up the phone or signal anyone in this restaurant, I will come back here and shoot you between the eyes." I then applied a little more pressure with the blade. "Get the point?"

"Yes…yes," he gasped in pain.

"Now go bandage that hand so that you don't bleed all over your customers."

Quickly, the three of us moved to the rear of the restaurant and through the hallway to the door with the red star on it. Politely, I knocked and in a few seconds the door opened. A large gorilla of a man with a bald head, a heavy, black mustache and an earring in his left lobe greeted us. He had the appearance of a circus strong man who obviously could have lifted a 500 pound barbell.

"What do you want?" he bellowed in a thick accent.

"We're looking for Mr. Yezhov," I responded.

"Who wants to meet him?" "Mr. Glock."

"Mr. Glock? Who the hell is Mr. Glock?"

I then stepped aside so that Mr. Clean could see that Mr. Glock was in Mr. Palmer's hand. The Russian lifted his hands a little and stepped back.

"Now turn around and walk us to where Yezhov is," I demanded.

Without word, the man did as ordered and we entered through the door behind him. At a table in the middle of the smoky room two men sat drinking shots of vodka and holding cards. I recognized them as Yezhov and Gordievski

"What is this!?" Yezhov barked. "Who are you people?"

I then pushed the big man forward and said "Sit down!"

After he took a chair with the other two, I sat down in a chair at the table opposite Yezhov while Palmer and Chuck stood with their Glocks trained on the three of them.

"Who are we?" I answered. "We are the guys you dispatched your comrades to kill last night. They shot my rental vehicle full of holes and smashed up my front end. Do you realize what kind of trouble that caused me with the rental agency?"

"Enough with the nonsense. Now who *are* you?"

"Somebody who will be working on having you and Mr. Gordievski here deported. Now why did you send people after us last night?"

"I don't like people following me. You are some kind of cops?"

"No," I replied. "Cops arrest people. We're not in that kind of business. We make people like you disappear."

Yezhov laughed loudly. "You are nothing but pesky gnats. You cannot come in here and threaten me. My people will cut you up in tiny pieces and feed you to the fish in Lake Michigan."

I ignored the comment. "What do you have going with Mitchell Lively, Mr. Yezhov?"

"What do you mean, and if I did know the man, what business is it of yours?"

"Don't play dumb with me, comrade. You were not at the bookstore last night to buy a copy of Doctor Zhivago. I know you and your business. You deal in women, drugs and guns, so why are you mixed up in domestic terrorism?"

"What makes you think I am, Mister...? I didn't get your name."

"And you *won't*."

Yezhov smiled. "It hardly seems fair that you know who I am and I don't know you."

"I'll tell you what's *un*fair, Mr. Yezhov…that the American people have to put up with Russian slime balls like you, extorting their money and living in fear, not to mention the facing of death and destruction when you and Lively set off your bombs in a few days."

Yezhov eyed me and sucked a piece of food from between his teeth. He then turned his head and spat it out on the floor. "We will not be doing that. We only have a business relationship with Mr. Lively. What he does is on his own."

"Well," I said, "let me make this as clear and succinct as I can, Yezhov. You go forward with your 'arrangement' to help Lively bring down buildings and kill innocent citizens, I will personally see to it that you, your wives and children disappear. Like none of you ever existed. You may think you're a powerful, bad-ass former KGB agent, but by God you have never crossed paths with people like us. Now you back out of this deal with Lively tonight, or I will set in motion a firestorm that will be felt by your grandmother in her grave."

Yezhov then leaned over the table toward me and snarled his lip. "You have no idea who you are threatening, asshole."

"This was a friendly visit tonight, Mr. Yezhov. The next one *won't* be."

Yezhov then looked at Gordievski and smiled diabolically. "These people dare to come to my place and tell me my business, Igor. What shall we do with them?"

Gordievski then snapped his fingers and suddenly from another door to the room two more goons appeared behind Palmer and Chuck, holding Uzis to the backs of their heads.

Yezhov laughed again. "What do you think now, brave

man?"

I settled back in my chair and glared at him. "I think, my Russky friend that you should look under the table where you will see the muzzle of my .40 caliber Glock aimed squarely at your balls. If your men so much as flinch, I will splatter the three parts of your Bohemian manlihood all over your shoes. My friends are always fully prepared to give up their lives in situations like these. Now, *your* friends have five seconds to place their guns on the floor…four… three…"

Yezhov quickly held up his hand to signal them. "Do as he says. My mistress will never forgive me if I allow my boys to get blown away."

Slowly and carefully, the goons laid the Uzis on the floor and Chuck kicked them away. He then motioned with his Glock for them to stand behind their boss. And I then brought my empty right hand up onto the table so that Yezhov could clearly see it.

"I've played a little poker myself over the years," I said. "I *told* you to look under the table."

Yezhov narrowed his eyes and grit his teeth. "Son-of-a-bitch."

I stood up and joined my two comrades. "You've been warned, Yezhov. Disassociate yourself from Lively now. If you don't, you will never see me coming."

We then backed out of the room, closed the door behind us and made our way quickly back through the restaurant. I didn't figure Yezhov would give chase, shoot up his place and risk nailing his customers…not to mention having to explain to the cops why there were dead dinner guests lying all over his establishment.

I knew as soon as we left the restaurant Yezhov would be on the phone to Lively, telling him there were Feds on his trail. It was a chance we took. It could in fact cause Lively to shut down his plan for the time being and/or move his operation to another location. But Groundhog Day was D

Day for the nationwide WUO mission and I figured he would still somehow attempt to put his plan into action simultaneous to bombings in other locations on that day. He had to know that the government was onto the entire WUO network, anyway, considering what went down outside of Lyons, Colorado. He would just have to be more vigilant.

Once the three of us pulled away from the curb outside of Ivanov's, Chuck said, "The food smelled pretty good in there, you know. We couldn't have eaten first?"

I smiled and shook my head.

Palmer had a gripe of his own. "Hey, you took a great deal of liberty back there with our lives, considering you didn't even have a gun in your hand."

Again, I said nothing and just continued to smile.

CHAPTER NINETEEN

After a mid-morning strategy session the next day, we knocked down a couple of beers and sampled some of Chicago's famous deep-dish pizza. It was then I realized that I was eating more than running and the waistline in my jeans was tightening. My apologies to the UNCF, but 'A waist is a terrible thing to mind.' Excuse the pun as well.

I called Carlos to see if he was able to establish himself with the postman, finding that in fact he and Baumann were meeting at the post office when Baumann finished up at the counter at 4:30. Carlos would accompany him to meet Lively at the book store at five. He said Lively was anxious to meet any friend of Tom Sperry's who he had met on several occasions in Colorado. I also told Carlos a few more things about Tom which would hopefully enable him to carry on a credible conversation with Lively. I then went over Tom's physical characteristics as well as those of the man called Doc and Karn himself. I also filled Carlos in on more specific information regarding what I had picked up about the new Weatherman order and Karn's agenda. Carlos told me what I had provided appeared comprehensive enough to bullshit his way through any dialogue that would ensue.I hoped it would, but knew that it would only take one wrong answer for Lively's antenna to go up.

I then called Jack to inform him we now had a man soon to be on the inside, providing everything went well, and that we would stake out the store again starting around four. He of course reminded me of the fiasco from two nights before that started out with a stake-out and ended up with a wild-ass chase leaving two guys dead. I assured him we would be more careful this time and wanted to not only make sure that Carlos got inside the store, but came out as well.

"Fine," he said. "How about if I join you all. I've got nothing going this evening. We can catch up on the past few months, and you know, hang out."

"Well, Jack, this won't exactly be a frat reunion…" "I'll bring donuts and coffee!"

"All right. Suit yourself," I replied without hesitation. "We'll be in a white Tahoe with dark, tinted windows."

"Gotcha. See you just after four."

When Jack signed off, I turned to Chuck and Jeff.

"We're going to have company this evening…Jack Fuentes."

Chuck shook his head. "Bruce, man. You know we don't mix business with the Bureau. Anyway, this guy seems a little green around the ears."

"He's bringing donuts."

"Well okay, then. Why didn't you say so?"

At a quarter past four, Jack found a parking space two vehicles behind where my Tahoe sat directly in front of the bookstore. True to his word, he carried a container in which sat four large coffees and a sack of Dunkin Donuts. As I watched him approach in my side mirror, I told Jeff to let him in on the passenger's side.

"Hey, fellas," Jack said as he entered the vehicle, sounding much like a schoolboy out for an evening with his chums up to no good. "I brought a variety…chocolate covered, jelly, and a couple of fritters. I didn't miss anything did

I?"

Chuck, sitting shotgun, glanced over at me with one of those 'is this guy for real?' expressions. I smiled and winked.

"No," I replied. "We didn't feel right killing anybody without you."

Jack leaned over the seat and jammed me in the arm with his finger. "Which is exactly why I felt it necessary to join you…to see that it *didn't* happen. And of course, to save my ass from getting fired because of you people."

"I don't see your cable company truck," I commented. "Have you tabled your surveillance?"

Jack took a swig of coffee and nodded with his head in the direction of a yellow van across the street and down two spaces. "We're now the North Central Gas Company. I have an agent and common guy in there."

"It's good that you're shaking things up with that. Are you in communication with them?"

Jack brought his wrist up to his mouth. "Tucker, you boys awake in there?" He then placed a finger to his right ear to assure he was receiving clearly.

"Okay, then. I assume you see where I am in the white Tahoe."

Another pause.

"Fine. I'll drop in on you later."

Well, my chums did have a donut or two, which would likely add another inch to each of their waistlines. As much as I craved one, I resisted. Something about trying to keep my rock-hard abs, which is an ever-increasing struggle at my age, not to mention a hell of a lot of hard work. And then to no one's surprise, Jack pulled out a half-dozen pictures of his two All American kids, including one that he was particularly proud of. Jack, Jr. in his karate outfit. After darting our eyes between us, we then placed them on the store front to take account of every head that entered.

"Besides seeing Carlos come and go, what do you hope to accomplish here tonight?" Jack asked.

"Just look for familiar or suspicious faces, especially after closing hours."

"What happens if they get onto Carlos?"

I then pulled from my pocket our standard issue Hammacher receiver. "He will send up the Bat Signal which will set this little deal off. Then we go in and get him."

"Nifty," Jack remarked. "Are these issued to just you guys or can I order some?"

"They come standard with the Junior G Man decoder ring, Jack. I'm surprised you don't have..."

I cut myself short to announce the arrival of Carlos and his new friend, Baumann. "There they are, gentlemen. Our guests have arrived."

Baumann, heavy-set and muscular, who filled out every inch of his postal uniform, led the way to the front door. Stopping momentarily, they both stepped aside to allow a shapely young brunette to exit. It was only five-fifteen and it would be a while before customers started being kicked out. I wasn't sure what kind of wait we'd have or whether there would actually be anything to wait *for*. However, as soon as Carlos came out, I would be waiting somewhere on the street to signal him for a rendezvous.

At about ten minutes till six, I caught in my rear view mirror the image of two burley-looking chaps approaching from the rear. They stopped for a moment to look around and then proceeded on. Non-customers I presumed.

"Bogeys at five o'clock," I said as the men came up onto my rear bumper. We watched through our heavily-tinted glass as the two men slowed at the door, looked around again, and finally entered.

"Looks like a meeting of the minds, my boys," I commented.

"Hmmm. At least four of them inside the store and one of Carlos," said Chuck.

"You think he can handle himself with those odds in case things go south?" Jack asked.

Palmer chuckled. "You don't want to know, Jack."

Jack spoke into his wrist again. "Did you get good shots of those guys, Tucker?"

A pause.

"Good. Out."

At six, what few real customers were left were shuffled out of the book store and the door sign changed to *closed*, an hour prematurely. A total of twenty minutes probably went by and then suddenly it was like something you'd see a stuntman do in the movies. Almost like in slow motion, window glass broke on the fourth story above us and a body flew out…unfortunately landing on the roof of my Tahoe. There was such a mash in the roof panel that the liner had caved in around our heads.

"Forget the Bat Signal!" I yelled. "Let's go!"

As all four of our doors sprung open we heard screams from a couple of women passersby standing frozen in disbelief. I glanced at the man on my roof to see that it wasn't Carlos. It was the mailman, thank God. And he was a mess. When he hit the roof, he spilled open like a Hefty bag filled with vegetable soup.

"Get out of the way, ladies!" I barked. The Glocks we were brandishing as we moved in caused one of the ladies to faint dead away, while the other backed up against the wall.

Jack, who was on my heels, yelled into his wrist. "Tucker! We're going in. Call the locals and attend to this man. Wait for my instructions!"

When we burst into the store, a young man in shoulder-length blonde hair and a dozen pieces of hardware in his brow, lips and ears began to run out. As he tried to brush by me, I snatched him by the frayed collar of his Army field jacket and slammed him against a bookshelf. Scores of books came tumbling down on his head.

"All right, punk, where's the door that leads upstairs to where we can find Lively?"

"I don't…"

Not giving him a chance to lie to me, I backhanded the lad across the mouth, tearing a silver ring from his lower lip. He yelped and then pointed toward the rear of the store. "There…up the stairs to the fourth floor to the door that reads 'private.'

I then grabbed the kid by his jacket again and half- ran, half-drug him to the front door, spilling him onto the sidewalk. Chuck and Palmer were already tearing toward the back of the store.

"Stay behind me, Jack!" I yelled.

So, we had three flights of stairs to negotiate. Like thundering hooves against the wood steps, we made enough noise to alert the bad guys; but as we hit the landing of the third set of stairs, I could hear enough of a clamoring going on inside the room straight ahead, that they probably didn't hear us coming.

I took the position on the left side of the door at the top of the stairs while Jeff took the right. Standing like a bull preparing to charge, Chuck counted to three and then dropped the door with one powerful kick. Jack followed him in through the threshold and yelled, "FBI! FBI!"

The two larger men we had seen entering the store somehow had subdued Carlos after Carlos had sent the postman via air mail out of the window and onto my roof. The goons' guns were trained on Carlos' head. So there we stood for about ten seconds, guns raised and pointed at one another, nothing being said. Two Mexican standoffs in as many nights.

Finally, the tall skinhead of a man who I took to be Lively spoke. "I assume this imposter here is one of you. If you value his life, you will drop your guns."

"That's not going to happen, chrome dome," I shot back. "Carlos knows the drill. You shoot him, then you *all* die."

Jack then took over. "You surrender now and *no one* dies. You'll face conspiracy and weapons charges. But you'll be alive."

One of the men whose gun was up against Carlos' right temple added his two cents and cocked the hammer. "They won't chance it, Mitch. They won't see their man's brains blown against the wall. I say…"

And then Jack shocked us all. With pinpoint accuracy he fired the round over Carlos' right shoulder that penetrated the gunman's right eye socket. Like clockwork, Chuck and Palmer fired several rounds into the other goon, but not before the man's .38 went off and struck Jack in the left chest. Jack went down immediately. I then wheeled to put a bead on Lively's forehead, but he threw up his hands and yelled, "I'm not armed! I'm not armed!"

I put the muzzle of my Glock between his eyes, cocked the hammer and replied, "When they find your body, you *will* be. Now put your hands behind your head and drop to your knees."

"Okay, okay. I'm done."

"No, you're *un*done, Lively."

My immediate attention then went back to Jack who lay with his eyes closed, flat out on his back. I could see though that he was still breathing. When I felt around for the bullet wound, my hand touched the Kevlar vest that he had had the foresight to put on.

Dazed, he finally opened his eyes and blinked. "Oh my God. I'm not dead."

And then I laughed. Partly because I was elated to see him still alive, but also because his reaction to being shot was actually quite comical.

"Come on, hero," I said, helping him to his feet. I then opened up his shirt and dug out the .38 slug. "Here's your souvenir. Good going, Jack. Your first kill was a good one."

I think he wanted to smile, but then he winced when he took a deep breath. "Damn. That's gonna leave a bruise."

With the two goons deader than doornails and the mailman spread-eagle on my roof, that left only Mitchel Lively who would be collected up by the Bureau's JTTF to undergo intensive interrogation. It was doubtful that Jack would concede his release to the State Department to undergo our post-911, new and improved 'techniques.' This of course would be Jack's collar.

As we heard the sirens in the distance, I asked Jack "How are you going to explain this mess, considering we'll be out of here in about thirty seconds?"

"I'll have an easier time explaining the three DBs than who *you* bozos are. Suggest you get out of here now."

"Tell you what, Jack. You go down and flash your badge to the cops. Just tell them that four of your agents are upstairs. They won't bother to check us for badges."

"All right. Tucker is coming up as well and I'm getting my crime scene team in here to turn this place upside down. I also need to keep the locals out of here. Not sure what all I'll tell them, though."

"Tell them the truth. Lively was part of a domestic terrorist plot to set bombs off in their city. Your team will uncover enough evidence to prove that. You'll come out looking like a hero on this. Maybe they'll put you on the Bureau fast track and send you to Washington."

"And I'm sure Mr. Lively here will be most pleased to turn over all his plans and provide locations of his devices. Won't you, Mitch?" Jack then slapped Lively on the back of his bald head.

I had to smile again. That's my boy.

As Jack was headed downstairs to meet and greet Chicago's finest, I said, "Hey, pal. What was that you said about *me* leaving a trail of dead bodies?"

"Yes."

"Well, thanks for contributing today." He then smiled and shook his head.

Jack was pretty smooth with the guys in blue and let them know in no uncertain terms that the FBI was there to take charge. In less than fifteen minutes his *real* agents were on the scene interrogating Lively and sifting through every piece of paper in the apartment. In all the activity, we nodded to Jack and slipped out relatively unnoticed.

Mitchell Lively, obviously scared poopless, sang like a canary. Jack and his team managed to nail down what they needed to convince the Attorney General's office and his Bureau highers that there was justification for the take- down of a terrorist element known as the New Order of the Weather Underground or NOW U whose agenda it was to bring down three Federal buildings and the Sears Tower in simultaneous explosions.

In a commercial garage on 145th Street, the Bureau Task force discovered crates of fertilizer and ammonium nitrate, boxes of C-4 and blasting caps, and a cache of small arms. A notebook with the names and addresses of sixteen other members of the New WUO was found in Lively's roll top desk along with structural blueprints of each of the buildings' construction vulnerabilities to include catastrophic probabilities. The goon that Jack killed was actually an architectural engineer who designed skyscrapers. He supplied the structural knowledge while his friend, a former Navy Underwater Detonation Team veteran, supplied the explosive expertise. It was all wrapped up in a nice, neat package for the U.S. Attorney General who would indict Mitchell Lively and the sixteen others for conspiracy to commit terrorist acts against the United States.

The reason that Lively had pounced so quickly onto Carlos was that he had a separate list of all members of the New Order from every state, and Carlos' name was not on it. The postman's job was to bring him to Lively to explain why it was not. Lively did not buy Carlos' story that he had only been a member of the group for less than thirty days. A phone call by Lively to a 'confidant' still out there somewhere in Colorado said there was no one by the name of Justin Barley who had just been brought in. He was sure of that. When Lively ordered the postman to take care of business,

Mr. Baumann then discovered he could not fly.

Jack would get all the credit for investigating and bringing down a dangerous and deadly terrorist faction spawned from the late Jonas Karn's Colorado WUO flagship. As usual, Team Zulu would hit and run, disappearing into the night as though we didn't exist. And as far as the general public was concerned, we didn't.

And Me? I had yet another damaged vehicle, the second in two days that I had to explain to the rental agency.

We met Jack the night before we took the State Department jet back to Washington at a popular pub on West Addison across from Wrigley Field for some cold ones. The waitress who brought us our brew was not just buxom; she could have carried her tray without the use of her hands. Anyway, we all let our hair down, told some jokes and laughed loudly at times. Jack said it made his ribs hurt and that we had to stop it. He had gone from a rather green, play-it-by-the-numbers field agent in Charleston, West Virginia, to a smart, seasoned agent-in-charge in a large metropolitan field office, baptized by fire. My friend Jack would make it just fine.

I called the Birdman to tell him the threat was over in Chicago. Mitchell Lively was in custody, and with his three sidekicks taking the celestial eternal dirt nap, we did not believe any bombings would be carried out. All the other players had been rounded up. This would take the gas out of the entire WUO network and would likely affect the February 2nd plans of any other local groups out there. However, even so, the Bureau would be following through and would work with the city to provide maximum security in and around all Federal buildings on the morning Punxsutawney Phil was coaxed from his hole.

"Great work, Bruce," Byrd replied. "I'm not sure how vast this WUO outfit is, but since their Denver and Chicago operations have been compromised, I trust that other major population centers will not see any activity."

"My friend Jack told me the Bureau offices in Los Angeles, Atlanta and New York will be collaborating with local and state law enforcement to maintain a high degree of vigilance," I said.

"Good. You guys go on home, Bruce. I guess *you* will need to start winding down the next couple of months. You have no idea how I'm going to miss you, my friend."

And that was about as sentimental a statement as stone man Lionel Byrd would ever be heard to make.

CHAPTER TWENTY

When Punxsutawney Phil came out and saw his shadow, the whole State of Pennsylvania sighed. Six more weeks of winter. But as the entire Federal Law Enforcement community had been holding its breath throughout the entire day of February 2nd, the sun rose on the 3rd without there being a single terrorist incident. And the Bureau, which had received all of the accolades for its accurate assessment and ultimate take-out of two major WUO operations, was beaming and basking in its glory. Lewis Pettyjohn and Jack Fuentes, Agents-in-Charge of the Denver and Chicago field units, respectively, received the FBI Medal for Meritorious Achievement.

As I sat on a Saturday morning in my apartment nibbling on a piece of buttered toast reading the second page of the *Washington Post,* I smiled when I saw the write- up about it. "Glad we could help out, Jack," I whispered. "Vaya Con Dios, amigo."

By March, most of Americahad fairly much recovered from the shock of 9-11, even though Ground Zero was still digging out and people were anxiously anticipating the warmth and glory of spring. It was now a time for rebirth and a rejuvenation of spirit. And there are few places in this country that can compete with the beautiful springs in

Washington, D.C. It was why my fiancée, Adrianna Wolf, waited until the first weekend in April, when the cherry blossoms were out in all their majestic radiance, to come to Georgetown so that we could select her ring.

On that lovely, brisk Saturday morning we strolled hand in hand among perhaps ten thousand people along the sidewalks around the tidal basins and Potomac taking in the grandeur of spring. As she lifted her head to gaze through the light pink blossoms into the cold blue sky, she occasionally took deep, exhilarating breaths that ended in happy sighs. A gentle breeze kicked up every so often to catch a wisp of her hair, causing it to feather against my cheek. Her face was as radiant as the sun, that lucky old sun that kissed her lips, causing them to break out into a smile. At one point near a small park on the bank of the Potomac where lovers lay close to one another on quilts, she stopped and placed her face close to mine, then said, "Kiss me. Make this wonderful day even better."

Although her lips were cool, her breath was warm and tasted of love. Any reservations I had mounted about marrying her these months we had been apart were now quelled. I knew that my life would not ever get any better until she was a part of it. As much as I had resisted becoming 'tamed', as Caroline said, I knew it was time to make myself a new life with someone like her.

We had a garbage dog at a vendor's stand which was a mall roach coach on wheels over which hung a red umbrella that read "Freddie's Famous Registered Hot Dogs." After gulping one down with a soda pop, I saw that Adrianna had only half-finished hers and couldn't digest another bite, the dainty salad-eater that she was. We then shed our jackets, since the noonday sun was quickly heating up the earth and walked briskly back to my Suburban. Looking as glamorous as a Hollywood starlet in her black woolen sweater, the pearls I had gotten her and jeans that clung delectably to every vivacious curve, she collected a few second looks from some of the male joggers who sailed by us. And I didn't mind it one bit. It actually made me feel good to be seen with a woman who clearly rivaled Washington's cherry blossoms for their beauty.

At just after one o'clock we stood over the tiffany case at Carini's of Georgetown looking for just the right diamond to put on her finger. The one she liked was over $3500, so she laid it gently back down on the velvet cloth and went to the case where the rings were less than a thousand. "That one will do," she said, pointing at a ring priced at $795. The prissy store manager with the pencil thin mustache and striped red bow tie shrugged and looked at me with raised, disapproving eyebrows and judgmental eyes that said, "You cheap bastard. Are you going to let her do this?"

And he was right, in his snotty little way. I placed my fingertips on her face, turning it toward mine. "No, my dear. That one will *not* do. I don't want you to have something this important that will just *do*. I want you to have the ring that you like." "But, it's very expensive," she protested. I then turned her attention to a rock in another case that was as big as a knuckle. It cost $25,000. "Now *that's* expensive. Mr. Clyburn," I said, "I think she would like the one you just put away."

"Excellent choice, sir. Will the lady step away with me and I will have that lovely little finger sized." He actually giggled like a school girl. I thought I might be sick.

"Skip, we shouldn't," she argued.

"Yes, we should. Now go with Mr. Clyburn."

After the jeweler had sized the ring to Adrianna's finger, we left for my apartment which was only a couple of blocks away. When we stopped at a crosswalk, she glanced down to see if it was still on her finger. "I love it, Skip. Thank you with all my heart."

We finished out the day with a nice dinner at Manfred's and then we turned in. Late Sunday morning I took her to Dulles, kissed her goodbye and returned to my lonely apartment to finish up her leftover manicotti from the night before. We would not see one another until the night before our wedding.

I had a lot of thinking to do. It was for sure that I would marry my dream girl, Adrianna Wolf, but I had still not committed to Lionel Byrd on his offer to accept occasional contract assignments for CTT. *And* it was something I had intentionally forgotten to mention to Adrianna. I supposed I was afraid she just wouldn't go for it and then call our plans off. But on the evening of May 14th, I finally called her to get it off my chest.

After a long, uncomfortable moment of silence, she said coolly, "And you held this from me how long?"

"Well, I didn't want to bring it up because I wasn't sure at the time whether I would commit to it or not."

"I believe you mean to say that you thought I may not agree to marry you if you stayed on with them."

"Perhaps that's part of it. But I really had not made my mind up until this week," I replied.

"And your decision?"

"Lionel Byrd speculates he would need me only as a part-time consultant, maybe to review cases with the rest of our team a couple days a month. And I would only be pulled in on significant missions where it was ascertained that terrorist elements were actually poised to strike."

"Which means you would be placed in danger and could get yourself killed."

"A better chance that a drunk driver could cross the center line and take me out on my way home from work."

"That's not the same thing, Skip. Please don't insult my intelligence and compare apples and oranges with me."

I had never heard that tone in her voice.

"Look, Adrianna, I've given this a lot of thought and ask you to at least do the same. You know that I will have problems adjusting to a sedentary life style. An occasional operation and collaboration with my team would be like me getting a booster shot of adrenaline."

There was another long pause and then she replied, "All right, Skip. I'll do what you ask…I'll *think* about it. But I *will* tell you this…if I continue having trouble accepting it, it just might affect my decision to marry you."

"And that sounds like an ultimatum."

"No, it isn't. I just cannot accept you going off on some dangerous mission in Kabul or some other place for a month or so, never knowing for sure whether you'll even come back to me. I can't bury another husband. I just *can't*."

Her last comment was a bitter pill for me to swallow.

Something for which I didn't have a response.

She continued. "We have a little over a month to sort this out. You have to believe I do understand what you're going through. I don't want you to ever feel like you're strangling or losing your sense of worth. But both of us have to come to grips with this issue one way or another. We both need to be happy and not have to worry about our future. And I do want us to have a future."

"And on that, my dear, I fully agree," I replied.

We talked for a few more moments about other things to include who would attend our simple ceremony, and then we said 'good night.' And so the long five weeks of contemplation began for the both of us.

I did know one thing. I would not put Lionel Byrd and my desire to continue as a CTT team member above Adrianna's wishes. If she decided she could flat out not accept my continued association with the team, even on a part-time basis, then the action man in me would just have to die.

On the 5th of June, even though we had still not resolved our differences over the issue, Adrianna went ahead and placed our *Wolf-McGowan* wedding announcement in both the Charleston Gazette and the Washington Post, the latter I guess because I lived there…like I had any friends who would read it. Anyway, it was short and sweet.

"Adrianna Marie Wolf of Greenbrier County, West Virginia, and Bruce Jackson McGowan, of Washington, D.C., will exchange vows in the gardens of the bride's country inn, Wolf Laurel, on June 22nd, 2002. The couple will leave for their honeymoon in Cozumel immediately following the ceremony."

It was official now. She was making all the arrangements, having fun with her girlfriends picking out flowers, the music, the cake and what she said would be a simple yet elegant wedding dress.

We talked every third night or so on the phone, her prodding me about my decision whether to completely distance myself from CTT, and me playing the equivocation game. In our June 15th conversation she dropped the big guilt anvil on my head.

"Bruce McGowan, if you go off some place and get yourself shot up, then you'd better *hope* to end up dead. I'm not going to have a man around here that I have to feed through a straw the rest of his life."

As frank as the statement was, it did tell me in other words that she had conceded. "Does that mean you'll let me go out and play with the boys every once in a while?"

For a moment there was only silence. "Today, I guess I'm having a weak moment. Maybe tomorrow I'll think about it again and change my mind." "About my working part-time with the State Department or the wedding?"

"Well, I'm not calling off the wedding, Mister McGowan. You're not escaping that easily."

"So the rest of the time do I help you run Wolf Laurel?"

"You can drive nails, repair roofs and paint sideboards; but no, the management of this inn is *my* job. So, have you thought about where you'd like to go to work?"

"I don't know. Maybe I'll teach high school."

"Uh huh," she replied rather sardonically. "You know

you can't slap kids around like you do bad guys. What happens the first time some kid shoots his mouth off to you?"

"Yeah, I see what you mean. Well, how about me working as an assistant football coach with Dandy Dan Laramie?"

"There is no way on God's green earth that will ever happen. He intends to keep as much distance from you as he can."

"And for good reason. How is he taking the news of you marrying the likes of me?"

"Well, if you must know, he actually snubbed me the other day when I ran into him at the bank."

"I hate sore losers," I said. "Just tell him the next time you see him to put on some big boy pants and get over it."

She laughed. "You're a bad boy. Of course, I've told you that a number of times. Makes me wonder how I could ever fall for a guy like you." "Obviously for my good looks, sexual prowess and oh, my humility."

"Goodbye, Skip. I'm still not over this contractor thing, you know."

"I know. It'll work out fine. You'll see. Love ya and see you in a week."

On my last day at work, Chuck and the rest of the Zulu boys were somewhere in Pakistan working on something hot. That just left the Birdman and Virginia to see me off. Virginia had made me a cake and given me a present of James Bond DVDs, all of which featured Sean Connery as 007. He was her favorite Bond.

"You still have a chance to change your mind, Brucie. It wouldn't take me an hour to pack up Tom's things and shove him out the door, you know."

"As tempting an offer as that is, my dear, I'd better stay with my plans. I've never made promises that I couldn't keep."

Byrd had a small sliver of cake, always watching his boyish figure, and then he asked me to come into his office. When we had sat down he pulled from his cabinet a bottle of cognac and poured us each two fingers worth in glasses. "Thanks, Bruce. It's been an interesting couple of years having you around. And I am damned pleased about the good work you did for this organization. But most of all, as hard as it is for me to say, I'm damned happy that you now have someone in your life. I'm sure Adrianna will make you a fine wife."

I clinked glasses with him and replied, "And I only hope to make her a good husband."

"Well, this is not 'goodbye'," he said. "As you have agreed, I will see you here once a month to review cases for a few days. And if and when a potential terrorist plot is either hatched or actually goes down, I will look forward to sending you out."

I nodded. "I do ask you one thing, though. Let me have a couple of months without any missions unless you have a dire situation. I don't want to jump into the fray immediately. I need some time with Adrianna. I don't want to give her the impression that this part-time contract work is more frequent than she expects it to be. It will also give me the time to get comfortable with this marriage thing. I've been out of practice for over twenty years."

"Granted, Bruce. Go enjoy yourself. You won't hear from me until sometime in September. How about we see you here the Tuesday after Labor Day for case review?"

"Good. How about my State Department ID? Do I keep it?"

"You keep it."

We then sat for a moment without saying anything further, both of us obviously uncomfortable with goodbyes. I then stood up and extended my hand.

"I want you to know, Lionel, as long as I was with the Bureau, I never learned more from any one person than I did you. You have my respect and admiration. If I could only have been a fraction of the policeman and statesman that you are, I would be a better man. Thank you."

For a second I thought I saw a bit of glistening in the Birdman's eyes. But he just nodded and pumped my hand.

"Now you get on out of here, McGowan, and go have a happy life."

I hugged Virginia on the way out the door. She then gave me a kiss on the lips and shoved me away. "Goodbye, 007."

"Goodbye, Moneypenny. See you in my dreams."

CHAPTER TWENTY ONE

On late Friday morning, the 21st, I stood by watching as the movers loaded up the last of my furniture and boxes of household goods. As my needs have always been simple, my belongings were few. It only took three hours for Atlas to box up everything and load it on the truck. The small Georgetown apartment had been my home for the previous six years…four with the Bureau and two with the Department of State. I had no real attachments to it and no memories to speak of, except the times Caroline occasionally stayed weekends. And only one other woman had ever spent the night there, and that was the first weekend in April. Well, maybe I *did* have one rather delectable memory after all.

As I sizzled down I-81 toward my destination, I wondered where all my stuff would go. My furniture wouldn't necessarily fit in with the Early American décor at Wolf Laurel. Would Adrianna make me give it to the Salvation Army or just put it in storage? I had a bunch of plaques and framed certificates from my Special Forces and FBI days. Where would *they* go? And then there was my Big Easy, as I affectionately called it…the over-stuffed leather recliner that had been my friend and comforter for more than fifteen years. Sure, it was well-worn and had a couple of rips in it. So what? I would be firm that it would become a fixture at Wolf Laurel…but not downstairs in the parlor where just anybody, include long-haired Burt would lay in it. Some things I don't share, two of which are my women and my chair. You see what things I had to think about just to have a permanent relationship with the woman I loved?

I was sure there would be a lot of things that needed to be sorted out when two people merge their lives. Things that neither of us had stopped to think about. Were all these thoughts about material items that were running through my brain merely symptoms of the pre-marital disease called 'cold feet'? Was I really 100% ready to give up my privacy, freedom, possessions, and full-time action man job, not to mention my swinging bachelor lifestyle? Well, the last item I just threw in to solidify all the cons I was comparing to my pros.

I pulled off in Lexington for a potty break, gas and a Diet Coke, then gave Adrianna a call. Before I went any further, I needed to hear her voice. The voice that would quell my apprehension.

"Hi, studly man. I love you," she said. Well, that was all I needed. I was no longer slipping out of the saddle. After a few sweet words from her lips that definitely worked their magic, I girded back up, took the reins firmly in my hands and continued at a gallop toward my destiny.

When I arrived, the moving van had not gotten there as yet. The first people to greet me when I walked into the lobby at Wolf Laurel were Adrianna's parents, the Randolph's, Bill and Gloria, fresh in from Florida. I certainly wanted to make a good first impression on them, so in anticipation of them being there, I had on my spiffy Navy blazer, a crisp, white oxford button-down and sharply-pleated gray slacks.

I had met these folks some thirty five or more years ago when ten year old Adrianna made a vow that she would marry me one day, but I didn't remember their faces. Although Gloria was still rather attractive for a late sixties dame, Bill had obviously not aged well. He was portly, nearly completely bald, supported by tacky red suspenders, and he wore his pants high above his mid-section where his zipper hit him right about his sternum. But he was a nice enough chap and had a crushing handshake, which I like in a man. Except I may never again be able to hold my Glock.

Gloria kissed me on the cheek, smiled and said, "So, you're the dashing rogue that stole my daughter's heart?"

I grinned and felt myself flush a little. "That would be me, except I normally keep the Eighth Commandment."

Bill answered for her. "I'm glad you do, my boy. Adultery don't set well with me."

Gloria shot him a laser-laced look. "That's the Seventh Commandment, Mister Know-it-All. He said he *stole* our daughter's heart."

"Oh, sorry."

"Well, then," I changed the subject. "Did you have a nice trip up?"

"We *would* have if Gloria didn't have to stop for a pee break every hour on the hour. A bladder the size of a golf ball."

I didn't respond, but in retrospect probably looked a little uncomfortable, looking down and shuffling my feet.

"Well, set yer luggage down, Bruce, and make yourself to home. It'll be yours anyway starting tomorrow. I 'spect Adrianna will be down in a few moments. She's upstairs primpin'."

I nodded and took a chair in the parlor alongside my future *in*-laws.

Bill continued. "Well, boy, I guess we don't have to tell you how we feel about our little girl, wantin' the best for her and all. So, you see to it that she's happy. That's all we ask…and to treat her right."

"Yes, sir," I replied. "We'll *both* be very happy. You don't have to worry."

We sat a couple of more minutes, each of us thinking about what to say next. I've never liked these kinds of moments. I looked toward the hallway. Where *was* Adrianna, anyway? Finally, I said, "I think I'll get on up there to let her know I'm here. It is great seeing you again after all these years…Mom, Dad." Now that was *very* uncomfortable to say, but I thought it both appropriate and opportune.

Gloria leaned in and grabbed my face between her two hands, then kissed me on the lips. "I was hoping you'd call us that, son. Now you go on. I know she's waiting." She then wiped a tear away with her fingers.

Well, it seemed I now had a mom and dad again, and if I say so myself, I made a pretty nice impression on them as their new son.

For probably the last time ever, I rapped a couple of times on Adrianna's door. Hopefully, I wouldn't have to keep doing that after we were married.

"Skip, darling," she greeted, kissing me where her mother just did. "You're just in time. I'm going over our seating list. I borrowed some folding chairs from Joey and think I have everyone placed."

"Okay, I'm listening, but can I grab a cold beer from the fridge?"

"Well, can you *not* get one right now? My parents are here and they don't condone the use of alcohol."

Uh, oh.

A bit disappointed, not to mention thirsty, I settled down with Adrianna on the couch. The list was short, as she intended it to be. I would be there of course, with Joey standing beside me as my Best Man. Adrianna's best friend, Suzette dePardeaux, from France, was her Maid of Honor. Officiating was the Reverend Davenport from the United Methodist Church. Two other of Adrianna's friends from town, Tracy Ann Bellamy and Krista Ellison, would sit with the remainder of the wedding party, her parents, Joey's family, and of course, Caroline McGowan.

"What? You didn't invite Coach Dan?"

She jammed a stiff finger into my chest. "You're being bad again." She then looked back at the seating chart. "Are we missing anybody?"

"I can't think of anybody else."

"The reception will be in the parlor and I have ordered a beautiful wedding cake, complete with bride and groom."

"Are any guests staying here this weekend?"

"Just a nice, middle-aged gentleman from Arkansas who said he would make himself scarce all day tomorrow."

"I thought maybe you would have blocked off the weekend to any guests."

"Well, I kind of did," she said. "But Mr. Carter is with the Country Inns of Americaand writes reviews for the annual publication. Greenbrier County was on his list this week. He stayed at the General Lewis a couple of days, then came here. I couldn't refuse the man who ideally will be bringing me more business."

"Guess not," I said.

She then took my hands in hers, looked into my eyes and smiled. "I can't believe our wedding day is here. There were times the last couple of months I didn't think it would happen. But tomorrow I will be Mrs. Bruce McGowan. Adrianna McGowan…has a nice ring to it, doesn't it?"

"Yes, it does. Then does that mean we'll be changing the name of the place to McGowan Laurel?"

"Nnnno, no. That *doesn't* have a nice ring to it." She then checked her watch. "We'd better get ready. Joey and Cora have opened up their house for a rehearsal dinner this evening."

"There's a rehearsal?"

"Not really. The dinner is just called that. I didn't think we needed a rehearsal considering the small, informal wedding we're having."

"Good. By the way, what time is the wedding tomorrow?"

"At two. And that's another thing. You need to stay at Joey's tonight and not be here *until* the wedding. You're not supposed to see me before hand."

"Really? I was looking forward to…you know…" "The 'you know' is not going to happen with my parents in the house. I think there will be ample opportunity along the way for that *after* we're married."

"Fine, then. Joey and I will put together a bachelor party tonight. One where girls pop out of cakes and guys get crazy."

"Just go ahead and have all the fun you want tonight and get it out of your system," Then she smiled. "Beginning tomorrow afternoon you get the old ball and chain clamped on you."

"Hmmm. Sadism. I think I'll like that. Will there be whips and leather as well?"

She then pulled me up to my feet. "Come on, perverted one. Let's get you downstairs before my dad comes up here to protect his daughter's honor. Stick around, though, for a few minutes while I chat a little more with mom about tomorrow's plans."

While Adrianna sat with her mom going over last minute ceremony particulars and Bill was pruning some branches along the pathway, I sat for a while on the veranda. I could smell the rain coming. The atmosphere, humid and balmy, hung like a dank blanket. My lungs struggled a bit to take in the heavy air. But it smelled fresh and earthy. It smelled like home. The showers which loomed over the Alleghenies to the west, would be upon us in a matter of minutes. It was the kind of afternoon that as I sat on the porch steps leaning into a banister took me back to the old McGowan farmhouse and the sweet days of my youth. Adrianna's B&B was not unlike our old Victorian in the country with its long veranda and shuttered windows. The farm of course belonged to Joey and his family. Had so for years. I had voluntarily given up my part of the house along with the funeral business years ago while I was still in the Army. As I was flitting around the world at the expense of my Uncle Sam and Joey had become well-grounded in the area running a business of which I wanted no part, it seemed only fitting that the house should go to him.

So, if I was feeling a little nostalgic sitting there, it was partly because Wolf Laurel reminded me so much of the place where had I spent such summer days during my younger years hanging out on the front porch with my grand-dad enjoying the intoxicating aroma of his Cherry Blend and leaning my head over the checkerboard strategically plotting my next move. Wolf Laurel would come with the wedding package when I married Adrianna, and I would again live in a beautiful, but ageing Victorian home in the lovely Greenbrier countryside.

Speaking of ageing, I suddenly felt the velveteen fur of fourteen year old Burt against my forearm. Rarely did he rub up against anyone except Adrianna, looking for a little stroking; but as he had apparently gotten used to having me around here and there, at least for longer periods of time than Adrianna's guests, maybe he was thinking I had become a more permanent fixture around the place. When he brushed my arm two or three times and started up his motorboat, I pulled him onto my lap and scratched him behind the ears. His motor then really revved up and he looked into my face and smiled. Yes, I tell you, he actually did smile.

"Well, old boy," I said. "I hope you don't mind sharing your digs here with the likes of me."

I think I saw him give me a nod of approval.

"And you know that means sharing your mommy's bed."

That prompted him to start digging his claws into my thigh. Well, actually it was just his natural response to the stroking. The kneading and purring continued until the rain came sweeping in, chasing us off the porch and into the house. Bill was close on our heels.

After feasting on Cora's magnificent country spread, Adrianna and parents left around eight, leaving Joey and me with our bachelor party that consisted of his cigar and my glass of Merlot on the front porch…our usual after- dinner oasis.

The rain had long departed and the last phase of the waning moon was dipping over the poplars in the western sky. A fingernail moon, Caroline used to call it. The evening was warm and a fresh breeze had just started up, carrying the sweet aroma of honeysuckle and jasmine onto the porch. I took a deep breath and drank into my lungs something that felt strange and intoxicating. It wasn't the honeysuckle on the vine. It was happiness. For the first time in a long time, I felt a sense of peace and contentment. And it wasn't just the evening air, either. It was all about love…love deep down in my soul. And it felt good.

"And so, my brother," Joey said, "the lion finally comes home domesticated."

"Domesticated, huh? Maybe so," I lamented. "I guess there will no longer be a sense of urgency…no pumping adrenaline. No knocking down bad guys."

"Is that a good or bad thing with you?"

I didn't respond for a moment, but took a swallow of the Merlot. "Good question. But it's a good thing. Hell, yeah. A *good* thing. I've been taking and giving blood for over thirty years. It's actually made me hate the color red."

"Yeah, I know what you mean, "Joey said, reflectively. "If it were not for keeping the family mortuary going, I'd have been out of my bloody business years ago."

"I just don't know how you've done it, Joey. It has always given me the creeps."

"I guess I got numb to it in time. Of course, Dad practically demanded that one of us continue on with the business. You were squeamish; I wasn't."

"And you took the bullet for both of us."

He grinned and took a final drag off his cigar before tossing it into Cora's yellow rose bush at the side of the porch.

"My big brother…getting married again." He then held up his glass of wine. "Here's to all the happiness in the world."

I clinked glasses with him, took a sip and said nothing.

I just looked up and smiled at the fingernail moon.

Caroline called me at dawn's early light on Saturday morning. She had flown in to her mom's the day before and was driving over as we spoke. She wanted to meet me for a hot dog at 11:30 at Jim's Drive-in. After piddling the morning hours away, I finally pulled into Jim's parking lot where there sat a Hummer, a couple of pick-ups, a blue Olds and a little green sports car. And that's when I did a double-take. I suddenly had one of those 'can't believe my sore eyes' experiences. There sat my 1973 Austin Healey 3000, looking as sweet as ever with its shiny, toothy grille and British Racing Green paint job, newly waxed.

Caroline sat off to the left at a picnic table in a pair of jeans, light jacket and a slightly visible shoulder holster that contained her Beretta 92. She waved me toward her.

I embraced her, kissing her on the forehead, then asked the question. "You're driving my Healey. What gives?"

"Don't I get a 'hello, daughter, great to see you again?'"

"Hello, daughter. Great to see you again. Now why are you driving my old sports car?"

"Mom sends her regards. She says she's very happy for you."

"Okay, I'm glad…I think." I scratched my head trying to figure out why she hadn't answered my question.

"She sent the car to you, Dad…with her congratulations and blessings."

"What? No way."

"Actually, neither she nor Ned wanted it, and she said she couldn't sell it, knowing it was a part of you. It's yours now."

If I hadn't been getting married to Adrianna and Darlene wasn't married to Ned, and I could stand living with her again, I'd marry her all over again, the saintly woman that she was. Mmmm, no.

"I can't believe it!" I exclaimed. "Why? Why the change of heart?"

"Well, I think it was more about *me* than anything. You dropped everything to go rescue me from the jaws of death…and then you got shot in the process. I guess it's her way of thanking you."

"It was something any father would do. But it pleases me that she feels that way."

Caroline then looked away for a moment and finally said, "You know, Dad. In her own way, she's still in love with you. Ned or not."

I dropped my head and nodded. "And whatever has happened to us in the past, I have always had feelings for your mom. In a historical kind of way, of course."

"Of course." Her face was now a bit sullen. "You know, Dad, for a long time I resented you both for breaking up. I probably resented you the most, even though she left *you*. Maybe it was because you were absent for most of my teen years. Important years. I guess I never told you because I thought it would hurt you."

I nodded again. "I was hurting enough for the both of us, my dear. But I'm glad you told me this."

She smiled and it was like the sun had come out from behind the clouds. "All water under the bridge and now I'm happy for my father. Whatever you are or have become, Dad, I want you to know that you have always been my hero." She then jumped up and took me by the hand. "Now, let's go get us a couple of those dogs."

"You're on," I said, taking a lingering moment to look back at the Healey. My baby had returned to me.

Caroline went on to Wolf Laurel in the Healey to finally meet Adrianna and to help her and her Maid of Honor get ready for our wedding…which would happen in two hours. After she left, I sat in the Suburban for a few minutes to allow the dogs to digest with the aid of a couple of Tums and then called Darlene. For some reason, the words I wanted to say weren't coming. All I could do was say, 'thank you.' But finally I did manage to say, "I wish you could have come to the wedding. It might have seemed to others as a bit unusual, but it would've been nice to see you again."

"Maybe we will see one another sometime," she replied. "Maybe when you're back in the northern neck area we can meet for a sandwich and cup of coffee."

"That would be nice." I paused a moment. "I don't know that I ever really told you this, but you did good with Caroline. She turned out to be a beautiful and compassionate young woman of character…" And then I laughed. "..even though she has her mother's tongue."

Then Darlene laughed. "Yes, that she does. I'm very proud of her."

"Well, again thank you for sending the Healey."

"It was always just in the way. I had to do something with it, and I didn't need the money it would bring. Ned did keep it maintained, as much as he disliked the fact that the car was yours." "Tell him 'thanks.'

"Goodbye, Bruce. Be happy." And then she was gone.

It was the nicest conversation she and I had had in twenty years. And I wasn't sure why. As many barbs as I had thrown her way over the years and made fun of my replacement, Ned, I never thought she would lose the anger. But she had weathered both me and my insults apparently without any residual hard feelings, which in a way hung another anvil of guilt around my neck.

CHAPTER TWENTY TWO

*We have all the time in the world time enough for life to
unfold*

*all the precious things love has in store. We have all the time
in the world.*

If that's all we have, you will find we need nothing more.

Every step of the way will find us

with the cares of the world far behind us.

We have all the time in the world just for love,

nothing more, nothing less, only love.

Louis Armstrong

When I arrived at Wolf Laurel with Joey and family, I saw that the wedding site was all set up…and so beautifully. At the beginning of the short footpath that led to the garden was a white trellis on which a long strand of freshly-cut clematis was interwoven. Planted near the angel fountain at the end of the path, showy snapdragons dwarfed by brilliant coleus and hollyhocks added magnificent color to the natural foliage of the woods. And so did the deep pink Rhododendrons and purple Mountain Laurel now in full bloom beneath the river birch and sprawling oaks. In a small open space under the trees, a ten by fifteen plot of deep green carpet grass provided the perfect setting for the exchange of vows and on which to place the dozen or so wooden chairs for the small gallery. Adrianna's friends, Tracy, a lovely, blonde feast-for-the-eyes, and Krista, also a loaded beauty, had already taken their seats beside Joey's ladies. I smiled and winked at them as I passed by.

As Joey and I approached, the minister who was standing in his white robe at the far side of the grassy area smiled and nodded. "Well, sir," he said to me. "You look mighty dashing in that tux. How are you feeling right about now?"

"Like I need to go to the bathroom in a huge way," I replied.

He laughed. "Those are just the butterflies working on you. Happens to every guy in this situation. So, do you have any last requests? Blindfold. Cigarette?"

I wanted to say, "Very funny, Parson." But I just stood there, smiled and shook my head.

Caroline, Gloria and the Maid of Honor, Suzette, were apparently still upstairs in the inn putting the last of the touches on Adrianna's make-up and wedding dress. I checked my watch. Two minutes till the hour. Even though we were standing in the shade in the understory of the woods, I started to perspire.

In a few moments at the head of the path near the trellis we heard the first notes of the Wedding March…played on an accordion. An *accordion* of all instruments. I wondered if this was somebody's idea of a joke. Maybe Joey's. He said he would handle the music. Joey just stood beside me and smiled.

First, Gloria entered the pathway and then sat in one of the chairs on the front row. Caroline followed in a pink dress and carrying a white clutch bag. She sat in the second row with Adrianna's friends. The pretty Maid of Honor came after her and took her place on the opposite side of the minister.

Finally, arm in arm with her father, quite frankly the loveliest specimen of beauty I had ever beheld, appeared from under the trellis and then walked gracefully toward me. She had on a knee-length white dress and white heels. A small wisp of a veil covered her dark hair. But most of all, she wore a smile so radiant that I swear I heard birds starting to sing in tune to the accordion music. There was no doubt about it. In spite of my hellious life of disobedience, the Good Lord above had sent me from Heaven the most beautiful of all angels to marry. And when that sudden sluice of sunlight broke through the trees and shone upon that angel, I saw the very breath of love on her face.

Bill trailed off to a chair beside Gloria and I reached out to take Adrianna's cool, dainty hand. She whispered, "I love you, Mr. McGowan."

As we stood with our hands locked together, smiling into each other's eyes, Adrianna's friend, Tracy, began our ceremony with one of my personal favorite Matt Monro melodies, *Portrait of My Love*. In just under three minutes she warbled the last of the lyrics:

…It would take I know A Michelangelo,

And he would need the glow of dawn That paints the sky above

To try and paint a portrait of my love.

Reverend Danforth then nodded to her with a smile and then to the accordion accompanist who's last rich, mellow chords rang euphonically throughout the woods. He began:

"My dear friends, we gather here to honor these two children of God who have cemented in their hearts for one another the sacred promises of faith, hope and love, those tenets of life so honest, pure and unrivaled…"

Either I wasn't paying any attention to the minister or Adrianna's beauty was drowning out his words. I didn't hear him after he finished his question to me, "…till death do you part?"

He chuckled and whispered, "Bruce?"

I was beyond embarrassed. Maybe we should have had a rehearsal. "Oh…I do. I do."

"And do you, Adrianna…"

My attention suddenly turned to a glint I saw through a large Rhododendron, which prompted everyone else to turn their heads off to the left side toward a man with a full head of white hair. As he walked from the woods toward us, the next thing I saw was the shiny, silver-plated pistol in his hand. I heard the ladies gasp and Gloria cried out.

Adrianna turned around to see the man as well and then exclaimed. *"Mr. Carter!"*

"No, Adrianna," I said. "His name is Jonas Karn."

Karn stopped within ten feet of us. "May I interrupt this nice little gathering?" A diabolical grin was on his face. "The dead sometimes come back to life, eh, McGowan?"

I felt absolutely naked without my Glock. Pulling Adrianna around behind me, I accosted him. The minister then stepped forward and said, "What is the meaning of this, sir? Do you dare come here to defile this sacred occasion? What in God's name do you want?"

I pushed Danforth back. "He wants to kill me, Pastor."

"Ah, I do indeed," Karn replied. He then aimed the gun at my chest. "My long-awaited day of reckoning is at hand. Goodbye, McGowan. Time for you to die. This is for my wife. See you in Hell."

Adrianna then whirled around in front of me with her back to Karn and screamed "No!" just as he fired. She immediately slumped from my arms and fell to the grass. As I bent down to her, a second and third report cut sharply through the air, echoing for several seconds through the woods. Karn's body jerked from both rounds and he hit the ground hard. I turned to see Caroline standing on the path, gun still aimed with both hands at Karn's body. A slight wisp of gun smoke trailed away from the muzzle of her Beretta.

Gloria screamed Adrianna's name and rushed to her side. Joey pulled out his cell phone and dialed 911.

I cradled Adrianna's limp body in my arms. The bullet had struck her in the left side of her back and blood began to quickly soak into her white dress and through my fingers. I felt her pulse and it was faint, if not failing.

All the ladies were crying. Reverend Danforth knelt over us and took Adrianna by the hand. He lifted his head up into the trees as his lips moved in silent prayer.

I then looked over at Karn who lay within three feet of us. He appeared to still be breathing. One of Caroline's bullets had struck him in the right side of his neck and the other slammed into his shoulder.

I suddenly began to shake as though I was freezing. All I could do was sit on the grass and rock Adrianna as she clung between life and death.

The rescue squad was on site in less than five minutes, which to me seemed like an eternity. When the EMTs rushed onto her, they pushed me away, quickly checked her pulse, and then hooked up oxygen. Joey came up and put his arm around me.

"Pull away, Bruce, and let these guys work," he said.

I stood with him, watching as the EMTs worked

feverishly to strap Adrianna to the gurney.

Caroline then drew near and said, "Dad, I'm so sorry. I took my gun from my purse seconds after I saw him, but didn't fire before he got his shot off. I was afraid I'd hit you or Adrianna. I should have reacted quicker."

I didn't respond, but nodded without looking at her. My attention was on Adrianna and the paramedics. I knew Karn was on us before anyone could do anything.

When I approached Gloria and Bill, they saw Adrianna's blood still on my hands. Gloria then began to wail even louder. Bill stood seemingly frozen in fear and disbelief with his mouth open.

While the EMTs were loading Adrianna into the back of the emergency van, I moved in on Karn. He was not conscious, but I knew he was alive since his chest was rising and falling. Caroline's first bullet had torn through the base of his neck near the clavicle, just missing the carotid artery. There was no exit wound which meant that the round had lodged somewhere in the cervical area.

"Give me your gun, Caroline," I said, not taking my eyes off of the large maggot lying in the grass.

"No, Dad. As much as I want to see this bastard dead, I can't stand by and watch you kill him in cold blood."

"You don't have to. Just walk away."

"A second ambulance is pulling in now. Let it go, Dad."

I turned and looked at her sternly. She was right. It couldn't happen in front of the people still standing around. And if she did hand me her gun, she would be an accessory to his murder. I nodded to her in resignation.

"Yeah. This is not the time or place." I paused and looked down at Karn again. His eyes were fluttering. "But this isn't over. And you know ultimately what I have to do."

"Go on, Dad. Adrianna needs you. Uncle Joey can take you and her parents to the hospital. I'll stay here to wait for the police, then join you later. They will need an account of what happened."

Joey quickly escorted us down the path to my Suburban and slid in behind the wheel. As we followed the EMTs down Seven Bridges, I kept my eye on the rear door of the ambulance. And I prayed that God was keeping His eye on Adrianna.

"Bruce," began Joey. "How the hell did this guy Karn know about your wedding?"

I almost didn't hear his question as I was still focused on the rescue squad vehicle and how slow it was going. What was happening inside? Was she still breathing? What could I have done differently to protect her from the mad man?

"What? Oh, I guess Karn saw it in one of the wedding announcements in the newspapers…the Gazette or the Messenger, I reckon. Maybe The Post. But he was going to find out about the wedding, anyway." I looked out the side window and shook my head. "Somehow, I knew he still had to be alive and I should have scoured the earth to find him.

After his hideaway was destroyed, he went underground. He was patient all right and wanted to give it enough time to make it apparent that he had died in the explosion. After everyone was then off guard and complacent, he would leave no stones unturned but to track me down…"

Gloria suddenly broke in on our conversation from the back seat. "Bruce, do you mean because this man was hunting you, our daughter ended up like this? How could you expose her to this kind of thing?"

Obviously, my status as their new son was in big time jeopardy. As I struggled for the words to answer, Joey interceded. "Ma'am, this was an entirely unpredictable situation. The FBI also thought this guy was dead…killed in a raid. Who could have anticipated it?"

She didn't respond. I turned my head around toward her, seeing the grief and agony in her face. Although Joey was correct, immense guilt was quickly setting in. Along with fear.

Joey, Reverend Danforth and Adrianna's parents sat with me in the waiting room as surgeons worked for over an hour to remove the bullet which had fortunately missed her spinal cord, but lay dangerously close to her heart. The Reverend prayed aloud as we all leaned forward, bowed our heads and closed our eyes. And I prayed separately that God would respond favorably to the words He was hearing. Why is it that when we talk to God, we're praying; but when we tell people God talks to us, we're schizophrenic? Anyway, I told God that if He did hear our prayers, my incorrigible soul would be His forever.

Caroline arrived at 3:30, sat beside me and picked up my hand.

"Any news, Dad?"

"No. The fact that they're still in there working on her says that she's still alive."

"The EMTs also brought Karn here, you know."

"Yeah. I understand he's down the hall fighting for his life, too. I've not only prayed for Adrianna to make it, but also for him *not* to. I guess the Big Guy up there is not very happy with me thinking that, but He's got to understand… Karn needs to go to Hell, *and* as soon as I can send him there."

The pastor looked up at me with disapproving eyes, but didn't say anything. He knew it was better that he didn't. He wouldn't like what just might come out of my mouth.

Caroline's eyes welled up and she cradled my hands in hers. "Dad, I…"

I looked at her and caught the guilt pangs still in her eyes. Whispering, so that Bill and Gloria would not get even more upset, I said, "Hey, you did the job, sweetheart. Thanks for taking that dog down. Good shooting."

"As soon as I saw him and pulled out my gun, I…" She shook her head. "If only it had been a couple seconds sooner," she whispered in return.

"Don't beat yourself up. You reacted as quickly as you could. How could anyone have realized something like that could happen? One moment we're all smiles. Life is good. The next, my wife is lying near death with a bullet in her." I then paused before saying, "You know, the hell of it is, she's not yet officially my wife."

"On the way over here, I thought about my shooting him. I didn't even have to think about pulling the trigger. And that scares me."

I squeezed her hand. "It shouldn't. It tells me your training was effective and prepared you well for a situation like this."

"I always wondered when it would happen. What would it feel like? How would it make me feel later?"

"And how do you feel?" I asked her.

"Kind of numb. Like maybe I dreamed it. I guess it hasn't sunken in."

I put my arm around her and drew her head into my shoulder. "Just know that you saved others' lives back there at the inn, including your old man's. There are people who deserve killing, and that bastard is one of them. He might not be dead, but now we both are vindicated."

Caroline then kissed me on the cheek. "I was saving that for you after the wedding."

I smiled down at her. "I needed that. Thanks."

At that moment the doors to the OR flew open and one of the surgeons half my age wearing green pajamas came out.

"Are you all the family of Mrs. Wolf?"

I jumped up to meet him. "Yes, we are. How is she, doc?" "Well, she appears to be out of danger, but we put her in a coma. She's also very weak from her loss of blood. All I can say is that the next twelve to twenty-four hours will tell the tale."

"Can we see her?" asked Gloria.

"I'd just as soon you didn't right now. Why don't you all go get some coffee and come back in three or four hours, and then we'll see. Hopefully, she will be coming around by then."

I shook the doctor's hand. "Thanks, Doc. I know you did good work."

"I did my best. That lady, though, is a fighter as tiny as she is. I heard this happened at your wedding." He then shook his head. "Horrible. But maybe that's why she's still in there fighting. She has everything to live for."

Bill and Gloria thanked the surgeon as well. "We'll be in the cafeteria, Bruce."

I nodded. "See you there."

I stayed for about fifteen minutes talking with Caroline and Joey, and then I asked Joey to take me back to Wolf Laurel to change clothes where I could clean the blood off of me and retrieve my vehicle. Caroline was to call Lew Pettyjohn to fill him in on what had occurred, and then contact Lionel Byrd. I appreciated her offering to do that. I was just not in the frame of mind to talk to anyone.

In twenty minutes, Joey and I were sitting in the parking lot at the inn. Before I exited the family car, Joey put his hand on my shoulder and said, "She's going to make it fine, Bruce. I'm sure of that."

"I pray you're right about that, little brother. Now go on back to your family and say a couple more prayers."

When Joey pulled away, I stood for a moment, looking back into the woods toward our wedding scene. The police were long gone and only the chairs and arbor of clematis remained. It seemed all so surreal, like it never happened. Like the little setting was still waiting for the wedding party to arrive. But I knew I couldn't stand there and dwell on it any longer. I had to clean up and get back to the hospital.

I took a quick shower and wiped the condensation from the bathroom mirror to take account of the man's face looking back at me. He looked haggard. The pangs of guilt and worry were fully apparent in his eyes. She *would* be fine, dammit. Joey had said it. The doctors had done their best. And God would work his magic.

When I returned to the hospital an hour or so later, I stopped by the cafeteria to talk with Adrianna's parents. I knew they were blaming me that their daughter had taken a bullet that was meant for me. And I didn't fault them for how they felt. I had unwittingly exposed Adrianna to something that had sprung from out of my past. And if she survived, maybe there was a chance she could be in even *more* danger being around me.

They were sitting at a table looking understandably somber and still in shock. Bill had not said much to me the entire time we sat outside the OR. I expected that he was angry at me. But then he opened up as soon as I sat down.

"You know, Bruce, our little girl up there has had to endure a lot of pain in her life, what with losin' Mason and our grandson before that. I'm just wonderin' if she will ever have a happy life again."

"She makes it through this, Bill, and I will see to it that she is happy the rest of her life. I swear to God Almighty that I will. She sacrificed herself to save my life. I…I don't know how to…"

Gloria then placed her hand in mine and said, "Bruce, I didn't mean to insinuate you're to blame for what has happened. It was just a mother trying to reason why it did. It's like it's not real…the worst nightmare ever. We can only blame that maniac."

Bill nodded in agreement. "And we're damn glad your daughter took him down."

"I'm just sorry it happened," I replied. "You were right to say that I exposed her to this. If I had known…"

"That's okay, son. Like Mother said, we're not blamin'

you."

I always hated it when a man calls his wife 'Mother.' But if that was the worst thing that I heard come out of Bill's mouth, I was sure we would get along just fine.

Adrianna did not regain consciousness that night, but she *was* moved from ICU to a private room. Her vitals were good, the doctor said, but it would be a while before she would come out of her medically-induced coma. He would try to bring her around in a few hours.

Karn was in a room on the floor above. And it was time for me to go up. When I stepped off the elevator, I saw where one of my friend Lieutenant Harlan Williams' troopers was standing with a coffee cup in his hand, making time with a sweet-looking nurse. As I approached them, the trooper then turned to look in my direction.

"You're Mr. McGowan, aren't you?" he quizzed.

"Yes. How did you know?"

"My lieutenant said you might be up here. And, you have the eyes of a government agent."

"What kind of eyes are those?" He smiled.

"I don't know. Maybe the kind that stare into you like laser beams…like yours do." He paused.

"So, why *are* you up here?"

"To see how my would-be killer is making it. Do you know?"

"Yeah, he's there in 425. They say the bullet severed his spinal cord and he's totally paralyzed. Can't move his head or anything from there down. But they said he'll live…if that's what you call *life*."

"Well, I guess there's no danger of him escaping. So why are you standing guard?"

"I wondered that myself," the trooper replied.

"But Williams saw fit to my being here. Maybe to see that no one got to him." Meaning *me*. I nodded.

"Well, all's well that ends well. That's all I wanted to know. Thanks."

He shook my hand and when I turned to walk away, he turned his attention back to Nurse "Goodbody."

But I wasn't done. I had to find a way to get into Karn's room. I had to see his face and he *definitely* had to see mine…that is, if he was conscious.

I stood for nearly fifteen minutes out of the trooper's sight about thirty feet away, peering occasionally around the corner. The nurse had returned to her duties, but he still watched her whisk about from her station to various rooms and back.

I then got the brainy idea as to how I would pull him away. Finding a waiting room on the same floor, I saw a phone on a table layered with a number of magazines. Taped to the phone was a hospital directory. Picking up the receiver, I dialed the front desk number. A voice with considerable age on it answered. "This is Mrs. Jones, may I help you?"

"Yes, Mrs. Jones. This is James in Security. I'm on the lower floor in the boiler area and I found some guy wandering around who shouldn't be here. When I tried to stop him, he ran. He's still down here somewhere and I need some help. Earlier I saw a state trooper on the fourth floor by the nurse's station. I need you to call there and tell them to send him down. This guy could be a lot of trouble."

"Oh, my", she replied. "I'll call right away."

In about thirty seconds I saw the trooper say something into the phone on his shoulder and scamper toward the elevator. When I saw the doors close, I then watched the nurse's station until I saw the trooper's girlfriend walk away and into a patient's room. There was another nurse sitting behind the desk, but as I strolled casually by toward Room 425, she didn't look up. The door was not completely closed and as I gently pushed it open and moved on in, I saw that the room was dimly lighted. I was also glad to see that it was a private room and there was no other patient there who would witness my act of premeditated murder.

And yes, I did have the foresight back at Wolf Laurel to holster my Glock beneath my sports coat.

There is no experience like killing another human being. I have taken lives of the enemy in battle, of bad guys in back alleys and of terrorists wherever they are preparing to murder the innocent. And then almost immediately afterward, after the thrill and the adrenaline have diminished, I search my soul, praying to God that it was a righteous kill. But, I didn't intend to talk to God after *this* kill. Whether He condoned it or not, it didn't matter. Somehow I think He would understand.

Karn looked wanly, even pitiful, lying there like a corpse, but with an oxygen hose affixed to his nostrils. His face was a sallow hue. The cardiac monitor beside his bed beeped away, the blips on the screen proving that he was indeed still alive. When I approached his bed, the slight nudge of my body against the frame caused him to open his eyes. Just what I wanted to see. His eyes slowly moved to the left in my direction, suddenly widening. I couldn't tell whether they were full of fear or surprise.

Our eyes pressed unwaveringly on one another for several moments without word.

"Hello, maggot," I finally said.

His lips parted slightly, but it was obvious that he couldn't speak. "So, here we are at last, eh Karn? Me standing here alive and well…you lying there like a slug all helpless and shit."

His eyes, wide and glistening, stayed fixed on my face. He didn't even blink. And I'm sure he did not detect one scintilla of mercy in *my* loathing eyes.

"You *know* what's coming. How do you want it…in the brain or in the heart?" I pulled my Glock and then retrieved the suppressor from my coat pocket.

Still, his eyes stayed glued to mine, unwavering.

After attaching the suppressor, I placed its muzzle against his left temple. I then flipped the safety off with my thumb and cocked the hammer. Applying gradual pressure to the trigger with my forefinger, I knew it was scantly a millimeter from exploding a .40 caliber round into Karn's brain. And then his mouth formed into a smile.

It took me a few seconds to realize exactly *why* he was smiling. It was what he *wanted*.

And then I smiled back. "Ah, yes. So, you *want* me to kill you."

Releasing the pressure on the trigger, I pulled the gun away from his skull and let it hang down by my side. Passion to kill this man had eaten away at my sense of logic and rationality. I would go to jail for a very long time and Karn would win out in the end. He wanted his life to be over and I would then sit in my cell as he had done for thirteen years. And I would be in jail because of *him*. That was what his smile was all about.

"Oh, I *will* kill you all right, Karn. By allowing you to *live*. You will be a prisoner in your own body the rest of your life…and I hope it is a very *long* life. When you lie there day after day in mental agony, unable to move, I want you to think about me. And about the woman you shot, who by the way will survive to live happily ever after with me. Yeah, Karn. I win…you lose."

The smile dissipated from his face and his lips began to quiver.

I detached the silencer and re-holstered my Glock. "Goodbye, Karn. Welcome to Hell…a *living* Hell. Now watch me walk…I said *walk*…out of this room." And I took great pleasure in doing so. I sat by Adrianna's bedside the entire next morning holding her hand and occasionally speaking to her, pleading with her to open her eyes. The doctor had not been able to bring her to a conscious state. She was extremely pale and I thought her lips looked purple. The doc said that was from the enormous amount of blood loss.

My senses seemed never as keen as they were while I sat watching over her. The rubber soles of the nurses' white shoes squeaked loudly on the tiled floor in the hallway. The whole place smelled clinical and sterile from the disinfectant. I watched as the glucose bag continued its steady drip… drip…drip. And I watched the second hand on the wall clock jerk second by second until it made a complete circle. Time would ultimately be the victor, no matter how it turned out with Adrianna. A hypnotic stillness had seized the room and as I watched the monitor become erratic at times, I feared more than once that her heart had stopped.

I was exhausted, not to mention emotionally spent. I hadn't really slept the previous night, slumping on the very uncomfortable couch outside of recovery. And of course praying like I was. My lids felt like they had ten pound weights on them. So, while still sitting in the bedside chair, I laid my head on the mattress by her hand.

It seemed that I was only out a few minutes when I awoke to something crawling through my hair. I glanced at the clock on the wall and saw that I had actually been asleep for about two hours. Some watchdog I was. The crawly thing on my head was Adrianna's hand.

"Hi, studly man," she said in a near whisper.

"Oh, thank God. I thought you'd *never* come back to me." I then leaned down and kissed her forehead.

"What happened? I remember seeing Mr. Carter with a gun and…"

"Shhh," I said, touching her lips with my fingers. "Save your strength. We'll talk about it later. Everyone's okay."

"Then why am I in a hospital bed?"

"You saved my life, sweetheart. That's all I'll tell you for now. You need to rest."

She smiled and nodded, then closed her eyes.

I left the room quickly and went to her parents in the lounge. "She's out of her coma," I said. "She's going to be fine."

Gloria stood up and hugged me, spilling out her tears on

my Polo golf shirt. "Can she see us?"

"Let's let her sleep a while. Why don't you just look in on her and then go back to Wolf Laurel to get some sleep as well. Caroline is still there."

Bill, whose face looked like the last rose of summer with his lack of sleep, said, "Maybe you're right. Come on, Mother."

I gritted my teeth, but figured I'd better get used to it.

Adrianna was out of it most of that day, but woke up again around eight and announced that she was hungry. She wanted a cheeseburger of all things. My salad-eating girl wanted a cheeseburger. And that's when I *knew* she would be fine.

"I'll have them bring something up."

She didn't get her cheeseburger, but as she ate the pudding the nurse's aide brought in, I began telling Adrianna what had happened the day before.

Her only question was, "Does that mean we're not married yet?"

"I'm afraid so. *I* said 'I do,' but *you* never got the chance."

"Then we must fix that right away. I want you to call Reverend Danforth and tell him to get his butt over here to marry us."

"Actually, he was just here. What say we wait until you're up and around and we'll try it again at Wolf Laurel?"

"I don't know. The last time we were there it didn't go so well. But maybe we can wait. We'll have the ceremony inside."

"It's a deal," I said.

Adrianna then caught sight of another figure lurking about in the doorway. As the man stepped forward, I smiled.

"Adrianna, I'd like you to meet my boss, Lionel Byrd."

While I shook his hand. Adrianna said, "Hello, Mr.

Byrd. Are you the man who has been keeping Skip away from me all this time?"

"Skip? Who's Skip?" he said. "Well, finally. Something that the man who knows everything *doesn't* know. That's me, boss."

Byrd formed his mouth into a wry smile. "I never figured you for a 'Skip.' How did you get that handle?"

"A long story, Lionel."

The Birdman then went over and took Adrianna by the hand and kissed it. "If you look this lovely in your sick bed, my dear, you must indeed be a beautiful creature when you are well. No wonder Bruce left me for you."

"Quite the charmer with the ladies, aren't you, Lionel?

I didn't know you had it in you."

"A lot you don't know about me, McGowan." And I was sure that was the case.

Byrd and I slipped out of the room for a few minutes to talk in the lounge.

"Thanks for coming, boss. I really appreciate…"

"Forget it, Bruce. Felt I had to be here. Look, don't worry about me calling you for a good long time. Maybe not even the rest of the year. Your new wife is going to need you to help her convalesce for a while. She doesn't need to be reminded of how dangerous our world can be. Every time you go off on a case for us, what happened yesterday is going to be recalled in her mind. She doesn't need any anxiety in her life. So you go on out and sell cars or teach school, whatever you need to do to sustain yourself. Then we'll talk about contract work after the first of the year."

"Fair enough. I'm sure by then both she *and* I will want me out of the house."

"You've got a fine woman in there. You do whatever it takes to keep her happy…and safe."

"Thanks, friend. Thanks for being here." I then clinched his hand warmly.

"Don't get all sappy on me, McGowan. See you around."

I watched in admiration as the distinguished, gray-haired man in the three piece Italian-made suit walked down the corridor. He was a dandy all right. The *real* Bond. It was for sure that the security of our country was going to be locked down tight for a good, long time, knowing that the Birdman was the President's most trusted anti-terrorist guru.

On July 20th in the parlor at Wolf Laurel, Adrianna and I greeted Reverend Danforth who would for the second time in a month officiate our wedding. Joey stood up for me and Adrianna's friend Suzette flew back in to stand with her. This time both of us finished our vows and said 'I do.' After the ten minute ceremony we were husband and wife.

She looked fantastic. Her color had long-since returned and her smile was as radiant as ever. But best of all, she was now nearly totally healed. And we had matching bullet scars on our backs.

We lost our vacation as both the airline and hotel costs were non-refundable. So, what's a couple thousand dollars and a tropical honeymoon when you can take your new bride for a top-down ride to Myrtle Beach in a beautiful Austin Healey 3000.

As we zipped along I-77 toward South Carolina, I couldn't help looking over from time-to-time at the lovely Adrianna McGowan who in her over-sized sunglasses and white scarf could have been Audrey Hepburn or Grace Kelly. There was a little of both in her. She looked back at me and smiled, showing the world that we passed by those perfect, white teeth.

"Are you happy, Mrs. McGowan?" "Perfectly happy, Mr. McGowan."

And it was all *very* perfect. It was then at that moment that I decided once and for all that Bruce McGowan, terrorist hunter, action figure, ruthless bastard feared by bad guys everywhere, and husband to the beautiful Adrianna McGowan would...

AFTERWORD

This was the second novel in the McGowan Series. Many of you who enjoyed the first in this series, *Wolf Laurel*, pleaded for a sequel to be written so that Bruce would not in fact end his relationship with the lovely Adrianna in order to continue his service as a counter-terrorist operative. I heard you. And yes, this *will* be a Series. Look for the third in the series, the ten year anniversary of 9/11. The McGowan Collection Series: Book 3, *A Hateful Wind,* out now.

THE END